THE END
OF
FICTION

Victor Thorn

The End
Of
Fiction
(or: How to get published without even trying)

Sisyphus *Press*

What follows is a work of fiction. The events described here are imaginary. The settings and characters are fictitious, even when an actual person's name is used. They are not intended to represent specific places or persons, or, even when a real name is used, to suggest that the events that follow actually happened.

THE END OF FICTION

Sisyphus Press
P.O. Box 10495
State College, PA 16805-0495
(814) 237-2853

First Printing July, 2000

ISBN 0-9701950-0-1

Printed in the United States of America

Dedicated to

THE PUBLISHING INDUSTRY

Cover Art: Paul Rupeka
        Ink Inc. Tattooing by Paul
        State College, PA

Thanks to Joshua, Lynnette, Marijo, and especially Kendall

Who Defines
Your
Identity?

Joan Jett
"Rubber and Glue"

I witnessed his sickness, his psyche, and his soul
swimming in circles
like sharks about to feast
on a midday meal.

1

"I'll rob a fucking bank," Ukiah snarled drunkenly, beer suds spilling from his lips, "if that's what it takes to start my own publishing company. And you ...um ... oh yeah, Chris. I forgot your name for a second. You're going to drive the getaway car."

"Me?" I objected. "I've only known you for two hours. Maybe less. I'm not going to be part of a heist, then spend the rest of my life in prison. No sir."

Ukiah hurled his empty beer can across the room, drops of yellowish brown liquid splashing in all directions as the aluminum container crashed against a plasterboard wall.

Crazed, he bellowed, "You're the one who picked me up. I wasn't even hitchhiking. And you're the one who came to a complete stranger's apartment. Now you cringe when the flame gets too high. Well, I'll lay it on the line. Whenever you lift a carpet and peek beneath, it's a safe bet you'll get dirt on your fingers." He paused a moment, then continued. "Anyway, who'd ever suspect you of being involved in a robbery?"

Offended, I blurted, "What's that supposed to mean?"

Ukiah laughed, "You're not exactly Bonnie or Clyde."

"I'm not exactly Romeo and Juliet either."

"That may be so," the man chuckled. "At least think about it." Ukiah then walked toward an unseen room, his voice echoing these final words. "We might have to butcher a few people, or gun 'em down in cold blood. But when it comes to getting published, nothing will stop me. Nothing."

I pondered my situation, then wondered how I could have gotten involved in such a predicament. The morning started as any other. I left work at 7:00 a.m. where I was the overnight manager of a data entry firm. And, as usual, I drove my Gemini along the Middlesex Parkway toward the suburbs of Latera Heights. Nothing seemed unordinary in any way. The morning rush-hour traffic was bumper-to-bumper, yet still moving smoothly. I listened to the same morning radio as any other day - The Glen and Glenda Show - essentially driving in a daze.

Then I noticed him walking along the road's shoulder. His pace wasn't rapid, nor was it slow. The man, whose black baseball cap partially covered dishwater blonde hair that tangled past his shoulders, merely advanced in a nonchalant fashion. I probably wouldn't have paid him a second glance, but traffic came to a halt, requiring me to momentarily stop. It was at this time that I took a closer look. The man, wearing blue jeans and a T-shirt, appeared to be quite average, at least physically - his only outstanding feature being that extended mane of hair.

For some inexplicable reason, I was instantly attracted to him. But why? What strange aura emanated from his body that so possessed me? Then I knew. This unknown character was different than anyone else, and different than me. Surrounding me were automobiles just like any other, with drivers just like me. They all had jobs to attend, car payments to make, and thoughts that never deviated from those of their next-door neighbor. They were all like me. We brushed our teeth that morning, raked leaves in the evening, and went to bed after watching a sitcom or football game.

But this man, for some reason, was cast from a different lot. I knew he wouldn't go home and follow the same routine as me. I'd cook two hard-boiled eggs, read the newspaper, then fall asleep after washing the dishes. But not him. This thin, solitary figure represented something beyond the norm, something that I sought for ages - freedom from the confines of normalcy.

It was at this point, with a car ahead of me, one behind me, and many to the left of me, that I acted in a strangely uncharacteristic manner. Rather than pressing the accelerator and following traffic, I veered from the slow lane onto the berm and pulled alongside this fascinating man. He wasn't thumbing for a ride, or in any noticeable need of assistance. He simply strolled along the parkway, not paying attention to the hustle and bustle around him.

My actions seemed strange, as if guided by an unseen hand. What was I doing? How could I, being thirty-three years old, approach a complete stranger to ask if he needed a lift? Hell, I was the type of person who, when going out in public, kept a vigilant lookout for people I knew, not so I could greet them, but instead to avoid them. The extent of my human contact was limited to occasional chitchat in the lunchroom, or passing glances at a supermarket. I could hardly be labeled a social butterfly, fluttering from one tryst to another. Now I was potentially placing my life in danger to a man who could be an escaped serial killer.

To my dismay, these thoughts didn't stop me from leaning across the bucket seat and opening the passenger side door.

"Excuse me, sir," I said tentatively. "Do you need a ride?"

Without saying a word, the man walked toward my car, then sat beside me on the gray vinyl seat.

Gazing in my rear-view mirror, I once again eased into the flow of traffic. The man to my right remained speechless as we ascended a slight upgrade, entering a fog bank.

Hoping to break our uneasy silence, I offered the following information.

"I'm not sure where you're going, but I'm rolling into town, past campus, then onto Halfmoon Acres. Oh, by the way, my name in Chris," I said, "Chris Edwards."

"Chris, huh," the man replied, looking straight ahead. "I once knew a Christopher, and also a Christina. Now I know a Chris."

Nervously, I continued, "Yup, that's me. Chris. What's your name?"

Without a hint of animation, the passenger responded, "You can call me Ukiah."

A repeated silence.

Questioning my decision to retrieve this man from the roadside, I hesitantly said, "I hate being so forward, but are you going anywhere in particular?"

"I'm sorry for being so quiet, but I have a lot on my mind. You can drop me at Transformer Towers."

Transformer Towers, I thought, what a dump. Nobody lives there except welfare cases, lushes, hookers, and derelicts.

But I didn't utter a peep. From what I gathered, Ukiah could have slipped a dagger from his hip pocket and slit my throat. He appeared, by all accounts, to be slightly deranged, with long, straight hair, an unkempt beard, a scarred Adam's apple, and blue jeans torn at each knee. From my perspective, Ukiah held the potential to become violent, and I had no desire to provoke him. In the same breath, though, my rider's face emitted a soft, gentle radiance. But this radiance couldn't be categorized as beauty in any classical sense of the word. Instead, Ukiah's appearance reminded me of an old cliché, "close, but no cigar." Stated differently, if his genetic mapmaker had switched a few chromosomes here and there, he may have been striking. But as such, his looks fell marginally short of the mark, lingering around the "what could've been" range.

Still, a magnetic force drew me to him - an energy I'd never felt before. What could it be? What type of mysterious guide was manipulating my mind? I couldn't decide, but Ukiah seemed oblivious to these thoughts. He sat stoically by my side, staring out the window as we entered Latera Heights. While his eyes surveyed the town and gown atmosphere, I desperately fought an urge to rest my hand on Ukiah's knee.

"What was happening to me?" I wondered as we drove through this typical college setting. To our right sat Latera University, a one-time agricultural school whose enrollment now peaked at 43,000. Then, lining the street's left side, were a host of businesses that the campus supported like Atlas holding a globe on his shoulders.

That foggy morning we passed sleepy pizza parlors, high-rise apartment buildings, souvenir shops, record stores, tattoo joints, and fashionable boutiques. As we zipped by these staples of higher education, I returned to my adolescence, when thoughts of growing older were more distant than orbiting planets.

Consumed by these thoughts, I momentarily forgot about my passenger, who likewise rode in his own private world. But this continuing silence unnerved me, so I made another stab at conversation.

"Are you hungry? Because if you are, we can stop at a diner."

"Thanks," he smiled, "but we're almost home."

Ukiah's dour resolve reestablished the mood. So I figured, "The hell with him. I won't volunteer any more of myself if he wants to stay so remote." But even though I felt rejected, I was still attracted to Ukiah. Without being obvious, I caught a glimpse of him from the corner of my eye. All of a sudden, as if communicated from beyond, I realized that Ukiah was controlling me. His non-verbal message rang like bells from a steeple, resonating through my ears.

"You're drawn to me, little moth, a flickering candle in the darkness. But I can't give light to every passerby. Get away from me. Be gone."

As if losing my mind, I mumbled silently, "Be gone."

"Your thoughts are absurd," Ukiah's alter ego persisted.

I could do nothing but create even more delusions.

"Why are you listening to me?" the voice asked. "Let your thoughts separate, then re-feed them to me. I know what your mind needs. I can give it nourishment. Don't be like all the rest. If you are, then I'll be forced to push you away."

My mind flashed three words. "Push me away."

"As I thought, you're just like all the others. And, because you are, I have to say goodbye."

"Chris. Chris. You just missed Splitter Street. That's where The Towers are."

"Oh shit, sorry," I apologized. "My mind was somewhere else."

"To say the least," Ukiah grinned, shaking his head.

As I maneuvered my Gemini through traffic and circled the block, I yet again caught sight of Ukiah's face. I wondered how old he was (probably in his early to mid twenties), and how he could have entered my mind. I mean, when overly fatigued, I had been prone to hallucinations in the past; but lately my sleeping had been normal. Maybe the problem lay hidden in my late night hours. The graveyard shift had finally drug me toward an incoherent state of paranoia.

"You can pull into that rear lot," Ukiah pointed, directing me along a faded redbrick wall. "Here it is. Home sweet home. Do you wanna to join me for a beer?"

"Now? At this time? It's only 7:30 in the morning," I observed.

"Morning, afternoon, evening. The beer still tastes the same. It's up to you."

The entire scenario could have been avoided that second if I had declined Ukiah's offer. But instead, without using an ounce of common sense, I shrugged my shoulders and said, "Why not?" The heavens only knew what awaited me.

After parking the Gemini, then double-checking each lock, I followed Ukiah around a corner that led to the Transformer's front entrance. Along the way, we sidestepped a fallen aluminum awning, broken boards with rusty nails sticking from their edges, and a patch of gangly weeds that crawled from the chipped red bricks onto a pot-holed alleyway.

After stepping onto Splitter Street, I looked up to see a paint-faded marquee that read "Transformer Towers." The building that supported this sign was in no better condition, like a cripple teetering on broken crutches. But prior to entering this structure, Ukiah wandered toward a corner newsstand that promoted an array of porno magazines, racing forms, and scandal sheets. A hand-scribbled banner hanging from two overhead metal poles read "Minella's News Shoppe." In addition, propped alongside an antiquated cash register, stood a small cardboard reminder that boasted: "You a steala oura stuff, we a breaka youra fingers."

Ukiah moved slowly toward an elderly gentleman who wore a shopkeeper's apron over his button-down shirt and khaki's.

"Salvatore, how are you?" my counterpart asked after extending his hand.

"Fine Ukiah, fine."

"How are your customers treating you?"

"All of them are paying just like they should."

"Very good. And how about your distributors? Are the magazines coming in according to schedule?"

"All but one, Ukiah. We might have to contact Mister Dubble across the water and remind him that certain deadlines are not being met."

"Very well, Salvatore. We'll talk later."

Ukiah parted ways with the senior citizen, leading me along a littered sidewalk toward the Transformer's main entrance. But instead of walking up its chipped concrete steps, Ukiah chose a side entrance that bordered a bar room.

"We'll go in this way," he mumbled. "Then we won't see the soaks panhandling for drinks in the lobby."

What was I getting involved in? Beggars, alchoholics, and bums blowing their social security checks on booze. And I couldn't be certain, but Ukiah and Mister Minella weren't talking about the trivialities of a corner newsstand. The net beginning to envelope me was undeniable. I could clearly read the words "TROUBLE" spelled out before me, but similar to an automaton being drawn toward its master, I couldn't alter my course. I entered Transformer Towers with open eyes, yet stumbled along blindly like a newborn kitten caught in a web.

If I thought the building's exterior was depressing, its interior was downright abysmal. Never before had I seen such bleakness and loss. Dozens of elderly men holding beer mugs in their wrinkled hands were meandering aimlessly along a narrow hallway leading to a bar. Unshaven, toothless, reeking like perspiration and arthritis medication, these desperate creatures were waiting for one last drink with a death-by-cirrhosis chaser.

Further along our trek towards Ukiah's room, we climbed a flight of stairs, then another. The aromas that filtered into my nose were unlike any others I had ever encountered, at least in one collective breath. I inhaled the acrid stench of urine, cooking grease, burnt food, stale beer, doused cigarettes, vomit, and one last intangible - that of poverty and depression. I apologize for the darkness of my descriptions, but to understand Ukiah, one must become acquainted with that which surrounded him. In other words, this world of stained carpeting, bloody walls, discarded cigarette butts, and unceasing decay was what he tolerated each day. I was no longer protected by suburban safety, office buildings, or tree-lined campus walkways. Ukiah's existence was certainly more brutal and unrelentingly morose, its mood far from being dreamy, cheery, or producing contentment. If one weren't on their toes every second of the day, The Transformer would swallow them whole without any possibility of escape.

We continued our climb up endless flights of stairs, a dump like this not equipped with the luxury of elevators. Finally, after reaching the seventh floor, Ukiah pointed to an open door and told me to proceed. It was hard to believe he would leave his door unlocked, let alone completely open. But there it was, a ready-made invitation for theft.

I entered Ukiah's apartment, which, in actuality, was more cramped than a pay-by-the-hour motel room. The only articles of furniture contained within his faded gray walls were a single bed, one chair, a cheap, rickety dresser, and a black lamp minus its shade. There was also one closed door, which presumably lead to a bathroom. Finally, a multi-colored banner hung defiantly from the wall overlooking Ukiah's bed, its graphic implications beyond my ability to describe. These meager furnishings were the extent of Ukiah's life - no refrigerator, no television, no washing machine, and no ironing board.

I gazed about my surroundings, then stepped toward the room's side window. As I waited for my host to return, I looked outside to the lot where I had parked my car. An aged woman in a plaid dress and pink sweater loitered alongside a Cadillac, tossing pebbles at an empty building with broken windows. Its walls were stained black from residue which filtered from a downspout, streaking a "No Parking" sign whose washed-out letters were barely legible.

I next peered alongside the building, its dull redbrick walls also stained from sulfurous orange and black residue. The fire escapes looked like they would crumble quicker than the paint that clung to their surface. Atop an adjacent roof, then, were ominous black exhaust ducts that hummed and rattled with the ferociousness of a blast furnace. Telephone wires and electrical lines were strung like spaghetti, while rusty pipes dripped sludge into open metal grates. Litter was strewn in every direction - beer cans on the fire escape, Styrofoam cups on the roof, and fast-food packets on the paint-chipped windowsills. Finally, to epitomize tenement life, ragged clothes hanging from nylon lines blew in the smoggy, fog-laced air. In all, Transformer Towers withheld a bleakness that was not suited for the weak of heart. Yes, this hellish hole was what Ukiah called home.

Gazing across the city, I was suddenly haunted by images that I would rather forget. The repetitive succession of grays and blacks triggered thoughts from childhood that made me shudder ... sleepwalking through the darkness, curled in a ball beneath the basement steps, huddled under a table with a blanket wrapping my feet ... my father's raised hand smacking my bare ass after I gouged my initials into a wooden desk in the cellar with a hammer and screwdriver ... the coldness of an oil-smeared garage floor, or screaming beneath the covers while trapped in another nightmare ...

Overtaken by nervousness, I started shaking as a novel sight emerged from the clouds. For the first time all morning, the sun broke free and shone with an overpowering brilliance. At precisely the same time, Ukiah strutted into his room holding a bucket of ice in one hand and an assortment of canned and bottled beer in the other. And, unlike his earlier silence, Ukiah now bubbled with a vibrant gregariousness.

After pouring the ice and beer into a plastic tub that he pulled from beneath his bed, my host exclaimed, "C'mon, grab a cold one! It's time to go go go."

Uncomfortable with this situation, I nonetheless twisted the top off a brown-colored bottle and slowly took a sip. Meanwhile, Ukiah tilted his head back to such an odd degree that the beer flowed down his throat as if it were a funnel.

Amazed, I blurted, "Do you usually drink this early in the morning?"

Not offended in the least, Ukiah smiled, drained his bottle, then simply answered,

"Yes."

I shook my head with disbelief as he popped his second beer and performed the same routine. This man would be with those other derelicts downstairs in a few years, loitering in the lobby and bumming spare change to buy another drink.

While I troubled myself with these thoughts, Ukiah leaped toward a cheap plastic cassette deck and pushed the play button, instantly producing a cacophony of noise.

"Did you ever hear this group?" he asked. "They're called the Yin-Yangs. It's their second album, called 'Split-Level'. They're fucking wild. Man, it's going to be a beautiful day," he then cheered, emphasizing the word beautiful.

After Ukiah jumped atop his bed and began springing up and down, beer splashing like a fountain, I realized that I had been lured into the clutches of a madman. I no longer had to worry about my life being boring and blasé. The unhinged figure before me guaranteed unlimited thrills and chills.

At song's end, Ukiah pushed the stop button, then sat on the floor beside his bed.

"So, whatta ya think?" he asked, retrieving a cigarette and lighter from his shirt pocket.

Unable to contain myself, I blurted, "Why do you live in this ... this shithole? It's not fit for a dog."

Howling with delight, Ukiah gushed, "Every dog should get fleas at least once in its life, then they'd know how good they have it after they're gone."

"But what if they never leave?" I prodded.

"Hmmm, I never thought about that. I suppose my glass, when used as a symbolic metaphor, is always half-full. If it weren't, I'd start getting worried," he assured me.

A symbolic metaphor? Where did Ukiah pull that concept? From the prize in a cereal box?

"Since you're in a questioning mood, what else do you want to know?" Ukiah sneered in a slightly taunting voice.

"Well, how much do you pay for this place?"

"Ten bucks."

"A month?"

"No. A day." Ukiah rolled his eyes at the foolishness of my response. "Just like motel rates. It comes to three hundred a month, in case your math isn't up to snuff."

"That's reasonable," I lied.

"What else? I'm an open book."

"Okay. This one's pretty personal."

"I like things that are pretty and personal. Let 'er rip."

"Where do you get your money? Do you have a job? I noticed you were talking shop with Mister Minella. I don't reckon you're in the magazine business."

"Hmm, quite perceptive," Ukiah joshed, swigging from his beer. "If you wanna know the truth, I work for Tattoo Blue."

"Tattoo Blue! He's the biggest mobster in town. Everyone knows that."

"They do, huh."

"Yes, they do. Why are you hanging out with a known criminal?"

"Why are you?"

"Why am I what?"

"Why are you hanging out with a known criminal?"

"What do you mean?"

"If Tattoo Blue is a known criminal, then so am I. And you're hanging out with me."

"But ... but I didn't know you were until now," I stammered.

"You're free to leave if you want," Ukiah motioned with his arm.

"But I don't want to."

"Then the matter is settled. Isn't life funny when you look at both sides of a coin instead of just one?"

Stumped, I sat motionless for a moment, then proceeded.

"What do you do for Salvatore?"

"I take care of business for him."

Fearlessly, but with respect, I asked swiftly, "Does that mean what I ...?"

Interrupting me, Ukiah responded, "Let's just say I make sure certain debts are paid on time. If I need to break a few thumbs, then so be it."

Perplexed by his admission, I countered, "Why are you telling me these things? What if I weren't trustworthy?"

"But you are."

"How can you be sure?"

"I know things. You're not the only perceptive person in this room."

"Perceptive?"

"Yeah, an ability to read people. It's like earlier when you picked me up. You're not the kind of person to even consider hitchhikers, let alone snag some stranger off the street. Yet here we are. You initiated our meeting. If it weren't for your needs, we would have never met."

"My needs? Really. Well, what are my needs?"

"That's easy. You were bored, wishing life wouldn't simply pass you by - the same old routine, the same rut that eventually gets most everyone. You couldn't bear one more day of it, so you brought me into your world. And once seeing me first hand, you were intrigued both physically and mentally ... even sexually."

Embarrassed, I sighed, "That's amazing. It's like you looked into a crystal ball."

"Nah, it's not nearly that complicated. Everyone is a crystal ball. All ya need to do is get past their defense mechanisms, beyond the facade, then interpret the pictures that surface from their subconscious."

"That's all it takes?" I asked.

"I'll show you. Look at my face. But don't just look at it - decipher it. What do you see?"

As rays of sunshine filtered through the window, I squinted, then commented profoundly, "I can't judge anything from your face. It's half bathed in light, and half concealed by shadows."

"Not good enough!" Ukiah yelled. "What do you see?"

Alarmed, I replied, "Well, there is a blemish."

"It's not a blemish. The damn thing is gigantic. Disgraceful. It's nearly a tumor! I can't even look at my own reflection. It's hideous and grotesque – maybe even cancerous."

I laughed giddily at his melodramatics, saying, "A tumor? It's nothing but a tiny mark. I hardly noticed it."

"Don't candy coat the situation," Ukiah demanded, popping another beer. "I could see this growth from a satellite. But that's all right. In a way, this tumor is the best thing that ever happened to me. At first, I was devastated when looking in the mirror. But a lotta times, salvation rises from the ashes of tragedy."

What in God's name was he talking about? Was he already drunk? The tragedy in question was merely a zit, a pimple. Ukiah made it into a life-threatening disease. Was he so self-centered that a simple blemish became a catastrophe? A tragedy? Hardly.

Hoping to change the subject, I asked, "So, what were you doing today when I saw you walking along the Parkway?"

After swallowing another mouthful of beer and lighting a cigarette, Ukiah replied, "Splitting up with my girlfriend. Or, should I say, being dumped by her. I would've driven home myself, but my car's in the shop getting inspected."

"Then the separation explains your earlier silence," I surmised.

"Partially. But I was more worried about whether that mechanic would notice the crack in my frame. Y'see, I usually take my car to Castor and Pollux on Division Avenue. They turn a blind eye to everything. But the law caught up with them, so now I'm on my own."

"That's too bad ... about your car and your girl," I said sympathetically. "Oh, by the way, what is that banner above your head supposed to mean?"

The poster I pointed to was a hand-painted creation teeming with splashy color. Essentially, it appeared to be a vicious serpent, tongue and fangs exposed, circled by a burning sun with flames and lightning bolts shooting from its core. With its mixture of reds, greens, oranges and yellows, it made quite an impression.

But Ukiah's response was enigmatic at best. He merely said, "That, dear friend, is my concept of creation."

"You painted it?"

"Actually, no. I designed the symbol, a tattoo artist perfected it, and a girl from my past painted it. The only thing she wanted from me was to sleep with her."

I stared with wonder at the symbol, imagining cracks of thunder, torrential winds, lightning flashes, comets, fireballs, and sunspots erupting across the heavens. The eternal void, blackened until that point, burst with fury as flames shot across the sky, the once calm ether now agitated by wondrous signs of life. Here on earth, tidal waves roared from the ocean, the ground quaked and divided, mountains spewed forth lava, trees were consumed by blazes, winds swirled in vicious circles, while snakes and dragons were pummeled with hellish pelts of hail. Yes, the ramifications of creation were quite profound.

While I daydreamed and Ukiah rose to grab another beer, I noticed an object that had thus far eluded my eye. Lying beneath a blanket alongside Ukiah's bed was a hard-cover book wrapped by plastic — the kind one would check out from a library.

Upon my host's return, I asked him about it.

"What is that book over there? Does it belong to you?"

"Ah, it's nothing," Ukiah shrugged sheepishly, averting his eyes.

"No, it's a library book," I jabbed good naturedly, not allowing him to change the subject. "Does it belong to you?"

Adopting the persona of a dim-witted Southerner with a drawn-out drawl, Ukiah cracked, "I cannn bare-lly reeead, leddda lone think. I'm jesss a dumm-ass backwards hillbilly."

"That's not true," I snapped, feigning anger. "Just a minute ago you mentioned meta-phoric symbolism. Now come clean. Lemme see it."

Ukiah tried to brush the book beneath his bed, but I reached over and snagged it.

"Hmmm, what do we have here? *A Dialectic Analysis of Twentieth Century Litera-ture.* Well, well, Ukiah, aren't we filled with surprises?"

"Whoever lived here before me must have forgotten it. I never even heard of Dianetics."

"It's Dialectics. You know full well what I'm talking about. So fess up. Spill the beans."

"All right, it's mine. Let's go downstairs and grab a beer. My treat."

"Not so fast. What are you doing with this book?"

Hemming and hawing, Ukiah finally confessed. "Okay, I'm a writer. Now you can laugh."

Straight-faced and serious, I said, "Why would I laugh? I think it's great. Why didn't you tell me earlier instead of playing that backwoods cracker act?"

Regaining his confidence, Ukiah replied, "I like people to underestimate me. That way, when I finally reach the big-time, they ain't gonna know what hit 'em."

"Wow. This's pretty wild. You're aiming for the top, huh?"

Gaining steam, Ukiah boasted, "I'm working on a book right now called *Blank Line* that's my masterpiece. After this novel, I'm done writing fiction. It's the end."

"The end?" I asked. "I don't understand. And what is *Blank Line* supposed to mean? Is there some secret message?"

"Don't worry about it. Just remember that every motherfuckin' author in this country better take cover, 'cause once I'm done with them, they'll never write again."

By this stage of the morning, or was it afternoon already, it was hard to tell, but I hadn't even finished my first beer. To the contrary, Ukiah had pounded at least a 6-pack, with no end in sight.

"But if I don't make it in two years," he continued, "I'm going out in a blaze of glory, and I'm taking a few motherfuckers with me."

In the matter of a few minutes, my impression of Ukiah went from that of being a down and dirty criminal to an embittered artist. He wasn't merely fighting through life, but a man whose mission, whose sole endeavor as a dedicated creator, was all consuming. He was countless times more serious than the poseurs who lollygagged through life pretending to be artists.

"Can't you see?" Ukiah asked desperately, "there's only one way out of this hole. I have to write my way to freedom. But fuck, nothing ever works for me. It's like I'm doomed. I need to become my own creator, my own ruler, my own God. And it's only through this fucking pen and paper that I can escape. But do you know what? The closer I get to being free, the more noticeable my ... my ... fuck. I can't even describe my frustrations, or how I can't escape the world."

"Don't get discouraged ..."

"Can't you see this sign on my face? This message from beyond? It was sent by a Muse who's telling me to get serious, or I'll never succeed. This woman demands absolute commitment - a complete surrender of my will to hers. But it's worth it, because I have only one purpose on this planet, and that's to get published. This's why, as an urgent reminder, Romlocon put her mark on my face. Can't you see? I need to step beyond the common and enter the annals of publishing history. If I don't make it, my entire life will have been a waste. Romlocon is calling me. Do I have what it takes to follow her?"

Ukiah emptied another can of beer, snatched a replacement from his rapidly melting tub of ice, then began a discourse that made my head spin.

"Over the last twenty years, the literary world has been injected with enough ennui to send it into a permanent coma."

"How so?" I asked, excited that I was being let in on a dark, guarded secret.

"Well," Ukiah began, focused. "We've all read that asshole Philip Prince, or Jackie Collins, James Michener and John Grisham, and each has risen to the top of their field. But when it comes to excitement, none of them, even Camille Paglia, bring a circus atmosphere to mind. The only personalities that pique the public's interest any more are movie stars, rock n' rollers, and sports figures. Shit, it's a sorry commentary when politicians are even more interesting than writers! Authors have gone the same route as sculptors, painters and philosophers - long forgotten by the past. But lo and behold," Ukiah chuckled, "I'm here to fix this situation."

The author's eyes hardened into a squint as I sat with rapt attention, amazed to be in Transformer Towers with this eccentric figure.

"Yeah, I'm going to become the most recognized writer of the 21st century. I also plan on saving the publishing industry, and becoming a spokesman for the new millennium. But sadly, I can't do anything until I'm famous."

Stupefied by Ukiah's outrageous claims, I blurted impulsively, "How many time have you been published?"

"None," he replied in a deadpan voice, an average man getting drunk in a diseased section of society's underbelly.

Continuing, I asked, "Have you ever tried to get published?"

"No, again," he admitted without delay. "I've never been read in books or magazines, but within the next decade, I'll publish more than any writer alive."

I listened with the attentiveness of a student under an ancient philosopher's wing, the world slowly drifting away until nothing existed except Ukiah's words. I was thrust into the midst of a man's dream, the entirety of his being. Obviously he had pondered these topics over and over again in his mind, possibly voicing them to me for the first time.

"Chris, you might think I'm trying to be a hot shot, but I'm not approaching the literary world like a novice with one book under their belt ... y'know, The Great American Novel ... then expecting to get their attention. No, over the past twelve years I've written 18 books that weigh a total of 57 pounds."

"57 pounds? That's incredible. Truly incredible," I said with amazement.

Impulsively, Ukiah bound from his seat to the floor and, while resting on his hands and knees, began digging manila envelopes from beneath his bed ... one after another ...

thick yellow packets stacked atop each other. After completing this maddening process, the envelopes stood at least two and a half feet high.

While panting for breath and chugging from a can of beer, Ukiah proclaimed, "There! Novels, novellas, poetry, fantasy, travelogues, a horror story, a play, suspense, straight dialogue, screenplays, a fairy tale, short stories, experimental prose, philosophy and correspondence.

"You wrote all that?"

"You got it. I'm 35 years old, live in a flophouse, harass deadbeats for a living, and drive a Chevy Celebrity with 203,000 miles. Knowing all that, I sit in my room at night and wonder what the fuck is going on. Why haven't I been discovered? I live in a medium-sized college town, but even though I'm this close to the ivory towers, I've educated myself. To hell with those university intellectuals, bathhouse poets, or isolated wordsmiths living on farms in New England. I can out write any of them. Better yet, I'm not genre impaired. I can write anything. So why am I still sitting in this dump getting drunk?"

Inspired by Ukiah's words, I jumped into the conversation.

"Maybe that's your problem. You're more concerned with getting drunk than you are with getting published. Wouldn't it be better to redirect you energies and let the world see your writing? You're the one who said you never even tried to get published."

As if struck by lightning, Ukiah's eyes lit up.

"You're right! I swear, Romlocon must have sent you from beyond. You're the one who's paving my way into the publishing world. You're the one who's delivering the message!"

Flattered, I blushed, then asked, "Did I hear you say you were 36 years old?"

"Yup, 36 a few months ago."

"That's hard to believe," I said, shaking my head. "I would have guessed mid-twenties, or younger. How do you do it?"

"Creation is the fountain of youth, baby! I'll never get old."

"This's incredible," I panted. "It's like I'm in the presence of ... of something spectacular."

"Now wait a minute, Chris. Don't inflate my ego too much! I never said I was a genius, but I do like that saying - the one about 10% being inspiration and the other 90% being perspiration. When ya get right down to it, I'm nothing but a bum sitting in a smelly room."

"But Ukiah, you could be so much more," I encouraged him, pointing to his stack of manuscripts.

"You're right, and that's what I'm going to show the world. I want every person on the street, at their jobs, or sitting at home to realize they can live their dreams to the fullest if they only put their minds to it and work their asses off. We don't have to settle for less. We can have it all. We just need to push our vision to the extreme. But most of us settle for less, just like me. But not any more. I'm not just a writer - I'm an industry! I have so many ideas that it'd take all year to describe them. The point I'm trying to make is this - do you remember when Jack Kerouac hit the scene and his publishers unleashed an onslaught of his material in rapid-fire succession? That's what I can do. Then, once the public gets a load o' me, my crazy train will never stop rolling!"

Dazzled by Ukiah's eloquence, I did notice an oversight in his presentation. So, at the risk of raining on his parade, I asked, "Won't the variety of your work be a problem? Society does have a way of compartmentalizing and labeling things by category. That way, when someone enters a bookstore or reads a review, they can call that person a horror, self-help, or science fiction writer."

Unfazed, Ukiah countered, "You have a point. But from my perspective, this problem won't be any trouble. If I use the media properly, and let the public see my vision, they'll definitely want to take a look at my books. I know this explanation is simplistic, but my diversity won't be a detriment. Instead, it's a benefit that can be exploited."

"In what way?"

"Well, anyone who becomes a public figure is always associated with their original claim to fame."

"In what sense?" I prodded, engaged by this discourse.

"Take Andy Warhol, for example. He was a painter, author, film director and musical producer; but to historians he'll always be a Pop Artist. Or more recently, look at Howard Stern. He's been a disc jockey, author, home video entrepreneur, hosted a television show, and is now a movie star. Hell, he could even start as quarterback for the New York Jets, but to the world he'll always be a shock jock!"

"Then what do you plan on doing with this stack of ... I don't even know what's in there."

"I see only one alternative. I need to publish my philosophy book first. That way, from day one, I can be taken seriously instead of as a run-of-the-mill novelist."

At that moment I shook my head in disbelief, wondering how I could have been so misled. Ukiah had impressed me so far ... but philosophy?

I didn't mean to sound sarcastic, but I declared, "What a blockbuster that should be. Let's look at the *New York Times* Bestseller List. Hmmm, no philosophy books are there. What a surprise."

I thought Ukiah would be rattled by this comment, but he casually lit another cigarette, sipped from his aluminum can, then commenced.

"Before jumping to conclusions, listen to my take on the situation. Historically, what has been the biggest problem with philosophers?"

"You can't read them."

"Exactly!" Ukiah replied. "Walk into a bookstore, stroll to the philosophy section, then choose any book and leaf through it. Most are so highbrow and boring that an average reader can't get past page two. Even the Grand Masters fall into this trap."

"And yours is different?" I concluded.

"Of course. Even though it covers psychology, religion, politics, conspiracy theory, sociology, and current events, not to mention all the brilliant minds throughout history, it's very accessible and marketable. I was careful not to fill it with the confusing mumbo jumbo that appeals to boorish academic types. No eggheads here, baby. Instead, this book was written for anyone with an interest in the world."

What was I getting involved in? Who was this outlandish man with the grandiose ideas? More importantly, what force had drawn me into his uninhabitable room? The entire scenario boggled my mind.

Not choosing to overstep my bounds, I timidly spoke.

"Do you really believe in this philosophy book?"

"Hell, yeah. It reads like a novel, exploring every avenue of philosophical thought, while unfolding with drama on each new page. It's funny, because I shadow box with the truth, dance around its edges, and bang my head until the very end. Eventually, every falsehood is put to rest as the ultimate truth emerges."

"And you plan on introducing yourself to the public with this book?"

"Once this book hits the shelves and my picture is on the covers of *The New York Times Book Review, Psychology Today, The Christian Science Monitor, Newsweek,* and *Rolling Stone*, I can assault the world with the rest of my arsenal. I'll be America's greatest overnight sensation," Ukiah proclaimed proudly, hoisting his beer can in the air.

Clearly, these were braggadocios claims for someone who had been writing for over a decade while never being published. Intrigued, I asked, "Ukiah, why haven't you ever tried to make it?"

With the directness of a shark, he answered excitedly, "In all honesty, if I had found fame in my youth, I'd be dead. As you can tell, I push myself pretty hard with the booze. And, being a student of pop culture who's researched all the greats, I understand my self-destructive tendencies. So, I vowed to never let fame destroy me like it did to Sam Kinison or Kurt Cobain. The only way I can make it is if I'm cleaner than a saint."

"But you're not, Ukiah. Your drinking is a ... I hate saying it, but a sickness."

"You're right, and that's why I'm quitting today. The cigarettes too."

"You're quitting, just like that?"

"Cold turkey. I'm going to keep getting ripped today, then I'm through."

"Can you do it?"

"Hell, I've been drinking since I was fifteen. But now Romlocon the Muse has called me. She's sent a message - this tumor on my face - and also a messenger - you. What could be clearer? Tomorrow I'm going to start finding an agent. But y'know, with as many books as I've written in my life, writing a letter to one of those bloodsuckers will be the most grueling exercise ever, even worse than laying off the booze."

"Why?"

"It boils down to the ugly concept of ego. Even though I've done it all day, I feel like a whore blowing my own horn. So, if I do prostitute myself, then that makes the agent my pimp. The way I see it, why should I keep groveling in the gutters when I can fuck in the clouds with all the other bigwigs?"

"It sounds intriguing," I said, "but what do you plan on doing?"

"I'm shooting for the top, baby, and need to devote myself entirely to writing. That's why it's so important to get published. Working full-time as a knuckle-breaker, then writing all night, doesn't cut it."

"Where do you plan on finding an agent?" I inquired, becoming wrapped-up in the drama.

"New York City, of course. The fucking world revolves around that place. I'm only afraid that once they find out where I'm from - Latera Heights - they'll think I'm a simple backwoods hick. But nothing could be further from the truth. The last thing I am is naive. I've been around the block enough times to realize that what I'm striving for won't come easy. In fact, they might even wonder if I'm ready to handle this action. But I'll tell ya, after assassinating a man, this is kids stuff. Becoming the most recognized writer alive is going to be a struggle, but I'm ready."

"Assassination?" I asked myself, subconsciously trying to block these words from my mind.

"What are you going to say to this agent?" I asked instead.

Buzzing with alcohol and excitement, Ukiah told me, "First of all, I'm finding a woman. I always open up easier with them. And what am I going to tell her? Basically, that I have the looks, the mouth, and the smarts to soar higher than anyone could imagine. I'll tell her to not simply read my words, but to feel them. Let them sink into her psyche. And don't just look at the photograph of me - absorb it into her soul. I'll tell her I'm the real thing, an undiscovered diamond in the rough; kind of unpolished, but with the potential to shine forever! By putting our heads together, we could take the world by storm and set it on fire! That's what I'll tell her."

"What if she doesn't buy it?"

"Then I'll rob a fucking bank," Ukiah snarled drunkenly, beer suds spilling from his lips, "if that's what it takes to start my own publishing company. And you're driving the getaway car. But what do I know about publishing?" Ukiah sighed. "All I can do is write."

Well, you know the rest of the story. It was at this point that the novel began. Ukiah threatened to pull a heist, even considering the possibility of killing a few bystanders if necessary.

So, a certain amount of trepidation filled me as I waited for Ukiah's return from the bathroom. He may have been boasting, but I believed him capable of, or already guilty of, murder. Why was I in such a predicament? And more importantly, how could I slip away without bodily harm? Time to ponder my alternatives had rapidly been erased, though, for Ukiah stormed into the room, heading directly for his ice-tub.

"Shit. We're out. Fuck!" he shouted ... no, roared would be a more apt description. "Did you drink all my fucking beer? Huh, did ya?"

Terrified, I stammered, "No ... nuh ... no. I only had one, had one."

Ukiah then smiled brightly and laughed with delight.

"C'mon, Chris, I was only kidding. And hey, no more literary talk, at least for today. How's that sound?"

"Fine with me," I grinned, waves of relief flooding my body.

Ukiah stumbled to his dresser, opening a drawer and pulling out a videocassette.

"I sure wish I could watch this tape," he said meekly, his voice laced with both sincerity and none-too-subtle manipulation. Was this man genuine, or a user who played on my naiveté and gracious nature?

Curious, I asked, "What's on the tape?"

"Oh, this," he replied absently, as if it didn't really matter. "Nothing but my kid's new band. They practiced the other night, but this time with a new lead singer. Usually he sends cassette tapes that I listen to in my car, but this one's on video. Too bad I don't have a VCR, or a TV for that matter."

"You have a kid?" I asked incredulously. "How old is he?"

"Sixteen. A junior in high school."

"Where does he live?"

"With his mom, about an hour and a half from here."

"That's amazing. You don't look old enough to graduate from college, let alone have a teenage son."

"Yeah, I started young," Ukiah said before laying the final blow. "I wonder how they sound? I'll bet my kid wrote some great new songs. Oh well, I'll watch it later. Maybe I'll rent a TV/VCR from the video shop sometime."

"If you want," I offered, "we could ride to my place. Believe it or not, I have a TV and a VCR. The wonders of modern technology. Go figure."

"No shit. You'd do that for me, Chris? You're wonderful. I won't be interfering with anything?"

"Nah, I'll sleep later in the day."

"Cool. Let's go. We'll stop downstairs at the bar for a six-pack along the way."

"Okay. I'll meet you in a minute. I'm going to use the bathroom, if that's okay."

"Sure. Meet you in the lobby."

As Ukiah left his apartment, I inched toward his stack of manila envelopes and, while looking to and fro, snuck one of the packets beneath a windbreaker that I folded over my arm. Then, walking from the premises with the guilt of a thief, I entered the hallway of Transformer Towers, leaving Ukiah's door opened behind me.

After replenishing our beer supply and sidestepping puddles in the littered alleyway, Ukiah and I slid into my Gemini, heading toward the bypass that circled Latera Heights. Fifteen minutes down the road we'd reach my quaint abode in Halfmoon Acres. Or so I thought.

Riding shotgun, with his son's videotape in hand (as if it were a guarded relic or a prized heirloom), Ukiah twisted the top from another beer and chugged it. Needless to say, I felt a certain apprehension when viewing this act, not cherishing the thought of explaining his antics to a police officer. Ukiah was oblivious, though; looking relaxed in blue jeans and a black-and-white checkered pullover shirt. He sipped yet again from his bottle, smiling while unrolling his window.

"Hey, does the radio work in this old gal?"

"Sure, turn it on if you'd like," I cringed, eyes on the road and hands firmly gripping the steering wheel.

Ukiah pushed buttons and fumbled with the knobs, finally deciding on W-A-I-F, a station that played cutting-edge rock n' roll. I had listened to it once or twice in the past, but my tastes swayed more toward easy listening music. The last thing I wanted when driving was an onslaught of wailing voices and screeching guitars. But Ukiah was a different story. Almost immediately he began rapping his fingers on the dashboard and tapping both feet.

"All right! What more could we ask for?" he yelled above the music. "A breezy autumn day, plenty of booze, and some cool tunes while we're rolling down the highway. Ya can't beat it."

I had my doubts. To me, driving was a necessary evil ... a means of getting from point A to point B. The quicker this task was accomplished, the better I felt.

"I'll tell ya, if I had my way, this car'd sprout wings and we'd fly straight into the sun. Wouldn't that be one helluva way to go?" Ukiah shouted. "Whatta ya think?"

"I like four wheels on the ground," was my timid response.

"Aw, c'mon. Just think how great it'd be to fly like a bird, soaring through the sky, swooping past trees, and gliding along a cloudbank."

After exiting the city limits, I flicked my turn signal and was about to hit the bypass on-ramp when a troubling sight caught my eye. Ukiah hadn't taken the necessary safety precautions after getting in my car.

Concerned, I asked, "Aren't you going to buckle your seat belt?"

Roaring, Ukiah replied, "Hell no. I don't like things holding me back."

"But what if ..."

"I don't wear rings, watches, chains, or underwear. Why would I strap a seatbelt around me? I need to be loose, baby. I need to be free. So let's go. C'mon. We don't have all day. Push that pedal. Go Go. Oh hey, cool. Listen to this tune on the radio.

It's a song by The Halves called 'Action/Reaction.' Turn it up!"

Ukiah was unrestrained in his enjoyment, abandoning himself to an afternoon filled with sweet-smelling breezes, loud music, and rivers of beer at high-speeds on the bypass.

Suddenly, he exploded with excitement. "Look at that car over there. They wanna race. C'mon, let's give 'em a go."

"I don't think so ... not today ..."

"What are you talking about, Chris? They're laying down the gauntlet. They're challenging you. We can't back away. Let this fucker roar!"

Instantaneously, as if prompted by a demon, I slammed my gas pedal to the floor and edged closer to the car ahead of us. Being unconcerned with such matters, I didn't even know its make or model. All I could see were blurring white lines beneath my wheels, and trees reeling past at increasingly rapid speeds.

"That's it, go go, more more," Ukiah squealed. "You have 'em. Don't let go now. Cut 'er loose."

I had never driven so fast in my life. What was I doing? The steering wheel vibrated in my hand as the Gemini quaked and rattled along the freeway. What if a cop stopped me? What if I lost control? 60 miles an hour ... heart beating faster, eyes frozen wide ... 65 ... foot twitching, body getting tense as blood gushed through each vein at an amazing rate ... 70 ... feeling nervous - going much too fast ... 75... the Gemini shaking and swerving about the highway, each bump and ripple on the road's surface magnified tenfold ... 80 ... hanging on for dear life ... losing control ... too much speed ... 85 ... I'm going to wreck ... 90 ... the car's going to fly off its hinges and we'll be splattered into bloody messes along the highway ... I'm losing control!

"Push it baby, push it! Look at 'em over there, eyes bulging wide, screaming. They can't keep up. Don't back off now. Stomp it one more time and drive a stake through their heart. I can see 'em shaking with fear. Don't let 'em off the hook. Crank it. C'mon. Go. Blow Blow Blow. Let loose, Chris. We have 'em!"

I felt like crying and screaming wildly at the same time. Holy shit! I was alive. I was on fire. This is what it meant to live life in the fast lane. Ukiah was right. I did want to lift-off the ground and drive straight into the sun. To hell with playing it safe. I was going to sprout wings and soar above the clouds, leaving behind anything that re-sembled normalcy or inhibition. I was gone ... gone!

"You did it Chris, you did it. Look in your rear-view mirror. That old eight-banger backed-down. They're turning off. You took 'em! Yes! Yes Yes Yes."

> *"Let's rip this bitch off of the wall on 96.9, The WAIF,*
> *your bastard stepchild radio station."*

After gearing down to 70, 60, then a steady 55, I shook my head and turned to Ukiah, who kept gulping beer and rocking to the radio.

"That was stupid," I hollered. "What if the cops had nabbed us? Or worse, what if I had lost control and slammed into a telephone pole? Then what would we have done? And you're not even wearing a seatbelt."

"Then the sun'd swallow us whole. What's the big deal?"

"What's the big deal? What we just did was so irresponsible that I'm ashamed to have been behind the wheel."

"Oh Chrissy, Chrissy. Pay attention to what just happened. You threw away your chains and experienced the joy of pure speed. Can't you see? Movement equals freedom - the faster the better. Who needs moss growing on their ass? Not me."

"But what if something terrible had happened?" I retorted.

After emptying another beer, Ukiah proceeded.

"Let me explain. I once had a cat that was supposed to be kept indoors. But guess what."

"You let it outside."

"Exactly. That bastard ran free and enjoyed life more than any other creature I'd ever seen. But everyone told me, 'he's going to get run over by a car, then it'll be your fault.' Well, whatta ya think happened?"

"The cat got hit by a car."

"Right again."

"Didn't you feel awful?"

"Of course, and everyone blamed me. But until it got squashed, that damn cat lived life to the fullest. He raced through the woods and across the meadow, laughing and squealing with joy. For me to have shackled him inside a house would have been a crime."

"But he'd still be alive."

"Would he? Not living life to the fullest. I disagree. He was only alive in his element - being free! To place restraints on that freedom for the sake of protecting his life would be nothing but selfishness. If taken one step further, how many parents do this to their children? And how often do the governing bodies that control society perform this very same role? We've allowed ourselves to be molly-coddled into a submissive state of cowardice because others assume they know better than us how we should lead our lives. Well, I'm saying to hell with them. I'm breaking the windows, sawing through the bars of my cell, and living life all the way."

Ukiah paused, then pointed, "There's the turnoff for Halfmoon Acres."

We soon rolled onto Reflection Alley, then into my unpaved driveway; Ukiah's eyes brightening at the sight of my spread.

"You live here?" he asked, noticeably impressed.

I was about to answer when I caught a glimpse of the stolen yellow envelope sliding free of my windbreaker in the backseat. It must have slipped out during our frenzied joyride.

Nervously, I coughed, "Yeah, c'mon. I'll show you around. It really isn't much. Oh, hey, look over there, a peacock in full-bloom."

As Ukiah stepped from the Gemini and gazed about, I hurriedly slid the envelope beneath my jacket, then rushed toward the front door. After fumbling to put my key in the lock, I disappeared inside.

After safely depositing the stolen manuscript, I walked outside, relieved that my theft had gone unnoticed.

"So, you're pulling a fast one on 'ol Ukiah," my guest said suspiciously.

"What? I don't know what you're talking about. I didn't take ..."

"There aren't any peacocks around here, are there?"

"Oh, that. Nah, I was just pulling your leg. Got ya!" I laughed.

"Yeah, you did. Lemme grab my beer and videotape, then show me around your place."

After doing so, Ukiah and I circled my home, passing two lilac bushes whose purple flowers had long since bloomed and fallen away.

"Your place is gorgeous," he said dreamily. "Look over there. That maple tree must be three hundred years old. What a sight. And all the land. How much is there?"

"Only half an acre."

"It seems like more."

"Probably because of the woods out back."

"Hey, who owns that place beside the meadow?

"The guest house? That's also mine."

"Shit. You have it made. Sunflowers, catnip, and three birdfeeders lining your eave. You own a little chunk of paradise."

"It is nice. I like sitting on the porch and watching the birds - blue jays, cardinals, morning doves, barn swallows, and regular old robins. You were right."

"About what?"

"Being a bird. I'd give anything to fly like they do."

"Now you're talking. C'mon, show me around inside."

The interior of my place was simple at best - a nondescript kitchen, a living room with three couches, a TV and stereo, plus two hidden bedrooms down a narrow hallway. I wish a more complete description could be given, but my place, similar to my life, was rather uninspired. I contented myself with the bare essentials and a fairly monotonous routine, leaving imagination for others.

Ukiah stepped toward my television set, which sat on a wooden shelf, then turned it on, instantly creating an array of colorful images. Staring with a child's wonder, he observed, "I guess I take the modern world for granted except for times like these."

"Here," he subsequently said, handing me the videocassette. "I don't even know how this contraption works."

I slid his tape into the machine, then pressed a few buttons. Within seconds, four teenage boys appeared on my screen, producing music that, despite its poor production value, was undoubtedly impressive. The tape's sound quality left much to be desired, as did its visuals, but none of these factors detracted from the band's talent. They performed in what appeared to be a garage, or attic, or spare utility room - its unfinished walls plastered with rock 'n roll posters and beer signs.

But a hardwood floor and naked light bulbs weren't my primary interest. Instead, I focused on the band, which consisted of a lead singer, guitarist, bassist and drummer. The music they played was reminiscent of WAIF - a power-punk sound mixed with elements of upbeat pop. I listened with rapt attention as the band leaped from one song to another, all of them lasting less than three minutes.

The members themselves consisted of a drummer, who was hidden from view, and a bassist who stood motionless in the shadows. The lead guitarist, also singing background vocals, bound about the room, adjusting knobs on each amplifier, and experimenting with the most rudimentary of rock 'n roll poses. From my limited experience with music, it was easy to tell that this kid held the band together. Finally, the lead singer was the group's obvious showman. With streaked, short brown hair dippity-doed into geri-curl horns, he stomped, jumped, twirled and thrust himself at the camera, aping about with the charisma of a seasoned television performer. The kid sang each song with vigor, belting out lyrics in a voice that combined both a harmonious lyricism and power-driven aggression. While singing, this young man closed his eyes, then stared toward the ceiling, producing a visual effect that was quite stunning.

Overall, even though I never considered myself a fan of such music, I found my feet tapping and body swaying to the catchy beat. It was then that I glanced at Ukiah, who sat only feet from the TV. No longer gulping beer at a torrid pace, he was instead fixated by the video, absorbing its presence. And then it struck me. Never before had I seen such love and unconcealed pride. The joy radiating from Ukiah's face was contagious, filling the room with an aura of relaxed contentment. I could not believe what was happening. Here was a hardened skid-row alcoholic – a man who clearly promoted his down n' dirty image - now exhibiting a tenderness that nearly made me cry. Who was this guy?

After eight or nine fast-paced numbers, the tape abruptly came to an end. As it did so, Ukiah broke into a spontaneous round of applause that echoed off the walls.

"Yes! Great. What a show," he cheered, even though their performance was only a rehearsal. "What did you think?"

"They're great. The best band I've heard in ages," I said sincerely. "Which one was your son?"

"Japhy's the guitarist and background vocalist. In his other band, he's also the lead guitarist and lead singer. Plus he writes all the music for each band, and most of the lyrics. He's a talented kid."

"I'll say. It's easy to see you're quite proud of him."

"Immensely."

"What's the name of his band?" I asked.

"Mirror Image."

"And where does Japhy live?" I pried, hoping he didn't say at The Towers with him.

"I already told you. With his mother, about an hour and a half from here."

"I'm sorry. It's been a hectic day. How often do you see him?"

"Regularly, especially since he started driving."

"That's great. I take it you're no longer with his mother."

"Divorced."

"All right then," I finally apologized, delighted by his response. "That's the end of my interrogation."

"You don't need to feel sorry," Ukiah assured me. "I'm an open book. You can ask anything you'd like. But, in all honesty, I should get home and call the mechanic about my car. Would it be a pain in the ass to give me a lift into town?"

"No, not at all. This day has been a blast. I usually do nothing but hang around here, then sleep all afternoon. Let's go."

"You better put your driving boots on, though, ya never know what we'll find on the bypass."

I froze at that point, then saw Ukiah burst into peels of laughter.

"Just kidding," he smiled. "I'll just finish my last beer and listen to the radio."

During our return trip, I asked Ukiah if Mirror Image performed live yet. He told me they still wanted to polish their act and tighten a few songs, but they were almost ready. In fact, Ukiah said he contacted a music teacher at the local high school who assured him that Mirror Image could play at one of their afternoon performances in front of the student body. Ukiah seemed especially excited about this prospect, due in no small part to his enthusiastic support of the band. He continued to talk about them the entire trip, a gentle tenderness in his voice that conveyed a special bond with his son. Finally, at Transformer Towers, I deposited Ukiah among the hookers, drug-dealers, vaga-bonds, and mental patients. It was a shame to see him wander among such people, but at least our farewell was rewarding. My newfound acquaintance told me that if I ever saw him straggling along the highway, feel free to stop. And then, with a sadness permeating my body, I watched Ukiah wander past the mud-filled potholes and litter, uncertain whether our paths would ever cross again.

While driving home, I felt a crushing sense of loss coursing through my veins. I had only spent half a day with Mister Ukiah ... hell, I didn't even know his last name. So why did I feel such a crushing emptiness? I'm sure Ukiah didn't suffer the same way. He may not have asked me a single question all morning or afternoon. So why did I become so attached to him? I was hardly a social being. I never dated, rarely went to parties, didn't hangout at bars, and shied away from lasting relationships. Indeed, I'd always felt freakish being a loner – as one so far removed from the norm. But then I saw Ukiah, who not only lived the same type lifestyle, but relished it, taking pride in the fact that he walked alone. While I saw myself as an oddity on the societal fringe, my sidekick cherished such a role - epitomizing the dark, solitary figure surviving apart from the mainstream.

Then again, Ukiah proved to be more than a degenerate. Admittedly, he exhibited an array of alcoholic traits, and whether he had the willpower to drop these tendencies remained to be seen. But the man was an author, writing 18 books that weighed 57 pounds. He also enjoyed a relationship with Japhy that exceeded those of most fathers and teenage sons. So why was he living in Transformer Towers, working for the infamous Tattoo Blue? Most likely, these questions would linger unresolved inside my mind, for I doubted Ukiah and I would ever be together again like we were today. As it stood, our chance encounter would probably never be repeated.

Disappointed by this prospect, I slowly pulled into my driveway, allowing the Gemini to idle a moment before shutting it down - a feeble attempt, I suppose, at clinging to the final vestige of my day. Then, as I walked toward the house, I noticed an alarming sight. My front door, which I always locked, stood wide open. I instantly feared burglarization, then remembered leaving it ajar before driving Ukiah home. What was I doing? I couldn't understand my motives, but the implications were riveting.

Still shaken, I stepped inside to see if anything had been stolen. Assured that everything was intact, I instinctively walked to the refrigerator and reached for my customary two eggs. But then I withdrew my hand and vowed to never again be a prisoner of routine. From now on, I would abandon my standard pattern - no more hard-boiled eggs at 2:00, no talk shows at 3:00, and no afternoon naps before supper. Today marked the beginning of spontaneity, irregularity, and a departure from the norm. So, as I reached for a pepperoni stick and a bagel rather than my usual eggs, I thought of Ukiah and instantly became excited. My life had been changed ... I would never be the same.

2

Miss Jennifer Ewen, my dearest loveliness. I gaze at the classy, gold-embossed capital letters that adorn our nameplate, then glide my tiny fingers with green painted nails across its slightly indented surface. Miss Jennifer Ewen - Literary Agent. The dignified title constantly reminds me of the ruse we perpetrate on a daily basis. This nameplate, which sits atop my mirror-finished mahogany desk, lends credence to an otherwise deceitful scheme. Miss Jennifer Ewen - Jenn to my friends. Jenn Ewen. Genuine. Yes indeed, Missy, you are genuine. A genuine mental case.

Look at the world that has opened its doors to you. A splendid suite at the esteemed Mason Turner Agency in New York City. My beautiful darling, your office is more spacious than the squalid apartments of those struggling artists who vie for your attention. You can lie on a gray suede couch whenever the mood strikes you, or sip whiskey from crystal jiggers as you dance around in fishnet and slippers on zebra-striped shag carpeting. My classy little lady, look around. Bask in the bounty of affluence and taste. The paupers forty stories below would grovel for your lot in life. You've made it honey - influence, prestige, a toast of the town. Cast your twinkling eyes on the city that flickers with wickedness and wealth below your picture window, each skyscraper possessing the perfection of a chess piece that maintains its proper order without needing to be moved.

Jennifer, look at yourself in the mirror. At fifty-four years of age, you could pass for thirty. You're gorgeous, honey, a striking middle-aged woman with her hair pulled back behind one ear in a flirtatious way that conveys teenage playfulness. Smile darling; imagine someone removing that choker from your neck, then kissing and licking ... but no. My suitors must stay away. They're much too dangerous. They only have one thing in mind. You know that blossoming flowers wither beneath the weeds that strangle them, or prick them with unwanted advances. You'll be nothing but a wilted rose that lost her elegance and vitality.

O Jennifer, such a gorgeous spectacle you've made of this life. Jennifer Ewen - Literary Agent. Jennifer Ewen - impostor. Your career has been nothing but a scam. Luckily, certain arrangements were made in return for your silence. Now our kissable lips and sensuous mouth must remain sealed, concealing a secret that covers our lack of literary expertise.

Dearest love, how did you get involved in this charade? How could you have forsaken your youth to live a nightmarish lie? How could you trade such a prized possession for these superficial wishes? Was it all worthwhile? The answer is obvious. You replaced meaning and substance with hollowness and falsehood. Look around. Nothing exists up here in the clouds of New York City.

You see the images that flicker in our rear-view mirror. We try to forget them, but their haunting regularity never allows a moment's peace. Oh Jennifer, how we yearn for that which is gone. But the longing never ceases, leading us into lands of abandonment and sadness. Regrettably, the tears are ever present, falling unnoticed as the world passes by.

"Miss Ewen, just a reminder that you will be meeting with management in twenty minutes," a voice from the telephone intercom declares.

No, it can't be. Did I subconsciously block this meeting from my mind, or deliberately overlook it? You're not prepared, Sweety. You never are. All of them will be snickering, whispering, or shaking their heads at our incompetence. Oh God, it's starting. Please make it stop. Okay, just settle down. Breathe. You're not going to vomit. Settle down. Phew phew. There. You'll be better. Those people are going to question you on sales projections and new literary prospects, and what will you tell them? You haven't contributed one dollar to this company's growth since you started thirty years ago. It's all been a farce. What am I going to do? Just hold it back. Don't puke now. You'll be all right. Settle down. Oh God, it's going to happen.

"Lola, could we reschedule this meeting?" I asked my secretary over our personal intercom.

"No, ma'am. You've already postponed it twice. I can't imagine any of the bigwigs being pleased with a third cancellation."

There's no escape. I'm trapped. What'll happen if I'm forced to flee gagging from the meeting like I did last time, then spew chunks of my stomach into the water fountain? I can feel it coming. Breathe, breathe. Take a drink of water. Better yet, how about a shot? That'll settle you down. But nothing will relieve me. I know it's coming. Look at yourself; sweat dripping from your forehead ... mind spinning ... blood gushing like pistons through your veins. Your blood vessels are actually expanding. I can feel them.

Why did you run? This catastrophe would have never happened. I can't go to that meeting. How can I get out of it? I'm going to burst. What if vomit spews from my mouth all over the conference table? I'll be gagging and bawling without excuse, then each of them will see how crazy I am. How could I have left without notice? The guilt is killing me.

Stop. Please stop. I beg of you, evil demon, get out of my body. Be gone. I promise to do better in the future. Squeeze your wrists, Jennifer. Stop the blood flow. I'm going to erupt. Take another swig of whiskey. I'm going to die. What an embarrass-ment. There's no air left in my chest. Breathe. Breathe. In, out. I can't function. How am I supposed to meet with these people? I'm a cripple, both emotionally and physically.

Oh, baby, lie on the floor and close your eyes. Curl into a tuck. I can see the face that haunts me. C'mon, please please, keep it under control. Don't puke. Don't vomit. You won't gag. It'll be fine. But what about my nonexistent reports? The board members will be expecting information. What should I tell them? The meeting will be a disaster. I'll finally be exposed. Where can I run? Everything's twirling. The pressure's building. Stop the blood. My heart is beating too rapidly. Here it comes. You're going to gag. You're swimming. Drowning. What can you do? Help me. Get away from me. I won't even be able to speak. The only thing that will come out of my mouth is a stream of vomit on the table, on my dress, on all the reports, and even on them. It's finally time. I can't hide any more. Here it comes. Don't pass out, don't faint. Keep calm, keep calm. You'll be fine.

"Miss Ewen, the board members are asking about your delay. They can't begin their meeting until you are present."

An extended silence.

"Miss Ewen, are you there?"

Don't puke now. Just keep your cool.

"Yes Lola, I'm here."

"Are you feeling okay? You sound ..."

"Tell them I'll be there momentarily."

This is it. There's no turning back now. Everything's a swirl ... Oh, Jennifer, grow up. You're fifty-four years old and still plagued by imaginary demons. Now stop it. I can't. I'm going to puke. Oh God, or whatever spirits can hear me, make it end. I'm going to explode. The tension is too powerful. I can't handle the responsibility. I can't ... I can't ... I can't catch my breath. The pressure is building inside. I can't deal with it. I can't face those people. What am I going to do? Please leave me. I'm not going to make it. I'm falling. Here it comes ... no no, please ... ahh, I can't continue ...

"Miss Ewen, your associates are becoming quite agitated and impatient ... ... Miss Ewen?"

3

Nothing could thrill me more than today's arrival. I knew that good-for-nothin' kid o' mine would crawl back begging to be bailed out. Chris was never able to stand alone, or be self-sufficient. Now look. All I see is a stranded orphan child sitting before me. It's hard to even call this individual an adult, because Chris acts more like a helpless infant.

"Dammit, stop fumbling with your napkin. It's making me nervous!"

"S.. sorry, Dad."

"Lena, why didn't you teach that lousy kid o' yours some manners?"

"You're right, honey, I should have raised our child better."

That woman doesn't love me, but she sure as hell knows how to follow orders. That's the mark of a good wife. Know your role, keep your yap shut, and spread those legs once in a while.

"So Chris, why in God's name did you invite your mother and me to this fancy restaurant? Lemme guess. Your car won't start?"

"No Dad, that's not it. Actually ..."

"Then I know. You defaulted on your student loan."

"No ..."

"What is it, Chris? Oh shit, don't tell me. You want to move back home. Can't cut it on your own, huh? Why else would we be sitting in a swanky restaurant like The Siamese Room? Look at this place. I can't afford to pay the prices at this ritzy joint."

"Actually, I'm treating you and mom ..."

"Some people have to actually work for a living. Unlike you, I can't sit around all night punching little numbers into a computer. I'm the man who actually designed those computers you operate. Did you know that before I retired, I was the most important employee at Halftone Incorporated? They didn't pay me enough, that's for damn sure, but they couldn't have functioned without me. I held that company together. I was ... what's that word ...?"

"... Indispensable, honey."

"That's right, Lena. I was indispensable! I'll bet you can't say that where you work, can you, Chris?"

"No, Dad, I'm certainly replaceable."

"Just as I thought. Not many people have what it takes to hold a position with the importance of mine. Halftone would have fallen apart without me. I always gave Chris a shining example to live up to, didn't I Lena?"

"You sure did, Norb. Your child always viewed you as a ..."

"Okay honey, we get the message. Now Chris, what rattled your cage? Why are we here?"

"Nothing's ... nothing's rattled me, I ..."

"Oh no, could it be? You're getting married."

"Not exactly ..."

"I should've known better. I'll probably never sit in a church and watch you exchange vows. And what about your poor mother? You know how choked-up she gets over those things. Are you even dating anyone?"

"No, not at the mo ..."

"It's a lost cause. I'll tell ya, why'd we even waste our time with this kid? You'll never get married, and your income hasn't risen in five years. Next thing you'll tell me is that you're..."

"Dad, please! I invited you and mom to The Siamese Room for a special reason."

"Jeez. Don't throw such a hissy-fit. Spit it out."

"Mom, Dad ... A couple of weeks ago I bought a house."

"Oh shit, what a catastrophe this is going to be. Do you remember that apartment you rented on Alter Street? You couldn't meet the payments, so six months later you crawled back to me like a wounded cat. Lena, do you remember that incident?"

"It was very sad."

"Now a house. Whatever possessed you?"

"I've been saving money, and feel comfortable that I'll be able to ..."

"What if the toilet leaks, or your hot water heater quits working? Do you know how to repair a faulty electrical panel, or replace a heating element on your stove? Huh, do you? I can fix all those things, but can you?"

"No, Dad, I can't. And do you know why?"

"Because you never had any common sense."

"No, Dad, it's because you never taught me. You could fix anything, but I ..."

"Good evening folks. My name is Lorelei, and tonight I'll be your server. Are we ready to order?

"Yes, sweety, I'd like a steak dinner with au gratin potatoes and broccoli."

"Very good, sir. And you, ma'am?"

"I'd like ..."

"My wife will settle for the meatloaf. Is that your special?"

"Yes sir."

The waitress turned her attention to Chris, and then I knew we were in trouble. That wishy-washy kid of mine hasn't been able to make a decision since childhood.

"I'd like ... um ... I can't quite decide. Let's see ... everything looks delicious. Maybe I should ... no ... how about ... could we have more time?"

"Of course ..."

"No, we're ready to eat now. Chris, quit fumbling with your menu and biting your fingernails. Now order, dammit, or we're leaving."

"But ... but. I'll have the same thing as my father."

"A wise choice. Your meals will be ready shortly."

"Chris, why do you embarrass us every time we go somewhere? It's a chore to even be seen with you in public. No wonder you're an only child. I was afraid we'd mess up worse the second time."

"I'm sorry, Dad ..."

"Apologies won't cover the shame you put me through. Do you remember the last time we dined together? It took you ten minutes to order. I thought you'd piss your pants with nervousness."

"It's just because you ... you frighten me, Dad."

"I frighten you. Quit being such a baby. How old are you, twenty-seven?"

"I'm thirty-three, Dad."

"He's thirty-three? Lena, when did that happen?"

"Dad, a lot happens that you never notice."

"Don't even think about getting smart with me, Chris Edwards. You may be in your thirties, but you're not too old to still go over my knee. And don't think I won't do it right here inside this restaurant."

"That's it! I've tried my best to be cordial, but it's no use. I'm leaving."

"Chris, sit down this instance, or so help me ..."

"No, Dad, I've had my fill of your shit. Mom, I'm sorry, but I can't tolerate him any more. He's all yours."

Can you imagine how disheartening it is to be belittled by a family member, particularly your own father? The experience is excruciating. But this incident in the restaurant was certainly not the first. His systematic debilitation of me began at birth, and continued to this day.

I had hoped for an enjoyable dinner with my parents at The Siamese Room, but naturally my expectations were ruined. Here I was, thirty-three years old, and the recent owner of a modest home. I maintained gainful employment, broke no laws (except for speeding on the bypass), and felt I made an adequate contribution to society. Why couldn't my father accept me as a quiet loner rather that an insignificant object of to be squashed beneath his feet?

I apologize for sounding so whiny, but once one's hopes have been diminished, another chunk of life slowly slips into the wind. Oh, how I longed for an enjoyable evening. I naively pictured this night as being perfect, with everything running smoothly. The Siamese Room could not provide a more pleasant atmosphere, with picturesque, floral-designed walls and high-backed hickory booths that insured privacy. As I arrived early and sat at our reserved table, the place settings were divine - pink folded napkins, polished sterling silver, and hand-painted yellow plates. Lastly, an arrangement of daffodils and daisies sat beside a shimmering candle that emitted soft yellow light.

I wanted the mood to be perfect, but feared a replay of our last dinner engagement -

the one my father alluded to earlier. Indeed, after landing my first apartment, I did run short on funds, and was then reduced to crawling back into the family fold on my hands and knees. The scene was dismal at best. My father, an absolute control freak, craved my helplessness like a leopard about to devour a fawn. This man sustained his existence with a need for power ... a power that feasted on another's dependence. My father's arrogance increased in proportion to how much someone groveled below him. He was sick, and his sickness only grew worse in the company of weakness.

As we sat years ago in that low-lit diner, I recalled the horrors that unfolded around me - my father looming with the presence of a general, my mother trembling and disconnected. I merely cringed at the notion of being a feeble spoke in my father's wheel of misfortune.

"I knew," he bellowed, the veins on each temple bulging, "that you were a failure. Ever since birth it was clear. You never had what it took to cut it. Now you're begging for money. I should have known you'd amount to nothing. You've never been able to make up your mind about anything."

The abuse continued endlessly, unreeling from my father's mouth like sheet music from a player piano. The humiliation on that day alone was so severe that it never left my memory. It burned like a hideous brand on my psyche, a lingering scar that will never be forgotten. Are you able to understand the direct infliction of pain by one who is supposed to love you? It stings to the core of one's being. Nothing ever satisfied that man, especially where I was concerned. To crawl back in such a reduced state was the final straw that crushed my facade of self-worth. After begging at his feet for help, I vowed to never again be placed in such a position. From that day forward I would stand apart - never subjected to anyone's tyranny or disdain.

And, you may wonder, what about my mother. Where did she fit into this dysfunctional family? In actuality, though I loved her dearly, she cannot be freed from blame. Why? Because her inherent weakness fueled my father's ruthlessness, enabling him to pursue me with increasing streaks of meanness. I can't believe these two were even married. Oh sure, they bore a child, owned a home, and belonged to the P.T.A. But my father was so remote and cold ... so impersonal; and my mother never progressed from being a doormat at his feet. I often prayed in bed at night that they would divorce ... hell, I even prayed for my father's death so that Mom and me could escape his spell. But it never happened. His spite was too strong for such happy endings.

Although I've spoken derogatorily about my father, during my youth I held a god-like reverence for him. That man was larger than life, and even now, retired, he could still inspire fear in someone. All it took was a nasty glance, a hardening of his eyes, or a single word uttered with enough negativity to make them cringe in their shoes.

Why did my father have such a desire for dominance and senseless aggression? I've asked myself that question many times, and it boils down to the concept of insecurity. This notion may sound ludicrous, particularly after the brief description I've given. How could this powerful man with an iron fist possibly suffer from insecurity? To be quite honest, I can't give an answer. All I can say is that he yearned for power to such a degree that the thought of me surpassing him in any way was unbearable. But I never wanted to be greater than him. I only asked for one thing, and that was love. Regrettably, I never received an inkling of this emotion.

Rather than gliding carelessly through childhood, I experienced the traumas of a journey through hell while being carried kicking and screaming in the arms of a demon. Lying in bed at night proved to be the most trying time of my still short life. Inconceivable images were triggered that sent me orbiting into the depths of despair.

My father, giant-sized, towered over me; a plethora of eyeballs (which sprouted from his head) glaring at me. I, of course, was pared-down to such an inconsequential size that I could have hidden in his hip pocket.

"Smack" - a slap across the face - screamed at for not following directions ... berated after church for not blessing myself properly - castigated in front of my friends and called names that even made them blush while being chased through the neighborhood with a leather strap, my sole offense —— being late for supper.

"Why is Pus such an asshole?" the kids would ask.

That's what everyone called my father – Pus - because his vindictiveness seeped like the yellowish/brown discharge from an open wound. I'd wake screaming in the cellar, a torn blanket wrapping my tiny body. In my dreams, I was still an infant, even during my adolescence. Smaller, smaller I became ... my father placing me over his knee, delivering a lecture that shot from his mouth like bullets - his lips twisting into a bazooka's barrel - a sulfurous residue swirling about his tongue, smoke fuming from his nose ... veins throbbing along his forehead ... every insane thought directed at me, a swaddling newborn in the skin of a teenager. How could he hit me? I was only a child, a beautiful creation cursed with an ugliness that is still traceable on my face.

I'd flee screaming into bed with my mother, but her protective arms could not shield me from my pursuer ... the voice - eyes - upraised hand - veins - metal flyswatters and twisted clothes hangers ... the positives were forever outweighed by negativity in our household.

Once in high school, I got a job at the local floral shop, but the humiliation I endured at this job was excruciating. Every day brought new forms of sadistic abuse.

"Look at this, here comes the little flower child. Why don't you sweep us some rose petals, my little daisy? Why don't you sprout wings from the side of your head like that delivery angel on TV? The post office delivers airmail, but our little flower child delivers fairy mail. Ho ho ho. Come here petunia, lemme sniff your ..."

"Mom, do something. Please!" I'd scream, but she couldn't help. My father's darkness outweighed the light she provided. Sometimes mom hinted at freeing us from our bonds, but the oppression was inescapable. My father's tyranny enveloped us, its parameters insuring our helplessness.

"You can't do anything for yourself. Where's your common sense? Get out of the way. I'll do it myself. If I want anything done right around this fucking place, I'm the one who has to do it," he'd scream.

And guess what. He was right. I never learned the most elementary skills, even though my father could fix anything. When it came to ingenuity, brilliance, and logic, he was incomparable. Through the years, I saw him repair most everything imaginable - radiators, the dishwasher, dripping faucets, light fixtures, an alternator on the car, or a section of roof that leaked. But his only child didn't possess the slightest hint of mechanical aptitude. Why? Because he never showed me how the world worked. By keeping these secrets, he hid his knowledge, guaranteeing that I would never advance beyond him.

I became a cripple who never learned how to walk through life. I was raised in a state of limbo, procrastinating at every step, unable to make the simplest decision. My father could sew, cook a gourmet meal, overhaul an engine, and bowl a 200 game. In contrast, I could barely boil an egg, catch a baseball, or drive a stick shift. I wanted to participate in these activities, but lacked the necessary skills. I was never allowed to operate a sewing machine, play tackle football, or tinker in the toolbox. Hell, I didn't even learn how to talk with members of the opposite sex, or the basics of intimacy.

Why would my father, who blossomed with knowledge, keep it all to himself? I became stifled, debilitated, my progress thwarted by a man who'd take all he knew to the grave. I often wondered, why would he bring a child into the world if it weren't for the sole reason of loving them, and to make their life better than his? I wanted to learn everything - to play football, go bowling, darn a pair of pants, or cook chicken cordon bleu. But my father was so worried about losing control that he forced me into being a feeble little person who couldn't even speak for fear of being castigated.

It was truly a sad evening ... sadder than most. I had such high expectations for our dinner at The Siamese Room, but I should have known better. Just when I started coming into my own and gaining self-confidence ... whoooosh, the rug was pulled from beneath my feet.

"Why didn't you become a doctor or lawyer, or at least a business executive?" he screeched at one point. "You never learned logic, science, or reason. What are you going to tell me next? That you want to be an artist like you were in high school? Well, I don't give a damn how good you paint. Artists are all freaks, fairies, or fanatics. I'm not letting a child of mine become a lunatic. Listen to me. I know what I'm talking about. Anything other than pure, cold-hearted science is unacceptable. If you want to become a success like me, get rid of your foolish notions. The next thing I know, you'll be arranging flowers and tiptoeing through the tulips ..."

The evening turned out to be a resounding failure. Dad ranted n' raved like a demented self-help guru on speed, mom cried as usual, and I fled from The Siamese

Room without eating my dinner. So much for the good news about buying a house. Instead, I walked along the darkened streets of Latera Heights, recognizing every landmark and point of interest, yet feeling strangely unfamiliar in my surroundings. The eeriness overwhelmed me to such an extent that at one point, as I passed The Karma Theater and caught my reflection in a plate glass window, I hardly recognized myself. Who was I? What was I doing? And more importantly, where was I going in life?

Once home, I looked forward to a carefree evening of reading and relaxation. But no sooner had I entered my living room and sat on the couch when a faint knocking could be heard at my front door. Resenting this intrusion, I rose from the sofa as an idea flashed through my mind. What if my father, regretting his crass behavior, felt remorseful and came to apologize? But then common sense convinced me otherwise. How could my parents visit when they didn't even know my address? So much for wishful thinking.

Clueless as to who would disturb me at such a late hour, I opened the windowless door to find my next-door neighbor standing on the porch.

"Hello Chris," he said meekly. "I was wondering if you'd ... well, first I should extend a greeting. Good evening. How are you tonight?"

"Fine," I replied blankly, not pleased with his company.

My neighbor's name was Woody Dewer, and he could possibly be the most pathetic human being I ever met. The man, a forty-five year old unemployed paramedic, was of medium height and slightly balding. None of these factors perturbed me. What did raise my ire was Woody's habit of bothering me at the most inopportune times (which was always). And, when doing so, he'd complain about an array of hypochondriacal ailments. Even though I had only lived in this neighborhood a few weeks, Woody told me he suffered from liver failure, heart disease, a bloated kidney, sleep deprivation, a blistered appendix, chlamydia, schizoid delusions, and a brain tumor.

The man stood at my door, almost begging to enter my premises, but I scowled at him with such contempt that he started stuttering and fidgeting nervously with his hands. I knew Woody wanted human kindness, but his weakness disgusted me. I couldn't tolerate looking at his sad, yellowy eyes, his sagging, choleric skin, or his drooping shoulders. What nerve he had bothering me. Why didn't he go home and talk to the walls, or chat with some other psychopath on the Internet? Or better yet, why didn't Woody read his medical journals and find a new disease that he hadn't suffered from yet? What a pathetic man.

"I was wondering if you'd like to go to a movie with me sometime?"

"Get out of here," I yelled. "You don't know anything about me or modern medicine? You're nothing but a sicko, and someone who's pathetically weak. Look at me. I'm strong and healthy. You're a wreck. Now listen. Go home, get your head together, and quit bothering me. I'm not ill, and I hate people who are. If you ever regain any semblance of normalcy, I'll consider socializing with you. But I can't be around people who don't live up to their potential. So go home and quit bothering me!"

Woody appeared to weep as I slammed the door in his face. What a cringing, desperate person. What nerve to actually think I'd befriend a sorry creature like him. I'm glad he was gone. Hopefully he'd never come back again.

4

Disillusioned by my inability to bond with my father, I walked to the Gemini one Saturday afternoon and decided to drive away from my problems. Without any particular destination in mind, I eventually meandered to the bypass ... the very same place where only weeks earlier I had exceeded the speed limit by at least 35 m.p.h. I suppose my actions were an unconscious desire to relive that afternoon, for my car was inexplicably drawn to the freeway by an unseen force. And, although I didn't break any more laws, Ukiah's spirit guided me along that four-lane highway. The link to my one-time companion was so strong, in fact, that I looked to my side and saw his manuscript lying on the passenger seat. I must have placed it there at some point, but for the life of me, I couldn't remember when.

After driving endlessly along the highway, I recalled reading Ukiah's material one evening after getting rid of my neighbor. Thankfully, his dismissal was forceful enough to prevent another repeat episode. Anyway, I gazed at the yellow manila envelope to my right, instantly returning to a ghastly land where reality was twisted into a tragic struggle for redemption among the brutal ruins of society. Entitled *Glitter Ghetto*, this book chronicled the life of a teenage sideshow freak that was exploited by his father in an inner-city tenement. As the story unfolds, we see our culture's dual nature exposed in regard to beauty and ugliness. And much to his credit, Ukiah never candy-coats life's seamier side by pretending it doesn't exist. With unnerving accuracy, he shows how certain people on this planet truly are, and not how we wished them to be. In the end, although I'm certainly not a literary critic, I scratched my head and wondered why this man wasn't a famous author. His material far surpassed those who were published simply because they created pleasing landscapes or sentimental moods. Ukiah was an observer whose brutal lyricism laid life to its barest.

While the numbers tumbled on my odometer, an anxious excitement built inside my body. Yet again, for some inexplicable reason, Ukiah's image presented itself to me. During the past couple weeks, not only did I think about him constantly, but I also began pondering how he would react in certain situations. My constant refrain became, "I wonder what Ukiah would do?"

Between the bitterness caused by my father and Ukiah's presence from afar, I became torn in opposite directions. I even envisioned a meeting between my father and Ukiah inside an ancient coliseum. The two combatants would square off against each other amid a throng of cheering spectators, both clawing and fighting unto the death, with the eventual prize being me. Yes, me! The victor would carry me away in his arms, forever cradling and protecting my tiny body.

Realizing the ridiculousness of this vision, and still unable to erase Ukiah from my mind, I decided to quit driving and visit the source of my infatuation. I knew that the dangers involved in this decision were immense, but I had to see Ukiah one more time. But what if I walked through his door to find gangsters ordering a hit, junkies shooting dope, or hookers turning tricks? What would I do? And worse, what if, after witnessing too much, they dragged me to an isolated scrap yard and dropped me in a vat of battery acid? Or else they'd beat me, gouge my eyes, or break my kneecaps. What was I doing? Why couldn't I erase Ukiah from my memory?

The parking lot behind Transformer Towers retained its crass lack of appeal, with discarded condoms, a worn tennis shoe, and broken glass dotting the urine-stained concrete. Why would Ukiah stay in such a sewer? He could live anywhere in Latera Heights. Why this dump? I didn't even want to walk around the building, let alone enter. If it weren't for Ukiah, I'd just as soon watch this hellhole burn to the ground. So, after concealing the manuscript I had stolen weeks earlier beneath a denim jacket, I inched toward a potentially life threatening situation.

After walking up seven flights of steps, I wandered along the narrow hallway leading to Ukiah's apartment, the sound of 1980's new wave music filtering through the darkened corridor. Upon approaching Ukiah's opened door, I realized his room was the source of these tunes. Gulping deeply and unsure of my motives (or whether I should knock at all), I tiptoed toward the door, then stood aghast at what confronted me.

Ukiah, in the throes of rock n' roll pandemonium, sat on his bed bucking his head back and forth wildly to a Cyndi Lauper song. While she sang about girls just wanting to have fun, Ukiah flailed his hair and jumped atop his stained and splattered mattress. Leaping and spinning in circles, eyes closed, the crazed man was consumed by Miss Lauper's music. The world, responsibility, consequences, and matters of circumstance had slipped into the distance, at least to Ukiah, for nothing appeared to exist except this moment.

At song's end, Ukiah collapsed on the mattress, still impervious to his surroundings or my presence. I lingered nervously outside his door, eavesdropping on his one-man party. Music continued to blare at a deafening level while Ukiah strummed an imaginary guitar and I stood frozen, certain I should leave before being detected, yet unable to draw myself from the spectacle. Ukiah was removed from reality to such an extent that his absorption was absolute. Singing, twirling, smiling, and performing to a nonexistent audience, Ukiah became a man unto himself, content within his self-created craziness.

Overtaken by Ukiah's spirited flight, I could no longer contain myself. After hurriedly setting my jacket and the hidden yellow envelope on the hallway's crusty carpeting, I burst into the cramped room without warning, dancing in unison with Ukiah as if we were a musical team. Shimmying my shoulders to and fro, then bowing my head before bobbing it up and down, I soon assumed the motion of a graceful daisy swaying in the wind. Upon seeing my uninhibited display, Ukiah chuckled, then flopped onto his bed while I continued to dance. The sensation filled me with an exhilaration I had rarely experienced - a freeing of my body, an unloosening of the doubts, and an overall feeling of release. No longer would I be consumed by self-consciousness. My feet had been unleashed, reeling about the room with awkwardness and speed, while my arms weaved intricate patterns through the air. Even my hair, which was stylishly short and dryer-blown, shot in all directions with electric frenzy.

At song's end, I abruptly quit moving and turned shyly from Ukiah. What was I doing? Prior to today, I had never even danced in my life. I could still remember my high-school socials where every other kid moved about freely. But not me. I recalled being mocked by the kids while trying to dance at an elementary sock-hop.

"Look at Chris. What a reject," they laughed. "It's like watching a shadow boxer trying to punch his own reflection!"

I raced from the dance floor that night, never again engaging in such foolish behavior. But this afternoon I let myself go, self-consciousness lost to unbridled physical expression. But why did I have to humiliate myself? Why hadn't I retained my quaint nature? At least then, nobody could laugh at me.

"Look at Chris, look at Chris," the kids mocked me years ago, their words still echoing true today.

Now I set myself up for Ukiah's ridicule. But rather than reinforce my suspicions, I heard faint applause emanating from across the room.

"How out of character," he chuckled sincerely. "I'll bet you even surprised yourself."

Feeling flushed, I hesitantly turned to confront my host.

"I'm sorry for barging in unannounced, then making an ass of myself. You're probably thinking ..."

"A dancer and a mind reader. Impressive."

"What?" I asked curiously.

"You must be psychic, being that you were going to tell me my thoughts."

"Oh, that. I didn't mean ..."

"You should leave the psychoanalysis to me."

"I'm sorry, Ukiah. I should have never disturbed your ..."

"Don't worry, Chris. You're perfectly welcome here."

"That's a relief. I thought maybe I'd find ... well, never mind."

"Someone tortured on a bed of nails, or a virgin being sacrificed on an altar."

"Yeah," I laughed.

"Those things can be arranged if you like," the man smiled.

"Nah. This suits me better."

As Ukiah sat before me, I examined his face to check the status of his blemish. Remarkably, it had vanished without a trace. I almost laughed out loud when remembering the fuss he made about that mark.

Not wanting him to decipher my thoughts, I quickly blurted, "How's your son's band doing? Did they land that show at the high school?"

Ukiah's face instantly hardened into a scowl as he sneered, "No. That motherfucking teacher hasn't returned my call in two weeks."

"Why?" I asked.

"Who knows? I've left messages on his machine, spoken with his secretary, and even with other teachers in his department. But so far Mister Doublet has ignored me."

The last thing I wanted was to get Ukiah riled, so I changed the subject.

"By the way, how is *Blank Line* coming along?"

"Fine. It's going slower than most, but ..."

At this point I tuned out Ukiah's words as a startling thought struck me. Before my impromptu dance, I set his manuscript, along with my jacket, in the hallway. What if, by chance, a corner of it snuck free and was now exposed? If Ukiah walked from his door and saw it, I'd be seen as a thief. Lord only knows what type of reaction this would trigger. He'd either backhand me, toss me from the premises, or ... or worse. Maybe a torture scene would result after all.

"Oh! Geez," I exclaimed, "I forgot something in the hallway."

Leaping instinctively, I burst from the room and retrieved my jacket. After coming back, I noticed a trace of curiosity on my host's face, so I continued my diversionary tactics.

"Y'know, I'm a bit parched. Could you walk downstairs and buy me a soda? ... Yeah,

I'm kinda thirsty. Would you get me a soft drink ... a pop ... y'know, a soda? I'm a little dry. A pop would do, a soda."

"Okay, quit babbling, Chris. I'll be back in a second," Ukiah said with an odd look on his face, detecting my suspiciousness.

After scooping a handful of change from his dresser, Ukiah stepped from the room. As he walked down the hallway, I sprung into action. Luckily his stack of manuscripts were set against a far wall, so I bound toward them and hastily hid my yellow envelope. Just as quickly, I returned to my chair and waited for Ukiah.

"There," he said minutes later upon return, his outstretched arm holding a bottle of soda.

"As I grabbed the cold, moisture-soaked glass container, I noticed three bright-red parallel lines slicing Ukiah's left forearm. The markings appeared to be scratches of some sort. But, being that my mind was occupied with other issues, I didn't give the matter further thought.

After untwisting the bottle's cap and taking a gingerly sip, I looked at Ukiah, who chugged from a jug of water.

"Did you really lay off the booze?" I asked with a tinge of hope.

"It's been two weeks plus," Ukiah replied triumphantly. "No cigarettes either."

"You quit cold turkey, just like that?"

"Not a single sip or puff. I'm clean, baby. I knew I'd eventually drink myself to death, so I made a promise to Romlocon. If she let me keep living, I'd never smoke or drink again. So there - no more drifting aimlessly through life in a stupor. From now on I'm focused on the goals at hand. I've left those senseless games behind. Just like I refuse to be a prisoner of possessions, I won't be held hostage to the poisons that ruled my life either."

Beaming with joy, I bubbled, "I'm so proud of you, Ukiah. In all honesty, I never thought you'd do it. But I'm glad you did."

"I like being underestimated. Oh yeah, can I ask you a question?"

"A question? Of me? Um ... sure ..." I gulped.

Point blank, Ukiah snapped, "What did you think of *Glitter Ghetto*?"

Waves of guilt washed across me as one word flashed through my mind. BUSTED! How did he know? The sensation reminded me of those times as a child when my father caught me doing something wrong.

"How dare you go to that swamp! What's wrong with you, Chris? Do you want to die? What if a monster sprung from the water and ate you alive? It loves to eat eyeballs, gargle with blood, and use children's spines for nail files. Would you like to be strangled with your own intestines? Maybe it would have been better if that beast ate you, 'cause right now I'm going to paddle your ass."

Ukiah had pegged me dead to rights. What were the chances I'd escape this nightmare?

"Glitter Ghetto? What's that?" I asked while looking away.

"It's the seventh packet from the top of that stack," Ukiah pointed.

"How did you know?" I blurted before realizing my admission of guilt. "Does your place have hidden cameras? You're amazing. Tell me, how did you know?"

Cracking a slight smile, Ukiah said, "I knew it was gone all along, ever since the last time you were here. Sooner or later you'd come back. It was only a matter of time."

"But how could you tell? Both times, when I took it and returned it, you were gone. It seems impossible. What did you do, count the packets?"

"No. I can tell by the energy they emit. When one is missing, everything is no longer in its proper order. That's why I know *Ghetto* is the seventh packet down. It's glowing."

"Glowing? But every envelope looks the same. They're all yellow, and none of them are marked."

"Then check," Ukiah directed with his finger. "Count seven down."

I did as he said, walking to the enormous stack of manuscripts, then counting seven down. After retrieving the packet, I opened its flap and removed the contents - the title page reading *Glitter Ghetto*.

"What are you, a magician? Where did you get this knowledge?"

"Where The Word is concerned, anyone can perform supernatural feats."

As Ukiah uttered this message, I once again felt an intruder entering my mind.

"No one on this planet is able to walk with me. You can jump from the highest mountain to impress me, but I won't notice."

"Let me change your mind. Don't be so cold and remote," I said silently.

"I've rejected hearts that beat more passionately than yours," the otherworldly voice told me. "I could walk alone for eternity and not be affected."

Rattled, I blurted, "Could I use your bathroom? All of this is ... is starting to weird me out."
"Sure. It's through that door. But don't expect much," he warned me.

Ukiah's words didn't settle well with me, nor did his facilities. Similar to every other aspect of Transformer Towers, his bathroom was an insult to the senses. The commode's porcelain bowl was stained a sulfurous orange, while its water ran endlessly - never shutting off. The sink, smeared with countless decades of discoloration, dripped from both faucets and the plumbing underneath. The bathtub, finally, was so nasty that I found it inconceivable that any human could use it. Even the hot and cold handles had been removed, replaced by rusty vise-grips that turned them off and on. I quickly tended to my business, then sped from the room.

"Why are you living here?" I demanded after returning to the main room. "This place is a shit-hole. How can you even use that bathroom?"

"I rarely do."

"Who could blame you? There isn't even a shower hook-up. How do you bathe? Inside that awful tub?"

"To tell you the truth, Chris, did you notice that kettle in there?"

"No, not really."

"Well, there's one beside the tub that I use to wash my hair. I wouldn't be caught dead inside that grungy tub."

"It's a mess."

"This room was so horrendous when I moved in," he continued, "that management hadn't even changed the bed sheets from the previous occupant."

Angered by his living conditions, I blurted without thinking, "Why don't you get out of here and move in with me?"

The words were shocking in their implication, floating in the air before me. Had I really spoken them? And more importantly, was there any possibility of getting them back?

But the moment had already passed, because Ukiah said plainly, "Okay."

"Okay. Just like that? You didn't even think about it."

"What's to consider? That is, unless you don't want me any more."

"Of course not. You can use the guesthouse. And anyway, the extra money would help pay my mortgage."

"Then it's a deal."

"And don't worry," I continued, "I won't be any trouble to you."

Wait a second. Why was I assuring Ukiah that I wouldn't be an inconvenience? It was my house. What was I getting myself into?

"It sounds great, Chris. It'll be great to get outta this dump."

"I should warn you, though, there is one drawback to my neighborhood."

"There always is."

"I have this neighbor, his name is Woody Dewar, and he's the most annoying man ..."

"Annoying?"

"Yeah. He has these mental and physical afflictions, like a palpitating heart, a tumor in his throat, and diabetes."

"I see. How else does he inconvenience you?"

"A couple of weeks ago he knocked at my door and asked if I wanted to go to a movie. But don't worry. I put that pest in his place."

"My God! The fiend," Ukiah shrieked playfully. "What a nuisance. We better notify the authorities and have that deviant arrested."

"You don't understand, Ukiah."

"I don't? It sounds like Mr. Dewer wants some company. Y'see, when someone is lonely, their need for companionship is mistaken for desperation. But instead of showing compassion, we abuse them, or turn a cold shoulder. But Chris, how does it feel to be abused, or not given respect?"

"How did you know about my father?" I exclaimed angrily.

"I didn't," Ukiah smiled. "But you've obviously learned this cruel behavior somewhere. C'mon, let's start hauling my stuff out of here. It should only take one trip."

As Ukiah began packing, I was carried away by a daydream. What if I didn't own separate guest quarters and had to rely solely on the main house? Then, some night after going to our respective bedrooms, Ukiah crept into my room and took sexual advantage of me. At first I'd feign displeasure, but deep down I'd submit to his intrusion ... even welcome it. Oh God, what was I thinking? Ukiah didn't find me attractive in the least. How could he? Even thinking such thoughts was so off-base that I began questioning my sanity.

Confused and disgusted by these visions, I regained my senses by asking a question that had troubled me for some time.

"Ukiah, I'm not sure if I told you last time, but I work as the manager of a data entry firm."

"That sounds like a respectable job."

"It's all right, but lately I've been having trouble with one of my employees. The situation has reached a point where I'm not sure what to do."

Appearing unconcerned, Ukiah kept packing, eventually asking, "What's the problem?"

"This guy, his name is Tom Twinson, has no respect for his co-workers. Not only does he show them little regard, but often he'll say the most asinine things you ever heard over the intercom. It's like he's an eighth grade kid with a C.B. radio. His idiocy disrupts the entire work force."

While cramming unfolded clothes into a suitcase, my counterpart began, "It sounds like Twinson is a real asshole. As the manager, what have you done so far?"

"Nothing ... nothing yet," I said.

Becoming more involved in the subject, Ukiah quit fiddling with his clothes and walked toward the window.

"Here's how you deal with a rabble-rouser. When is your next employee meeting?"

"Coincidentally, next week."

"Good. When all your employees are gathered around, you need to mention this intercom problem. Then, after explaining how detrimental it is to your work atmosphere, ask if any of them would like to take responsibility for this immature act. If Twinson stands and admits fault, your problem is solved. But, knowing what type of cowardly person would pull such stunts, Twinson will probably ignore his duty. This is where you enter the picture. Do you remember being in school and having to tolerate the class asshole, or a playground bully? This kid is always the ringleader, and has a bunch of guys around for protection. So, to end this situation before it gets out of hand, you need to zero in on the problem. In this case, Twinson is your version of the schoolyard bully. So, what should you do? Being the boss, you have to take a hatchet and chop this fucker down to size."

"But I don't know how to handle these situations," I interrupted with exasperation.

"The solution is simple." At this point Ukiah's voice rose with animation. "During this meeting, focus on Twinson by first telling him to stand before his co-workers. Then embarrass the hell out of him. You have to slam it to this son of a bitch with both barrels." Ukiah now yelled his words. "Knock this fucker out at the knees. You have to make him cringe ... wanna crawl under his desk ... berate that bastard. Be unrelenting. Become so forceful that he'd give anything to just sit back down and mind his own business. Then, after the others see how you handled this situation, none will want to get on your bad side."

"But what if ...?"

"There can't be any buts. If you're not willing to take the upper hand and blast this asshole out of the water, then don't use my advice. If you get wishy-washy and refuse to exercise your authority, you'll surrender every ounce of respect. Your employees will run roughshod over you."

"What happens next?" I asked, feeling empowered.

"Everyone returns to work, with Twinson understanding that these shenanigans won't be tolerated. In other words, you need to make him aware of what is expected, and if he doesn't listen, then the axe falls. You're giving Twinson an ultimatum – one more chance. If he fucks up, he's gone."

Excited, I blurted, "It might work!"

"Of course. And here's why. People don't like being told what to do, but they love being led by the hand. When you put Twinson in his place, the others will see you as someone who doesn't take any shit. There's nothing to it. Now c'mon, let's get this junk in my car."

As I struggled with two compact boxes and Ukiah lugged a suitcase in each hand, we started carrying my new tenant's belongings to his car. Along the way, I thought about the advice he gave in regard to my workplace. It seemed as if, reminiscent of our joyride on the bypass, Ukiah was pushing me beyond my normal parameters. Instead of avoiding risk at all costs, he urged me to confront my fears. While I adhered to a policy of avoidance, my new acquaintance told me to attack the world rather than being passive. But to do so required an entirely new frame of mind, a move I was currently ill equipped to make.

After descending seven flights of steps, walking through a dusty lobby, then circling the building and parking lot, we finally reached Ukiah's Celebrity, my arms sagging like melted rubber. In contrast, my counterpart threw his two suitcases into the car's backseat without any noticeable effort.

After doing so, he asked, "What are you doing today? Are you busy?"

"I don't have anything on the agenda," I told him.

"Then why don't you cruise with me to your place? We'll have a chance to talk, and it'll be safer that way."

"Safer?" I asked, fearing Ukiah may be the target of a mob hit.

"Yeah, we don't need a repeat performance of your hot rod driving on the bypass," Ukiah joked, a broad grin forming on his face.

I chuckled with relief, then sat alongside my partner as he rolled through town. After checking out the sights, Ukiah asked me a question.

"You never did give me your impression of *Glitter Ghetto*."

Touched that Ukiah was concerned with my opinion, I responded, "I'm not a literary critic, but your story showed life the way it really is."

Ukiah remained silent for a moment, then proceeded while making a left turn. "I've never pretended that we live in an idyllic world, or that mankind has his brother's best intentions at heart. To think that way is naive and unrealistic. I suppose my stories are somewhat clouded by this outlook, but I try to keep them truthful, with an ever-present tinge of hope."

"Well put," I beamed, tickled by Ukiah's explanation. I continued, "Would you tell me more about something you said earlier today?"

"Sure," he told me, turning onto the bypass.

"You said ... 'where The Word is concerned' ... and then I can't remember what else. What did you mean?"

Focused, Ukiah began, "The Word is an author's primary ingredient. Like the relationship between a sculptor and clay, a writer is continually drawn to, inspired by, and reliant upon The Word. Without it, he could never create, or reach his ultimate goal, which is to burst through the gates of publication. The Word is basically a conduit, like the pigskin to a football player. Before scoring a touchdown, a running back first has to grab the football and run with it into the end zone. The same concept applies to writers. Without The Word, they'd never enter that cherished land of publication."

"That's interesting," I commented, feeling honored to hear these words. Who else in the world spoke of such topics? When they talked about football, it usually concerned college polls, final scores, statistics, or playoff pictures. No one used it to analyze the publishing world.

I followed with this inquiry. "Do you remember mentioning a Spirit the last time we were together? How did she enter the picture?"

"You have a good memory. You must mean Romlocon, the Muse."

"Yes, that's it!"

Ukiah continued driving at a rapid pace.

"I'm trying to understand," I said hesitantly. "Where does Romlocon live?"

Ukiah laughed good-naturedly, then explained. "Romlocon doesn't live anywhere. She comes from Creation itself, serving as a messenger to deliver The Word to her subjects. Without her inspiration, an author would never become a true Artist or Creator. She's the source for all we do."

Trying to make sense of this information, I asked, "How does someone communicate with this Muse?"

"To maintain a relationship with your Muse requires absolute devotion. You have to make a commitment. If you're only going through the motions, or acting like it was a hobby, then forget it. The Muses demand all or nothing, and they can tell which path you choose."

"You said Muses. Are there more than one?"

"Of course! The only problem is, there are many Muses who aren't the real thing. Take the science-fiction writer Philip Prince, for example. That hack is the most recognized author in America, but he still writes shit."

Fascinated, I kept pursuing Ukiah. "How did you discover these secrets?"

"My past artistic incarnations must have accumulated enough goodwill to let me look beyond the veil of ignorance."

"What! You've lived before?"

"We all have."

"Who was I? Why don't I know this stuff?"

"You could, Chris, but first you need to get in touch with your Muse. Luckily, I've done this by using the gifts given to me. By understanding the symbolic aspects of my personality, the world, and the myths around me, I was allowed to see the hidden treasures held within my mind."

As Ukiah finished his sentence, he pulled into my driveway.

Disappointed that our conversation was ending, I protested, "I don't want to quit talking. Hearing you speak is like being let in on a magic trick."

"Thanks, Chris," Ukiah said. "We can continue on the way home, as soon as we unload."

"Don't forget where you were," I suggested.

In a stern, matter-of-fact tone, Ukiah spat, "I never forget anything."

After grabbing his suitcases and boxes, we strolled through my yard, our feet kicking piles of multi-colored leaves that fell from the trees. I enjoyed this time of year more than any other - the cool autumn wind, aromas of harvest and decay, and the general climate of festivity associated with Halloween, Thanksgiving, Friday night high school football games, and darkened evenings playing hide-n-go seek when the sun set at an early hour.

We soon entered Ukiah's new residence, his guesthouse exhibiting the simplicity of a Spartan monastery. The three-room bungalow had a kitchen (furnished with an economy-sized refrigerator and an electric range), a cramped bathroom, and a general living/sleeping area that sported a foldout sofa/sleeper. The cottage couldn't compare with mansions on the hill, but it sure as hell beat Transformer Towers by a long shot. So, after setting Ukiah's possessions on the kitchen floor, we returned to his car.

Fidgeting with anticipation, I blurted, "Okay, who were you in previous lifetimes?"

"Chris, Chris, at least let me start the car," Ukiah joshed before turning his key in the ignition.

After pulling from Reflection Alley onto the main road, Ukiah continued his discourse. "In this life, I've been graced with the souls of both the French writer Louis Ferdinand-Celine, and also a beautiful female empress who horribly abused her power. Because of this woman's brutality, and her reliance upon looks to further her career, I've been sentenced to an incarnation of 'what ifs.' I was almost beautiful, I was almost a famous author, and I would have seized the reigns of power had everything fallen into place. But by facing the fuck-ups of my earlier lives, I've been reduced to a struggling writer with barely a pot to piss in. I hate complaining, but knowing this stuff frustrates the hell out of me."

Amazed, I shook my head and said, "I'm not sure ... or, I'm not even able to comment on what you've said. Do you really believe you're being penalized for a series of mistakes in a previous lifetime? It sounds incredible."

As we sped along the bypass, Ukiah responded, "The visible and invisible exist on very intimate levels. There's more occurring in this world than you could ever see. All of us are able to communicate with beings from other dimensions. And they, in turn, involve themselves in our affairs."

Considering the lunacy of his words, and how Ukiah drove at 75 miles an hour, I nervously shook my head to and fro. "You have to excuse me, but this information is overloading my brain. It's all too much. Do you really think you're cursed by a supernatural being? It sounds so strange."

"Chris, how do you explain this world? I've been spoken to, so I know. Can you say the same?"

"No, and I'm not trying to criticize you. I'm just ... blown away."

"I see," he replied, exiting the bypass.

"Don't get mad, Ukiah. That's the last thing I want. Tell me about this queen and Louis Ferdinand-Celine." I felt tears welling in my eyes as I choked on these words, the thought of being ignored by Ukiah too much to bear.

"If you wish. But remember what I told you about lifting a rug and peeking beneath it. You're gonna get dirt on your fingers."

Without notice, Ukiah slammed his hands on the steering wheel and violently veered around a corner.

Enraged, with the level of his voice rising, he bellowed, "Life is more than sweet nothings and pillow whispers. I'm in the middle of a fucking ordeal, and you're making light of it. How would you like to be damned from the start just because some psycho-queen tortured her subjects, or because her beauty stopped Time itself? Mix in a dash of Celine's tragic life, and that's what I have to deal with. It's no wonder I'm irate. I might even run this fucking car into a telephone pole."

Covering my eyes and pushing both feet to the floor (as if pressing an imaginary brake pedal), I squealed with fright, "Don't do it, Ukiah. I'm not ready to die."

"I don't give a damn what you say! I'm tired of being tortured because of a crazy old lady from the middle ages and an embittered author."

Ukiah wove through traffic like an ambulance driver, except he didn't have any lights or sirens to warn the other vehicles.

"I'll run this fucker right into Doppelganger's Tavern," he screeched, voice on fire.

"Please, I beg you, don't kill me. There has to be some escape ...."

At that instant, Ukiah eased off the gas pedal and let loose a blood-curdling shriek.

After returning to normal speed, he shouted loudly, "You didn't really think I'd wreck, did ya? C'mon Chris, that was just fun n' games."

"Fun n' games! We could've been killed. That's twice now - both times I was with you - that I've been scared to death."

"Yooo-hooo! You're right, we've been living, baby! What a blast."

"Just pull over and let me out. I'll walk to my car."

"C'mon, we're almost there. I just wanted to loosen things up a bit. We were getting too philosophical. Whenever that happens, it's cool to crank up the speedometer and blow a 'lil carbon from the tailpipe."

Breathing easier, my anger subsided as I asked Ukiah, "What about all that other stuff, y'know .... the past lives. Were you just pulling my leg? Because if you were ..."

"Do you want it to be true or not?"

"I don't know. You're confusing me."

"Settle down, Chris. Let me explain the way things are. I'm a smart guy - one helluva smart guy. Being gifted, I realize that if I am cursed, one of two things could happen. First, if free will is simply wishful thinking, then I'm doomed. But if it does exist, and I was born under a black cloud, I'm still able to fight this fate and realize my chosen destiny, which is to enter the halls of publication. So, if I walk around moping all day, whining that I'm jinxed, then I might as well slit my wrists and be done with it. But I don't buy into that pessimistic shit. I'm no victim. Instead, I believe the Muses intimately affect the artistic aspects of our lives. So if I surrender my Being to Romlocon, and WILL her to enhance my creativity, then I can defy my previous incarnations. To hell with the queen, and to hell with Celine. But there's only one problem with my theory."

"What? Tell me. We're almost to Transformer Towers."

"In a nutshell, I know Romlocon requires total devotion from me. This much is clear. And, being that I'm aware of this fact, am I only devoting myself to her to get something in return? Namely, to get published. So, to satisfy Romlocon's demands ..."

"Out of curiosity, what are her demands?"

"Well, instead of acting in my normal self-serving manner, I need to change my very nature. But will knowing this secret keep me from being published? If I am able to change myself and submit to Romlocon, will I still enter the cherished land of publication knowing that I'm only doing it for my own self-benefit?! It's nothing but a vicious cycle."

Before I could answer, Ukiah rolled into the parking lot of Transformer Towers.

"I'm sorry, Chris, but business calls. I'm going to grab my bed clothes, check-out of this cesspool, then meet with Tattoo Blue. We'll talk later. And don't worry, I won't shit where I eat, if ya know what I mean."

With those parting words, I stepped from Ukiah's car and slowly walked toward mine. As he rounded the corner and disappeared from sight, I started my Gemini and drove from the pot-holed lot, hoping to never visit this dilapidated structure again — no more beggars hitting me for spare change, or prostitutes propositioning me for sex. I'd never even been to a hooker before. If the truth be told (and I've never disclosed this embarrassing point to anyone), I've never even had sex in my life. I'm still a virgin!

I certainly didn't feel like stewing over this point, so I cruised through Latera Heights, burdened by an array of conflicting opinions concerning my new tenant. In one sense, I envied Ukiah with every bone in my body. He was everything I wanted to be. But how could I ever be like him? Even though his ideas were screwy, he believed in them whole-heartedly. Muses, reincarnation, vicious queens ... he was out there. But me, I was indecisive and hesitant about everything.

My entire life was marked by avoidance. I shied away from people, conflict, danger, risk, and intimacy. The way I viewed the world was, if I never confronted anything, hopefully nothing bad would happen. I developed this technique during my youth as a defense mechanism against my father's tyranny. I figured his ability to strike or berate me was limited if I couldn't be found. So I hid. I hid and became a coward. Yes, a coward. I feared fights, people, words, and life. Life in general created fear within me, and to avoid it at all costs became my primary goal.

But from all appearances, Ukiah didn't fear anything. He'd have sex at the drop of a hat, drive 100 miles an hour, break a man's kneecap for refusing to pay a debt, or even defy the gods with his brashness. All I wanted to do was live in a fantasy world of make-believe games.

Since I'm telling secrets, I may as well include this one, the most embarrassing of all. My greatest passion is to live in a fantasy soap-opera world. I'm sure you're laughing at my pathetic existence, but I've invested a great deal of time inventing (and reinventing) this artificial world. What do I mean? First there are the characters - Mister Torcher, the sadistic abuser, Mama Woom, the protector, Baby Baller, who's a social misfit, and finally No-Sho the Hero. Every day after work I'd write new scripts and dialogue for the actors, design their outfits, and ... I hate to say it, I even went so far as to buy actual costumes and play-act their roles before a mirror. This is how far I've plummeted ... the life of a failed actor.

I'm sorry if you find me worthless, but when I'm in the midst of the Dewel family saga (that's what I've entitled it), I'm no longer shy, fretful, or afraid to talk with members of the opposite sex. I can roar like Mister Torcher and kick my kids around, or comfort them like Mama Woom. Or else, if the mood strikes me, I can curl in a ball and whimper like Baby Baller. But in the end, No-Sho The Hero always arrives to save the day.

So, certain that I've already disclosed too much personal information, I'll sign off for the moment and stand naked in front of my mirror, deciding what the Dewels will do next.

5

I recently created a new imaginary character - Ukiah the suicidal dive-bomber who drops from the sky to save my family. Even when No-Sho The Hero is defeated, Ukiah arrives in the nick of time to battle evil (while also delivering equal measures of it). He is no doubt my most complex character to date. I even went so far as to make a rag doll/action figure in Ukiah's likeness, complete with long, dishwater blonde hair and a body bathed in both light and shade. At night, when thoughts of Ukiah proved too powerful, I'd rub the doll along my naked body while lying in bed. Needless to say, my soap opera's plot line took a novel turn, one that made me blush on a daily basis.

I couldn't tell Ukiah about my secret world - neither the play-acting, nor the perversions performed on the doll made in his image. Likewise, something happened at work that would cause my friend a great deal of disappointment. After listening to his advice concerning my problem with Tom Twinson, I did an about-face and resigned from my position as overnight data entry manager. Rather than confronting my fellow employees, I moved to day shift as a data entry operator. In the transition, I lost my title, seniority, suffered a pay cut, and surrendered a week's vacation. But at least I didn't have to deal with personnel problems, or account for my department's success. Rather than face the world, I fled once again.

Resigned to this sorry life, I looked out the back window late one afternoon to see Ukiah walking through the fallen leaves toward me. The mere sight of him caused my heart to flutter. With my breathing short and labored, I wondered why this enigmatic man intrigued me to such an extent. Whatever the answer, I found it impossible to look away from his gray corduroys or black-and-white checkered shirt.

After rapping on the door and entering my house, we exchanged a few pleasantries before Ukiah asked, "Are you busy tonight?"

"Not especially," I told him.

"Well, do you want to watch me drive at the stock car races?"

Surprised, I burst, "You're a race car driver? I should've known by the way you fly around town. Sure, I'd love to go. When is it, tonight? Where's the track?"

"I race at Duality Speedway."

"Up on the mountain?"

"That's the one."

"When are you leaving?"

"Right now," Ukiah said. "My car's already there. I just need a lift to the track."

"All right. Let me grab a few things and I'll be ready."

While we zipped through Latera Heights, Ukiah asked if I could stop at a grocery store on the outskirts of town; he needed to buy a few items before continuing on to the track, which was about an hour away. Naturally I agreed, and soon we were darting through the aisles of a supermarket.

At one point Ukiah, who was pushing a cart and loading it with various items, asked, "Have you been paying attention to how much this stuff costs?"

"Paying attention to the prices? No. I never do."

Ukiah grabbed two apples, placed them in a plastic bag, then weighed them.

"That's too bad," he said after doing the same with a tomato. "I hope I have enough money to cover it all."

"You didn't bring enough money? How much do you have?" I asked desperately.

"Forty bucks."

"That's it. You'll never have enough," I said as we reached the checkout counter.

"Oh, well. I guess we'll have to let this gal ring it up, then take back whatever goes over."

"You can't do that," I whispered as Ukiah loaded his goods onto the checkout counter. "It's embarrassing."

But Ukiah didn't pay attention to me. Rather, he placed product after product on a narrow conveyor belt, then flirted with a cashier who appeared to be in her mid-40s.

"Hi, Ukiah. I'm still waiting for you to stop over and mow my grass," she said softly. "It's been a long time."

"It has, Anna," my counterpart replied, laying his apples, tomato, and lunch meat on the counter.

I watched the woman swipe each item across her scanner, the prices and sum total appearing on a display unit attached to her cash register.

$19.62 ... $21.12 ... I hoped he didn't go over forty dollars, because a line of shoppers formed behind us.

"Y'know, when my grass gets too long, I start getting uncomfortable," Anna winked, her wicked smile conveying an unabashed sex appeal. "I could always get someone else to cut my lawn, but I like the way you do it best."

As Anna continued to swipe and weigh products ... $25.26 ... $28.77 ... $33.36 ...I noticed that none of her fingers held rings.

$35.10 ... $36.44 ...

"I'll stop by one of these evenings, Anna ..."

"When?" she purred. "My lawn is in desperate need of attention."

Five items remained on the belt. There was no way Ukiah's order would stay under forty dollars.

$36.90 ... $37.21 ... $38.06 ... $38.90 ... $39.86 ...

"Okay Ukiah, that'll be $39.86," Anna smiled.

How did he do it? Ukiah was only fourteen cents away from exceeding his total, then we would have had to start taking things back. I couldn't believe it.

As Ukiah pulled two twenty dollar bills from his left front pocket, a droopy-lidded teenage boy with greasy hair and facial piercings absently placed each item into thin plastic sacks. While I marveled at Ukiah's mathematical skills, he paid Anna with the nonchalance of a high stakes gambler. I found it incredible that someone could buy not only specifically priced items, but also taxable products and intangibles like fruit and vegetables which had to be weighed and didn't have a set price. To come within fourteen cents of forty dollars was amazing. He either got lucky, or Ukiah's mind was always working.

As I drove the Gemini from town, Ukiah rummaged through his sacks and made a makeshift supper for himself. At first he wrapped slices of lunchmeat and cheese into cylinders, then ate them with a tomato. I could only roll my eyes at his peculiar choice of foods.

As he chewed, I asked, "How did you do that in the supermarket?"

"What?" he said after swallowing.

"Come within fourteen cents of forty dollars."

"Oh, that. All you have to do is pay attention. It's the same with life in general, or even writing. Everything matters, but too often we ignore the world. That simple exercise in mathematics proved the point. Our minds should be active at all times, not passive lumps of sludge. Hell, I could even use this episode in one of my stories."

"Speaking of which," I continued, "why did you become a writer? The discipline and time requirements are enormous."

After eating another cylindrical roll-up, Ukiah said, "If you wanna know the truth, during my youth a series of foster families raised me. I never knew my biological parents."

"You never had a real mother and father? Holy shit! You must have been devastated."

"I don't feel like talking about specifics, but there is one motivating factor that has fueled my entire life. Do you know what it is?"

I shook my head.

"I'm going to prove to my parents, wherever they are, that I'll become a success despite their abandonment. Whoever those assholes are, they'll know me once I'm famous. Then I'll lure them into my web by pretending to love them. Once we're reunited, though, I'll kill 'em both. How dare they discard me like a pile of shit? I'm not a failure. I'll show them."

Ukiah growled his words by this stage.

"Can you imagine living your entire life for one moment? I can't wait until I'm on the cover of *Newsweek*, or when I'm on *The Tonight Show*. Then they'll come crawling to me, trying to reclaim their prize and milk my money. But screw 'em. After I kill both of them and cover it up, I'm going to buy a remote island, then live according to my own laws. The only monkey on my back - that of my parent's abandonment - will have been erased by their deaths. Then I can live as my own island-god, saying 'fuck you' to The System while stealing fire from the sky. As it stands now, my existence doesn't amount to anything. But things will change. Everyone will see, especially my parents."

Ukiah ate his final meat and cheese roll-up, then began routing through another bag when he lost his temper.

"Fuck! Son of a fucking bitch," he roared. "Where is it? Stop the car. Stop this second!"

"What?" I panted, veering to the berm. "What did you lose?"

"That fucking bag-boy forgot to pack my apples. Damn him. Turn the car around, we're going back," he demanded.

"But we can stop anywhere along the way for apples..."

"Turn this fucking car around and drive back to the market."

The finality of Ukiah's words conveyed the importance of this matter to him. I wheeled the Gemini around, then drove silently back to the supermarket. Once there, I parked, then followed him as he stormed into the store.

After reaching the customer service desk, I witnessed an explosion that rivaled The Big Bang. Ukiah confronted a bespectacled man whose name badge said, "Store Manager." Without introduction, he verbally assaulted the poor guy.

"I was shopping here a while ago, and spent forty dollars on groceries. One of the things I bought was two apples. Then after I left and drove out of town, guess what I wanted to eat. Guess!"

"Your apples, sir."

"Yes, my fucking apples. But guess why I couldn't eat them. Because they weren't in the fucking sacks that your derelict bag boy packed because he's so fucking stupid that he doesn't even know what planet he's on."

"I'm terribly sorry, sir," the manager chirped, cringing from Ukiah's tirade. "If you'll wait here, I'll walk to the produce section and get two apples for you."

As the manager stepped from behind his perch and entered the store, Ukiah followed closely on his heels.

"Do you know what man's most important commodity is? I'll tell you. It's time. And because you're so cheap that you can't hire competent help, you've wasted approximately half an hour of my time. My valuable time," he repeated, stressing the word valuable. "With all the competition among grocery stores, you'd think this one would hire someone who at least knew what planet he was on."

"Sir, I'll inform our baggers to be more diligent in the future," the manager replied, hoping for nothing more than to retrieve Ukiah's apples, then escort him from the store.

"A meeting won't return half an hour of my life, will it? Just so you know, I'm none too pleased with this episode."

"There sir, two apples," the manager said, handing him two shiny red pieces of fruit. "Once again, I apologize."

Ukiah stormed from the produce section, but not before settling one more score. He proceeded to the checkout area and, upon seeing the dim-witted bagger, snarled, "Hey asshole. Do you know what these are?"

The bagger stared at him blankly.

"These are just like the two apples you forgot to put in my bag half an hour ago. Start paying attention, you moron."

The kid scratched his head with confusion, unable to decipher Ukiah's message.

As he left this area (like a tornado that swooped-down from the sky, wreaked havoc on everything in sight, then twisted into the distance), Anna the checkout woman echoed, "Don't forget about mowing my lawn, Ukiah."

The next time my friend went shopping, I vowed to let him do it alone.

After returning to the Gemini, Ukiah still bubbled with rage.

"Did you see that dopey piece of shit bag boy?" he bellowed while I maneuvered through the parking lot. "What an ignorant ... Hey! Look out!"

From nowhere, a purple Cadillac screamed from between two stationery cars, nearly bashing into ours. I violently slammed my foot to the break, creating a screeching sound that echoed across the lot. Prior to my Gemini reaching a complete stop, Ukiah swung open his door and stormed toward the lavender car.

"What's the big idea?" he screamed, flailing his arms. "You damn near hit us. Why don't you watch where you're going?"

Upon hearing Ukiah's abuse, a lanky man wearing garishly designed threads and a floppy velvet hat stepped from his Cadillac. The intensity of his glare filled the air with tension - so much so that I actually shifted my car into reverse and considered leaving the scene. What if he yanked a knife from his black leather trench coat, or held a gun to Ukiah's head? I couldn't stand watching my friend get gutted, or filled with bullets. Why couldn't he just let this incident slide? Then we'd be on our way. But not Ukiah. Standing a full head shorter than this chain-draped, open-collared man, Ukiah continued to glare into his eyes, refusing to back down.

The stand-off persisted for a full minute before the taller participant grabbed his own crotch and snarled, "Hey man, sorry for the hassle. I'll start driving more cautiously."

With this apology, Ukiah nodded his head and returned to our car. For a second, I thought I would see flying fists, bloody switchblades, broken arms, or a white chalk outline surrounding Ukiah's body. A horrible childhood memory then popped into my mind.

"Don't make me stop this car, you little bastard," my father threatened, "or you'll be sorry you ever opened your mouth."

The next thing I knew, my pants were hanging around my ankles while a thin black belt pelted my ass. For the remainder of the trip, my tiny ass stung as it rubbed against our upholstered seats.

But Ukiah never cringed from the ghosts of his past. Rather, he approached his conflicts with the savvy of a war-wearied general, releasing his frustrations like a pent-up volcano. Why couldn't I be fearless instead of a trembling lily in a rainstorm, or a frightened pussycat running from its shadow?

Other than exhaling deeply, Ukiah seemed unaffected by his showdown. He simply sat quietly beside me while I drove from town. Reminiscent of our first meeting, I felt an awkward uneasiness when riding in silence. And, at moments such as these, I soon became subject to Ukiah's mind control.

"I'm content with my own company," the voice informed me, slithering through the deepest recesses of my mind.

A glistening image then appeared to me - a magnificent alabaster mansion with a neon sign in its front lawn repeatedly flashing a solitary word - AUTONOMOUS ... AUTONOMOUS ... AUTONOMOUS. After noticing Ukiah's face in one of the windows, I rushed toward the house and began banging on its door.

"Let me in, please. I need to be with you."

Instead of allowing me in, a voice boomed from the mansion.

"You don't have the type of love I desire ... the type of love I require. That's why you must stay outside. Your heart doesn't beat with the passion I demand. Unless you're willing to plunge a stake through your chest and lay your heart on a platter, your sacrifice will not be enough."

"I will. I'll kill myself for you," I whispered while driving along a freshly paved blacktop road. What was wrong with me? What force had taken hold of my mind?

The voice refused to leave me alone.

"I'm free from you, and all those like you. Although I live in this house, my company never ends. You, and others like you, can't understand my urge to be pure. So condemn me if you choose, but your heart will never beat inside my Hall of Mirrors."

A Hall of Mirrors! Stakes through the heart! What was happening to me? Was I actually losing my senses? In psychological terms, I'd be labeled hallucinatory, or subject to delusions of grandeur. Could I be psychotic, or just plain nuts? How could I even drive with such insane thoughts in my mind?

Desperate to empty my head, I asked Ukiah a question that would surely break the silence.

"How is *Blank Line* coming along? Maybe you'll let me read it someday."

"Maybe, but it's moving pretty slow. The amount of concentration needed to fit every piece into the puzzle is extraordinary, especially while working for Tattoo Blue. I'd love to be like those hotshot authors who do nothing but write all day. If I were them, I'd finish ten books a year."

"I can't imagine working forty hours a week, then writing in the meantime. Speaking of which, what else do you write about, other than what I read in *Glitter Ghetto*?"

"You name it," Ukiah said, adjusting his seat to the backward tilt position. "There's so much going on around me; y'know, suicides, drunkenness, crazy people, and saints."

"Lemme guess, everything's autobiographical," I joked before wishing I had bitten my tongue.

"Chris, are you saying I'm a psychopath?" Ukiah asked while looking straight ahead.

"Not at all. I ... I ..."

How could I change the subject without upsetting Ukiah's fragile emotional balance?

"I was wondering how you ever became a race car driver."

"A race car driver. Who wouldn't want to be one? Shit. Compared to writing, getting behind the wheel is a breeze."

"Where did you get the car? Who pays for it?"

"In the racing world, sponsors foot most of the bills. So, since we need to spread a little money around ..."

Launder it, I thought.

"... let's just say stock car racing is a good place to hide it."

"I can't wait to watch you. I've never been to one of those races. Do you ever win?"

"Here and there," Ukiah laughed. "Usually more than less."

"Super. Since we're talking about winning, is there any other reason why you want to get published other than to murder ... I mean, to contact your parents?"

"Isn't it obvious?" Ukiah replied. "An artist has four purposes. One, he must create, that's a given. Second, he needs to maximize his freedom. If a person can't get up each morning and not owe the world a damn thing, it'll show in their work. Third, it is a must for artists to procreate, so their genetic energy can flow from one incarnation to another. Finally, and most importantly, the artist should become one with their Muse."

Once again, Ukiah mentioned his Muse. I wondered if he thought this being was real? The entire concept sounded absurd. Who could ever believe in an invisible Being that allowed you to write better? To even consider it was sheer lunacy. Romlocon, huh? Ukiah felt compelled to please this unseen creature. How would he handle having a real cross to bear, like the thought of my father in his mind twenty-four hours a day? As I drove, I realized that the source for every action I had ever taken was my father. His face, words, fists, and regulations patterned each move I made. And somehow, Ukiah picked up on these fears and used them to manipulate me. I had only mentioned my father once, but Ukiah knew ... at times I thought he knew everything in the universe.

Troubled by these thoughts, I cruised along a striking mountain pass, the fall foliage becoming more colorful the higher we got. Ukiah had been talking the entire time, finally closing with these words.

"... from my perspective, an artist should not only feed off adversity, but let it fuel their creative drive. Without grains of sand irritating them, oysters would never make pearls."

Disappointed with myself for ignoring Ukiah's monologue in favor of my own paranoid thoughts, I took a stab in the dark with the following question.

"How does one go about getting published?"

Laughing, Ukiah responded, "I'm glad you asked me a simple question. How does one go about getting published? First, I need to clarify a few points."

My passenger spoke with an authority that transcended others whom I had met during my life. Their talk about politics, sports, and gossip only reinforced my status as a loner.

"To become a published author, ya have to always worry about being tarnished in the process."

Yet again, I couldn't grasp Ukiah's message.

"Tarnished?" I asked.

"Yeah. For me to get published, I need to purify The Word, and not get tainted while doing so."

"Tainted?"

"If even one aspect of my Self is compromised, then I've soiled The Word's purity."

"But how do authors dirty The Word? I'm not following ..."

"Listen! If you're reduced to sucking dick, calling in favors, writing phony formula pieces, or surrendering your freedom, then you've already sold your pound of flesh. How do you benefit by getting published if The Word has lost its purity in the process?"

"And you?"

"I want it all, baby! I've refused to approach the artsy literary magazines who've ruined more authors than they've helped. Instead, I see myself being the greatest overnight sensation since Elvis Presley. When I finally hit the literary world, their heads will spin."

"Have you tried to find an agent?" I asked after noticing a sign for Duality Speedway.

"Actually, I wrote my first two letters last week."

"You did! Why didn't you tell me? Ukiah, if we're going to be friends ... we are friends, aren't we?"

"Of course, Chris."

"Then you should start telling me these things. That's what friends do. So what did you write?"

"In my first letter, I reiterated everything we talked about during our first conversation. In the follow-up, I told this agent in New York City that if they didn't contact me soon, every day that passed was another one pissed away."

"It sounds like your letter had a sense of urgency."

"It did! The plans that are bouncing around inside my head are ready to explode. I made it clear that time is of the essence. It would be different if I were a hack writer with only one book under my belt. But I have such a huge body of work that to keep wasting time is inexcusable."

"I agree," I said, fretting that we were nearing the speedway. Although I anticipated the races, I also dreaded the end of our conversation.

"Did you tell this agent about the diversity of your work?"

"Yeah, but I'm not sure my descriptions were accurate. I mean, how can fifty-seven pounds of material be compressed into two pages? To compensate, I told this agent that my output was even more detailed than Jack Kerouac's. Here's what I want to do - line all my books up side by side, then let each reader start at one end. By the time they reach the other end, they'll have learned about my entire life. So, just like Jack Kerouac, my undertaking hints at an egotism gone mad!"

"Did you send any excerpts, or a few pages for the agent to read?" I asked, turning from a four-lane mountain highway onto a dusty dirt road.

"It would be impossible to give a reflection of my overall work by sending a few random samples. Suppose I were talking about acting, and the subject was Robert

DeNiro. How could I summarize his career?"

"You'd splice together a few clips from his movies."

"True. But with my work, I wouldn't feel comfortable being pigeon-holed by a few samples."

"So, instead of listening to the opinion of others ..."

"... I'll follow my own instincts," Ukiah laughed. "But what's it matter? They'll only settle for mediocrity anyway. While I'm staring at the stars, those assholes in New York can't see past their sun visors."

"That's a heavy rap you're laying on them," I commented while bouncing along the dirt road.

"Is it? Are we so progressive nowadays? I went to Splitting Image Bookstore the other day and leafed through a book that outlined the history of philosophy. This work covered all the heavy-hitters through history; then, for some reason, came to a stand-still after the 1940s. My first reaction was, 'whoa, you mean for the last fifty years there have been no advances in critical thinking?' I was astonished, and disappointed with our recent generations. It was as if we've lived in a void for the last half century. How could this lapse in creative thought be justified? What the hell is going on? Are we returning to The Dark Ages?"

"How far is the track?" I asked, my Gemini taking a beating along the way.

"Only a couple more miles." Then, not missing a beat, Ukiah continued. "The same applies to literature. Look at France during the 1920s and 1940s. It was vibrant and alive with The Word. Likewise, 1950s America bubbled with creativity, spawning another burst of talent in the 1960s. But take a critical glance at 1990s America. There ain't nothing going on."

"How do you plan on changing this situation?"

Amped with energy, he shouted, "I'm going to gas up the Maserati and burn down the highway to fame. There sure as hell won't be any congestion. I could blow the world away in five categories - philosophy, religion, literature, politics, and the sociology of popular culture. And believe me, Chris, I didn't brag to this agent when I told her I had the potential to be the next decade's most prolific author. To become a star in this country, all ya have to do is lay your bloody, neurotic perversions on a plate and let the morbidly fascinated lick it up. And baby, I'll be the biggest freak they've ever seen."

"You're wild ... insane!" I yelled with delight.

"I believe in my vision more than anything on this planet. If my words didn't make this agent curious, they better check their pulse to see if they're still alive."

With this braggadocios close, I pulled my Gemini into Duality Speedway, wondering if Ukiah were a genius (as he professed), or simply a deluded, arrogant man who'd lost his marbles. Hopefully, I'd find out one of these days.

After entering the speedway gates, I drove the Gemini across a huge dirt lot that had enough ruts, gullies, potholes, mounds, and crevices to make it feel like we were riding a surfboard, or in a sailboat being tossed about a wave-swept ocean. My shock absorbers worked overtime as we bounced and rocked through this veritable minefield. In addition, the dust being kicked-up by other automobiles made the struggle similar to driving through a bowl of soup.

We finally arrived at a grassy meadow that served as the parking area. A tiny aluminum-framed ticket stand stood before us, while a set of wooden bleachers loomed in the distance. The distinct echo of revving engines could be heard by all, a sure sign that the first race was ready to begin. So this was it - Duality Speedway.

As we strode toward the bleachers, Ukiah pointed excitedly.

"Look over there, its Japhy and his girlfriend!"

Holding hands and grinning broadly, a young couple approached.

"How are ya, buddy?" Ukiah yelled. "What are you doing here?"

"I wouldn't miss your last race of the season," Japhy replied.

After greeting both of them, Ukiah introduced me.

"Japhy, Gina - this is Chris Edwards. We came here together."

Following a round of hellos, the four of us proceeded toward the track. As Japhy and Ukiah chatted, I took a closer look at the teenage couple. Physically, Japhy resembled his father, both possessing thin, medium-sized frames. And although their hair color was different (Japhy's being brown), facially they mirrored each other. Even their voices sounded the same. It was also easy to tell from their conversation that they had a lot in common. So this sixteen year old boy was Japhy ... damn, I still didn't know Ukiah's last name. What was wrong with me?

On the other hand, Gina was a girl of exceptional beauty. Somewhat shorter than Japhy, she sported straight brown hair with bangs, and a face that drew people in like a Siren's song. Bestowed with statuesque cheekbones, straight white teeth, and a pouty smile, Gina was definitely a catch.

After reaching the grandstand's entrance, Ukiah declared, "Okay, I gotta go. Chris, you can sit with Japhy and Gina. I wanna hear some cheering up there."

"Kick their ass, Dad," the teenager shouted as his father strolled toward the pit area.

As dusk enveloped the rural setting, we climbed the bleacher's black metal steps, then sat on splintered wooden slats as floodlights illuminated the half mile track. A slight chill rippled through the autumn air as I gazed about the grounds. The bleachers were approximately half-full, with the majority of men wearing flannel shirts, jeans, cowboy hats, and western-style boots. The women were essentially dressed the same, minus the cowboy hats. The focus of their attention was an oval-shaped asphalt track with broken white lines marking each straight stretch. Prior to race time, the track's infield monopolized our attention. Dozens of late-model automobiles littered the pit area, each with dented fenders, smashed headlights, glassless windows (except for the windshield), and battered doors. They were also splashed with flashy paint and an array of stickers that promoted their sponsors.

As mechanics fine-tuned their engines, the unmistakable smell of exhaust fumes and gasoline permeated the thick, smoky air. But even more noticeable were the sounds that filtered across the track - revving engines, clanging tools, acetylene-cutting torches, and tires burning around corners as the racers took practice laps. The assault on one's senses was incredible - intoxicating aromas, shrill, penetrating noises, and the visual whirl of cars racing in circles. A part of me wanted to flee from the track and return to my Gemini - by night's end I'd either suffer permanent hearing loss, or die from asphyxiation.

Prior to the first race, I summoned the courage to start a conversation with Japhy and Gina.

"Do you go to many of these races?"

"Almost every Saturday," Japhy laughed. "I gotta make sure my dad doesn't get killed."

"Yeah," I smiled, "he is a crazy driver."

"I don't mean that. He's the best racer on the circuit. I meant that some of the other drivers want to kill him."

"Why?" I asked with concern.

Gina chimed in, "Last week after Ukiah won the trophy, they set his car on fire."

"They set his car on fire? Who?" I panted.

Japhy explained, "There's this racer named Wendall Krause. He's the dirtiest driver goin'. One week my dad got hung-up on the wall, and guess what Wendall did?"

"He bashed right into the side of his car," Gina answered.

"My dad sat there like a duck in the pond when WHAM, Krause smashed into his rear quarter panel."

"Why would he do that?" I asked.

"Jealousy, pure and simple. See, my dad never has the hottest car on the track, but he makes up for it with sheer racing ability. Now Krause's sponsor is a big money high roller, so he lands a speed-demon every week. But my dad shows him. Wendall hasn't entered victory lane in fourteen races."

"What number is Wendall's car?" was my next question.

"It's double zero because he never wins," Gina giggled.

"Yeah, Wendall is the biggest cheater on the circuit. A few weeks ago he smuggled a bucket of grease into his car, then when my dad was ready to pass, he poured it out his window and made him spin."

"How about the time he threw those roofing nails under your dad's wheels," Gina added.

"He does that?" I asked with disbelief. "Why don't the officials penalize him, or disqualify the bum?"

"These guys are just Saturday night roundy-rounders. They don't have an official rules commission or anything like on TV. They just go out there and bang away. But my dad got Wendall last week."

"What'd he do?"

"Well, he had his mechanics rig a spiked pole into his left front tire that sprung out if ya pushed a button. When Krause tried to pull one of his tricks, my dad pushed his button and this spear popped out and punctured Wendall's tire. It was great."

"You should have seen him swearing!" Gina cried. "He was so mad."

"That's when he lit his car on fire, when dad stood in victory lane. But don't worry, he has something planned for him this week, too."

"What? What?" I begged.

"I'm not sure, but earlier he whispered that near the race's end, when Wendall usually pulled his stunts, he'd be ready."

"I can't wait," Gina shrieked with excitement.

As I pondered the sanity of these racers, I noticed a hill that overlooked the speedway's far corner. Atop it sat a large contingent of pick-up trucks and sports cars, a few campfires lighting their surroundings.

"Who are those people over there?" I asked.

"That's the beer drinker's hill," Japhy told me. "They sit there all night guzzling from a keg and downing whiskey. It gets crazy by night's end. And boy do they hate Wendall. When he starts cheating, they'll pelt him with beer cans, or splatter his windshield with eggs. It's a howl!"

As Japhy and Gina laughed, a husky-voiced man howled over the speedway's public address system, "Gentlemen, start your engines!"

As motor's fired and roared with life, a deafening wall of noise rolled through the grandstand. It felt as if packs of growling beasts were unleashed from the jungle to run roughshod across the bleachers. I was certain I'd never be able to hear again.

While the first set of racers circled the track, I didn't notice Ukiah's car.

"Where's your dad?" I yelled to his son.

"He doesn't race until later. These are the Outlaws. After them come the late-models, the midgets, the pure stocks, then the sprint cars. Finally, when they're all done, the major leaguers hit the track. That's when my dad races."

Just then a teenage girl walked past yelling, "Programs. Programs for sale."

Hoping to understand this sport a little better, I bought one ... then an insightful thought entered my mind. I would finally learn Ukiah's last name! I hurriedly leafed through the pages until finding the following section:

Car Number	Make	Sponsor	Driver
888	Chevy	Minella's News	Ukiah Rhymes

Ukiah Rhymes! That was his name.

A few lines down I noticed the following information concerning his nemesis.

Car Number	Make	Sponsor	Driver
00	Ford	Double Helix Delivery	Wendall Krause

As the Outlaws geared-up near the far turn, a man at the start/finish line waved a green flag and the evening's first race began. Each car screamed down the front stretch, maneuvering for position and pulling kamikaze passes around the turns. Where earlier I had been distracted by the smells and noise, this spectacle now came alive! I remembered the rush I felt on the bypass a few weeks earlier where every ounce of life was focused on the task at hand - to keep from wiping-out. Now these guys were racing like that lap after lap, with a dozen other cars doing the same.

In no time the first collision occurred, two cars trading paint, then connecting bumpers as they veered into a concrete retaining wall. Yellow lights began flashing around the track as a wrecker arrived to haul away the demolished vehicles. Soon after, the racers were once again screaming under a green flag. As we watched these Outlaws, then the late models and midgets, I wanted to leap from my seat and race with those guys. How great would it be to fly at 90 miles an hour ... to feel your blood gushing with such intensity that you feared every vein in your body would burst ... adrenaline pumping like water through a fire hose ... eyes riveted to a track that was blanketed by flood-lights ... speed gushing speed — cars veering to your right and left, spinning passing blasting toward you ... hit the gas and crank it even faster, motor roaring - tires squeal-ing ... go go ... heart pounding ... so intense ... faster, everything a swirling whirl rushing past - blurry. Gas brake steering wheel - a vacuum of deafening silence - someone wrecks in front of you, quick turn to the left, then right, avoid an accident - but then … no - the wall approaches ... slam bam, head against the steering wheel, twisted metal, a flattened tire ... ...

A catastrophic accident did occur when two late-models collided, their momentum carry-ing them straight into the wall. Being that the impact was so direct, one of the cars actually catapulted into the air over the other's roof, then straight into a metal guardrail. His velocity was so great that his car nearly flew over top the wall. Luckily, his car sailed back onto the track where two other racers T-boned him in succession. The man looked like a pinball on the track - getting slammed in one direction, then violently in the other. To compound matters, gasoline leaked from his fuel cell, spreading onto the track where an errant spark from the twisted metal ignited it, soon starting a dangerously intense fire. In no time, a fire engine sped onto the scene and extinguished the blaze, soon followed by an ambulance and tow truck.

The result of this crash was an entire section of guardrail had not only been damaged, but completely torn away. An eight-foot stretch of metal was decimated by these stock cars careening through the air. A horrifying vision then entered my mind. What would have happened to Ukiah and me had we lost control going 90 miles an hour on the bypass that day, especially with no roll cage or safety equipment? My bones would have resembled the twisted wreckage laying on the track. I didn't even want to think about it.

During the interim, as a new section of metal was welded onto the guardrail, the race promoters held a burnout contest to entertain the crowd. If you're like me, you're probably wondering, "What is a burn-out contest?" Basically, the master of ceremo-nies announced to the crowd that anyone was allowed to drive their personal vehicle onto the straight stretch to see how far they could burn rubber down the track. That was it - a burnout contest.

Before I knew it, a line of cars circled Duality Speedway waiting for their turn to lay rubber. You should have seen these crazy people in their souped-up muscle cars - Camaros, Corvettes, GTOs, and Furys - beating the hell out of them. Over time, the amount of smoke they generated became noxious, so I asked Japhy how they did it.

"What they do," he began, "is use a technique called power braking."

"Never heard of it," I confessed.

"All ya do is stomp on the brake, then punch the gas. What happens is that your back tires start turning, but since you're also humping the brake, all they do is spin in place, creating the screeching effect. Then, when you release the brake, your tires, due to the overblown r.p.m.'s, scream down the track, causing a burn-out."

"But where does all that smoke come from? Some of those cars are so consumed ya can't even see 'em."

"That's a little trick. What these guys do is soak their tires in bleach. Then when they burn out, the effect is magnified."

"I see."

"Why don't you try it, Japhy," Gina coaxed him. "C'mon. I wanna see a burn-out."

Ten minutes later, Japhy's gray van was squealing along the track, laying marks with the best of them.

It was hard to believe what these people did to their automobiles - they could tear up a transmission, blow a motor, or drop their rear ends, not to mention the tire damage. But who cared? It was a riot to watch. These souped-up muscle cars idled on the track, then suddenly the drivers gunned their engines, back wheels spinning violently in place. First the cloud was negligible, but after a few seconds the bleach kicked in and the entire car became smothered in its own smoke - r.p.m.'s gunning higher, tension increasing, then SCREEEEEECH, the hot rod emerged from the fog — squealing tearing ripping and roaring down the track, a trail of burnt rubber, smoke, and exhaust fumes left behind. What a blast.

Half an hour later the guardrail was repaired, just in time to finish the late-model's final heat; then on to the main attraction - Ukiah's division! As these speed demons took their practice laps, I checked out Ukiah's #888 racer. Being that Salvatore was his primary sponsor, the black Chevy's hood was painted with the following logo:

Minella's Newsstand
"Where Everything You Read Is True"

Behind him ran Wendall Krause's Double Zero Ford, an imposing machine that enjoyed the privilege of being that night's most expensive automobile (if the intricacy of one's paint job was any determinant). Whereas the other cars settled for makeshift designs and flat colors, Wendall's Ford sparkled under the floodlights.

Here it was - the night's most anticipated race - forty laps, the winner able to claim bragging rights for the entire winter. As Japhy returned to his seat beside Gina and me, the green flag dropped and twenty stock cars sped across the starting line. Being at the end of the pack, it took about seven laps before Ukiah maneuvered through the crowd to join Wendall near the lead. These two racers then fought and clawed for ten, fifteen, twenty laps - neither able to successfully pull from the other.

Being that Wendall's car had an engine of slightly higher quality, he tried to pull ahead of Ukiah. But to his credit, Japhy's father did everything in his power to keep him in sight. By lap 30, these two had lapped every other competitor, the race boiling down to a ten lap shoot-out.

Ukiah tried everything in his power to pass Wendall - first he'd hold a high line, then pull from a turn and swoop down low. But the #00 car was there to block him, so Ukiah tried a different line. Nothing worked, and laps quickly slipped away on the half-mile track.

Lap 36, 37, 38. Only two more to go. Then they crossed the start/finish line as a white flag furled in the wind. The final lap!

"Don't worry, my dad said he had a surprise for Wendall when the going got tough," Japhy yelled as he rose to his feet.

And that's when it happened. On lap 40, as Ukiah executed a slingshot maneuver off the first turn and pulled near Krause on the outside, Wendall thrust his Ford to the right and bashed into Ukiah, nearly sending him into the wall. Miraculously, Ukiah kept control of his car, still running side by side with Krause. Frustrated, Wendall once again pulled the same stunt, this time even more blatantly. WHAM. He slammed into Ukiah full force, but instead of trying to avoid this collision, an unbelievable event transpired. With only one hand holding the steering wheel, Ukiah extended his left arm from the window and ... what was he holding?

"Look, he has a baseball bat!" Japhy exclaimed.

Sure enough, as these two rivals passed the drinking hill and volleys of aluminum cans showered down on them, Ukiah crashed into Wendall's car and then - I don't know how - he SMASHED the Ford's windshield with his baseball bat, sending shards of broken glass into Wendall's driver's compartment. Every person in the crowd leaped to their feet and cheered (especially those on the hill) as Wendall lost control and skidded headlong into Ukiah's Chevy. At first I thought my friend would maneuver around him, but the impact was too ferocious. In a passing second both drivers slammed their brakes, creating a tremendous cloud of smoke around them. Then WHACK, they hit the wall with the force of a locomotive ... but instead of getting hung-up, both cars slid down the track as lapped traffic passed them. Being that they were all one lap down, each car had to once again circle the track to catch Wendall and Ukiah. These two leaders were only one straightaway from the finish line, but both were coasting - their fenders, bumpers, and doors dented in every direction.

Both were rolling, stalled, trying to refire their engines. Each had enough momentum to cross the finish line, and being that Ukiah managed to rebound off the wall in front of Wendall, I thought for sure he would emerge victorious. Slowly, ever so slowly, he rolled toward the finish line, only fifty yards away. Yes, he would win! BUT then — NO — it couldn't be. Wendall refired his engine, revved it once or twice, then sped in front of Ukiah to win by the nose of a car. Broken windshield and all, Wendall Krause would remain champion all winter long.

6

"Grab your coat and let's go," Ukiah panted one evening after rapping impatiently at my door.

"Where? Where are we going?" I replied, adrenaline bursting through my body.

"Joan Jett and the Blackhearts are playing at The Dies Infaustus Bar. How could I have forgotten that show?"

"What's that?" I asked, "What's a Joan Jett?"

But Ukiah refused to answer.

Sixty seconds later we rushed from my house like dust devils spinning through piles of fallen leaves. With Ukiah, nothing was ever commonplace, or based on pre-planned normalcy. It seemed like we were forever confronted with catastrophes, matters of utmost urgency, or impending disasters waiting to occur. One thing I never needed to worry about was a hardening of the arteries. With Ukiah, my blood was always flowing.

A short while later we parked in downtown Latera Heights, then walked briskly toward the Dies Infaustus, the area's premier nightclub. Once inside, after descending two spiral staircases, a vibrant anticipation shot through the bar's dark, smoky air as patrons crowded every inch of the club. There were so many fans, in fact, that after we strolled through the front door, two bouncers locked it behind us. The bar had reached (and probably surpassed) its maximum occupancy - a throbbing, sweaty collection of revelers crammed into this glittery underground hall.

The Dies Infaustus' stark, unfinished walls were plastered with velvet rock n' roll posters, while black metal fixtures holding multi-colored lights hung from a ceiling whose skeletal rafters were deliberately exposed. A rectangular mirror-lined bar highlighted one section of the club, while small circular tables and chairs lined the walls. The dance floor was nothing more than an open pit packed with anxious fans whose bodies radiated claustrophobic closeness.

Being the last two patrons allowed into the club, Ukiah and I stood near the pit's stairwell, directly facing a stack of amplifiers only fifteen feet from the stage. Not one to frequent such venues, the proximity of bodies filled me with a slowly rising surge of anxiety. I would have preferred the contentment of my protective living room ... but ...

The entire nightclub lost its lighting as shrieks of delight and raucous applause erupted from the crowd. The loud, heavy, heart-penetrating thump of a bass drum created an aura of tribal anticipation - THUMP ... thump thump thump ... THUMP. This bass drum laid the foundation ... Thump, THUMP — then a set of blinding technicolor lights flashed atop the stage to expose a petite woman with short-cropped flaming red hair and an intense pale face. The crowd gushed with enthusiasm as Joan Jett strummed a white guitar and growled her lyrics into a twitching microphone. This slight yet athletically framed female hit the stage with such an intense energy level that I felt her vibes fifteen feet away. As I stared at her through a sea of bobbing heads and flailing hands, I soon realized that Joan projected an image unlike anything I was accustomed to. In addition to her shocking red hair, Joan's eyes were lined with jet-black mascara, while her alabaster skin glowed with ghastly brilliance. Her stage attire consisted of nothing more than a low-cut sleeveless leather vest that exposed her navel, and tight black jeans wrapped by a thin, silver-studded belt. In all, an aura of unmistakable androgyny emanated from this charismatic rocker - a short, boyish haircut, nearly nonexistent breasts, and straight, compact hips. Even the stickers on her guitar highlighted this enigma, with one declaring in bright red letters, "Gender Fuck."

The crowd went crazy for Joan and her band, which consisted of another guitarist, bassist, and drummer. Their music - no-nonsense three-chord power-pop spiked with elements of punk - had every fan cheering and rocking in place. Even I got used to the sensory overload - amplifiers blasting with powerful fury, their sound ricocheting off the walls like a rubber ball. The concert became viciously energized - faster, with pulsating drums, a thumping bass line which kicked each listener in the chest ... ear-shattering feedback that pierced my brain with the torturous intensity of burning needles ... stomping feet - clapping hands ... shrill whistles and crazed banshee wails ... occasional guitar solos that sizzled with speed, and Joan's ability to burn down the house with frenzied delirium.

I looked at Ukiah at one point to see him bouncing up and down in place, bobbing his head to the beat. Cramped tightly against those around us, Ukiah's eyes ... his complete Being ... was fixed on Joan Jett. I couldn't tell what impact she made on him, but Ukiah's entire focus revolved around this searing, diminutive rocker.

As a pulsating throng of partiers slowly pushed toward the stage, I was overcome by the manic experience - unrelenting music, lights flashing with the brilliance of a hallucinatory rainbow ... a drum beat continually thumping into my chest – the smell of spilled beer and cigarette smoke wafting through the dense air, and a buzz ... a buzz that rose with vibrant life.

Joan pushed the crowd, lead them, urged them to wilder heights ... then I saw a horrifying sight only rows from me. A drunken, shirtless man with psychopathic eyes began thrusting his arms in circles around his head, hitting anyone in the vicinity. Girls squealed tearfully as men in the crowd tried to subdue this maniac ... but there was no stopping him.   The drunken wild man randomly threw punches at anyone within reach.   As he moved toward me, I feared being hit by bloody fists, or having this nut case bite off my nose.   His behavior was sheer insanity ... an amok gone mad.   As I readied myself to race down the stairwell, two bouncers shoved through the crowd.

"Get your fucking hands off me or I'll kill you," the lunatic screamed as each bouncer clutched his body and dragged him from the dance floor.

As they did so, only inches from my trembling body, I watched this madman clench his teeth into one of the bouncer's arms and bite with the ferociousness of a wolf.   The bouncer instantly loosened his grip, then yanked a beer bottle from someone's hand and smashed it over his sweat-drenched head.   Upon impact, the psychopath gurgled an incantation of such evil that I truly thought he was possessed.   Partially freed, he swung one arm viciously through the air before two other bouncers arrived on the scene.   Four of them now held the man as they hauled him kicking and screaming from the premises.

As he passed me, the delirious creature (grunting and gasping for breath) snarled, "I'll kill you too, freak," his face so near mine I could see the spittle flying from his lips.   If released, I'm sure he would have murdered me with his bare hands.   Following his eviction, I glanced sideways to see if Ukiah was scared.   To my dismay, a broad grin crossed his face, as if he enjoyed the mayhem.   While I stood utterly petrified, Ukiah craved the chaos.

As this melee ensued, Joan Jett and the Blackhearts didn't miss a beat, opting instead to continue their frenetic onslaught.   During one number, Joan set aside her guitar and sang about the joys of bondage and discipline, wrapping the microphone cord around her wrists in a blatantly sadomasochistic fashion.   The symbolism did not escape me.   Following this song, Joan did an about face and, rather than churning out another ball-burner, sang a touching ballad called *Crimson and Clover*.   Of all the songs she performed, this was the only one whose lyrics I could understand.

Joan ended her set with four rousing encores, then raced from the stage dripping in sweat, about to drop from exhaustion.   The crowd's standing ovation lasted for at least three minutes before they finally dispersed.

After stepping from the club into the cool autumn air and trying to shake the sensory imbalance from my head, I shouted to Ukiah (due to my ears buzzing with such clamor), "What a show!"

"Joan is the most gorgeous woman alive," he proclaimed.   "What a knockout!   I'd marry her on the spot."

Laughing, I commented, "You might need a sex change to land Joan Jett."

"I'd do it," Ukiah boasted, "if that's what it took to see her play guitar every night!"

We both laughed at this prospect, then walked along a sidewalk bathed in calm, fluorescent light. While doing so, my head echoed with an eerie hollowness, similar to the sensation one gets when putting a seashell to their ear. In addition, my body tingled with a rubbery looseness that made my knees weak. Yes, by concert's end, I was bouncing and swaying with everyone else in the crowd.

While the subject of music lingered in my mind, I broached the topic with Ukiah.

"By the way, have you heard anything from that high school teacher about Japhy's band?"

"No, but I got a cassette tape of his band a few days ago, so I sent it to Mister Doublet."

"Is he the same one you've been trying to contact?" I asked.

"You bet, and I'm going to keep pestering that son of a bitch. There's nothing like a good dose of tenacity and perseverance. Yeah, this tape Japhy made was incredible. Although it was recorded on a four-track while they practiced one night, it sounds professional."

"Oh, before I forget," I chirped as we reached my Gemini, "do you remember that author you're always talking about ... the one you hate?"

"Philip Prince?"

"Yeah, he's the one. Well, Prince is on *The Tonight Show* this evening."

Excited, Ukiah snapped, "What time does it start?"

"Midnight," I told him.

"What time is it now?"

I checked my watch. "11:45."

"C'mon, hurry, we can still make it," he urged. "Oh, sorry, um ... can I watch the show at your place? I still don't have a TV."

"Sure. Hop in. On second thought, maybe you should drive," I suggested, tossing the keys to Ukiah. "I wouldn't want to be responsible for missing the show's beginning."

With that vote of confidence, Ukiah placed my key in the ignition, fired up the Gemini, then roared through the foggy streets.

As Ukiah burst though the darkness, ignoring speed limits with blatant disregard, I gazed across the seat. Becoming better acquainted with him, I wondered if I needed professional help. At times it seemed as if he were the only person that mattered to me, and nothing could be done to distance myself from him. Ukiah seemed to live atop a pedestal, an idol resented by the worshippers below. His subjects were once flattered, adoring their object of desire. But now they accused him of selfishness for not making their dreams come true. But how could Ukiah please them? The only thing he was ever fascinated by was himself. The commoners used to love him. But their love turned to hatred. In his presence, their once barren lives were replaced with meaning - if blind adoration can be called a legitimate emotion. But Ukiah never noticed. He rose above them ... callous, vain, and insensitive. Nothing mattered except his own reflection - one that he stared at endlessly each day. He withdrew from them, and subsequently his subjects plummeted into madness ... a madness that dominated their lives.

After pulling into my driveway from Reflection Alley, I returned to reality and considered my thoughts. Was it really Ukiah who put himself on a pedestal, or did I give him this important position? Similarly, were the subjects who felt ignored by their idol actually symbolic of me? Was I the pathetic worshipper who felt shunned by this inaccessible idol? Actually, Ukiah probably never stood on a pedestal at all. He simply lived as a loner in his own private world. There wasn't anything remarkable about this stance ... Ukiah just kept to himself. And where did this realization leave me? I remained a faithful slave at his altar, waiting to pray when he allowed it.

*　　*　　*　　*　　*

Philip Prince's Daily Journal: (Subject - Tonight Show with Jay Leno)

"So Mister Prince, tell us about your new book, 'Prince of the Earth,' the host asked me.

Displaying the brilliance of a polished public speaker, I conveyed to Jay that my latest novel ... well, let me see, how many have I actually written? Let me count. Thirty-two novels, five short story collections, nine screenplays, and one study of the science fiction genre. If I do say so myself, I truly am America's most prolific author.

I was witty beyond words this evening, far superior to the petty audience who felt honored to share my presence. How I must have enlightened them with my repertoire of anecdotes and literary allusions. Those lucky fools, so close to the greatness of Philip Prince.

"Philip, tell us about your new book, *Prince of the Earth*."

"This extraordinary tale takes place in a realm called The Twin Cities. In it ... wait a second, Jay. I want to tell you about my garden."

"Your garden?"

"I'm growing the most wonderful flower, a strain of New World bulbous herbs that originate in the Amaryllis family. Related to the daffodil and jonquil, these paper-white pretties bear clusters of small, yet extremely fragrant pure white blossoms ...."

"Listen to that idiot. What a phony," Ukiah yelled. "He's booked on TV to promote his latest novel, and what does he talk about? His fucking flowers. What an asshole."

I seconded the motion by adding, "He is boring."

"Boring. It's no wonder I won't buy a TV. These talk shows are so absurd ... blah blah blah all night long. Nobody has the balls to talk about anything important. I swear, if that man goes on a book tour and speaks at Latera University, I'll murder him. I'll shoot him right between his beady eyes."

"Turn that fucking TV off," Ukiah cursed as he rose from the floor. "The sight of that phony gives me the creeps. He reminds me of a professor I read about who published a book concerning obsessive-compulsive disorders. In this article, he talked about going to a public relations seminar before his book signing tour so, get this, he could sound like every other author. His exact quote was, 'All my answers should be identical to everyone else's.' Can you believe it? The bullshit that came from this professor's mouth is what I'm rebelling against. Rather than being a clone, I want to be unique ... real ... different from those nobodies who peddle their crap. Writers," Ukiah sighed, "sure are a sorry lot."

"Why do you say that?"

"Look at what we endure. The final product is nothing but words on a page. How boring. And the process is excruciating - eternal isolation, grueling concentration, and all the revisions. I'd give anything to be a painter, or moviemaker. At least then I could get some satisfaction from the final product."

"In what way?" I inquired.

"Look at those other craftsmen. Painters can hang their murals on a wall and admire them. Sculptors can use their creations for ashtrays or plant holders, while a cinematographer can watch his movies over and over. But what do we have? Black letters on a white page. And I'll tell ya, after preparing each novel, slaving over it for months, editing and revising, typing it, then proofing the damn thing, who wants to sit in a room and read these run-on letters? The worst part of writing involves our Muse."

Oh no, not this Romlocon nonsense again.

But Ukiah didn't notice my misgivings. He simply kept rambling.

"Think about the penance we have to pay to be granted ... yes, given the privilege to write. An author never knows when their Muse will call them home by taking away their inspiration."

"I don't understand."

"Writers rely on The Word as their life blood. If the Muse decides their time has come, she revokes her presence and the author becomes like any other mortal staring at a blank white page. The Word no longer flows - the magic is gone - and then there's writers block."

I shook my head as a blank expression painted my face.

"We've reached a point where most people don't even believe that a Muse exists. If I told ten people on the street what I'm telling you, they'd think I was crazy. It's all part of a plan to eliminate the Muse from an artist's life."

"I still don't follow."

"Do you know anything about my relationship with Romlocon? It's very intimate. But most artists today have no pact with their Muse whatsoever."

"Why is that?" I asked.

"Y'see, in simpler times, man enjoyed a much closer relationship with their Muse. But as we progressed technologically and scientifically, placing more emphasis on rational thought than artistic inspiration, we distanced ourselves from these Beings. We're actually nearing a stage where one could say the Muses have vanished, and no one would argue."

"Of all the people on this planet, why were you chosen by your Muse?"

"Because sometime soon Romlocon will reappear to deliver The Word. See, literature has lost its importance in this day and age. Sure, books keep getting published, but the majority don't have a message, or any inherent value. But once the Muse reawakens our dormant spirit, The Word will become an integral part of our lives. And I ... I've been chosen to sound a trumpet that will herald the Muse's arrival."

Rattled by Ukiah's grandiose explanations, I switched subjects by asking, "While we're talking about writing, are you still working on *Blank Line*?"

The living room remained quiet.

"The process is painstakingly slow, but I'm making headway," Ukiah commented. "At times, I wonder if my efforts wouldn't be better served elsewhere."

"Why?" I asked, surprised by Ukiah's loss of confidence.

"You watched *The Tonight Show*," he began, "and saw the difference between Philip Prince and me. He's polished, professional, and phonier than the tooth fairy. Publishers aren't looking for a whippersnapper like me who'll expose their lies. They'll stick with some old fogey like Prince."

"How old do you think he is?" I wondered aloud.

"Probably mid-fifties. He's ancient," Ukiah quipped.

Brimming with encouragement, I told him, "You can still break though their walls. What about The American Dream? You'll show 'em."

Ukiah shook his head and laughed.

"Let me tell you how the world works," he began dejectedly. "Suppose I had a rose bush that only sprouted one flower a year. People far and wide adored this rose, and wanted to possess it. When it finally blossomed, I could decide who got this prized beauty. Let's also say an old girlfriend planned on visiting me, and her stay coincided with the rose's maturity. Plus, she promised certain favors if I gave her the rose. Now I remember how fine those favors were, so who will I choose when it comes time to clip this flower? My former girlfriend who will sweeten the deal, or a complete stranger who's written from who knows where? This is how those vipers in New York City operate. And I'll tell ya," Ukiah shouted forcefully, "I'm not sweetening any fucking deal!"

Ukiah stood for a moment, then excused himself to use the bathroom. While away, I fretted over his frustrations. Although he saw himself as a realist and a survivor, Ukiah still had a thread of idealism that caused his spirit to be crushed on a daily basis. Due to this utopian streak, Ukiah couldn't understand why his efforts were constantly foiled. But could the entire publishing industry be as ruthless as he imagined? Worse, would it deliberately deny a genuine artist their chance at fame? The premise sounded too cold to be true.

My observations quickly dissolved as Ukiah stormed into the room with a head of steam.

"When Philip Prince polluted your television set with his gardening tales, I should have ran next door and grabbed my gun, then emptied an entire clip into the screen. What a jackass. Do you know what my new goal has become?" Ukiah shouted disdainfully.

"No ... no. What?" I stammered, fearing that tone of voice and look in his eye.

"I plan on destroying the literary world as we know it, then starting all over again. There's not an author on this planet that I look up to — none of them are what they seem. So my new purpose is to destroy writing. C'mon, let's get out of here."

"Get out of here?" I asked. "Where? I have to work tomorrow morning."

"C'mon, aren't you hungry? We didn't even eat after the Joan Jett concert."

"My stomach has been growling ..."

"Then grab your coat ..."

Ruing the fact that I was riding in Ukiah's Celebrity instead of lying in bed, I sat silently as we pulled from the driveway, then spontaneously exploded with rage.

"Shit! Damn!" I yelled.

Ukiah continued to turn his steering wheel without uttering a word.

"Keep going. Don't stop for anything," I told him.

Ukiah refused to listen. After proceeding a few feet, he saw a man wobbling along the darkened alleyway, weaving between potholes like a punch-drunk boxer.

"Who's that?" Ukiah asked as he pulled toward the disoriented man.

"Nobody," I lied, trying to avoid my neighbor Woody Dewar.

"Nobody seems to have X's for eyes," Ukiah laughed, pulling beside the man.

"Hey buddy, you're not lookin' too good," Ukiah said softly from the window.

"Pat left me," Woody moaned, slurring his words. "For somebody named Allen, or Ellen .. I'm not sure. Plus, I'm suffering from a fatal case of hermaphrodysuria."

"Well hey, buddy, why don't we get you home to bed. It looks like you could use a good night's sleep."

With those comforting words, Ukiah lead Woody to his front door, then disappeared inside for a few minutes before returning.

Boiling with rage, I snapped at Ukiah after he sat inside his car.

"Be careful, you'll be nursing Dewar every day."

Ignoring my sarcasm, he replied, "Woody just needs some friendship and understanding. The poor guy's lonely."

Unable to understand what Ukiah saw in my neighbor, I asked, "Where are we going to eat?"

"How about The Spectre?"

"I thought that place was only open during the day," I said.

"No, it's open at night, too."

As we drove, I considered Ukiah's statement about destroying literature, then asked, "Could you tell me more about the publishing industry, and why you're so disillusioned with it?"

"Another easy question," he laughed. "Essentially, this system is like any other in that its primary goal is self-preservation."

"Continuing into the future?" I queried.

"Exactly. To insure its existence, they have to bar their doors to anyone who refuses to toe the line."

"How do they do that?"

"By choosing lackeys who aren't ballsy enough to be dangerous. Now writers, especially those without any functional skills in the world, aren't ones to start trouble. How could they? What else can they do? Dig ditches or stamp parts in a factory? Hell no! Most are too feeble for the real world. What would you rather do - sit in an ivory tower or an air-conditioned skyscraper, or fix sewer lines in twenty-degree weather? The answer is obvious."

"How are these authors controlled? There must be certain techniques," I asked.

"Chris, rules are created for Art ... certain formulas which lay the groundwork. By following these rules, the artists lets their creative process be controlled. So, once they've been indoctrinated into the system ..."

"Indoctrinated?"

"Yeah. We're first molded during our grade school years, then shaped even further in college and grad school. If you move beyond this point into the shadowy world of manipulation ... where you meet with lawyers, editors, accountants ... well, the creative process has already been tainted ... even destroyed. From a very early age, The Word has been reduced to exactly what these people want it to be. Personally, I wonder how The Word can be perverted into anything other than what it is - a message of purity. The Word, which represents freedom to an artist, actually becomes the very device that enslaves them ... the controller's primary tool of manipulation. Anyone whose creations aren't an expression of their true Self ..."

"Becomes like Philip Prince," I burst.

"Yes! If they compromise their Art to make it sell, they're destined for a life of submission, obedient to the demands of a power hungry publisher. Today, money is the key that fuels the system and keeps these artists locked inside a web of lies. In essence, they become addicts to the publishing industry."

"Like drug addicts?"

"One in the same. By allowing their Art to be compromised by the powers that be, they assume the role of junkies, while the agents and publishers become their dealers. If their Words aren't approved by the publisher, they'll suffer withdrawal symptoms. Can't you see where it leads? It's a vicious cycle. The Word lends itself to Language, which Mankind becomes parasitically attached to as a host. This Language either grants freedom, allowing Man to flourish beyond his wildest dreams, or it constitutes an extremely powerful tool of control. Any artist who sacrifices his freedom for money becomes enslaved by the controllers … a destroyer of our creativity."

As Ukiah pulled into a darkened parking lot, I tried to comprehend the maze of information he laid on me. At least we'd be eating soon. Maybe the food would help clear my mind.

The Spectre, a non-impressive all-night diner whose storefront was highlighted by a plate-glass window stocked with intricately-designed cakes and pastries, was located across the street from Latera University. Its interior consisted of nothing more than high-backed plastic booths surrounding hardwood tables that sat on a crusty linoleum floor. The actual wallpaper could not be seen, for years of colorful graffiti marked every inch of space. In all, the café's atmosphere was typical of any college town hangout.

While passing the front counter, Ukiah bought a copy of *The New York Times Book Review*, folding it in his hand as we walked through the diner and found a table. Not accustomed to the nightlife, I had expected the eatery to be deserted, but instead it teemed with activity. Each booth held diners from every walk of life - students cramming for exams, partiers stopping off for a snack after boozing at the bars, long-haired dreary-eyed stoners, juvenile delinquents, hookers taking a break from the street, homeless men sipping from bottles hidden in brown paper sacks, wild-faced maniacs and freaks, and an array of late-night workers winding down after their shift. When I worked graveyard, the thought never crossed my mind to eat at one of these places. I simply drove home and hibernated in my house. Due to my limited social life, I never imagined such a thriving subculture. It felt as if I had encountered an entirely new world – darkened, halogen-lit streets, the smell of alcohol wafting from underground bars where bluesy music filled the frosty air, and a variety of subterranean werewolves and vampirish oddities.

As we sat in one of the booths, Ukiah unfolded *The New York Times Book Review* to find a full-color photograph of Philip Prince on its cover, the headline above it in bloody red capital letters declaring:

PRINCE OF THE EARTH RULES PLANET

At the sight of his smirking, sinister face, Ukiah erupted. "I swear, if that motherfucker comes to Latera Heights on a book tour, or lectures at the university, I'll gouge his fucking eyes from their sockets. My new purpose in life isn't to get published, but to murder that prick. But I'm not going to simply kill him. First I'll torture that bastard. Look at him gloating. I'll wipe that smile off his face. Maybe I'll pour battery acid across Prince's cheekbones, then make him watch his face melt in the mirror. How can I do it though? How can I get at him? I could shoot him, but then I'd get busted. Who wants to die in prison because of that asshole? If I can somehow hijack his limo, or get at him backstage, then I could get away with it. Or, maybe a bomb in his hotel room would do the number. The best though ... the best would be to kneel on his chest and strangle him until those beady eyes popped from their sockets. Even better ..."

The case was now closed - Ukiah had turned into a psychopath. No longer did he simply froth at the mouth and make idle threats. He planned on killing Philip Prince ... or worse.

"... that way maybe he'd just be a cripple for the rest of his life."

Ukiah finally quit plotting the author's demise, choosing instead to leaf through his newspaper. "Look," he chimed after reading page two. "Allen Ginsberg is dead. Shit," he chuckled, "if I were one of those flowery authors, I'd write a splashy poem about birds flying over the ocean with his spirit in their wings."

"You weren't a fan of Ginsberg?"

"I didn't agree with his politics or agenda, but he did have a vision that had a dramatic affect on the world. Yeah, I admired his persistence and tenacity. If only he could've written poetry as well as he promoted himself."

As Ukiah flipped through his newspaper, I asked, "What else is happening in the book world?"

"Let's see," he said vacantly. "Here's a two-page spread on the latest wave of literary lions."

"What's do you think of them?" I inquired, becoming interested in this exercise.

"The article looks boring, and the authors even more boring. I hate sounding negative, but I went to a bookstore last week and checked these guys out. In no time, after leafing through each of their novels, my suspicions were confirmed. Every book was written from a cookie cutter mold, without a hint of creativity or originality."

"They were that lame?"

"They reminded me of a few authors from the 1980s. Do you remember 'The Brat Pack'?"

"Not especially," I admitted, quite limited in my knowledge of literature.

"Well, you didn't miss much. These kids weren't writers, they were fireworks - a lotta flash, little substance, then they quickly burnt out. The same could be said about the newcomers in this article. They've essentially graduated from writing college papers that they got A's on to writing expanded, novel length versions of these term papers.

But that's all they'll ever be. None of them possess brilliance, vision, or greatness. That's why they'll be forgotten like last week's laundry. Oh sure, there will always be more laundry, but none of these flashes in the pan will be around for the long run."

As Ukiah's dissertation drew to a close, a college-aged waitress approached our table and handed us flimsy cardboard menus. Just as quickly, she scooted toward another table, a surprising bundle of energy at this late-night hour.

"They sure aren't much on rushing the customer along," I commented, inspecting a menu that was splattered with jam, egg yolks, ketchup, and hot dog grease.

"Nah, they figure if you're still out at two in the morning, ya got lots o' time to spare."

2:00! Damn. I had to be awake at 5:30 to begin my shift at 7:00. As it stood now, I'd only get a couple hours sleep. But Ukiah didn't care. He kept bitching about his book review.

"Speaking of novelty acts, last week I read about the literary world's newest sensation. I can't remember her name, but she wrote about having an incestuous affair with her own father."

"Are you serious?" I asked.

"Yeah, and because of morbid curiosity, the book will probably sell. But will she still be on her feet to answer the bell for the fifteenth round? Not a chance. She'll be like those gimmick songs from the 1970s - pure hype with no substance."

"Are you against hype?" was my next pointed question.

"Of course not. Without it, how would we ever get anyone's attention? I just don't want to be linked to a group of one-hit wonders who make a quick buck, then hibernate until they get hungry again."

"All right. What would we like to order?" the waitress chirped after returning to our table.

"A burger and fries," Ukiah replied.

"Um ... I'm not sure ... maybe a ... no ... how about a ... wait ... let me think. Could I get a ... no ... I'll have the same as him ..."

Shaking her head at my indecisiveness, the waitress zipped away like a brisk autumn breeze.

Laughing at my uncertainty, Ukiah continued his line of reasoning.

"Do you remember years ago when an ingenious marketing plan was used to promote

William Kennedy's *Ironweed* trilogy?"

Again I shook my head.

"Well, all three books were published at the same time. And to the best of my knowl-edge, it was done with class, and made money. But what has Kennedy done since becoming rich and famous? Nothing. I remember him being interviewed on *60 Minutes* after this event, and Kennedy was quite blunt in saying that he'd probably never write anything as potent as these three books."

"Why?"

"Because fame and fortune had already softened him. He wasn't hungry any more. But me, I'm starving, and plan on staying that way until the day I die!"

While my counterpart sat silently, I gazed about The Spectre, noticing an artsy-type crowd gathered at a nearby table.

"Do you know what?" Ukiah blurted. "If I can get all eighteen of my books published in five years, that record will stand forever ... unchallenged!"

Lured into Ukiah's trap, I asked, "What will your books look like?"

How could I be so naive to ask this question? A clock on the wall read 2:10 a.m., and I fueled the dreams of a knuckle-breaker who suffered from delusions of grandeur. It was like enabling an alcoholic, or giving chemicals to a mad-scientist. How could I continue this nonsense? Ukiah had never been published, yet acted as if he were more famous than Philip Prince. I should have been in bed dreaming about The Dewel Family, and how No-Sho The Hero saved our rocket ship from a gigantic pair of galactic scissors.

"Here's how I see the process," Ukiah burst, filled with manic energy. "I'll publish one book every three months. We'll make them paperbacks, and keep them simple. And, due to the wide variety of my writing styles, it'll be like eighteen different authors were being published."

"You're going to print cheap, throwaway books?" I asked, scratching my scalp.

"No, you're getting the wrong impression, Chris. I just want to make my books accessible to the public."

"Here ya go, two burgers with fries. Enjoy," the waitress smiled.

After greedily eating a few bites from my burger, I asked Ukiah, "Do you see that artsy crowd over there? Have you ever been associated with any particular move-ments?"

"Are you kidding? I wouldn't go anywhere near 'em! In fact, I've created my own literary style."

"Really," I said, outwardly impressed. "What's it called?"

"Solipsism."

"So what ism?" I coughed between bites from my burger.

"Solipsism," he repeated, none too pleased with my ignorance. "It's a Latin derivative of two words - 'alone' and 'self'."

"I get it."

"Solipsism means that the self can only know itself. So, the self is the only thing I can write about. Artistically, then, what I create is purely and solely ME. In this regard, I see myself leading a group of unknown authors just like myself - those who write painfully autobiographical material, yet are isolated from others in the artistic community. We're Soloists."

I had planned on asking Ukiah where his Muse and previous incarnations fit into this picture, but suddenly a ruckus broke-out at a table next to ours. An obviously drunken young woman dressed in jeans and a T-shirt staggered into The Spectre and sat in a booth beside us. A waitress politely tried to accommodate her, but every attempt at kindness was countered by abuse.

Finally fed-up, the waitress hollered, "Listen, Missy, why don't you take it outside and play hide n' go fuck yourself?"

"You want me to fuck myself?" she retorted. "Listen you bitch ..."

At that moment, Ukiah rose and walked toward the frantic lady. I instantly feared the worst, with fingernails tearing flesh, hair being pulled, wild shrieks, tears, torn clothing, screams of rape, and kicks to the groin. But Ukiah simply grabbed the girl's shoulders, then put his mouth to her ear. The young lady instantly settled down, looking like an overly medicated mental patient. He spoke a few more words to her, then returned to our booth without incident.

Beaming with pride, I gushed, "How did you do that? It was remarkable."

"A few well-selected words can ..."

"You fucker! Don't ever get in my face again," the girl screeched, racing toward Ukiah.

Beside her stood a burly college kid who was likewise drunk and wobbly.

As she clenched her fists, Ukiah stood without saying a word, reared-back, then punched her boyfriend square in the jaw, sending him spinning like a top.

The girl momentarily froze, then fled from the premises.

"Get this trash out of here," Ukiah finally told the waitress, pointing to the half-conscious man moaning on the floor.

Returning to our booth, Ukiah didn't say a word as he dipped a French fry in a pile of runny ketchup.

Rattled, I demanded, "What's going to happen now?"

"About what?" Ukiah sniffed, eating another fry.

"That guy. You walloped him right in the kisser."

"He asked for it."

"I know, but ... but what about the cops? Won't you get arrested?" I stammered.

"Nobody saw anything."

"But I ..."

"Did you see anything?"

"No."

"Okay then. Actually, that drunken broad is kinda cool in a way that relates to my writing."

"Cool?" I panted, unsure whether I heard him correctly.

"Sure. See, I try to make every story a reflection of the crazy life around us."

"As usual, I don't follow," I nodded, still trembling.

"The way I see it, life's greatest enemy is sameness. That crazy broad represented a departure from the norm. Can't you see? Repetition is boring. That's why I get so pissed-off at the art world."

"I don't have any idea what you're talking about," I confessed, too shaken to eat.

"It seems like once a creative person finds their niche, they become imprisoned by it. So, instead of pushing the boundaries and challenging themselves, they settle for the least common denominator."

"Where do your stories fit into the picture?" I asked eagerly.

"Well, there are common themes that run through my work, but I try to make every book different from the rest. And, although these stories relate specifically to my own life, I also try to make them universal."

"I wish we had a tape recorder," I said after Ukiah finished his latest explanation.

"Why?" he asked, eating his last French fry.

"Your critiques and observations are exactly what you should be telling that agent."

"I do! Believe me. Oh, I'm glad you reminded me. What's your address on Reflection Alley? I need to tell that agent."

"It's 3704."

"Thanks. Do you know I counted how many times I've moved since 1980, and this will be the twenty-fifth time."

"Wow. You've been around the block. What did you do to support yourself through all those moves ... that is if you don't mind my asking."

"I've been a janitor, gardener, computer operator ... let's see, a warehouse manager, stock boy, taxi-driver, and a factory hack. Plus, during one stretch when I lived at a cheap motel, I did maintenance work and painting during the day, then worked the motel's front desk at night."

"It sounds like you've seen your fair share of the world."

"I've met a lotta crazy people - alcoholics, pill freaks, conmen and thieves, pimps and hookers, plus some holy rollers, sex fiends, and psychics. Yeah, those moves and jobs taught me not only about life, but also human nature. In terms of writing, the world shouldn't be a remote subject researched from afar, but instead an intimate friend investigated each day."

Somewhat saddened, I said, "It all reverts back to writing, doesn't it?"

"Chris, it's all I have. I feel destined to enter the gates of publication, and due to this inescapable fate, I'm preparing myself for the celebration. I can't take lightly what I've been preparing for my entire life. Why do you think I quit drinking and smoking? I'm back in fighting shape, plus my mind is clear. Most importantly, my mouth is ready to roar!" Ukiah looked around casually, then smiled, "C'mon, let's get outta here. Why are you keeping me out so late?"

My alarm would ring two and a half hours later.

7

Yap yap yap yap yap. Jennifer, how can you even be employed at the same literary agency as that horrible man? We should get our gun and blast a hole right through the television screen. At least being crazy, there's something real about us. But look at Philip Prince. He's even cheesier on TV than in person. He makes my skin crawl. I can't watch him. How can Jay Leno even let him on *The Tonight Show*? It sickens me to be in the same room as him.

*   *   *   *   *

Jennifer, what possessed you? Look at this apartment. Every corner is crammed with flowers, while the ceiling hooks hold enough hanging plants to start a biosphere. How could you have stolen these things in such a brazen manner? Even worse, you took them from the greenhouse next door. Once the owners discover their missing plants, all they have to do is walk next door and catch you red-handed. It looks like a jungle in here.

Baby, what's driving you to these extremes? You're fifty-four years old, employed at The Mason Turner Literary Agency making $120,000 a year, and you're stealing plants from a greenhouse. Imagine the scandal and embarrassment that would result from your arrest. Sweety, your scam would surely mean our demise.

But I must admit, an exhilarating rush of excitement coursed through our body while those thefts were occurring. Dressed entirely in black - a tossle cap, sweatshirt, leotards and boots - I snuck from my apartment in The Village, slipping through the bushes like a ghost.

Oh God, if any of the neighbors had seen me, they would have run me out of town. What a sight I must have been, creeping across the parking lot, then dodging between parked cars whenever a flashing light or errant sound was heard. I was alive - heart pumping rivers of blood, veins expanding to the diameter of dimes ... eyes bulging with peripheral awareness, vision so acute I could see rain gullies on the moon. What a sensation! I was so in tune with the surroundings that I heard train whistles twenty miles away. I had never been this alive.

At first I thought I'd chicken-out, so nervous that buckets of vomit bubbled inside my stomach. But the excitement could not be denied. I crept through the greenhouse aisles, overwhelmed by the aroma of freshly cut flowers, bountiful bouquets, and thriving, mist-dampened plants. This concept may have been the key to my actions. For years I was plagued by thoughts of deterioration and death ... the nervous anxiety, puking, and ever-increasing tension. But these flowers represented life! I had never even owned a plant, or knew the first thing about maintaining them. But now I was ransacking a garden house.

What insanity! I raced for dear life across the spooky, fog-laden parking lot, three spider plants in one hand, a potted fern in the other. What were you thinking, Jennifer? How could you have been so foolish? But nobody saw a thing. I wheeled into my apartment with the glee of a master thief. I made it! Nobody saw me. So what did I do? Count my blessings and lock the door? No. I returned to the greenhouse for more thrills.

What an escapade. For the first time in decades I wanted to leap from the ground and squeal with delight. Rather than stagnating, or letting life pass me by, I started living! I shimmied through the shadows with the cunningness of a fox. The final prize, these potted plants, didn't even matter to me. I didn't care about them. I just wanted to steal ... to steal more and more ... to inject myself with invigoration and anticipation. What if I triggered an alarm, or janitors hid in the darkness? Realistically, a squad car could be patrolling the area, or a group of concerned citizens could band together and tackle me as I fled through the sleepy streets.

The headlines trumpeting my demise would be disastrous:

Bookworm Booked
Literary Agent's Secret Life Exposed

Jennifer Ewen, 54 year old executive at The Mason Turner Literary Agency, was recently arrested for stealing potted plants from a local greenhouse ....

What were you thinking, little lady? Why place your entire life in jeopardy for a momentary rush of excitement? But even when I stole those bushes, bonsai trees, planters and perennials, I felt compelled to make one last stab at infamy. I had to get that gigantic cactus in the hand-painted clay pot. But why? Pushing my luck in this fashion dramatized the sickness that compelled gamblers to play one more hand - dealt with all or nothing odds - after they had already won a million dollars. Who would accept such wagers? The stakes were too high.

But after whetting my appetite, I craved the taste of danger. I crawled yet again into the night, a willing participant in this sinister mission. I lurked among the devils of deceit - those whose consciences were emptier than Satan's soul on Judgment Day. At this point I may have robbed a bank, carjacked an armored transport, or knocked-over a convenience store ... anything to keep the blood coursing through my veins.

The neighborhood's unremitting silence enveloped me like a deprivation chamber, while the clamor inside my mind filled me with paranoia. Each step toward the greenhouse carried additional fear ... police sirens, flashlights beaming in my eyes, attack dogs chasing me along an alleyway, or handcuffs slapped around each wrist as I'm dragged toward a rat-infested cell. Why was I behaving this way? I didn't even want that ugly cactus.

But I kept inching closer, ever vigilant, senses alive and on guard. Then I saw that prickly plant, the prized feather in my hat ...

Dearest love, how did you ever escape? Your luck was miraculous.

"Hey lady, drop it. Get back here. I'll call the cops!"

I'll never get away. He has me. Oh honey, what are you going to do? Stomping feet in the distance ... nearing, getting closer ... his panting breath becoming louder.

Sweet Jenny, in the past you were simply neurotic. But now, look at what has happened. You're actually crazy. Was this debacle a subconscious desire to get caught? You saw that look on your face after ducking through the bushes, then rounding the corner and losing your pursuer. The looking-glass spoke volumes — a pale, startled face, trembling lips, bulging eyes and flared, heaving nostrils. Don't ever put yourself through that torment again. You could have lost everything. Or is that what you want? Why sacrifice everything? Was it all worthwhile? Who knows? But I must admit, it does smell fantastic in here, like a tropical rain forest.

You're so gorgeous, darling. The mirror never lies. Look at yourself. If I weren't me, I'd kiss you in a heartbeat. With all we have going for us, why is our life in such shambles? You draw a respectable salary at Mason Turner, yet we still live in a one-bedroom apartment. Other than the plants, this place is nothing more than a dump in Greenwich Village, its bleakness reflecting our barren life. Speaking of New York, how do we entertain ourself in the world's most thrilling city? We don't. We're virtual prisoners living in a nuthouse. And who could this boarder be? It's us! We're crazy, Sis. Out of our minds whacko!

We're supposed to be on top of the world. In theory, you're a top-level literary agent. Naturally we know your entire career has been a ruse, but most everyone else in the world doesn't know about this sham. Why can't we enjoy life rather than cringing with fear? Jenny, how long has it been since we've had a man? It seems forever. You could land a partner without batting an eye ... but that face from yesterday still haunts us. We see it every day. You could actually be living in a mansion with some million-aire ... but the only lover we know - Oh Jenny, our only pleasures are given by the long, sweaty fingers of self-gratification. Why can't the past leave us alone rather than haunt us with constant reminders? You've abandoned intimacy to wallow in a lonely cell of despair. Oh honey, what will we do?

8

Autumn's annual fashion revue took center stage, showcasing its colors in the form of fallen foliage that had accumulated across my backyard. As I raked the damp, colorful leaves into randomly sized piles, I marveled at the beauty surrounding me. With the temperature at sixty degrees and gray clouds blotting the sky, I performed this task with gusto. A soothing breeze carried in its midst the wonderful aromas of this season - jack o' lanterns being carved by rambunctious children waiting for Halloween, dried catnip decaying beside once green weeds and partially naked trees, or the smell of a gentle rainfall creating mud-puddles across the October landscape. There was no other time of year that equaled autumn's magical brilliance.

While hastily sweeping leaves into piles, I saw Ukiah leaving his cottage. Other than our trip to the races or a concert at The Dies Infaustus, our paths rarely crossed. I still worked daylight hours at the data entry firm, whereas Ukiah ... if the truth be told, I didn't know how he spent his time. And being that ignorance is not only bliss, but also an insurance policy against getting one's kneecaps shattered, Ukiah's business remained his own. I often wondered, though, how my tenant spent his time. I assumed he wrote on a daily basis, but his affiliation with Tattoo Blue troubled me. It would be different if Ukiah simply ran numbers or laundered money, but breaking thumbs was another ...

"Howdy, neighbor," he smiled upon approach. "Do you have another rake?"

"Sure," I told him, welcoming the help. "There's one over there."

After Ukiah returned, we stood side-by-side and raked leaves while chatting on this cool weekend afternoon.

Following a few pleasantries, my boarder asked, "How's Woody? Is he feeling any better?"

Even hearing his name made the blood boil in my veins. I don't know why, but every time I thought about Woody Dewar I felt like screaming.

Reluctantly, I answered. "Woody stopped by this morning for a few minutes, but as usual, he's sick."

"I hope nothing serious," Ukiah said with genuine concern.

"It shouldn't be. Woody diagnosed himself as having either spinal meningitis or Hanta virus."

"Hanta virus? What's that?"

"He said it comes from the fecal droppings of mice that migrated from southwest America to the Poconos. If someone gets this virus, they're usually dead within twenty-four hours. So no, it's nothing serious."

"Maybe we should check him into a hospital."

Losing my temper, I yelled, "There's nothing wrong with Dewar. Can't you see? He's a hypochondriac who sits home all day reading medical books, then thinks up imaginary diseases. He's a crackpot."

My sudden burst of anger seemed to alarm Ukiah, for we raked in silence a few moments before he volunteered a rare glimmer of personal information.

"Afternoons like these take me back to my grandmother's farm ... well, my foster-gram's farm. She wasn't a biological grandparent, but still ..."

"You were raised on a farm?"

"Not actually, but I spent a little bit of time at one as a kid. I can still remember that woman's face. I called her Gramma Moo because of a speech defect that I had, plus there were all these cows on her farm - so she became Gramma Moo."

"Tell me about her," I said softly, overjoyed to finally peek behind his veil.

"There couldn't have been a simpler woman on earth. Gram was an ol' farm gal who milked cows, grew her own food, and weaved carpets on a loom. Oh, the memories I have of her house. Cobwebs clung to every rafter and dusty corner of her basement, while canned goods stocked every shelf as an old coal furnace spitted and sputtered from a cold dirt floor. To even walk down her cellar stairs scared the hell outta me. The rickety wooden steps were lined by musty granite walls that were slippery and slimy. At the bottom of this stairwell hung a naked light bulb that swung from an electrical cord. Every time I walked down those creaky planks I was sure a monster would jump from the corner and swallow me whole. But once I reached the bottom everything was fine because Gram was always there, smiling as she wove carpets on her loom or washed clothes in a metal basin."

"What wonderful memories," I sighed, hoping Ukiah would tell me more.

"That farm was a slice of paradise. I can still remember Gramma Moo and me feeding goats, pigs, and chicken in the barn, then running across her meadow to a brook that sliced through a tree-lined hillside. There we'd splash water on our feet and catch crayfish that tried to pinch our fingers before we tossed them back into the stream. I'd laugh and giggle with glee as Gram hugged me dearly, or held my hand as we picked blueberries from a bush."

"What a fantastic woman," I reiterated.

"Then at night, when we were finally played-out ... isn't that a great child-like concept ... to be played-out ... you're too tired to play any more. Those were the days," he said longingly. "Anyway, as the sun went down behind the mountains, Gramma would cook supper for me. The smells in that kitchen are burned into my memory - freshly butchered roast beef, lumpy mashed potatoes with mounds of butter, special recipe onion and mushroom gravy, and green beans picked from the vine. Finally, Gramma always had homemade bread steaming from the oven. What a treat! We'd eat so fast that gravy dripped from the corners of our mouths to our chins, our fingers were all covered with butter, while pieces of meat and beans clung to our faces. To this day, I've still never eaten meals that compared to those at Gramma Moo's. Afterward, we'd wash dishes in this old-fashioned sink, then bake apple pies or chocolate chip cookies that melted in our mouths. Y'know, I can honestly say that those days spent at my Gramma's were the only one's of my life where I've been happy. I've done everything to recapture those times, but it has always proven fruitless. I wish Japhy could have enjoyed that farm, but Gram died while I was still young ... my childhood ended by the realities of adulthood."

Touched by this heartfelt confession, I tried to lift Ukiah's spirit by mentioning his son's band. But asking whether he'd had any progress with the high school teacher who promised to let their band play only brought sadness and rage.

"I've called Mister Doublet at least twenty times after sending Japhy's cassette, and haven't heard a word from him."

"What do you think is bothering him?"

"I'm not sure, but this morning I typed a letter to him."

"That's a good idea. What did you say?"

"Here, I printed an extra copy for you to read."

Ukiah pulled a folded piece of paper from the pocket of his checkered flannel shirt, then handed it to me. I propped my rake against the house's vinyl siding, then read this letter:

> Dear Mr. Doublet,
>
> My name is Ukiah Rhymes. I spoke with you in the middle of September about a band named "Mirror Image." At the time, I mentioned a Halloween show they were filming, and thought our conversation went well. We even-

tually agreed that after I received this tape, I would forward it to you.

But recently, to no avail, I have been trying to make contact with you, via messages with personnel at your office, and also on your answering machine. But these attempts have not proven successful for some reason. I know you're busy with school, so if I'm somewhere on your list of things to do, I understand. If, on the other hand, you've had a change of heart to this band, I'll understand. These kids only want a response. I don't know if I did something wrong in the interim since our last conversation that has made you ignore my messages; but, if so, hopefully I can alleviate this situation. Whatever the case, if you feel "Mirror Image" is not a band you care to deal with, please let us know one way or the other. These kids are all big boys. They can handle whatever you decide ... except silence. They don't understand that, and I hate to keep them hanging in the balance. They worked extremely hard preparing for the Halloween show, and also making these tapes. I just want to let them know where they stand - for better or worse.

To close, we're all very nice people. If I offended you in any way (I can't imagine how), but if I did, please let me know. It certainly wasn't intentional. I am certain, though, that you would be impressed with this band, and would be proud having them perform at one of your shows. Mr. Doublet, please get in touch with me. All I'm trying to do is be a good father to my son, and help him with his band. These kids all work very hard. Please let us know one way or the other.

Thank you,

Ukiah Rhymes

After reading this heartfelt plea, I asked, "Why is Doublet such an asshole? All he has to do is call you and ..."

"Doublet won't get many more chances," Ukiah snarled, returning to the leaves before him.

As he labored quietly in the cool autumn air, I recalled an observation Ukiah once made. He said that every day spent on this planet ripped another small chunk from his heart. At first I didn't understand, but after being abandoned by his parents, suffering through Gramma Moo's death, and being separated from his wife and son, I now saw how personally he took the world. Of course, Ukiah never let casual observers see his vulnerable side. He always acted as if he didn't care - as if nothing bothered him. But I knew it did, especially after remembering a line in his letter to the high school teacher. He said, "All I'm trying to do is be a good father to my son." Think about the stark, confessional qualities of that statement, then getting a cold-shoulder in return. I could see the vultures tearing another chunk of flesh from Ukiah's heart.

In the same breath, I recalled my thoughts of Ukiah standing atop a pedestal. While he stood above his subjects, those who idolized him continued to be neglected. One by one, his followers abandoned him, some even asking the powers that be to wreak havoc on Ukiah. Could these ludicrous thoughts be linked to his belief in past incarnations? Were those who idolized him actually real-life subjects from a previous time when he lived as a vicious empress?

What was I thinking? My thoughts were crazy. Could Ukiah be controlling me to such an extent that I believed him to be a reincarnated ruler? But then another thought entered my mind. During this hallucination, I offered Ukiah my undying love, but he selfishly rejected me. Disappointed, and on the verge of suicide, I laid on his doorstep each day, begging to be allowed into his house. But Ukiah ignored me until handing me a present one day. Overjoyed, I tore the paper to discover ... a sword. A sword! Devastated by this gift, I plunged the weapon into my chest and bled to death on his stoop.

At this stage in our relationship, I began getting scared. Had I become so attached to this man that I was afraid of committing suicide if rejected? What was wrong with me? And more importantly, how did Ukiah exert such an influence on my life? I wanted to run from him, but his body, words, and mind attracted me with the force of a hypnotist's spell. It was impossible to break free. I wanted him to leave this very second, yet such thoughts drove me insane. I needed him more than anything ... and I hated him more than anything. It was easy to see Ukiah's manipulative ways, but then I'd consider his sadness, and that look of melancholy (not only in his eyes, but surrounding his entire being) when caught at rare, unguarded moments.

"There, all done," Ukiah yelled from across the lawn.

While I daydreamed, Ukiah finished raking the leaves all by himself. Even more unsettling was the fruit of our labors. My leaves laid scattered in all directions, while Ukiah's piles reflected an ordered neurosis that bordered on insanity. Each pile was exactly the same as every other, reflecting his philosophy that, "Everything must be in its proper order." I couldn't believe my eyes - each pile was in a perfectly straight line and of such uniformity that if I were to count each leaf, I doubt they would have varied by more than half a percent. The ramifications of his perfectionism extended well beyond raking leaves.

As we stood and admired our handiwork, Ukiah turned toward the woods that circled my backyard.

Leaning against his rake, he asked, "What's back there?"

Disinterested, I replied, "Who knows? I've never followed any of the paths. It looks like a gigantic swamp to me."

"Well, let's do some exploring," Ukiah suggested.

"Back there? Um," I said, before feeling an unexpected surge of courage. In the past I would have resisted his offer in a heartbeat, but today I blurted nervously, "Okay, why not?"

"Great. We'll get rid of these leaves later."

Woody Dewar called the wetlands behind my house The Marsh. As we walked between the trees and weeds, the ground definitely squished beneath our feet, but also welcomed us like an old acquaintance waiting patiently for a visit. And what an invitation it made. The woods thrived with life - rain-soaked leaves lying like plush carpeting, thick-barked trees resonating with strength, plus various weeds and bushes whisking along our pant legs or placing unexpectedly wet kisses on our cheeks. I noticed squirrel nests high atop the branches, plus ivy and moss nearer to the ground. I don't know how I could have avoided this place for so long.

Ukiah must have read my mind, for he was also overwhelmed by nature's simple gifts.

"These woods are what I was talking about a few days ago when I said that men used to enjoy a closer relationship with their Muse. Too often we neglect this part of our lives in favor of concrete, exhaust fumes, and the twisted metal framework of modern society."

I nodded my head in agreement.

"I can't believe I almost hopped in my car and took a spin on the bypass. Now don't get me wrong, speed does have its merit, but we get too caught-up in the damn rat race. It's cool to just relax and enjoy nature's elegance and perfection."

Ukiah did have a knack for summing up certain situations.

"Oh, by the way, Chris, I wanna apologize for my comments last night concerning the literary world."

"In what way?" I asked, breaking a fallen branch into a walking stick.

"I was too negative and critical, but you have to understand the motivation."

"Which is?"

"When an author is consumed by the act of writing ... of creating ... and it all CLICKS ... the sensation is magical ... otherworldly. The joy of this experience lets them communicate with their Muse. And if you want to know the truth, this rush is even better than sex. That's why I hold writing in such high esteem. It's man's only chance to approach their Muse on equal terms. But after seeing this privilege abused by authors who don't give a damn about their craft, I start losing my mind. I'm not trying to put myself above them, I just hate the way they squander their gifts."

"That sounds fair enough," I said, poking my twisted branch into a lily pad that sat alongside a pond. "Is that why you were so mad, or is there more?"

While walking along an overgrown path, Ukiah continued. "Writing always goes back to The Word. As I said again today, earlier artists were much closer to their Muse than we are today. Hell, The Word has been all but eliminated. We're losing our creative forces, turning instead to alternative arts and suspicious forms of communication with phony Muses."

"Why?" I asked, absorbed by Ukiah's attempt to make sense of his world.

After hesitating a moment, he responded, "In the upper echelons of the artistic community, there is a secret organization known as S.W.A.N. Have you heard of it?"

"Swan?" I inquired, "like the bird? No, I haven't."

"The acronym stands for Single Word Authorial Nation, but, unlike a real swan, this group doesn't have any redeeming qualities."

"As usual," I interrupted, "I'm not following your ..."

"Swans are symbolic for two reasons. First, their white color represents purity - a departure from man's more sinister pursuits. This concept leads to our second example — and why the swan has become so legendary. In more magical times, swans were associated with song. This is why an artist's final composition is called their swan song. So, the swan became symbolic of both purity and creation. But today, S.W.A.N. is doing everything in its power to destroy our language."

Unable to understand him, I jabbed my stick into a mud puddle, making it unnecessary for me to voice my frustrations.

Sensing my loss, Ukiah slowed his frantic pace.

"S.W.A.N. is like commercial radio in this country. I'm sure you've heard enough of it, Chris. So lemme ask - what kind of music creeps from your speakers? It's all the same bland, pre-programmed shit with the same format that's heard in every other city across America. Even with names like 'The Revolution,' they're still generic and unoriginal. Do you wanna hear the same canned music day in and day out? Of course not. But the world of literature is steadily moving in that direction. Did you know that a single U.S. book publisher, one who merged with an overseas company, now controls 26% of all book sales?"

"Really? Who is that?"

"Cygnus Publishers. They've recently become the world's third largest media conglomerate. Speaking of outsiders, did you know that four of the top seven publishing companies in America are foreign owned? The industry has become so dependent on bottom-line financing that a large house like Cygnus has to sell at least 15,000 books to break even. Being pressured by their greedy investors, publishing has become an industry dominated by money rather than quality. There's no room any more for unknown writers who've surrendered their life for art. This shift in emphasis is one reason why the agent I've been trying to contact is ignoring me."

"Ukiah, after all this time, I still don't know anything about this agent. Who is he, and who does he work for?"

"This he is a she, and her name is Jennifer Ewen."

"A woman? Who does she work for?"

"The world-renowned Mason Turner Agency. I told you I was shooting for the top," he said with excitement, dancing in place.

"The Mason Turner Agency!" I exclaimed. "Don't they handle Philip Prince?"

"They sure do!"

By now Ukiah was hopping in circles, so enthused that he nearly stumbled over his own feet after hopping atop a log.

"Don't you think you should ...?"

But I wasn't allowed to finish my sentence.

"Don't you think you should set your standards a little lower?" Ukiah sang, parroting my words. "No! No, I don't. I'm shooting for the top, baby! I'm the One, and nobody's going to stop me!"

Ukiah shouted his words to the trees, the sky, and the universe, so inspired that he bounced up and down in place, then leaped over rocks, splashed through puddles, swatted at low-hanging branches, and finally jumped into the arm of a tree. I'd never seen anyone beam with such vigor.

At the risk of raining on Ukiah's parade, I asked, "How did you find Miss Ewen? I mean, of all the literary agents in this country, why her?"

"I guess it happened to be her lucky day," Ukiah joked. "Seriously, I knew Mason Turner would be my agency ... why settle for anything less than number one? So, I went to the library one day and found a blueprint for their corporate structure in a reference book. Y'see, Mason Turner is enormous. So, the big question became, of all these literary agents, who should I choose? I started researching them until I found that Jennifer Ewen was the only one who graduated from Latera University."

"Right here in town?"

"Exactly. So, without any other reason, I chose her as my target ... or should I say ..."

"Nah, I'd leave it at target," I laughed.

"You're probably right," Ukiah chimed in, realizing the irony of his Freudian Slip. His mood then turned serious. "I suspect, though, that Jennifer may be working for S.W.A.N."

"Why?"

Before he could answer, Ukiah pointed into the distance and yelled while running away from me, "Hey, look over there, what is that?"

I gazed across the swamp to see a dilapidated cabin sitting inside a cluster of trees.

"C'mon, Chris, let's check it out," Ukiah hollered, scurrying with the joy of a young boy playing Cowboys and Indians.

Upon approach, the cabin reminded me of an old beagle lying beneath a weeping willow tree. Its exterior consisted of irregularly shaped boards nailed together at odd angles, with throwaway slats and plywood used to cover the open spaces. Its slanted roof was covered by shingles that appeared to have been stolen from a construction site. With only one window, overgrown by weeds and fading with age, this fallen hut had seen better days.

After pushing through a tangle of vines and hanging branches, Ukiah and I entered the darkened shack, then stared with curiosity and wonder. The cabin's ruddy dirt floor was littered by rusted beer cans, burnt firewood, crumbled cigarette packs, a porno-graphic magazine, soda bottles, a beanbag chair with its stuffing falling out, and a fire ring. Meanwhile, its walls were spray-painted with enough graffiti to end any specula-tion as to what this hut was used for. Green marijuana leaves were scrawled on the unfinished planks, alongside phrases such as "Party Hardy," "LSD for Life," "I like to get drunk and fuck," or "School Sucks/Drugs Rule."

Ukiah laughed at these messages as he sat atop a cinder block and began leafing through the wrinkled porno mag. I milled about uncomfortably as he did so, continuing to look around the cabin.

"Man, I remember these kinda places in my wilder days," Ukiah said longingly. "Those were some good old times. No responsibility, no pressures, no tomorrow. Only the moment - another buzz, another beer, and another lost night. But not now. Today I work for Tattoo Blue and write letters to an agent who doesn't even care that I'm alive."

"How many have you sent without getting an answer?" I asked, curious as to Ukiah's motives.

"Four," he told me.

"Why do you keep trying to contact ... what was her name?"

"Jennifer Ewen," Ukiah smiled after unfolding a tattered centerfold. "You don't mind ... do you?" he wondered aloud.

"Well ..."

"Okay, I'll put it away .... Anyway, I keep trying with her because these letters have become a type of freedom for me."

"Why?" I said quietly, looking from the cobweb-riddled window.

"Because I refuse to toe the line. Everyone else has dollar signs in their eyes, but not me. Y'see, publication represents something more ... something extraordinary. So these letters to Jennifer are an expression of my Self, of my Life."

"Why won't she answer? Is Jennifer that swamped with work?"

"That's a good question, but I only know one side of the story. I can tell her what's on my mind, but I can only wonder what she's thinking. What is on Jennifer's mind? How does she spend her time at that agency? And most importantly, what does she want from an author? I wish I knew, but I'm lost. I don't have a fucking idea what Jennifer, or the industry in general, is looking for."

"What did you say in your last letter?"

"I started by telling her about a 19 year old female college student who recently sold her first novel to a big name publisher. The deal, which included foreign and television rights, reportedly topped $800,000."

"Almost a million dollars," I declared with disbelief, "for one book?"

"Can you imagine?" Ukiah asked, kicking a chunk of firewood. "With that kind of dough, this young lady will definitely lose her hunger and drive. Money kills the creative process, and I'm sure she's not immune to it. But before I get too negative, let me lay this disclaimer."

While watching a squirrel leap from limb to limb, I wondered about a curious phenomenon – how many other people needed to present disclaimers in normal conversation?

"I'm sure this woman put a lot of work into her book, which deals with the life of a middle-aged, widowed housewife. But when it's released, nobody will know her name. And five years down the line, she'll have amounted to nothing more than a forgotten footnote."

"How can you be so sure?" I asked, amazed at Ukiah's audacity.

"Essentially," he began, "this kid doesn't have an EDGE. Her novel will probably be made into a television movie, and will air on a Saturday night behind *Doctor Quinn*,

Medicine Woman. Every viewer will say what a fine show it was, and the world will keep spinning on its axis."

"But this won't happen to you," I surmised, confident Ukiah would run with my comment.

"Hell no! When I enter the arena, the other players will wake up and take notice. Every dull bulb will be extinguished as I shine in the limelight. Most of them won't cheer me on, but I guarantee they'll be on their feet."

"How can you be so sure?" I asked, slowly retrieving the tattered porno magazine from the floor.

"Because I'm betting everything on a single hand, and that hand is me! Confident gamblers don't make these kinda bets unless their opponents know they're not bluffing. Well baby, I'm sitting on a full-house, ready to raise the ante!"

I momentarily tuned-out Ukiah's claims as I leafed through the worn edition of *Seedspiller Magazine.* The folded pictures looked strangely familiar to me, yet also utterly foreign. Nearly every photograph involved naked men and women in the throes of passion. I gazed at these stills with cautious curiosity, wondering how I would fit into such an arrangement.

Ignoring my fixation with the magazine, Ukiah proceeded with his usual bravado.

"Jennifer should realize that I'm not blowing smoke out my ass. I just wish she knew what she had with me."

"Don't you think she's able to tell what you're all about?" I replied vacantly.

"Who knows? I once wrote a story about a man who searched the world over for riches, then came home to a dilapidated shack. After he died penniless, his house was in such sorry shape that a construction crew had to level it. Underneath the foundation they discovered an immense goldmine that was larger than anything he could have found elsewhere."

"A lesson in irony, I see."

"This man scoured the planet for riches, while all along he sat on top of more than he could ever imagine."

Somewhat naively, I asked, "If Miss Ewen can't see your brilliance, why is she an agent?"

Ukiah moved toward the cabin's door as darkness slowly enveloped the sky.

"Jennifer is an agent for three reasons. First, of course, is to publish books. The second is to make money. But most importantly, the Mason Turner Agency forces her to reflect their company's vision."

"Part Three lays some heavy vibes," I commented, beginning to worry about the sun being swallowed by night. "Where do you fit into the puzzle?"

"Regarding point A, I'll sell more books in the next decade than any writer in America. As to point B, not only will Jennifer get rich, but she'll also become the most recognized agent in America. When the history of twenty-first century literature is written, her name will be at the top of the list."

Even though Ukiah beamed with confidence, he remained calm. He didn't try to convince me, or feel the need to win me over. Ukiah simply spoke as one who was convinced of what he said, and to hell with what others thought. But I continued to prod him.

"Where do you stand on point C?"

"All I can say is that I have my own priorities, and won't compromise them for anyone."

I should have known before asking.

As we loitered silently for a moment, the rapidly approaching darkness filled me with dread.

"Ukiah, don't you think we should start heading back? In another hour it'll be dark."

"What're you worried about, Chris? Didn't you hang-out in tree cabins as a kid, then wait until dark so you could prowl through the woods?"

"No," I exclaimed fretfully.

"I thought you had a normal childhood," he then said with a smile.

"It was anything but," I told Ukiah, hoping he would take an interest in my life. But he was more concerned with personal matters ... matters that involved him.

"Although I moved a lot between foster families, one place I stayed during my teenage years was a town where factories were king."

"What kind of factories?"

"Powdered metal. Most every person that lived there was a beer drinking, blue collar, card carrying union member. Their lives consisted of graduating from high school, buying a truck, getting married, and slaving away in those factories until retirement."

"Did you work at one of those sweat shops?"

"Twice, and I got to know the routine real well. It was abysmal. During the summer, room temperature was 140 degrees. The air was filled with powdered metal dust, exhaust fumes, and smoke from the ovens - their flames shooting ten feet high. Plus, try to picture a line of presses pounding out parts, each one more deafening than the next. The place was also poorly lit, adding to its gloomy aura. The experience was like going to hell, with only a lucky few able to escape."

"What did you do there?" I asked, watching the darkness slowly consume our light.

"I ran a press in a part of the plant called Production, and was once given a job for one million parts."

"A million? I can't even conceive ..."

"Try to imagine the Sisyphean implications of this task. My day consisted of nothing more than sitting at this machine and stamping out parts."

"That's it?"

"The press was fully automated, so I didn't even have to push any buttons. I'd just fill a bin with tiny gears, and when it was loaded, a forklift hauled it away and brought me a new one."

"I'd lose my mind."   (darker, ever darker).

"I followed this routine for eight hours a day, minus twenty-seven minutes for lunch. The only way to interrupt this maddening boredom was through quality control. That's where an operator checked their parts for consistency."

"How did you do that?"

"We had this tool called a micrometer. Usually the procedure was futile, but every once in a while a press went haywire and threw its parts out of variance. These malfunctions were the day's highlight because the machine had to be shut down for maintenance. Once it was fixed, though, the worker went back to stamping and stacking."

"I thought my job was boring," I told Ukiah as I fidgeted nervously over the onset of nightfall.

"Their lifestyle is grueling, but I'm not trying to criticize these workers, or their place of employment. In fact, I admire their fortitude. Without them, none of us would be able to drive, run a washing machine, or use disposable lighters."

"It's not surprising that your town was alcoholic. After eight hours of mind-numbing madness, it's a wonder those folks didn't slit their wrists."

"It's true," he said sadly.

"Shouldn't we get going, Ukiah? It's getting late."

"In a second, but first let me finish my explanation."

"That's right, we were talking about writing. What does your explanation have to do with the publishing business?"

"Well, I'll use Andy Warhol's philosophy as a starting point. He created his art to reflect popular culture's tendencies toward mass production and consumerism. Repetition became symbolic of our migration toward sameness."

"Like his soup cans stacked in a museum," I beamed, proud to finally know something.

"Yes. Even his studio was named, 'The Factory'."

"Which leads us where?" I asked, hoping Ukiah's response would be brief.

"Well, I understand Warhol's satirical reflection of society, and his method of exposing our fixation with stardom. I even agree with his stance that Art is nothing more than a product. But here is where I disagree with him. To me, our culture's greatest enemy is the uniform sameness that surrounded me in those factories. There's no surer way to destroy one's spirit than through uniformity. That's why I'm so intent on creating literature that can't be classified by genre. Variance - the breakdown of a machine symbolizing the mechanistic confines of an industrial society - is the only salvation that will spare us from becoming homogenous automatons."

"Ukiah, I still don't know what you mean. And please, can we leave?" I whined, almost begging. "It's getting dark, and I don't feel like being trapped in this cabin. I'm ... I'm getting scared."

"We'll leave in a little bit," Ukiah told me without fear of being challenged. "Just let me finish my train of thought. Okay, where was I? Oh yeah, what I'm trying to say is this - I still believe in The American Dream. I know this concept may be passé, or a mere cliché, but without it I might as well sit at a press for the rest of my life. It's this need to succeed, ingrained since being abandoned as a child, that keeps pushing my pen across the page."

I wanted to join his conversation, but my fear, anger, and pent-up frustration wouldn't allow me to speak.

"To some, writing may seem absurd. But to me, the challenge of becoming not only published, but king of the hill, is a supreme test of Will. I want to make it, without compromise, solely on the basis of my talent. The problem with this quest is best summarized by another cliché: 'no man is an island.' I've always tried to be self-sufficient - to never ask anything from anybody. But in this case, as much as it sickens me, I'm forced to ask for Jennifer's help in getting published."

"Can we leave now? Look. It's almost dark."

"It's only dusk, Chris. Sit down and relax."

"I don't want to relax. I want to leave."

"We will ... shortly. But first I want to tell you about three famous authors."

Resigned to my fate, I plopped on the beanbag chair and almost started to cry.

"Have you ever heard of William Burroughs?"

"No," I spat with resentment.

"He was a career college student for much of his younger life, then worked briefly as an exterminator and petty thief. His main source of income, though, was a monthly stipend from his wealthy family who invented the adding machine. Now I'm sure you've heard of F. Scott Fitzgerald."

"Sure, everyone has."

"Did you know he never worked an honest day in his life except to write? Luckily, he got published at the age of twenty-three."

Unable to control my growing anxiety, I once again took a peek at the *Seedspiller Magazine* lying beside me. In a glimmer of fading twilight, I turned to a section that showed an array of transsexuals - some looking like men, others predominantly female. Shocked, yet also intrigued, I noticed that facially, one of the models looked exactly like me! Shaken (quite literally), I instantly tossed the magazine over my shoulder (and subsequently out the window).

"Finally, there's Jack Kerouac. Despite making romantic stabs at employment, such as on the railroad or as a field hand, he only worked until the novelty wore off. Much to his disappointment (and the source of his immense guilt), ol' Jack's primary source for money was provided by his mother, who worked her fingers to the bone in a shoe factory."

Dusk had settled across the forest, quickly followed by nightfall. But the loss of light didn't bother Ukiah. His monologue could well have taken place on the moon. Speaking of which, the moon, being nearly full, would be our only hope of exiting this jungle.

"In contrast to the above writers was Charles Bukowski, who may have been hired and fired from every job on the earth. What impresses me about his life, and differentiates him from the others, is that after slaving for ten hours in a warehouse or factory, Hank went home and wrote. He was filthy, exhausted, and fed-up with the world, but he still closed himself in a grimy room to write all night. It was these flophouses, shitty jobs, and the unending desperation that fueled Bukowski's creative drive."

Other than moonlight filtering through the window, darkness had completely engulfed the woods. With it came the eerie rustling of trees, chirping bugs, hooting owls that hadn't flown south, and other sounds that filled me with dread. Whereas earlier I wanted nothing more than to go home, now I feared for my life if we did leave. If only I could stay by Ukiah's side, then I'd be safe.

"Are you listening, Chris?" he asked unexpectedly.

"Of course," I blurted, lying through my teeth. I hadn't heard a word he said in the last ten minutes. "I'm just waiting for the climax."

"Just as I suspected," his voice echoed. "I'll keep going then. With the above reasoning in mind, I arrived at a dialectic that conveys the point I'm trying to make."

Dialectic? Where have I heard that word?

"To start, we have our thesis, which is the blue collar worker - rooted, realistic, with an understanding of man's plight. In contrast stands the antithesis, represented by the artist - aesthetic, ethereal, hoping that man can live up to his potential. Finally, when the two are combined, we arrive at a synthesis, symbolized by the Labored Creator - a working class hero."

Dialectic, I remembered joyfully. That word was on the cover of Ukiah's library book in his room at The Towers. I wonder if he ever returned it.

"I'm not sure if my descriptions reflect what I'm trying to say. It's a difficult concept to capture. As writers, we're constantly torn between two opposing forces - work, and the art that results from it."

As Ukiah closed his latest literary dissertation, I sat in the darkness - cold, lonely, frightened - when all of a sudden ... it couldn't be ... a slithering object crept along my leg.

"Snake! Snake!" I screamed, leaping to my feet and hopping in circles, trying to brush the intruder from my body. "Get it off me!"

"Chris, settle down. There aren't any snakes in here."

"Ukiah," I demanded, "we're leaving right now, and I mean it."

"Okay, relax. Why didn't you say something earlier? Look, it's already dark. We have things to do tonight."

"We do?" I asked nervously. "Like what?"

"Joan Jett is back in town."

"But she was just here."

"The club she was supposed to play at tonight burned down yesterday. So, since Joan and her band were in the area, they decided to return."

"And you're going?"

"Of course we're going," Ukiah informed me excitedly. "Now c'mon, let's try to find our way back to civilization."

I wished Ukiah hadn't phrased his words in such a doubtful manner, but at least we were leaving. As he fumbled toward the door, I gingerly grabbed hold of his flannel shirt.

"I can't wait to get home. It's spooky," I whispered. "At least the moon is almost full."

Ukiah remained quiet as we left the cabin and inched through the forest. In actuality, we really weren't that far from home (my house was less than a mile away). Still, the distance seemed eternal. I could feel my heart doing backflips as I followed Ukiah, relieved that each step brought us closer to home.

"Ahhhh, it has me! Help. Get away. NOoooooooo!"

Ukiah screamed with abandon, then raced urgently into the woods.

"What is it?" I squealed, terrified to be alone. "Come back. Where are you?"

I stood frozen for a moment, then frantically shuffled along a darkened pathway. Separated from Ukiah, I walked alone, exposed and vulnerable. If a ferocious animal wanted to pounce on my body, I wouldn't be able to defend myself. Except for my tentative steps, the woods were silent ... deadly silent. The silence became so unnerving that I swore the moon started buzzing like an electric razor. Oh God, I didn't want to be alone. Where was Ukiah? Maybe he was eaten by a bear, or mauled by a mountain lion? What if I were next? I didn't know how to fight. I didn't have a weapon. What would I do?

Then I heard it ... a slithering, a rustling of branches, a creeping along the ground ... its breath heaving ..."

"Ukiah, where are you? Help! I'm going to die. It's going to get me."

Its presence neared me ... broken twigs, crackling leaves, an errant rock kicked across the ground ... more breathing – I heard it inhale, then exhale deeply – the sound like silent winds blowing sand across the desert.

"Chris, run!" Ukiah bellowed. "It's coming your way. Go - fast!"

Oh my God. It's coming my way. Run! Run!

"Hurry. It already got me. Now it's closing in on you. Get away before it's too late."

I was going to die, or be eaten alive. Why me? Run! Quit thinking, run faster. I'm too young to die. What if it didn't kill me, but just mutilated my face with its claws? Save me, please, anybody. I could hear it coming.

"Run faster, Chris, it's right beside you."

This is it, I'm dead. No no ...

"Help me, Ukiah, I hear it."

"Keep running - go go go," he urged me.

I bashed into trees, scraped against branches, scratched my arm on briars, and felt logs and rocks kicking against my shins. But I didn't care. I just kept running ... running, then whooooosh, my feet slid across a wet patch of grass near the swamp ... the next thing I knew I was lying on my back. I hadn't been injured, but a far worse fate awaited me. The sound of an approaching beast was now atop me ... only feet away, bursting through the bushes ... lumbering, slobbering, its breath diseased and sickly ... stomping — licking its chops ... the final branches separating me from this monster began parting ever so slowly.

I closed my eyes... the end was near - my final demise.

"GROOOOOWWWWLLLL," I heard, "GRRRRRR."

I winced and curled in a ball, grabbing at anything that would shield me from the predator.

"GRRRR ... GROOOWWWLLL ... where's the ketchup? I never eat humans without ketchup."

I opened my eyes to see Ukiah standing over me, the moon forming a halo behind his head as he howled with delight.

"You son of a bitch!" I screamed. "What's the big idea? I almost had a heart attack."

After extending his hand (which I resentfully took hold of), Ukiah said, "You didn't think I paid attention, did you?"

"To what?" I asked, struggling to my feet.

"Your childhood," he said, steadying me.

I opened my mouth, but no words came out. Ukiah had startled me to such an extent that I couldn't even speak.

"Did I capture the terror of your youth when Big Daddy haunted you with abuse?"

"How did you know? I never told you."

"Not in so many words."

"I can't believe you did that to me. I almost died of fright."

"C'mon, we have a show to see," he laughed, leading me along the path. "And next time I talk about writing, start paying attention. It'll do wonders for your health."

"When did you get interested in Joan Jett?" I asked as Ukiah drove toward The Dies Infaustus.

"I've followed her career for years. The first time I saw her was in the tenth grade. She played guitar in an all-girl group called 'The Runaways.' Joan was only sixteen years old."

"Sixteen and touring America? Wow," I sighed. "How old is she now?"

"Thirty-eight, I think. Thirty-eight and still gorgeous."

In no time, we once again stood in our same spot near the steps watching Joan Jett and the Blackhearts crank out their ferocious brand of rock n' roll. Although Joan wore the same stage attire, she had drastically changed her appearance. Rather than being neon red, her short-cropped hair was now colored a stylish blonde. The sight of her new hair-do, and also being more accustomed to the surroundings, had a calming affect on me. During the first show I was racked with fear, but now felt relaxation washing over my body. And, being that I could enjoy the show, I took a closer look at Joan Jett.

I must admit, Ukiah was right in his opinions concerning beauty. Joan's face glowed with knowing confidence, her huge brown eyes set inside wide, almond-shaped sockets highlighted by thin, pencil-lined brows. Joan's chiseled cheekbones were offset by her pale flesh, and lips that anyone would love to kiss, even me. Now I saw what Ukiah had known for twenty years – Joan Jett was undoubtedly the coolest and most gorgeous woman in rock n' roll. What a sight they would make walking down the aisle - Mr. Ukiah Rhymes and his bride, Joan Jett. But the thought horrified me. Even though Ukiah was a prick who almost scared me to death, I prayed that the day he left me would never arrive.

9

Incredibly, Ukiah invited me to attend yet another Joan Jett concert, this one at a venue near the town of Polarville. Being that I rarely saw him during the week, any time spent with Ukiah was anticipated, even if it meant watching the same group three times in one month. The show's locale, an outdoor amphitheater nearly eighty miles away, appeared an unlikely selection considering its 8:00 o'clock starting time this late in the year. The predominant factor that prevented this concert from becoming a disaster was a welcome spell of Indian Summer. Daytime temperatures peaked at seventy-five degrees, while at night they settled at a comfortable sixty-five. Had the mercury dipped to a seasonal forty degrees after nightfall, we could have been in for a chilly evening.

As Ukiah greeted me late that Saturday afternoon, we hopped inside the Gemini - me driving, him riding shotgun. Brimming with excitement as I pulled from the driveway onto Reflection Alley, Ukiah shattered any possibility of spending time alone with him.

"Wait a second," he said. "There's Woody. Let's invite him along."

These words burned into my mind like fiery torches searing each eardrum. In fact, even hearing Dewar's name caused me to punch the accelerator. I would have kept driving to Polarville had Ukiah not opened his door to catch Woody's attention. The last thing I needed were Ukiah's legs mangled beneath the wheels of my car. Damn him. Why couldn't Woody just leave me alone?

"Woody, what's happening?" Ukiah yelled across the yard.

I envisioned a burnout similar to those at Duality Speedway, with Dewar's head ground into hamburger beneath my wheels.

"Nothing much," Woody said. "Just putting up my storm windows to keep out the viruses."

"Do you wanna go to a show in Polarville?"

Say no. Please say no.

"Who's playing?"

"Joan Jett and the Blackhearts."

You're too old for rock n' roll. Say no, then go home and listen to the swing-kings.

"Joan Jett. Sure, I'll be there in a minute. Let me grab my medicine bag."

Ukiah closed his door, then chimed, "Cool. The more the merrier!"

I don't know if Ukiah invited Woody to spite me, or if he simply didn't notice the man's annoying habits. Whatever the case, I fumed with silent rage. What began as an exciting trip now held the potential to be an endless nightmare.

"What's wrong, Chris?" Ukiah asked as we waited. "You seem ..."

"You know I hate Woody. Why did you invite him?" I seethed. "The entire trip is ruined."

"You don't like him?" he asked with such feigned ignorance that his facade was almost believable.

"If I never saw that pain in the ass again it'd be too soon. In fact, if Woody dropped dead today, I'd be the first person to dig his grave."

At that instant, I caught my neighbor's reflection in the rear-view mirror as he passed behind the Gemini, then crawled into my backseat. As he sat, wearing white jeans and a faded green medical smock, I noticed a black leather bag with two handles (the kind doctors carried) resting on the seat beside him. This man was beyond hope.

"Let's go," Ukiah yelled, removing his black-and-white checkered flannel shirt.

After laying his garment on the consul between us, I looked at Ukiah's left arm and again saw three parallel lines, similar to scratch marks, lining his flesh. They looked identical to those I saw a month earlier.

"Let's roll," Woody chimed in. "I feel like getting drunk and fucking! Whatta ya say, Chris? Do you wanna join me?"

I curled my upper lip and rolled my eyes without justifying his question with a response.

"Maybe we can stop along the way and buy a six-pack," he continued from the backseat. "I'm not supposed to drink due to cirrhosis of the liver, but what the hell. Ya only live once!"

The sound of his abrasive voice scraped against my ears like sandpaper to a grater. How would I endure a three-hour round trip with this man? Then I remembered Woody crooning, "I feel like getting drunk and fucking." Where had I heard those words? I knew! At that cabin in the swamp. Its graffiti was nearly identical - "Get

Drunk and Fuck." I wonder if Woody had been the one who painted it years ago.

"Chris, I forgot to tell you," Ukiah blurted. "Yesterday I bought a used television set. It's only black-and-white, but it still works."

"Pretty soon you'll be using an electric can opener instead of that hand-held model."

"I don't know. That may be getting carried away," he chuckled.

"Or else ..."

Woody interrupted by declaring, "Did you know that the grungy brown build-up in the metal rollers of a can opener are responsible for the spread of clostridium botulinum?"

"It's responsible for claustrophobia?" Ukiah laughed. "You mean it'll make you afraid of being in a room full of can openers?"

Ukiah and I laughed as Woody tried to make sense of my passenger's joke. As we drove from Latera Heights, darkness enveloped us as streetlights were replaced by darkened trees and blacktop highway. Ukiah fumbled with the radio dial before settling on a station that played country western music from ages past - the type where hillbillies, moonshiners, cowboys, and outlaws sang about heartbreak, loneliness, and living off the land. We listened to the soothing tunes for quite some time before Woody's shrill, nasal voice ruined the mood.

"Have either of you noticed that toe jam which hasn't been flicked away for a couple days leads to respiratory problems?"

The temperature of my blood neared the boiling point. Even Ukiah, who usually sympathized with this man, became noticeably perturbed by Dewar's intrusiveness. But rather than exploding, Ukiah showed restraint, retaining his slouched position in the bucket seat.

"How have you been feeling, Woody? You look to be in good health."

"I feel fine, but a few days ago I might have caught something from Chris."

Unable to keep silent any longer, I snapped, "From me? What did you catch from me?"

"Don't get offended, neighbor," he snickered guiltily. "Any of us can be carriers ... even Ukiah."

Even in the darkness I saw Ukiah grimace as his body became tense.

"Let me get this straight," he began. "Are you saying I might be transmitting germs and disease?"

"Anyone can be a catalyst for infection. You might be an agent for some element or group ..."

"You're talking about S.W.A.N., aren't you?" Ukiah roared. "You're one of their spies."

"What? Wh ... What are you talking about?" Woody moaned nervously from the darkened backseat. "I'm not a bird, but some aquatic birds, when not properly cooked, have been known to cause paratyphoid fevers."

"Don't try to snow me, Dewar. I'm onto your code words."

"What code words?" he exclaimed, fidgeting behind me.

Ukiah sat erect in the seat, then turned to face Woody.

"When you mentioned a catalyst for infection, that was a slang term for the virus that is infiltrating our language, wasn't it? Then your allusion to agents for some element or group ... it's obvious you're pointing to O.W.L. - One Word Literature."

"Owls?" Woody whined. "What're you talking about? You're mad. Stop the car and let me out."

Ukiah, now propped on his knees and directly facing the backseat, screamed, "Who are you working for? Tell me! Who sent you to steal my ideas?"

The tension rose dramatically as Ukiah's blistering interrogation of Woody started scaring me.

"Ukiah," I coughed, clearing my throat, "Maybe ..."

"Shut up and keep driving," he demanded. "This argument's between Dewar and me."

Then, as if defying the laws of physics, Ukiah sprang from his knees to land in the backseat beside Woody. Towering over him as Dewar cringed, Ukiah continued his verbal assault.

"I've known all along that you were a spy for S.W.A.N. Who's financing you? Was it someone at Mason Turner?"

"I swear U ... U ... Ukiah, I'm not a plant."

"Don't make me beat the hell out of you."

"Please," Woody begged, "leave me alone."

"Ukiah," I pleaded, teeming with fear, "this situation is getting out of hand."

Ignoring my request, he focused his wrath on Woody.

"I swear, my books won't fall into the wrong hands. Just because you work for a group of men who plan on destroying our language doesn't mean I'll surrender The Word to them. Do you hear me?"

I wondered whether stopping the car would be wise, then thought of Ukiah turning his vengeance on me. I decided to keep driving in silence. Woody lay prone on the backseat behind me, his feet pushing against the rear passenger door. Ukiah knelt atop him, out of his mind with insanity.

"You've been trying to erase our ability to communicate for ages by obliterating The Word. But I promise ... the signal will continue to be sent. Is that clear?"

"It's clear," Woody whimpered, his throat clogged with phlegm. "Why are you doing this? I haven't done anything to you."

I heard the distinct sound of fists hitting flesh, then Woody's cry for help.

"I won't surrender anything where The Word is concerned. Am I understood, Woody?"

"Please, no. Don't hit me again," he wept.

"You have one last chance, motherfucker," Ukiah snarled, his voice scratchy and deep. "You better answer correctly."

I peeked in the rear-view mirror, catching brief glimpses of violent activity. A nauseous feeling bubbled in my stomach as the taste of vomit rose through my throat.

"I'll try to ans ... answer ... I'll try to answer right," Woody cried.

"Do you think that I'm in direct contact with my Muse?" Ukiah growled.

"Yes, I do," Woody bawled. "Just leave me alone."

"And do you believe Romlocon can help me save The Word from S.W.A.N.'s efforts to destroy our Language?"

"Yes .. yes," Woody screamed.

"Then you're ready to die, motherfucker," Ukiah howled at the top of his lungs.

"No ... no ... I beg of ..."

"Ukiah, don't," I pleaded. "Don't kill him!"

I heard a chorus of heavy breathing, gurgled moans, gasps, whimpers ... ... then one last final sigh emanating from the backseat. It couldn't be. They must have arranged this routine as some sort of practical joke. How could a murder occur when only ten minutes earlier we were riding along listening to country western music? Woody was dead — in the backseat of my car! This nightmare couldn't be happening. Murder. Murder. I just heard a murder being committed. A fucking murder! What the hell was going on?

I cautiously peeked in the mirror to see Ukiah sitting upright in the backseat - his wide eyes staring directly at the reflection of mine. They appeared the size of silver dollars, with the whites so bright I swore miniature flashbulbs were hidden behind his pupils. Their callous, unblinking nature freaked me so badly that I lost control of my arms and steered the Gemini toward a low shoulder along the road.

A darkened stillness enveloped us at that moment - the air vibrating with electric para-noia ... surrounding us with the full implications of this act. A murder, the most brutal and irreversible of human acts, had occurred in my car. Any attempt to escape its consequences would be futile.

Trembling, I sniffed, "What happened?" before resting my head on the steering wheel.

Still in the backseat, Ukiah spoke evenly, without answering my question, "No wonder Woody was always sick. His illness reflected a disrespect for The Word."

Bawling uncontrollably, I yelled, "Get off it, Ukiah. What is all this mumbo jumbo about spies and The Word? Woody wasn't an agent for some secret group that tried to ruin the human language. Look beside you. He's dead. It's not very likely that this worthless, unemployed hypochondriac could be a high-level ... oh shit, what're we going to do?"

"About what?" Ukiah asked, a steely-edge in his voice that froze my blood.

"About what? About this murder," I screamed, lifting my head. "You're going to spend the rest of your life in prison, while I ... who knows what will happen to me. But I don't feel like being on my knees for the rest of my life ... scrubbing floors or God knows what else for some psychopathic inmate. I wouldn't last long in the penitentiary."

"We should probably do something with the body," Ukiah replied calmly.

"How did I ever get involved in this mess?" I wailed, about to collapse.

In a confident voice that made me take notice, Ukiah demanded, "Drive back that dirt road over there, the one beside those pine trees."

Without using my headlights (not wishing to draw undue attention from passing motor-ists), I drove to this clandestine location. I envisioned a shallow grave with Dewar's still warm body covered by dirt. Even more terrifying were the thoughts of this murder. I pictured Ukiah straddling Woody, his long hair falling in all directions as he covered his victim's mouth and nose. Woody gagged and coughed, pleading for breath, while Ukiah badgered him with questions.

"Do you wanna die?"

"Yes ... yes," Woody coughed.

"Why are you ready for death?" Ukiah gurgled in a scratchy voice.

"My body's been marked," Woody cried. "I can feel it every second of the day - even when I'm sleeping. The mark is poisonous. I've been chosen to die, and you're my deliverer."

Peeking beneath the trees, still without light, I saw Woody draw his last breath as blood splattered my face. Before I could wipe away the crimson fluid, Ukiah drove my Gemini while I was atop Woody, both hands strangling his scrawny, chicken-flesh neck. I was killing him! But I wasn't the one who smothered Dewar - Ukiah was. My involvement ... I had no involvement. Yet there I was, in my own mind, choking the life out of Woody Dewar.

"Where should I go? I can't see a thing. What are we going to do, Ukiah?"

My passenger told me to stop, then delivered the following plan.

"To cover our tracks, we'll throw Woody in the trunk, then go to the Joan Jett concert. We should still be able to catch her opening number," Ukiah told me.

Exasperated, I squealed, "That's all! What about the police? What about a dead body? All you're worried about is a concert."

"Look, Chris. If we act suspicious, the cops'll start nosing around. But we'll stick to our plan by going to the concert. That way we have a clear-cut alibi - the ticket stubs."

"What about the body?" I panted. "This is a nightmare. Nothing makes sense."

"After we get back to Latera Heights, we'll take Woody inside his house and put him to bed. Your house and his are the only ones in the neighborhood, so nobody will see us moving the corpse."

"That's all we do?" I asked, feeling somewhat relieved.

"Everyone knew Dewar was a hypochondriac. To find him dead in bed would be no surprise. Plus there's no evidence, like a bullet hole or knife wound. Smothering him was clean and easy."

"It might work," I said softly, then somewhat louder, "it just might work."

"Of course it will. People get away with murder every day. So hell, let's toss that body in the trunk, then rock n' roll with Joan Jett and the Blackhearts!"

"I'm with you," I cheered a bit too enthusiastically. "But there is one thing I'd like to know," I added.

"What's that?" Ukiah asked.

"I wonder if Woody painted that message on the cabin wall. Y'know the one, let's get drunk and fuck."

"Who knows?" Ukiah said grimly. "But he won't be doing either for awhile."

Even when Woody's body stopped bouncing in the trunk, I could still feel its presence. Although a possibility existed that we might get away with this deed, the thought of a corpse rotting in my trunk was creepy. At least nightfall had arrived. To have witnessed this murder, then moved the body in broad daylight, may have been too much to bear. So, I drove without saying a word as Ukiah sat to my right, his silence reminiscent of our initial meeting.

As we neared Polarville, I asked Ukiah what he was thinking about. His answer filled me with both alarm and sentimentality. He began slowly, pointedly choosing each word.

"The last time Death entered my life, my cat Deuces died. You should have seen this cat, a purebred Persian with thick white fur and a luxurious tail. He was more beautiful than anything on earth, even though he usually came home with briars, jaggers, and earthworms in his fur. But Deuces didn't mind. That cat ran from the time he woke up until I brought him in at night - stopping only long enough to eat and catch a drink of water. I can only imagine the adventures he had in my old neighborhood that had a woods behind it, just like yours, Chris."

"It's too bad I never saw him," I said softly.

"You would have fallen in love at first sight. I fell head over heels for that cat, but not for the reasons you'd expect."

"How so?"

"Deuces never went for the typical affection routine. He just wanted to run wild, and the only place he could do that was outside. So when it came to being petted, or sleeping in bed with me, Deuces had nothing to do with it. He needed to run. The only time he ever let himself be loved was when I brought him in the house at night. After he ate supper and drank his milk, Deuces laid down to sleep. It was only then that he'd roll on his back and let me pet his belly or stroke his fur. You should have heard him purring, or cooing like a morning dove. Deuces would finally let his defenses down and accept love. I'd pet his long white coat and try to pick the jaggers from his fur; but mostly I just ran my fingers along Deuces' body and listened to him purr. After a while, Deuces fell asleep. I'd lay my head on a pillow beside his chest and listen to his displays of love ... the soft gentle meows, the swaying of his tail, a look of contentment, and an ever-present purr. The next morning, Deuces would be ready to run wild again, having long forgotten his need for affection."

Pausing for a moment, I finally bolstered the courage to ask, "Whatever happened to Deuces?"

Ukiah sat stoically as I drove through the darkness, then replied. "One morning, as usual, he ate a can of tuna, then rambled on his merry way. That night, Deuces came home with his ass splattered with what looked to be mud. After checking closer, I discovered it was diarrhea. But instead of smelling like shit, this wet substance smelled like sulfur. I could tell that Deuces wasn't his normal self. He was dying right before my eyes from a disease called F.I.P. In the matter of twelve hours, this strong, loving cat went from life to death. His storybook existence ended. Now, some folks may say Deuces wasn't much of a pet anyway, 'cause he did nothing but run all day. But that's why I loved him. Deuces epitomized freedom - living life to the fullest. How could I make him something he didn't want to be? I loved seeing him race along the yard, chasing birds or squirrels, rolling in piles of catnip, or hiding behind bushes to play hide n' seek with me. Man, I loved that cat. His senseless death made me question our very existence. I may have understood this tragedy had he been sick over a long period of time. But Deuces never even sneezed during his life. How could he have been taken so quickly? It didn't seem fair. But then I came up with an explanation. Deuces' existence did serve a purpose, one of the most important of all time."

"He had a mission?" I asked without trying to sound doubtful.

"I asked myself - how could his life be taken so unjustly? Deuces never hurt anyone. There wasn't a mean bone in that cat's body. Even his color reflected his gentle nature. What is white symbolic of?" he finally asked.

"Goodness?" I replied naively.

"Purity! Whiteness is symbolic of our attempts to rise through the levels of existence until we're no longer corrupted by the world."

"When you mentioned a purpose, how did it relate to Deuces?"

"Deuces was sent by Romlocon as a sign to let me know I better get my shit together, because when she arrives to deliver The Word, it'll be my time to enter the annals of publishing history. But if I'm not ready, the opportunity will pass me by. Deuces was a sacrifice sent from my Muse to show me that none of them had forgotten my mission."

"I'm not following ..."

"Deuces had lived many lives on this planet, bettering himself each time until he only had one last incarnation - to deliver a message of purity and love. He was sent directly to me as a wake-up call. Following his death, I couldn't understand why he had to go. Its suddenness wasn't fair. Then I felt Romlocon's presence for the first time. Before this happened, I never understood my writing. Why did I always scratch this pen across the page? It didn't make sense. But then Deuces opened my eyes. An entire spirit world exists just beyond our reach. To make contact with it requires a special messenger. So, ya see, Deuces paid his final penance. The rest of his existence will be one of absolute purity."

Confused by Ukiah's split personalities - on one hand a heartless murderer, the other a spiritual artist - I asked pointedly, "What about Woody? You murdered him. An hour ago he was living just like Deuces. Now he's bouncing around in my trunk. How does this 'mishap' fit into your picture of reincarnation and past-lives ...?"

I wasn't allowed to finish my sentence, for Ukiah interrupted my closing words.

"All I can say is that Dewar's death was not a coincidence, or random act. He died at the right time." Then, as if batting a fly, he pointed toward the windshield, "Look up ahead, a sign for Polarville Meadows. That's our exit."

Soon we would be watching Joan Jett and the Blackhearts.

To find Polarville Meadows, one needed more than a map, they had to rely on a sixth sense. The rural amphitheater sat hidden in such a remote section of forest that early explorers who blazed trails across this nation would have had trouble finding it. We eventually followed a two-lane cattle path (Ukiah called them turkey tracks) past junkyards, a one-room schoolhouse, dilapidated country churches, dairy farms, and state game lands dotted by rows of silos held behind barbed-wire fence. In the late autumn darkness, this scenery assumed the surreal characteristics of an aged painting, or a black-and-white movie that time had forgotten. Somehow, like a divining rod drawn to water, we reached our destination.

The amphitheater's parking area was nothing more than a rolling meadow situated near a cluster of trees. Being that Woody's dead body still laid in my trunk, and fearing that it would soon start smelling, I drove the Gemini to a remote corner of the lot, far removed from any other vehicle.

After inspecting the backseat for any obvious signs of mayhem, we hiked toward the stage area that was located at the foot of a hill. Considering the Indian Summer's balmy temperature, concert-goers largely ignored their campfires, instead drinking beer, or tossing glow-in-the-dark Frisbees. The amphitheater definitely resonated with life, and soon winter would unleash its fury across the countryside. But for the time being, everyone was enjoying the season's final bash.

While we wandered among the revelers, an image of Woody's stiffened body (arms covering his head against attack), refused to leave my mind. Ukiah and I were like criminals who murdered an entire family, then sat at their kitchen table and ate a meal before leaving. Less than an hour earlier a man's murder took place in my presence, and now I was ready to watch a rock n' roll show. If the authorities caught wind of these extenuating circumstances, they'd fry us.

From all appearances, Woody's death had little impact on Ukiah. He quietly wandered through the crowd, absorbing every sight like a newspaper reporter covering his beat. At one point, Ukiah motioned for me to follow, and soon we strolled toward the stage. Unlike The Dies Infaustus, where screaming amplifiers, glitter, neon, strobes, and tightly-packed bodies produced droves of claustrophobic commotion, the amphitheater reflected the laid-back style of rural life. The crowd lounged on blankets, smoked weed, and chatted under a crescent moon. Without effort, we walked right to the front of the stage, separated from it by only a chain-link fence and one row of spectators. Nobody fought for space or bumped into those around them. They merely stood contentedly ... waiting.

Reminiscent of their two earlier concerts, a tribal drumbeat and cacophony of feedback trumpeted the band's arrival on stage. Suddenly, an array of lights exploded, bathing Joan in glimmering shades of color. Being only five feet from the stage, I witnessed Joan intimately - her alluring, dark brown eyes, drops of sweat mixing with pancake make-up, thin sexy hips wrapped by tight black jeans, and perfectly formed breasts peeking from her sleeveless black leather vest. Her performance, as usual, cast an invigorating spell on the crowd, filling them with an infectious energy that wasn't easily forgotten. As for Ukiah's reaction, he obviously fell in love once again, floored by the sight of a gorgeous woman playing an electric guitar.

Following a number of rousing encores, the stage lights dimmed and we returned to our car. The journey home was generally uneventful as we listened to old-time country music on the radio, our thoughts monopolized by a certain complication in my trunk.

"You grab his hands while I hold his feet," Ukiah instructed after I parked the Gemini behind a bush in my driveway.

"What're we going to do?" I asked, my heart beating frantically.

"We'll dump Dewar's body in his bed, take his clothes off to destroy the fingerprints, then cover him. Sometime tomorrow, we'll snoop around in here to see if there's any evidence pointing to us, like a note. Other than that, we'll bide our time until his corpse is found. It's a good thing you two weren't close."

"Why is that?" I panted, the weight of Woody's body sapping my strength.

"Being that you never socialized, there's no excuse to notice anything out of the ordinary. Does he have family in the area, or close friends?"

"Who knows? I never had anything to do with this ..." I was about to call Woody an asshole, but with his blue lifeless face and open eyes gazing up at me, I figured respect for the dead would be wise.

If someone had told me six hours earlier that I'd be involved in not only a murder, but also its cover-up, I'd have said they were crazy. But unbelievably, I stumbled through the darkness holding a cold, clammy corpse in my hands. I feared that the weight of Woody's body would overwhelm me and I'd be forced to set him on the ground, but an intense burst of adrenaline fueled my strength.

Once reaching Dewar's back door, we set his body on the porch step, careful not to let it thump against the concrete, causing post-mortem contusions.

"How are we going to get in?" I pleaded. "The door is locked."

"I'm sure he has keys in his pocket," Ukiah snapped, his patience wearing thin.

"I'm not sticking my hand in there," I gasped, feeling the heebie geebies.

Shaking his head, Ukiah dug into Woody's hip pocket and sneered, "If you were calling the shots, we'd both be in prison by now." He continued to dig, then whispered, "Ah ha, here they are!"

After jingling the keys lightly, Ukiah continued his instruction.

"Once inside, don't turn on the lights."

"Why?" I asked, numbed and confused.

"Because if an autopsy is performed, the pathologist will determine Woody's time of death as sometime earlier this evening. But if a passerby notices lights on at two o'clock in the morning, don't you think they'd get suspicious?"

"Sure," I whispered, realizing why Ukiah worked for Tattoo Blue and I didn't.

Understanding what needed to be done, we hauled Dewar's cold, stiff corpse through his house to a pitch-black bedroom. Without the luxury of light, our motions were laboriously slow.

"Okay, let's get him on the bed," Ukiah commanded tensely, both of us sighing with relief after completing the task.

"Now what?" I asked nervously.

"We'll strip him down to his shorts."

Certain my words would rattle Ukiah, I delivered them anyway.

"I ... I don't feel like touching him any more. It's too creepy."

Furious, Ukiah spat, "Okay. Get out of the way. I'll do it."

As he peeled articles of clothing from Woody's rigid body, waves of paranoia crept through my mind. The darkness certainly didn't help matters, for soon I pictured police cruisers approaching Dewar's house, lights flashing and sirens blaring. I raced through the house as the black-uniformed officers chased me, crushing my skull with billy clubs, then handcuffing me. Dragged away kicking and screaming, they'd eventually toss me in a cell riddled with blood-sucking ticks and venomous vipers.

"Ukiah," I whispered urgently, "I hear something. It might be footsteps."

"Shhh," he demanded, struggling to remove Woody's pants.

"I'm serious. What if it's the cops?"

"There. Nothing left but his underwear. We're almost done."

Turning to Ukiah, I was shocked to see him removing his own T-shirt.

"What are you doing?" I shrieked a bit too loudly.

"Listen! Keep quiet. I'm taking my shirt off because how else will I pull his sheets down without leaving fingerprints? The doorknobs can be wiped clean, but not a comforter. I was going to ask you to take your shirt off, but I'm sure that would have been too embarrassing."

"I'm glad one of us is thinking."

Ukiah slowly pulled-down Woody's sheets, then positioned the corpse into a normal sleeping position. With his hands wrapped by the T-shirt, he finally pulled the bedspread over Woody's body, ruffling it slightly to look slept in.

"There, we're done. I'll put these clothes in a bag, then we'll get out of here," Ukiah sighed, sounding exhausted.

"Don't forget to wipe the doorknobs," I reminded him as we slowly walked along the darkened halls of Woody's house.

Unable to sleep, I paced through the rooms of my house, obsessively replaying the night's grizzly scenes - Ukiah's outrage, the way he suffocated Woody, how we hid the body in my trunk, then created an elaborate cover-up. Would we ever get away with this hare-brained scheme? Were the Latera police naive enough to believe Woody died of natural causes in his own bed?

Then a horrifying thought filled me with doubt. Did Ukiah forget to wipe his fingerprints from an antique dresser in Woody's bedroom? I distinctly remembered him touching it at one point. Shit. This oversight could foil the whole plan.

Not willing to risk such a glaring error for even one night, I looked from my window to see Ukiah's lights still on. I had better tell him about this circumstantial evidence before a detective found it.

Retrieving a jacket, I crouched from my back door and snuck through the gloomy yard. Being that the air was still quite warm, I noticed one of Ukiah's windows partially opened. Figuring I'd peek inside to see if he were still awake, I saw a sight that blew my mind. As I hid behind a lilac bush and peered through the open window, I watched as Ukiah held a pair of vise-grips over an open flame. Clenched in its jaws was a single razor blade, its sharpened edge glowing orange. As if on a mission, Ukiah withdrew the blade from its heat source, then wiped it clean with an orange towel. To my disbelief, he lifted the vise-grip/razor blade device with his right hand and pressed it against the flesh of his left forearm, producing a ghastly red gash.

What was he doing? He was insane. Who in their right mind would deliberately press a heated razor blade into their flesh? No one. No one except a man who'd lost his mind. But not only did Ukiah mutilate himself once, but two more times, producing three parallel lines on his forearm. At least now I knew where the marks came from that I had been periodically noticing.

But my neighbor's insanity did not stop at this bizarre form of flesh-art. Still unaware of my presence, Ukiah knelt beside a flowery brown couch, clasped his hands in prayer, then beckoned an unseen spirit.

"Dear Romlocon, you can see what I'm willing to do for you. Why doesn't anything ever work for me?"

What if Ukiah noticed me? If he saw me now, while lamenting his lot in life, I'd surely be lying dead beside Woody Dewar.

"Why do you let the world torture me? What have I done so wrong to be here? And why ... why won't you let my writings be accepted?"

My heart beat faster than when we hid Woody's body beneath the sheets. If it continued this way much longer, I'd have a heart attack. But as I watched Ukiah praying, a realization dawned on me. Even though I'd never say this to him, I saw that while he pretended to be callous and tough, on the inside he bubbled with softness and sensitivity. His rough, unpolished exterior was nothing but a facade.

"Oh Romlocon, I don't understand your motives. Why are The Muses conspiring to oppress me? I'm here to save our Language, and prevent it from being destroyed. The Word doesn't stand a chance without me. I can take it back from those who are using it for their own greedy purposes. Please, let me give these readers hope. Soon they'll be blinded, unable to read anything but the most basic symbols. Let me lead them, Romlocon. Don't keep tying my hands. My words shouldn't be locked in a box while maggots and termites eat at their pages. Romlocon, you have the power to free The Word. Don't defy me. My gift will only last so long, then it'll be gone. I welcome the struggle before me, but not if its only reward is frustration. Why do I have to wither beneath your all-knowing eyes? Oh Romlocon, Oh majestic daughters of Memory ... Oh inspirers of comedy and tragedy, of poetry and lyricism. I've created a legacy for people to embrace as their own, to share with history and the heavens. You see me every day. Why do you treat me so unfairly? I promise to be a better author. I'll do anything for you. Just let me enter the gates of publication."

Ukiah then rose, stumbled toward his black-and-white television set, and turned it on. He glanced at the screen, then moaned, "Mom and Dad, where are you? I'm all alone. I'm so sad. Why did you abandon me? Please come home."

Freaked out of my mind, afraid of being seen, and unable to watch any more of this emotional meltdown, I raced from Ukiah's window, not stopping until I had locked every door in my house behind me.

10

The need to distance myself from Ukiah became apparent the next morning. I even considered severing our relationship completely. Why? The list of reasons was longer than a yardstick. My only acquaintance (or best friend?) could be characterized as a nihilistic murderer with self-destructive tendencies. In the brief time I'd known him, he nearly killed me on several high-speed joy rides, and now, I potentially faced a long-term prison sentence.

What was I thinking? I'm not the kind of person to get involved with someone like Ukiah Rhymes. Even from afar, one could tell he was trouble. In fact, he defined the term. Let's examine his life. How did Ukiah earn his income? By illegal means, none of which I cared to become familiar with. Where did he live before moving in with me? In the town's sleaziest, most crime-ridden neighborhood. The pizza joints even refused to deliver into that war zone. Plus, he always drove twenty miles an hour over the speed limit, and his business associates included gamblers, drug runners, prostitutes, and thugs. If these factors didn't sway one's opinion, last night he smothered a man to death in my car – a cold-blooded murder resulting from his paranoiac delusions concerning a literary conspiracy and a fictional Muse who he prayed to after masochistically burning his flesh. What was I thinking? I had to sever our ties, the sooner the better.

Sadly, with the above reasoning in mind, the last thing I wanted to do was end my friendship with Ukiah. How could I distance myself from him? Before meeting him, I plodded though life, stifled by boredom. But Ukiah was breath! Life! Whereas fear and insecurity were my only acquaintances, Ukiah taught me how to live my life without bowing to anyone. And, even though I hadn't followed his advice, a seed had been planted. Without him, I would remain locked in a cage while he soared through the clouds. I couldn't say goodbye, or kick him out of my guesthouse.

What would I do? How could I choose between ennui and ecstasy, stagnation and exhilaration? Did I want a life spent behind bars, or in my own self-imposed prison of fear? This conflict led to a fork in the road. Would I choose the safety of normal, everyday life, or take a stab at darkness and danger? To even ponder such a decision proved that my suspicions of Ukiah were well founded. I had to move forward and eradicate him from my life. The future may be boring, but at least I'd live to see it.

After opening my outside door, I leaped with fright when seeing Ukiah standing on my porch, hand raised as if to knock.

"I see you're not in prison yet," he said seriously, his sunglass-covered eyes peering directly into mine.

"For what ... what?" I sputtered, taken by surprise.

"For what? Woody's murder, of course," he snarled.

"His murder? I didn't kill anybody. You ..."

"The mind is funny when it tries to rationalize," he began, tapping his foot on the step. "It comes up with a lot of excuses, such as whether we should betray someone, what is important in life, and if we'll take responsibility for our actions."

"What are you talking about?" I asked, stepping outside.

"Follow me. We better check Dewar's house to make sure you don't go to jail without any chance for parole. Here," he then said, "put these gloves on."

Dumbstruck, I did as he instructed, then followed Ukiah as he walked between a row of bushes to Dewar's house. After unlocking his back door with the same key he found last evening, we entered his residence. Even after only one night, death's presence filled the air like the sickly sweet cologne worn by a mortician. Sunlight filtered through Woody's stained, tattered drapes, an ironic phenomenon in that this symbol of life was squandered within these faded walls.

While Ukiah rifled through kitchen drawers, looked under a coffee table, and performed a general search of the house, I peeked from a window in case somebody tried to interrupt us. The morbid absurdity of this situation did not fail to make an impression on me. Only one room away, Woody Dewar lay dead in bed as rigor mortis set in.

After finishing his search without finding any incriminating evidence, Ukiah made a beeline toward Woody's bookcase. I watched as he scanned each book, then read their titles.

"Look at this crap," he whispered. "*Illness Is Your Enemy, Good Health Bad Virus, I Told You I Was Sick But You Wouldn't Listen,* and *Don't Cough, Breathe, or Sneeze Near Me - The Germophobe's Bible.* What a nutcase. Not one literary book."

Suddenly, remembering my fear from the night before, I blurted, "Ukiah, did you wipe your fingerprints from that dresser in Woody's bedroom?"

"Yeah, I wiped it clean."

"I didn't see you do it."

"Chris, there's plenty you miss during the course of a day," he commented flatly. "C'mon, let's get outta this morgue."

After returning to the porch of my house, Ukiah sighed, "It looks like you'll get off scot-free."

"Ukiah, I didn't do anything."

"That's the attitude," he laughed. "If the authorities do question you, keep acting that way."

Not believing my ears, I stated adamantly, "Ukiah, I didn't kill Woody. You did."

"Me! You must be out of your mind," he countered.

"I sure didn't do it."

"You're saying that I did?"

"Of course you did," I told him.

"Chris, traumatic events have a tendency to mess with people's minds. I'm sure you're suffering from denial. But you're with me - Ukiah. So, come clean, level with me."

"But I didn't kill him. Seriously. You did!" I burst. "I'd never do such a thing. You're the killer, not me."

Unruffled, Ukiah methodically dissected my position.

"Chris, who hated Woody Dewar?"

Reluctantly, I said, "Me."

"And who liked him?"

"You did."

"And who ... who wished him dead, even going so far as to say they'd be the first to dig his grave?"

"Me."

"Chris, aren't you the one who said this fiasco seemed like a nightmare ... that nothing made sense?"

"Yes, but ... but how could I have killed him? You were the murderer."

"How could I have been the killer? I drove your car."

At that moment, a terrifying memory flashed through my mind, one where Ukiah drove the Gemini while I straddled Woody, then strangled him. I clearly saw my hands gripping his neck and the look of terror on his face. Could I have been responsible for this horrible crime?

Terrified, I pleaded, "Ukiah, did I really kill Woody?"

"You did."

"But how? Why?"

"In my opinion," he said rigidly, "you always wanted Woody dead, but never had the guts to do it. But last night your subconscious impulses took control — and you turned into a killer ."

"Did you actually hear me wish for Woody's death?" I trembled.

"Chris, it's useless to run from the past. Every finger points in your direction. The murder happened in your car ... it was your wish fulfillment ... I even have Woody's clothes and medical bag in a box at the guesthouse with your fingerprints on them. The most important thing at this point is how to keep the law from getting you."

"It can't be me, it can't be," I lamented, slumping to the porch step. "How could I have done such a ...? I'm a murderer. A murderer!"

"Cool it, Chris. Nothing's going to happen. Trust me."

"How can you be sure?" I moaned, face cupped in my hands.

"Because I'm an accomplice," he reminded me. "I watched you kill Woody, then didn't report the crime. I'd also serve time."

"Then what're we going to do?"

"Keep living!" Ukiah told me. "If we lead our lives as if nothing happened, no one will suspect us."

Somewhat reassured, I asked, "How do we do that?"

"Since we saw Joan Jett last night, this evening we'll go to the wrestling matches on campus at the Bryce Splycer Center."

"Wrestling matches? You must be kidding?"

"No. Wrestling's a howl. Plus, it'll reinforce our alibis as people who don't have anything to hide."

"Professional Wrestling?" I frowned.

"You'll love it. Japhy and Gina are coming too. They're driving here tonight." Ukiah looked about, then continued. "There's also something I want to look into at the arena."

"What's that?"

"Since you killed your enemy, I figure it's time to get in on the act."

"No! No more killing," I declared. "One was enough."

"I'm disappointed in you," Ukiah told me sternly.

"In me? Why? What did I do now?"

"You're the one who killed Woody, and I'm helping you stay out of prison. But when it's my turn to off somebody, you start acting selfish."

"Who, Ukiah? Who do you want to kill?" I whined, so confused that my brain did back flips.

"Haven't you heard? Philip Prince is speaking at the Splycer Center in a few weeks. It'll be the perfect chance to snuff that bastard. As a matter of fact, let's drive up there now and start snooping around."

"How? They'll never let us in."

"Sure they will. I have a couple work shirts in my car that we'll put on. I'll tell 'em we're plumbers, and you're my apprentice. They'll be none the wiser."

"I don't think so, Ukiah. I've already taken one human life. I don't want to be involved in another."

"It's up to you, but it'd be a shame if that bag of clothes fell from my car in front of the police station - the one with your fingerprints ...."

"Okay, I'll go. But after this killing, no more."

"It's a deal," he told me, laughing as we strolled to his car.

As Ukiah steered through traffic, a light mist fell from the sky. Overwhelmed by my part in Woody's death, I tried to remember last night's events. I clearly recalled my vision of strangling Dewar, but vaguely remembered Ukiah smothering him also. Did he really commit this act, or was I compensating for my guilt by pushing the blame on him? I heard Woody moaning, and saw Ukiah on top of him. But for some reason, I now thought of myself as the killer. I did despise Woody, and longed to see him dead. I really could have been the murderer. Why not?

At that moment, I felt empowered. I was a murderer. Yes, I WAS a murderer! For some reason, rather than resenting this fact, it strengthened me, enabling me to assume a more important role in society. Instead of cringing, my spirits soared. I was a killer, a real-life killer, and I'd get away with it!

Gushing with newfound confidence, I blurted, "Did you say Japhy and Gina were coming tonight?"

"I sure did," Ukiah replied, pulling into the arena's parking lot.

"Whatever happened with that high school teacher, Mister Doublet?"

"I still haven't heard a word from the fucker," Ukiah spat, "so I scheduled an appointment with the school's principal Monday morning."

"Good idea," I said. "What are you going to tell him?"

"The whole story, how Doublet's an asshole. I'm not letting that fucker off the hook," he cursed, parking.

"I don't blame you."

"Yeah, that son of a bitch won't fuck with my kid's future. There's already too many things in the world that control us."

"Such as?"

After yanking a metal tool chest from his trunk, then two blue uniforms, Ukiah spoke passionately.

"What controls us? Are you kidding? The list is endless," he snarled, buttoning his work shirt.

He then proceeded to reel off a litany of factors that comprised our control.

"There's genetics, parental influence, the media, religion and false gods, community standards and neighborhood mores, laws, government impositions, taxes, nationalism, consumerism and The American Dream, status, death, male and female role playing, unseen evils, love, work, time with all its alarms and bells, offspring, language, money, thought, even intangibles such as what is expected of us."

"I never knew there were so many things controlling us," I replied, slipping into the loose-fitting uniform.

"What I mentioned is only the tip of the iceberg. There are a lot more. But do you know the one element that links all of them?"

"No," I replied as we approached the arena's loading dock.

"Fear. Fear is always the key."

"In what way?"

"Look at any of the above examples. Fear is the only constant. What do parents hold over their child's head?"

"Punishment."

"Of course, punishment based on fear. The church tells us to stay in line or we'll go to hell. Don't let your grass get straggly or the neighbors will shun you. Fail to pay your income taxes - boom - a prison sentence, or your wages are attached. Every marriage could end in divorce. Don't do an upstanding job at work - get fired. And then there's The American Dream. Every citizen has to own a mansion, drive a fancy car, wear the fanciest clothes, and make sure their appliances are up to date. If one falls short in these aspirations, they're a failure. Turn on the TV, it'll confirm every point. You've heard those commercials - your kids won't love you unless you buy new Double Chocko Cereal, a new bicycle, a new dollhouse, a new blah blah blah. Ringing bells mean you're late - don't return to your car before a meter runs out - wham, a ticket. And if you don't pay the ticket ..."

"I get the point. Kill an innocent man, fry in the electric chair."

"You catch on quick, Chris."

"There was one factor that might not pertain to fear."

"That was?"

"Genetics."

"But it does, Chris, it does. Y'see, genetics equals destiny, and destiny equals death. To be born a product of your genetic makeup in and of itself implies fear. We emerge from the birth canal screaming, and at that precise moment when our consciousness becomes aware of our mortality, every motivation revolves around the fear of death. Until the genetic engineers eliminate that aspect of our predetermined code, we'll always have this personality quirk."

"Then how do we even function?" I asked.

"Through a combination of defense mechanisms, sublimations, and repression."

"I've heard of those terms. What do they mean?"

"In simple language, they refer to a redirection of our attention from that which troubles us. In other words, being mortal, we'll do anything to avoid the concept of death."

At the loading dock, we met a bored security guard who lounged in a lawn chair doing a crossword puzzle in the daily newspaper.

"Howdy folks. What can I do for you today?"

Ukiah strode forward with the confidence of a television preacher.

"We're from Double Flushers Plumbing. Have you ever heard our commercial? A royal flush always beats a full house."

"Yeah, I think so," the guard chuckled. "How can I help you?"

"We've been sent to fix a clogged toilet in the star's dressing room."

"Really?" the guard asked apathetically. "All stars are full of shit anyway. Here, I'll show you the way."

"Don't bother," Ukiah told him. "We'll be fine."

"Suit yourself."

As we walked into the arena, the guard hollered, "By the way, what's a seven letter word for self-love?"

"You got me," Ukiah hollered without looking back. "I'm just a dumb plumber."

While strolling through The Center - past scaffolds, beneath ventilation ducts, and across iron-grate catwalks - we entered the headliner's staging area.

"Man, look at this joint," Ukiah marveled. "A fucking dressing room that's bigger than my whole apartment at The Towers. What a place."

Ukiah's amazement was well founded. The room we were in had every perk imaginable - a hot tub, training area, pinball machine and video games, plush velvet couches, a full-bar, massage table, vibrating water bed, and a refrigerator stocked with beer and soda. Even its full-length mirror outshone your standard run-of-the-mill models; the glass so perfect that even a troll would look beautiful.

"In a couple of weeks, Philip Prince will be standing inside this room," Ukiah said absently. "I hope you've been paying attention to all the little nooks and crannies," he told me. "You never know where a well-concealed bomb could be hidden."

I hadn't been keeping an eye out, but lied and said otherwise.

Ukiah continued, "The satisfaction I'll get from torturing Prince will be great. Think of the ways we could inflict pain in here – a waterbed electrocution, massage table enemas with a barbell, smothering him with a velvet pillow, or drowning him in a whirlpool. Prince will rue the day he agreed to speak at Latera University."

Still rattled by last night's madness, I longed to change the subject. Regrettably, the other thoughts on my mind weren't much rosier.

"Ukiah, when you mentioned those psychological terms in the parking lot, and how people redirect their attention to avoid unpleasant thoughts, what did you mean?"

Still inspecting the room, Ukiah explained, "To compensate for their fears, humans do a lot of things to elevate their sense of importance, the primary one being power enhancement."

I shook my head and continued to loiter about the room.

"Instead of feeling helpless, humans resort to that which gives them a sense of control. Ruling other people is a perfect example, or manipulating them. Can't you see? It's all about fear."

"How else do we cope?" I asked, feeling this information shouldn't even be discussed.

"Escapism is the basic form of denial."

"Escapism?"

"Yeah, living in fantasy worlds that divert our attention. There's booze, drugs, television, gambling, sexual addiction, soap operas... the list is endless. But so many other alternatives exist for people to hide from the truth. Some try to save their souls, or become so attached to riches and status that they fool themselves into thinking they can buy their way out of death."

"And you?"

"I'm just a lowly writer who's trying to find immortality through his art. I've seen enough in here. Let's make tracks."

After leaving the stars dressing room, I asked Ukiah, "It's obvious that you understand the world better than most. So, why does it seem like you're constantly struggling with your existence? Who are your enemies?"

Ducking into a boiler room with scores of churning furnaces, Ukiah told me, "First of all, I'm battling my parents, whoever they are and wherever they may be. Their abandonment will never give me any peace. Secondly, I'm struggling with the way society restricts my freedom every day."

"Do you really think society has that much influence on us?" I asked, examining a cooling unit.

Speaking as if I were naive beyond belief, he began, "Let's pretend you never left your yard. It'd be a pretty safe bet that the world would leave you alone, don't ya think?"

"I'd say so."

"Well, what if you wanted to run around naked at midnight? You'd be arrested for indecent exposure, but that example is ludicrous. Say you wanted to build an extension onto your living room. The first obstacle confronting you is the zoning board, then environmental regulations. You might not even get a permit. In the winter, if you owned sidewalks and they weren't shoveled after every snowfall, you'd be fined. And, if you failed to pay your school, property, and real estate taxes, you'd be imprisoned and your house repossessed. You haven't left your property yet, which you own by the way, or done anything that directly harmed another person. But all of the above constraints have been imposed on you."

"That's scary," I replied as we reentered a long hallway and walked around. "Are there other things that contribute to your rebellion?"

Ukiah sneered, "Yeah, those bastards who run the publishing houses … them and Philip Prince."

"You never told me why you hate him."

"If you wanna know the truth, Prince is a symbol for every hack writer who has surrendered The Word in exchange for easy money. I went to a bookstore the other day and counted eighty-three books written by Prince. I began leafing through them at random and couldn't find one worthwhile sentence. The Word had been corrupted. But do you know what irritates me more than anything? Work, or should I say, the concept of work."

"Is it Tattoo Blue?"

"No. I actually don't have a problem with him. In terms of work, it's easy and the money is good. But I need more. I crave freedom, and the ability to spend my time how I see fit. I don't want to be a fucking Donald Trump. I just want to escape from their drudgery."

Ukiah reencountered the security guard, who was still sitting in a lawn chair doing his crossword puzzle.

"All right buddy, we're finished. Maybe you'll see us again sometime."

"Take 'er easy," the guard grumbled. "Hey, what's a ten letter word for erotic feelings derived from one's own body and personality?"

"I told ya, fella, I'm nothing but a poor, stupid wrench. I kin hardly even read."

Both the men laughed heartily as we retraced our steps across the parking lot, the drizzle long since dissipated.

"Do you see what I mean about work?" he said pointedly.

"That guy has it made. I've never seen an easier job in my life," I responded.

"Chris, my explanation doesn't have anything to do with a job's difficulty, its pay, or its duties. I'm talking about time. Anything we're forced to do is work, the antithesis of art."

"Again I'm lost."

"Can't you see? That poor bastard's languishing within a system that controls almost all of us, myself included. We're forced to work, leaving less time to create."

"Why is art so important?" I next inquired.

"To be among The Muses, one must become like The Muses. Being that they inspire creation, so must we; but those who control access to The Muses, in my case the gates of publication, will do anything to divert people from their proper course. Chris, I've said it before. Getting published is my only escape from this fucking system of control. Most people have been so ingrained with the idea of work that it doesn't even irritate them. But I've figured out their system, and can't handle it any more. I'm ready to drive off a cliff. Art is nothing if not discontentment."

After hopping into Ukiah's car, I marveled at his ability to stroll into the arena with the ease of a safecracker. He did have a way of getting things done. I asked, "If you don't mind, what did you do before meeting Tattoo Blue?"

Cranking his ignition, Ukiah replied, "I endured a lifetime of humiliating labor. The last job became so unbearable that I resorted to recycling aluminum cans every Monday afternoon to buy a pound of cheap lunch meat and a package of day-old buns."

"What were you doing?"

"Stocking shelves in a grocery store. This fucking job was so ludicrous that management actually timed us putting cans on the shelf. Here we're pulling minimum wage, and they roll a skid ..."

"A skid?"

"Yeah, a pallet. They'd roll this bastard down the aisle with a forklift - I worked graveyard by the way - and it held thousands of cans. I'd start stocking the shelves with green beans and sweet corn, and some asshole would time me with a stopwatch, filling out an efficiency log. For minimum wage! Can you believe it? So I chucked that job after three weeks, then drank beer all day and collected aluminum cans."

"What other kind of things do you do for Tattoo Blue?"

"I'm a jitney man."

"A jiminy? Like Jiminy Cricket?" I laughed.

"No, jitney. I run his hookers around town, or bail them outta jail when the law nabs 'em."

"That's it?"

"Essentially. Whatta ya think I did, kill people?"

"Oh no ... no," I lied, "the thought never crossed my mind."

"Yeah, I deliver Tattoo's women to their street corners, then work on *Blank Line* before I have to get another batch. It's not real shameful, and the scenery is pleasing to the eye!"

"Have you heard from your agent at Mason Turner?"

"No, but I mailed my fifth letter to her a few days ago."

"No response? That's amazing," I said as we pulled into the driveway.

"It looks like we'll be raking leaves again," Ukiah observed while walking toward my porch.

"It does. I wonder why that agent won't answer your letters?"

"Who knows? Sometimes I wonder if it's worth the effort."

"Of course it is," I said energetically.

"I'm not so sure. I can see myself being sixty years old and still hauling dirty clothes to the laundromat. My biggest fear is that I'll still be stocking shelves until I retire. The thought fills me with horror. We're only given so much time in life. Why squander it on something as unappealing as work? I keep writing and writing, but lately it doesn't make sense. Am I just a nobody with big dreams who sees himself being special in his own mind, but is nothing more than a talentless, regular old Joe? I'll grab the rakes and we'll do this yard one more time."

As he wandered toward the back of my house, I felt a tinge of sadness bathing my body. Ukiah's usual bravado seemed to wane, leaving him in a peculiar frame of mind. How would I describe him at times such as these? Angry? No. Embittered? Slightly. Miserable? Absolutely not. Frustrated? That would be the appropriate word. I knew Ukiah wanted nothing more than to be free, to be alive, to spread his wings and fly across the universe. But slowly each of these dreams was fading away before his very eyes. To him, his entire life would be a failure if he didn't get published.

Ukiah returned with two rakes in one hand and a library book in the other.

He cursed, "I checked the mailbox and still nothing from Jennifer. I know that bitch is plotting against me. I'll bet she poisoned every mind at Mason Turner."

Taking a rake from him, I asked, "What did you say in your latest letter?"

"I began with a critique of Thomas Pynchon. Have you ever heard of him?"

I shook my head back n' forth while trying to rake leaves into tidy piles.

"He once wrote a book called *Gravity's Rainbow*, and has now given another one of his masterpieces to the masses."

Ukiah placed special emphasis on both the word "given" and "masses," then continued in a sarcastic voice.

"We must all be thankful that this enigmatic man has been generous enough to en-lighten us. Without intellectuals like him parading their knowledge, how would we - mere commoners - be able to interpret the minds of those who write pretentious prose? How would we ever learn to identify the literary elite?"

My sidekick's voice returned to normal as he raked leaves into piles that were much more uniform and exact than mine, even though I made a concerted effort to be more precise.

He continued, "Don't mind my sarcasm, but when I read a review of Pynchon's newest novel, *Mason and Dixon*, in *Time* Magazine, it epitomized everything that I rebel against. In the same breath, it also reinforced my three main credos for good writing."

Curious as to what Ukiah found important concerning his craft, I naturally questioned him. He responded as such.

"The first lesson to remember is - get to the point. Begin every story with a bang. Secondly, be readable. Finally, above all else, don't bore your audience. Don't be-come a member of the masturbation on paper syndrome. Pynchon's *Mason and Dixon* not only falls victim to each of these pratfalls, it blatantly exploits them."

"Explain."

"Better than describing his style," Ukiah said after dropping his rake, "I'll show you."

Ukiah retrieved his library book from atop a cinder block, then showed me its cover. The title 'Mason and Dixon' was blurred, the only readable letters being 'MAS ON."

"Open this book to any page, then start reading," he told me.

I turned to page 123, then read aloud the first full paragraph:

> The Pilgrim, however long or crooked The road, may keep ever before him the Holy Place he must by his faith seek, as the American ranger, however indeterminate or unposted his Wilderness, may enjoy, even at his Back, the Impulse of Duty he must, by his Honor, attend.[1]

What is this shit?" I gushed with disbelief.

"It's only one of many run-on sentences! How would you like to read a whole novel of this trash? One third of the book, approximately 250 pages, is devoted to the main character's lives before they even start any action."

"Who buys this crap?" I asked, still unable to understand a word I had read.

"Not me. The man who wrote the article in *Time* said, 'The author renounces contemporary English speech altogether and casts the entire narrative in the eighteenth century diction allegedly spoken by a clergyman.' The reviewer concludes by asking, 'Are today's literary patrons capable of engaging in the mind-numbing torture that Python's illegible verbiage requires?'"[2]

"I'm not!" I cheered.

"Me neither, Chris. I'll even speak for every laborer, businessman, clerk, and student by saying NO, we're not willing to devote our valuable time to such nonsense. Mr. Pynchon may have time to toy around with being a wordsmith, but most of us don't. After working eight hours a day, we have to mow the lawn, clean the bathroom, look after our children, cook supper, and fix the car. When we DO have a few spare moments to indulge in the luxury of reading, none of us will rush to buy this book."

"I agree. We don't have time for that high-fallutin' crap."

"Chris, I'm not trying to belittle my fellow man by saying the only publications we read are grocery store scandal sheets. That's the furthest thing from my mind. What I am trying to say is that when readers choose to be challenged or enlightened, they at least want to do it with something they can relate to. *Mason and Dixon* doesn't come close to filling that bill."

---

[1] Thomas Pynchon, *Mason and Dixon*, Henry Holt, 1997.

[2] Paul Gray, *Time Magazine*, May 5, 1997.

"It'd take me three years to read that book," I added, awed by the novel's length.

"At 773 pages, the novel is way too long. My philosophy towards writing is similar to visiting whorehouses. Start with a flourish, finish with a bang, then get the hell out. I don't waste time on roses, foreplay, or pillow talk. I have a job to do, then it's out the door."

"Would it be safe to say this author's not on your list of favorites?"

"After doing a hatchet job on Pynchon, I should say that I do admire his reclusive lifestyle and rock n' roll attitude. Years ago, he was smart enough to carve his own niche which differentiated him from the others."

"Your compliment almost sounds sincere," I said, continuing to rake leaves.

Breaking a sweat, Ukiah admitted, "I respect anyone who can capture the public's imagination. I've been studying the media for twenty years, and am fascinated by those who find a place for themselves."

"You should be able to do it," I deduced.

"I know! I could be a P.R. man's wet dream. I'm not approaching Jennifer with one novel, or collection of poems. I'm sitting on fifty-seven pounds of material. I'm the type of human-interest story that makes a marketer see stars. Imagine the spin they could put on me, a solitary man who traveled the country living in shacks and mobile homes, quietly writing eighteen full length books."

"Ukiah, you're a cottage industry waiting to be exploited."

"Exactly! Being as prolific as I am, the possibilities are endless. I don't want to be a flash in the pan, or an underground author with a cult following. I have too much talent to be limited."

"Then what do you want?"

"To reach the pinnacle of both commercial success and historical significance. I'm not striving for mass-market appeal like Philip Prince, or seeking an intellectual audience like Thomas Pynchon. Both ends of this spectrum seem silly to me. I want to transcend time and trends."

"It looks like we're finished raking leaves for another year," I observed, noticing that my haphazard piles didn't compare to Ukiah's perfected ones.

"I suppose so. Let's grab the wheelbarrow and haul them into the woods."

"I was wondering, Ukiah," I tentatively began, "what if your agent is asking herself, 'how can this man make such outlandish claims? Where does he get the gumption to put himself in the same realm as The Masters?' What would you say?"

"I've been writing for seventeen years, and have captured my entire life in these books. I've spent years getting ready for the limelight. As for the books, anyone can watch my life unfold - every influence, bad habit, peak and valley."

"What do you mean?"

"In the early days, I thought being a writer meant using fifty cent words and complicated phrases. I then entered my dope-smoking days, the boozing days, and so on. Also, I started writing allegories, philosophy, poetry, and plays. The entire process is contained in those letters to Jennifer."

We began scooping armfuls of dampened leaves into a lopsided wheelbarrow.

"It's amazing that you've written for so many years. The sheer volume blows me away."

"The only missing piece to this puzzle," Ukiah sighed, "is a masterpiece. Hopefully, *Blank Line* will fill that gap. I am encouraged by the fact that Hermann Hesse wrote some amazing books during his life, but didn't win a Nobel Prize until the very end."

"With all you've written, why don't you have a masterpiece?" I asked, beginning to tire from gathering leaves.

"I'm not making excuses, but the simplest answer is time, or a lack thereof. I've been so concerned with fitting each piece to the puzzle that I neglected to look at the overall picture. I'm not saying my previous works aren't good. It's just taken one helluva lotta time to reach this point. Yeah, it's been a long journey, with every book being a struggle."

"But there isn't a masterpiece?"

"Not like Kerouac's *On The Road*. I recently read another biography of 'Ol Jack, and found he only spent a total of five months writing his eight most famous books. Many people would say it showed!"

"And your opinion?"

"When Kerouac was ON, there weren't many writers who could touch him. But as was often the case, booze, weed, and speed took their toll. And no artsy, academic rationale can explain away the fact that much of his later work was the self-absorbed ramblings of a demented genius. Kerouac will always be my favorite author, but Truman Capote's remark about him being a typist rather than a writer hit the mark more often than many scholars realize. But that's enough for now. Whatta ya think."

"I'm bushed."

"All right, I'll see you tonight before the wrestling matches. Tattoo Blue snagged us front row seats."

I didn't know if that was a good sign or not.

I didn't have the slightest idea what to expect from professional wrestling. The only aspect of this "sport" I had any familiarity with was its supposed fakery. I didn't even bother to watch it on TV. I never understood the attraction of gorilla-sized men in tights jumping around a ring. At least I'd get another chance to talk with Ukiah, Japhy, and Gina.

When it was almost time to leave, I looked from the kitchen window to see a dented gray van parked in my driveway. This tank must have been what Japhy used to transport his band. Somewhat later, the three of them arrived at my door, bubbling with excitement while talking up a storm.

"... how many kids were there?" Ukiah asked excitedly.

"Probably eighty to a hundred," Japhy told him.

"What did the stage look like?" Ukiah followed up.

Gina told him, "It had about fifty different colored lights flashing on the band."

"No shit. It must've looked like a real concert."

"It was so cool, Dad."

"Where did you play?"

"It was an old high school gym," Gina blurted joyfully. "There were basketball hoops at each end, and above the floor, circling it, was a track where people could run. I'd never seen such a place."

"What other bands were on the bill?" Ukiah triggered, absorbed by every detail.

"The Alter-Egos, Doctor Jeckyl and Mister Hyde, and The Irrational Thoughts," Japhy told him.

"Where did you fit into the line-up?"

"They were the headliners!" Gina declared, hugging Japhy.

"The headliners! Holy shit. I'm so proud of you, buddy. How were you guys compared to the other bands?"

"We kicked their asses! You should have seen Hawke."

"Is that the lead singer?"

"Yeah," Gina took up the story. "He had the place rockin ..."

"... stage-diving into the audience, then jumping around like a madman ..."

"All the while Japhy's crankin' out monster chords as Atomic Aaron's banging his drums."

"It was our best show ever, Dad."

"One of these days I'll get to see you guys again," Ukiah assured his son.

"Hey, whatever happened with that high school teacher? Did he like our tape?" Japhy asked.

"I don't know," Ukiah told him. "That asshole never called."

"Why? Doesn't he like us?"

"Not a chance. Mirror Image is the best band around."

"Then why hasn't he called?"

"I'll find out Monday. I'm meeting with the school's principal," Ukiah stated matter of factly.

"You are?"

"Sure. I'm not letting some asshole ignore my kid's band. Hey, we better get going. You guys remember Chris, don't you?"

We reacquainted ourselves, then walked toward Ukiah's car. The night air blew across my yard, catching a few errant leaves and swirling them in circles. The cool autumn air, when combined with a creepy darkness, filled me with memories from childhood ... racing through the neighborhood after sunset, scarf blowing in the breeze, with the smells of rotting leaves and pumpkins floating through each nostril. Unlike other seasons, when darkness fell in autumn a magical feeling permeated the air, creating an atmosphere of wondrous mischief. Naturally I loved Halloween, but also the high-school football games on Friday nights held under glowing fluorescent lights, or playing hide n' go seek as we ran between scarecrows and dried corn stalks. The ground was cold and hard beneath our feet, the grass stiff and unforgiving. Autumn certainly had a contradictory element to her nature (harvest versus decay), but it also provided our last chance to celebrate before winter set in.

While enjoying these pleasant memories, I saw Woody Dewar's darkened house. To the best of my knowledge, not a soul had visited him today, or discovered his rotting corpse.

Despite my uneasy feelings toward him, I was now overcome by sadness. It didn't seem right that the four of us would have fun all night while Woody lay dead in bed.

I couldn't let my sorrow affect the others, though, especially Ukiah, whose mood changed from earlier dejection to a current state of delight. If I didn't know better, I'd swear he was two different people.

Ukiah eased his Chevy onto Reflection Alley, then acted in an uncharacteristic manner by apologizing to me.

"Sorry for our heavy talk today while raking leaves. Whenever I think about my art, I tend to get overly serious."

"Don't mention it," I told Ukiah. "I enjoy your literary discussions."

Meanwhile, Japhy and Gina tussled with each other in the backseat, laughing and squealing wildly.

"Who's wrestling tonight?" Japhy asked at one point.

Gina added, "Are these matches going to be live on TV?"

"They sure are," Ukiah told them. "They're supposed to be the biggest matches of the year, with Stone Cold Steve Austin laying his title on the line against Cactus Jack."

As Ukiah fiddled with the dials of his radio, I asked, "How did you ever get interested in professional wrestling?"

"I used to watch the matches with Gramma Moo on the farm. We'd sit in her living room every Saturday night and cheer for all the old-time grapplers. I still remember those guys - the champion Bruno Sammartino, and all the bad guys like 'Superstar' Billy Graham, Ivan Koloff, Killer Kowalski, and Blackjack Mulligan. We had a great time. Throughout the years, I've gone to matches all over the country - big city forums, high school gymnasiums, war memorials, or at college arenas. It's the best show in town."

Soon I would discover for myself. We parked in a crowded lot at the Bryce Splycer Center, then zipped toward the arena. Surrounding us were thousands of fans ranging in age from elementary school students to senior citizens. Most of them wore brightly colored T-shirts that flaunted their favorite superstars - those with names like The Undertaker, Chyna, or Ric Flair. But no endorsement appeared more than Stone Cold Steve Austin's - a scowling, bald-headed man who seemed to be a psychopath. Many of the kids wore rainbow face paint or ghastly masks, plus a variety of costume accessories like spiked shoulder pads (fake), Styrofoam hand claws, or black-striped plastic chest protectors. Even the old grannies were decked-out in wild attire. If I didn't know better, I would have sworn we were going to a Halloween party.

Once inside the arena, an usher escorted us to front-row seats near where the wrestlers were led to the ring. The spot wasn't exactly ringside, but at least we'd be able to see the wrestlers as they approached the squared-circle.

"How did you get such good seats?" Japhy asked after we had taken our places.

"Let's just say I have connections," Ukiah smiled.

With show time quickly drawing near, I gazed about the arena to see every seat filled. There must have been 15,000 spectators jammed into The Splycer Center, a frantic anticipation electrifying the air. Banners hung from the cheap seats, while most of the fans waved makeshift signs written with colorful magic markers. I had no idea professional wrestling had reached such a mainstream audience. I saw it as strictly a cult phenomenon, with matches between hairy Neanderthals in smoky gymnasiums.

A ring was set up in the middle of The Splycer Center with bright red turnbuckles and a fluorescent green drape covering it. Because the matches were being televised live, a crew of cameramen surrounded the ring. An extended ramp led to the ring, with a lengthy rectangular stage at its highest point. Finally, a gigantic video screen stood above the ramp, flashing an assortment of wrestling highlights. There was enough room between the screen and stage to permit a curtained walkway through which the wrestlers entered. This sport had definitely evolved since the olden days.

Suddenly, the arena dimmed as the sound of broken glass blasted from the sound system. The audience exploded with glee, leaping to their feet as fireworks soared from hidden compartments in the stage. Sparklers erupted in all directions, followed by soaring red balls of light, flames, lasers, flashpots, smoke bombs, and spinning streamers. The intensity of these pyrotechnics became so intense that I closed my eyes, the heat nearly searing my skin. No one else seemed affected, though, for they screamed in unison, 15,000 strong, as their hero, "Stone Cold" Steve Austin, lumbered toward the stage. Passing within inches of us, separated by only a chain link fence, I had an opportunity to see a wrestler up close. With sweat seeping from his muscular, well-defined body and a glistening gold championship belt strapped about his waist, this scowling man cast quite an imposing shadow.

Once inside the ring, surrounded by deafening applause, Austin grabbed a microphone and jumped atop one of the turnbuckles, issuing a challenge to his opponent.

"Listen, Cactus Jack, you crazy 'sum bitch. Let's cut through the crap and get right to it. For our last match o' the night, I'm puttin' a barbed wire steel cage around the ring. That's right, a Flesh Or Death Match. Whoever surrenders or dies first is the loser! And do you know why? Because Stone Cold said so."

With those venomous words, Austin threw his microphone to the mat while every fan whooped and cheered. I glanced to my side to see Japhy standing on his seat, while Gina jumped up and down in place. Even Ukiah howled with delight, a broad smile crossing his face.

As the evening proceeded and we participated in (as opposed to just watched) a series of matches, I saw almost every sight under the sun. The first bout involved The Undertaker, an ashen-faced zombie with long, tangled black hair; versus Kane, a seven-foot maniac wearing a leather mask. Following them we saw acrobatic jumping jacks, tag teams dressed in spiked shoulder pads and studded boots, a gigantic Olympic power lifter, a freakish alien wearing a gold-lame bodysuit, two lady wrestlers, an obese pig farmer in overalls, midgets, body builders, and a villain who dressed like a Satanic biker.

In all honesty, the parade of wrestlers was nothing more than a freak show. But none of the spectators seemed to notice. They immediately recognized each character - cheering if he was a good guy, hissing if he was a heel. The spectacle was so well choreographed that each wrestler had their own distinct music, lighting, and legion of fans. When one wrestler, The Guard Dog, entered the arena, every fan barked and tossed Styrofoam bones. Another one, the Snake Charmer, drug a live cobra into the ring and taunted the fans.

Ukiah laughed with such glee that I knew he was having a blast. Along with Japhy, Gina, and the other fans, he jeered the bad guys, cheered the favorites, and howled uncontrollably when one of the midgets bit another one's butt.

Inside the ring, these wrestlers were the toughest men (and women) I'd ever seen. They executed piledrivers, hammerlocks, power bombs, suplexes, spinning toeholds, figure-four leg locks, sleeper holds, and eye gouges that made my spine tingle. I learned the proper terminology by asking Ukiah what happened after each match. He, Japhy, and Gina were so wild-eyed by the final match that I feared one of them, or any fan for that matter, would hop the fence and start clawing at the bad guys.

The matches became a rousing exercise in fan participation, a morality play of good versus evil. More importantly, they showed what power the cult of personality had in this country. The mere sight of these wrestlers produced instant displays of loathing, adoration, and worship. I had never seen such devotion. These gigantic men strutted within inches of us, playing their role to the hilt. The dividing line between adulation and hatred had never been more defined. The ancient Greek playwrights had nothing on the men who wrote these storylines, with heavy doses of drama, tragedy, comedy, and suspense. They created a soap opera universe where the line between good and evil was permanently blurred. In a twisted way, the production reminded me of an imaginary family saga that unfolded in my head each day - the one where No-Sho The Hero constantly saved the day.

As if watching a circus-train being unloaded, the final match arrived as a barbed-wire cage was lowered from the ceiling to cover the ring.

"What is a Flesh Or Death Match?" I asked Ukiah, a certain anticipation building within me.

Breathing rapidly and smiling with glee, he replied, "It's a no-holds barred, pinfalls anywhere bout."

"What does that mean?"

Manic, he beamed, "Anything goes. The only reason there's a referee is to count one-two-three."

"Someone could get killed ..."

The lights once again dimmed as a grotesque, hunchbacked creature with straggly hair wearing a partial leather facemask emerged from behind the curtains. Raucous rock n' roll blared from the loudspeakers as Cactus Jack's likeness appeared on the overhead video screen. The 300-pound man wore an unbuttoned brown sleeveless vest and black stretch pants. Growling ferociously and pulling his own hair, Cactus looked more like an escaped mental patient than a professional athlete.

With attention focused on Cactus Jack inside the steel cage, the arena lights were extinguished a third time as Austin's signature sound - breaking glass - pierced the air. 15,000 maniacal fans stood in unison as Stone Cold raced down the ramp toward the barbed-wire cell. In a matter of seconds, the two wrestlers locked horns and started beating the hell out of each other.

Beside me, Ukiah, Japhy, and Gina pressed against the restraining fence, so intent on the match that an atomic bomb could have dropped beside them and they wouldn't have noticed. A vibrant buzz swept through the air, elevating every spectator to a frenzied peak.

Inside the cage, Cactus Jack pummeled Austin with a series of closed fists, then executed an atomic knee drop. Stone Cold slumped to the mat as the villain landed a bionic elbow. He next lifted the champ, threw him into the ropes, then ... a hush swept across the crowd. Cactus took Austin's baldhead and began raking it across the barbed-wire fence. Instantly, blood gushed from the champion's skull, dripping down his face to the mat.

Enraged by the taste of his own blood, Austin retaliated by pummeling Cactus Jack with a barrage of rights and lefts, then threw him from the cage through an open door. In a matter of minutes, both combatants had climbed atop the twenty-foot high cage, belting each other with vicious blows. The next move defied what the human body should be able to withstand. Near the cage's edge, Stone Cold lifted Cactus by the throat, then threw him from the cage! Cactus Jack fell - back first - twenty feet through the air and landed on the announcer's table, crushing it in half. A collective gasp quieted the crowd as Cactus lay crippled on the splintered table.

For years I'd heard wrestling was fake, but how could they fake a 300-pound man landing back-first on a wooden table after being thrown from a twenty-foot cage? I was flabbergasted. Cactus Jack laid motionless while a team of paramedics rushed to his side.

"What was that?" I panted.

"I don't know," Ukiah answered, a concerned look crossing his face. "I've never seen any shit like that."

Miraculously, Cactus Jack rose from the floor, hobbled in circles, then — unbelievably, climbed again to the top of that damned cage! There he met Stone Cold, who still had blood dripping from his head. The two pounded each other for a few moments until the champ lifted his weakened opponent and — it couldn't be - slammed him through the cage's roof! Cactus Jack sailed toward the mat, then WHAM, landed flat on his back, nearly snapping his neck.

Twitching uncontrollably, Cactus lay prone while Austin climbed inside the cage, then crawled beneath the ring. Where was he going? What was he doing? The champ returned shortly thereafter holding a burlap sack filled with thumbtacks that he emptied around the ring. Then, with sadistic glee, Stone Cold scraped Cactus Jack's face across the sharp metal objects, drawing rivers of blood from every inch of flesh not covered by the leather mask.

With his challenger nearly paralyzed and comatose, Austin pounded his boot on the canvas, then waited for the crowd's response. Every fan cheered with bloodthirsty excitement.

"Why are they clapping?" I yelled to Ukiah.

"Austin's going to give him the Stone Cold Stunner!"

"What?"

"You'll see!"

Austin grabbed his challenger's head, then violently slammed it to the mat, causing Cactus Jack to quiver in spasms. Stone Cold then leaped atop him while the referee counted one-two-three! Austin would remain champion until his next brutal match.

I figured the festivities had ended, but not a single fan left their seat. Wondering what would happen next, my curiosity was soon put to rest.

Stone Cold grabbed a microphone from the ring announcer, then addressed the crowd.

"Did you see how I treated that crazy bastard? How many of you folks would love to do that to your Boss at work?"

Uproarious applause.

"How about a teacher, or neighbor, or some bureaucratic asshole at the DMV?"

Insane laughter and unanimous encouragement.

"Well, if you're fed-up, and don't feel like taking any more crap, here's what ya do."

Austin dropped the microphone, then bent over and pulled down his tights as the crowd - 15,000 strong, chanted in unison, "SCRATCH MY ASS," then gave the champion a standing ovation as he exited the arena.

I couldn't believe my ears. I'd been to college football games in stadiums that held 97,000 fans, and they didn't make half this much noise. The phenomenon was amazing.

Once outside the Splycer Center, the four of us were so pumped with adrenaline that we raced across the parking lot through the chilly nighttime air to Ukiah's Celebrity. We weren't the only ones filled with such life! Countless fans ran through the darkness, engaged in mock wrestling matches, or simply letting loose uninhibited howls. It looked like they were possessed, or at least empowered, by Austin's speech. These regular, everyday people, who worked boring jobs forty hours a week and took shit from their bosses, now felt like kings of the world, at least for a few fleeting moments.

Once inside the car, Japhy blurted, "Dad, can you drop Gina and me downtown? There's no way I can go home now. I feel like getting crazy and running wild."

A few minutes later, after Ukiah weaved through traffic with the precision of a big city taxi driver, he left his teenage son and girlfriend on a darkened street corner.

"What?" he asked after turning his car around and noticing my concern. "I'm not his baby-sitter."

"Like father, like son," I laughed.

"So, did ya enjoy the matches?" Ukiah asked, slowly rolling down a back alley.

"In all honesty, I haven't enjoyed myself this much since ... well, since the Joan Jett concert. It was a madhouse inside that arena. Pure bedlam."

"Yeah, they do get crazy."

Rather than following the main highway, Ukiah navigated the darkened alleys and side streets.

He continued, "Once we went to the matches in L.A., my buddy and me plus his three sons, to see a blood match between Ric Flair and Hulk Hogan. What a riot. Those kids got so crazy at intermission ..."

While he told this story and drove along the alleys, my body and mind were overpowered by the strongest sexual feelings I had ever experienced. I wanted to rub my hand along Ukiah's leg, past his knee to his thigh, then massage his crotch. I was forced to actually fight my impulses ... but they were so strong, so powerful, so urgent. I wanted to strip him naked and put his dick in my mouth. I'd then suck on it until he came all over my face.

Oh God, what sick, ugly power was controlling me?

"... and we're buying beer when I see all these people crowded around a stairwell. I told my buddy, who, by the way, committed suicide a few years ago, that we should check out the ruckus. When doing so ..."

Ukiah mentioned his friend's suicide with such passing casualness that I'm sure true craziness didn't bother him at all. To him, suicide, drug addiction, or prostitution were the same as professional wrestling. He watched with baited interest, then went to his next attraction. But I was being sucked into his twisted whirlpool ... slowly consumed.

"... we see that of all people, its this guy's three sons, and they're beating the hell out of each other - one brother leaping from the steps to hit the others with flying elbows and noggin' busters. These kids were a riot. I nicknamed them The Wildcats, and they definitely earned it. Finally, after watching his sons stir the crowd into a frenzy, my buddy shoved through the people and dragged them away, each still throwing cheap shots at the others. I couldn't quit laughing."

As Ukiah pulled into our driveway, I flashed-back to my earlier sexual thoughts, then pictured my friend's reaction.

"I know you, FREAK. Get your hands off me! I'd rather die in a pool of piranhas than let you touch me."

I cried, "Touch me."

"Stay away from me," Ukiah demanded.

"Stay away ... stay away," I begged.

"We'll never unite as one," he stressed.

"Unite as one."

"I'll say it again. I'd rather die than give up control."

"O ... O ... give up your control."

"I can't even talk to you," Ukiah snarled. "You never start an interesting conversation, or maintain one either. And remember. Never touch me! Don't hug me! I'd rather curl up and rot away than become intimate with you."

"Become intimate with you," I cried, voice trailing into the distance as Ukiah strolled toward his cottage in the darkened backyard. The only words I imagined him saying were, "Freak - freak - freak," as they echoed through the oppressive air.

11

Freak. The concept haunted me since childhood ... now I may have inadvertently planted the notion in my counterpart's mind. I know that the scenario concerning my sexual attraction to Ukiah, and his subsequent reaction, were mere fantasy, the product of an over-active imagination. But what if he sensed my growing infatuation that bordered on obsessive compulsion? How would he react? If only I weren't such a coward. Where was my courage ...

Standing naked before a full-length vertical mirror, I lamented a lifetime of disgrace. Look at my body. Who would ever want me as a sexual partner? Certainly not Ukiah. He could find anyone more pleasing than me. Who needed a sexually inadequate misfit? Nothing seemed right. I reminded myself of a puzzle where none of the pieces fit together. My friend always harped about everything being in its proper order. What would he think of me? He would call me a misfit ... nothing but a freak!

I can still remember kids taunting me as if it were yesterday. Given the name Chris Edwards, some of the children called me Eddie, while others referred to me as Edwina. Or, due to my father's nickname being Pus, they'd taunt me in the school cafeteria - "Pus, Pus, Eddie Pus. Run home so your mommy can fuss." I'd get bullied everyday by both boys and girls, one young lady even challenging me to a fight in the seventh grade. Rather than square off against her, I raced home to my mother as the kids threw stones at me.

Who could blame them? Children have a disturbing ability to hone in on freaks like me. Regrettably, the damage they inflicted could never be forgotten. I became so aware of my condition that by high school it took up permanent residency in my mind, similar to a debilitating disease that coursed through one's veins. Nothing mattered except my freak-ishness. Any attempt to make myself like those around me was impossible.

I'm not sure if most people can relate to these descriptions of being different, but the effects were emotionally debilitating. The horrors I experienced in the high school locker room led to overwhelming bouts of suicidal despair. How could I defend myself against such deliberate abuse? Didymus High School became a nightmare, especially when being forced to shower after gym class. I'd cringe in the corner, trying to hide my inadequacies, but it never helped. I'd watch my classmates in the shower, all of them healthy and normal. Then I'd catch a glimpse of myself in the mirror and run for cover. Why was I so different from them? How could anyone love an abnormality like me?

One student especially disliked me - a dislike better described as hatred. His name was Rusty Skelple, and every afternoon in the schoolyard he taunted me with a distinctive brand of surrealistic spite.

"Eddie Pus, Eddie Pus, little baby Edwina Pus. Wash your head with pee-pee juice, wipe your hands on mama's ass."

None of his sayings made sense, but I learned to avoid not only Rusty, but also the entire world so they'd never again hurt me with their words. Who was I, and how did I get this way? Could my father be faulted for hating me? I deserved his abuse. He knew full well that I had broken the mold. I couldn't hide it from him or my classmates. Luckily, due to a necessary resourcefulness over the years, I became more adept at concealing the truth about myself.

But at what cost? My shyness became so debilitating that prior to meeting Ukiah, I rarely spoke to another human being. I suffered from such crippling insecurity that my SELF never allowed a moments rest? Every conscious thought focused on my inadequacy. Why did Ukiah even befriend me? No one else ever took an interest. The only acquaintance who ever accepted me was No-Sho The Hero, and as we all know, he wasn't even real.

Following last evening's traumatic bout of sexual yearning, I became filled with fear. I longed to be intimate with Ukiah, but the odds of consummation were less than winning the lottery. So, I pondered my appearance in the mirror. What could I do to draw Ukiah's attention? I didn't have a clue. I certainly couldn't rely on my past experiences for any help.

Past experiences - what an embarrassment. We attended the eighth grade together, Chris Dibbuk and myself. I'm not sure if it was because of our same first names, but Chris became the only friend I ever had. One weekend evening I slept at Chris' house, and soon curiosity led to experimentation. Chris's father hid an entire cache of pornography in their cellar, so when his parents went to the theatre, we rifled through the drawers with bated breath.

Such sickness, such depravity, such unbridled lust. We paged through each magazine with the eagerness of a bride and groom on their honeymoon, soon removing our clothes in the basement's fruit cellar. In no time, both of us, stark naked, were massaging our genitalia and soaring into novel realms of joy when ... it couldn't be ... the Dibbuk's came home early and barged in on our masturbatory excursion. Needless to say, I was never allowed into the Dibbuk household again; my brief friendship with Chris ending quicker than a porn star's premature ejaculation.

I never experienced such sexual arousal until decades later with Ukiah. My only resort were private fantasies ... lumbering men and petite women having sex with each other.

I replayed these scenes over and over again, wondering where I'd fit into the picture. I had been rendered incapable of actual relations with other human beings, deprived of any chance to regain my self-confidence. While scores of normal people surrounded me, I laid alone like a severed limb from its body.

How could I change myself to augment what little attractiveness I had? Staring at my peculiar body, the alternatives were certainly limited. What if I grew my hair longer, or had plastic surgery? Or, if all else failed, what if I underwent the most extreme surgery of all - genital transformation? Would Ukiah find me attractive then? With a body like mine staring back at me, it seemed a lost cause.

What a pathetic reflection. I'd surrender my life for Ukiah, but he'd only brush me away. To even sneak a peek at him caused my heart to flutter, the way he'd saunter through the yard each morning with drops of dew falling from the trees to kiss his lips. If this man lived on a mountain in the clouds, I'd climb it to wash his feet.

Naked to no one except myself, I felt certain I'd follow Ukiah anywhere. We'd sit beneath weeping willow trees and talk in soft voices, then fall asleep in caves or along mountainous cliffs. But none of these delusions would ever come true. I'd sit in this house for the rest of my life, consumed by grief until my body rotted like ...

At that moment, an extraordinary sensation entered my mind ... a vision of Woody Dewar's body being moved from his house. I raced to my living room window to see an ambulance from some bygone era sitting in my neighbor's driveway. Lurking behind a curtain so as to not be seen, I watched as two white-uniformed men pushed a gurney along the sidewalk. As they loaded the corpse into this antiquated vehicle, I felt as if I were viewing an event from the past. This ambulance with rounded fenders and peculiar headlights didn't seem a fitting end for this man. It was too old, too hokey, and too low-rent to carry bodies. But maybe, just maybe, Woody had been so alone that no one forked over enough money to arrange a proper funeral. Now I witnessed his body being carried from the premises ... me - the one who took his life - his murderer. I wanted to rush across the frost-laden lawn and admit my guilt, but knew such a move would be foolish. So I hid in the shadows, wracked by guilt.

As the ambulance pulled-away and Woody's presence faded into the distance, I was swept away by such grief that it made every inch of my skin tingle. Only minutes earlier I had lamented my inability to connect with Ukiah, now a precious human life that I had ended was being carried to a lonesome grave. Woody's bones would rot in the earth, nothing remaining but his memory in my mind. I then began wondering - if I died today, would Ukiah cherish our times together, or would my fate resemble Woody Dewar's? My voice would cry into the distance, then fade to nothing, joining the other unrequited lovers throughout history.

I wanted to become one with Ukiah, but even mentioning this desire would shame me beyond words. I'd be forced to hide beneath piles of leaves, or cringe in an undiscovered cavern. Periodically, I'd sneak from this cave and follow Ukiah in the shadows, a furtive, yearning soul never to be comforted. But as I approached him, the more intensely the flames of passion scorched my heart. Even if I never crept close enough to touch his long, flowing hair, or kiss his sweet, moistened lips, I'd cling fast to Ukiah's image.

Oh, how the rejection pained me. I saw my naked body in the mirror, then saw myself running back to that cave. I'd become emaciated, my color and vigor slipping into the wind. I prayed to hear three words emerge from Ukiah's mouth – "I love you". I'd hear this phrase every day - the trees whispering "I love you" as winter winds blew through their branches, or whistled by snow-geese flying south for the season.

Every time I heard those words, I'd sing aloud in unison – "I love you, I love you." But these words never entered my ears, because, as usual, my imagination only provided false hope. To compensate, I huddled in my cave, heartbroken and disillusioned, the phrase I longed to hear haunting me for eternity. In the end, nothing existed but my freakish reflection looking back at me in the mirror. With such a companion, was it any wonder I was losing my mind?

12

How dare she disobey me? The nerve of that tramp. I knew Lola would never live up to what I demanded from a secretary. Look at how she's dressed, like a slut trying to outshine her boss. But in all honesty, Jennifer, even though you're fifty-four, you're more beautiful than any woman working here. No one can compare to you, especially Lola in her low-cut blouse.

"How many times do I have to correct you? If an author doesn't live in New York City, we won't even consider them at Mason Turner. Do I have to pound this idea into your head with a jackhammer?"

"But Miss Ewen, this man from Latera Heights may actually be on to something. His first five letters were amazing. Maybe you should read them ...?"

"I'm not paying you to think, Lola! Should I paste a sign on your computer - type, don't think! Do what you are told, and nothing more. You know what is expected, now follow orders. The next time I have to repeat myself, you'll be fired. Lola, you've terribly upset me by mentioning that letter from Latera Heights. I can barely think. See what you've done?"

"But why, Miss Ewen? You look so sad."

"Years ago I went to college at Latera University ... Oh, so long ago. The very thought troubles me ... Lola, when our prospective author ... what is his name, anyway?"

"Plebius Baseborn. His first novel is called *Spurius*."

"Yes, when Mister Basenji arrives, send him into my office."

"Very well, Miss Ewen."

Eighteen years old with the entire world opening its arms to me. If only I could return to those cherished days of my youth - homecoming queen, valedictorian, the high school prom princess, voted prettiest girl in the senior class yearbook, plus most likely to marry a wealthy man. Everyone wanted to know me and be me - dating the first-string quarterback, accepted to Latera University with a full-scholarship, dazzling looks, a petite, knockout body, and dreams of a bright future bouncing through my head.

How could I have let these aspirations slip through my fingers? We owned the world, Jenny, then you moved to Latera Heights and it all went to hell. Oh, how those girls loved you in the freshman dorm, each of them clamoring to be your friend. How could we forget those walks across campus on warm September afternoons? Every boy turned to stare, while the professors begged for our phone number.

Your dreams could have come true in the bat of an eye - a handsome husband, riches galore, a fifty-room mansion, cars, mink coats, and beautiful children who looked like their mother. But then disaster struck that fateful evening - everything turned dark, our bejeweled tiaras replaced by a crown of thorns ... our yellow brick road leading to a pitiful dead-end.

Oh baby, look out that window – New York City. Instead of staring at the power, glitter, and fame, you could have been controlling it. Our ambition to become a recognized author was well within reach. At eighteen years of age, all you needed was a four-year degree and time to write that groundbreaking novel. But nothing worked according to plan. You've been reduced to peddling the work of sub-rate authors who can't hold a candle to what you could have accomplished. If only circumstances had been different. Instead of being studied by scholars, you get letters from idiots in Latera Heights who have the talent of houseplants.

Damn! The past has slipped away, and soon the future will bring nothing but sickness and the loss of my looks. Time will ravage my beauty. Then what will become of me? I can't let this travesty continue. Hope is slipping away, Jenny. What will you do? I'd like to bomb every building in this city and reduce their dreams to rubble just like mine. I want to kill the young, ruin their aspirations, and obliterate any chance of making their dreams come true. If I can't get published, no one should be allowed to either.

Oh baby, why are you so miserable? Life can't be that bad. You draw six-figures a year, enjoy good health, and sit in an office more luxurious than most apartments. But none of it satisfies us. We need more! If only Philip Prince would accept our manuscript. That rotten bastard has the power to open the doors of publication. But he never took you seriously. That arrogant monster struts through these halls like a peacock parading its feathers. Why won't he accept me as an artist rather than simply a ...

"Excuse me, Miss Ewen, Mister Baseborn is here to see you."

"Send him in, Lola."

The author approached my desk with the fresh-faced excitement of an adolescent on Christmas morning. His gray pinstripe suit held a fluffed red handkerchief in the breast pocket, and silver cufflinks on each sleeve. His slacks must have been pressed only minutes earlier, while his black leather wingtips looked as if they were still wet with polish from a shoeshine cloth.

"Have a seat, Mister Baseball."

"Thank you, ma'am, and uh, that's Baseborn."

"I'm sorry. The agent who initially handled this deal was promoted to management, so I've been elected to handle the formalities. It seems this type of busy work is all I'm qualified to do, but that's beside the point. So tell me about yourself."

With an unblemished complexion and short brown hair parted meticulously on the side, he began, "I'm twenty-four years old, I live in New York City, my favorite author is F. Scott Fitzgerald, and I graduated from college with honors while editing my fraternity's newsletter."

"Is that so? Why do you like Mister Fitzgerald?" I asked.

"Because his novels revolved around wealth. It became obsessional."

"And you?"

"I want to get published so I can lead a life of luxury like F. Scott did."

"How interesting, Mister Baseborn. How many novels have you read that were written by Fitzgerald?"

"Only his famous one, *The Great Gatsby*, but I did write a term paper on him for an English class."

"Then you don't know that Fitzgerald died while in his forties after suffering from chronic alcoholism and a series of mental breakdowns?"

"No, not at all. I thought he patterned his life after Jay Gatsby and the other jet-setters in his book."

Unable to take another minute of this banal exercise, I pulled a legal contract from the author's file and slid it toward him.

"Here, sign this, sir."

After momentarily scanning the form, the young writer joked, "Why? Am I selling my soul to the devil?"

I didn't reply, instead pushing the contract closer to him.

Becoming edgy and noticeably nervous, the author stuttered, "Wait ... wait a minute. I'm not, not signing this paper unless ..."

"Unless what, Mister Bashful?"

"Unless I know its content. Aren't there any other alternatives?"

"All our authors sign this paper," I told him flatly.

Trembling, he asked, "But ... isn't there anything else I can do?"

"There is one other option, Mister Baseborn."

"What? I'll do anything."

"The owner of this company, Mason Turner himself, is in that office. Would you care to discuss the matter with him?"

"Sure. Anything but signing that contract," he smiled, a distinct sign of relief crossing his face as he stood.

"Oh, before leaving, you better take this," I suggested, placing a plain brown paper bag on the desk's mirrored surface.

Taken aback, Plebius asked frightfully, "What's in there?"

Grinning, I laughed, "Let's just say it's something to help grease the wheels with Mister Turner."

Snatching the bag, then removing its contents, the author squealed, "Lubricant! You're sending me in there with a jar of Vaseline? What kind of nuthouse is this?" Outraged, he continued to voice his displeasure. "I'm not signing your contract, and I'm not greasing any wheels. When I get published, it'll be with a shred of dignity."

"Dignity!" I shrieked. "Nobody works in this business and keeps their dignity! What are you, a fool?"

"No, I'm ..."

"You're not an artist, Mister Baseborn, and you don't give a damn about literature. The only reason you're in this business is to reap the rewards. Now get the hell out of my office. There are a thousand other schmucks on the street who'll sign these papers. Now scram," I demanded.

"Wait ... wait a second," Plebius whimpered. "Let me reconsider. If you give me the boot, who knows how long it'll take to land another deal."

"Decide Mister Baseborn, or I'll tear this contract into a million pieces."

After tapping his left foot and gnawing viciously at his thumbnail, the writer blurted, "Okay, gimme the damn contract. I'll take it into Turner's office myself - this very second."

The young man turned and walked toward the door when I ushered him back for one last dose of indignity.

"Mister Baseboard, you forgot this tub of grease. Whenever Mister Turner hears an author bucking the system, he prefers that they carry both the contract and the lubricant. It seals the deal, if you know what I mean!"

The young man begrudgingly grabbed each item, then limped from my office with the demeanor of a prostitute being lead to her pimp after stealing the entire night's profits. Soon I would hear the protests, painful squeals, and the final anguished cries associated with one's loss of self-respect. This author's face would eventually appear on the back of a dust jacket, but his soul will have long since departed. C'est la vie. Another day in the publishing industry.

13

When I sleepily opened the windowless front door to my house that morning, two unexpected sights greeted me. I knew the first would come sooner or later - winter's first snowfall. The second nearly knocked me from my socks. A blue-uniformed police officer stood on the steps leading to my door, a stern look painting his face. Holding a metal clipboard and tapping his toe, the youthful detective, sporting a crew cut and mirrored sunglasses, introduced himself.

"My name is Officer Idem. Is this the Chris Edwards' residence?"

"It is," I replied, wearing nothing more than a chartreuse bathrobe and red socks, one with a hole in the big toe.

"May I come in?" he asked.

"Certainly," I coughed as a lump rose through my throat.

After tracking bootfulls of snow onto my kitchen carpet, the officer proceeded with questioning.

"Did you know that your neighbor Woody Dewar recently passed away?"

Ever since that incident occurred, I had been preparing myself for this event. Every potential question, followed by my response, was replayed inside my mind. In addition, I had prepared for this interrogation by rehearsing my answers as if I were Ukiah. Had any of this insanity occurred before we were friends, I would have crumbled under the scrutiny. But this morning I reacted with a coolness that even surprised me.

"Yessir," I replied groggily, rubbing my eyes dramatically.

He followed-up, "Did Mister Dewar recently complain about any medical problems?"

Poised and confident, I said politely, "I'm not sure. We never visited except for a passing hello."

Curiously eyeing my bathrobe, the officer ended his questioning with this piece of evidence.

"Nothing seems out of the ordinary with Mister Dewar's death, but his family did tell us that the deceased constantly carried a black medical bag. Strangely, none of them were able to find it when cleaning his house. Could you help us with this matter?"

Rattled for the first time, I turned away guiltily and said, "No sir, I haven't the slightest idea."

"Very well. If you happen to remember anything, please contact us downtown."

I turned and led the officer to the door, assuring him I'd call if anything developed.

As Idem walked from my porch, I expected him to return to his cruiser. But rather than leaving matters well enough alone, he complicated the situation by turning toward Ukiah's cottage. What if he found that damn evidence box? I didn't feel like spending the rest of my life in prison.

"Why did it take so long?" I asked later that morning after rapping at Ukiah's door.

"Don't sweat it, Chris, everything's cool," he replied while flipping fried eggs in a skillet. "Come in, it's cold out there."

After I entered his house, Ukiah continued. "I have to say, you handled yourself very well. That policeman didn't suspect a thing."

"I did all right, but he pressured me about the medicine bag," I informed my accomplice.

"Don't worry. I have that sack hidden where no one will find it."

"I hope so. I couldn't stand one second behind bars."

"Do you want a couple of eggs?" Ukiah asked, scooping them onto a plate.

"Sure, if there's enough."

"There's plenty," he smiled, long hair falling in tangled strands about the sides of his unshaven face.

After eating a few bites, I asked, "Where have you been keeping yourself? I haven't seen you in days."

"Workin' and writing like a madman."

"That's good. For a minute I thought you were mad at me."

"No, I don't watch TV, go to the movies, or goof around any more. I'm serious about this project. I can't let my writing be a hobby, pastime, or sideline. It's all work. In the past month, I've written 280 pages."

I continued to eat, amazed at Ukiah's work ethic.

"Someday you should let me borrow a few of your books. All I've read so far is *Glitter Ghetto*."

"Sure. Remind me before you leave."

"You got it. How's progress coming with *Blank Line*?"

"I'll tell ya, there aren't any toboggan rides, birthday parties, or get-togethers with long-lost friends any more. It's nothing but work. But *Blank Line* is coming along well."

"How do you stay so focused?" I inquired, scooping the last bit of eggs into my mouth.

"I'm like a machine that constantly needs to run or it'll seize up and quit stamping out parts. Ya gotta keep oiling that fucker and keep 'er churning. I never know when Romlocon will remove her spirit and fade away. When that day comes, the game is over. If you wanna know the truth, I'm afraid to stop. That's why I make every second count. Writers always have to pay attention to their Muse and never take them for granted. If they catch you sleeping, or not using your gift to the fullest - BAM - it's gone. If that happens, the gates of publication will close and your time has passed."

Half laughing, I commented, "You do live by a different set of rules."

Ignoring this observation, Ukiah walked toward a chair and grabbed a folded newspaper.

"Did you see yesterday's *Latera Daily Times?*"

"No, sorry."

"Check it out."

Ukiah opened the newspaper to its front page, then held it before me.

Philip Prince To Speak At Latera University
Prince of the Earth Conquers Literary World

Excitedly, Ukiah proclaimed, "He'll be in town next Saturday to lecture on campus. That's when I'm doing it ..."

"Ukiah, you're not ..."

"I'm taking that fucker out!"

"No! You'll get caught," I told him.

"Far from it, Chris. There's no chance they'll nab me. I have it all planned out. Do you wanna hear ...?"

"Not really ..."

Once again ignoring me, Ukiah began, "After his lecture, Prince will return to his dressing room. I considered the odds of him signing autographs or answering questions, but that bastard doesn't want anything to do with the common reader. He's much too conceited for us. So, I'm betting he'll make a beeline straight for his dressing room, then I'll strike."

"It'll never work, Ukiah ..."

"Wait and see. Do you remember that metal grate above air-duct number seven in the boiler room?"

"The what?"

"Right before the end of Prince's speech, I'll sneak from the auditorium and go into that boiler room we found when we were at The Splycer Center. To avoid suspicion, I'll wear my plumber's uniform when I duck into the boiler room and crawl through the air duct leading to Prince's dressing room. By the way, air-duct number seven was the one beside that fire extinguisher with the cracked cover."

Overwhelmed by this information, I asked, "How do you remember those things?"

"You were with me, Chris. All ya have to do is pay attention."

"What are your plans after the murder? Someone can't kill a famous author, then drive away like nothing happened."

"In fact, that's precisely my plan."

"What!"

"Chris, don't worry about the details. I'll tell ya more next weekend."

"But ..."

"We have more important matters at hand. Did you notice the snow outside?"

Feeling foolish, as if Ukiah thought I were an imbecile, I said, "Of course."

"Do you know what it means?"

"That winter has officially begun?"

"No. It's the beginning of our annual Crash n' Burn Demolition Derby."

"A demolition derby?" I asked. "In winter?"

"It's a tradition in this little town called Cymeez."

"What happens at this event?"

"Rather than describing it, why don't you come along? It's the weekend, so you don't have to get up early tomorrow morning. Plus, Japhy and Gina will be there."

"Okay. When are we leaving?"

"Later this afternoon."

"A demolition derby at night? I can't picture it."

"Just wait n' see."

The sight of Ukiah's driving made me realize I should have stayed home. He tore from the driveway spitting snow and mud from his tires, then spun a donut while turning onto Reflection Alley. Within minutes he fishtailed around a curve, burned rubber on the main highway, and punched his accelerator with such force that my neck snapped against the headrest. To think, I could have been relaxing in my living room watching TV.

Hoping to save my life, I tried calming Ukiah by talking about writing. He usually became so intent on this subject that hopefully it would keep him from driving like a lunatic.

"Y'know, you keep talking about your book *Blank Line*, but you've never really told me anything about it."

Ukiah stared straight ahead, saying, "Really?"

"Yeah, really. Who are the main characters, what genre is it, and what's the story about?"

"I'll tell you someday," Ukiah replied, turning onto the bypass.

"Why not now?"

"Because now I want to drive. I want to fucking fly!"

Ukiah, wearing brown corduroy pants, a red-checkered flannel shirt, and a denim jacket, stomped on his gas pedal, cranking the Celebrity into overdrive.

"I want to go faster than I've ever gone before!"

Unable to object, I grabbed both sides of the seat as gravitational forces gripped my body.

"Yooo-hoooo! I'm going to fly off the edge of the fucking world. Sixty, bam bam. ... Seventy, bang bang. C'mon bitch, go - go! Yeah yeah."

Stricken with fear, I sat frozen in my seat as Ukiah passed a string of cars by weaving between the fast and slow lanes. While he hooted with joy, clutching his steering wheel in both hands, I panted for breath while emitting helpless squeaks of desperation.

"C'mon, take off. Eighty, Ninety ... go go ... push it all the way. Get off the ground you son of a bitch."

Suffering from vertigo as cars, trees, white lines, guardrails, and my life whirled past, I squealed, "STOP!"

"One hundred! I'm going to bury this bitch at 120. Don't try to fight me, baby, you're mine."

I glanced across the dashboard to see a red needle quivering at 110. The entire car shook like we were on a creaky wooden roller coaster, my mind repeatedly screaming, "You're going to die - you're going to die."

"110! Go baby go, crank it. Yow yow yow. Whoo-hoo! Give it to me baby, give it up. You're mine now. Don't try to fight. Just lay back n' enjoy the ride. Ow Ow. Open up, baby. C'mon, don't resist. We're almost there. Go go - Oh yes, that's it. Whoooo - 120. Fuck, we did it!"

Instead of backing off the throttle, Ukiah kept it pegged to the floor, his Celebrity whining, shaking, rattling ... life and death rushing past - cars to the left and right crawling along in comparison - engine revving, pleading for relief, so fast - faster. Oh God, make it stop.

"Slow down, we're going to explode," I pleaded, nearly sobbing with hysterics. "Please."

Consumed by the rush, I'm not sure if Ukiah even knew I was sitting beside him. After I continued to plea, though, he took his foot off the accelerator.

"Damn," he sighed. "If I still smoked, I'd light a cigarette."

Barely able to breathe, let alone complain, I slumped in my seat while still clutching its upholstered veneer.

Winding down to sixty miles an hour, Ukiah asked with the ease of a professional lecturer, "What were we talking about this morning? Writing?"

"How can you act like that?" I asked in a displeased tone.

"Like what?"

"Like nothing happened."

"Oh, that. I just got our blood flowing - a little jump start," he laughed, not exhibiting a trace of craziness.

"I don't like jump starts," I told him curtly. "And if you keep driving that way ..."

"Okay, Chris, I get the point." Ukiah then assumed the voice of a sideshow barker. "Until next time, ladies and gentlemen, your host will drive like a respected member of The Senior Citizen's Club."

I managed a slight chuckle, feeling more at ease than I had minutes earlier. An extended silence then passed before I broached the subject of literature.

"Have you heard anything from that agent in New York City?"

"Not a word," Ukiah sneered, obviously perturbed.

"Have you written to her lately?"

"I wrote my sixth letter to her this afternoon. The envelope's sealed and in the mailbox."

"It's unbelievable that you've written that many letters with no response. Have you considered a different agent?"

Agitated, Ukiah grit his teeth. "I'm sticking with Jennifer until she writes back and accepts me."

Silently questioning his blind persistence, I asked, "What did you say in your last letter?"

Settled into a comfortable driving mode, Ukiah began, "I asked Jennifer, 'When was the last time the literary world had a sex symbol?'"

I grinned, "A better question would be, has the publishing industry ever had a sex symbol?"

"Well, Jack Kerouac's appearance on the back cover of *On The Road* was quite striking with his tasseled hair and Christian cross. In fact, when meeting Kerouac, Salvador Dali became so enamored that he said, 'You are more beautiful than Brando!' But 'ol

Jack was so reluctant and withdrawn that he cringed from the spotlight."

"Were there any other candidates?" I asked.

"F. Scott Fitzgerald lit the stage early, but lost his looks by the second act. Henry Miller scored his fair share of women, but he couldn't be included in the same league as movie stars. Even today, is there anything happening on the writing scene that excites the masses?"

I shrugged my shoulders, at a loss where literature was concerned.

Ukiah continued to ramble, his right hand slumped over the steering wheel.

"I see a new bunch of authors on the talk shows, plus a few of the old stand-bys, and they strike me as either being arrogant elitists or bumbling eggheads. I get the impression that they'd rather sit in dark corners typing at their personal computers than actually setting the world on fire."

"I sense your disappointment. Could you fill the bill as a sex symbol?" I asked, trembling at the question's implication.

Ukiah howled with glee at this proposal. "Not as I am now. But with a little ... okay, with a lotta work, I could."

"What type of work?" I inquired, extremely curious.

"Look at me. I'm almost handsome, but my old man, whoever he was, must not have given my mom a full load when impregnating her."

I remained silent, giggling to myself at Ukiah's self-absorption.

"My head's tilted, nose is too curvy at the end, my eyes are screwy, complexion is too marred, plus I need higher cheekbones. So, if I could get these things fixed, I might have a chance!"

He did constantly think, I had to give him credit. But who knows what else occupied his mind?

"It's a shame that whenever these writers are given a chance - the talk show circuit being their forum - none show any electricity. It's like they stumbled onto the set with only one goal in mind - to put their audience to sleep. Boring, boring, boring."

"When given your chance to shine ..."

"I'll take full advantage of it. I'm going to show the whole world how to act. It's too bad that the concept of cool has all but disappeared from our culture. Turn on your television. Who are we supposed to emulate? Dennis Rodman, Marilyn Manson, or movie stars who shove rodents up their ass. Whatever happened to old-time cool?"

"You have a point. How did this state of affairs develop?"

Excited, Ukiah explained, "Most people on TV don't know how to walk, talk, or dress themselves. They're all so phony. But I'll give the world a course in Coolness 101. After the initial shock, they'll get used to my lessons, then we'll start a more complex study."

"Ukiah, what are you trying to say?"

As darkness set across the countryside, my counterpart began, "Let's use Madonna as an example. Early in her career, how did she make such an incredible rise to the upper echelon of fame? Was it due to her dancing? No. Her abilities were average at best. Did she have an astounding voice? Hardly. Were her songs earth shattering in their originality? Not a chance. And lastly, was she irresistibly gorgeous? Unlikely."

"Then why did this little Italian girl from Michigan become such an icon?" I inquired, suddenly interested.

Ukiah told me, "My first answer is superficial at best. Madonna's rise to the top can be explained as follows. She unleashed the right look at the right time on a culture that was willing to accept it at that moment. This opportunism, coupled with a heavy dose of attitude, gave us Madonna."

"How about the nonsuperficial answer?" I urged him.

"I don't know if I have time to explain it."

"Why, Ukiah?"

"I'm not naive, that's why my explanation would have to delve into what happens behind-the-scenes of not only the political arena, but in the artistic world as well. The two are, in every sense, inexorably linked."

Getting caught up in this drama, I blurted, "Why was Madonna chosen as a cultural icon when other women were more talented?"

We climbed a mountain highway, gradually rising to 2,400 feet. When we left Latera Heights, three inches of snow lay on the ground. But here, as we rose toward the treetops, at least six inches of snow covered the rugged landscape.

As I gazed at this gorgeous country, Ukiah responded to my question. "Here's the answer. Madonna, like other artists through history, was selected to promote the hidden agenda of a certain power elite."

"Like the one you mentioned before? What was it called?"

"S.W.A.N."

"That's it. Are they really calling the shots?"

"I realize that by hinting at this secretive group, I run the risk of being called paranoid. Despite these consequences, I'll continue my line of reasoning. The three main reasons why someone is picked from the litter are: creativity, hunger, and anonymity. In regard to Madonna, she was an unknown musician from the streets whose thirst for success was unquenchable. In other words, she had all the characteristics required by the high-rollers."

Confused, I asked, "Is being chosen a good thing or bad? On the surface it seems fantastic to be discovered, but now I'm not so sure."

"Unbeknownst to her, like so many others who were destined to shape our popular culture, Madonna joined the ranks of Jack Kerouac, Bob Dylan, and Kurt Cobain. The only problem was, none of them, at the time of their discoveries, realized they were puppets whose strings were being pulled from behind a curtain."

"Give me an example," I told him.

"As I've done before, I'll use Jack Kerouac to illustrate my point. When he first gave *On The Road* to his publisher in 1950, America wasn't ready for drug use, illicit sex, and nihilistic migration to find one's self. Hell, we still had to elect Dwight Eisenhower. So, for seven tortuous years, Kerouac labored at his fruitless love - creating his Legend."

"I hate to show my ignorance," I apologized, "but when did he finally get published?"

"In 1957, a revised version of his novel created a tidal wave on the literary scene. The American people, amid a stifling surge of conservatism, were now deemed mature enough to handle such matters. Kerouac, who was by now a right-winger and very square compared to his friends like Allen Ginsberg, hardly resembled the frantic protagonist from his youth. America expected a wild man, but instead got an introverted alcoholic who wore checkered lumberjack shirts. What *On The Road* did accomplish, though, was to establish a foundation that laid the groundwork for what would follow a decade later."

"What happened to Kerouac?"

" 'Ol Jack became an unwitting pawn in a game far more complex than he ever imagined. He became tangled in a web that would snag many like himself. 'Ol Jack was already embittered and despondent by the time he was published, and would die of cirrhosis in 1969. Others like him suffered similar fates, even if the circumstances varied. Bob Dylan reached this realization, changing from an angry protester to a disillusioned troubadour. John Lennon went from a social commentator to a heroin addict and total recluse. Then, when making a comeback, he was swiftly murdered. Finally, there's Kurt Cobain. He created a new kind of music, then became martyred as a suicidal casualty."

With more snow falling from a darkened sky, I said, "I understand your premise, but how does it affect Jennifer and your writing?"

"Can't you see?" Ukiah roared. "I'm the most dangerous man in America because I have the right look, attitude, and creative energy to lead the literary world. Once I hit the big-time, I'm going to attack S.W.A.N. with every ounce of vengeance in my body. Not only will I restore The Word to its rightful position, but I'll open the gates of publication to every person on earth."

"You told this to Jennifer?"

"Not exactly," he stated, sensing my misgivings. "Don't think I'm paranoid. I'm just aware. I'm sure you doubt the above premise, but you have to agree it's possible."

"Do you think a literary agent wants to hear these theories, even if they are true?"

"Chris, I'm not stupid. Those people at Mason Turner aren't concerned with genius, art, or appearance. The only thing they care about is if a writer can make money. But with all I've told you, we both know more is at stake than mere wealth. That's why I think Miss Ewen is plotting against me with S.W.A.N. They know I won't be a dupe in their conspiracy to destroy The Word."

"What are you going to do? Your situation sounds bleak."

"Not so fast. I didn't lay my entire hand out to Jenny. I still might be able to salvage my career."

"I don't follow."

"For appearance sake, we can generate money as an illusion for the uninitiated. That's why I plan on breaking every literary record on the books."

"Records?"

"By setting records, the world will have to take notice. Nothing grabs the public's attention quicker than when records are shattered. Chris, I'm not going to be a hack writer who ekes out a living working day jobs, then supplements his income by writing novels on the side. It's all or nothing with me. I'm not content with mere recognition. I need more than money. I see my name becoming synonymous with literature and change! I don't want to bury my predecessors, only improve on their work by opening the gates of publication to everyone. I guarantee that all those who follow S.W.A.N. will be buried in the dust."

"How will you accomplish these goals?" I asked, wondering how much further into the sky we had to climb. Darkness had completely engulfed the barren surroundings, while a quiet solitude blanketed the ground. At least the snow had quit falling.

"By creating an obsessive audience that can't get enough of my product. And I don't simply mean in America. I see the whole world falling under my spell. Once people become addicted to something, whether it's drugs, sex, hobbies, or people, they become powerless to deny the urge for more. They need to collect, inject, or amass until their source has run dry. This's why my output has to become machine-like."

Ukiah's confidence was unparalleled. He had his game plan all figured out (at least in his own mind), then let his ego run wild.

"All we need to do is drop a few well-placed quotes in the media, and soon the initiated will devour my work like flies on shit."

"Who are these 'eaters' you're talking about?"

"We need to start with the outsiders - The Soloists - those who are hip enough to appreciate cool."

"How would you define an outsider?" I asked, noticing a sign for the Village of Cymeez.

"They're the one's who live beyond the boundaries of everyday life. They're the enlightened students, urban trendsetters, and street-smart partiers who are into their own individual scenes. They're hung over waitresses who want to be actresses, taxi drivers who write poems between calls, and those who are still up when others are in bed. There's a fascinating subculture of fringe-dwellers who are far wiser than the establishment gives them credit for being. These Soloists are starving for something new. They're going to be our target audience. Once we corral them, the rest of America, and eventually the world, will follow suit. Hey look, there it is - Cymeez Fairgrounds. It's time to crash and burn!"

Ukiah parked in a rutty, pitch-black, snow-covered field; our only hope of finding civilization being an aura of light peeking from a distant hill.

"Everybody's down there," Ukiah pointed toward the distant light. "We better hurry. The first round should start any time."

As we trudged through ankle-deep snow, a curious thought entered my mind.

"Ukiah, what do you plan on driving in the demolition derby?"

"I'm not sure."

"You're not sure?"

"Japhy's supposed to find a car, then drive it here while Gina follows in his van."

"I see. What kinds of people enter this contest?"

"The Crash n' Burn is by invitation only. That means only selected drivers are allowed to compete."

"Where do you find them?"

"Most are drivers from the speedway that want one final bang before winter sets in."

After reaching the crest of this hill and looking into the valley, I momentarily froze when seeing the sight before me. Dozens of floodlights set on tripods bathed the clearing with enough rays to illuminate a baseball stadium. As I peered at this amazing sight, a feeling of transcendence overtook me. We were standing on a mountain in the middle of nowhere, staring at this dazzling vision which filled both of us with awe.

Overcome by fear as I descended the slippery slope, I couldn't help but be fixated by the festive gathering at the base of this hill. At least fifty canvas tents were pitched in the snow, while partiers gathered around a beer keg lit by red and orange spotlights. Set in the middle of this bustling party was a snowy, mud-bogged pit encircled by used tires that served as the demolition derby's battlefield.

As frosty air emerged from my mouth and each foot slid along the icy hill, I asked Ukiah, "Why are people camping in the snow? Won't they get cold?"

"Just wait and see," he told me as we neared the temporary campground.

What I saw will stay with me until my dying day. These thick, canvas tents, each identical to the next, rested atop cinder block and wood frames on ground cleared of snow. Rigid metal poles, used to support the structures, were plunged into the earth. With simple flaps serving as doorways, I peered into the roomy tents to view an entirely different world. Drawing energy from gas-powered generators, these tents had carpeted floors, lamps, a television and VCR, refrigerators, paintings on the wall, kerosene heaters, a couch and chairs, an efficiency grill, plus miniature beds. For a second, I thought I had walked into The Twilight Zone.

"What's going on with these people?" I asked my counterpart, flabbergasted by their comfortable arrangements.

"They do it every year," Ukiah said, nodding his head and smiling to each passerby.

"But who are they? Who camps out in the middle of winter?"

"It's tradition, Chris. These folks are racers, family members, fans and friends. They come here to have a good time."

"It must be thirty degrees. Don't they get cold?"

"Not with those space heaters and an electric blanket. It's great to be wrapped in a thick comforter, lying beside a heater, while it's freezing outside. They're just like pigs in a blanket!"

"Have you ever camped here?"

"Of course. In my drinking days, I'd get wasted, bang around in whatever car I planned on demolishing, then sleep if off with some broad in her tent. Those were the days."

A voice suddenly resonated from the darkness.

"Dad, where have you been? The first round is about to start," Japhy said anxiously.

"Hey, buddy! Hi Gina. How are you two doing?" Ukiah cheered.

"Ready to see some ass-kicking," Japhy replied.

"What's the line-up tonight, kiddo?"

"First are the four-bangers, then the mini-trucks, followed by the full-size cars. In between each heat they'll have snowmobile jousting. Finally, you'll be ready to roll in the Destruction or Death Heat."

"Okay, now the big question," Ukiah asked. "What kind of vehicle did you find for me?"

Bouncing with excitement, Japhy answered, "A 1953 Zebra Bagel truck. It's built like a tank."

"You should see it," Gina added, "we covered it with black primer, then painted a white skull n' crossbones on each side!"

"Cool," Ukiah sang. "I can still remember Zebra's logo on the radio - 'They're hard and crusty on the outside, but soft and tender on the inside.' I wish we didn't have to wait for the final round."

Disturbed by this discussion of skulls and crossbones, I blurted, "What's a Destruction Or Death Heat?"

Japhy, pent-up like a jumping bean, answered, "Do you remember that anything-goes cage match between Stone Cold and Cactus Jack?"

I nodded my head.

"Just picture it with any type of vehicle on the road," he continued.

"What kind of vehicles?" I inquired, feeling uneasy about such a contest.

Gina followed-up, "Last year there were delivery vans, hearses, an old ambulance, a dump truck, and even a miniature cement mixer."

"Cement mixers at a demolition derby?" I shrieked. "Someone could get killed!"

"That's why every contestant is given a white flag," Japhy told me.

"For what?" I asked

"That's why it's called Death Or Destruction," Gina said. "The only way you're eliminated from the contest is if your car won't start or you surrender."

"People actually surrender?"

Gina continued, "Last year, the only two vehicles left were a panel van and a cement mixer. These two were banging it out when the van got stuck in a snow bank. So this cement mixer bore down on the van at full-speed when the driver waved his white flag at the last moment."

"Ukiah!" I declared. "You're going to drive in this … this fiasco?"

"Hell yeah! I was the one in the cement mixer last year!"

Before I could protest, a voice hollered from a distant loudspeaker, "It's shatter shatter shatter time!"

"Yes! Yes!" Japhy proclaimed. "Can I do the honors this year, Dad?"

"Sure thing, kiddo. Lead the way."

The four of us, along with hundreds of others, migrated toward the demolition derby vehicles.

As we walked, I whispered to Ukiah, "What's shatter time?"

"None of the cars are allowed to have any glass."

"Why?"

"For safety purposes. Ya couldn't have shards of glass flying in all directions whenever two cars hit. So we alleviate that problem beforehand."

"How?"

"You'll see."

As we continued along our way, I contemplated their convoluted logic. These drivers worried about broken glass when fifty-ton cement mixers were barreling toward them at full speed.

I soon discovered what shatter-time meant. A burly man holding a microphone and wearing orange fluorescent pants, a brown camouflage hunting vest, green rubber hip boots, and a red, white, and blue top hat screeched in a fake English accent, "Ladies and gentlemen, commence to handle thine devices."

Dozens of people dressed in winter clothing, Japhy included, bent to the ground and grabbed sledgehammers. Twirling them about in their hands and fingering them anxiously, I saw what would soon happen.

"Okay gentlemen, and I haven't forgotten you ladies," the colorfully clad emcee pronounced. "What are we waiting for? Let's shatter some glass!"

Japhy reared back with his sledgehammer ....

"One, two, three - GO!" the master of ceremonies hollered.

... and let loose with a violent swing as his sledgehammer smashed through the driver's side window. The impact sent shudders through my body, but not only because of the noise. Scores of men and women were gleefully smashing windshields, headlights, mirrors and sunroofs. Japhy, excited by breaking one window, ran around to the passenger side and did the same to the other. Crazed, he leaped atop the bagel truck's roof and, with a ferocious roundhouse motion, lambasted the vehicle's windshield, sending triggers of glass in every direction. After jumping to the ground, he handed his hammer to Gina, who completed the job by blasting both headlights. Riotous whoops, hollers, and cheers of joys filled the air as cars, trucks, and vans were assaulted in similar fashion. The noise created by this exercise was similar to a hall of mirrors during an earthquake, every pane of glass exploding with fury while people shrieked and stomped their feet. I had never seen such blatant disregard for property.

As soon as this madness ended, the four-cylinder cars fired their engines and proceeded to the demolition area. This arena was enclosed by used tires and shaped like a football field. Its surface, considering the recent snowfall, lay untouched with pristine whiteness. This tranquility would soon be disturbed, for the compact cars circled the arena, then waited until the emcee waved a green flag in the air.

The insanity unleashed within this pit unfolded like an apocalyptic disaster. With the floodlights illuminating their way, the drivers began moving their vehicles in reverse, bashing at each other like battering rams. I asked Ukiah why all the cars drove in reverse and used their rear bumpers to make contact. He told me it protected their radiator from taking a direct hit, and thus being punctured. Once a car lost its antifreeze and overheated, it was done for the night.

I watched eagerly as the dented autos circled the pit, eyed a mark, then gunned their engines to strike. Their primary target was a car's front end, but they'd bash an opponent in the rear quarter panel, passenger side door, or trunk. Any section of the car was fair game except the driver's side door. For obvious reasons, that area was off limits at all times.

The four cylinders spun in every direction - crinkled fenders, rear tires spitting rooster tails of mud, slush, and snow ... bashed in doors, head-on collisions, spilled antifreeze and columns of smoke rising from their engine block, flattened tires, T-bone crack-ups that sent cars flipping on their sides, and the predatory nature of a driver moving in for the kill. The stalking manner of these men reminded me of a chess game, or a more powerful animal closing in on a crippled foe. Nature itself was reflected in this demolition pit - one driver acting as the predator, the other feeble and immobilized, trying to bide time and seek shelter. But similar to animals in the wild, the stronger often won over the weak. The crowd cheered wildly as the apparent victor gained speed by driving around the pit's perimeter, then zeroed in for his final kill. BASH, he smashed the debilitated auto dead-on, sending it toward a tire pile as smoke poured from its hood.

Even more intriguing was what happened after the first event. A slew of wrecked automobiles sat inside the pit, and before round two could begin, something had to be done with them. To remedy this situation, four wrecking trucks began dragging the dented cars toward, of all things, an actual hydraulic crusher. Disabled vehicles were loaded into this device, their frames crushed within seconds as powerful pistons compacted them into scrap.

"Who brought the crusher and tow-trucks?" I asked Ukiah.

"Volunteers from up in the hills. The man who owns the crusher has been hauling it here for thirty years. Yeah, everything's free - no admission fees or entry dues. People just come here to have fun and drink beer."

They did drink with a passion. Once one keg was kicked, someone instantly tapped another, which was soon surrounded by drunken revelers.

After the four cylinders were dragged from the pit, a crew of snowmobilers raced onto the scene, each equipped with a helmet and jousting stick. I found it hard to conceive of these men flying at high rates of speed trying to knock the others from their machines with padded sticks. But sure enough, snowmobile jousting equaled, even surpassed, medieval horseback jousting, for rather than focusing on a single foe directly in front of them, there were dozens of snowmobiles zooming from every direction. I couldn't understand this insanity, but these folks cheered to the heavens as men were sent reeling head over heels from their machines.

As this competition ended and other heats began, Japhy told Ukiah about his latest concert.

"It went all right, but the youth center doesn't hold enough people. There were kids out on the streets that couldn't even see us."

"I have good news," Ukiah told his son, beaming with pride. "I visited the school principal last Monday, and he said he'd speak with Mister Doublet. I expect a call any day now."

"Cool," Japhy exclaimed. "When we play Latera Heights, we'll kick some real ass!"

"You got that right. I can't wait to see you guys perform live."

Japhy then changed the subject, asking, "Dad, when am I allowed to drive in the demolition derby?"

"I'd let ya enter tonight, but you know the rules. Ya gotta be eighteen years old."

"I know, but I still wanna go out there rockin' and rolling."

Aghast, I asked, "You'd let your son drive in this ... this death battle?"

"Why not?" Ukiah asked, blowing on his hands to warm them.

"He'd get crushed to ..."

Before I could finish, a medium-sized man approached our group and sneered, "He'd get crushed to smithereens, just like his old man is going to get crushed tonight."

Ukiah turned slowly to face an angry-looking fellow with an overly round head, receding hairline, and wire-rim glasses.

"Wendell Krause. What are you doing here?"

"Ukiah, I'd like you to start calling me the driver's champion."

Krause than pulled a gold victory cup from behind his back and held it over his head.

"Revenge was sweet in our last race at The Speedway. Now tonight, Ukiah, your laughing will turn to crying."

"Why don't you go to hell?" Gina unexpectedly spat. "Get out of here."

"I'll be leaving shortly, hon', but not before asking this has-been if he's seen my machine."

"No, I haven't Wendell. What are you driving?"

"An old REO fire engine ..."

"Who cares about a fire engine?" Japhy told him.

Confident, with one hand polishing his trophy, Krause bragged, "What about a fire engine with a cowcatcher?"

"Hey! Cowcatchers aren't allowed," Gina objected. "You know that."

"I don't know any such thing," Wendell laughed. "I just know I'm saving you for last, Ukiah. So long."

The four of us stood silently until Japhy asked, "What're you going to do, Dad? That old bagel truck can't beat a fire engine."

"Especially one with a cowcatcher," Gina added. "Why does Krause always have to cheat?"

Ukiah remained lost in thought as mini-trucks, snowmobiles, and finally the full-size cars bashed, crashed, and banged inside the tire-lined pit. While they were hauled away and pulverized by the hydraulic crusher, the final round arrived. Being that the vehicles in this heat were expensive, only six participants entered the contest.

"Go get 'em, Dad, especially Krause. You can take him," Japhy smiled.

"Yeah, he's all yours," Gina said encouragingly.

I didn't want Ukiah to even enter this contest, let alone face a man who had a definite advantage. Ukiah didn't seem worried, though; in fact, he smiled wickedly before walking to his black bagel truck with a skull and crossbones on its side.

The six combatants soon rolled into the pit - a fuel delivery truck, a battered milk van, a UPS truck, a gold Cadillac, Ukiah in his bagel mobile, and Wendell Krause manning his fire engine with a cow-catcher and red flashing lights.

The odds were stacked in Wendell's favor as he drove around the pit, still waving his gold cup out the window to taunt the other drivers. The master of ceremonies then waved his green flag as the crowd applauded under a pocket of exhaust fumes, flood-lights, and frosty breath.

Japhy and Gina paced nervously as the six combatants circled each other, searching for an advantage. It didn't take long for Wendell to strike as he stormed headfirst toward the gold Cadillac and laid a lethal blow with his cowcatcher. The luxury car, unable to escape, rolled weakly in the slush as Krause shattered its front grille, causing plumes of smoke to rise into the darkened sky.

Meanwhile, Ukiah disabled the delivery truck by backing into its rear bumper and sending it over the barricade. Unable to engage its rear wheels, the brown van sat idly by the wayside. The fuel tanker and milk van were similarly disposed of in rapid fashion by Wendell, who enjoyed a distinct advantage over the other competitors. Where they were forced to drive in reverse to protect their radiators, Krause could barrel ahead in drive due to the cowcatcher which shielded his grille. Because of superior equipment, it looked like Wendell would once again emerge victorious.

I may have spoken too early, though, for Ukiah circled the track, peering intently at his foe. With steely determination, Ukiah threw his truck into reverse and bashed directly into Krause's rear quarter panel. The impact on Wendell's fire engine was negligible, while Ukiah's rear-bumper became dislodged in the process. Ukiah drove forward, gained a head of steam, then slammed into the fire engine's passenger side door, this time completely ripping the bumper from his bagel truck. Shaken, but not deterred, Ukiah spun in the slush, rounded the pit, then backed into Wendell's rear bumper. Being that the rear of Ukiah's truck was now unprotected, he crinkled his frame quite severely.

"Look," Japhy blurted upon impact. "My dad punctured his gas tank. We better do something."

Before Japhy could leap over the tire barricade, Krause cranked his fire engine into drive, circled the pit, then aimed his machine at Ukiah's disabled vehicle. Wendell crashed head-on into his opponent, sending Ukiah reeling in the driver's seat. It was clear this contest had reached its conclusion, for Krause reversed direction, then again raced at Ukiah.

"Holy shit! There's gas pouring from my dad's car. He's going to blow up!"

"Stop!" Gina screamed, but with both trucks revving their engines, no one could hear her.

Wendell barreled into Ukiah's passenger-side door, sending his truck spinning 180 degrees.

"Dad, throw the white flag!" his son pleaded.

But Ukiah's truck remained intact, at least for the time being. He managed to creep ahead slightly as Wendell got ready for the kill. Flooring his fire engine and aiming directly for the driver's side door, he sped toward Ukiah.

"He's not allowed to do that!" I cried helplessly.

"That son of a bitch," Japhy cursed.

Krause didn't pay attention to the rules. He blatantly hammered into Ukiah's driver's side door, sending him careening to the truck's floor. Due to the violent impact, sparks leaped from the two trucks, some of them landing in a pool of gasoline that surrounded Ukiah's vehicle. In a split second, flames ignited around the bagel truck, consuming its rear end.

"It's going to blow," Japhy screamed. "I have to save my dad."

"No, Japhy, wait," I pleaded, but he had already sprung into action.

Japhy hurdled the barricade and raced across the sloppy pit as Wendell Krause bolted from his fire engine and ran for cover. Pandemonium swept through the crowd as they carried buckets of water to the fiery scene.

"Run for cover," one of them warned, "it's going to be a powder keg."

Japhy had almost reached the bagel truck when Ukiah crawled from the passenger side door and hobbled toward his son.

With blood dripping from his forehead, Ukiah grabbed Japhy and hollered, "It's gonna explode."

As they stumbled through the slushy mud and snow, Ukiah's truck burst into a bright-orange ball of flames, sending columns of smoke into the hazy air. Along with dozens of others, we raced toward Ukiah and his son to find them shaken, but uninjured. With a deep laceration marring his forehead, Ukiah bled into the snow and smiled at his son, the need for words unnecessary. The crowd helped Ukiah to his feet as the demolition derby came to an abrupt end.

After Ukiah said goodbye to Japhy and Gina, we sorrowfully parted ways.

On the ride home, as I drove the Celebrity down a series of winding mountain roads, I asked Ukiah, "What'll happen to Krause for cheating like that?"

Still disoriented, my passenger replied groggily, "Who knows? I'll see him again next summer on the circuit."

"You're still going to drive after what happened tonight?"

Ukiah didn't answer. He simply looked out the window and held a makeshift bandage to his head.

Unnerved by the silence, I said, "It was nice to see Japhy and Gina again."

Ukiah nodded his head.

"I'm sorry for not asking about the high school principal. Your meeting with him completely slipped my mind. At least something positive came from your discussion. Japhy's a special boy. You're lucky to have been gifted with such a wonderful son."

My friend responded gruffly, "Yeah, he is a joy. Y'know, everyone's been worried about his future ... being from a broken home and all ... but not me. All of us are able to realize our dreams. All we need is a Will to succeed. That's why I've always let Japhy be his own person. While a lot of parents use fear to raise their children, I've always had faith that Japhy would make the right decisions. I guess I've been lucky."

As Ukiah slouched in the passenger seat, I noticed he didn't speak with the same bravado that usually marked his speech.

Concerned, I asked, "Are you disappointed about tonight's defeat?"

Ukiah snorted, "Nah. I'm just touched by Japhy trying to save my life. At times like these, I get sad about how I blew everything in the past."

"Ukiah, if you don't mind my asking, what happened to your ex-wife?"

Our darkened surroundings and rural setting created a touching atmosphere for Ukiah's heartfelt words.

"Lana tried ... she really tried to make our marriage work. We were both so young, eighteen years old with a child, and I was ten times wilder than I am today. But, instead of appreciating the good things of our marriage, I rebelled by lashing-out at every turn. Even though I loved Lana, I constantly regretted what I wasn't able to do. I felt trapped, and the concept of never having sex with another woman killed me. I was eighteen years old and had never flown on an airplane, visited a prostitute, or traveled across country. The idea of white picket fences and birthday parties every other weekend was unacceptable. I'd been shuffled from dozens of foster families, then ran away for years. Now I had to support a family and act like a responsible husband. Other than my Gramma Moo, I'd never been loved by anyone my entire life. Now I found myself thrown into a life-long relationship. I'm not trying to pass the buck, but I didn't do too well."

Hoping to learn what Ukiah found appealing, I asked, "How would you describe Lana?"

Soft-spoken, my friend began, "When we first met, she equaled me in wildness. Our craziness could have set the world on fire. But when Lana discovered she was pregnant, she completely changed her ways."

"And after you were married?"

"She tried to keep our marriage alive, but I repeatedly pushed her away. I remember one instance that particularly broke my heart. Lana never considered herself very bright, and felt insecure when discussing certain matters with me. So one day I came home to find Lana reading *Newsweek* magazine, something she had never done before. When I asked why she suddenly took an interest in this magazine, Lana said, 'So I can make myself smarter for you.' The only problem was, I never bettered myself for her. So, after four years of living with a selfish, non-committal man, Lana called it quits. In all honesty, who could blame her?"

"I'm sorry, Ukiah."

"Maybe I'm feeling sorry for myself, because there were plenty of good times. I'm sure Lana would have made a wonderful wife had I been mature enough to realize it. Do you know that by the time of our divorce, I had changed into such a stark-raving lunatic that I threatened to kill Lana if she ever came after me for child support? And do you know what? She believed me! The worst part is, I may have killed her."

I continued to follow a darkened mountain road, commenting, "It sounds like you miss her."

"Yeah, I do. I even know why I treated her so badly. It's not that I didn't love her, but at eighteen years of age, I kept fretting over all I hadn't done in life. Being married seemed like the ultimate shackle. Here I had a sexy little teenage wife, and I was worried about not being able to fuck hookers. I definitely didn't have my priorities straight. Plus, now we're really delving into my twisted mind - while we were married, I never thought Lana was pretty enough to be an adequate reflection of me. But I see her now and wonder how I could have been so stupid. Lana's beautiful - gorgeous. But this syndrome became habitual. I've always wanted a woman more when she was unobtainable than when she was mine."

"Why, Ukiah?"

"Because in my mind, if a woman has lowered herself by being with me, there must be something wrong with her."

"Wrong with her?" I asked.

"Yeah, she must be a freak, or mentally unbalanced, or ugly. But then when they dump me, I begin to appreciate their gifts and see how pretty they really were. It's as if by choosing me, a shadow of hideousness is cast on them. After Lana, this crazy affliction plagued me ... hell, it still plagues me today. No woman is good enough when they're attached to me. They always lack something."

The difference in Ukiah's mood, perception of himself, and outlook on the world had changed so dramatically between our trips to and from the demolition derby that a casual observer may have concluded that Ukiah suffered from multiple personality disorder, or an emotional imbalance of some sort. Earlier he had been active, aggressive, and self-aggrandizing. Now he slouched passively in his seat, lamenting his problems.

Intrigued by his thoughts concerning a suitable partner, I asked, "I've noticed that you don't have a steady girlfriend."

"I have a girlfriend," he said softly.

"You do?" I gulped, devastated.

"Yeah, her name is Romlocon. Seriously, between working for Tattoo Blue, then spending every other second writing, women, like everything else in life, take a back seat. My Muse requires total devotion. Even if I did decide to play the field, I doubt I'd settle on a steady."

Hurt, I asked, "Why?"

"At this stage in life, I don't see the payoff."

"What do you mean?"

"How could a woman fit into my life with the amount of creation that is required of me? How would she benefit my life? I cook and clean for myself, and whenever I need sex, Tattoo Blue's hookers are there. Other than that, I can't see the payoff."

Amazed at Ukiah's coldness, I blurted, "How about companionship? Don't you get lonely?

"Lonely!" he laughed. "There's so much shit on my mind I could never be lonely. Chris, I'm my own best friend. If I had to choose a woman, though, she couldn't just be a fuck. She'd have to be perfect - a glimmering reflection of myself. And even though I'm not perfect, I continually look for that ideal. In fact, if I were a woman with tits and a pussy, I'd make a perfect girlfriend for myself!"

"Ukiah, you're so different from any person I've ever met. Don't you ever want to be normal?"

"Do you know what I want?" Ukiah asked fervently, rising in his seat. "I want to land enough money to guarantee that Japhy won't be forced to lead the same type of life I do. If he doesn't get a break, he'll be forced to put up with the same crap as everyone else. Once I reach the gates of publication, all my material needs will have been met. The only thing I want is to lift Japhy from the same gutter I've lived in for thirty years."

"He really does mean a lot to you, doesn't he?" I queried, finally back on flat land near Latera Heights.

"Japhy saved my life. Back in my drinking and drugging days, if it hadn't been for him, I would have overdosed or committed suicide. Not only did he try to save my life tonight, he's been rescuing me since birth. I'm just glad he didn't turn out like me - confused, addicted, and crazed by whatever red flag was waved in front of him. I wish we could be together more often - it's the only time I'm able to let my defenses down and be myself. That, Chris, is the only sign of love I know."

"So it's either nonstop work, or an occasional break with Japhy and me?"

"Japhy's always a ray of sunshine, and believe me, I appreciate it."

As we pulled into the driveway from Reflection Alley, my opinions varied concerning Ukiah. He was undoubtedly a man of many faces – someone with a death wish, the crazed wild man, a focused artist, a compassionate father, an unrepentant lawbreaker, a rampant egotist, and the insecure son abandoned by his parents. With these conflicting characteristics, it's understandable why Ukiah needed nights like these to meltdown … or to let his vulnerabilities show.

As he stepped from the Celebrity, still holding a bloody bandage to his forehead, I remembered something from earlier that morning.

"Ukiah, I know it's late, but can I step inside your place and pick out another manuscript?"

"Sure. Follow me."

As we walked to his guesthouse, I asked, "What should I take?"

"Whatever," he replied drearily.

Reading the apathy in his voice, I scurried inside Ukiah's house and rummaged through a towering stack of manuscripts, each yellow manila envelope identical to the next. Unable to tell what was in each packet, I decided on a title scrawled in thick black letters - *Beneath the Weeping Willow*. As I did so, Ukiah flicked on his portable black-and-white television set, then walked to the kitchen. As I moved toward the front door, I heard a woman's voice beaming from one of those late-night psychic call-in shows.

> As Teresias, your personal fortuneteller and seer into other worlds, I predict you will live long into the future under one condition. Never know yourself, and never capture that which you truly love.

"I'll see ya, Ukiah. Thanks for the reading material."

"Don't mention it. We'll get together next Saturday for the Philip Prince lecture. Be ready to spill some blood."

Gulping, I left his tiny house and wandered across the yard. As a brisk breeze blew through the trees, I looked up to see a full moon peering back at me. Incredibly, the face in this glowing yellow orb so closely resembled Ukiah's that I felt compelled to rub my eyes. Was I influenced by this man to such an extent that even planets looked like him? I didn't feel brainwashed, but a definite sense of possession overwhelmed me.

"Why are you punishing me with a fate I can't control?" I whispered to the moon.

But like all my unrequited pleas to Ukiah, the moon stared at me with cruel indifference.

14

I dreaded Saturday more than death-row inmates awaiting the electric chair. My fears may have even surpassed those of convicted criminals, for at least they knew what would eventually happen. But in regard to Ukiah and Philip Prince, I didn't even know why he wanted to kill the author. Worse, how would I be implicated in this murder? I had already killed one man. With any sense, I'd refuse to be Ukiah's accomplice. But considering his help in covering up Woody Dewar's murder, I felt obliged to help in return for his silence (regarding my neighbor's medical bag). If only I could make time stop. Why did Philip Prince choose our university?

In the meantime, I read Ukiah's novel, *Beneath the Weeping Willow*. I am by no means a literary critic, but I do know what piques my interest. And, although I can't provide heady explanations or in-depth analysis, I can tell if a certain piece of art has merit.

So, I read *Beneath the Weeping Willow*. The tale revolves around an incredible summer weekend where a metropolitan female physician visits a small town to attend an arts festival. Amid a flurry of activity, this woman seduces a man she'd never met before. Their tryst takes place in a trailer park beneath a cluster of weeping willow trees that sit along a residential street. The writing style celebrates life and the simple joys contained within it. But this novella is not a mere exercise in hedonism. It also exposes the freedom of responsibility in contrast to the feeble state of victimization.

The story focuses on this doctor following her night of passion with the protagonist. She eventually abandons the medical profession and moves in with this man. But, due to complications surrounding marriage (she was for, he against), they end their relationship. As the story ended, I was curious as to the woman's identity. Was she the one Ukiah mentioned when we met? If so, my friend definitely showed some maturity. He could have performed a slash job on her, but instead treated the doctor with tenderness and respect. Instead of being negative, he transformed the situation into one of affirmation. From what Ukiah told me, years ago he may not have exhibited such restraint, instead going straight for the jugular.

If someone asked about Ukiah's writing style, I'd say it possessed a sense of urgency, as if time were rapidly slipping away. Why did his work reflect this notion of time being lost? I can't be certain, but I would bet he wrote that way due to his self-destructive lifestyle. It seemed like Ukiah needed to chronicle his entire life before he died. Rather than patiently completing each project, he rushed into them with wildfire abandon.

In all (using my limited abilities to critique such matters), Ukiah's story stood head and shoulders above those currently sitting in the bookstores. I'd even say reading these tales was akin to actually being with Ukiah - his art and his SELF becoming one. I couldn't help but wonder, assuming his stories were autobiographical, if this female physician fell under the same manipulative spell that had so much control over me.

Despite my pleas to prevent its arrival, Saturday did come, carrying with it snow flurries and brisk winds. Also, as anticipated, Ukiah (a horizontal scar from the demolition derby marking his forehead) stormed into my house with the energy of a tornado eyeing a trailer park.

"The lecture starts at three this afternoon. C'mon, let's go. We have things to do."

Sacrificing my pride, I begged, "Please, Ukiah, isn't there another way? We'll never get away with killing Philip Prince."

Impervious, Ukiah snapped, "You're driving. We need a rental car."

Fearing the authorities could link us to this automobile, then trace our identities, I complained, "A rental car? Can't you think of a better plan? Maybe we should forget the whole thing."

Every vein in Ukiah's forehead throbbed as he glared at me with burning eyes.

With his voice booming angrily, he demanded, "Chris, if you want to stay in your little closed-off world, say so now. I don't have the time or patience to play these games. In a few hours, I plan on killing a man. Being that you've already taken a life, you should understand my plight. I'm serious about this mission. One slight fuck-up and we'll both spend the rest of our lives in prison. Are you with me or not? If you're afraid, say so now. But if you stick with me, it's all or nothing. Prince and his cronies are erasing The Word from our consciousness, and I'm not taking it any more. Now, are you with me?"

Trembling, I squeaked, "I'm in."

"Then let's go. We're not fucking around. This is serious."

Once inside the Gemini, I nervously drove through Latera Heights. Unable to believe what was happening, I wondered how I let myself get suckered into these situations. I wasn't stupid ... or was I? Later in the day, I'd be in prison with depraved criminals eagerly pawing at my ... oh, I couldn't even think about it.

Hoping to alleviate these thoughts, I mentioned Ukiah's manuscript as we entered downtown Latera Heights.

"I finished reading *Beneath the Weeping Willow*."

Distracted, Ukiah peered out the window while sniffing, "Really? What did you think?"

Trying to sound educated, I said, "You write on a variety of levels, triggering a lot of emotional reactions. If ... I mean, when you get published, I can see your readers laughing, crying, screaming with terror, or leaping with joy."

Pleased with my commentary - maybe even happier than he'd ever been with me - Ukiah smiled, "Why should someone keep swimming up the same creek when there's so many other ways to cross the stream?"

"Will you tell me something about the book?" I asked, weaving onto campus.

"Anything," Ukiah replied, looking around.

"Did you really have sex with that doctor under a weeping willow tree?"

"All my stories are fiction," Ukiah laughed, a twinkle in his eye.

"Tell me more about this story. Fill in the blanks."

"Well, I wrote it in ten days."

"Ten days! It takes me two weeks to decide what CD I'm going to play on the stereo," I chuckled, slightly embarrassed.

Not paying attention to me, Ukiah continued, "This piece was a departure from a collection of short stories I had just finished, and also a recent screenplay. I wanted to write this book in an experimental fashion, told from the doctor's point of view. I called the process 'cognitism,' but when I started writing this way, I realized her perspective would be far too unsettling. So, I started all over, using this woman's neurosis as the foundation. By the end, every character involved, including the doctor, appreciated life to its fullest."

I wished we could have kept talking about literature, but knew it wouldn't solve the matters at hand.

Resigned, I asked, "What are we going to do?"

In control, Ukiah told me, "Swing by the Splycer Center. We'll see what kind of crowd is milling around, and how tight security is. After that, we'll get a rent-a-car at Crossgrain Plaza."

I followed orders, slowly circling the arena as my accomplice inspected every detail.

"Here's the plan," he shot pointedly. "We'll rent the car, then go to Prince's lecture like we were fans. I decided not to wear the plumber's outfit because it'd draw too much attention. Instead, I wore my regular clothes. Then, somewhere near the end of his speech, I'll slip from our seats and sneak into the boiler room."

Feeling ill, I summoned enough courage to ask, "What will I be doing in the meantime?"

"Stay until Prince's lecture ends, then don't waste any time getting back to our car. Listen closely now. Drive to the rear loading dock. All of the other cars will be heading toward the main exit, so you'll be able to sit there without any trouble. Then, when I run from The Center, we'll zip out through the lower gates. There might be a few traffic diverters blocking our way, but we'll bash through 'em."

"What about you?"

"After creeping into the boiler room, I'll crawl inside the cooler unit, then follow that air duct towards Prince's dressing room. Once there, I'll just wait for the son of a bitch."

"What if there are security guards in his room? It'll be impossible to kill Prince with other people around."

"Chris, just have the car idling by the loading dock. Leave the rest to me."

With those chilling instructions, I meandered through traffic until reaching Clotho Rent-A-Car. After leasing a maroon sedan with fake I.D., we returned to the stadium. With Ukiah driving, he unleashed the vilest diatribe I had ever heard.

Growling, he began, "Philip Prince is crawling here like sewage seeping into an infested ocean after being processed at a shit refinery. That rat-eyed rodent won't smirk with phoniness on my television set any more. I can't believe how people applaud his awful responses. Plus, y'know how he parts his hair in the middle. I'll pluck every strand with a pair of pliers. Yeah, he likes to be the science-fiction king, huh? I'll stab that fucker's eyes out with a pen, then shove 'em down his throat until he pukes."

Ukiah continued ranting with Hitlerian rage.

"I see him staring at me - a vague familiarity, as if this familiarity were a breeding ground for contempt. He may have smiled in the past, but now, when seeing me, Prince will suddenly turn silent. The words that flowed so freely will now only be whispers, squeaks, or gasps for breath. In Prince's make-believe universe, he controls the plot — alien tentacles, mind control implants, galactic viruses, extraterrestrial surgery, and deadly laser beams. But soon, he'll be strapped to a table - helpless - submissive - his burning eyes weakened into submission. I'm going to love seeing his ego surrender to my Will. I'll burn him alive with flames kindled from the pages of his very own books. How ironic, don't you think, Chris? A man whose primary goal is to destroy The Word is eliminated by those very same words."

Ukiah slammed his hands on the steering wheel while turning into the Splycer Center's parking lot.

"Prince, who's really in control? You or me? I'll tell you. I am. I'll crush your skull with a dumbbell, saw your nose off ..."

At this point, I had to shield myself from Ukiah's outburst. He was a lunatic. Trickles of spittle actually formed around his mouth while his eyes bulged maniacally. How did I get myself in this situation? Please, somebody, help me.

I peeked across the seat at Ukiah. What possessed this "creature" with such hatred? What had he become? His rage turned into unrecognizable ugliness - vicious, permanent ... scary. Ukiah scared me to the core of my soul. How could I be associated with this madman? Would he really rip Philip Prince to shreds, then eat his flesh while sucking on his carotid artery?

Just run, Chris, run faster than you've ever run in your life. Run ... run ....

*   *   *   *   *

Jennifer, we were so beautiful when we lived in Latera Heights. But so much time has passed since those fruitful days of our youth. How many years has it actually been? But here you are - the place where it all started - the beginning of your downfall - a once promising life shattered by irreversible realities.

The limousine ride through town reawakened memories and horrors that had laid dormant for so long. Many of the same businesses stood along Latera Boulevard, some with different names, but their architecture still identical. I gazed with sadness at bustling taverns I'd sneak into on Friday nights, the quaint pizza parlors that served piping hot slices for a dime, or the all-night diner where us girls would study, gossip, and act silly.

Oh, baby, you thrived. You were in your prime during that time. Life was wondrous. It seemed as if you tiptoed on the clouds, everything happening according to plan. But then ... there it was ....

"Driver, please stop," I pleaded as the limousine pulled alongside The Latera Shrine.

It stood regally, towering, observing all that passed beneath its view.

The Latera Shrine – usually called The Breached Circle. While other universities had lions, eagles, or peacocks as mascots, Latera's mysterious symbol filled me with fear.

There it stood - anchored, eternal - surrounded by weeping willow trees with slender, drooping branches - an enormous granite sculpture with an obvious crack down its middle.

The sphere was symbolic of an ordered universe where the entirety of creation became one, then suffered a disastrous split. Until the severed halves of this circle reunited, we were destined to lives of imperfection.

I stepped from the limousine to stare at this enormous structure. The thought of that fateful night still filled me with dread. The nightmare occurred at this precise location so many years ago ... my fall from grace into the clutches of despair.

The Breached Circle. Oh why, why? You've ruined my life, you bastard. I hate your very presence. Die! Whither away! Shatter into a thousand pieces. You destroyed my hope. Look at me. I'm a wreck because of that awful night. You're evil!

"Driver, get me away from this abomination."

*   *   *   *   *

With my blood pumping like water through a fire hose, Ukiah and I circled the arena's interior, my partner observing every minute detail. The Splycer Center's ceiling was adorned with banners representing every college in its division - teams with mascots such as badgers, gophers, and wolverines. Oddly, Latera's team, The Circlets, used a simple sphere pierced by a lightning bolt, its significance lost on me. In addition to these banners, a trophy case teeming with mementos lined one of the corridors. Finally, food vendors and souvenir peddlers hawked their wares to fans waiting to hear Philip Prince.

My anxiety built to where I was afraid of vomiting to death in a bathroom stall. I would have gladly chopped off one of my hands instead of going ahead with this ludicrous plan. In two hours, I could be imprisoned as an accomplice to murder. How did I let myself get suckered into such a predicament? I was doomed, swept away in a whirlpool beyond my control.

After Ukiah cased the arena, we took our place inside the 15,000-seat arena (approximately three-quarters full), to watch America's best-selling author.

"I'm often asked, Mister Prince, when did you want to become a writer? The answer may be embarrassing, but a silent force invited me into this magical world of literature one morning shortly after my eighteenth birthday. I won't bore you with the details, but I had made love to a young girl who looked like another girl I dated before her. Although one gal sported blonde hair and the other brunette, the two could have been twins. Anyway, I woke the next morning in what could possibly be one of the oddest, spookiest locales ever. It was at that moment, with sunlight filtering between low-hanging tree-branches, that my Muse extended her hand and lead me toward a cherished land ....

He tells me, Jennifer, come on, let's get out of New York for the weekend. You haven't been anywhere for ages. Watch me lecture. Then, of all places, he brings me to Latera Heights. Why here? He knows how I'm haunted by the memories of this place.

There he is, S.W.A.N.'s god -king. Look at him standing behind that podium – glowing, regal, so proud and larger-than-life that it's going to be harder to kill him than I thought.

.... I eventually wrote a novel called *The Princess Twins* that went on to become a mainstay of the science-fiction genre. I never saw one of those twins again, but the other is still part of my life ...

That bastard acts like he owns you. Jenny, sweet baby, why do you let him use you? He hasn't tried to sell your manuscripts, or even read them for that matter. Darling, he's been stringing us along for ages, and all we get in return is a meaningless position at Mason Turner. Philip has never taken you seriously, or respected you as an author.

His smugness repulses me. Why does Prince inspire such negativity in me? If the tables were turned, I'd act just like he does – probably worse. In fact, it's almost like looking in the mirror when watching him. The arrogance, when watching him. The are all part. of your literary diatribes.

What's going to happen? I know Ukiah's going to blow it, probably when he's in the car with me. Worse, what if he kidnaps Prince and drags him to our rent-a-car? I'll be the getaway driver! Our photos will be plastered all over the country, especially on the local news. What if my father sees it? Not what if - he will! If the police don't kill me, he'll do it for them. "You worthless, good-for-nothing horse's ass," he'll scream at me through the prison bars ....

.... let me read a speech that was written by someone unknown to all of you. It begins - 'This student was a pleasure and a surprise right from the start. He asked of me what no other student asked ... demanded of me what no one else did ....'

How can you let him control your entire life? Jenn, are you insane? He doesn't consummate his love, but stands over you and jacks off while you writhe in pain. He's never going to publish your books. Just quit Mason Turner, even if you're forced to live on the streets. I can't stand that man.

When you finally confront him, how will you do it? Smothering Woody worked well, with little resistance or evidence. But Prince needs a more profound statement. Look at the vanity seeping from his body. I can't stand that man.

"… A kidnapper, huh, you little moron. I knew you were a waste of time." He'll glare at me behind those iron bars … and do you know what? I almost hope we get arrested for Philip Prince's kidnapping just so I can spite my father, that rotten bastard. I'll actually laugh with glee as he curses me, then spit in his face while being dragged to the electric chair. See what type of monster you created, father dear!

'…. This student grabs his learning, like a great chef pouring in a little of this and a little of that, seeking sources and inspirations to create far beyond my expectations, challenging his peers to do the same ….'

What an asshole.   What an asshole.

What an asshole.

'…. this student possesses a quiet wisdom for which I am grateful. I once heard an existential philosopher say that we don't need to make a lot of noise to prove what we know ….'

Tonight, Jennifer, when he takes his clothes off in our hotel room and starts jacking off, grab that pair of scissors from your purse and butcher him …

Here we go, Ukiah. The killing time has arrived. Bloody that fucker with such vindictiveness that the world will take notice. Or, if we kidnap this prick and hold him hostage, we'll force S.W.A.N. to bow to our demands …

'….This student's perception of the world, how it works, and the people in it, deepens on a daily basis. When he is ready to voice his realizations, as he currently does in his writing, the literary world will stand and listen. This award is his testimony.' My adoring audience, do you know who that speech was written about? I'll tell you. It was me … yes, me! And why did one of my college professor's feel compelled to write it? Because I'm the greatest fucking writer in the universe! I'm the king, baby, The Prince of the fucking world! I want to become God of the literary world!"

"This's it, Chris, I'm splitting," Ukiah sneered beneath his breath. "You know what to do."

The rental car's engine idled too highly as I sat near the Splycer Center's loading dock. Without even pressing the gas pedal, the motor revved so intently that I knew something was wrong. What if the engine overheated, then melted-down? Worse, what if I shut-off the car, then couldn't restart it once Ukiah ran from the arena with a crew of armed guards following him? I could even flood the engine, then we'd be forced to sit while the authorities arrested us.

Where was he? The temperature gauge steadily climbed to half way, then three-quarters. I could smell antifreeze seeping from the radiator, and see small plumes of smoke rising from beneath the hood. Hurry, Ukiah, please. This damn car could burn at any moment. The gauge continued to rise, tapping against the redline, causing a panel light to flash "overheat - overheat - permanent engine damage possible." Where could he be? What should I do? The last thing I wanted to do was draw attention to us. Now huge amounts of gray smoke rose from my purple car. Should I drive around and cool the engine, or just turn it off? If I did, it'd never start again.

The red needle buried itself inside the temperature panel, while another light began flashing - "Abort immediately - turn engine off." Billowing clouds of smoke rose from the hood, clouding my vision.

Damn! What should I do? My heart pounded more intently than ball bearings trapped in an overheated pressure cooker. I sweated profusely, mouth dry, eyes darting maniacally in all directions, gnawing at my fingernails ... where was he?

Unexpectedly, a bear-sized hand shot through the smoke and began rapping at the window.

Panic stricken, I unrolled the window, unable to speak.

"Is everyone all right in there?" a man asked. "Your car's going to start on fire."

Unable to cope, I slumped headfirst against the steering wheel. Let the security guards arrest me - I didn't care.

Overwhelmed by confusion and paranoia, I leaped with fright as the passenger door opened and someone jumped in the car.

With the burly man still standing to my left, I looked beside me to find Ukiah panting rapidly.

Aware of my predicament, Ukiah said calmly, "We should be going."

As I shifted the car into drive, the concerned citizen asked, "What about your radiator?"

I didn't bother responding, choosing instead to leave him standing in a cloud of smoke.

After pulling away from the man, Ukiah snapped, "Get lost in traffic. Make yourself anonymous."

"But I thought we were going to sneak out the delivery exit ...."

"Chris, get this fucking car lost in that traffic jam. The authorities are gonna fly from that loading dock any second now."

Ukiah's rapid words relayed a sense of urgency I'd never heard before. Not wasting a second, I wheeled my car into the heart of a snarled traffic jam. At any other time, Ukiah would have told me to dodge left, slip between two cars, zip toward a short cut, or throw 'er in reverse to find an alternate way. He'd drive backwards down one-way streets, hop over curbs, or knock down plastic pylons. But today he sat quietly, so consumed in thought I feared his head would explode.

In no time, hundreds of automobiles surrounded us as the rental car's temperature gauge returned to normal. Other than his initial words, Ukiah remained silent, an energy radiating from him that made my hair stand on end.

I repeatedly looked in the rear-view mirror until seeing a dreadful sight. Distant police lights flashed across the parking lot as darkness fell on the area. Luckily, the squad cars stayed near the loading dock as we approached our exit. Once we left the crowded lot, I figured we were safe. But what if one of the flagmen told us to stop? What would I do? Bash through their barricades like they did on TV, or surrender against Ukiah's objections?

Once again fate smiled on us as we left the Center's parking lot. I stared straight ahead, catching sight of a patrolman eyeing us suspiciously. Was I just paranoid, or did he suspect us?

In the clear and unable to tolerate the suspense any longer, I blurted, "What happened? Did you kill him?"

Ukiah sat uneasily in his bucket seat, then said modestly, "Everything went as planned. I slipped from the lecture hall, then eased my way into the boiler room. No one was around, so I slithered into the cooler unit and crawled through the ventilation duct."

Ukiah gazed in the rear-view mirror, swept the hair from his face with a brush of his hand, then continued as I drove through town.

"The part of the plan that most troubled me was whether the heating duct lead directly to Prince's dressing room. If it were blocked, my access to him would be shot. But luckily, a few minutes later I stared through a plastic grate into the star's dressing room. I made it, and no one was in there. With a few quick turns of my pocketknife, I unloosened a few screws, then found myself in a prime position to kill! All my preparations had paid off."

"Speaking of preparations, I was too worried to ask earlier, but did you take a gun or knife into the Splycer Center?"

"I considered it, but figured if I were nabbed somewhere along the line, a concealed weapon wouldn't help my situation. So, once inside his dressing room, I had to remedy this situation. After a quick inspection, I noticed a set of free-weights, y'know, dumbbells. What a perfect weapon. I quickly unscrewed the nuts that held the weights in place, then pushed them aside. I now held a twenty-four inch metal bar in my hand. One shot over the head with that fucker and Prince would see stars."

By this time I had returned to the parking lot of Clotho Rental Cars. Other than overheating, the car worked fine for us. So, after paying the bill, we drove my Gemini home. Although I had drawn a considerable amount of attention to myself for a brief period, no one seemed to suspect us.

Ukiah, now driving, continued. "I didn't have to wait long for Prince to arrive."

"What were you thinking inside that room? You must have been going nuts."

"Patience has never been my strong suit, so yeah, my adrenaline was pumping. I only had one loose end to wrap up."

"Which was?" I inquired, my heart suddenly throbbing as if this event had not yet happened.

"I pulled a black hood from my back pocket and put it over my head."

"A black hood?"

"Yeah, like an executioner's hood, with two eye slits! What did you think I'd do, attack Philip Prince without a disguise?"

"C'mon, tell me what happened. Did you murder him? The suspense is killing me!"

As Ukiah drove through the congested streets (obviously due to traffic still flowing from the Splycer Center), I noticed some of the very same people we sat with less than an hour before.

"Thunderous applause echoed through the halls, so I knew the lecture had ended. Ducking into a closet, I waited anxiously for the author to arrive - heart beating like crazy, waterfalls of sweat under the black hood, my fist shaking as I held the dumbbell, and jittery knees attached to rubber legs. Then he walked through the door - alone. All the fuck alone! As Prince sauntered into the bathroom, I seized the moment, quietly sliding from the closet to lock the main door. That fucker was mine! With the hood hiding my identity, I stood out of view until Prince left the restroom, then BOOM! I cracked that prick on the head just hard enough to send him reeling to the floor, but not with enough force to kill him."

"Why, Ukiah? Wasn't that what you wanted to do?" I asked as we entered my neighborhood.

Intently involved in retelling the story, Ukiah proceeded. "I wanted to talk with him first ... to see what made him tick. So as Prince gasped and fell to the floor, I pounced atop his chest, glaring with hatred into his stunned face.

"Who are you?" Prince coughed, a slight trickle of blood flowing from his temple.

"I'm Atropos, and I've come to do Atropos' business."

"No! Why me?"

"Shut up, asshole. Don't make me bash your skull into mush."

"Okay ... anything," he whispered. "Why now? Why do you want to kill me?"

"You belong to S.W.A.N., don't you?"

"No, I don't have any pets. I don't even like animals."

"Don't play stupid with me, Prince," I demanded, raising the iron bar above my head.

"I'm not. You're confusing me."

"Are you pushing an O.W.L. agenda on the literary world so you can destroy it?"

"No, no. Birds scare me."

"You fucker, you're lying."

BAM, I cracked him in the mouth with my fist.

"Answer me, Prince. Why are you trying to banish me from the halls of publication?"

"I don't even know you, Atropos."

KNOCK KNOCK.

"Mister Prince. The door is locked. Are you all right?"

"Answer him. Say you're fine or I'll pulverize you."

"Yes ... um ... yes, I'm just lying down. I'm tired."

"Fine. Call us if you need anything."

"Very good, asshole. Now tell me, Prince, who's calling the shots for S.W.A.N.?"

KNOCK KNOCK.

"Open up, Philip. Let me in."

"Who is it? Get rid of her!"

I heard the jiggling of a key, then saw the knob turn ever so slowly.

"Where'd she get a key? Tell me, Prince."

"It's a special guest key."

I bound from Prince's body as a woman who appeared to be in her late thirties, but may have been older, tentatively entered the room.

"Who was it?"

"I'm not sure, but we stood frozen for a second, this gorgeous woman staring through the slits in my hood - right into my eyes. And do you know what?"

"What?"

"We connected for a moment. Time actually stopped as we gazed ... pupils merging as one - the whites of our eyes converging ... her sight became mine, and mine hers. The experience reminded me of looking into a mirror at close range. I became her, and she became me."

As Ukiah pulled into my driveway, I asked, "Didn't she notice Prince lying on the floor, or scream when seeing a hooded man with an iron bar in his hand?"

"Not immediately. That's what I mean. For a brief moment we connected in a ... I'm not sure, but then all hell broke loose."

"How did you get away?" I asked, stepping from the Gemini.

"I barreled past this woman, tore off my hood in the hallway, then fled to the loading dock. Luckily, the overheated car created enough diversion to draw attention to you rather than me. When I hopped in the car, no one had even seen me."

"What happened to Prince, and that woman?"

"Who knows? I should have killed the bastard instead of taunting him. Now he'll live to see another day."

"Ukiah, I don't mean to worry, but aren't the authorities going to track us down? I know we slipped away, but you have to admit this wasn't the cleanest job in history."

"Prince doesn't know me from Adam, that's for sure. He could never identify me in court."

"Because of the hood."

"Exactly. But do you know what? As I knelt over top that man, I knew him."

"Of course you did. He's the most recognized author in America."

As the sun set on a cool winter evening, Ukiah answered, "No, Chris, I knew him. I couldn't tell if it was his ego slipping-out between drops of sweat, or the messiah complex hiding behind his fear-riddled eyes ... but I identified with him."

"Probably because you're both creators ...."

"Who knows?" Ukiah shrugged, walking to my porch. "The sensation became eerier every second. I had him right there, dead to rights. He was mine. But I couldn't land the final blow. Those beady rat eyes and quivering jawbone ... they horrified me. I've been close to death quite a few times - drug overdoses, alcohol poisoning ... and I've looked into the mirror to see beyond the flesh of my face – past the skeletal remains where death itself stared back at me. That's exactly what I witnessed when looking at Prince. I saw my own death reflected, as if his dying mirrored my own mortality. I could see the thread of life spinning, its length determined by my hand - but then, strangely, I stepped out of character and let him off the hook. It was an odd sensation - the nauseating fear in his eyes, the sweat, blood ... death never presents herself in the most pleasant light. It was weird. So, anyway, I'll catch ya later, Chris," Ukiah finally said. "Determining one's destiny takes its toll on a person."

15

Local, national, and tabloid news organizations converged on Latera Heights with the eagerness of bats attacking a herd of cattle. An area television station became the first to broadcast the assassination attempt on Philip Prince.

> Announcer:
> (Latera University's "Breached Circle" behind him)
>
> World-renowned author Philip Prince was nearly murdered late this afternoon in a dressing room at the Bryce Splycer Center. Thea Orestes is on the scene.
>
> A thin, fragile, female news reporter with brunette hair:
> (inside the star's dressing room)

Thank you, Dan. Earlier today, a man identifying himself as Atropos savagely attacked Philip Prince. The perpetrator may be affiliated with a radical pro-logging organization protesting the preservation of endangered bird species such as the cob swan and bubo virginianus, also known as the great horned owl.

Split Screen

(dramatically) "Thea, could you describe precisely what happened this afternoon?"

"Dan, it appears Mister Prince had finished his lecture and returned to his dressing room when Atropos, wearing a black executioner's hood …"

"An executioner's hood?"

"Yes, Dan. A local police artist has drawn the following composite sketch which was based on the eyewitness testimony of Mister Prince and an unidentified female."

ATROPOS

"Thea, how exactly did the author escape from this intruder?"

"According to police reports filed by Officer Daniel Lachesis, plus interviews with the author himself, the trespasser lunged at Mister Prince with a lead bar. After being repeatedly struck about the head, Mister Prince retaliated by striking Atropos with a series of blows to the stomach. Using superhuman strength, the author fended off the attacker and was able to save his own life."

"Incredible. Mister Prince must be commended for his courage. You mentioned an unidentified female. Do you have any information as to her role in this unfortunate incident?"

"No, Dan. Understandably, for her own protection, the authorities are withholding this woman's name."

"Thea, do law enforcement officials have any further leads at this moment?"

"Only that a smoke-colored sedan was waiting for the attacker outside a loading dock at the Splycer Center."

"Was the getaway driver also male, or wearing a disguise?"

"No, Dan, the driver wasn't wearing a hood. As to the accomplice's gender, no additional information is available."

Later that evening, a similar report appeared on the network news, further promoting Philip Prince's heroic role in fending off his attacker. As each of these stories flashed across my television screen, I realized I would no longer be able to live in an isolated fantasy world. What had I been thinking? How did this insanity unfold at such an alarming rate? Why hadn't I stopped it? I wasn't living in a movie, playing games, or reading about fictional characters in a book. I killed a man with my bare hands, and now Ukiah's likeness appeared on the national news after he tried to assassinate the country's most beloved author.

My life began to resemble those of serial killers on TV. Conceivably, this crime could make us famous in the annals of modern literature. Similar to John Hinckley, who watched *Taxi Driver* thirty times, then fell in love with Jodi Foster before trying to kill Ronald Reagan, we would also be seen as unhinged lunatics. I was living history! We hadn't simply killed an anonymous hypochondriac without notice. Ukiah made a stab at killing America's best-selling author.

How many of us actually create history during our lifetime? Previously, my existence held the importance of a feather falling into the ocean. I hadn't even made a ripple. Now I helped mastermind a diabolical plot. I would become recognized as a notorious cult personality - Chris Edwards - getaway driver.

The seriousness of this act struck me with the impact of a wrecking ball toppling a skyscraper. My world crumbled around me as I considered the ramifications. First, rather than dealing with inept policemen who ignored Woody's death, the FBI could enter the picture. These detectives wouldn't overlook clues, bumble leads, or view witnesses as innocent-until-proven-guilty. They'd track our rental car, interview those on the scene, and eventually nail us. In the end, a federal penitentiary would be my home.

I continued to flick through the channels, finding further snippets of breaking news.

> "Author Philip Prince, recuperating in a sequestered Latera Heights hotel room, has issued a $50,000 reward for any information leading to the capture and prosecution of his would-be assassin."

Becoming more panicked each second, I had to tell Ukiah about these recent developments. So, grabbing a coat, I fled from my house into a calm winter night. Enjoying the cool breezy air, I marveled at the season's mild temperatures. In fact, I couldn't remember an autumn that lasted so long.

Instead, the temperature neared fifty, its unseasonable warmth bathing me with comfort. While kicking a few leaves as I strolled toward Ukiah's house, the unmistakable groans of female passion filtered through the air. Filled with both intrigue and envy, I crept along a darkened path to a partially opened window. Reminiscent of an earlier eavesdropping episode, I snuck behind a lilac bush, then spied on my neighbor.

The sight before me was hardly startling, but to actually see Ukiah thrusting his manhood into a woman caused a cannonball to lodge in my throat. Lying prone on the sofa bed, legs spread wide and eyes closed, the woman emitted passionate moans like a kid blowing bubbles in the air. Lying atop this lady, Ukiah (facing away from me) ground his lust deeply into the woman, causing her to squeal with wild abandon.

Hidden in the shadows, I felt a surge of sexual excitement. I wanted nothing more than to massage my groin, to feel it and rub it and fondle it until my fingers were wet with love. Why couldn't I be the one lying beneath Ukiah, stomach pressed against the mattress as he satisfied my desire? Why couldn't the willing victim on that mattress be me? I'd prop my glory in the air for Ukiah to take advantage of - I'd bite my pillow, claw at the bedspread, and plead for more pleasure and pain. Squeals of passion would slither from my lips ... a wet, dripping eagerness to make every sinful desire come true. I'd become Ukiah's slave, lapping at the emissions which shot from his ...

The woman beneath Ukiah, face glowing with ecstasy, moaned and groaned appreciatively, then surrendered her will as orgasmic spasms rippled through her body. Ukiah, grinding piston-like into her willing hole, soon withdrew his love and came on her stomach. His lover cried with delight as Ukiah remained silent.

Dripping with excitement, I stared longingly as Ukiah and his date untangled their bodies, then lay without shame. The woman by his side had mounds of curly brown hair and layers of makeup. Quite thin and undeveloped, it was easy to tell that she earned her living in the dark.

While I pressed my ear against the window and watched from the corner of my eye, the woman kissed Ukiah, then cooed, "Baby, what's wrong? You know any of us girls would quit the business in a second if only you'd let ... ... Oh darling, why are you so sad? You're so innocent, yet filled with coldness ... so detached and remote. None of us can ever penetrate ..."

Ukiah pulled the sheets over his body, lying quietly in the dim, romantic light.

"Honey, why are you so unhappy? We just made the most fantastic love ..."

"Sweety," Ukiah grumbled, "my keys are on the kitchen counter. You can drive my car to the parking garage downtown. It's the Chevy Celebrity ...."

"Can't I stay longer?" she complained, pouting noticeably.

Ukiah shook his head, then buried his face in the pillow while the hooker got dressed. After she left, he rolled from bed still naked, clasped his hands together, then pleaded desperately while closing his eyes.

"Romlocon, please listen. I'm sorry for fucking that whore. I try to stay pure, but I'm too weak. Please give me another chance. I'll do better - I promise. Why do I always ruin my chances of entering the realm of publication? I'm going crazy - everything's out of control. I'm losing my fucking mind."

Ukiah rose, threw a pillow against the wall, then continued to lament his existence.

"Why can't things be in their proper order? Romlocon, I see so many fucked up things in life every day, and though I try to put them right, they only get worse. I can't control the disorder. Why can't life be the way it should be?" (pause) "I'm no different. You've given me proof of your existence, but I still act horribly. Look at me. I fucked this hooker tonight after promising I'd stay true to you and live in a way that'd make you proud. Romlocon, what's wrong with me? Give me another chance. I won't ruin it. Oh, who am I kidding? You know I'm lying through my teeth. I can't control my carnal desires. What should I do? Romlocon, send me one of your virgins - a fifteen-year-old girl who has never lived, who has never been touched - a living, breathing, gorgeous girl with no family, no friends - unattached, orphaned – an innocent bride living in a land of timelessness. Send her to me, Romlocon. Let me mold her into perfection like a warm piece of clay. I promise to respect her virginity. I do. But as it stands now, I'm possessed by lust, and can't escape. My appetites are uncontrollable. You see it. Send me a virgin who is beyond reach ... beyond this world ..."

Ukiah wandered in circles, tugging at his hair with one hand while scratching his ass with the other.

"Romlocon, what if I knocked-up that prostitute? I can't be responsible for another innocent life. I deserve to be penalized, but don't let it be pregnancy. This frail human life doesn't deserve a wretch like me. Romlocon, I'd mirror the ways of my parents. It's a miracle that Japhy turned out as well as he did. Don't make me try to repeat this feat. I'm going crazy. I'd abandon my child. Romlocon, keep this tragedy from happening. I promise to be better. Give me strength. I want to be good. Why am I imprisoned by these earthly pursuits? If only I surrendered to you, the gates of publication would open to me."

Ukiah slumped to the floor, the gash on his forehead still visible, then begged for forgiveness.

"Romlocon, I'm not good enough in this incarnation. I'll never be good enough. If you want, kill me now. Take my life. Then put my spirit in someone else so I can have another chance to write my way from this prison. You know I'm trying, but I've gone as far as this incarnation will allow. I can't be any better inside this body. But I want to be good with all my heart. I know you love me, so do whatever's necessary to let me enter the gates of publication. I love you, Romlocon. Take me. I'll willingly die this second if it meant I could meet you. Kill me, Romlocon! Take me. I'm ready to die for your love and acceptance ..."

With tears streaming down each cheek, I snuck from the lilac bush and stumbled blindly across the lawn, unable to watch my friend in this condition. While shuffling across my yard, an eerie vision from Woody Dewar's window caught my eye. Unbelievably, I saw a figure pass behind his curtain, then walk out of sight. Terrified, I ran home at breakneck speed, then locked the door behind me.

16

Honey, you promised to never let him degrade you again. But look at us. What kind of control does he have over you? You're tied by one wrist to a hotel bed, wearing nothing but a crotchless French maid's outfit, torn fishnet stockings, a red garter on your thigh, and knee-high black leather boots with stiletto heels. Plus, look at the makeup he forced you to smear on your face - blue and purple mascara, thick black eyeliner, false lashes, cheap rouge, and whorish red lipstick. The clothes and makeup drive him wild, but what about us? What do we get from this situation other than humiliation?

Oh, Jenny, why? We have too much self-respect for this abuse. You've become a slave to his fetishistic behavior. We can't even move ... nausea building within our throat. What if we start gagging, then choke to death on our own vomit? Why are we such a mess? He enjoys your defenselessness, and how you puke in an ice bucket over the bedside. It turns him on to be your master, your lordly controller. But how can we change our life? How? We just give in to Philip's wishes, and get nothing in return.

> **Flash** - Late breaking news concerning the Latera Lunatic.
> Author Philip Prince, America's favorite writer and creator of the number one best-selling novel *Prince of the Earth*, whose savage attack this afternoon has outraged fans, recently granted an interview to network anchor Peter Palter. We must warn our viewers that Mister Prince's facial contusions and lacerations incurred during the melee are not for the weak of heart. Parental guidance is advised.
>
> Interviewer: Mister Prince, congratulations on a courageous testament to the human spirit. Your death-defying battle against adversity in thwarting this hooded assailant known as Atropos will receive my vote for heroic act of the year.
>
> Prince: (A dozen purple bruises marring his cheekbones, plus a black eye and numerous red slashes on his forehead and chin) Thank you, Peter. I apologize for my appearance, but I owe my fans an explanation.

Interviewer: Will you confirm the rumors of an alleged $50,000 reward for the capture of your assailant?

Prince: On my behalf, the money will be given to anyone providing information leading to this man's arrest. But more importantly, Peter, (his voice rises as he faces the camera) right now I am issuing a challenge to this cowardly anti-environmentalist named Atropos. You snuck-up behind me with an iron bar to get an advantage. That's the way sissies fight. But I'll battle you mano a mano - anytime - anywhere. Just show your face, you spineless piece of trash.

Interviewer: Your bravery must be applauded, Mister Prince. In a different vein, can you offer any reasons as to why this enigmatic figure known only as Atropos chose to attack you?

Prince: In my current novel, *Prince of the Earth*, available at local bookstores, I include a scene where The Great Horned Owl, the story's protagonist, takes control of the Earth. This bird, along with a family of swans who support his goal of uniting the planet into a global family of animals, are attacked by an organization known as The Ugly Ducklings. I feel Atropos, being a pro-logging advocate and ugly duckling himself, used this opportunity to malign not only me, but also this noble idea. But I have news for that faceless coward. Bubo Virginianus, The Great Horned Owl, will reign supreme on this planet.

Interviewer: Thank you, Mister Prince. You have certainly set a shining example for the youth of this nation.

What a load of rubbish. I always knew Philip was the phoniest person alive, but this report is ridiculous. Where did those bruises and scratches come from? Philip told me his attacker only punched him once in the face after knocking him down. From his appearance on TV, everyone will think he fought an entire motorcycle gang.

Isn't this nonsense par for the course, Jenny? The world-famous author basks in the spotlight, and where are you? Tied to a hotel bed counting ceiling tiles. What a disgrace. He's destroying our self-respect. There has to be a better way.

Baby, we need to change our life. How absurd is this picture? You're shackled to a bedpost, your only company being the television set and a painting on the wall. You're tied to the bed - sickened, vomit welling in your throat. Damnit, I'm tired of this humiliation. Start sticking up for yourself, baby. You're worse than a common whore. This is no way to live. I should claw that bastard's eyes out.

"Philip, where have you been? Untie me. I'm fed-up with this game."

Look at his arrogant swagger, like the only rooster in a pen full of hens.

"For your information, I've been satisfying my public. I need a washcloth to wipe this makeup from my face. How did I look on TV? Did the bruises and lacerations look real?"

He makes my skin crawl.

"Philip, how can you justify this fakery? You know what really happened."

"You bitch, don't ever emasculate me again, or use that tone in my presence. I'm engaging in this charade to quench the public's thirst for excitement. Without person-alities like me, they'd be forced to face the daily tedium of their miserable lives. I'm a welcome diversity, a glimmer of hope in an otherwise mundane universe."

As Philip removed his expensive clothing (a long-sleeved yellow silk dress shirt, a thin purple flowered tie, and pressed gray slacks fastened by a white cloth belt) to reveal his soft flabby frame – I replayed the dressing room scene in my mind. There he lay, a trembling, pathetic man whimpering for help. A slight trickle of blood dripped from his lower lip, but otherwise Philip looked like he did on the back of his dust jackets.

Jenny, can you remember your initial attraction to him years ago? He swooped down on you like a cherub, but appearances were deceiving. Dear lady, how could you have been so mistaken? His innocent façade led to a brutal savagery that erupted into full-blown sadism. Look at his smugness, the all-knowing attitude, the arrogance hinting at self-deification. You sure know how to pick 'em, Jenny. What a sick, repulsive creep.

How can I end this relationship? Philip will never allow it. Every time you think about leaving him, he glares at us with those menacing eyes shielded behind wire-rim glasses - penetrating, otherworldly, hypnotic. In regard to looks, sweet Jenny, we could have done better. It's not that he's ugly; he's just not very handsome.

Even now, as he takes off his underwear, Philip doesn't excite me. If only he could be gentler, but the thought of him saying "I love you," cuddling, or buying roses is out of the question. Baby, he doesn't have any feelings. Look at the vein that runs across his left temple. Every time he gets mad, it pulsates wildly, sending his jaw into a locked position that reflects his harsh nature. But those eyes are the worst. I can't even look at them. Oh, Jenny, this ritual is worse than being licked by a pack of rats. Oh, those eyes - so scary - beady, rodent-like, sickly, scary, alien ...

"I'll say whatever I damn well please, Philip. If it weren't for me, that psychopath would have murdered you. I saved your life. Now untie me!"

"Untie you! We haven't even begun, my little trollop. We must finish our evening with a round of frivolity."

"I hate your guts. I'm not putting up with these sick games any more."

"Jennifer," he growled, grinding his jaw, "don't make me wrap that telephone cord around your neck. I single-handedly beat my attacker within an inch of his life. Don't make me turn the tables on you. Now look at this big thing in my hand that I'm stroking. Do you like it?"

"It's not big, you freak!"

Philip backhanded my cheek with such force that I felt my teeth crack against each other. The taste of blood seeped across my tongue as my lips swelled with numbness. This man doesn't care about us. When will you finally admit it? Philip has been dishing out the same abuse for years. He'll hit you, draw blood, leave actual bruises (as opposed to his fake ones), or spit in your face. Wake up, Jenny. This man thinks your garbage, a piece of meat to get pleasure from.

"You know what I like. Now play with your toy. That's it ... I like what I see."

I'd rather be dead than subject myself to this torture. I feel ill. If only I could free my other hand and snag that pair of scissors from beneath the mattress. I'd stick him right through the heart. Oh baby, kill him, get loose, free yourself from this abuse.

"Tell me I'm the greatest writer of all time. That makes it real hard."

"You're the best, Philip."

"Say it like you mean it, bitch. C'mon, I need some help with this thing."

"Your prose elevates me to unheard of levels ... ecstasy, sheer delight."

The words sickened me.

"Yeah, Jenny, keep circling your finger around it - yes, like that. Now slip it inside. Flick it a little. Ooooh, look at this monster growing like a skyscraper."

Get loose, Jenny, little by little. Don't let him see you loosening the knot. Just slip free. Be subtle. Easy does it. Nice n' easy. That's it.

"I'll mastermind the greatest literary coup of all time with this attack by Atropos. What better luck could a writer have? Free publicity! Pretty soon I'll have those morons believing I tracked that fucker down and captured him myself. Tell me, Jenny, you love my writing, don't you?"

Just play along, Sweety.

"You're fantastic, dear. I need your prose more than breath itself."

"Oh yes, yes! Keep playing with it. I love to watch. Yeah, with your middle finger, right around the edge."

Here it comes, Jenny - the padded dog collar. He's such a sick monster. The only way he gets off is by autoerotic strangulation. Perverse little man – immature, childish boy. Keep stringing him along. You're almost loose. Just a few more squirms and wiggles. He has the collar fastened around his neck ... now the rope. I can't believe he makes me tug on that cord each time, cutting the blood-flow along his carotid artery. What a depraved thrill freak.

None of this nonsense will matter after you gut that bastard. Who needs his job at Mason Turner anyway? It's not worth it, Jenny. Even if you're convicted of murder and forced to spend your dying days in prison, at least you'll have your own identity. Now just slip free. You're almost there. Easy does it. Shhhh. Don't let him see you.

"Sweet Jenny, it feels so good. I love to watch you play with your toys - those two little perky, almost non-existent titties - that's it, keep circling your finger around them. They're so tiny, so cute, so attentive. Oh baby, you're making me feel good. Now lower ... pet your kitten. Treat her nice. Let her lick your finger. Yes, now another, and another. Show how much you love her. Kiss your fingers, then let them kiss your kitty. Such a precious little girl."

There's more to life than this twisted misery. But where can I turn? I hate myself. Jenny, what's wrong with you? Why is this perversion allowed to continue? Look what you're doing to yourself - what he's forcing you to do. Philip Prince is standing above you with a dog collar wrapped around his neck while engaging in a sick, masturbatory ritual. Once we escape this hell, things will change.

"Deeper Jenny ... now start pulling the cord. I'm almost there. You know how to do it ..."

Just a little bit more. Pull your wrist through the opening, there!

"There! There! Keep pulling. Harder - harder ..."

Now go for the scissors ...

"Harder ... Oooo baby ... I'm going to ... hey, what the fuck are you doing? Scissors?"

Kill him. Ram it through his chest, right into his heart.

"I hate you, Philip. Now you're going to die!"

Wobbling toward me, his onanistic exercise interrupted and temper flaring, Philip's eyes possessed the fiery evil of ...

"Damn your soul! How dare you ... the nerve ..."

"Don't hurt me, please. You're scaring me, Philip. I didn't mean it. Leave me alone. I want to live. Not again. Please, I beg of you. Ouch. No, not there. You're killing me. I'll do anything, just leave me alone. I can't take any more. Why me? I can't breathe. It hurts. Oh ... Oh ... Agggghh, raaalllphhh ... Ohhhhhh ... no more. Let me go. I'm going to die. It's killing me. Don't stick it in there, please. I'll be a good little girl. I'm sorry, I'll let you do anything to me, just not that. Don't hurt me. I apologize ..."

"You ungrateful, wretched whore. After all I've done for you."

His ugliness repulsed me - a flabby, hair-covered stomach, short, flaccid penis, pudgy legs.

"I should have fired you from Mason Turner years ago. What would you do then? Die on the streets, because you're worthless. You couldn't find literary talent if it bit your cute little ass."

"Philip," I bawled, "why did you ever bring me to Latera Heights? You remember what happened the last time we were here. I hate this place."

"I'll take you wherever I want. Do you know why? Because I own you. You're my property."

"But Philip, you don't even make love to me."

Honey, we can't see a thing. Wipe the tears from your eyes.

"You know what happened last time," he groaned, towering over me.

"I'm miserable, Philip. This madness never ends. I used to love you, but now I realize you're sick. You need help. I can't take any more ..."

"What were you going to do with those scissors? Tell me."

"I WAS GOING TO KILL YOU! ... ... I was going to kill you, Philip. I hate you so much."

"Jennifer, Oh sweet little Jenny. You'd never kill me. I'm much too ..."

"I wanted to claw your forehead, slit your throat, then scratch your eyes out. Philip, I even considered cutting your dick off and shoving it down your throat until you choked to death. You don't give a damn about me — me or my writing."

"You write?"

"You asshole! I've been writing for thirty years, and telling you about it every time we meet. But you never listened, or cared about what mattered to me. I've written my heart out while being forced to stagnate at Mason Turner. I can write better than anyone who's walked through those doors, yet no one's read a single word. Why haven't you given me a chance?"

"Let's get one thing straight. There have only been a handful of adequate female writers through history, and those were the ones who killed themselves."

I hate him even more than the vomit that spills from my mouth.

"Now that this annoying topic has been settled, why don't we finish the task at hand? I'll let you man the throttle, if ya know what I mean, Jennifer."

Yet again we're reduced to trash, little lady. As I service his needs and Philip pants with pleasure, our desires are ignored by a man who cares for us less than used condoms in an alleyway. What are we going to do? This vile activity makes my skin crawl. It's not right. Jennifer, please straighten out your life. Find a more meaningful path. You can't live in such a disgusting fashion. But what can we do? I can't quit working at Mason Turner. I'd starve to death. And what else are we qualified to do? Nothing. You've been insulated from the world for too long. What few skills you did possess are long since gone. We have to get away from this creep, that much is certain. But how? You should have killed him when you had the chance.

"That's it, Sweety, just a little bit more! Yes, yes! Whooo Hooooo! Awww baby, you sure know how to make a man feel good!"

17

I hadn't spoken with Ukiah since his attack on Philip Prince. Events were unfolding so quickly that if we didn't keep a handle on the situation, both of us would wind up in court. Visions of being arrested monopolized my thoughts. I remembered when David Berkowitz terrorized New York City two decades earlier. After his arrest, the stalker's sheepish face plastered the covers of every newspaper and magazine in America.

What if I were to follow in his footsteps? I didn't look like a serial killer. People would laugh at my mug shot. But I still pictured the headlines:

Chris Edwards
Murderer, Accomplice, Conspirator

My father would get the morning paper from his doorstep, unfold it, then read those bold black letters. My face (already a bane to his existence) appearing below the caption would immediately send him into orbit.

"Lena, look at what trouble that kid of yours got into this time."

My mother stares at the photo, then covers her mouth while gasping.

Meanwhile, my father, eyes burning with rage, jaw quivering, snarls, "First there was Chris's screwball clothes ..."

"Norb. That costume was part of a fantasy game that Chris played ... something with a superhero."

"How about the time we found Chris playing with ... I can't even think about it. Right there, in the middle of the afternoon. Fiddling with that ..."

"Norb, all teenagers experiment with those things at one time or another."

"Lena, quit making excuses for that rotten kid. Chris has done nothing but spite me ever since slithering like a freakish aberration from your womb. Where did I go wrong? All I wanted was a normal child. But what did I get? A cape-wearing misfit with pink boots who fiddles with ... it's too horrible to picture. Now that ungrateful freak turned into a criminal. The next time I get my hands on ..."

The thought of my father's disgust filled me with self-satisfaction. I actually smiled when pondering Pus's reaction – the muscles trembling in his cheek like a palsy patient, the way he'd ball his fist as if ready to strike me, or that habit of mussing his hair like the feathers on a rooster. He'd snort like a sow at its feeding trough, squint his eyes, then BOOM, a volcano would erupt. I enjoyed the scenario so much that I considered a T-shirt that I'd wear for my arrest. The left side would have a picture of my father, while the right showed a photo of a horse's ass. Finally, the logo would declare: "Why aren't these two ever seen together at a party?"

I could only imagine my father's reaction as he plopped onto his tattered brown re-cliner with a bowl of chili and a ham sandwich. He'd take a bite from his sandwich, loudly slurp (as he always did) a spoonful of chili, then complain about taxes and sleazy politicians. Then, unexpectedly, a TV newsman would announce, "an accom-plice in the Latera Lunatic case has been apprehended." Spotlights and television cameras would focus on me as I removed my jacket to show this T-shirt comparing my father to a horse's ass. I could see him now. He'd be so outraged that chili beans would shoot from his mouth while a chunk of ham lodged in his throat. I almost started praying to be arrested!

These amusing thoughts only delayed certain matters at hand. I needed to speak with Ukiah about our plan of action. So, hoping he wasn't with another naked prostitute, I walked across the lawn and knocked at his door.

A minute passed, then another, until Ukiah finally answered. Obviously fresh from a shower, Ukiah's dripping hair hung in tangled strands across his face, while beads of water dotted his body which was covered by a thick red bath towel. My heart fluttered passionately as he invited me into his house, my greatest hope being that his terry cloth wrap would fall to the floor, exposing the remainder of Ukiah's wet, glistening torso.

After excusing himself for a moment, then returning, hair combed and fully-dressed, Ukiah questioned me.

"What's wrong, Chris? You look upset."

"Ukiah, we need to talk. Things are spinning out of control."

"Things?" he asked, wrapping his hair in a ponytail.

"Yes ... things," I said softly, turning away. "Last night I saw someone in Woody Dewar's house."

"Is that so?" Ukiah asked, unconcerned. "When did you see them?"

Not wanting to reveal my whereabouts, I lied, "Oh, I um, I looked out my window and saw a shadow passing behind his curtain. I couldn't tell who it was, but what if the FBI is on our trail, or they're putting surveillance cameras in Woody's house. Isn't it strange that Dewar's house hasn't been placed on the market? I'll bet the cops are bribing Woody's family to let them use it until they've collected enough evidence to arrest us."

"Or, maybe this apparition was actually Woody's ghost returning to haunt you and avenge his death. It's like an old Hollywood horror movie. You'll enter the house late one evening when wham, from nowhere, a gigantic slimy germ cell carrying a medical bag will leap from a corner and cough all over you. Ooooo, it's so spooky."

"I'm serious, Ukiah. What about the news reports covering Philip Prince's attack?"

Ukiah grabbed his car keys from a counter, then said, "C'mon, let's go. I need to get a package from the post office."

As we strolled through the yard, Ukiah began, "Let's look at the Latera Lunatic case. First, nobody in the world knows where I live. Secondly, due to an overheated radiator, the authorities couldn't even tell what color our rental car was, or its license plate number. Third, because I wore a hood, no one ever i.d.'d me. Lastly, we both have alibis."

"We do?"

"Yeah. We were walking together through the woods. Don't you remember?"

"Oh yeah, right. I get it. I'm still worried."

"That's the difference between us. You worry, which gives you ulcers, while I get mad. By being pissed off and taking action, I get results."

Yeah, the type of results that lead to imprisonment.

After entering Ukiah's Celebrity and proceeding along Reflection Alley, I asked, "What about your package at the post office? I'll bet they know your address."

"Wrong again, Chris. I had it sent 'General Delivery' to a Mister Ambrose Benoni. All I have to show 'em is another fake driver's license."

"What about the police officer who questioned us after Woody's death?"

"Let me think. If my memory serves me correctly, that day I was Laban Concelare. I'm telling you, Chris, no one has found me yet. No lawmen, tax collectors, polling officials, or postal employees. If they do, I'll just keep movin' on."

"Wait a second. How about your agent? I remember you asking for my address."

"You're right, Chris. Jennifer Ewen is the only person who knows my address. When she decides to contact me, all my problems will be solved."

"You still haven't heard from her?"

"Not a word. To Jennifer, I don't even exist."

"Have you written to her lately?"

"I'm working on a letter, but haven't finished it yet."

As Ukiah drove through downtown Latera Heights — past college students bundled in winter jackets, bicyclists dodging traffic, and double-parked delivery trucks — a troublesome thought entered my mind.

"Ukiah, how many letters have you mailed to that agent?"

"Six."

"Being that Mason Turner represents Philip Prince, what if Miss Ewen rereads your letters and connects you to him? The possibility isn't inconceivable. He was attacked in Latera Heights, the same place postmarked on your letters."

"Well, Chris, I hadn't written anything offensive in those letters, but, yeah, if Jennifer looked deep enough, and had a suspicious mind, she could follow a trail leading to me."

"Holy shit! We're busted!" I yelled, suddenly panic stricken.

"Settle down, Chris. We're in the clear. For all we know, Jennifer might be feeding every letter into her shredder, or using them to line her parrot's cage."

"How can you stay so calm, Ukiah? The world's closing in on me. I'm sure that Jennifer's calling the cops, probably as we speak."

"Chris, let me explain how these agencies work."

Before doing so, Ukiah pulled into a downtown-parking garage, circling each level with nerve-wracking speed until pulling into an extremely tight stall, then stopping on a dime. After sliding five quarters into a meter, we strolled toward the elevator as revving engines, car alarms, squeaky brakes, and slamming doors echoed through the cavernous structure.

After pressing the "down" button once, then again and again, Ukiah proceeded with his explanation.

"Jennifer, being a lowly literary agent, doesn't make any important decisions at Mason Turner. She's been relegated to an artistic scrap pile - a mere conduit in the creative process."

"I'll bet she'd love hearing those words," I laughed, shaking my head.

"She'd agree, because S.W.A.N. has grown into such an impersonal organization that the employees and writers get lost in the shuffle."

Ukiah pushed the "down" button at least six more times in rapid succession, commenting, "It makes the elevator come quicker if you do that."

"Obviously," I smiled.

A few seconds later, the elevator doors parted and we stepped inside.

As it descended, I told Ukiah, "If you want to know the truth, I still don't understand S.W.A.N., or what they're trying to accomplish."

Intent on explaining his ideas, Ukiah pointed to a speaker in the elevator's ceiling.

"Do you hear that?"

"What?"

"That Muzak. Were you paying attention to it?"

"No. I hadn't even noticed."

"Precisely! That obliviousness is what S.W.A.N. wants to accomplish. They plan on reducing literature to such a generic state that it resembles this canned, preprogrammed music."

The elevator doors opened as we exited at the garage's ground-floor level.

"Why, Ukiah? What purpose would that serve?"

"Remember what S.W.A.N. stands for. Single Word Authorial Nation. And O.W.L. stands for One Word Literature. Can't you see the similarities?"

"A single Word?"

"Yes! Our Muse gave The Word to every artist, asking of them to not only cherish this gift, but also share it with mankind. The Word is able to lift Man from being a common animal to one who's trying to rejoin their Muse. Look how easily animals are controlled. Even elephants and lions can be caged and trained. So, in our lowest animal form, man is also slavishly dominated. But with the Word comes knowledge ... and with knowledge comes freedom. Take, for example, a person filled with self-confidence and wisdom. Try to control that individual. Try to halt their progress. It's impossible. What differentiates the animal from a man with purpose? The Word! Can't you see? When I try to become like my Muse by entering the gates of publication, I refuse to be a cog in S.W.A.N.'s machine. That's where the One Word aspect of this equation enters the picture. By limiting The Word, they want Language to become like the Muzak in that elevator."

Passing storefronts, video arcades, and bustling eateries, I asked, "How does S.W.A.N. plan on accomplishing this goal?"

"By compartmentalizing, labeling, and forcing all writers to conform."

"I still don't understand."

"In the past, artistic movements flourished in not only this country, but the entire world. Authors, poets, painters, sculptors, and filmmakers crossed every line, refusing to be pigeonholed into one specific style or genre. But today, an author won't even consider it. Take Philip Prince, for example. That imbecile can't write anything but science fiction. In the future, even titles such as horror, mystery, romance, and fantasy will be eliminated as the range of creative expression is narrowed. Literature will digress to such a sorry state that we'll pay less attention to it than we do to music played in shopping malls."

Nearing the post office, I pleaded, "Why? What end does it serve?"

"By destroying literature, our primary forms of communication - Language and The Word - will be eliminated. Rather than moving toward our Muse, we'll be controlled like animals. Y'see, our Muse is alive - intelligence personified. The Word breathes Life into our lungs, letting us grow and find what is important. Now, if you reverse this picture, without The Word, what do we become? Slaves! Robotic, mechanistic, meaningless cogs in a hopeless wheel."

"How does S.W.A.N. destroy our creative spirit? It seems impossible."

"Impossible?" Ukiah sighed, passing a used-record store. "Vinyl. Those were the days," he commented, distracted momentarily. "For your information, Chris, the process of destroying The Word has already begun."

"It has? How?"

"Via the computer."

"The computer is responsible for destroying mankind's hopes and aspirations?" I asked.

"Yes. A direct link to our Muse was eliminated when the computer was invented."

"It doesn't make sense."

"Look at literature throughout history, when man had a bond with their Muse. How did they write The Word? With a pen. Their ink flowed like blood on the page, and blood equals life. Those authors had ink on their fingers, on the page, on their desk, and on their sleeves. The first move away from the pen was found in a typewriter, but those machines were acceptable because their manual nature still allowed a special communion with our Muse. They were noisy and cumbersome, and writers had to pound their fingers to death in order to create. But then S.W.A.N. gave us the computer, a noiseless, sterile device with no clanky parts or mess. Instead of getting calluses on your fingers, or rapping at a stiff keyboard, we can sit in a comfortable chair and tap our merry hearts away. The following analogy is a good example. Look at modern cars that have cruise control. It takes the fun out of driving. I need my foot on the gas pedal, another on the choke, a hand on the stick shift, and one foot always ready to hit the brake. Can't you see how involved driving is with a regular car? You become one with it. With cruise control, ya might as well hire a monkey to drive, then fall asleep until the trip is over. The same applies to vinyl records versus compact discs. Records have an inherent coolness - a needle, stylus, tone arm, and turntable — plus there's the album itself with its artwork, scratches, skips, and hisses. A CD is sterile, pristine, and passive. It all revolves around personal involvement ... with being ALIVE! I want to scratch out mistakes when I write, feel the pressure in my right forearm, and watch calluses grow on my middle finger. I need to smell the ink, rub my palm on the paper, and draw arrows and carets. Who needs fancy display screens, cursors, or a mouse? Screw it. If authors keep falling for S.W.A.N.'s technological nonsense, they'll become indistinguishable from each other. Instead of talking intimately with their Muse, they'll be reduced to pushing their Mouse across a rubber pad." Ukiah caught his breath, then said, "C'mon, let's grab my package from the post office."

Like every other time I went to the post office, a line extended from the service desk past a rectangular counter, then through a set of double doors into the lobby where rows of postal boxes were located. It'd seem after years of this inefficient routine, the postal service would find a better way to serve their customers. But I guarantee if I came to this same office in five years (barring life imprisonment, of course), the waiting line would be the same.

I saw the collective face of impatience standing in front of us - an angry, disgruntled crowd that pondered an endless list of better things to do with their lives. They had, essentially, been pushed to their limit. But behind the service desk, another story unfolded. Of the six available stalls, four were closed, one was manned by a postal employee, and the last was vacant – the woman supposed to be working there instead gossiping with the only worker who was waiting on those in line. From where we stood in the lobby, it actually looked like the end of creation would arrive before we reached the service desk. To me, such a wait seemed inconceivable; but to Ukiah, this inefficiency threatened to make his head explode.

"Whatta ya think?" I asked from the corner of my mouth.

Ukiah remained silent.

"It looks like we'll be waiting all day," I continued.

No response.

"If I had known about this line, I would have brought a pillow," was my next complaint.

Unable to wait another second, Ukiah burst through the double doors, then stood in the lobby, directing his scowl and burning eyes at the two employees loitering behind the service desk.

Knowing what would happen, I began a silent countdown.

Like a ticking time bomb, Ukiah's disgust bubbled into madness. Surrounded by frowning, unhappy people, his patience reached its end.

"Excuse me," he asked in a loud voice, his words aimed like a bazooka at the postal employees. "Is there any reason why we have to wait this long?"

The people waiting in line, filled with resentment, suddenly turned to Ukiah for inspiration - a source of escape from their helplessness.

"Sir," Ukiah continued, speaking to the man who actually worked behind the desk. "Why, when there are six windows and a line of customers stretching until tomorrow, don't you open a few more of them? Let me count the people ... instead, I'll let them to count themselves beginning with number one. Go ahead, ma'am, you're first."

An elderly black woman, somewhat shy, said meekly, "One."

The man behind her, snapped, "Two."

A young female college student, holding an arm full of textbooks, chirped, "Three," while the others behind her fell into place.

"Eight - fourteen - twenty-one - thirty - thirty-six," — all the way back to me.

I yelled victoriously, "Forty!"

"Forty customers are waiting in line, and what do they see? Four closed windows, plus an inconsiderate woman who'd rather chitchat than help these people. This is worse than watching road-construction crews where eight men stand around drinking coffee and smoking cigarettes while one shovels dirt."

"You tell 'em," one man shouted from somewhere in line.

"No," Ukiah said proudly, "I think we should ALL tell them! Whatta ya think?"

"Yeah," the crowd cheered while those behind the desk squirmed uncomfortably.

"How many windows should be open?" Ukiah asked with a smile.

"Six," the crowd responded in unison.

"And what should this lady do who's been gossiping all afternoon?"

"Get back to work!"

"Okay sir," the postal employee interrupted, "I get the picture. Bob, Ray, Sue and Joe, get out here - pronto," he yelled over his shoulder. "And Muriella, quit gabbing and start working!"

The crowd cheered while stomping their feet and clapping, patting Ukiah on the back as he returned to the end of the line.

In less than ten seconds, all six windows were opened for business, the line moving smoother than cheese through a grater.

At 5:50 p.m., ten minutes before closing time, I followed Ukiah to the next available window - the one occupied by Muriella.

Displaying the foulest expression I had ever seen, she snorted, "Yes ... sir. How may I help you?"

"I called earlier today about a package for Ambrose Benoni - General Delivery. I was told it arrived."

"Let me check," Muriella replied flatly, expressionless.

The large-hipped woman walked behind an adjacent counter, shuffled through a stack of yellow slips, then smiled with a joy usually reserved for wedding days or Christmas morning.

Returning to her post with a skip in her step, Muriella beamed, "Mister Benoni, you cannot pick-up this package until tomorrow morning."

"Tomorrow morning?" Ukiah asked, a slow simmer apparent in his face.

"Yes. It says right here on your yellow slip - pickup after 8:00 a.m. Tuesday morning. It is now 5:58 p.m. Monday evening. I'm sorry. Next."

"No! Not next. I've been waiting for forty-five minutes and you're telling me I can't have my package? Why didn't they tell me that on the phone?"

"Rules are rules, sir."

"Where's my package?"

"Out back with the others, of course."

"Then why can't I have it?" he asked, a touch of desperation mixing with rage.

"Because the slip says tomorrow."

"Ma'am, let me explain ..."

"Sir, I'm an employee of the United States Government. If you even hint at threatening me, it's a federal offense. Would you like that?"

Ukiah leaned closer to Muriella, his mouth nearing her ear, then said, "Ma'am, I'm not leaving without that package."

"Sir ..."

"Muriella, I'm not leaving. In fact, I'm going to sit my ass on this floor until you get my package."

Unbelievably, Ukiah sat cross-legged on the grimy tiled floor beneath the service desk.

"Now Muriella, I know there's nothing more you'd rather do than quit work at six o'clock and go home. But if I keep sitting on this floor, you'll have to call the police. I figure it'll take at least half an hour for them to get here. Then they'll try to arrest me, but I'll throw a fit over your treatment of me. After I'm finally hauled away, you'll have to give a statement to the officers and ... hell, I'll bet you won't get outta here until eight o'clock. Is that what you want? Or would you rather walk out back and get my package? It's all very simple."

Outraged, Muriella snarled, "You son of a bitch," then disappeared behind a row of green metal shelves. Upon her return, she handed Ukiah an oblong box wrapped in plain brown paper, glaring at him with veinous red eyes.

"Don't ever come to my window again, Mister Benoni."

"Have a pleasant evening, Muriel," Ukiah smiled while rising to his feet.

Finally, as we waltzed from the post office, Ukiah grumbled, "Do you see why another chunk of flesh is ripped from my heart each day? I can't believe the shit I put up with."

Returning to the parking garage, Ukiah, clutching his plain-wrapped package, noticed an ice cream store that also served as a magazine stand.

"Let's see if they have any new magazines," he told me, ducking inside the store.

As Ukiah shuffled toward a magazine rack, I found the lure of chocolate-chip ice cream in a sugar cone irresistible. My mouth actually watered as a young girl with pigtails scooped the treat from a deep metal bin. After taking a few licks from the icy cone, I strolled toward a glass-topped table with curved metal legs and took a seat while Ukiah rifled through a pile of reading material.

Upon seeing me, he moved in my direction, a collection of newspapers in one hand, his package in the other.

"Do you want some ice cream?" I asked after swirling my tongue around the cone's edge.

"I don't eat sweets," Ukiah told me, more concerned with the newspapers in his hand.

"What do you have?" I inquired, pulling a chair towards him from another table.

"Look at this rubbish," he snapped, tossing the newspapers, scandal sheets, and a magazine on the table. "These headlines boggle my mind."

Prince Pops a Pauper

The Author Known As Prince
A Profile in Courage

Prince Single-handedly Thwarts Latera Lunatic

"Even *People* has Prince on its cover, and this supposed tragedy only happened two days ago. Who knows what glory *The New York Times Book Review* will shower on Philip."

"Ukiah, we shouldn't be talking about this inside an ice cream parlor," I whispered. "Let's go back to your car."

Once outside, I asked, "Did you see Philip Prince's interview on television the other night?

"Of course," Ukiah replied, still steaming.

"What happened to his face? I thought you only punched him once."

"I did," Ukiah bellowed, his voice animated. "It's all a ruse. That phony bastard smeared makeup on his face to make my attack look more serious. Do you know what I accomplished in that dressing room?"

I shrugged my shoulders.

"Nothing! Instead of murdering that creep, I made him even more popular. Soon he'll join the WWF and challenge me on national television. I can't believe how my plan backfired."

Intrigued by this unintended turn of events, I asked, "What do you think about this nonsense concerning your affiliation with an anti-environmental organization, plus Prince's explanations about a fictional group of owls and swans? He even called you an ugly duckling."

Bubbling with rage in the dark evening air, Ukiah began, "Here's my theory. Prince may have been in shock from being whacked on the head and thought I was talking about real birds when mentioning his group. Or, more likely, he was covering for S.W.A.N. by playing stupid and throwing the reporters off track. Y'see, it's no accident that Prince included The Great Horned Owl and a flock of swans in his novel."

"Why?" I asked as we passed the local library, a group of homeless men loitering under its soft fluorescent yellow lights.

"Because Philip is communicating in a secret language to other members of S.W.A.N. He can't blatantly state their missions or directives, so he uses symbols and allegories. Did you notice how that bastard made the story's protagonist - an owl - the world's controller?"

"I did."

"Owls will never rule the planet, but this plot twist was Philip's way of telling S.W.A.N. that they'll assume control of The Word. Now can you see their subtle nuances and word plays?"

"Holy shit!" I blurted. "It does make sense."

At that moment we passed a simple stone church, the sign on its front lawn declaring, "The truth will set you free."

Ukiah, tossing his package in the air, then catching it, explained further, "S.W.A.N. will go to great lengths to conceal their true identity and motives. This is why they communicate in secret codes. As you can see, Language has retained its power over the masses. But once they've fragmented and confused it into a meaningless collection of babble, then those bastards will finally conquer us."

We eventually reached the parking garage where Ukiah repeatedly pushed the "up" button until an elevator arrived. After reaching our car and driving back home, I gazed at him as streetlamps cast both shadows and triggers of light across his face. While impulsively switching from one radio station to another, he steered through traffic like a gentle breeze. For some reason, Ukiah's first two novels trickled into my mind. I read them a considerable time ago, and since then so much had happened. Why did his words still hold such power over me?

Ukiah's stories showed both tenderness and compassion, yet in daily life he was distinctly cold. His world revolved around regular installments of hostility and desensitization. Weakness was not only frowned upon, but despised. How could this man also write prose of such softness and beauty? How could he reconcile his job, which promoted brutality, with the incredible sensitivity that lurked inside him?

I wanted to ask Ukiah about these discrepancies, but at the moment he seemed impervious to the world. Not wanting to disturb him, I wondered what thoughts occupied his mind. To a casual observer, Ukiah may have looked bored, but this facade only increased his mysterious presence. I wanted to burst through his walls, but what would I talk about? Ukiah either became quickly disinterested in my conversation, or else enraged to the point of filling me with terror. More often than not I felt as if I were walking on eggshells in his company.

As Ukiah pulled into the driveway with a quiet self-assurance, he turned the car off, then grabbed his oblong package.

Unable to maintain my curiosity, I asked, "The suspense is killing me. What did you get from the post office? It doesn't even have a shipper's name or return address."

Ukiah laughed, "Let's just say it's something you would picture arriving in a plain brown wrapper ... something I've been planning to use for a long time."

With that evasive response, Ukiah and I stepped from his Celebrity. Following a tepid farewell, he returned to his cottage while I stood on my porch gazing at a crescent moon lying low in the sky.

"Tell me, please," I whispered to the hazy orb. "What should I know about Ukiah? Enlighten me. I beg of you, I'm lost. You spoke with me once before. Please give your wisdom to me."

A cool winter wind whipped across my lawn as an unexpectedly eerie movement caught my eye. Turning toward Woody's house, I once again saw an apparition shuffling behind his curtains. As shots of adrenaline and fear burst through my veins, I heard a faint voice echoing in the wind.

Straining to hear, I still couldn't translate its message.

"You crazy old moon, answer me. What secrets can you tell me about Ukiah?"

Listening with every ounce of attention, I finally heard a response.

"Whoever shuns the advances of those who adore them will never be able to adore their Self. Whoever scorns these adorers will never be able to adore their own. Instead, what they see they will never possess despite the yearnings of their own eyes. These visions of lustful adoration will be nothing more than a mockery. The allure of their own Self will never bear fruit."

"What are you trying to say?" I begged. "Please. I don't understand."

Without further clues, the wind disappeared while ominous clouds covered the moon. Frazzled and confused, I barricaded myself inside the house.

Had I actually been receiving messages from the wind and the moon? What was I thinking? A cool evening breeze in the middle of winter does not talk with people, nor does the moon. If I told this to a psychiatrist, they'd call me insane. What was wrong with me? I was asking the moon for advice. But where did those words come from? Was it all fantasy? Had Ukiah monopolized my mind so completely that I actually started hearing things? For all I knew, even those shadows inside Woody's house were figments of my imagination. What was real? I no longer knew. I knew I'd never been firmly rooted to reality, but lately I questioned my very sanity. Fact and fiction merged to such an extent that ....

While pondering my mental state, I heard a crash, followed by muffled shrieks outside my window. I instantly feared a S.W.A.T. team invasion, or special agents rappelling onto my roof from a tree. Racing to a window facing the backyard, I peeked through the curtains to see a strange car sitting in the driveway, then two men dragging someone toward Ukiah's cottage. As my heart beat intently, I looked closer to see that one of the abductors was Ukiah, while I didn't know his assistant or their abductee. In fact, after squinting into the darkness, I realized their captive wore the very same hood that Ukiah adorned during his attack on Philip Prince.

What in God's name was happening? Ukiah assured me he would keep his business separate from my property. Now that son of a bitch was dragging ... who knew what into his guest cottage. What would follow? Police officers, helicopters with search lights, bloodthirsty dogs, shootouts, tear gas, handcuffs, and the electric chair. Damn him. The madness never ended. Each day brought more insanity. How could I escape? Would I ever escape?

As the boisterous trio stumbled into Ukiah's house, I knew there was one thing I shouldn't do. I had to stay away from this incident, sheltered in my own home. But an irresistible force drew me toward danger. I wanted to stay put ... I needed to stay safe ... but I soon put on a jacket and walked toward the lilac bush beside Ukiah's window.

Chris, CHRIS! What are you thinking? Listen to your heart. It's thumping so hard that you'll have a heart attack. I actually became lightheaded while sneaking across the lawn, my blood flow so great that I saw stars and felt my head spin. This idea was more ludicrous than those cliff drivers who jumped into the ocean off of rocky crags. At least if they made a mistake, death came quickly. But if Ukiah saw me outside his house, he'd torture me before taking my life.

None of these thoughts prevented me from lurking outside his living room window. Fueled by curiosity, I inched my head around the bush and over the windowsill, focusing on a perilous scene. Ukiah, with honed muscles rippling beneath a tight black T-shirt, shoved the hooded man (eye-slits facing backwards) onto his unfolded sofa bed -

the same place where I saw him having sex with the prostitute.

His associate, a medium-sized man with blue tattoos running the length of each arm, unbuckled a set of handcuffs from his belt, then attached the prisoner's wrists to the sleeper's metal frame. The tattooed figure appeared especially brutal in his actions, grinding the hooded man's face into the mattress before backhanding him across the head. Judging from the designs on his biceps and forearms, I deduced that he was Ukiah's employer, the infamous Tattoo Blue.

Blue was the same height as his employee, wearing scuffed brown cowboy boots, faded blue jeans torn at one knee, tight black leather gloves, and a tie-dyed T-shirt covered by a brown-suede jacket. Sporting a goatee, two scars on his left cheek, and brown hair wrapped in a ponytail, it seemed Tattoo Blue made a conscious effort to play his outlaw role to the hilt.

With their victim shackled to the sofa, Ukiah approached, ripping the hood (along with a few strands of hair) from his head, then began a caustic diatribe.

"Why the fuck haven't you returned my phone calls or answered my letter, you prick? I even visited your fucking principal."

I now knew the shackled man's identity - the high school teacher who agreed to let Japhy's band play at a student assembly, then repeatedly reneged on his promise by ignoring Ukiah. The teacher, whose name I could not remember, sat awkwardly on the mattress, his shattered wire-rim glasses hanging from one ear. The trembling, terrified individual, with short, sandy-colored hair and a delicate complexion, begged for release.

"I'm sorry. My actions were inexcusable ..."

"Doublet, you motherfucker," Ukiah bellowed. "Nobody fucks with my fucking kid, you fucking prick."

BAM. Ukiah belted him with such ferociousness that even though his window was closed, I could still feel the impact of bone striking flesh. The teacher's mouth was nearly torn from his face, a spattering of blood dripping from both lips. As Ukiah reared back to land another blow, I felt surges of nausea bubbling in my stomach. This wasn't staged TV violence, or the choreographed theatrics of professional wresting. SMACK. Ukiah punched this defenseless creature across the cheekbone with the force of a jackhammer chiseling at concrete. Doublet slumped to his side, but due to the handcuffs strapping him to the bed, couldn't let his body to fall in a lump. Instead, he dangled over the bed's side, a feeble, broken man ... sobbing, bruised, bloody, shocked, and terrified.

"Get up, you fucking sap," Ukiah hollered. "Tell me, Doublet, why didn't you return my calls? I left at least two-dozen messages. I want an explanation."

"I'm sorry," he cried, slobber hanging from his chin.

"Am I some kind of fucking chump? Huh? Do I look like a chump? Tell me?"

"Please ..."

"Obviously you don't give a shit about me or my kid, do you?"

"It's not that!" Doublet whimpered, his cheeks red and tear-stained.

"Hand me that box," Ukiah said to his accomplice.

Tattoo Blue grabbed the unopened, plain-wrapped container, smiling deviously while handing it to his partner. Ukiah pulled a silver knife from his pocket, slit the package's seal, then pulled a vise from inside as piles of green Styrofoam floated in the air. This vise, though, was not the kind found in neighborhood workshops. Rather, one of the clamps had a thumbtack welded to it, while the other clamp was padded with fur. What kind of torture tool did Ukiah order? I would soon learn, for Ukiah strolled toward Mister Doublet, twirling the vise around his index finger.

Only inches from the teacher's face, Ukiah snarled, "I gave you every fucking chance to do the right thing, but you refused. Why, you fucking dick-fuck?"

"I don't know," Doublet sobbed, trying to turn from his tormentor.

"I know why," Ukiah bellowed. "Because you hold a position of power as a teacher, and you figured it'd be easy to fuck with some dumb fuck like me, didn't you? Who gave a damn if you ignored twenty phone calls, a typed letter, and the principal's intervention? You were in the driver's seat, so to hell with me and my kid's band. But now, guess who has the upper hand? Me, you fucking gutter fuck. Now I'm going to show you what frustration feels like."

"Please, I beg of you, not that."

Ukiah strapped the clamp on Doublet's forearm - the fur-side underneath, spiked-side on top jabbing into the teacher's flesh. I couldn't believe this man, who I considered a friend, planned on torturing another human being. What was happening? Torture didn't happen in this day and age, did it?

"All right, fucker," Ukiah snapped, the thumbtack resting on Doublet's forearm. "I want you to taste the rage that ate through my brain every time I left an unanswered message on your machine."

Doublet screamed in agony as Ukiah twisted the tension lever, clamping the device lightly on his arm.

"You haven't felt anything yet, cocksucker. I'll bet you got quite a bit of enjoyment shining me on. You were hot shit ignoring me, riding on a wave of power. You probably thought, 'that asshole and his son's band don't matter.' Well, fuck you."

Ukiah twisted the metal tension bar another turn, causing the needle-like device to puncture Doublet's flesh and send a stream of blood - an actual stream of blood - into the air. Upon seeing this horror, my hand instinctively rose to cover my mouth as sickness bubbled inside my stomach.

"You'll never fuck with me again, will you Doublet?"

"No, I promise."

Twisting the press even tighter, Ukiah, with fire burning in his eyes, declared, "Then here's what we're going to do. Next Tuesday, 'Kiss' is performing at The Splycer Center. Being that my kid and his band are all skipping school and going to the show, I figure that'd be a perfect chance for them to play at Latera High. What do you think, Doublet?"

"It's fine. Anything."

Relieving the clamp's pressure, Ukiah smiled, "Now wasn't that easy? If only you would have shown the same courtesy and returned my calls in the first place, we could have skipped this messy extracurricular activity."

Drenched in sweat, blood smearing his face and forearm, Mister Doublet exhaled with relief.

Ukiah continued, his tone steady and pleasant. "Teach, there's one last matter to discuss. Naturally, in a short time we'll unshackle you, then drive you home. The first inclination for many people would be ... what?"

Tattoo Blue replied jokingly, "To call the cops?"

"Correct," Ukiah answered, his voice reminiscent of a television game show host. "Partner, why don't you tell our contestant what'll happen if he decides to snitch on us."

Tattoo Blue moved within inches of the teacher's face, then began cordially, "I swear on my mother's grave and all that is holy, if you rat on us ..." His voice then assumed the growl of an attack dog. "I'll kill you. Let me repeat," he said, deliberate in his delivery. "I'll — fucking — kill — you." Tattoo then planted a kiss on the teacher's sweaty forehead. "That, my friend, was your kiss of death. If you even consider going to the cops, I'll track you for the rest of my life. I'll pulverize your skull with a sledgehammer, but not before torturing you so severely that it'll make this episode look like a day at Boy Scout camp. I'll rape and butcher your wife, plus ... well, your kids, let's just say you don't want to know. Now look into my eyes, you fucking prick. Do I seem like someone who's fucking around? I'll go to the electric chair just to murder you. This ain't a fucking television show or movie where the lawmen hide you in a witness protection program. If Ukiah or me don't personally track you down, one of our associates will. So, here's the plan. Japhy's band will play at the high school next Tuesday. Is that understood?"

"Yes," he squeaked - bottom lip quivering, tears welled in each eye.

"And from this point forward, you'll act like nothing ever happened between us. You never even saw us. Because if you fuck up, Doublet, I'll kill you. I'll fucking kill you twice. I'll gut you like a deer, then strangle your old lady with the entrails. I'll scoop your eyes out with a melon-scooper ..."

Queasy, dizzy, scared and sick, I began retching behind the lilac bush ...

"... how would you like to have your dick shaved like a piece of whittling wood? Hey ... did you hear something?" Tattoo Blue yelled.

Shit! What am I going to do? I'm dead.

"Like what?" Ukiah asked, walking to the window directly above me.

Don't move an inch. Don't even breathe. Stay low. Don't move. Oh shit.

"I don't see anything out there," he replied, only inches away.

"Go check it out," Tattoo demanded. "I'll throw this sniveling little piece of shit in the car."

Go - Go! As Ukiah walked away from the window, I leaped to my feet, raced towards Dewar's house, circled it in the darkness, then stormed toward my front door, making sure not to slam it. Hyperventilating, I dropped to the floor, then crawled into the living room on my hands and knees. What if Ukiah knocked? He'd see my rapid breathing, sweaty face, and dew on my shoes. He'd instantly know I'd been spying on them.

What should I do? Don't knock, please don't knock. Just lay there quietly. Don't let him see you moving around. If he catches you ... a vise to the fingers, thumbtack through the pinkie ... Oh God, don't let him knock. You'll be safe in here ...

KNOCK — KNOCK.

Oh no! It's him. What will I do? No, no, it's only the wind knocking over one of my garbage cans. Phew. What a relief. Stay calm. That's it, breathe deeply. I'm so tired. What kind of lie should I make up? .... I'm so tired.

So very sleepy ...... close your eyes ....

18

Over a week had passed since last seeing Ukiah. I hadn't spoken to him, or even seen him during our separation. Naturally, I noticed his house lights at night, or heard his car pulling from the driveway, but not once did we actually meet. The hiatus was a well-needed break from our recent bouts of lawlessness and insanity.

Considering all that had happened in the past couple weeks - I murdered a man while Ukiah assaulted another and tortured a third - one would think such an interlude would be welcomed. But quite honestly, I quickly began longing for excitement. I hate admitting it, but before meeting Ukiah, my life was so boring that it was hard to tell one day from the next. In fact, my entire existence had been a series of disappointments. For seventeen years, I cringed under my father's fist as he berated and belittled me at every turn. After escaping that nightmare, I entered college, graduated with a degree in computer science, then began a faltering career at the data entry firm where I currently stagnated.

Working became nothing more than a tedious waste of time. Rather than soaring toward goals and plateaus, I wallowed in misery - a self-defeating underachiever who'd lost interest in the American Dream. As I sat in my cubicle, glancing at others like myself, I realized the only aspect of life that thrilled me were those spent with Ukiah. Sure, I'd probably spend my remaining days in prison, but at least a glimmer of excitement would have shined on my otherwise meaningless life.

While entering text into a word processor at work, I remembered Ukiah's theories concerning computer technology and scientific advancement. Unlike workers in the past who became one with their immediate surrounding - coal miners with pick axes chipping at blackened walls, a farmer digging radishes from the dirt, or leather-skinned women washing clothes in a stream - I showed no such affinity to my environment. My job made me a machine. Whereas blacksmiths, seamstresses, or moonshiners derived intrinsic pride from their trades, I felt nothing but emptiness ... an emptiness compounded by my demotion from management.

To compensate, as the day went by, I slipped deeper into the fantasy world of No-Sho The Hero. I saw myself being an aberration of the modern age - a retarded child born to a cretinous father and a mother who drank household cleaners. Unable to get sympathy from my parents or the world, I was reduced to being a filthy carnival freak

- a deformed child with stunted nubs for arms, a nonfunctioning voice box, and tentacle-like flippers that wiggled whenever I shit myself. A human oddity, the multitudes gathered around me each evening to snicker, whisper, and chastise me. Following each show, I'd sleep on a bundle of straw alongside the other sideshow freaks. All seemed hopeless until No-Sho The Hero, wearing a flowered cape and pink boots, flew down from the sky and cradled me in his arms. From that point forward, even if society shunned me, No-Sho would protect me.

The data-entry job became so boring that I doubted my very sanity. With fantasies involving No-Sho taking place on a daily basis, I came to a conclusion one afternoon while gazing at my terminal. I enjoyed the excitement that Ukiah created. I wanted to drive at ninety miles an hour, peek into windows at midnight, or murder people who rubbed me the wrong way. It didn't even matter who they were - a decrepit woman who stood at the bus stop, a fellow employee who chewed with his mouth open in the lunchroom, or ... or the greatest thrill of all. I'd kill Ukiah himself! One day, after letting him fuck me, he'd lie on the mattress, depleted from orgasm. Then, from nowhere, I'd thrust a knife through his heart, watching as blood gurgled from his mouth.

I needed a change ... desperately.

Early Tuesday morning, the day of both Japhy's high-school show and Kiss's appearance at the Splycer Center, an impatient rapping sound echoed against my front door. While getting ready for work, I opened the door to find Ukiah standing on my porch, a broad smile on his face. I invited him into the kitchen, then asked about his cheerful mood.

"Great news, Chris. Mirror Image is playing today at Latera High! I finally got a hold of Mister Doublet."

Being that we hadn't talked in over a week, I should have had no idea about this event. But, unbeknownst to Ukiah, I saw his brutal emasculation of the high-school teacher.

"Fantastic," I exclaimed, feigning surprise. "How did that happen?"

"Once I got to speak with Doublet, I persuaded him to see things my way. There's nothing like healthy dialogue," Ukiah laughed. "Oh," he then asked, "have you noticed anything weird happening around here?"

"Weird?" I asked, turning away while pretending to look for something in a cupboard.

"Yeah, like prowlers, odd sounds, or ..."

Interrupting him, I blurted a bit too eagerly, "I did hear what I thought was a cat burglar last week, but it turned out to be the wind knocking over my garbage cans."

"Your garbage cans?" Ukiah repeated, expressionless.

Wondering whether he knew about my voyeuristic activities, I reiterated, "Yes, garbage cans."

"That explains it," Ukiah said without elaboration. "Anyway, can you take a day's vacation from work? We have a lot to do before Japhy's show."

"We do? Well ... um ... I could call in sick."

"Do it."

"If you say so."

"I'll meet you here in an hour."

Just like that, after being away from Ukiah for over a week, we once again began a series of events he had planned far in advance.

"Here we go," Ukiah cheered, tapping his steering wheel while I crawled through the Celebrity's passenger side door.

"Where are we going?" I asked, feeling like a guinea pig.

"Look in back," Ukiah pointed, pulling onto Reflection Alley.

Six plastic laundry baskets filled with dirty clothes were stacked on the seat and floor, while a tattered notebook sat between us.

"There's three more loads in the trunk," he added, "plus my bed clothes."

"When was the last time you did the laundry?" I inquired, amazed that anyone owned that many clothes.

"Fifty-one days ago," Ukiah stated matter of factly.

"Fifty-one exactly? You counted?"

"Of course," he told me. "I have fifty-two shirts, twenty-six pairs of pants, twenty-six pairs of socks, and twenty-six towels. It all fits into a formula."

"A formula, for laundry?"

"Can't you see?" he asked as if I were a dimwit. "I wear each pair of pants and socks twice, and change my shirt every day. Plus, I'll dry with a different towel every two days. That way, everything works out perfectly."

"Everything in its proper order!"

"You're catching on, Chris."

Once again, Ukiah amazed me. Who else used such an intricate system for laundry? If Ukiah washed his clothes once every fifty-one days, that meant he only did laundry seven times a year. Incredible. To even consider the thought involved in this under-taking boggled my mind - a remarkable combination of efficiency and neurosis.

Amused by this preposterous concept, I gazed at Ukiah, noticing a change in his de-meanor. Over the past month, his face exhibited signs of such stress that I feared he would collapse. What do I mean? Well, had a stranger on the street seen my friend, they wouldn't have noticed anything wrong. Ukiah always erected a calm façade ... a coolness hinting at boredom. But I started seeing cracks - a slow, simmering frustra-tion that threatened to explode into full-blown psychosis. He radiated an intensity that reminded one of walking into a brick wall - a brick wall spray painted by a martyred man on a mission.

After pulling into the laundrymat, I saw a blazing display of speed that made my head spin. Ukiah unloaded the nine baskets of clothes, then zipped into action. He first fed quarters into the slots of fourteen machines, then slammed their lids to begin the wash cycle. He then grabbed an industrial-sized container of detergent and poured one heaping scoop into each washer after reopening their lids. I almost asked if I could help, but decided that any deviation from his system would be a hindrance. So, I marveled as he loaded arms full of laundry into each washer, slammed their lids, then scurried to the next. After fourteen machines were loaded, he stuffed two double-loaders with bedclothes that he removed in a ball from his trunk. Ukiah slid quarters into their slots, poured soap into a hinged opening, then stacked the empty clothesbaskets in uniform rows. In all, he readied seven weeks worth of laundry in the span of ten minutes. With sweat rolling from his forehead, we returned to the Celebrity and continued our journey.

"What's next?" I asked, hoping I hadn't missed an entire day's work to watch him run errands.

"The post office," he told me.

"Oh no, not again," I replied, fearing another confrontation.

"Don't worry," he assured me, "There won't be another scene. That last episode will stay in their memories for a while. Once those bastards saw someone sticking up for themselves, it set an example for the future. They'll forget about it somewhere down the line, but until then, things'll run smoothly."

"I'll never forget how you sat on the floor in front of that window. What a riot."

"From now on, I'm sticking up for myself. I'm not going to get dicked over without saying something. I'll set an example rather than stand back and say things should be different. But I'll tell ya, Chris, sometimes I wonder if it's all worthwhile. The frustrations are killing me. Then I'll speak with Romlocon about my writing, and she'll tell me that if I think these battles are tough, what'll happen when I try to dethrone S.W.A.N. and save the literary world? So, little incidents like those at the grocery store or post office are just preparations for the real war."

After buying a book of stamps, we hit a bookstore, a pet shop (where Ukiah bought a fifty-pound bag of sunflower seed to feed the birds), the library, then returned to the laundrymat where he threw his clothes into a row of dryers. After finishing these errands, we drove through the garishly decorated downtown streets (being the Christmas season) to a nondescript diner. In no time, we ate a delicious breakfast of bacon, eggs, and fried potatoes.

"You still don't understand that episode inside the post office, do you?"

Unsure of what to say, I shrugged my shoulders while buttering an English muffin.

Ukiah continued, "Do you remember those folks standing in line? All of them were disgruntled, seething with anger, and ready to explode. But what did they do to change their situation? Nothing. They just stood there and accepted their fate."

"Why?" I asked.

"I'm not faulting these people, because I'm sure they work hard for living. But one element is missing from their lives."

"And that is?"

"Due to an ongoing effort over the years, their passion has been stripped like ore from a mountainside."

"Ore?" I asked, again confused by Ukiah's explanations.

"I'm sure you've seen hillsides that have been ravaged by strip mining. These plunderers go into an area, tear out the trees, burrow through the earth, then take all the natural resources. After they leave, the area has literally been raped of its original glory. The same concept applies to the process of stripping mankind of its passion."

"I still don't follow."

"Let me explain. Name man's three most burning passions."

"Um ... hunger, shelter ..."

"No, Chris, those are needs that keep us alive. I'm talking about the fire beyond our daily requirements."

"Oh," is all I could muster as a response.

"I'm talking about art, sex, and violence."

"Of course," I replied, cluelessly.

"Do you remember that time I mentioned our governments attempt to control our lives?"

I nodded my head.

"These same people look at passion as a negative force, like wildfires blazing across a field. With this in mind, what is the first thing ya do when a fire breaks out?"

"Extinguish it."

"Right! The same applies to our passions. Let's look at my life in regard to these three pursuits. First, there's art. How does society view a person who's written fifty-seven pounds of material without earning a cent from them?"

"They'd call him crazy ... a crackpot."

"Exactly. How do you rationalize this answer? I'll tell you. In a materialistic culture, we value producers, not creators."

"What do you mean?" I asked, consumed by both Ukiah's insights and the breakfast before me.

"The essential element of capitalism is consumption. To consume, one must produce. So who is more highly prized - workers who stamp out parts in a factory, or an artist who creates ideas, characters, and philosophical theories?"

"The laborer is a more integral part of this system."

"Exactly. So, rather than encouraging people from an early age to develop their artistic passions, we're told to abandon such foolishness. So, creators become outlaws, enemies of a society where products such as leather wallets and automobiles are the height of success. Now how about sex. Who do we think leads normal sex lives?"

"Married people?"

"Correct. Every other option falling outside these parameters is judged abnormal. Now don't worry, I'm not going to tell you what I think is moral or immoral. I'm just saying that our identities are molded by societal forces we don't even recognize. Finally, look at violence. This act is the most frowned-upon by any culture. Those in control tell us that no human being should ever attack another. If somebody does cross this line, they'll be swiftly imprisoned or executed. But go home tonight and watch TV or go to a movie. What does society present in the form of entertainment and news? Violence! Can't you see the hypocrisy? Their behavior is acceptable, but if we act the same way, the judicial system locks us up."

"What are you trying to say, that we should let anarchy run rampant?"

"Of course not. But like art and sex, violence in regard to passion is unacceptable. Instead of promoting our natural reactions, we're forced to act like those people in the post office - our passions eliminated like a strip-mined hillside."

As canned Christmas music filtered through the diner, I asked Ukiah, "The holiday season is here. Should I buy you anything ..."

"Don't even finish your sentence. Christmas is nothing but a conditioning tool."

Knowing what sent Ukiah into fits of rage, I quickly changed the subject.

"How is *Blank Line* coming along? I haven't seen you in a week, so I figured ..."

"Between my latest letter to Jennifer, and ..."

"You sent another letter to her? Great. She'll answer one of them, I'm sure of it."

"I'm not," Ukiah frowned. "I know she belongs to S.W.A.N., and is doing everything in her power to confuse our language. But I won't quit."

"Good."

"The Mason Turner Agency is like a huge stepped temple that I have to climb. And, like the nine levels of Hell, this building also has nine stages; only they rise instead of descend. So every day I start all over again, trying to reach the tower's summit. But like any ordeal, I have to scratch and claw every step of the way. Y'know, when I first started this battle, I thought I knew how it would go, but during the climb, all I heard were confused cries, indecipherable voices, and misunderstood languages. The entire process has been disillusioning beyond words. But in the end, I've learned something about creation."

"You have?" I asked, finishing my meal.

"Yeah. I've found that contented people haven't been dragged through Hell enough to produce meaningful Art. At the core of Creation is discontentment - a deeply scarred psyche and soul that can only be healed by discovering what is needed to enter the gates of publication. This discontentment is pure darkness, creation being its only light. I need the struggle before me. I need it to keep creating. If the darkness and displeasure are taken away, I'm through. I need agony."

"Check, sir?" our waitress asked Ukiah.

Ukiah nodded, then smiled at the young girl, a gesture that reflected his respect for her.

After paying our bill, we encountered an unseasonably warm December morning.

"I can't believe it's almost Christmas, and we've only had one snowfall."

"I hope we keep it at only one," Ukiah joked.

While returning to the Celebrity, I asked, "What did you say in your last letter to that agent?"

"I told Jennifer I'm not playing any more cat and mouse games. I don't simply want to get published. I have too much material and too many revelations to squander on one petty contract."

"Then what do you want?" I asked as we entered Ukiah's car.

"I'm shooting for my own publishing house!"

"You want that woman to give you an entire publishing house!"

"That's right. I want my own subsidiary, complete with presses, editors, operators, and the whole shebang. I can't be bothered with the incidental bullshit that other authors have to put up with. When Jennifer finally decides to get the ball rolling, we have to storm headlong into production with no looking back. It's all or nothing!"

While he drove through Latera Heights, I blurted, "You have such a sense of urgency in everything you do. Why?"

"There are two reasons. First, it becomes clearer every day that I need to save the literary world. Jennifer has become an important part of this process, but the details are so complicated that I can't talk about them now."

"What's the second reason?"

"I need more time to write *Blank Line*. This book will make ninety-nine percent of what has ever been printed look like the scribblings of a preschooler. It'll be very readable, yet more complex and symbolic than The Sphinx's riddles. I almost feel sorry when people read this monster. They'll be disfigured for the rest of their lives, and the damage will be irreversible! Getting published is my way of escaping the drudgery of life. When those nuisances are gone, I can complete my legacy, which is the culmination of my entire life up until this point."

"Ukiah, you still haven't told me what *Blank Line* is about."

"All I can say is that it deals with Possession in a variety of different forms."

Ukiah pulled into the laundrymat's parking lot, unloaded his clothes and blankets from each dryer, then put them in his car. With this job done, he reached into his pocket and removed a wad of bills.

"Here, this should cover next month's rent and utilities."

"Thanks. Speaking of which, can we hit the electric company, then pay our cable bill?"

"Sure. Japhy and his band won't get here until noon."

As we drove toward Twinborn Power, I asked, "What else did you say in your letter?"

"I took a few quotes from the Sunday paper given by a local woman who had her first romance novel published. Here is her pearl of wisdom:

Publishing is not a business for sissies or impatient people.

"She said that?"

"Yeah. So I told Jennifer to listen closely. I don't resemble the first part of her quote. But as for the second, I plead guilty. I can't stand wasting time to even take a piss, let alone be bothered by other things in life."

"So the last four months you've spent waiting for her response ..."

"Have been torture. Enough is enough. I told Jennifer to brush the clutter off her desk, disconnect the phone, and pay attention to me. Why should she waste her time on a bunch of sleepwalkers when we could set the world on its ass?"

"What else did this romance writer say?"

"It concerned her day-to-day routine. Here's how she described life with her husband." At this point, Ukiah's voice took on the characteristics of a frumpy old housewife. 'At night, we watch public television, listen to opera, or sit in separate rooms talking to each other in our favorite Internet chat room. We rarely leave our secluded cabin in the woods ... we're so mundane.' Ukiah's voice returned to normal. "I get so frustrated with these boring authors who are a constant embarrassment. It's stumblebums like her who give ME a bad name. Here she is, a representative of our field, copying all the other writers I see on TV. She's boring ... BORING," he yelled. "But if Jennifer lets me enter the gates of publication, I'll have people's heads spinning." Ukiah became hysterical as he concluded, "I'm ready - anytime, anywhere! I just wish Jennifer could see another side of me rather than this raving, egotistical asshole."

Speeding into Twinborn Power's parking lot, Ukiah waited as I ran into the office and paid our light bill. Then, when driving toward the cable company, I asked him another question.

"What's in that notebook you brought along?"

"The handwritten copy of my letter to Jennifer," he replied.

"Can I read it?"

"No," Ukiah laughed, "I never let anyone see me prostituting myself. But I'll let you glance at it."

At a red light, Ukiah opened the notebook, then held it against the driver's side window as I looked across the seat. What I saw was the oddest display of illegible chicken-scratch that any human being could ever conceive. I swear, without exaggeration, that not a single word could be read, even if I were close enough to see them. When Ukiah told me he wanted to become one with his writing, he didn't stretch the truth. In the few seconds I had to glance at this mess, I saw words and complete sentences hastily scratched out and revised, circled words attached to arrows, swirled lines jutting between fragmented passages, carets with illegible words above them, four different colored inks, diagrams and faces drawn in the margin, scribbled notes, and weird symbols that appeared to have no meaning. The page looked like the demented scribblings of a mental patient. I found it hard to believe that anyone could read this mish-mash, let alone type it. The process had to have been harder than translating a prehistoric language found buried in the desert.

"I call it an abortion on paper," Ukiah joked about his creation. "You have to admit, it is different."

We soon reached the cable company, where I paid another bill.

Returning home, I asked, "How do you actually write? What does the process involve? It's so visual. Did you learn to do it in college?"

For some reason, Ukiah laughed uproariously at this question.

"Chris, I've never taken a writing course in my life. In fact, I'd tell every aspiring writer in America to stay away from creative writing courses, bookstore fiction groups, or studying critical essays on how to write. They'll ruin a writer every time."

"Then what should they do?"

"Two things. First, be themselves. Don't try to write like an author from the nineteenth century, or the way a professor tells you to. Follow your intuition, and the voice that your Muse has given you."

"And the second is?"

"If you've been paying attention, you'd notice that I rarely read fiction these days, especially books currently on the market. But in the past, I made it a point to read at least a hundred novels a year."

"Why did you quit reading contemporary material?" I asked as Ukiah sped through traffic.

"So I could stay pure ... untouched ... virginal. After devouring what I considered essential reading material, I began creating rather than following. This way, I wouldn't be influenced by trends, styles, and specific genres. Who wants to read twenty pages describing a fucking hotel room, or wallow in a sappy novel that creates a certain 'mood'? Those books waste my time. I want the writer to enter my mind, say what they have to say, then get the fuck out. I may have told you my three main credos for writing, but here they are again:

1) start with a bang
2) get to the point
3) don't bore your audience

When all is said and done, the most fundamental point to remember is this: don't masturbate on paper."

"I've noticed that you mention genre quite a bit. Why?"

"Because genres are another shackle in our lives - a loss of literary and creative freedom. Once the public knows a writer, their publishers want them to stay in familiar territory, so they frown upon experimentation. But shouldn't writing, or creativity in general, reflect every aspect of our personality? Why limit ourselves to one fucking mode of expression, like that asshole Philip Prince? All he's ever written is science-fiction, which in and of itself isn't bad, but when you're pigeon-holed by these limitations, you might as well stamp parts in a factory."

"That makes sense," I told Ukiah as we pulled into the driveway. "What else does the creative process entail?"

Stepping from the Celebrity, then stacking one laundry basket on another as he unloaded them, he began (as I followed hauling one basket), "My entire writing style can be summed up by The Boy Scout's credo - be prepared."

"In what way?" I asked, setting the clothesbasket inside his door, then following him back to the car.

Ukiah explained, "When working on a novel, the story's seed has already been planted in my mind before a single drop of ink touches the page. As the idea germinates and begins to bear fruit, I'll scribble notes on anything imaginable: matchbook covers, napkins, the margins of a newspaper, or the back of a notebook. I keep collecting tidbits of information pertaining to plot structure, lines of dialogue, and character development until I'm finally comfortable enough to start unscrambling them."

After Ukiah's clothes were unloaded and we sat on his front stoop, I asked, "What does this unscrambling process involve?"

"I set every scrap of paper on the floor, then start rifling through them. Each sheet that has more than one idea is cut with a pair of scissors until it only holds a single concept. After this's done, I start putting the jigsaw puzzle together, cramming the strips of paper into separately labeled envelopes. Once nothing else is left on the carpet, I'm ready to start writing."

"You put the notes in individual packets?" I inquired, watching a blue bird eat seeds from its feeder.

"Yeah, then each of these envelopes is emptied - the notes laid out before me and deciphered. Once everything is in its proper order, I start writing like a madman, not worried about spelling, grammar, or punctuation. Nothing matters except the Moment - those exhilarating flashes of creativity that temporarily make life meaningful. Then, after this foundation has been laid, I start editing. I do this to both the handwritten draft, and also while typing. The entire process becomes a combination of styles used by three authors I mentioned earlier."

"Which three writers?" I asked, embarrassed by my lack of memory.

"To begin, my scissors and jigsaw puzzle description is a spin-off of the 'Cut-up' method used by William Burroughs. Next, my stream of consciousness on the initial draft is reminiscent of Jack Kerouac's 'Spontaneous Prose.' Finally, the editing is reminiscent of F. Scott Fitzgerald's obsession with endless revision. So, although I like these three writers, I improved on each of their techniques. Burroughs 'Cut-up' gave the world a different way of viewing The Word, but many of his novels, like *Naked Lunch* or *The Soft Machine,* were literally unreadable. In terms of Kerouac's 'Spontaneous Prose,' when he was 'on,' his work made readers come alive with excitement. But as was often the case, especially in his later life, this holiness of The Word led to nothing more than self-indulgent ramblings. Finally, Fitzgerald could turn a phrase like few others. But his perfection of The Word often left the overall work feeling stale and labored. Sometimes he'd rewrite a chapter seventeen times. Luckily, I've seen the errors of their way and won't fall into the same traps."

"Basically then," I said, trying to understand, "you use a complex process of preparation in order to create?"

A brilliant ray of sunlight peaked from behind a cloud prior to Ukiah's response.

Choosing his words carefully, Ukiah began, "I should clarify the process that I use to create. I may have given you the wrong impression when speaking of the work's methodical nature. I admit to being very prepared in regard to my novels, certain to include details while keeping everything in its proper order. But my poetry and short stories have none of these laborious tendencies. Instead, I start with a single word, line, or idea, then let spontaneity follow its course."

"Tell me more," I said as a cardinal fluttered toward Ukiah's feeder.

"Let's say the concept of multiple personalities was included among a list of potential subjects. I'd then run with this idea, writing about a little girl who got abused as a child."

I nodded my head.

"I use the same principles when writing poetry. The exhilaration of these open ended works is probably the greatest joy the creative process can provide. I'll tell ya, you should see how different these tales look compared to the scribbled pages I showed you earlier. My poems, especially, are one-shot wonders - a frozen, spontaneous snapshot that reflects my particular mood at a given moment. But hey, who cares about all this writer's talk anyway? I have a few things to take care of inside, so I'll see ya when Japhy and his band get here."

I said goodbye, then returned to my house, excited to be free from the drudgery of work.

"Hurry. Throw your coat on," Ukiah panted after rapping at my door.

"Why? What's going on?" I asked while doing as he said, then following him to the car.

"Japhy and the band were delayed, so he called and said that they drove straight to the high school. Their show starts in fifteen minutes."

"What happened?" I asked as Ukiah spun tires and kicked gravel while tearing from the driveway.

"I don't know. Japhy called and told me they were setting up their gear." Ukiah zipped through traffic with the speed of mice through a maze. "By the way, which building is the senior cafeteria in? North or South?"

"Beats me," I told Ukiah. "I went to Didymus High, not the public school."

"You went to a private school," Ukiah asked, screeching into the high school's senior parking lot.

"Yes. My father thought it would increase my chances of getting into medical school ..."

"He wanted you to be a doctor?" Ukiah laughed as we sped from the Celebrity.

"Can you imagine? Doctor Edwards needed in surgery. I feel faint when thinking about a flu shot, let alone slicing somebody's spleen. Oh well, another disappointment in a long list of many according to my father."

"Where's the cafeteria?" Ukiah frantically asked a janitor in the hallway.

"Da Slop Hole?" the custodian grinned while leaning on a broom. "Follow dis corridor straight to da end."

In no time, we burst into the cafeteria to see a student wearing white and black make-up exclaim, "Straight from Twin Falls, the best damn band in the land - Mirror Image!"

Approximately four hundred kids burst into applause as Japhy's band cranked into their opening number.

"Look, over there, near the window. It's Gina," Ukiah said gladly, leading me toward her.

As we stood near a row of folded tables stacked against a purple wall, the sight before us epitomized what rock n' roll was all about. Even though I had never followed music, I was moved by this event. Mirror Image performed directly in front of the cafeteria's serving area, which luckily was shut off from view. The band didn't even have a stage or fancy lighting. They simply set their amplifiers, three mike stands, and a drum kit on the floor, then let loose a barrage of ear-piercing rock n' roll. Behind them, serving as a backdrop, was a brown paneled wall, a row of vending machines, green plastic garbage cans, a water fountain, and a clock hanging from the ceiling.

Staring directly at the band, only inches away, were throngs of bouncing teenagers dancing in place and hopping wildly.

I found one aspect of the student's appearance bizarre. Many of them painted their faces with the same white and black makeup as the kid who introduced them. Some wore painted stars and bat wings over their eyes, while others looked like space men or alley cats. I wanted to ask Ukiah why they all looked so strange, but he was already talking with Gina.

"What happened to you guys?"

Gina told him, "We were half way here when Looney said, 'Uh guys, I forgot my bass.' No one could believe it. We had to drive all the way back to Twin Falls."

The band, meanwhile, sizzled with ferociousness. Their lead singer, Hawke, served as Mirror Image's main energy source. Wearing a green and red Christmas sweater, a tight-fitting silver chain around his neck, torn green shorts, and no shoes or socks, Hawke definitely presented an offbeat image. With his short, light-brown hair formed into horns (using mousse), and sporting silver hoop earrings from each lobe, Hawke bounced about the linoleum floor with uninhibited frenzy.

Their bass player, Looney, was a short, stocky kid who wore black wraparound sun-glasses, a black hat, black leather wristbands, while a silver chain hung from his belt. Thrusting his right fist into the air between notes, Looney nearly equaled Hawke in his animated stage antics.

The drummer, Atomic Aaron, actually had the most unique look of all. As if preparing for the high school prom, he slicked back his black hair with grease, then wore a white ruffled dress shirt with a red bowtie, red cummerbund, and black tuxedo pants.

Finally, Japhy stood calmly to Hawke's right, not leaping about or drawing attention to himself, but simply holding the band together with his guitar work. Flaunting a white Godzilla T-shirt and black jeans, Japhy adjusted the group's amplifiers between songs, told them what number to play next, and provided background vocals during each chorus.

Following one rousing number, Hawke yelled into his microphone, "This song is about what every kid fears most. It's called 'Knocked-Up!'"

As Atomic Aaron banged his drums, the crowd exploded with wild cheers. I'd never experienced anything that sent such chills down my spine. The kids before me - crazed, unleashed, spirited - danced and twirled with such freedom that I finally knew what rock n' roll was all about. Here were four high-school kids with cheap amps, a used drum kit, and two guitars, playing songs that sent their peers into fits of delirium. At one point Hawke sang:

> Please don't tell me that you're knocked up
> Please don't tell me that you're knocked up

Could any song deliver a more direct message? The kids, many wearing garish kabuki makeup, sang in unison while stomping their feet, cheering, or dancing in circles. Soon, every person in the cafeteria fell under Mirror Images spell - girls standing on eight-foot folding tables, cheerleaders in the back row, and even a few teachers who filtered in from the hallway.

"All right," Hawke yelled into his microphone after finishing the above song. Random whoops, hollers, whistles and cheers filled the cavernous cafeteria. "Here's a question for you. What is the President's favorite game to play at The White House? Give up? It's called Swallow The Leader!" The kids laughed in unison, eating from Hawke's hand. "Now," he panted, "here's a number about something all guys like to do at least once a day, but never admit to. It's called 'My Daily Task.' Let's rock n' roll!"

Kids pushed toward Hawke's monitors on the floor, crowded into Japhy, and patted Looney's back with encouragement as he plucked his bass. During one of Japhy's guitar solos, Hawk stormed into the crowd, then began slam dancing with the rowdy teenagers, twirling in circles, then hopping up and down in place. The scene grew so wild that I couldn't tell the band from the crowd. Swarms of teenage bodies whirled chaotically, while music emanated from somewhere inside the madhouse.

I looked sideways to see Ukiah beaming with such pride that it can't be adequately described on paper. Bobbing his head in rhythm to the music while trying to sneak a glimpse of his son, Ukiah's radiance could have lit a stadium.

"Why are those kids wearing makeup?" I yelled.

"In tribute to Kiss. They're probably going to the show tonight."

From Ukiah's tone, he must have thought I grew up under a rock.

By now, kids actually lifted other kids over their heads and passed them around the cafeteria. Meanwhile, Japhy's band kept playing ... pushing the crowd to its limit. Kids leaped from tables, whooped indiscriminately into the air, spun on the floor in circles, and bounced around without worry. Hawke urged them to greater heights while Japhy cranked out chords, or put his guitar in front of an amplifier to create deafening shrieks of feedback.

I thought the cafeteria would actually collapse as the noise and delirium peaked, but then I turned to see Ukiah glaring at something from the corner of his eye. Following the path of his invisible glance, I looked across the lunchroom to see ... Oh no ... Mister Doublet, the teacher who Ukiah and Tattoo Blue had tortured. With a bandage on his right forearm and a bruise marking his cheekbone, Doublet stood meekly in a corner beside two other teachers. Obviously, he hadn't mentioned last week's incident, or Ukiah would have already been arrested. On the other hand, were school officials simply waiting for the show's finale to prevent a riot? Whatever the case, Ukiah's defenses had been erected. Periodically, he'd throw a piercing glance at the teacher to let his presence be known.

To close the show, Hawke caught his breath, then addressed the maniacal mob pressing against his chest.

"Let me hear. Did we enjoy this afternoon's performance?"

Thunderous applause.

"That's what I thought. The only thing I can't figure out is why it took so long to bring us to Latera High. So our last song is dedicated to Mister Doublet. It's called 'Piss Off.' Hit it boys!"

As the band launched into their final number, a group of students noticed Mister Doublet hunkering near the cafeteria's rear exit. Crazed with excitement, three of them rushed toward the teacher, then dragged him onto the dance floor. To my amazement, two of them held Doublet's arms behind his back while three more smeared Kiss-style makeup on his face. I couldn't believe it. Doublet, obviously humiliated, didn't even try to resist. He simply stood passively while the kids dabbed makeup on his cheeks. To make matters worse, two cheerleaders entered the picture by slathering his mouth with red lipstick. To finalize this embarrassing episode, another cheerleader set a pompom on Doublet's head and sprayed him with silly string while a candy striper snapped pictures of the trembling teacher.

The ordeal traumatized Mister Doublet, but so much activity kept happening that hardly anyone noticed. Pandemonium ensued in every direction - a stomping, clapping, hooting and hollering let your hair down free-for-all. The band, meanwhile, chanted in unison with the students:

Piss off - piss off

The concert reached its end when Atomic Aaron leaped from his drum kit, then began throwing pieces from it into the brown wall behind him. The kids wanted to join this destruction, but a series of bells were triggered while school officials rushed the scene and dispersed the crowd. The cafeteria actually looked like a riot zone. Now when people scream, "Hail, Hail, Rock n' Roll," I know what they mean!

As order was restored to the cafeteria, Ukiah sped toward the band, shaking hands with each member, then hugging his son. To watch Ukiah react in such a manner touched everyone in attendance, especially me, because he usually showed the tenderness of a cactus. I couldn't even imagine Ukiah embracing another human being, let alone holding them close to his body for an extended period of time. Oh sure, I watched him with a prostitute one night, but what he did to her couldn't even be called making love. Ukiah simply fucked that woman, then threw her out the door. To witness such warmth was certainly a change from his standard behavior. But then again, who did Ukiah actually have in his life? No parents, relatives, wife or siblings. Of course, many of these hardships were of his own making, but all Ukiah had was his son.

After releasing his embrace, Ukiah joked to the band, "I used to think the only group in America better that Mirror Image was Kiss. But after this afternoon's show, you may have stolen their crown!"

We went in all directions following the show - Japhy, Gina and the band celebrated downtown after their triumphant appearance; Ukiah got our tickets from Tattoo Blue, while I drove to the grocery store and bought snacks for our post-concert party. As I wandered through the supermarket, I remembered an episode that took place as we loaded the band's equipment into his son's gray Chevy van. Japhy told Ukiah that Mirror Image wanted to produce a demo tape and send it to East Coast record compa-nies. Being that Japhy wrote the music and lyrics of every song, this news obviously thrilled Ukiah to no end.

Even though Ukiah and his son rarely got together, they instantly clicked every time I saw them. They joked and discussed personal issues as if an unspoken trust would never be broken. When with his son, I saw a side of Ukiah that never surfaced at any other time. He became, for lack of better terms, responsible. At any other time, he existed in a nihilistic world where the consequences of his actions were only considered after the fact. But with Japhy, Ukiah actually used forethought before acting. Oh sure, he'd keep racing and entering demolition derbies, but at least he didn't speed at ninety-five miles an hour along the freeway, or attack people who crossed him.

Another aspect of Ukiah's personality that changed was his interest in Japhy's life. In regard to other people, myself included, Ukiah rarely found much that interested him. One almost gathered (considering he had tasted every experience in life), that Ukiah settled into a jaded state of disinterest. After drug addiction, alcoholism, unlimited sex, life in the gutters, and cross-country travels, Ukiah felt removed from daily life. I certainly bored him ... at least that's the impression I got. The only notions that concerned him were those revolving around the gates of publication.

But this attitude changed when Japhy visited. Ukiah asked questions concerning his son's innermost feelings, inquired about his studies and hobbies, or checked on his ex-wife's well being. He seemed so different from the man whose sadistic streak sent waves of terror through his victims. If only we could turn back time and start all over, with no crime connections, murders, or assaults. What a life we would lead, never being forced to look over our shoulders.

But these fantasies were wishful thinking. Ukiah didn't give a damn about me. I doubt he'd even care if a cement truck crashed into my Gemini on the way home. Even after all we'd been through together, plus the horrors I saw outside his living room window while hiding behind a lilac bush, I still felt a deep affection for Ukiah.

As I passed a frozen-food cooler in one aisle, then looked inside to see TV dinners, instant pizzas, and ice cream sandwiches, a bizarre image formed in the reflective glass. Taking shape before my eyes was Ukiah bending over a gleaming silver tray. This plate was unlike any other - untouched by meats or vegetables, garnishes or fruits. Its virgin surface was polished by the invisible fingers of a swirling wind, making the platter so shiny that no one dared to taint its surface. That was until Ukiah saw this tray, staring into it like a sorcerer casting spells in his looking glass. Ukiah became so enamored with the platter that he actually floated above it ... hovering like a ghost obsessed with seeing its shadow. As if magically, time stopped as Ukiah and the silver tray became absorbed with each other ... complimented each other ... and fanned each other's flame. Ukiah's interest grew so great that he even began speaking to the plate.

"Dearest to my heart, I forget myself when consumed by your spellbinding charm. Your glistening image attracts me like a mother's bosom. But to be enchanted by that which you reflect is a state I cannot, or will not, resist."

Dumbfounded, I rubbed my eyes to find nothing inside the cooler's icy glass case except frozen vegetables, pot pies, and popsicles. I had to quit thinking about Ukiah or I'd lose my mind.

Seven of us piled into Japhy's dented gray van - Ukiah driving, his son and Gina riding shotgun, and the rest of us in back sitting on spare tires, amplifiers, or wooden equipment crates. Waves of excitement washed across the van, some of it still an adrenaline rush from that afternoon's show, the rest in anticipation for this evening's Kiss concert.

"You should see 'em," Japhy told his band mates. "We saw 'em years ago at The Civic Arena, then last fall at The Splycer Center. They're the greatest show on earth!"

"Did you see what we did to those kids in the cafeteria?" Hawke chimed in. "We set the place on fire. Hey Looney, we could even kick your last band's ass. What were they called?"

"The Self-Mutilators," he replied.

"Yeah, we'd even blow them off stage."

While pulling into The Splycer Center's parking lot, Ukiah asked, "What's it feel like being on stage? It must be great!"

Hawke responded eagerly, "It's the greatest. Pure exhilaration. When I looked into that crowd and saw nothing but enjoyment and insanity, it's like the world quit turning. It's like I wasn't even standing on the floor, but actually floating above those kids, like a god or something."

"We had so much power over those kids," Looney chuckled, "that we could have told them to kill every one of their teachers, and they probably would have done it. What a rush!"

"How about you?" Ukiah asked Japhy while paying a parking attendant. "How did it feel?"

"I was so focused," he said, "that I forgot about the world. Nothing existed except the moment. There were no tests, responsibilities, or bad news. Then I'd look over to see Gina smiling and bouncing around ... I knew we were kicking ass."

"I just wanted to fuck," Atomic Aaron blurted unexpectedly, causing everyone to laugh.

"How about those kids ganging up on the teacher who kept blowing us off," Hawke gloated. "Did you see 'em spraying that geek with silly string, then painting his face? What a loser."

They all roared with enjoyment when recalling the scene ... everyone except me. After seeing the expression on Doublet's face - one of utter defeat and a loss of hope - I started worrying. After being tortured by Ukiah, then humiliated by his own students, Doublet could crack at any moment and call the cops. Ukiah would then be arrested for that incident, plus Philip Prince's attack. Nothing good could come from it.

"Let's rock n' fuckin' roll," Atomic Aaron cheered as we piled from Japhy's van into the chilly night.

While walking toward The Center, our attention was drawn to four inflatable Kiss balloons that were anchored to the arena's roof, each more colorful than those at a Thanksgiving Day Parade. With spotlights illuminating each character as they swayed in the wind, I realized that Kiss would never settle for anything less than being larger-than-life. Plus, their fans reminded me of those at the wrestling matches, each displaying their allegiance to a particular grappler. Tonight, they all turned into bat-lizards, star-children, space-men or alley cats.

After walking around the lobby, a group of high-school kids, all wearing black-and-white makeup, approached Japhy and his friends to exclaim, "Hey, Mirror Image! Cool, dude. We saw you at the high school today. You kicked ass!"

Another added, "Keep Rockin'!"

All four members of the band beamed with pride at being recognized so far from home.

"You better cut that demo tape pretty quick," Ukiah laughed. "Your fans can't wait."

Gina, teeming with enthusiasm, asked, "Where are our seats?"

"Twelfth row on the floor," Ukiah smiled, obviously pleased.

"How do you get such good tickets?" Japhy asked as we entered the hall and found our seats.

Ukiah simply patted him on the back and grinned.

After watching the warm-up band ... a group called Powerman 5000 ... we all stood, clapped, and stomped our feet as the arena lights dimmed and Kiss took the stage. Amid blinding explosions, smoke bombs, fire gushing from hidden jets under the stage, and sparks dropping from the rafters, Kiss made an entrance that secured their status as being the greatest show on earth. Before us, only a few yards away, were three monstrous superheroes and a drummer. Perched atop seven-inch platform heels, these men cranked out music at such a deafening level that I thought the roof would collapse.

"Holy shit," Atomic Aaron screamed, out of his mind with delight.

It was hard to tell who made more noise - Kiss with their wall of amplifiers, or the 15,000 crazed fans standing on their feet.

Standing right in front of us was Gene Simmons, a towering figure with bat-wing eyes wearing a caped, black leather costume with spiked shoulders and a black silver-studded codpiece. This animated demon, performing a series of comically lewd pelvic thrusts while strumming his bass, also wore black gloves with spikes protruding from each knuckle, plus black leather boots with silver studs and gangly spikes.

Beside him at center stage was Kiss's primary front man who painted a single black star and bright red lipstick over his otherwise white painted face. With mounds of curly, shoulder-length black hair, an open-chested (to his navel) black jumpsuit, and a red rose tattoo on one bicep, Paul Stanley pushed his sex-appeal for all it was worth. He even wore a black feather boa around his neck while dancing across the stage in silver platform boots.

The third band member, Ace Frehley, dressed like an alien, complete with silver makeup, silver lightning bolts emblazoning his black spandex jumpsuit, silver rings around each shoulder, and black circles dotting his silver platform boots.

Finally, all that could be seen of Peter Criss, the drummer, was his makeup, which cast him in the role of a cunning alley cat.

To witness this spectacle may surpass any other form of entertainment on the planet. Flash pots erupted at random ... fans chanted every song in unison with the band ... Gene Simmons spewed blood from his mouth and spit fire ... crushing power chords reverberated through our chest, then rumbled through our stomachs ... an elevated drum kit was lifted by mechanical risers ... a smoking guitar levitated toward the rafters after shooting fireballs across the stage — hydraulic cherry pickers transported each band member over the audience ... more flash pots and pyromania, smoke bellowing from the floor ... flame throwers - explosions, flashing multi-colored lights, falling confetti, smashed guitars ...

By concert's end, my body had surrendered itself to sensory overload ... throbbing, shattered ear drums, blinded eyes, racing heart, and shaky knees. But do you know what? Japhy was right when describing the rock n' roll experience. During this show, I became so engrossed in the music, theatrics, and outlandish props, that for two hours nothing existed except the four men on stage. To accomplish such a feat, especially with all that had been worrying me in recent days, was miraculous. Rather than sitting home alone, consumed by thought, I was LIVING, rockin' n' rolling, soaring into orbit while catching glimpses of pure, unadulterated excitement! Mirror Image was an exciting band, but Kiss will reign supreme as the greatest show on earth. I looked to my side and saw Ukiah, certain he felt the same way.

19

If the concept of work could be eliminated, I'm sure my outlook would improve drastically. Forty hours a week was intolerable, especially toward late afternoon. The minutes passed slower than hours, the hours moving nowhere as if they were forever. And due to my loss of seniority, I didn't even have a vacation day until the following year. Passing time assumed the utmost importance. To alleviate this boredom, I frequently found myself slipping into No-Sho The Hero's fantasyland.

On this particular day, I gazed into my computer screen to see myself as a wind-up doll, the type with no clothes and smooth, nonexistent features. With a metal crank in my back that was turned by an unseen hand, I stumbled robotically through nightmarish lands of surreal terror. Schoolchildren pulled my matted blonde hair, policemen jabbed needles into my plastic feet, while Pus fried me over a skillet of sizzling piss. The abuse reached unendurable heights when a posse of computer terminals brandishing silver handcuffs strapped me to a guillotine. While the silver blade reflected slivers of light above my neck, the computer terminals flashed a collective message across their screens: "CHOP IT OFF."

The situation seemed hopeless until I looked to the sky and saw No-Sho's flowered cape flapping in the wind. As usual, he once again came to save the day.

Sensing my imminent rescue, the computer terminals reiterated their message: "CHOP IT OFF."

As No-Sho landed before me, I peered up to thank him when ... No, it couldn't be. Dressed in No-Sho's costume was none other than my dead neighbor, Woody Dewar!

"What are you doing here?" I pleaded. "Where's the real No-Sho?"

"He's sick with whooping cough, plus is suffering from depression associated with his bipolar condition."

"No-Sho's never been sick a day in his life. What did you do to him?"

CHOP IT OFF.

"How did you get in my daydream?" I demanded, still strapped to the guillotine.

"You didn't think a simple murder would get rid of me, did you?" Woody chortled in an annoying voice. He then pulled a wooden stick from his pocket and walked toward me. "Stick your tongue out and say Ahhh, little doll baby. I want to check your tonsils for choleric spores."

CHOP IT OFF.

"Get away from me, you asshole."

"Now, Chris. Is that any way to talk to your hero?"

"You're not my hero, you imbecile. I want the real No-Sho."

"I'm the only one who can save you from the guillotine. Now c'mon, tell me how much you've missed me.

"I wish you were still dead. Get out of my mind."

"Those computers plan on dropping the blade any second now. Just gimme a little kiss, then I'll free you."

"Go to hell! I'd never kiss you, Dewar."

Woody loomed above me, then gloated, "Now, Chris, what would you rather do? Stay mad at me, or die when they drop that blade?"

CHOP IT OFF.

"I'd rather die! Get out of my mind. Won't you ever leave me alone?"

"Here it comes, Chris. Quick! Give me your hand," Woody screeched.

"No. Leave me alone."

"It's going to chop your head off ..."

"Chris ... Chris. Get with it," my boss growled. "You haven't entered a shred of data for the last ten minutes. Get with the program, or you'll be daydreaming in the unemployment line."

Damn. Even dead, Woody Dewar was still a thorn in my side.

As the day crawled to an end, I left work to wander the darkened city streets. Christmas passed without celebration, and other than a brief meal with my family, the season had been noneventful. Decorations were being removed from the buildings and trees, while snowplows cleared the streets. In all, winter had virtually ignored Latera Heights, much to my pleasure.

After entering the same ice cream parlor that I had visited weeks earlier with Ukiah, I passed a newspaper rack to read the following headline:

High School Teacher Dies In Automobile Accident

Overcome by dread, I scanned the adjoining article, my eyes glassy and unfocused.

> High School Science teacher Gideon Doublet died late last evening after his automobile careened over a mountainous stretch of road ....

Panicked by this information, I stumbled past the circular metal tables where I had eaten an ice cream cone the previous time. Confused, my initial suspicions were that Ukiah had been involved in this accident. I remembered Mister Doublet's terror when Ukiah and Tattoo Blue strapped him to the bed, then pierced his arm with a torture device. Worse, how would his students ever respect him after that humiliating episode in the cafeteria where they sprayed him with silly string and smeared his face with makeup? His final days had been marked. For the moment, I could only question Ukiah's involvement in this matter.

Still rattled by the stark black headline, I circled aimlessly through the ice cream parlor, passing a shelf of sleazy magazines, bumping into a postcard rack, ignoring rows of paperback novels and toiletries, then glancing at a stack of scandal sheets before returning to the dining area. The notion struck me as odd that an ice cream parlor, which supposedly catered to children, would supply, only feet away, rows of pornographic material.

Pondering this contradiction, I gazed sideways to notice a large photo of Philip Prince on the cover of *The New York Times Book Review*. Prince's face looked identical to when he appeared on a television news program following Ukiah's attack. With black-and-blue bruises, scratches, a bloody scar across his forehead, and a puffed, bloody lip, Prince glared from the periodical, his rodent-like eyes causing me to look away. Following the initial shock of this sight, I grabbed a copy of the book review, then walked toward a cash register. There, standing beside a counter stocked with cigars, chewing gum, and lottery tickets, I overheard two elderly women discussing a matter of great importance to me.

The first whispered, "Did you hear the latest scoop on that high school teacher's death?"

"No," her counterpart replied, a carton of Marlboros in one hand, a lit cigarette in the other.

"Well, Mabel told me at the beauty salon that there were no skid marks on that mountain road before he crashed through the guardrail."

"You're kidding," her friend gasped, ordering an ice cream cone after dousing her butt in an ashtray. "What does that mean?"

Resting a box of stool softeners and a tube of arthritis medicine on the counter, she replied in a scratchy voice. "The news isn't saying so, but being there were no skid marks, the authorities think this accident may have been an autocide."

"How horrible ..."

Paying for *The New York Times Book Review*, I walked from the ice cream parlor, stunned by the news of this high school teacher's calamity, and the explanation presented by these senior citizens. Folding the newspaper beneath my arm, I whisked along the chilly streets, wondering if Gideon Doublet's life had plunged to such unbearable depths that he deliberately drove his automobile through those steel rails. Considering all that had happened in the past few weeks, the evidence pointed in that direction.

Welcoming the return to my Gemini, I slowly returned home after another trying day in the world. It would seem, after thirty years, I'd get used to life's traumas and trials, but in all honesty, it only got worse. I wanted to live in a cocoon ... distanced from everything except my safe, tiny universe.

Winter continued to blanket the landscape with its dark, depressing presence. Bitterly cold temperatures, frigid winds, a lack of sunlight, and ominous skies only made my return more urgent. As I stepped toward my front door, I once again saw a distinct movement inside Woody Dewar's abandoned house. Angered by his constant memory, I acted on impulse and sped toward his house. Hoping to solve this mystery, I inched toward the porch when a flicker of light glimmered from the kitchen window.

Holy shit! Woody rose from the dead! Damn, he's returned to seek vengeance on me! Get the hell out of there!

Paralyzed by fear, I tried to run when an unseen hand grabbed hold of my shoulder from behind.

Letting loose a shriek, I screamed, "I'm sorry. I didn't mean it."

"What didn't you mean, Chris?" a voice asked, the grip on my shoulder tightening.

I turned, dread-filled, to find Officer Idem standing behind me.

"What ... what are you ... you doing here?" I stuttered, obviously rattled.

"A more important question is, what are you doing here, Chris?" the policeman asked sternly.

"I saw, saw movement over here, so I figured ... well, why not ... check on, investigate ... see what's going ... who was over here."

Oh shit, I was blowing it. My guilt in Woody's murder was apparent. Damn. How did I get into this situation?

"Chris, what are you sorry about?" Idem asked menacingly, staring into my eyes.

Somewhat shielded by darkness, I instantly envisioned Ukiah, then said, "What are you talking about?"

"You said, 'I'm sorry. I didn't mean it.' Obviously you were referring to something," Idem growled.

What would Ukiah do?

"I thought you were a burglar. I must have been scared. I didn't want him killing me, so I apologized."

"That's it?"

"What else would I mean, Officer?"

"You seem suspicious, Edwards. Are you withholding evidence?"

Acting like Ukiah, I felt in control of the situation.

"Officer Idem, I'm surprised by your insinuation. I'm just a responsible citizen who fulfilled my civic duty by investigating a possible burglary."

"All right, Edwards. I'll be keeping an eye on you."

"Sir, I'd keep both of them open." Then, resentfully, I snapped, "Why are you here anyway, if you don't mind my asking?"

"Mister Dewar's family is troubled by the disappearance of his medical bag. Until it's found, they refuse to close the case."

"If I stumble on anything, I'll be sure to let you know," I assured him, my voice cracking again to raise his suspicion.

"Something's not right around here, and I'll get to the bottom of it," Idem finally snarled before leaving.

As he stomped toward his police cruiser behind Woody's house, I knew Idem would be trouble. If Ukiah or I made one false move, he'd nab us.

Strolling through my front yard, I remembered the last time I had spoken with Woody, prior to the night of his death. This occasion was the one he referred to when telling Ukiah I may have been responsible for spreading an illness to him.

Woody tapped at my door, then stood on the porch steps while we talked. I never welcomed him into my house.

Anyway, Dewar invited me to another movie, then winked his right eye and said softly, "Let's share our sicknesses together."

Alarmed by his double-entendre, I slammed the door without response.

Ever since moving into this idyllic neighborhood, Dewer had been, and continued to be, the bane of my existence. If only someone had killed him before me, none of these troubles would have arisen.

Finally safe inside my house, my sanctity was short-lived, for six rapid-fire gunshots, originating from Ukiah's cottage, shattered the silence.

Did Officer Idem question Ukiah, uncover our guilt, then try to arrest him? I knew he'd never surrender, or be taken alive. Had he killed Idem, or vise versa? Worse, what if both lay wounded, waiting to reload? I'd walk across the darkened lawn, then be riddled by bullets from both men. What in God's name was happening? Actual gunfire burst across my yard. First Ukiah brought a hooker to his cottage, then tortured a man. Now weapons were fired. What would I find at his house? A law officer's body filled with lead, blood gushing from his temples or chest? What if Ukiah was hurt? How would I endure such a tragedy? I couldn't watch my best friend's death. Why did he insist on making life such a perilous drama?

I ran beneath my maple tree, heart beating rapidly. Where was he? Nothing but silence blanketed the property. How could the grounds be so quiet when only moments earlier blasts of gunfire echoed through the darkness? Where was he?

I tapped lightly at Ukiah's door, then walked around his cottage.

"Ukiah," I said guardedly. "Ukiah. Where are you? Are you all right?"

Terrified that he may be lying dead or bloodied, I scrambled about the property until seeing him sitting beneath an oak tree in the woods.

"Ukiah!" I squealed. "What happened? Are you hurt? Who fired those shots?"

Choosing not to speak, Ukiah lifted a black revolver from the ground, then pointed it at his head. Before I could object, he squeezed the trigger, but luckily the cartridge had been emptied.

"What are you doing?" I demanded. "You could've killed yourself! The cops were just here snooping around Woody's house? What are you trying to do, get us arrested?"

Still silent, Ukiah handed me an envelope.

"What's this?" I asked, receiving the thin, folded letter.

"Read it," he sneered.

"Here? It's too dark. Let's go to your house."

After doing so, I examined the envelope's upper left hand corner to read a black-lettered return address bordered by blue lines:

The Mason Turner Agency.

Centered on the envelope's face was Ukiah's name.

Realizing he had gotten a response from his potential agent, I opened the envelope and unfolded the letter while Ukiah sat dejectedly on the floor, back against the wall.

> Dear Mister Rhymes:
>
> Thank you for your letters.
>
> Unfortunately, I must inform you that, due to my heavy workload and an obligation to current clients, I cannot take your material on for representation. I have noted from your many letters that you are an extremely prolific writer who seeks to leave his mark on the world. As such, I encourage you to submit your work to someone who can give it the attention and enthusiasm you feel it deserves.
>
> I wish you the best of luck with this and all your future endeavors.
>
> Sincerely yours,
>
> *Jennifer Ewen*

"I'm so sorry, Ukiah. I don't know what to say ..."

"I know what to say," Ukiah snarled, leaping to his feet. "Including my last letter, I've mailed that woman fifty-one pages of material, and she can only give me five sentences in return. I'll show her! I'm driving to New York City right now. I'll kill her. I'll bash her head across the desk, then rape her before I murder her. Where are my keys?"

"Wait, Ukiah. Hold on! You're not thinking rationally," I said forcefully. "Just settle down."

Ukiah scrambled frantically around his cottage, rummaging through his drawers and throwing things while searching for his keys.

"Where the fuck are they?" he demanded, his voice seething with rage.

"Listen," I interjected. "If you drive to New York City tonight, then try to kill Miss Ewen tomorrow, you're going to get arrested. Then what'll happen? They'll also pin Philip Prince's attack on you. You will have accomplished nothing but spending the rest of your life in prison."

Gathering his senses, Ukiah plopped on his bed, then moaned, "It'll never happen. I'll never get published."

"Yes you will," I said, sitting on a brown tattered recliner. "Instead of focusing on a single agent, why don't you start writing to other ones? Y'know that old saying - there's more than one fish in the sea."

Ukiah rested his head on a pillow, then lamented, "What do you know, Chris? Things are so easy for you."

"Easy? For me? You must be kidding."

"You've never had to struggle for anything. You lead a sheltered existence. To you, life is simple - something to float along without strife, challenge, or confrontation. But I've had to struggle for everything. Life has been a war for me. I've had to fight every inch of the way."

"But why, Ukiah? Why is life such a struggle? You do it to yourself."

"Can't you see? It's me versus them! Jennifer has teamed up with S.W.A.N., and now she's preventing my publication. If I rollover and play dead, they'll get complete control of The Word, then try to kill my Muse. That's why I've had to claw for everything. No one at S.W.A.N. will give me a helping hand. Those self-centered bastards only want one thing — their own preservation."

Ukiah rolled over on his mattress, put another pillow on his head, then returned to a seated position.

Clearly disturbed, he continued, "I'm sorry for lashing out at you, Chris. I didn't mean to attack you personally. I'm simply ... jealous I suppose."

"Jealous? Of me? That's ridiculous."

"Is it? Do you know how frustrating it is to be constantly denied? I've never succeeded at anything in my life. I've been a loser since day one."

"That's not true. What about your writing? That's something to be proud of — a true accomplishment."

"My writing is nothing but toilet paper until it's published. Nothing more. What's the use?"

"Don't get down on yourself ..."

"I know what it is. I haven't shown enough virtue or devotion. My Muse is telling me to purify myself. But I'm so worried about Jennifer that I've ignored her. Well, things will change. From now on, all my energies will be focused on entering the gates of publication."

"Ukiah, you might not be able to ignore the world, because we have trouble. Officer Idem investigated Woody's house again tonight."

"Why?" my counterpart asked, obviously disinterested.

"Dewar's family won't close the case until they find Woody's medicine bag. He never went anywhere without it, so they think it's suspicious that it wasn't found after his death. (Pause) I hate to ask, but do you still have it?"

"Huh?" Ukiah asked, eyes closed and head leaning backward.

"I'm serious! Do you still have that medicine bag?"

"Of course," he told me, pained in his expression.

"Maybe we should sneak into Dewar's house some night and hide it in a secluded location ... just visible enough to be seen by a snooping detective."

Ignoring me, Ukiah said vacantly, "I should make Romlocon more aware of my love for her. To battle S.W.A.N. and Philip Prince, I'll need every weapon at my disposal."

"Oh, speaking of Philip Prince," I interjected excitedly, "I picked up a copy of *The New York Times Book Review* with his photo on the cover. Have you seen it?"

"Yeah, I read that rag last night. What a load of shit."

"What did the article say?"

In a disgusted voice, Ukiah said apathetically. "How much bravery Prince showed in defending himself against my attack ... how superb he is as a writer, and the supernatural road to recovery he's following. He then started popping off about wanting to fight me — anytime, anywhere ... even saying he'd shove that hood up my ass. Why didn't I kill him when I had the chance?"

Hoping to steer Ukiah away from matters of violence, I asked, "Did you say you wrote another letter to Jennifer before getting the ... oops, I'm sorry."

"My rejection letter? Yeah, I wrote to her again."

"What did you say?"

"I began by wondering how the other half lived."

"How the other half lived?" I asked, puzzled.

"Here was my eighth letter to Jennifer, with my heart and visions bleeding on the page, and I didn't even know what she looked like. So I told her it would be nice to attach a face to the nameplate on her desk."

"I see."

"But next, I told her there were probably three possibilities regarding her status."

"You're really confusing me, Ukiah."

"Even though I know Jennifer's age, due to my research at the library, I said she could either be:

A) A twenty-seven year old Ivy League phenomenon who was intent on taking the world by storm;
B) A sixtyish socialite who'd been in the book business for ages; or,
C) Best of all, a classy divorcee in her forties who's not dating anyone.

I then said that if option C were the case, the next time I went to New York, I'd ask her out on a date."

"You propositioned a literary agent at The Mason Turner Ageny? Ukiah, are you out of your mind?"

"Not at all. I know New York is her stomping grounds, but I rolled through there enough times with Japhy to show her how WE run around the city. We'd hit Times Square, then The Village, and eventually wander over to Saint Mark's Place. What a time we'd have!"

No wonder she finally decided to mail a rejection letter. I'm sure this woman, who earned six-figures a year, thought she was dealing with a stalker, or a psychopath. Jennifer probably told her receptionist - "if a Mister Ukiah Rhymes enters the lobby, call security. He's a homicidal maniac." Naturally, I kept these theories to myself in fear of triggering another reaction in Ukiah.

"We'd have a blast on our date, eating at little restaurants, then bouncing in and out of the local shops. But the only problem is, I don't know a thing about Jennifer. I never even played the Latera angle with her in my letters. Being that we've both spent time here, it might have been helpful."

"She could be happily married with ten children for all you know," I joked.

"You're right," Ukiah smiled. "Ideally, I could do more research and find out, but it's more intriguing this way. Staying in the dark, though, does present a major problem. I don't know where her head is, but I sure as hell know where mine is! And, by trying to penetrate her walls with these letters, I'm like a race car driver who's in second place with ten laps to go. He knows the leader can be passed; it's simply a matter of finding the right line. So he follows the front-runner through each turn, jockeying for position while trying new tactics and techniques until finally, when the time is right and a small hole opens, he seizes the moment and enters victory lane." Ukiah paused for a minute while looking out the window, then said, "Speaking of racing, let's go to the arcade downtown and play a video game called 'Daytona U.S.A.'. Japhy and me play it every time he visits. I have to warn you, though, I'm unbeatable at this game, so watch out. You don't stand a chance."

"Okay," I said meekly, not telling him that I was a whiz at video games as a youngster. I figured that by playing it cool, I'd have a better chance to surprise Ukiah.

"Let's go. I'm ready to kick some ass," he bragged.

Once inside his Celebrity, I asked, "What else did you say to Miss Ewen?"

Flicking on his lights as we pulled from the driveway, Ukiah began, "I asked - WHAT ARE YOU AFRAID OF? Why are you so hesitant? I know she's busy, and has to deal with established authors, but couldn't Jennifer tell from these letters that I'm not a schmuck with nothing to offer? I don't know much about her world, but she should have a clear picture of mine by this time. And y'know what? I never bullshited her."

"Do you think Miss Ewen thought she was dealing with something special?" I inquired.

"Who knows? I gave Jennifer a once in a lifetime opportunity. Why did she keep playing the delay game?"

"Maybe she couldn't figure you out," I said as Ukiah drove through town. "You are quite enigmatic at times. Maybe she couldn't see through your veils?"

"What are you saying? That Jenny couldn't put her finger on me? That's bullshit. She might not have believed everything I wrote, but my arguments were legitimate. I went for broke. That's my attitude toward life. I gotta do everything on a large scale. It has to be bigger and better, or not at all." As an aside, Ukiah drove past a darkened apartment building in the business district, commenting, "There's the whorehouse I went to last night."

Hurt by this remark, I thought about my appearance. If it were altered, and I made myself more attractive, would Ukiah pick me at a whorehouse? It would be so exciting to sneak in some evening, then be Ukiah's selection for the night. I'd lie on the mattress while he ...

He continued, obliviously. "I admitted to Jennifer that I was an extremist. From my earliest days, I can remember doing things in a big way, with no holding back. When-ever I was interested in something, I tackled it with full-bore intensity. I read about this balls to the wall attitude the other week in a book about Kiss. When buying it, I thought the book was about their wild lifestyle and road antics. But instead it was about their business affairs. So, I got a first hand account of their marketing ploys, financial troubles, logistics, and legal entanglements. This book wouldn't make me CEO of Pepsi, but it did confirm my theories on how to get famous and not settle for second best."

"In other words ..."

"To enter the annals of history, we have to become larger than life. That means turning the volume past ten, revving the engine until it redlines, and climbing to the top of every tree. I know we can do it!"

"What do you plan on doing?" I asked.

Before Ukiah could answer, an important thought entered my mind that I had forgotten about earlier.

"Ukiah, did you hear about Mister Doublet's death?"

"Sure. What do you think happens when we're not together? That I sleep under a rock?"

"No, but ... but what about the suicide angle?"

"Suicide?" he asked, lowering the radio's volume.

"You didn't hear? The authorities didn't release these details, but there weren't any skid marks on the road before Doublet slammed through the guard rails."

"Autocide. How did you hear?"

"Two old ladies were talking about it at the ice cream shop."

As Ukiah flipped through the dial, this news blurb echoed from his radio:

> Authorities are now questioning the accidental nature of high school teacher Gideon Doublet's death. Although more details are pending, his mother did show law enforcement officials a final note written by her son, with whom she lived. On a lighter note ...

Ukiah turned off the radio, then howled with laughter. "That little pussy still lived with his mother! What a riot."

Terrified by this news, I yelled to Ukiah, "I think you're missing the point. This is serious. What if that note ..."

I then bit my tongue, remembering that Ukiah didn't know about me standing outside his window while he tortured Mister Doublet.

"What if ... what, Chris? Why would we be in trouble?" he asked suspiciously.

"Oh. Well ... I just thought that um ... maybe if they found your letter to him ... somehow ... possibly ... they could implicate you."

"Don't be absurd," he said flippantly.

Even though Ukiah made light of this fact, I could tell he had already pondered a thousand scenarios in his mind. He didn't survive this many years on the street without being crafty.

It seemed like I was getting used to changing the subject these days. So, hoping to cover my knowledge of Doublet's torture, I said, "You were telling me about your Grand Plan."

Rather than driving directly to the video arcade, Ukiah meandered aimlessly through the streets.

"First, after *Blank Line's* publication, I want to put out eighteen more books in six years. We'll print 100,000 each, then distribute them according to regional calculations and promotional tours. They'll have the same print style, font, and cover design, with one exception. Each book will be slightly different in color, varying along shades of the spectrum." Ukiah veered into an alleyway, then concluded bitterly. "I wrote a lot more to Jennifer. But now, who cares? She thinks I'm a dreamer. The whole process seems pointless."

Ukiah drove into a municipal parking lot, grabbed a ticket from its mechanical dispenser, then found an open space.

"C'mon, let's do some racing," he cheerfully declared, excited by the prospect.

I followed Ukiah, finding it incredible how rapidly he breezed through situations. Initially, as the night began, I found him firing a pistol in the woods, then plunging into his deepest depression to date. He next threatened to kill the agent who rejected him, dismissed Officer Idem's inquiries at Woody Dewar's house, ignored a suicide note that might implicate him in the torture of a high school teacher, seriously considered attacking Philip Prince, then tried to set up a blind date with an agent he'd been writing to for five months. In lieu of these crucial matters, Ukiah placed the most emphasis on, of all things, video racing. What was he thinking?

"Here we are," Ukiah panted with anticipation. "Daytona U.S.A. The greatest video game ever made."

We sat at separate consuls, inserted quarters into a slot, then waited for it to begin.

"Okay, the object of this game is to cross the finish line first," he laughed with self-assurance. "The gas pedal is to your right, brake on the left, and the shifter is on top. If you see me passing from behind, don't worry. It just means I've lapped you. Ready - set - go!"

Unfamiliar with the track's layout, I sputtered at first as Ukiah jumped to an early lead. Getting more comfortable, though, I quickly gained my bearings and started catching up. Alarmed, Ukiah's casual technique turned to one of intense concentration.

We battled lap after lap - banging into each other, swerving through turns, jockeying for position, and avoiding major collisions. I actually lead by the last lap, causing Ukiah to curse beneath his breath. After rolling through the first turn without incident, I sped along an extended straight stretch. All that separated me from victory was the final hairpin turn. An overpowering excitement coursed through my body - heart thumping, legs twitching, fingers executing a death-grip on the steering wheel.

"Just hold on. Don't make any mistakes," I told myself. If I won this race, it'd be the first time I ever did anything better than Ukiah.

"Don't blow it. Keep 'er steady."

I barreled along the straight stretch, eased into the turn gracefully, then stomped on the gas while eyeing the finish line. There it was. So close, I have it! It's mine. But ... at the last possible moment, Ukiah executed a perfect pass, flew past, and crossed the checkered line before me. He won.

Ukiah slumped with relief, then rose from his seat.

"C'mon, let's race again," I demanded, amped with adrenaline.

Appearing troubled, Ukiah replied, "Nah, I hurt my arm last week. It's still sore. I'm only running at twenty percent capacity. I can hardly even turn the steering wheel."

"What? You never mentioned your arm before. Let's race again," I declared, not moving from my seat.

"Nah. I read a lot last night. My eyes are sore," he moaned. "It's hard to focus on the track. I could be declared legally blind."

"I thought you spent last night at a whorehouse," I quipped, not letting him off the hook.

"This was after the whorehouse," he said, turning toward the door.

Reluctantly, I followed Ukiah from the video arcade, deriving a moral victory if not an actual one.

Once we reached his Celebrity and hopped inside, Ukiah gunned the engine. Then, when turning the wheel, he groaned, "Oooooh yeah, that shoulder sure is sore. It's a wonder I could even finish one race. Miraculous."

I knew Ukiah was snowing me, but considering his earlier rejection, I let him slide.

Instead, I asked, "What else did you say to Jennifer in that last letter? It's not like you to stop in mid-stream."

Ukiah paid a portly parking attendant, then said, "Let's see. What was I talking about? Oh yeah, the most important part of a star's mystique is the element of mystery. So, after my initial press conference where it would be announced that I finalized the largest signing bonus in literary history, I'd disappear for a while."

"What do you expect to gain from this press conference?"

"First, the media will go WILD over my outrageous claims. They may not believe me, but I'll sure as hell catch their attention! And, by not being available after this choreographed affair, a feeding frenzy will ensue among the various media outlets to reveal my identity. Every reporter will clamor to be the one who cracks the case by making an important disclosure to the public. But, being that I'm unpublished and unknown, they won't have any clues to follow. Of course, I'll be pulling strings from behind the scene by throwing a few bones to the dogs while I'm away from their prying eyes. Remember, Chris, nothing sells like MYSTERY! People are starved for what they don't know. So, periodically we'll push the human-interest angle by leaking a few details. The public and media will all be wondering, 'Who is this guy, and where did he come from?' I can see the headlines splashed across *The New York Times Book Review* and *The National Enquirer*! All this hoopla leads to our primary objective - we need to get both the highbrow press and the tabloid rags on our scent. This way, we can overcome one of the fundamental problems facing the publishing industry. Right now there's a division between the intellectuals - those who read serious literature, and the commoner - those who read romance novels or mass market thrillers. But by creating excitement for EVERYONE, we'll be ahead of the game with a united audience rather than a fractured one. So, we can't alienate anyone. Instead, our marketing plan should include every person in the country."

By this point, Ukiah had cruised a number of streets and alleys.

"Do you wanna keep going?" he asked.

"Where?" I replied.

"Wherever. We'll just keep going."

"Sure."

Overjoyed, Ukiah drove his Celebrity toward the city limits.

"Finally, after whetting the public's appetite, we'll give an interview to one of the network news magazines. By doing so, we'll show the public this coolness I talked about earlier. There are so many elements to this plan - airing date, lighting, advertising, question content - that I couldn't possibly mention them all. The most important thing, though, is to stay anonymous for two, maybe three weeks. That way our product will have already been introduced into each market. As a result, the public's pump will have been adequately primed. Plus, a dash of notoriety wouldn't hurt either."

Amazed by Ukiah's mind, I said, "You have it all figured out, don't you?"

Not listening, he rambled on, "Once a mystique has been created, the next stop involves barnstorming the country to make sure the books keep selling. In three and a half years, I'm going to hit 2,000 cities from Bangor, Maine to Baja, California. Along the way, I'll give interviews and make myself available to every television station, newspaper, fanzine, art publication, and whoever else wants a piece of me. Plus, I'll also go to the larger markets and be on programs like *The Tonight Show*."

"How many times do you plan on criss-crossing the country?" I asked as we passed an unlit dairy farm.

"I figure after three marathon tours, we should be able to blanket it. Try to imagine the questions they'll ask as new books are published every three or four months. It's mind-boggling! We'll also get scores of coverage from the national magazines, even letting a few of them tag along."

"What kind of magazines?"

"*Vanity Fair* and *Rolling Stone* like this type of article. Another possibility would be an article for *Sports Illustrated.*

"I don't think literature and sports go together."

"Believe me, the two are related. I've written lots of sports-related material. The same can be said for movie magazines or literary digests. The point I'm trying to make is this. It's important that I make myself accessible to the media and the public by expanding every horizon and making our target audience all-inclusive."

"You're going to hit the road for three and a half years?" I asked as we drove into nondescript areas of the countryside.

"At least. But there's also another part of the formula that's important - product marketing."

"What do you mean?"

"I want to make T-shirts and other paraphernalia. Chris, I don't simply wanna be a writer. I want to become a cultural icon. How many people wear T-shirts with author's faces on them? A few dead writers seem to have caught the public's imagination, but none of the living ones are popular. I'll change that by becoming someone that the common man can rally around. I want my face to be beside basketball players, movie actors, and even Madonna herself."

As Ukiah spoke, a compelling thought entered my mind. If he did become successful and entered the public consciousness, many would wonder what he did before hitting the big time. What did Ukiah Rhymes do before he was famous? Then it hit me. Sure, Ukiah showed signs of certifiable craziness - violent tendencies, misguided notions, and self-destructive behavior. But these conversations (or monologues) were him at his truest. Try to imagine someone's all-consuming obsession - those of mental patients, serial killers, or geniuses. Rarely, if ever, do we get to peek inside such minds. But here, seated beside me, was one of these individuals.

The more I pondered this phenomenon, the clearer Ukiah's picture became. Who else could he talk with about these dreams and ideas? Tattoo Blue? Hardly. How about someone at the library? They'd call him nuts in five minutes. I was the only one left. So, as Ukiah drove past unlit pastures, nothing existed except his words and the purr of his engine. Here we were - somewhere in rural America on a cold January evening ... winding blacktop highways — the car's heater emitting waves of warmth ... and Ukiah's voice - steady, strong, and direct.

"Finally, we need to find a famous writer to chronicle our odyssey. It should be something like Tom Wolfe's *Electric Kool-Aid Acid Test*, or the way Robert Frank did *Cocksucker Blues* for the Rolling Stones."

"Why do you want this to be part of the formula?" I asked, leaning back in my seat.

"So we can show the public what it was like to be on the bus with us."

"You told all this to Miss Ewen in your letter?"

"Yeah, and I'll bet she said, 'Does this jerk have any idea what the world is all about?'"

"Do you?"

"I think so. I even told Jennifer I wouldn't do things with reckless abandon or a careless attitude. I've been preparing my entire life for the limelight."

"What do you mean?"

"The other night I watched a movie called *The Mechanic*. Charles Bronson played a hit man whose father was as a judge."

"A real judge?"

"No. He was the man who settled disputes between members of the mob. His word was law. So, Bronson learned everything from his father. He didn't act like a ticking time bomb. Instead, his decisions were well planned, with the consequences heavily weighed. It was due to this careful course of action that his peers held him in high esteem. I want the same respect showered on me. Chris, I want to change the world. My ideas are above and beyond ANYTHING being promoted in our society. I'm not content with being a mere author. I want to make an impact on history – both now and in the future."

Slowly rolling through the woods along a dirt road, I realized that Ukiah spent every moment thinking about how he could enter the gates of publication. His plans were so detailed that they became the most important thing in his life. All he wanted was to get published and live for eternity with his Muse. And y'know, the more I thought about it, the more I realized Ukiah was right. Try to imagine anything that is special in one's life. Was it easy to get, or did it take a huge amount of effort? Now picture something countless times more wonderful than what we have ever known. This is what Ukiah wanted.

"How are you going to do it?" I whispered, gazing from the window at bare trees and fallen limbs.

Bouncing over potholes along a country road, Ukiah told me, "Don't you know that ya get power in this world through behind the scenes manipulation? That's why I need Jennifer's help. Only by putting our heads together can we come up with a strategy that will push me to the forefront of popular culture. I made it perfectly clear that I wasn't afraid of what would devour me."

"You're not?"

"No! I want to meet the controllers and see how they wield their power. I want to feel the sensation, then exert some of my own. I guarantee the world will remember me, because I'll leave an indelible impression on it."

"I'm not trying to be critical, Ukiah, but your convictions probably scared that agent?"

"Maybe. But I'm not watering down my vision. If Jennifer can't stomach these rites of passage, why didn't she give my letters to someone at Mason Turner who was more receptive? I'll tell you why! Because they're all plotting against me. S.W.A.N. is trying to silence me, but I won't back down or change my ways. I'll come out swinging as I expose the hypocrisy and weakness that permeates every element of society. And trust me, no one will be spared." Ukiah actually screamed as he spoke these words. "Nothing on this earth is sacred. I'll fight the corrupt politicians, phony religious leaders, elitist professors, then expose the anemic, talentless art critics. I'll topple the whole fucking house of cards!"

Out of his mind with rage, Ukiah slammed both fists against the steering wheel.

While he stewed, I commented, "I hope you know that a lotta people won't be happy with your ideas."

"Fuck 'em," Ukiah sneered. "I'll tell 'em I know what makes the world go 'round - BULLSHIT. Without lies, fakery, and illusion, mankind would self-destruct. But I can't perpetuate this phony myth any more. I'll smash their system into a thousand pieces. That's why I'm the most dangerous man alive! The worst part is, Jennifer and S.W.A.N. know it. That's why they're trying to prevent my publication."

"You're still shooting for the top, huh?"

"The Mason Turner Agency doesn't care about money, and fame is nothing but a novelty to them. What fuels their fire is POWER. And by being in such a position, they see me as nothing more than something to toy with for amusement." He paused, then continued with burning intensity. "If you want to know the truth, that's good enough for now - at least until Jennifer meets me. Then she'll see I'm not a simpleton that can be brushed aside like a piece of shit."

"Are you going to keep writing to Miss Ewen, even after her rejection letter?"

"You're damn right! I even know what I'm going to say."

"You do?"

"I've been thinking about it ever since I got that damn rejection letter."
"What are you going to say?"

"My letter's gonna be brief, straight from the cuff, with no notes or safety net. First, I'll thank her for writing back, then say the obvious."

"That her response wasn't what you expected?"

"Exactly. Then I'll say I know how busy she is, but by ignoring me, she's showing a definite myopic tendency. But to redeem herself, all Jennifer has to do is schedule a fifteen-minute meeting with me. What could it hurt?"

"Nothing," I said energetically. "She wouldn't be disappointed."

"How could she be? I'm not giving up on her, Chris. But y'know what? I am going to follow your advice and try different ways to get published."

"I know what else you should do," I offered. "Ask Miss Ewen if she could give your name to another agent. I'm sure, after reading your letters, she has a good idea what you're trying to do."

"Are you crazy?" Ukiah snarled angrily. "Haven't you heard a word I've said for the past five months? Jenny won't help me get published. She's the enemy. Shit. I can write like a madman, but what good does it do if nobody reads me? I don't know a thing about their sick little world except this - not one of those assholes will lend me a hand. I realize Jennifer doesn't know me from Adam, and she has no obligation to do me any favors ..."

"But if she could find it in the kindness of her heart to throw you a bone," I said, "it'd be greatly appreciated."

"Let me know when you quit holding your breath," Ukiah growled with disgust.

"I'm serious. Miss Ewen must know hundreds of agents in New York. Why can't she send ONE SIMPLE NAME? Imagine what a great team you'd make if you found a hungry go-getter who's willing to take chances and have a blast. You'd be indebted to her forever."

"You still don't have a clue, Chris. Those people never show compassion. Jennifer's heart is made of stone, and her blood's colder than ice water. I know my words are strong, especially since I'm an unknown writer talking about a bigwig at a famous talent agency. But I'm also a realist. I know I'm dealing with prime timers, and that the odds of getting through their door are stacked against me."

"Why shouldn't she give you a shot?" I asked, pained that Ukiah kept beating his head against a wall.

"I'm like a kid standing outside the gates of an amusement park, and Jennifer's inside spinning on every ride. Why should she let me in? What can I offer her? My situation is like a sandlot ballplayer walking into Yankee Stadium and expecting to play with the pros. Why should they let me on their field ... the same field where the ghosts of Babe Ruth and Mickey Mantle still trot the base paths ... when I don't even have a number on my jersey?"

"Ukiah, why don't you bend a little to please them ..."

"Never!" he bellowed. "I'M THE REAL THING! I'd rather stay poor and unknown. I'll never sell-out. To enter the gates of publication, I have to be completely PURE! I won't be demeaned, or lessened. I'll make my mark, even if it means killing that woman. I'm going to shape the literary world into something other than the embarrassment that it currently is."

Exasperated, I pleaded, "Why are you so intent on changing the literary world and the human condition? Most people ignore the big picture and focus on their petty, insignificant problems. But not you. What's driving you?"

Somewhat calmer, Ukiah responded, "I have a soft spot in my heart for creators and lawbreakers. Neither accepts our condition as it is. In this sense, I consider myself an artistic outlaw. The world doesn't satisfy me. It's begging for attention. And when I hit it big, I'll start giving it the medicine it needs. The status quo isn't good enough any more. Mankind needs to advance beyond being a bastard stepchild that's been tormented for eternity. We need an artistic revolution to heal our wounds - one lead by a true visionary."

"Lemme guess who that is," I joked.

Laughing, Ukiah declared, "I know where mankind should be in the next millennium. That's the purpose of my Art. Money and fame are irrelevant. My Muse knows what is important and what Art should represent. She's who I'm trying to be like. Beyond that, nothing else matters. All I care about is creation."

Still confused, I blurted, "I don't understand your ideas about publication. In one sense, the gates of publication are an author's primary goal. But then, in the next breath, you criticize writers for being phonies. How do you differentiate one from the other?"

"Actually, Chris, when you're talking about writers, it all boils down to one simple question. Has an artist surrendered their life to their Muse in order to enter the gates of publication, or are they just doing it for material gain by bowing to their agents and publishers? Most of these authors have sold their soul to get published. But what did they get? Nothing. They've been bought and sold ... sucked in by a process they don't even understand. And I'll be honest, Chris, the temptation exists ... sometimes very strongly ... for me to do the same. All I'd have to do is sign on a dotted line and I'd see my name in print. But by doing so, I'd lose contact with my Muse and wallow in a pit of despair. So, no matter how crushed, defeated, or desperate I become, I'll stay true to Romlocon. Only through her do I have any chance of getting my books in print for the long run."

By this time, we emerged from a darkened forest to once again see Latera's lights.

Reinspired, Ukiah suggested, "Y'know what I feel like doing? Hitting the bypass and cranking this baby all the way!"

Naturally, I said, "I don't ... ... ," then waves of excitement flashed through my mind, canceling the initial reaction. "... I don't mind in the least. Yeah, let's do it."

"Let's do it?" Ukiah said questioningly. "All right, let's do it!"

Moments later he stormed toward the on-ramp, then drove his Celebrity onto the bypass. Slamming his foot to the floor, the automobile purred as it hit seventy, eighty, ninety, one-hundred ... one ten ... Ukiah buried his car at one twenty as glimpses of a slower moving world swirled past. Traffic signs, other vehicles, trees, dotted lines, and guardrails all looked different - less important - with less impact on my life. At one hundred twenty miles an hour, the mind becomes so in tune with an alternate universe that billboards or direction markers become meaninglessness. What really mattered were our own personal worlds. We were alive - life on the line - speeding ... seeing things in a different light ... flying ... close to death ... looking into lands unseen by most ... everything else moved too slowly ... lacking inspiration or excitement. It almost seemed dead, motionless, inert. We were on fire - the ones who burned and churned with wildness, denying an ancient world – then replacing it with novelty and newness - new views, new sights, new visions, and new perceptions. We were there!

As Ukiah returned to normal speed, I breathed deeply with satisfaction, then let loose an inspired whoop. Ukiah, on the other hand, smiled slyly, a look of contentment on his face. He no longer cared about inconsiderate agents, conspiratorial publishing houses, or power hungry elitists who twisted the knife after plunging it into his gut. He didn't even care about his narrow victory at the video racing game. Although he didn't show his displeasure, I knew deep down his slight victory ate away at him. The only emotions he felt now were those of complete release, and the subsequent relief that followed.

"Do you know that I've spent my entire life trying to recapture those days at Gramma Moo's farm?" he said as the speedometer's needle wavered at sixty.

"That explains the freeway ..."

"Those were the only moments of pure, unimpeded freedom I've ever felt. If I could only go back to those innocent days. The whole world was shut out back then ... nonexistent. Why can't I recapture those moments forever, not only for just a few fleeting seconds?"

Ukiah drove along the bypass toward home, asking, "What came over you tonight, Chris? I expected you to complain as usual when I stomped on the gas pedal."

"In all honesty, so did I. But lately, a change has washed-over me. Life is something to be lived, not ignored. I think you're starting to ..."

"What, Chris?" Ukiah asked. "I'm starting to what?"

"I just see so many differences in our lives."

I expected Ukiah to interject, but he remained silent, awaiting my explanation.

"I noticed that, without any baggage, you experience life to its fullest. But me, I've been so hindered by the past that I've been conditioned into submission. You were right, Ukiah ... right about our identities being defined and controlled. You never had family, neighborhood, church, or regular schoolmates to mold you into a proper little automaton. But I've been ruined by all the above and more. I was raised to be defeated, while you strive for absolute freedom."

Pleased, Ukiah asked, "Do you wanna hear a funny story about Japhy's upbringing?"

"Sure," I said as we pulled off the bypass.

"When I was still married, I drank and smoked like a demon. Japhy must have been three years old, and he'd always try to sneak drinks from my bottle of beer, or puff from a cigarette in the ashtray. One night a buddy of mine named Mack Keegan came over and Japhy tried to be a hot shot and drink from my bottle. But instead of telling him, 'No,' I said, 'Okay, kiddo, go grab a glass and you can party with the big boys.'

Excited, he came back with a brown plastic cup shaped like a football. I filled his container with beer, then told him, 'Drink up, boy!'

Japhy chugged that cup, asked for another, and gulped that one. After about four rounds of this game, he started to get woozy and turn green.

'C'mon,' I told him, 'Let's drink!'

But Japhy said he didn't feel good, then stumbled to bed where he got the spins. A few weeks later, the same thing happened, this time with cigarettes. Japhy tried to fish a butt from the ashtray when he thought I wasn't looking, so I told him 'Forget about them. I'll give you a real one.'

I told Japhy to put a cigarette in his mouth, then grabbed my lighter and lit it.

'Suck it in, boy,' I laughed. 'This is how we smoke.'

Japhy inhaled deeply, then coughed like crazy, his face red and eyes watering.

'Whatcha waitin' for, boy? C'mon, smoke up!'

Japhy coughed again, then doused his cigarette in the toilet. But I'll tell ya, to this day, he hasn't smoked or drank. Can you see the point I'm trying to make about a person's upbringing?"

"Kinda," I replied as we pulled into my driveway.

"Instead of trying to control a kid with negative responses and fear, let 'em be their own person. Most kids smoke and drink out of rebellion towards their parents - not because they like sucking smoke into their lungs or getting dizzy. Do you know how many lung cancer deaths and alcoholics are created for this very reason? Millions. So I figured with Japhy, if he wanted to do something that badly, I'd show him the realities of it. With the sneaky feeling removed, he saw that cigarettes and booze weren't all they're cracked-up to be."

"That's amazing," I replied.

"Well, I'm going to call it a night. Catch ya later."

As we stepped from the Celebrity and walked toward our separate residences, I pictured Ukiah as a child frolicking at his grandmother's farm - bright eyes flashing with delight, long hair circling the outline of his healthy face, rounded kissable cheeks, parted innocent lips, and a smooth ivory neck. It would have been great to be his father or mother. I would have given anything for the chance.

With these melancholic thoughts galloping through my mind, I stepped on my porch, unlocked the door, then swore I saw Woody Dewar's curtains moving as I entered my house.

20

Not already. Why now? It can't be 5:31. Didn't I just go to bed a few minutes ago? Whoever invented the alarm clock should have burning torches shoved through their eardrums. Why can't I stay in bed until the world stops turning? 5:32 - hurry, you'll be late.

Don't cry, honey. I know you'd like to, but we have to get up. Oh, Jenny, we didn't think life would be this way during our freshman year in college. You should sleep-in, be served breakfast in bed, then lounge until the maid rings a bell for lunch. Keep dreaming, little lady. Damn, it's still dark outside, and the air is so cold. 5:33.

C'mon, start moving honey - Mason Turner awaits. The floor is freezing. Now close your eyes - the bathroom light is too bright. First things first. Sit on the toilet, tinkle, then wipe three times - always forward. Toothpaste on our toothbrush. Bottom molars on the right side - one hundred brushes. Bottom molars on the left side - one hundred brushes. Upper right molars - one hundred brushes. Upper left molars - one hundred brushes. Front teeth, from right to left - two hundred brushes. Right side canines - one hundred sixty brushes. The right side is always first. Left side canines - one hundred sixty brushes. There - done. Spit three times in the sink.

Now the shower. Hot water first, then the cold. It's freezing. I wish I were still in bed. Okay, grab the soap. Lather your right arm first, then the left. Now your body - first the right breast, then the left. They feel so nice and soft ... tiny but inviting. Now the right leg, then the left. Oooh, now my little girlfriend. She's been lonely for much too long. Nobody is allowed to visit her except me. I wonder if an intruder will ever enter her again, or if my fingers will suffice for the rest of our life? At least she's pure, not an impure breeding ground for ...

Different soap for the face. First scrub our forehead - fifty circular clockwise motions. Never use a washcloth, they're a whorehouse for germs - the bacteria copulating and reproducing in that damp, squalid wasteland. Now the right side of your face - up and down twenty-five times. Rinse. The warm water does feel refreshing.

Wash your hair honey, keep going. If you stop now, we'll never make it to work. One palm full of shampoo. Put your hair under the shower's warm, invigorating water, then begin shampooing — fifty-five tiny circles. Gently massage your scalp. A quick rinse, then the conditioner. One squirt into the palm of our left hand, then lathered along the front of our head. Then one squirt to the right side - one squirt to the left. There, now we're ready to rinse. Where's our wide-toothed comb? There it is. First brush the right side, then the back, then the left side, finally the front.

Now again, our face – we can't let the conditioner's greasy residue mar our complexion. Thank goodness for makeup. Three cotton balls doused with green astringent cleanser. Brush the hair from your forehead, then twenty-five circular clockwise swipes with the cotton ball. One more thing to do. Grab the other bottle of clear astringent cleanser. Three more cotton balls. First the right side of our face - fifteen circular clockwise swipes.

I'm still so tired. At least the filth has been washed from our body. Turn off the water - right faucet first, then the left. Pull your hair into a ponytail, then squeeze the remaining droplets. I'm cold. Quick, grab the towel. Throw it over your head. I love these thick, cottony-towels - they smell so fresh and clean. I couldn't imagine reusing one of them after they've been dirtied. Nothing equals cleanliness. Fluff your hair, then dry your face. Now the right arm, then the left — across our chest, first the right breast, then the left. They're both cute ... cute but lonely. Down to our girlfriend. Don't let any moisture hide in there ... around the edges, then underneath. Next my right leg, then the left. Finally, our back. Now bow you head, wrap the towel around your hair, then flip it back.

Hang the towel from a silver hook, then sit on the commode. Pull two tissues from a floral container. Place one on the toilet paper roll (which should always unravel from the top), blow your nose with the other. Three forceful blows ... clean the right nostril, then the left. Discard that tissue, then retrieve the other to clean our ears. First the left one - six separate swipes through the lobe - then the right ear, six swipes with our pinkie inside the tissue.

Pull a moist towelette from its package, then thoroughly clean your bottom. I'm not sure if most people realize its seriousness, but the butt can be a very unsanitary region. Toss the stained towellette into the trash, wipe with a ball of toilet paper, then push the final drops of pee from Little Missy.

There we are honey, the mirror isn't foggy any more. Look at you. So gorgeous. Even with wet hair and glistening perspiration, you're still quite striking. It really is miraculous - fifty-four years old, and you could pass for thirty-five. The best part is, you've never been reduced to plastic surgery, nips, tucks, or facial reconstruction. Your beauty is natural ... so natural.

Oh no, why did you come back? Please go away ... Mommy, I can still see you in the mirror. Your face is mine. Your sickness is mine. I'll never forget the traumas you experienced during your short, troubled life.

"I can't leave the house, I'll puke. I feel the gags rising through my throat. I'll never make it to the bowling alley. Please don't force me ... I'll stay home. I'll be safe here."

The look of terror in your eyes is burned in my mind ... the same expression of fear that crosses my face every day before leaving this apartment.

"I'm going to lose control. Here it comes. I can't hold back the vomit. I'll puke on everything. People will see my craziness firsthand."

"Mommy, mommy! You'll be all right. I'll help you."

"Get away from her, Jenny," Poppa barked. "It's all in her head. There's nothing wrong with her. It's all an irrational fear. Now Sela, walk out that damn door."

"I can't ... I can't ... I'm going to vomit. Somebody help me."

Oh Momma. I'd never seen anyone look so terrified in my life ... eyes of utter fright ... trembling ... pure horror — body twitching, pupils darting traumatically.

"Mommy, let me make you feel better."

"Sela, get out of this house ... now."

"Please don't make me go. I can't."

The sight of her helplessness never left my consciousness ... mother started gagging uncontrollably, then vomited in the sink, spewing a chunky, light-brown liquid on the dishes, over the counter, and onto a circular throw-rug covering the floor.

"Mommy, mommy, are you going to die?"

"Quit bawling, Jenny," Poppa barked. "Get back in your bedroom," he directed, pointing his finger. "Sela," Daddy then continued. "What in God's name is wrong with you? Clean up that mess, then fix me a pot pie when you're finished."

I cried, Momma sobbed, and the entire world seemed hopelessly fractured. I later tiptoed into Momma's bedroom to find her sprawled on the mattress, head hanging over its edge. I could tell she'd been weeping for some time, as the whites of each eye were veinous red, while tear gullies marred the smoothness of her otherwise flawless cheeks.

"Mommy, what's wrong? Are you going to die?"

"I don't know, Sweety. I'm so sick," she wept, bottom lip quivering. "Oh dearest Jenny, I wish I never would have had you."

"Why, Mommy?" I cried, heartbroken. "Don't you love me?"

"Precious love, it's not that. I just hate to see you suffer through life ... like me."

"Maybe I won't, Mommy."

Rising weakly, then brushing my long brown hair, she cried, "Dearest love, can't you see? We're all trapped. Genetics is destiny."

Deeply affected, I whimpered, "What do you mean? Is that why Aunt Lana's in that ... that scary place with all the troubled people?"

"Regrettably my love, it is. For some reason, we've been cursed. I don't know what our ancestors did, or if we somehow brought this affliction on ourselves, but there's no escape. We're doomed. Sweetheart, I'll never leave this house again."

"Mommy, don't talk like that. I'll help you. We'll see a doctor."

"If only it were that simple, my darling. But in this house, we never talk about our problems. We don't expose our dirty laundry." Momma appeared pained beyond description, sobbing, "We're all haunted ... each and every one of us. Once we're put in these bodies, we can't escape."

Quit thinking about it, Jenny, you'll only make yourself sick. Now Sweety, get your act together. If you don't hurry, we'll be late for work. That old grouch Mister Turner won't be pleased with our tardiness.

What was I doing? Oh yeah, gargle with mouthwash. One medium-sized gulp, then gargle, swish it in your mouth. Tilt your head back - gargle -swish - tilt your head back - gargle - swish - six times ... there, now spit three times.

Time to get dressed ... but first, look at your full-length bedroom mirror. So slender, sweet darling ... hardly a curve, and definitely not an ounce of fat. You're perfect, my dear. But enough of that, get dressed. First your panties, right leg first, then the left. Now your stockings - right toes in the little hole, then roll it up. Now left toes in the little hole, then roll them up. Okay, then your little bra, both cups like tiny protective hands. Hurry, hurry, you're running out of time. Slip on our skirt, now the blouse ... bottom button - in the hole, out of the hole, now through the hole - next button - in the hole, out of the hole, now through the hole.

Sweet baby, you're running out of time. C'mon, hurry. Roll on deodorant - right pit first, lift up your arm, then your shirt, ten circles. Now the left - ten circles. Spray your hair with detangler - two squirts in front, two squirts on the right side, two squirts to the left side. Finally your hair brush - one stroke in front, two, three, four, five, six - now the right side - one stroke, two, three, four, five, six ... same for the left side - one swipe, two, three, four, five, six.

With that done, now your makeup. Into the bathroom, flick on the overhead light. Oh Sweety, if we had more time, we could look at ourself all day. So many women in their fifties are worried about wrinkles, bags, and sags. But Jenny, dear Jennifer, you're pretty enough to kiss.

Okay, first the foundation. One dollop of cream in my left hand, put it on with the right. Three circles for the forehead, four circular motions for the right side of my face, then one, two, three, four circles for the left. Eyeliner ... three swipes to the upper right lash, three swipes to the lower. Now a little rouge, two touches to the right cheekbone, two touches to the left cheekbone. Finally my lipstick ... turn it up a bit, bright cherry red — start at the right side on top - one full application, then back from the left. Now the bottom lip - start at the right side - one full application to the left, then return in the opposite direction. Kiss the tissue, honey - only one time.

All right little lady, you're almost ready. Turn on the alarm clock for tomorrow morning. Still set at 5:30. Pull out the button in back. Push it back in. Pull it back out. Push it back in. Now pull it out. The third time is always the charm ... now it's set. Oh, before you forget, write a note to check the alarm clock tonight. Where's my pen? Never use a pencil. Not permanent enough ... too erasable. Write another note to remind us of tonight's watering chores. Why are all my plants dying? I don't feel like stealing more of them from the greenhouse. Okay, staple the two notes together. Never use paper clips - not permanent enough ... can slip off.

All right ... the journey's last leg. There's my shoes, right where I put them last night in their correct location. Sit on the sofa - right shoe first, then the left shoe. Hurry honey, you can't be late for your meeting with Mason Turner. Here comes the nerves ... waves of sickness ... it's going to be hellatious ... to complete the picture, a dab of perfume - one squirt, two squirt, three ... now rub your wrists together six times ... should I wear baby powder today? What will I do when the sickness overpowers me? Oh God, I hate being cursed.

Wash your hands before leaving ... eradicate the filth. One scrub - rinse. Second scrub - rinse. Third scrub - rinse. Fourth scrub - rinse. Fifth scrub - rinse. Final scrub - rinse. Damn, the drain's clogged again. It must be backed-up from washing my hands two dozen times a day ... all that disgusting soap scum.

Oh sweety, I dread this meeting. We'd do anything to sneak out of it. Here it comes ... I feel it rising. I can't face them. What if I puke all over their conference room table? Please momma, I beg you, don't let your sickness visit me today ... ...

21

Days unceremoniously passed into weeks ... weeks of little or no contact with Ukiah or the peripheral madness of his world. Although this respite proved beneficial to my mental stability, I still fretted over the circumstances that drew us together. Had Ukiah been questioned by the authorities concerning Woody's death? Did the federal case involving Philip Prince move in a new direction? Worse, had Ukiah tipped our hat in his letters to Jennifer Ewen? I found it ludicrous that she hadn't linked Ukiah to this famous author. To compound matters, winter had finally arrived in Latera Heights, periodically dropping layers of snow across the county. Being that my footsteps were now detectable in the snow, I couldn't even sneak through Ukiah's backyard and eavesdrop on him.

My freedom from legal entanglements came to an end one Saturday morning when Officer Idem rapped at my door. The sight of him, toting a compact, rectangular cardboard box, sent shivers through my body. Considering the number of visits he paid me over the past few months, it was clear that I had been targeted as the prime suspect in Woody Dewar's murder. Pondering this delicate situation, I quickly assumed Ukiah's persona, then opened the door.

"Good day, sir. How can I help you?" I asked nonchalantly.

After stepping into my kitchen and stomping dirty snow on the carpet, Idem began rudely, "Edwards, if I decided to, I could arrest you on the spot. But ..."

"Arrest me, sir?" I asked, a lump in my throat.

"Don't play coy with me, freak. I'm onto your sick, twisted, perverted game. Do you want to come clean with me, or should I haul your demented ass downtown?"

Hardly expecting this type of interrogation, I stuttered, "I'll, I'll, I'll ... prefer ... here. I'll be ... what would you like to know, sir?" All attempts to keep cool vanished as Idem seized control.

"Edwards, could you tell me one more time what type of relationship you had with Woody Dewar?"

Idem stared at me intently, refusing to divert his burning gaze.

Frantic, I blurted, "I told you before, we didn't have one."

Grabbing a black pen and a palm-sized notebook from his breast pocket, Officer Idem scratched a quick note.

"Very well, Chris. Would you care to look at the contents of this box?"

"If need be," I said nervously, feeling ill.

Officer Idem squatted to his knees, opened the box's folded flaps, then pulled ... Oh God no! It was Woody's black medicine bag! How did he get that piece of evidence? Why was Ukiah setting me up? What was he thinking? The scam had ended. It was all over. Idem knew I was involved in Dewar's murder, and now was toying with me until I confessed.

Setting the black handled leather bag on my counter, Idem curled his upper lip and snapped, "Does this look familiar, Chris?"

Drawing on my innate survival instincts, I muttered, "Kind of."

"Kind of?" Idem barked. "Explain!"

"I ... I saw Woody carrying it to his car. That's all."

What happened to Ukiah? Maybe the cops arrested him while I was at work, confiscated the bag, and were now awaiting my confession.

"And, may I ask, are you familiar with this bag's contents?" Idem inquired, confident in his approach.

Trying to look innocent, I replied, "No, not at all."

Without saying another word, Idem unzipped the leather bag and removed its contents. The sight before my eyes was truly bizarre. Officer Idem initially pulled an enormous flesh-colored rubber dildo from the bag - set it on my counter - then continued to remove an array of sexually related paraphernalia - a battery-operated vibrating vagina, a set of ben-wah balls, an ejaculation pump, fur-lined handcuffs, lubricating grease, pornographic videos and magazines, another dildo (two-pronged, colored black), and a few other devices whose function I couldn't determine. In all, the collection looked like the inventory of a back alley porn shop, or the stash of a hard-core pervert.

Unable to respond, I stood speechless, gazing at this menagerie of gratification tools.

"Edwards, is there anything you'd like to say about these ... these things?" Idem growled, absent-mindedly snatching a dildo from the counter and stroking its shaft.

Realizing my freedom depended upon this response, I said softly, "I'm not sure how to answer, sir. It looks like Mister Dewar was a ... why candy-coat the situation? It looks like he was a sex-addict."

"A sex-addict!" Idem bellowed, massaging the dildo's head. "Don't snow me, freak! How were you involved with Dewar? Tell me." He inched closer, then panted, "Lay it on me, degenerate. Don't hold back."

Shaking with fear, I mumbled, "I wasn't involved with him. I told you."

Grabbing the hair-lined vagina from my counter and fingering its labia, Idem snapped, "Then how do you explain the photograph?"

"Photograph?" Oh God, is this a nightmare? It couldn't be. "What photograph?" I asked, petrified.

Idem, still preoccupied with the hand-held vagina, produced a white legal-sized envelope, then opened it to retrieve a blurred, instamatic picture of me! There I stood, partially naked from the waist, standing inside my bedroom. What was happening? The entire affair seemed unbelievable. I'd never been photographed nude in my life. Now a police officer pawed a half-clad picture of me.

"How do you explain this ... this abomination?" Idem sneered, waving the Polaroid before my eyes.

"I don't know what to say," I whimpered, cringing as I turned away.

Roaring, Idem demanded, "I want some answers, sicko. Were you making it with Woody Dewar?"

"No."

"Were you lovers?"

"No."

"How many times a week did you engage in sexual relations?"

"None."

"How many of these sex-toys did you two use on each other?"

"None."

"Then you did it without the use of marital aids?"

"No."

"Ah-ha! So you're admitting to being a deviant," Idem declared. "Spill it, Chris. Were you and Woody a couple? Were you kissy kissy close?"

"No."

"Is that why you killed him? Tell me. Did Dewar start withholding sexual favors from you, and in a moment of lustful frustration ..."

"No! No! It wasn't like that at all."

"Then you denied him sexually, and in a fit of terror murdered him ..."

Overwhelmed, I staggered to the living room, plopped on the sofa, then moaned, "I didn't kill him. Please understand."

"You're lying, Edwards," he barked, following me into the parlor.

"I am not."

"Then explain this," Idem snapped, yanking a folded piece of pink paper from the medicine bag while replacing the photo and other items.

"What is it?" I panted, head spinning from the dizzying implications of this surreal affair.

"As if you don't know," Idem laughed sarcastically. "First the sex tools, then an erotic photograph, and now ... the final piece to your sordid puzzle. An unsent love letter from Dewar to you. To YOU, Edwards. Now come clean. What was your involvement with Woody? Was he porking you?"

"No," I gasped, leaning my head against the sofa's arm.

"Then why would he write this steamy letter to you? To practice his penmanship? Spill it, Chris. You murdered Dewar, didn't you? Maybe you can cop a temporary insanity plea, or get a reduced sentence for killing him in a fit of passion."

Delirious with fright, I coughed meekly, "May I see that note?"

"Why? So you can relive those glorious days of love with your stud?" he sang in a girlish voice. "Oh Woody, smooch smooch, I want you. I need you. Here, you sickening freak."

Shaking like a Parkinson's patient, I grabbed the pink piece of paper, then unfolded it. The handwritten note began:

> Dear Chris,
>
> When seeing you, my heart flutters like a butterfly in flight. I long to ...

I erupted with burning rage, but not for the obvious reasons. The note's content disturbed me, that's a given, but it was the form that made my blood boil. Scrawled in black ink rather than being typed, the words before me were strewn with arrows, carets, scratched-out deletions, and circled words attached to squiggly lines. I instantly knew this chicken-scratch belonged to Ukiah. He wrote the note! Had I been nothing but a pawn in his twisted scheme? Or, was he actually a police informant, clandestinely arranging my arrest? Damn him!

"Edwards, have you finished your little love letter?" Idem asked impatiently, looming above me.

Rattled, yet strengthened by uncovering the author's true identity, I regained my composure to declare, "Officer, have you shown this note to Mister Dewar's family?"

"I'll ask the questions around here," he snapped bitterly. "But no, no we haven't. Nor have we revealed the medical bag's contents. They've already suffered enough."

Standing firmly while returning the letter, I began confidently, "Officer Idem, I'm not sure what kind of person you're dealing with in Woody Dewar, but I'll tell you one last time - I had nothing to do with his death. In addition, I never had personal contact with him except for passing hellos. From my perspective, it looks like this man had numerous problems, none the least being sexual addiction and misdirected affections. So, if you have any further questions, arrest me and we'll continue this interrogation downtown at the station. You have no evidence linking me to that pervert, so in my eyes, this matter has been resolved."

Trembling with anger, Idem pointedly said, "I'll decide when a matter is closed, not you." He then paused, red-faced, and concluded, "This investigation is currently closed ... for the time being. But I'll be watching you. Something doesn't add up in Dewar's death, and I'll get to the bottom of it."

Walking toward the kitchen door, I opened it and smiled, "Good day, sir."

After returning the medical bag to its cardboard box and stepping to the porch, Idem cursed, "Damn freak. Mark my words - I'll get you. You haven't heard the last of me."

No sooner had he pulled from the driveway - exhaust fumes dissipating in the wind - than I raced toward Ukiah's cottage. After only a few steps, though, a precautionary thought entered my mind. Turning around, I walked into my kitchen, pulled a paring knife from the plastic drying rack beside my sink, then slid it into the front hip pocket of my sweat pants as I followed my original route through the snow-covered yard. Within seconds I reached my boarder's front porch, rapping at his hollow, wooden door.

Moments later, a lump formed in my throat as the door slowly opened and reality struck. For the first time in my life, I was about to angrily confront Ukiah Rhymes.

Dressed in black jeans, black boots, and a green flannel shirt, Ukiah looked outside and declared cheerfully, "Chris! Long time, no see. C'mon in."

Determined not to crumble, I hesitated by kicking the snow from my boots, then entered his house.

"How have ya been ...?"

"What's the big idea?" I demanded, fondling the knife in my pocket while glaring into his eyes. "Why are you trying to set me up?"

Unaffected, Ukiah stepped toward his stove where a frying pan filled with chopped ham, onions, peppers and cheese was cooking. Grabbing a plastic yellow spatula, he stirred the contents, then asked in an even voice, "Set you up?"

"Don't play stupid with me, Ukiah. You know what I mean. I could be in jail right now. Why didn't you tell me about Woody's medical bag?"

"Oh, that," he laughed. "I suppose those morons finally found it. Do you want a plate of food?"

"Don't change the subject! Why did you do it? Why didn't you tell me you returned the bag to Woody's house?"

Turning off his stove, Ukiah smiled, "Weren't you the one who told me life was for the living? You're the one who wants more excitement in life, so I obliged."

"By getting me arrested!"

"Chris, you're not behind bars. You're in my house. Now settle down. Here, take a seat. Have some brunch. You'll feel better."

"Don't patronize me," I said less forcefully, sitting at his bar. "If it weren't for some quick thinking, I'd be in jail right now."

"Aw, Chris, spare me the melodramatics," Ukiah retorted, scooping piles of ham and cheese onto a white plastic plate.

Still not satisfied, I snorted, "What's going through your mind? Do you want to spend the rest of your life in prison? Don't forget, you're still an accomplice in this matter. I can't ... I can't for the life of me understand why you'd replant evidence at a crime scene after it had already been removed. What motivated you?"

Placing the plate before me, then preparing one for himself, Ukiah began, "You told me the authorities wouldn't close this case until the medical bag was found. Being that I can't live with things hanging over my head, I alleviated the problem."

"What about the contents of that medical bag? Did it actually have all those ... atrocities?"

"Hell no," Ukiah chuckled. "The bag was originally filled with the usual things a hypochondriac would carry - a stethoscope, thermometer, bandages, pills, gauze, a blood pressure instrument ... you name it. But by filling it with sexually-related paraphernalia, don't you see the situation's charm?"

Beginning to eat, I said, "No."

"Start thinking," Ukiah told me. "Not only do the local city officials shy away from scandal ..."

"Why?" I interrupted.

"Why? Due to college enrollment. The University runs this town, you know that. This's why every rape, murder, or drunken rampage is swept under the carpet. If parents started seeing Latera Heights as an unsafe location, they'd send their kids to a different college."

"I see."

"That's why everything looks, at least on the surface, so squeaky-clean. It's all a facade. If you take this idea one step further, try to imagine the family's reaction when Idem told them Woody's medical bag had been found. This is the same one he took to their houses on Thanksgiving Day, or for their children's birthday parties. And what was inside this bag? Dildos, rubber pussies, pornographic videos, and hot love oil. It's a riot. Once they saw its contents, they'd drop the case quicker than ..."

"Now I get it," I hollered joyfully, inadvertently spitting a chunk of ham in the air. "But out of curiosity, where did you get those things? I didn't even know what half of them were for."

"Do you remember Mister Minella?"

"The newsstand owner?"

"Exactly. He also runs a porno shop on the side. Let's just say I supplemented his income one evening."

"How do you explain the photograph?" I then asked, once again becoming angered.

Ukiah found this question amusing, for he laughed, "I thought the situation needed a personal touch. You seem to forget, Chris, I'm an artist. I can't simply create generic situations, or let them be blasé. So, I visited Tattoo Blue one day and borrowed a telephoto lens camera. Y'see, he fences stolen goods at his pawnshop, so I had quite a wide selection. Then, I snuck into Woody's house and snapped a picture through your window when you came home from work. I could have shot it from my window, but the camera angle would have been wrong."

Finishing my meal, I said, "I didn't find the love letter entertaining in the least."

Sensing that I had finally settled down, Ukiah chuckled, "That love letter was a howl!"

"At least one of us thinks so," I smiled, unable to conceal my amusement. "What if I had blown it and confessed to Woody's murder?"

"I guess we wouldn't be sitting here together, would we?" he laughed.

I had hoped Ukiah's answer involved bail money or hiring a lawyer, but he didn't consider those options. Instead, he took my plate, put it in the sink under a trickle of water, then asked me a question.

"What're your plans today?"

I was (due to Woody interfering with my daydream by wearing No-Sho's costume) going to buy a ream of material to make a new cape to wear; but being embarrassed by these thoughts, simply said, "Nothing."

"Great. The Splycer Center is having a monster truck rally tonight. Japhy and Gina are driving down, and I bought an extra ticket for you."

"Monster Trucks?" I asked.

"Yeah, you'll love it. But now we have more pressing matters at hand."

"Like what?" I tentatively asked.

"Considering how well you bamboozled Officer Idem, I've been thinking about bringing you into the operation - on a part-time basis, of course."

"Me! In the ... I don't even know what to call it," I said, bubbling with excitement. "The Mob, or The Family."

"Don't get carried away, Chris. That's only on TV." Ukiah grabbed his car keys, then continued. "Seriously, that episode with Idem was a test. And I have to admit, you passed with flying colors. So, I'm going to need your help this afternoon when I track down a rummy that's been skipping on his debts to Tattoo Blue. Once in a while, I could use another hand, y'know."

Teeming with anticipation, I blurted, "Where are we going? Who is this person?"

"You'll find out. For the time being, why don't you hop in the Celebrity. I'll be out in a minute."

Letting my guard down, I rose from the bar stool to feel the paring knife slide through my hip pocket toward the floor. I'm not sure if the blade sliced a hole through the material, but before I could react, it bounced on the floor directly in front of Ukiah. A frozen moment of silence passed as the object glistened in the light.

Looking suspiciously at the black-handled knife, Ukiah asked, "What's this, Chris?"

"Oh, it's nothing," I replied, hurriedly retrieving the utensil.

"You're in the habit of carrying concealed knives in your sweat pants?"

"No, I just ..."

"You what, Chris?"

Intimidated, I blurted, "I just thought if you framed me with that medicine bag, I might need to defend myself. I'm sorry."

"That's interesting. Why don't you wait in the Celebrity. I'll be out shortly," Ukiah instructed me in an even voice.

I followed orders, sitting in the passenger seat while pondering this turn of events. Before seeing that knife, Ukiah thought I was worthy of becoming a member in his gang. Me! Chris Edwards. I'd never been a part of anything. I'd get to escort prostitutes, terrorize debtors, or transport drugs. Now, who knew what Ukiah would do? Only then did the truth hit me. All of these activities were illegal ... plainly illegal. If convicted, I'd get thrown in prison. How could I have been so happy? I actually agreed to become a criminal. What was I thinking? Breaking someone's kneecap because he owed money to a loan shark wasn't the same as daydreaming about No-Sho The Hero. This was the real thing! What's wrong with me? Get out now ... before it's too late, or you'll end up in prison. Get your act together.

"All right, here we go," Ukiah beamed, sitting in the driver's seat, then cranking his ignition.

Tell him. Don't be afraid. The rest of your life is at stake.

After shifting his Celebrity into reverse and turning on the radio, Ukiah said, "Well, I took your advice."

"Ukiah, I have to tell you something."

"In a minute," he told me, pulling from the driveway. "Aren't you going to ask what advice I took?"

"Okay, what advice?"

Proudly, he stated, "I wrote to a bunch of literary agents other than Jennifer Ewen."

"You did! Fantastic!" I said encouragingly as we neared the highway.

"Even better, I got a positive response from one of them."

"Ukiah! You do this every time!" I shrieked.

"What?" he replied blandly.

"You never tell me your good news. That should have been the first thing you said when I visited today."

"If I remember correctly, you were too worried about other matters."

"Well, you should have told me after our discussion. Anyway, congratulations! Fill me in on the details."

Before doing so, Ukiah turned up the radio's volume to hear Carly Simon singing, *You're So Vain*. Following that song, a radio promo announced, "And now, back to *The Shelly n' Michelle Show*."

> Shelly (perturbed): It looks like our intern, Dimwit Dan, didn't crawl outta bed for work again this morning.

> Michelle: This is the third day in a row. How should we deal with this problem?

> Shelly: Let's prank his mother!

> Michelle (excitedly): Perfect! Do you have her phone number?

> Shelly: Right here.

> Michelle: May I do the honors?

> Shelly: Naturally.

> Michelle: It's ringing. Okay, she's picking up. Mrs. Seuse.

> Voice (sleepily): Yes, this is her.

> Shelly: My name is Shelly, and I'm calling about one of your family members. Do you have a son named Dan?

> Mrs. Seuse (intently): Yes. What'd that little <<Bleep>> do this time?

> Michelle: Well, the matter at hand ...

Shelly: ... no pun intended.

Michelle: ... is rather delicate, but last night at a restaurant, we saw him sitting alone at a table masticating.

Mrs. Seuse: (shrieking): Doing what?

Shelly (seriously): Ma'am, he was masticating, right there in public.

Mrs. Seuse (screaming hysterically): Damn him! I caught him doing that last weekend in his bedroom. Won't he ever stop? Maybe I should take him to a psychiatrist. Wait till his father gets home. I'm sorry, I have to leave now. I'll get that lazy bum outta bed and cut-off his ... bzzzzzzzzz ....

Michelle (roaring with laughter): For those ... oh gosh, what a riot. For those listeners who don't know, masticate means "to eat."

"Those gals are wild," Ukiah howled, finding a considerable amount of hilarity in this routine.

"They are funny," I added, "but tell me. What did the agent say? No, first, what did you say in your letter?"

Cruising the Latera streets, Ukiah began, "The letter looked like a resume, with my name, address, and age on top, then ... let me remember ... okay, the first centered heading said: 'Aspiration.' I told them I wanted to become the most recognized author of the twenty-first century, on par with F. Scott Fitzgerald. Then I said I didn't want to just be a writer. My ambition was to transcend the field of literature by becoming larger than life ... a cultural icon."

"Hmmm, you used subtlety," I laughed.

"What else would you expect?" Ukiah grinned, joining in on the laughter. "I next told 'em about my fifty-seven pounds of material, and that I wasn't a wacko, dreamer, schemer, or con-artist. Instead, I'm a realist with unbelievable visions for the future. I listed those two sections under 'Works' and 'Disclaimer'."

"Then what?" I asked excitedly.

"Under the 'Motivation" section, I said I was tired of wallowing in poverty and anonymity. After working full-time and writing for the past fifteen years without trying to get published, I now wanted to succeed like no other person alive. The only problem was, even though I could write like a madman, I didn't know the first thing about getting published. So, this drawback explained the generic form letter with a resume appearance."

"Anything else?"

"I also included a 'Strategy" segment, then ended with my 'Recommendation,' which said that if any of these agents had a hunch about unpublished authors, let them revolve around me. I'm hungry, pissed-off, serious, and honest to a fault. I want to get rich, famous, and change the world so badly that it scares the hell out of me. All I need is someone to help me along the way. I finished by urging them to write back, promising they wouldn't be disappointed!"

On the edge of my seat, I blurted, "One of them responded? Who was it?"

"A woman named Marcy Hewer from ... shit, I can't even remember the name of her agency."

"What'd she say? C'mon, tell me."

"She returned my resume with a note scribbled along its bottom margin in blue ink telling me to send a query letter describing one - underlined - one project that I thought was salable."

"Fantastic! You're on your way, Ukiah. You're finally going to get published!"

"Not so fast, Chris. What are you so excited about?"

"What am I excited about? Are you kidding? You finally got your foot in the door. I told you to play the field. Why stick with just one agent?"

"Well, I'm not sticking with this one."

"What? Why not? What'd you do?" I begged.

"I wrote Marcy a letter this morning and declined her offer."

"Are you crazy? Why?"

"I couldn't follow her advice."

"Oh my God, are you nuts? What advice couldn't you follow?"

"The part about submitting a query letter regarding a project I found salable."

"I hope you didn't sound disrespectful."

"Chris, you don't understand. I don't have any aspirations to be a standard run of the mill ham n' egg writer. I want to be historic! This's why I can't think small, or jump through hoops."

Disappointed, I told him, "I hope you know you slit your own throat."

"That's a risk I'm willing to take. I've been planning my strategy for the past decade, and promised to do things my way, even if it meant wallowing in anonymity for awhile longer."

"Ukiah, most people would think you're arrogant beyond words."

"I could care less about that shit. I'm doing things according to my vision. If I stay true to my Muse and The Word, I can set the world on fire."

Frustrated as we meandered aimlessly through town, I replied, "I'll bet Miss Hewer always gets letters from writers who think they're hot shit."

"Yeah, it does seem to be an affliction among us. But believe me, I've differentiated myself from those other hacks. I have eighteen books under my wing, with my master-piece *Blank Line* in progress. How could I possibly send one sample, or a brief outline, that would be representative of the whole? I'm not looking to start small. I want to hit the big-time running, with both feet flying off the ground. What I need is an agent who thinks the same way. I'm one hundred percent certain my vision could make both of us rich and famous. But she, like every other agent, no longer believes in The Word. They think my assurances aren't enough. They want proof. Well, when I enter the gates of publication, my Muse will lead me - and all those who believe - without the need for examples or samples. Actually, I ended my letter on this note, saying we could be like everyone else in this business and follow the rules, or we could shoot for the stars. I'm a diamond in the rough that's waiting to be discovered! If only she'd hear my Word without needing query letters or samples, we could make it all the way."

Fearing he'd squandered an opportunity to get attention, I asked, "Did you mail that letter yet?"

"This morning," he replied, preoccupied by events on the street.

"I hate to say it, but I think you made a big mistake by not mailing your material to Miss Hewer."

Ignoring me, Ukiah said, "Do you know what really irks me? Look over there."

"Where?" I asked, scanning the street.

"Right there - that girl walking down the sidewalk wearing headphones."

"What's wrong with her? Don't you like her clothes?"

"No! She's wearing headphones in public."

"So?"

"Can't you see the irony? This woman is obliterating one of her primary senses -

hearing - by blocking the world with those headphones. Instead of absorbing the sounds around her, she's made herself deaf, deadening her brain with artificial noise. Rather than grooving to the world, her brain is bombarded by the shit coming through those headphones. It's like walking into an art museum wearing blinders. Can't you see how this woman's act is related to the world in general? We're all numbing ourselves - living in artificial worlds - with computers, videos, mood-altering drugs, television, and booze. Reality is being lost on the masses. We're all hiding in one form or another."

"You got all that from a girl walking down the street wearing headphones?" I laughed, amazed at Ukiah's perception of the world.

"Every second of life holds the potential for more writing material. Why should we deliberately block any of the sources?"

"Life revolves around creation, doesn't it?" I said affectionately. "I still don't think you should have ignored that agent."

As Ukiah reached the outskirts of town and approached a four-lane highway, he admitted, "If you want to know the truth, I could rant n' rave all day about my artistic vision, or how Jennifer Ewen and S.W.A.N. have blackballed me in the industry. But in all honesty, there's another reason why I blew off Marcy Hewer's request."

"There is?" I asked.

"Yeah. I've never written an outline in my life. Shit, I wouldn't know where to start. The thought of even choosing one book from fifty-seven pounds of material sent me into orbit. I know how to write. But when analytic descriptions or synopses enter the picture, I'm at a loss. Fuck, I blew it. I might not ever get another shot at getting an agent, especially with Jennifer plotting against me."

"Don't worry, Ukiah, there'll be others."

Uncharacteristically vulnerable, Ukiah said sadly, "Do you know how it feels to go through every second of existence thinking you're a failure ...?"

... As a matter of fact, I did, but kept silent. Ukiah didn't let down his guard very often.

"...I want to enter the gates of publication more than anything in life, but my writing is still too impure. I've finished over half of *Blank Line*, but my words still look dirty on the page."

"What do you mean?" I asked as we drove from the city past snowy farms and leafless trees.

"Last week Tom Wolfe published a new book – y'know, that guy who only wears fancy white suits. Anyway, it took him eleven years to write this piece of shit - eleven years to describe how pigs fuck, and twenty-page descriptions of hotel rooms. But authors like him get published without batting an eye because they live in the towers of privilege. He hobnobs with the literary elite, follows every grammatical rule, and is convinced he's worthy to enter the gates of publication. But in reality, those who set phony examples, or say that only the privileged are worthy of publication, are the same ones who've lost sight of The Word's purity."

As a shimmering noonday sun glistened off frozen lakes and sheets of virgin snow, I said, "You always speak of purity and The Word in the same breath. How are they related?"

"Try to picture the first man who ever grabbed a writing device and wrote a Word. I don't know what he scribbled, but imagine the purity of that Word. I mean, he didn't use a pencil or pen, more like a piece of chalk, or a stick of graphite, or even a colored rock. But the result of this act was absolute purity. He had been untouched by publishers, manipulative thoughts, fame, influence, or money. His Words were like my time at Gramma Moo's farm. I'd run, swim, and frolic with such joy that it seemed I was the only person on earth - a true Soloist. I was free, alone, alive, and filled with joy. But similar to my life, that man holding his piece of chalk found trouble after discovering The Word's purity. He would write and write, becoming more proficient at his craft, when BAM, all of a sudden an unseen force took control of his hand, wrapping itself serpentine-like around his writing implement. Now, instead of enjoying pure expression, devious thoughts entered his mind. 'Maybe I could earn a few pearls for this material, or get the attention of that purdy gal over yonder. Even better, that caveman in the valley has been bullying our tribe. I could write a nasty note on this rock calling him a sheep-fucker, then he'd be discredited by his people. Just think, I'd be known throughout the land ... keeping my memory alive for all time!' So, just like my Gramma's death and the end of my childhood, this conniving force that twisted around that man's hand also caused The Word's purity to be lost forever ... at least until our Muse returns The Word to man. This way, every person will have a chance to enter the gates of publication, not only the privileged few who guard this cherished realm as if it were their own. S.W.A.N. has taken over the role of that negative force leading the first writer away from purity."

"Wow," I said, amazed. "Where do you get these ideas? You boggle my mind."

"I'm not trying to sound like a hot shot, but I've been given the gift of perception."

"Perception?" I asked as the highway stretched endlessly.

"Yeah, I can read people's minds. I know what makes them tick. I can discern their motives, fears, and aims like I'd read a comic book."

"How can you do it?"

"How?" Ukiah laughed, tickled by the notion. "By being born completely human, with every human attribute imaginable - both positive and negative - especially negative. I'm petty, vindictive, selfish, jealous, proud, and greedy. I KNOW the way people think because I'm so fucking human. But ya see, I'll never find The Word, or purify myself like The First Author, if I keep chasing selfish goals. Instead of discovering the purity of expression, I'm more like a black cauldron. No matter how hard I try to clean it, the tar stays at its base, unwashable and out of reach. If only I could cleanse myself ... but to do so means I have to completely change myself. Chris, genetics is destiny, and to become pure, I need to get rid of every genetic disorder passed on from my father, his father, and every father before him. Eventually, if my aims are true, I could be like The First Author - a purified Solipsist of the highest degree."

"When you say solipsism, what exactly do you mean?" I asked, wondering where we were going.

Driving effortlessly at eighty miles an hour, Ukiah began, "Solipsism involves:

A) Purifying oneself;
B) Becoming one with your Muse;
C) Chronicling one's life in its entirety as if nothing else existed.

Once these goals have been accomplished, one can be a Soloist like The First Author." Ukiah paused momentarily, then continued, "Do you know who I can't quit thinking about?"

"Who?" I asked, filled with anticipation.

"That woman walking along the street wearing headphones."

"Are you still worried about her?"

"No. It's just that she looked like a woman I'm destined to marry if I get famous. Did you look at her face?"

"No," I said meekly, disappointed that I never noticed anything.

"She looked like someone I'm going to meet in the future — the most manipulative woman in history."

"Who?"

"She'll make every femme fatale before her pale in comparison. This woman will not only know what she wants, but exactly how to claw, kick, scratch, bite, and lie to get it. Then she'll set her sights on me ..."

"I can't imagine you having a girlfriend, or a wife for that matter. You seem so alone."

"Well, this lady'll eat me alive, steal my heart, then crush my spirit ... Oh no, FUCK!"

"What? What happened?" I squealed, filled with terror.

Ukiah punched his gas pedal, sped over a hill, then skidded to a halt along a dirt road.

"Quick! Change places with me. That cop zapped me with his radar gun. He has me. Hurry!"

"What should I do?" I shrieked, panicked.

"Don't ask questions. Just sit in the driver's seat."

Scatter-brained, I crawled over top Ukiah as he slid beneath me, then removed his black baseball cap and sunglasses, handing them to me.

"What should I do with these?" I asked.

"Put 'em on. What else?"

As I did so, a squad car, red and blue lights flashing, pulled directly behind our Celebrity.

"What should I do now?" I panted.

"Do you have a driver's license?"

"Of course. Right here in my jacket," I said, breathing deeply.

"Great. Just play it cool. We'll see if the cop cites you or not. Don't admit to anything."

"Cites me! You're the one who should be ticketed! What the .... I can't believe ... damn ... How'd I ..."

Unfrazzled, Ukiah said calmly, "Chris, the officer has just left his car and is walking toward us. Relax."

After unrolling my window, a bespectacled state policeman with a deeply pockmarked complexion stared at me with both intensity and curiosity. Was it Ukiah's ill-fitting ball cap that caught his attention, or the sunglasses that slid from my nose?

"License, registration, and proof of insurance, please," he said, frosty breath hanging about his face, eyes scanning my body.

After giving these articles to the patrolman, I sat quietly as he inspected them.

"Chris, which of these addresses is current - the one on your license or your registration?"

"Registration, sir," I said evenly.

"Do you know you have fifteen days to notify DMV after relocating?"

"I'm sorry, sir."

"Do you know why I pulled you over?" he asked sternly, still eyeing me suspiciously.

"No, sir. No I don't."

"You were operating this vehicle, weren't you?"

"Yes, sir."

"Chris," he began icily, "I clocked you doing seventy-two in a fifty-five mile an hour zone. Rather than ticketing you for that offense, though, I'll only give you a warning for not properly notifying the state as to your change of address. Do you know what I'm doing for you?"

"Yes, sir. I appreciate your kindness."

"Wait here. I'll return shortly."

As the officer left, I wiggled in my seat with excitement.

"I can't believe he let us off. How'd you know?" But before Ukiah could answer, I got mad again about being placed in this situation. Noticeably angered, I sneered, "Why'd I take the heat for you anyway? What do I have, 'Sucker' written across my forehead?

Softly, in a business-like tone, Ukiah explained, "Chris, you now belong to The Organization. That means making certain sacrifices for fellow members. Can't you see? The only people who know my address are you, Tattoo Blue, and the literary agents I've written to. I can't let the cops know where I live. I've been pulled over enough times to be arrested on sight, even if I did have a valid license. Now cool it, here he comes."

The officer promptly returned, handing me my papers.

After staring at my chest, he told me, "Being that you have a clean driving record, it's been noted that a written warning has been issued to the driver of this vehicle. One last question."

"Yes, sir," I squeaked.

"Where is the owner of this automobile?"

Unsure of a proper answer, I looked at Ukiah, then the officer.

"The owner?"

"Yes, a Miss Sheila Dualis of Splitting Lane. Where is she?"

Knowing that a correct answer would end this situation, I said calmly, "Sheila's currently incapacitated."

"Very well. Let's slow 'er down from now on."

"Thank you, sir," I replied, sighing with relief.

After pulling slowly back onto the highway, I turned to Ukiah, smiled with pride, then said, "How was that?"

Nodding his head, Ukiah replied, "Very evasive. I'm impressed. You've passed another test. If that cop woulda popped me ... well ... all I can say is ... it coulda got ugly, very ugly."

"How many times have you been pulled over in your life?" I asked, keeping the car at fifty-five miles an hour.

"I asked myself that same question back there, and the answer is an even dozen."

"Twelve times. I've never been cited in my life, not even a parking ticket. What did you do wrong?"

"Speeding, possession of alcohol while driving, speeding, failure to stop at a stop sign, speeding, an illegal U-turn and reckless driving, failure to stop at a stop sign, speeding, speeding, driving through a restricted access area, speeding, and finally, speeding."

"How many times did you get off?"

"Let's see. The first three offenses happened two months after I got my license, so I won't count them. Of the other nine infractions, I got two full tickets, both of them on the West Coast; two reduced citations, and nothing for five of them."

"Not too shabby. You should start slowing down, though," I suggested.

"Actually, being pulled over today was a blessing in disguise. Romlocon set it up."

"Romlocon! Your Muse?" I asked with disbelief.

Ignoring my reaction, Ukiah told me, "Yeah, she sent a message, reminding me that finding purity isn't a game, or a part-time hobby. It's serious. If I don't purify every part of my life, dire consequences will result in relation to my writing." Abruptly changing the subject, then, Ukiah pointed to his right, saying, "See that country market over there? Pull into the parking lot."

I did as he instructed, asking, "By the way, where are we going? We're in the middle of Hicksville."

"We need to see some rummy who works at a logging outfit down the road. We'll be there in a few minutes. Do you need anything?"

"I'll come inside and take a look. I don't get many chances to shop at these mom and pop operations."

Before I could step inside the market, a startling sight leaped at me from a coin-fed newspaper machine. The following headline was printed in bold black letters:

High School Teacher's
Suicide Note Released

Mister Gideon Doublet's death last month in a late-night automobile accident has officially been ruled a suicide. This ruling coincides with the release of a chilling death note written only hours before his car plunged through a set of guardrails lining a winding mountain pass. This note was found by the teacher's mother, with whom he lived.

Granting full permission for its release, Mrs. Gideon also issued a plea for any information regarding the tragic death of her son.

What follows is the full text of Mister Gideon's suicide note:

> You know who you are. You've destroyed me. You've stolen my self-respect and will to live. I'd confess your identity to the authorities, but such an act would only endanger my mother's life. You've ruined me. Why? For what? You are the most wicked person I've ever met. I hope your soul rots in Hell.

Anyone with information regarding this matter is urged to notify the Latera Heights Police Department.

Holy shit! After finishing the article - feeling both shocked and frozen - I looked up to see Ukiah walking from the market with his own copy of the newspaper. Exhaling frosty breathes of air that circled his head, Ukiah appeared shaken, as if the teacher's final words struck a tender nerve.

After sitting in the passenger seat, Ukiah spoke with deliberate slowness. "What does it matter any more? I can't purify myself. I'm the residue that lies at the bottom of a sludge pit. Get this fucking car on the road, Chris, we have things to do."

Still unaware that I saw him torturing Mister Doublet, I let the matter slide without further mention. By no means did I want to infuriate Ukiah, have him murder me, then bury my body in an abandoned coal shaft.

"Turn right at that wooden fence," he said curtly, burning with silent frustration. "Now pull to that log splitter behind the sign and stay put. Don't move this car. If you see a man running from me, stab him through the chest with your paring knife."

Before I could answer, Ukiah saw a one-handed man sitting atop a screeching log splitter. Leaping from his car, he sprinted through the snow, then yanked the man by his coat and pulled him from the device.

"Turn this fucker off, Charley," Ukiah yelled. "It's making too much noise. Good. I want you to hear my words. Can you hear me?"

"Yeah, Ukiah, loud and clear."

Although I could barely see either man behind the wooden sign, their words echoed through the crisp winter air.

"Charley, you've run on me three times. You know Tattoo Blue doesn't like waiting for his money. I'm not particularly fond of it either."

"I'm sorry, Ukiah, really."

"Sorry doesn't feed my fucking bulldog, does it? Are you gonna make me to do what I did last time?"

"No ... please, no, Ukiah. I need this hand to work ..."

"And to throw the dice too, huh, Charley."

"I've been on a losing streak. You understand."

"Do I?"

"My wife and kids have been sick, too."

"And lemme guess, your house burned down and the moon's falling from the sky."

"I'm serious, Ukiah. Things have been tough."

"I agree, Charley. Things have been tough for me, too. Y'see, when Blue wants his money, and I can't collect it, who looks bad?"

"You do."

"And guess who doesn't like looking bad, Charley."

"You, Ukiah."

"I'm glad we see eye to eye. Now let's cut the nonsense, you old rummy. Do I shove your other hand through that log splitter, or do you pay me some money?"

"Okay, okay. Here's fifty. It's all I've got. I swear."

"Fifty, Charley? You know we need a lot more money in the future. I can't keep driving into the middle of nowhere to track your sorry ass. To me, time isn't just a concept, it's a commodity ... as a matter of fact, my most valuable commodity. So, to fuck around with a measly-ass nobody like you is costing me money. Can you see my point?"

"Crystal clear, Ukiah."

"Good. Now hand me that hammer over there."

"The hammer? No ... please no."

"Okay, Charley, I'll let you go this time, only because I feel sorry for you. But don't mistake my kindness for softness, or for permission to keep screwing Tattoo Blue. Next time I have to track your ass, you won't have any hands. I'm trying to be a nice guy here, Charley. Don't make me do an about face."

"I'll start hittin' ya with money every Tuesday, you can count on it, Ukiah."

"Good man, Charley. I'll see you then."

"See you then. Stay warm."

Moments later, Ukiah returned to his Celebrity, sliding into the passenger seat. After blowing on his hands, he snapped, "Let's get the hell outta here."

While waiting for Ukiah that evening, I peeked through the curtains to see nothing but blustery gusts of snow swirling about the grounds. It felt good not being stuck in that mess. Winter was the worst of all seasons - bitter temperatures, treacherous roads, snowdrifts, and hypothermia. I remembered the terror-filled episodes of my youth - numbed fingers and toes, bruised elbows and forearms after sled-riding over The Camelhumps, falling through the ice while skating on a pond, or almost getting my eye jabbed out by a falling icicle. In regard to winter, I always thought bears had the right idea - hibernate for three months until spring arrives.

Ukiah burst into my kitchen, interrupting these troublesome memories.

"All right! Are you ready to see some stompin', chompin' and clawin'?" he perked, removing his boots. His attire consisted of simple black jeans and a white T-shirt.

"Sure," I smiled. "When are Japhy and Gina coming?"

"Soon. Japhy had to work one of his two jobs after school."

"He's in high school and has two jobs?"

"Yeah, he's a worker. He works as an apprentice accountant at some legal firm, then washes dishes at night."

"Plus he plays in a band ..."

"... and bowls in the bowling league once a week."

"He sure keeps busy."

"I'm glad. At least he's not getting drunk and doing drugs every night like I did. I'm pretty proud of him."

"You should be. In fact, I was proud of you today, too," I told Ukiah while walking into the living room, slightly embarrassed by my admission.

"Proud of me. For what?" he asked, following me.

"The way you were kind to Charley at the sawmill, letting him keep his dignity. I guess that traffic infraction and Romlocon's message about purity made an impact on you." I cringed as the above words slid from my lips, horrified that I referred to Ukiah's Muse the same way he did.

"You're right, but part of me still thinks I should have rammed his hand into that saw blade," Ukiah snarled, pacing about the parlor.

"Is that really how he lost his other hand?"

"Whatta you think?" Ukiah responded, looking out the living room window.

"I think you felt sorry for Charley because he was so far in debt."

Turning toward me as he knelt on a couch, Ukiah snapped, "Let's get one thing clear. The reason I feel sorry for Charley isn't because he's in debt, but that he's been conditioned to live that way."

"Conditioned to live beyond his means?" I asked. "I thought he was a gambling addict."

"He is, but why do so many of us accept living in debt as a natural part of life? I'll tell you why. Starting in adolescence, we're bombarded with images that tell us to buy buy buy at any cost. The process begins with cartoons, which are nothing more than non-stop commercials. Add neighborhood expectations, peer pressure, and The American Dream; and soon, by adulthood, we aren't defined by our honesty, how well we can paint, whether we can tell a story, or if we believe in a true Muse. No, we're identified by our job title, what kind of car we drive, the label on our jeans, and the size of our house. Yeah, we're told that education is the most important thing in life, but to enroll, what do we have to do?"

"Get a student loan?"

"And go into debt. Then, after graduating and landing a job, we have to buy a fancy car, a washing machine, then max out our credit cards. Women are even more suscep-tible than men. They judge us on our purchasing power rather than our fidelity or truthfulness. Everything else is secondary - even appearance - as long as we can pay the mortgage."

"I hate to admit it, but you're right, Ukiah," I said supportingly. "But is this why Charley owes Tattoo Blue so much money? When you called him a rummy, didn't that mean that he's an alcoholic?"

"You're fulla excuses for 'ol Charley. Maybe you should be his counselor."

"It was just ...."

"I don't buy these excuses for irresponsibility. If anyone had a drinking problem, it was me. You saw my sickness first-hand. I acted that way every day, even worse on weekends. I'd leave work on Friday afternoon, then instantly start drinking. I'd annihilate myself that night, then wake up dying Saturday morning. To ease the pain, I'd run to the store for more booze. I'd pound beer all day, pass out, then wake that evening for more of the same. By Sunday, I'd barely eaten, didn't shower, or even bothered to wipe my smelly ass. All I did was drink, puke, sleep, drink more, and gag."

"I never knew your problem was so bad."

Speaking solemnly, Ukiah began, "During that final year of boozing, I almost died three times."

"Three times! You should have quit after the first time."

"Nah, I'm too damn stubborn. I need to learn the hard way." Ukiah rose from his sofa, paced in a circle, then said, "I wonder what's taking Japhy and Gina so long? They should have been here half an hour ago." Ukiah looked through the curtains once more, then continued. "Yeah, I was scared shitless a couple times."

"Tell me about it," I said, squirming on the couch.

"The first time, I spent the night with a girl at her apartment. But before getting there, we stopped at a pizzeria and bought three cheesesteak strombolis. Those bastards must have weighed two pounds apiece - nothing but dough, cheese, and grease. We even called them heart attack food. Anyway, I'd been drinking all morning, afternoon and night while watching football, then ate two of these strombolis. Two of them! Well, after clogging my arteries, I slipped into a food coma and passed out with this girl in bed. Later during the night, I woke with excruciating chest pains, certain I was having a heart attack. I'm thirty years old and on the verge of death! So, I got outta bed and paced around, which seemed to help after awhile. But, what happened was this four pound stromboli lay like a bolder in my stomach, then lodged against my chest cavity, causing my heart to pump so fast that it finally quit working. I was lucky to survive."

"Holy shit! After something like that, I would have quit drinking instantly. What happened the second time?"

"I was with a different girl, and we went to an art museum one morning after a huge night of drinking. On the second floor, while she looked at paintings, I felt light-headed and couldn't breathe. Unable to stand, I had to sit down. A few moments later this lady turned to say something, but couldn't find me. She looked all over the museum, then found me slumped on a mahogany bench, clutching my heart. Alarmed by my frail appearance, we trudged from the museum, this girl helping me as we walked downtown. She wanted to call an ambulance, but we went to a bar instead. Once inside, I ordered a beer, gulped it, then sighed weakly, glad to still be alive."

"That girl must have thought you were insane, nearly collapsing from cardiac arrest, then racing to a bar for another drink." I shook my head, then said vacantly, "You must have been a wild one. What happened the third time?"

Without answering, Ukiah leaped from the sofa, exclaiming, "There they are, finally!"

He stormed into the kitchen, put on a pair of boots, turned on the light, then went outside.

I followed, hearing Ukiah bellow, "Damn! What happened?"

The entire front passenger side quarter-panel and light assembly on Japhy's van were demolished beyond repair.

"I was rolling through Union City," Japhy began, still rattled, "cruising along that straight-stretch by the old Double Dip Ice Cream joint, when all of a sudden a buck jumped onto the road and bam, I clipped him."

"What'd you do?" Ukiah immediately asked.

"Nothing. I didn't even have time to swerve. I just slammed on the brakes ..."

"What'd you do?" Ukiah asked Gina.

"I was sleeping when I heard the brakes squealing. I opened my eyes to see a deer about six inches from my face. I let out a scream ..."

"You shoulda heard her," Japhy laughed. "I think the deer was more scared than she was! But y'know what? It's a blessing that this van is flat-nosed instead of the kind with an actual hood. If it'd had an extended nose, I would have hit that buck straight on."

"Then it would have flipped over your hood, smashed the windshield, and Lord knows what else," Ukiah concluded. "You were lucky."

"Yeah, we were," Japhy said, shaking his head.

"I didn't like it at all," Gina added innocently, the little girl inside her momentarily emerging.

"C'mon, we better get going," Ukiah said, leading us toward his Celebrity.

Once situated (with Ukiah driving, me riding shotgun, and Japhy and Gina in the backseat), we fishtailed from my snow-covered driveway.

"Hey, Japhy," Ukiah yelled as we spun onto the highway, "since your van has seen better days, do you want the Celebrity?"

"Do you mean it, Dad?" he said excitedly. "I've been worried ever since I hit that damn deer."

"It's yours," Ukiah told him.

"What are you going to drive?" Japhy asked with concern.

"I'll use the van for awhile until ... well, until I find something else. Your car's registered to Sheila Dualis, but I'll take care of that."

"Thanks, Dad."

While zipping through a residential neighborhood, Ukiah turned on the radio, tapped his fingers on the steering wheel, then unexpectedly veered into an unplowed church parking lot.

"Whoo-hoo! Hang on," Ukiah hooted, slamming his gas pedal to the floor.

Without time to protest, I grabbed the dashboard as Ukiah sped forward, spiked his brakes, and turned his steering wheel violently to the right. Skidding uncontrollably toward a brick wall, Ukiah straightened his car, thrust his wheel again to the right, then spun two donuts only feet from the wall.

"Yow!" Japhy howled. "Do it again, Dad."

"Yeah, spin another one," Gina agreed.

Without further encouragement, Ukiah gunned his engine, roared toward a light pole, then cranked two more donuts.

After stopping, he panted, "Once, when I was a teenager, I stole a car and did the same thing in a church parking lot. I was flying through the snow, spinning donuts with this gal by my side, when I saw a man at the end of the lot. Geared with excitement, I raced toward him, cut the wheel, and skidded into another donut. After coming to a stop, the girl yelled, 'Whoa, get going! It's a priest running toward us swinging a cane!' It was a riot."

"Lemme try it, Dad," Japhy suggested, and within seconds he spun a series of donuts that almost equaled Ukiah's.

After he stopped, Japhy howled, "C'mon Gina, give 'er a try."

Just like that, Gina giggled and kicked her feet as she spun the Celebrity in circles around the snowy parking lot.

We laughed with glee as Gina brought the car to a halt, then hopped from the driver's seat as Ukiah was about to take over.

Disappointed that he hadn't asked me to spin a few donuts, I cleared my throat with noticeable disapproval.

"Oh, did you wanna give 'er a whirl?" Ukiah asked, stepping around the car and riding shotgun as I sat behind the wheel.

Pumped with adrenaline, I gunned the engine, pressed the gas pedal to the floor, then hung-on tightly as we raced toward the same brick wall Ukiah had avoided. The Celebrity roared as our speed increased — faster, faster ... I thought we were going to fly off the ground when I saw us nearing the wall with frightening momentum.

"Chris, hit the brakes!" Ukiah screeched, covering his head and ducking.

Holy shit! What am I going to do? Hit the brakes. Quick! We're going to crash, cut the wheel. Hurry! Pump the brakes. Oh no!

I swerved left to the best of my ability, but wasn't able to swing the Celebrity quickly enough. BAM, the car's rear bumper smacked against the brick wall, bringing us to an abrupt stop.

"Shit," I cursed, humiliated beyond words. "I'm sorry, Ukiah. I'll pay for the damages."

Laughing, Ukiah told me, "Don't worry about it. This car's built like a tank."

"Good driving, Chris," Japhy snickered with delight.

"Yeah, Chris, you drive just like Wendall Krause!" Gina shrieked joyously. "Maybe even worse, if that's possible."

"Here, Ukiah, you better do the driving. I never was very good behind the wheel."

"You did your best, Chris," Ukiah chuckled condescendingly. "That's all that can be expected."

We reached the Splycer Center only minutes before the Monster Truck Rally started. Ukiah hurriedly paid the parking fee to a bored looking attendant, then pulled into the lot. Without warning, he abruptly stopped, staring at a row of orange pylons.

"That's where I want to park," he pointed. "It's right next to the exit. We'll be the first ones to leave. I ain't waiting in no traffic jam."

"It's blocked by those pylons, though," I interrupted, stating the obvious.

"Not any more," he snarled.

With frenzied spontaneity, Ukiah dashed from the Celebrity and, in full view of the parking attendants, moved the pylons. He then returned to his car, shifted it into gear, and pulled into the spot he wanted.

"What're you doing?" I gasped. "You can't do that right in front of those attendants. I can't believe you just did that."

Ukiah smiled as he turned his key in the ignition, shutting off his car.

As we stepped outside, I shook my head with amazement. "What if the police tow your car, or put a ticket on the windshield? I can't believe you moved those pylons."

Meanwhile, Ukiah, Japhy, and Gina inspected the Celebrity's rear quarter panel and bumper.

"Well, son," Ukiah boomed in a fatherly voice, "you've only owned this car for ten minutes, and already it's dented!"

"Hey, Dad," Japhy replied, "you should let Chris join the demolition derby next winter."

"Why's that?"

"Because Chris and Wendell Krause'd demolish everything in sight!"

"Who needs to wait?" Ukiah answered, "Chris drives that video game – Daytona U.S.A. - the same way - ramming into every wall and car on the track. You should have seen how easily I won our last race. The next time, I'll wear a blindfold to make things more even."

All of us laughed good-naturedly - even me - the brunt of their jokes. But after slamming into that wall, I figured the jabs were well deserved.

We eventually took our seats in the arena, soon watching an array of larger-than-life exhibitions. First, go-carts sped around an obstacle course on the concrete floor, zipping like hornets in a flowerbed. Following them were a host of souped-up quad-runners squealing tires in every direction.

The feature attraction was the monster trucks, and soon they entered the arena to overwhelming rounds of applause. These behemoths were incredible, with oversized tires, fire-breathing exhaust pipes, kaleidoscope lights, and flashy paint jobs that displayed names like Predator, Metal Muncher, and Terrorizer.

These monsters leaped over ramps, crushed cars, and spun donuts on the cement with such ferociousness that the entire arena was filled with exhaust fumes, burnt rubber, and the sound of squealing tires. The audience leaped to their feet at these sights ... then I finally knew what turned Ukiah on. The three main variables were speed, volume, and destruction. In other words, he liked things fast, loud, and violent. These trucks were all three and more. They breathed fire, squealed tires, backfired, left heaps of twisted metal, and created an ungodly racket. At one point, amid much hoopla and fanfare, a scantily clad woman was shot from a cannon (with accompanying explosions and fireworks) across the arena into an awaiting net. The spectacle was amazing, and by night's end, all of us were thoroughly entertained.

Throngs of spectators filed from the Splycer Center into a chilly winter night, each of them scurrying toward their vehicles. But we didn't have to worry because our Celebrity was parked beside the restricted set of pylons. Amid mischievous laughter, we instantly left the lot without delay. I could tell that Ukiah got a huge amount of satisfaction from this tactic.

Once we hit the main highway and entered Latera Heights, Japhy and Gina asked for permission to run around before catching a taxi home. Naturally, Ukiah extended his blessing, dropping them at a video arcade. So, for the rest of our short trip home, I rode shotgun while Ukiah drove along the alleys and side streets.

While doing so, I inexplicably had a daydream about Ukiah crawling into an underground tunnel where he began mining, of all things, diamonds. The thought was ludicrous, but it wouldn't leave my mind. I saw Ukiah, with pick ax in hand, stumble toward an unmarred pool of diamonds. Struck by its magnificence, Ukiah dropped his ax and bent toward the diamonds. At first glance he became noticeably self-absorbed, staring at his reflection as if it were a mirror. Kneeling on all fours, Ukiah clung to the natural wonder, transfixed and motionless.

He then said, "Oh sparkling Wonder, you present the most perplexing reflection in creation. I am undeniably beautiful, but how long will it last? Who would have known I'd find you in such a way? I've been searching my entire life for you ... oh, how the blood courses through my veins, my heart doing somersaults in my chest. But my quest has been worthwhile. A lover whose beauty equals mine now stares back at me ... but please, why won't you speak? Tell me how much you love me."

Ukiah stared at the diamonds, his straggly blonde hair falling about his face. I could see his gruff face melt like wax from a candle, his entire being consumed by the fires of desire.

Ukiah continued, "I want to kiss you, but will you return my gesture? Please tell me. Your silence is infuriating. I've waited a lifetime to meet you, but what do I get in return? Silence! Why? Don't you love me? Haven't you waited for this day, too? Oh, what should I do? Kiss you?"

Ukiah leaned toward the glistening pool, then tried to kiss it. But with unexpected fury, a stalactite dropped from the ceiling, barely missing Ukiah's head. As it shattered his diamond looking glass into a million pieces ... Ukiah's reflection vanished ...

At this moment, as Ukiah drove without notice and I fantasized about his self-absorption, I wanted to become one with him more than at any other time in my life. I can't explain my motives ... I just wanted to be with him for eternity.

22

Regrettably, the preceding day's activities prevented me from telling Ukiah that I wanted to leave his illegal organization. So, as prearranged, I was to meet him at eight o'clock for another secretive mission. What did he have in mind - unloading drugs from the cargo bay of a plane, slicing an informant's tongue from his mouth after snitching to the cops, or laundering money from a gambling casino? Needless to say, none of these thoughts filled my morning with sunshine.

I'm not sure if living in No-Sho's fantasy land had insulated me from the realities of life. Maybe I just couldn't fathom the implications of a given situation. Yesterday alone, Officer Idem interrogated me, a state patrolman nearly ticketed me, a high school teacher (whose torture I witnessed) had his suicide note published in the newspaper, plus a federal investigation continued in Philip Prince's attack. How many other warning signs did I need? Without doubt, a prison sentence waited if I didn't change my life.

Chris, what are we thinking? Our affairs no longer revolve around a make-believe fantasy figure that wears a cape and saves the day. How will you react when handcuffs are shackled around your wrists? The bars in prison are made of iron - every cell crawling with cockroaches that breed inside the dank, cinder block walls. Try to imagine how those depraved inmates will treat you. Someone like you will be slaughtered. The defiled acts awaiting us are so grisly that to even think of them ... we'll be raped with broom handles, forced into orgies, bent over a commode, or laid spread eagle ...

Chris, do something - now! You know this life isn't suited for you, yet each day you fail to break free. These diversions will soon turn to perversions of the worst sort. Your quaint, secluded fantasy world will become one of screams, nocturnal terror, and sadistic wickedness.

Horrified, I burst from the door, vowing to change my life. Ukiah would no longer spin me like a helpless fly in his web. I'd take responsibility for my actions, following a virtuous path rather than a disgraceful one. Elated by this decision, I walked across the backyard to find Ukiah's van missing from his driveway. Alarmed, I rushed to his door, finding a message attached by a piece of gray duct tape:

Chris,

I left. I can't wait around to play your little games. Start being on time.

I instantly looked at my watch, which read 8:06. I was only six minutes late. What a jerk. But, when thinking about it, Ukiah was right about my tardiness. For years I tried to deny this problem, but finally realized my habitual lateness stemmed from a condition rooted in youth where my make-believe world took precedence over all else. I wanted to stay hidden so badly that I delayed leaving until the last possible moment ... so late that I never arrived on time. This practice extended to work (nearly causing me to be fired on several occasions), appointments, and probably even my own funeral. Ukiah finally got tired of this nonsense and left without me. For all I knew, my name was probably on a hit list for failing to meet my obligations.

Disappointed that I let Ukiah down, I returned to my house, hearing the phone ring once inside.

"Hello," I said tentatively, fearing someone named Guido wanted to know my where-abouts.

"Chris, this is your mother. I have terrible news."

Panicked, I gasped, "What happened?"

"Your father's in the hospital," Mom told me, her voice trembling.

Without answering, I pictured my father lying unconscious on a gurney, tubes attached to every part of his body. As I stood over him, the EKG beeped a few times, then flatlined until my father drew his last breath. For some reason, while thinking these thoughts, fireworks exploded inside my mind, followed by a parade where everyone smiled and clapped wildly. On closer inspection, I realized that each of these revelers was ME! I hopped about joyously in place, waved a pompom, lit sparklers, and banged a drum. A radiant sun burst from behind a cloudbank as flowers sprung from the ground. More fireworks exploded, the parade continued with cheerful activity, and everyone celebrated riotously.

"Chris ... Chris. Are you there?" my mother asked, breathing rapidly.

"Yes, Mom. I was simply shocked. Did Dad have a brain aneurysm or a stroke? Does he have cancer?"

"No, Chris, your father has an ingrown toenail that got infected."

"That's all?" I shrieked with disbelief.

"Is that all! Chris, ingrown toenails can be serious, even life-threatening. I think you should visit your father. It may be the last time you see him alive."

"Aw, Mom, you know I don't like ..."

"Chris, I want you there this morning. Your father's the one who brought you into this world. You should show him some respect."

Resigned, I moaned, "All right, Mom, I'll be there in a little while."

The thought of talking with my father filled me with dread, especially when he was in a hospital bed, complaining about his treatment. The notion sent me reeling with despair. I didn't want to see him in one of those light blue gowns, a name band snapped around his wrist and a progress chart hanging from the bed. I didn't even want to be with him in a more comfortable setting, like his own living room.

As I readied a few items around the house, thoughts from my youth re-entered my mind. I recalled a family camping trip when my father told me to find out what time church started Sunday morning. I wandered toward a bulletin board in the recreation building, looked at a confusing list of activities, then returned to tell my father. The next morning, the three of us walked to this building at the time I suggested, finding no sign of a congregation or mass. Rather, at 10:00 a.m., a beanbag contest was being held. My father damn near blew up. But before he could, one of the activity counselors finagled him, my mother, and me into joining a beanbag competition. The sight of my father wearing his Sunday best in the middle of a gnat-infested field on a humid Sunday morning - tossing beanbags all the while - was priceless. I could hear him swearing beneath his breath as he tossed each sack through the air, the goofy camp counselor, dressed as a clown, chiding him to try harder. I nearly cried with laughter as Bozo harangued him, then cried actual tears afterward as my father screamed at me.

"What am I, some kind of sideshow freak? Do I need to buy floppy feet and a rubber nose to get your attention? We should have been praying to the Lord. Instead, you made an ass of me. What should I do, squat down on all fours and bray like a donkey while taking a shit in a pile of straw? Would that make you happy? Someone needs to learn respect for their elders. You wanna make a fool o' me? Fine ..."

My father began a twenty-minute diatribe about my worthlessness. Although the above story may sound funny, to have this maniac screaming in my face was a daunting experience. My father actually SCREAMED at the top of his lungs at me on literally hundreds of occasions. What could I have done so wrong, a six or eight or ten year old child, to merit such outbursts? I mean, I never chopped off his foot with a hatchet, or threw our dog in a bonfire. Okay, I mistakenly read the incorrect time for Sunday mass. Did this oversight necessitate a brow beating that scarred me to this day?

I remembered another time where I was humiliated beyond words. Every fall we visited a camp with my uncles where all of them played cards and drank beer in front of a roaring fireplace. I'd usually run through the woods during these getaways, pretending that grizzly bears trapped me in their lairs, only to be rescued at the last moment by No-Sho The Hero. The part I hated, though, was when I needed to use the bathroom. To reach it, I had to walk past all these drunken gamblers.

"Hey, don't stink up the whole place, pip-squeak."

"Yeah, last time it smelled like a skunk died in there."

My father should have protected me from these attacks, but instead, he joined the others in embarrassing me.

"You should smell the shitter at home after Chris is done. The damn paint peels off our walls!"

Not wishing to subject myself to this abuse, I snuck to a secluded tree behind the camp, squatted near the ground and unburdened myself. Unbeknownst to me, these men were watching from a second story window. So, while defecating in the weeds, I looked up to see them.

"Hey look, Chris is shittin' in the woods like a dodo bird," one of them hooted.

"No wonder I saw those geese flying south," another added to uproarious applause. "They caught a whiff of Chris' pile."

There I sat, hunched over a pile of leaves with a load of crap sliding from my ass, and these drunken men were mocking me, even my own father.

"Hey Chris, why don't you play 'Switchboard Operator' when you're finished. Shove one finger up your ass, put the other in your mouth, then Switch 'Em!"

My uncles screamed with laughter while I felt like digging a hole and burying myself.

The worst experience, though, happened after a particularly brutal spanking at my father's hands. Aching, dejected, with my pride at its lowest point, I stomped from the house to search for a smaller neighborhood kid who I could terrorize. I finally found Little Joey, pushed him to the ground, then pinned him down as I sat on his chest.

"I'm going to spit a big hocker in your face," I threatened, finally feeling superior to someone else.

"No, don't," Joey cried, half my size.

"I'll do it. A big green slimy spitball - right in your face," I continued.

"Please, don't do it."

"Okay, I won't," I told Joey, "but because I'm so nice, you have to kiss my ass."

"No ... I won't do it," Joey whimpered.

"If you don't, I'll ..."

Just then I looked up to find my father holding a bicycle horn that he honked when calling me for supper.

"What the hell is going on?" he screeched, face beet-red.

"Chris wanted me to start kissing ass," Joey plead hysterically.

"You little asshole," Pus yelled while pulling me from Joey. "Get off him." He then spoke to my would-be victim. "Joey, get all the neighborhood kids and tell them to come here. I want to show them something." Pus then directed another tirade at me. "How dare you pick on someone smaller than yourself? You have some nerve. You should be ashamed of yourself. I oughta beat your ass right here."

At that point, Joey returned with a dozen neighborhood kids, each of them clamoring with anticipation.

"Okay, Mister Pus, here are all the kids," Joey cheered, feeling vindicated.

"Very good. Now Joey, since Chris wanted you to kiss ass, I feel it's only right to turn the tables. Do you think that's fair?"

"Sure, Mister Pus," he said with a broad smile.

"Okay Joey, pull down your pants and kneel over there," my father told him. "And Chris, get your smoocher ready. You'll see how it feels to kiss ass."

The neighborhood kids danced with such excitement that they nearly fluttered off the ground.

"Dad, please don't make me do this," I whispered. "I'll never live it down."

"Chris, you wanted to be a hot shot, picking on little Joey. Now get down and kiss his ass," my father roared.

My peers giggled with the glee of ... well, with the glee of those seeing one of the most absurd sights of all time.

"Please, Dad," I begged, "don't make me do it."

"Do it, Chris, or I'll take my belt off and beat your ass first," Daddy snarled, clenching his fist.

So, with tears welling in my eyes and rolling down each cheek, I knelt to kiss Little Joey's ass while the kids taunted me with names like "suckerfish" and "liplock." Understandably, I never forgot the experience.

While driving to the hospital, I recalled my reaction, or lack thereof, to the above degradation. As a child, the fear of my father grew so large that I was literally unable to speak. I went through life as a mute, my suppressed words turned inward. I became so sensitive to criticism that my thoughts were never spoken. Every social situation, especially those involving my father, became an exercise in futility. My entire life seemed like a round of shadowboxing against the man who created me. My father's reflection loomed above me - towering, omnipotent, savage - but regardless of what I did, I could never get rid of his shadow.

My father became a god-like figure, his presence intimidating me, stifling my advancement, and ruining my life. But during this cruise to the hospital, I vowed to never let him interfere in my affairs again. Instead, I would slip into my Ukiah alter ego and beat my father at his own game. This strategy had already worked with Officer Idem and the state patrolman. Now I'd face my father in the ultimate showdown, trying to recover my last vestige of self-respect.

I entered Dykotemee Memorial Hospital, instantly overpowered by the odors of sickness, death, and disease. After finding the location of my father's room, I strolled along the sterile corridors, inhaling a variety of aromas that made my head spin. After trying to bolster my courage with a silent pep talk, I still stood on shaky knees.

I eventually walked past senior citizens in wheelchairs, grim-faced nurses, and gray-lit rooms that housed patients whose afflictions I did not want to become familiar with. Then I saw the number outside his room - 888 - the mere thought of his presence creating a sense of unbridled fear.

Unable to imagine any alternatives, I summoned my courage, then entered the room, extending a cheery "hello" to both him and my mother.

Dad didn't look nearly as feeble as I had envisioned. I had pictured him being very small, frail, and curled in a fetal tuck with his eyes bulging from their sockets, a light-blue hospital gown draping his withered frame as tubes protruded from his arms and legs. But this afternoon, Dad looked ready to run a marathon, which scared the hell out of me.

"How are ya feeling, Dad?" I asked meekly, quickly losing my nerve.

"I've been better," he snarled, obviously displeased with his situation.

"Aren't you glad Chris came to visit?" my mother suggested, trying to put us at ease.

"Thrilled," my father responded.

Off-guard, I commented, "Mom says you have an ingrown toenail ..."

Agitated, Pus snapped, "Damn doctors. What do they know? There probably ain't even nothing wrong with me ... Hey Chris, do you remember the last time I had an ingrown toenail? It was the day you skipped around in that flowered cape pretending to be a superhero. So I snuck around the couch, and when you flew past, I planted a foot right in your ass. Whoa-ho, what a riot! I couldn't quit laughing as you rolled head over ass across the room. Those were the good 'ol days."

Infuriated, I relived yet another humiliating experience from my childhood.

Trying to appear undaunted, I said, "Yeah, those were the days."

Sensing my unease, Mom asked, "Chris, how have you been? Are you feeling well?"

"Yes, I'm fine."

Feisty, my father snapped, "Chris, are you still the little manager of that data entry firm?"

Jittery, I admitted, "No, I resigned from that position, and am now just a data-entry operator."

"Good God, Lena, page a nurse! I'm having a heart attack. Chris just stuck a dagger through my chest."

My mother streaked toward the door, then realized my father was exaggerating to embarrass me.

"You resigned from a managerial position to be a lowly operator? When will this disappointment end?" Pus lamented. "In my day, I ordered people around with such an iron-fist that their knees knocked. You could have done the same thing, Chris, but what did you do? I'll tell you. The same thing as always - crawl in a hole and hide. What's wrong with you? Why did you make such a decision?"

Unhinged, my original plan of being like Ukiah had all but been forgotten. Instead, I blurted, "because ... be ... because I couldn't handle the pressure."

"Lena, quick! I'm having a seizure. Call the doctors!" he again exaggerated. Once calmed, my father sneered, "Pressure? I ate pressure for breakfast, then spit nails by lunch. Pressure. Ha. I worked best under pressure."

An extended silence blanketed the room as my mother fidgeted with her needlepoint, Dad gazed out the window, and I paced uncomfortably.

Finally, Mother asked, 'Well Chris, how is everything else in your life? Have you made any new friends?"

"Better yet, have you gotten married, or found any prospects?" my father said disdainfully.

Unable to connect with Pus or gain his respect, I let the following comment slip. "As a matter of fact, I have found someone."

Overjoyed for the first time, my father exclaimed, "Fantastic. Maybe you'll be all right after all! Fill us in on the details."

"Yes, Chris, please do," Momma chimed.

Gazing at my father, his eyes bright with pride, I reluctantly said, "Well ..."

Sensing my hesitation, Pus's elation quickly faded. "Oh no ... what kind of freaky scene are you into? It's not another catastrophe like that time in high school with Chris Dibbuk, is it?"

"No, Dad, it's not ..."

"I don't like the sound of this news," my father snapped. "First, tell me, is your lover male, female, or some freakish aberration in between?"

Exasperated, I shouted, "That's it! I can't handle your comments any more. I'm outta here."

While racing toward the door, my mother cried, "No, Chris, wait."

Stopping abruptly, I panted, "Mom, you can deal with this asshole, but I'm not putting up with his shit any more. Goodbye, forever."

23

Sweety, we need to make drastic changes in our life. Look at us. We're hiding in a bathroom because Philip Prince is in our living room. The last time we were together, he strapped you to a hotel bed and anally raped us while we gagged in a trashcan. Life hasn't been rosy for years, but now we've hit rock bottom.

Look at yourself, honey. The mirror doesn't lie. We're still beautiful, but the constant degradation and sickness are beginning to erode our looks. It's frighteningly apparent that we need a different path. But where can we turn? Oh Jenny, look inside yourself - look at your face. You know the answer.

Oh, Mother, there you are. I can still see your face hidden in mine. Why did you leave when I was just a child? I know you were sick, but I could have helped.

"Mommy, let's get out of bed and play today. We'll do somersaults, pick flowers, and dress my baby dolls. C'mon, Mommy, you can get up."

"Oh Sweety," she said softly, head on the pillow. "I wish I could, but my condition hasn't improved. The world frightens me, baby. It overflows with such ... oh honey, I can't even leave the house any more."

Jenny, we can't live like mother - so weak that we can't even get out of our nightgown in the morning. But then again, maybe she was right about the world. Look at us - we're literally trapped in a bathroom by our supposed lover - a sadistic abuser who couldn't care less about us. The way we treat authors at Mason Turner is no better. Just think what they must do to find fame and fortune.

"Mommy, Mommy! I'm home from school. C'mon, let's play ... Mommy, where are you? Mommy. There you are. Why are you sleeping at this time of day? Mommy, wake up. Let's play. Mommy? ... No ...!"

Mother, how could you have committed such a deplorable act? I don't blame you, I just can't understand. Try to imagine what you did to me? Even today, every time I look at a person's wrists, I see your blood flowing from them. You didn't even say good-bye. What were you thinking as the blood washed across your arms? What can I do, Mother? I'm lost and confused. How will I ever escape this nightmarish world?

Mother, please tell me. Can't you see me staring at you through the looking glass? Don't you even remember me?

"Oh honey, I haven't forgotten my precious little girl. I'll always keep a special place in my heart for you."

Mommy, I knew you would come back. Please tell me, what should I do to get rid of the horrors in my life?

"Little Girl, to destroy the negative, one must turn to creation ..."

"Jennifer, what are you doing? You've been in there for half an hour," Philip demanded, pounding on the door.

Oh baby, why won't he leave us alone?

"Don't worry, I'll be out. Quit knocking."

Mama, please come back. What did you mean - to destroy, we must create? I need some answers.

"Jennifer, get your ass out here. I don't have all day to play these silly games."

Open the door, darling, you have to confront him sometime.

"What? What in this world is so important, Philip?"

"Don't sass me, woman. I'm the most famous author in this country. Don't forget it."

"How could I?"

"Drop the sarcasm, Jenn. We need to get our stories straight before talking to the police. I want to nail my attacker's ass to the wall so badly that, until he's caught, I won't enjoy a moments peace."

"Oh, I see. You want me to tell the cops how you, with tears dripping down each cheek, laid on your dressing room floor until I rescued you."

"You're a nasty woman, Jenn."

"Only when I'm with you, or while working at that agency which promotes your lousy science-fiction novels."

"Shut up! If it weren't for me, you'd be eating from dumpsters and living in a cardboard box. You know it's true. You're helpless on your own ... where'd you get all these ugly plants anyway, Jennifer? Look at them, they're withered and dry ... nearly dead ..."

Mommy, what did you mean about creation and destruction?

"... You should at least water them once in a while."

"Philip, mind your own business! Just leave me alone."

"I'm serious, Jenn. We need to get our stories straight about that night in Latera Heights."

"What night are you talking about, Philip?"

"You know which one. Don't even mention that other time. It never happened. It doesn't exist. Just remember, hon', I'm the one who hired you at Mason Turner. I can also arrange your firing."

"I'm sick of you holding that job over my head. I'll quit if that's what it takes to get away from you."

"You'd die on the streets."

"Would I? What if I called a reporter at *The New York Times Book Review* and spilled the beans on you? How would you like the tables turned?"

"Don't even consider it ..."

"Mister Philip Prince, America's favorite author, exposed as an abusive, rapist adulterer. Philip Prince - coward. You bamboozled every reader in this country with your supposed heroics, when in reality you cringed like a Girl Scout beneath your attacker. I'll bet they'd love to read the true story."

"I'm warning you, Jennifer ..."

"How about your wife? I'm sure she'd love her husband after discovering his affair for the past thirty years."

"Don't make me ..."

"What, Philip? I saw you on *The Tonight Show* bragging about your gardening, and what a good father you were to those three darling children. You're such a phony. I can't wait until your wife discovers the truth."

"This is the last time, Jenny."

"Or, how could we forget that infamous night in Latera Heights so long ago? Ooooh, that would make some juicy reading ..."

"That's it! You've pushed me too far," Philip gurgled.

Oh Jenny, look what he's done to you. A fist to the midsection ... how symbolic ... you're buckled over in pain … it hurts so much, honey. But then, what would you expect? The man you once loved - now reduced to continual abuse. Rather than comforting us, that asshole bit our arm. It has to end, Sweety. Can't you see? Things will only go downhill from here. There's no saving this dead-end relationship.

"Why are you so wicked?"

> to destroy the negative,
> one must turn to creation

"Jennifer, you've pushed me too far this time."

"I'll get even with you. Believe me, I will."

Look at those beady eyes - rat-like - veinous - only inches from yours - burning with fiery spite.

"Listen, and listen closely, Jennifer. I'm not playing games with you. Too much is at stake. I can't let some dizzy broad ruin all I've built over the years. You might try to shame me in public, or report my activities to Mason Turner, but at some point, you'll be alone. All alone. And when that time comes, I'll be there to pounce ..."

"Why do you always need to have power over me?"

"Baby, if you try to fuck with me, or damage my reputation, I'll kill you. I swear, I'll corner you some day when you're all alone, then slit your throat. Mark my words! You're nothing but a worthless little girl who schemed her way into my life. Now look at how you've benefited. You're a senior agent at the most esteemed agency in New York City. And how did you get there? With a falsified resume and no credentials. All because you got to know a struggling author while attending Latera University. Well, you've kept your mouth shut, and subsequently received a lucrative position. So far, everything has paid off for both of us. But if you rock the boat, Jenn, I'll stop at nothing to eliminate ..."

"Why are you such a prick? Tell me! Every time I ask, you ignore me. Now open up, Philip. I want to know why you're such a creepy bastard."

"Do you really want to know?"

"Yes, Philip. I'm tired of being treated like a mindless object. If you realized I had some intelligence, maybe we could reach a mutual level of understanding."

"Okay. If you like. My problems stem from a simple concept related to my parents."

"A simple concept?"

"Yes, a simple concept relating to The Word."

"The Word?"

"My parents were both geniuses - my father a linguist who spoke a dozen different languages, my mother a pioneer in revising the English dictionary. To them, Words were the fundamental building block that permitted mankind's advancement. They loved words ... adored them - fascinated by their definitions, origins, and interactions. The world could change around us, but The Word remained unaltered and true ... rooted to creation. I constantly heard Words all my life - not simple chitchat or inane conversations, but exhilarating exercises in the true meaning of our language. In our household, The Word was larger than life, the center of attention. As I grew older, I wanted to follow in my parent's footsteps. I wanted more than anything to take hold of The Word and embrace it as dearly as they had. I admired, yet also envied, their simple understanding and fluent mastery of the language - their ability to accept The Word's purity. But as I matured, The Word became more of a hindrance than a form of inspiration. I couldn't live up to my parent's expectations in regard to The Word, so I rebelled against it by writing science fiction. In time, I met other authors and publishers who despised the truth and purity found within The Word. This group was like modern artists who didn't have the talent to actually create, so they splattered paint on a canvas and called it Art. So, we've devoted our lives to preventing the masses from enjoying literature by giving them an array of substandard genres. Our plan has progressed quite well; but for every mystery, suspense, romance, western, horror, or science-fiction novel on the market, there's always an unknown writer who has mastered The Word and promotes its purity. It is this Artist who must be eliminated before he or she reminds the reading audience of our language's true origin."

> to destroy the negative
> one must turn to creation

"Philip, I never knew about the turmoil inside your mind. There's so much more we could discuss, but can I ask one simple favor?"

"If you must."

"Will you consider the writings I've accumulated over the past few decades? I think you'd be impressed with them."

"No. Absolutely not! If I couldn't live up to my parent's expectations regarding The Word, I'm not going to give you the satisfaction of capitalizing on the purity of this endeavor. Do you know what my parents dying words were? 'Surrender yourself to The Word.' I've considered myself a failure ever since. So, we'll only publish those authors who are intent on destroying The Word. The purists, loyalists, and faithful are our enemies. And that's final."

> Oh sweety, you need to make drastic changes in your life. This man is detrimental to
> your advancement, and any possibility of ever reaching the state of publication.

24

I started reading *The New York Times Book Review* every week, venturing to my favorite ice cream parlor to buy a copy along with a vanilla cone. While eating this treat, I'd leaf through the book review, reading about contemporary authors, past classics, and upcoming titles. Considering how often Ukiah spoke of this subject, I figured I'd better familiarize myself with it.

Of particular interest was any news concerning Philip Prince's attack. Coincidentally, in the book review's current edition, I noticed the following article:

A Thorn In His Side

Recognized as the country's best-selling author, Philip Prince has derived little satisfaction from the runaway success of *Prince of the Earth*. Instead, he prowls the streets at night near his New York City penthouse like a modern day Caped Crusader searching for his attacker - a hooded figure known only as Atropos.

In a recent interview, Mister Prince vowed that after locating his assailant, he would not act as mercifully as he had during their initial confrontation.

Prince guaranteed bitterly, "I'll beat this cretin within an inch of his life. I'll kill him - mark my words. If I'm forced to spend the rest of my life in prison to protect the fine people of this country, I'm willing to make that sacrifice."

Although federal investigators have not uncovered any recent leads in the case, scores of vigilante-type fan clubs have sprung up across the country, calling themselves "Prince's Minions." Combining typical book club elements with fantasy role-playing, the phenomenon has attracted national attention. Sporting makeshift masks depicting his recent novel's protagonist - Bubo Virginianus - The Great Horned Owl - and wearing T-shirts showing Philip Prince standing atop our planet with a pitchfork in hand and the slogan "Atropos Must Go" beneath, the Minions have begun a weekly Tuesday night ritual of blanketing the streets of their local community.

When asked about this cult-like response, Mister Prince, facial scars still visible, responded, "My Legions will continue to grow until we eliminate our foe and control the globe."

Laughing at Philip Prince's megalomania and theatrical use of deception, I paged through the front section of our local newspaper, unexpectedly finding an article about Mister Doublet's suicide. It seemed that recent events warranted the teacher's mother to drop any further investigation into the matter. Without hesitation, I instantly pictured Ukiah, wondering how he had affected this decision.

After eating my ice cream cone, then drinking a mug of hot chocolate topped with marshmallows and whipped cream, I drove through Latera Heights, marveling at spring's early arrival. In fact, townspeople started bragging about "the winter that never was." Other than a few snowfalls and an occasional drop in temperature, the months of December, January, February and March passed without incident. Now into the opening weeks of April, I figured we had winter licked. The following statement may sound absurd, but if this is global warming, I'm all for it!

As I turned onto Reflection Alley and neared my house, I saw the worst sight imaginable. Parked in my driveway, squad car emitting plumes of bluish gray smoke, was none other than Officer Idem. I considered pulling a U-turn and racing from the neighborhood, but knew such a move would only delay the inevitable. Officer Idem had finally arrived at an obvious conclusion - I was Woody Dewar's murderer.

Pulling beside his white cruiser, I shut off my car, then stepped into the warm, midday air. Doing the same, Idem strolled slowly toward me, his usual grim look replaced by a more humane expression.

Still fearing the worst, yet somewhat relieved, I said, "Good morning, sir. Beautiful day."

Eyeing my body from top to bottom, Idem began, "Chris, may I have a word with you?"

"Sure. Follow me."

Once inside my house, Idem didn't waste any time. "Chris, I should apologize for my recent accusations in connection to Mister Dewar's death." Nervously brushing his pressed blue uniform, he continued. "After divulging the contents of Woody's medicine bag to his family, they told me to immediately end the investigation into this matter. Although they couldn't prove it, they suspected Mister Dewar was a ... well, a degenerate. In retrospect, my past brow beatings of you were both unnecessary and extreme. So," he concluded, humbled and sincere, "I trust you will accept my apology."

Touched by this tender display, I spoke calmly, "Apology accepted."

Officer Idem then extended his right hand, which I held, before he said, "One last thing, Chris." As we shook hands for an uncomfortably long time, with Idem drawing me closer all the while, he said, "Y'know, I still have Woody Dewar's medical bag. I was wondering ..." he pulled me even nearer, "... if you'd like to get together some evening and use the contents of that bag on each other. I even found a pair of edible ladies undies that one of us could wear."

Repulsed, I screamed while pulling my hand from his, "Get out of here, you creep! Leave me alone!"

Reverting to his old self, Idem sneered, "freak," then stormed through the door in a huff.

Rattled, I momentarily gathered my senses, then left the house, heading toward Ukiah's cottage. After letting me in, then listening to my story about the police officer, Ukiah howled with amusement, saying I was lucky I hadn't been arrested. Who knows what would have happened inside the holding cell.

Humiliated again, I changed the topic to Mister Doublet's suicide.

"Have you heard the latest news about that high school teacher? It seems his mother put a halt to the investigation. I wonder what happened?"

Washing dishes, Ukiah commented, "I might have played a minor role in that matter."

Proven correct, yet not letting on, I said, "How so?"

While scrubbing a Teflon-coated frying pan, Ukiah confessed, "A couple months ago, an assistant and myself escorted Mister Doublet to my cottage."

"Here?" I asked, playing dumb. "What did you do?"

"Essentially, because he was such a prick, we tortured that son of a bitch for not answering my letters."

Acting surprised, I gasped, "Torture?"

"I won't go into the details, but after this matter was resolved and we set Doublet free, I found an engraved gold chain attached to a medallion that had slipped from his wrist. I didn't think much of it at the time, but then, when reading that suicide note in the newspaper, I realized that an investigation could lead to me."

"That's true."

"So, to cover myself, I came up with a plan."

"Oh no," I said, closing my eyes.

After rinsing his silverware, Ukiah continued. "I wrote a note to Mrs. Doublet saying that I - name undisclosed - was the person her son referred to in his suicide note."

"You? Who?" I asked, confused.

"I'll get to that, just hold on. Anyway, one of Tattoo Blue's hookers is a transsexual ..."

"You mean one of those ..." I interrupted.

"Yes, one of those. So, one night, while driving this ... this person downtown, I asked him ... or her, if I could take a picture of them naked. Being that they all love me, she ... or he ... let me do it. So, I snapped a few photos from the neck down that didn't show their face, but had everything else hanging out. Then, in this letter, I said I had been Doublet's secret lover for the past three years. But, since he refused to have a sex-change operation to please me, I left him. Devastated, that's why the teacher killed himself."

"Ukiah! You're horrible!" I yelled. "Try to imagine his poor mother. She must have been devastated."

Surprisingly calm, Ukiah ignored my outburst, then continued his explanation. "To add a personal touch, I included the gold chain and medallion - the one personally engraved, 'Gideon Doublet' in cursive lettering." He paused a moment, then said, "I didn't read today's paper, but I'm glad my plan worked out all right." Ukiah washed a final soup bowl, then asked, "Hey, what're you doing today?"

"Nothing."

"Great. Do you wanna take a cruise to Tooferville? Japhy's band is playing there tonight at a youth center."

"Sure," I replied excitedly. "Where's Tooferville?"

"It's an old coal mining town up in the mountains. It'll be a nice drive." Then, abruptly changing his line of thought, Ukiah snapped, "Anyway, Doublet was an asshole. Being that his mother brought him into the world and let that inconsiderate bastard live with her, I figure she must be just as bad. She should have taught her son some manners, like answering letters and phone messages. None of this would have happened if he had shown a little courtesy. Now it's them or me. C'mon, let's roll."

As we walked outside, waves of joy overcame me. For months, I had fretted about evidence, arrests, and court cases. Now, miraculously, it looked as if these clouds had been lifted. Philip Prince's federal case had stalled, Doublet's suicide fiasco reached an end, and Woody Dewar's murder investigation had been terminated. Somehow, Ukiah landed on his feet again.

"Can we take your car?" Ukiah asked politely. "I fixed Japhy's van, but the headlamp is still outta whack."

"Sure, but it needs gas," I told him.

"Cool. We'll stop at Kwikky Pump. I know a cute girl that works there."

I hopped in the Gemini, drove from Reflection Alley to a local service center, then started pumping gas. With Ukiah standing beside me, describing the hurdles Japhy's band had to overcome to get this gig, I kept squeezing the pump's lever until it stopped. When it finally clicked at $12.23, I pulled the pump from my gas tank.

"What are you doing?" Ukiah asked, eyes open wide with disbelief.

"What am I doing? Putting the pump back," I told him, rattled by his inquiry.

"You're not done yet," he continued, a sour look on his face.

"I'm not? Why? The pump stopped by itself."

"But you didn't top it off at an even number."

"So?"

"So! Look at the total - $12.23. Ya never stop at an odd number like that," he told me, as if speaking with a fool.

"Why? What's wrong with that number?"

"Ya always stop at an even total, like fourteen dollars, or six dollars ... never at $12.23."

"What does it matter?" I asked, amazed that we were even having this conversation.

"It matters that $12.23 is not an even number. Everything isn't in its proper order. It's like putting a roll of toilet paper on the holder feeding from the bottom. Ya never do it that way. The roll should always come from the top. That's its proper order."

Unable to comprehend this convoluted logic, I shoved the pump back into my gas tank, squeezed its handle, then stopped when it reached thirteen dollars even.

"There. Are you satisfied?" I asked sarcastically.

"No."

"No! Why not?"

"You can't stop at thirteen - that's an unlucky number."

"You're nuts, Ukiah. Completely nuts!" I shrieked with disbelief. "What should I stop at?"

"Make it $13.50, that's even enough," he told me.

Squeezing the handle yet again, I ran my total to $13.50, then walked inside to pay the cashier.

Upon returning, I shook my head, then started the car.

"$13.50. I can't believe it," I laughed. "I'll never understand you."

Smiling, Ukiah remained silent until I pulled onto the bypass, then remarked, "I mailed another letter to Jennifer yesterday."

"Why, Ukiah?" I asked, disappointed. "I thought you were finished with her."

"I can't quit that easily. I still might have a chance. What if her first rejection was a test to see if I had fortitude, or if I'd just quit after one try?"

"It's possible," I said blandly. "What did you say this time?"

"I started by talking about *Blank Line*, then asked her a question that's been killing me. Why is it so hard to get a literary agent and keep one's dignity at the same time? I've worked my fucking ass off writing eighteen books. And y'know what? I KNOW these books, which sit unread in my closet, are fantastic. But I'm afraid they'll keep gathering dust because I can't sell them."

While following a four-lane highway out of town, I asked, "Why is it so hard to promote yourself?"

Pouncing on this question, Ukiah began, "Before telling you why, I want you to know I'm not trying to play the role of victim. That's the furthest thing from my mind."

"I understand."

"The way I see the world is that a man should stand strong, be self-sufficient, and rarely ask for help. To do so is a sign of weakness. People shouldn't talk about their problems, either, or blow their own horn. They should be recognized for their actions without needing to grovel, kiss ass, or call in favors. That's why I hate writing those letters. I feel like a whore reducing myself to that level. Plus, when I'm forced to brag about my abilities, it comes across as phoniness, because I don't act that way in everyday life ..."

"Except for video racing," I joked to myself.

"... a person's greatest strength is their ability to get self-respect from both the way they lead their lives, and through their creative output. Success can't be appreciated if this balance is compromised."

As miles of pleasing scenery passed outside our window, I asked, "I think we're on the same page, but how do your views relate to the printed word?"

With an acute (or at least unique) understanding of our fragile universe, Ukiah began, "My philosophy toward literature is different from that of the mainstream publishing houses."

"How?" I asked, passing skeletal trees that recently began adorning themselves with leaves.

"Well, let's look at two books that were recently released – Don Delillo's *Underworld,* and Caleb Carr's sequel to *The Alienist.* The reviews for both novels have been favorable, and they're both fine pieces of writing. My problem with them is that they're period pieces, set in distant eras that can be dated. My output is different though – it's pure, timeless literature that isn't hindered by actual places, calendars, or historical bias. My works exist solely in their own self-created world."

"Interesting."

"I gotta tell you about a book by Ernest Hemingway that I recently tried to read."

"Tried to read?" I asked.

"Yeah, tried, because *To Have And Have Not* was one of the worst examples of prose I've ever read. Now don't get me wrong. I'm a fan of Hemingway, and enjoy his work. But *To Have* was awful. And this from a man who is supposed to be the standard-bearer of twentieth century American Literature. I'm not trying to be overly critical, but if he's who we're trying to copy, we're in trouble."

"Even the masters aren't sacred," I laughed, trying to keep my speedometer below the legal limit.

"Wait until you hear my opinions on academia and literature."

"I can only imagine how they irritate you."

"These folks are so concerned with playing fancy word games that their work becomes sterile, effeminate, and unapproachable. Two examples would be Vladimir Nabokov, and Camille Paglia.

"Who is Vladimir Nabokov? I never heard of him."

"He was a Russian author who wrote about butterflies and little girls, but that's not the point. Y'see, the common man doesn't care about these eggheads. Walk into a bookstore and pick ANY novel, flip to page one, and tell me if it grabs your attention. I've performed this experiment hundreds of times, and usually I can't get past the second paragraph. It's like I'm staring at Creative Writing 101 ... nothing but phoniness dripping into my hands. But by promoting these elitists, the publishers perpetuate the system. The way I see it, literature, like rock n' roll, should come from the streets - simple and without pretension. In other words, the real thing."

Confused, I interrupted his discourse. "As usual, I have no idea what you're trying to say."

With a full head of steam, Ukiah said, "The point I'm trying to make is this - those in their ivory towers don't give the common man enough credit. That's why their books are so detached and inaccessible. But they'd be surprised by The Soloists ... those of us who can articulate our feelings ..."

"Ukiah, your writing is accessible to everyone!" I exclaimed, finally seeing his point. "The process must frustrate the hell out of you."

"For the past fifteen years I've been writing like a man possessed. If it weren't for this HOPE, this last stab of salvation, I'm sure I'd be insane by now. I can't understand people who go through life without creating. What is their purpose? Why doesn't this crazy fucking world drive them mad?"

"Do you mean the gates of publication ...?"

In his own world, Ukiah rambled loudly, "Every day brings me closer to the breaking point. I don't know how much more I can take ... the mundane tasks, inane conversations, absurd situations, and all the misguided, misdirected energy that is needed just to survive. The only thing that makes it livable is the dream of escape ... so I keep pushing my pen across the page."

I knew Ukiah was slipping into a pit of despair, one that was hard to escape from.

"I'm isolated in my seclusion," he lamented, "the best damn writer in this country. I epitomize the abandoned man - alone, so alone. My cats are dead, I live alone, don't have a girlfriend, belong to no clubs or organizations, and aren't a member of any literary clique. I don't go to picnics in the park, and never shop at the mall. I'm all by myself."

I continued to drive silently along a four-lane interstate.

"But guess what. I do know how to write. Why can't Jennifer see? Doesn't she feel the hunger leaping from each line? Doesn't she hear the passion when I tell her writing and The Word could be lifted to a higher plateau instead of being so boring? Authors should be important members of our culture rather than socially inept geeks. When I'm interviewed on *The Tonight Show*, it should be an EVENT! Rock stars, actors, criminals and politicians - the last two examples being redundant - shouldn't be the only ones capturing the public's imagination. What if everyone who knew Vincent Van Gogh had told him not to paint with such fiery passion? That he should tone down his style and get rid of the demons that raced through his soul. Then he could use a slower, more methodical process for his creations. Or what if Van Gogh's paintings had been left in an old barn for eternity? Wouldn't it be a disgrace if his works were erased from the landscape of nineteenth century art?"

Ukiah's voice boomed as he lost his bearing, at one point talking directly to Miss Ewen.

"Jennifer," he pleaded, "I'm not good at much, but I CAN write like a madman. During the past twelve months I've written 1072 pages of prose, over 1700 in the past year and a half. I can't understand why you keep ignoring me. What if I am better than F. Scott Fitzgerald and Ernest Hemingway? I'm not saying I am, but I could be as accessible to the public as they were. Can't you see my vision? It can't be denied. Jennifer, just work with me. It's impossible to relay my vision on such a nonpersonal level. Imagine Jackson Pollock trying to describe his paintings to someone in a letter. He'd tell them about splattering paint on a canvas, and the reader would think he's insane. But guess what? Pollock caught on, eventually finding wealth, fame, and critical acclaim."

Ukiah paused for a moment, realizing he had plunged over the deep end by speaking so intimately to this literary agent. Unfazed, and certainly not embarrassed, he said to me softly, "Chris, even though it might not seem like it at times, I know I'm not the only writer on this planet. My ego isn't that outta control! But the way I see it, Jennifer has three alternatives after she gets this letter. She can keep ignoring me, arrange a meeting in New York City, or shuffle me to one of her underlings."

Touched by his dedication and faith, I said, "It's easy to see that you're a prolific writer. Why would Miss Ewen let the competition get their claws into you? It doesn't seem like a prudent business decision. Hell, even if they hid you for awhile, wouldn't that be better than letting another agency steal you away?"

Appreciating my input, Ukiah moaned, "Thanks, Chris, but I'll probably just drift into the sunset. It's such a shame, though, because I could become an actual Industry. Considering my ability to produce, Jenny could reap benefits for years to come. But she wants to follow the same path that has already been laid. I could expand into areas that the industry never thought imaginable. All she needs to do is open the door. Why won't she welcome me? It'd be one helluva ride. I even sent another picture of myself. Jennifer probably thought - at least he doesn't have to rely on his looks to make a living."

Laughing at this final observation, I asked, "What are you going to do, Ukiah?"

Gazing out the window with a distinct sadness bathing his face, Ukiah said, "I've written eighteen books so far. As a whole, each story takes on meaning as an autobiographical document - each a piece to the overall puzzle. People could then ask - what importance do they hold? Being so close to the subject, I'm not sure of an answer. All

I've done is create a Legend – filling in all the blanks. Who knows? Maybe my legacy has no more merit than an old-timer in a retirement home putting together a puzzle."

"I'd say your books are more important than a jigsaw puzzle."

"I'm beginning to wonder," Ukiah said with resignation. "I thought life would be so different when I started writing. By now I'd be famous, rich, with a gorgeous wife and a nice home. Huh, look at me. I'm a fucking bachelor, a thug, and a nobody author who not only isn't published, but can't even find a lousy agent. I've always had a plan. Don't think small, don't leave a paper trail, and shoot for the top. But now I'm getting desperate. This plan may have been nothing more than a pipe dream. If only one person in the world believed in me ..."

While exiting the interstate after Ukiah pointed to an off-ramp, I told him, "I believe in you. Even if I'm not allowed to read your letters until you get famous, the imperative phrase is 'until you get famous.' If Jennifer, or any of those other agents, believed in you like I did, you'd be well on your way to publication."

After directing me toward a blacktop highway, Ukiah perked, "Y'know, Chris, you may be onto something."

"What?" I asked, distracted by the scenery.

"I'll make you my agent!" Ukiah said excitedly.

I was so alarmed by this prospect that I actually tapped the brakes of my Gemini.

"Me! I'm not a literary agent. What do I know?"

With the wheels of his mind spinning in overdrive, Ukiah boasted, "Don't worry, Chris. Just listen to me. I'll tell you what to do. Hell, two heads are always better than one. This is going to work great! I can't wait to get started."

"I'm not so sure, Ukiah. I've never ..."

"Don't worry. After you start mailing letters, everything will fall into place."

"But I can't write letters. I don't have any experience."

"Chris, I thought you believed in me," Ukiah challenged. "What? You don't think my idea is any good? Do you doubt me? Are my words just bullshit to you?"

"No, but ..."

"Then listen to what I'm saying. Think! Putting everything in its proper order means getting your priorities straight. Don't let your mind get cluttered with a bunch of meaningless fluff. You have to set goals, then eliminate everything else. It's all or nothing, Chris. There are 50,000 other asshole writers who want the same thing as me. That's why, now that you've agreed to be my agent, you need to focus 110% of your energies on this goal. Entering the gates of publication can't be a hobby or part-time endeavor. It takes complete devotion and an all-consuming passion. Nothing else should be important. What do you get from all that other shit, anyway? Nothing! Chris, focus your energies on publication and forget everything else. I'm talking about dedication and commitment. Have faith in me. I'll lead you along the right path. This is the best idea you've ever had. I'm so glad you thought of it." Beaming with joy, Ukiah finally told me, "Turn right at that barn. This's where Japhy's band is playing."

A short while later we entered Tooferville, a one-stoplight town near an oval-shaped lake. The setting made me reminisce about an era long since passed, one I was too young to remember, yet still lingered in my collective unconscious. Quaint, Victorian style mansions lined the lake, while a boardwalk connected each house. Tooferville's business district - a dairyette, pizzeria, fire hall, gas station, butcher shop, church, and funeral parlor, sat on a hill beside the lake, keeping vigilance over the water.

After driving through town, I thought about Ukiah's words regarding the state of single-mindedness needed to become his agent. Although he hadn't really chided me, my client (how hilarious is that concept, the blind leading the insane) did deliver his message in a firm, direct manner. Such a fatherly tone hurt my feelings, but I figured it was better for him to yell at me than sever our relationship. This way, at least Ukiah paid attention to me rather than abusing and ignoring me like my father had. I even imagined our friendship ending and how depressed I would become. Devastated! In the same breath, though, I didn't think it would bother Ukiah at all. He'd remain untouched, cold, passing through another day without second thoughts. He could be a heartless ogre at times.

Traumatized, I asked blankly, "Where is this place? Do you even know?"

Before answering my question, Ukiah said, "You seem down. What's wrong?"

"Nothing. Just thinking," I told him.

"Okay. Well, we're looking for the V.F.W. I have no idea where it is ... hey, wait a minute, there it is, behind the fire hall."

Sure enough, we pulled into an asphalt parking lot to find scores of teenagers standing near the club's entrance smoking cigarettes and sipping from jugs of wine. I initially thought there weren't even fifty people living in Tooferville, let alone enough to make the show worthwhile. But once we stepped inside the Vets Club and found its dance floor, I was astounded to see hundreds of kids.

"I'm surprised this place is full," I told Ukiah.

"Not me. These kids up here in the mountains ain't got nuttin' to do 'cept drink beer and joyride. Whenever a show comes to town, they flock from everywhere to attend.

I wonder if Japhy and his band are here yet?"

As he left to look for his son, I sat on a table near the back wall and surveyed the club. The first thing I noticed was that a stage didn't even exist, so the first band set their equipment on the floor and started tuning their instruments. If the particulars had been different, I could picture myself at a bar mitzvah, or a Polish wedding reception. Everything about the hall called for a return to the 1950s. I saw aged vets dressed in ill-fitting suits holding mixed drinks in plastic cups while their wives danced to a swing band. In the parking lot, girls wearing poodle skirts would snap their bubble gum as guys with slicked back haircuts puffed cigarettes and sat inside Edsels, Falcons, or Studebakers. Following the dance, they'd cruise to a drive-in diner, then listen to jukebox music as waitresses whisked by on roller-skates.

Today's crowd was a far cry from those innocent days. While an American flag, war mementos, and framed photos of veterans hung on the cheap paneled walls, these kids wore dopey-looking hats, oversized shirts, baggy pants with chains hanging from their pockets, and untied tennis shoes. The boys had haircuts that looked like they'd been forced to sit under a bowl while someone hacked at their heads with lawn shears. The girls, meanwhile, deliberately underwent a process of uglification that boggled my mind. I could honestly say that this generation was the first in history to systematically worsen their appearance. These females chopped their hair, wore old-fashioned eyeglasses, and draped their bodies with clothing that removed any hint of sexuality. The phenomenon was quite unsettling.

Shortly thereafter, Ukiah, with Japhy's girlfriend Gina close by, found me at the rear of the dance hall.

"The band got here a few minutes ago," he told me. "They're unloading, and will hit the stage after the first two bands are done. Who are those guys up on stage, anyway?" he asked Gina.

Dressed in a blue pullover sweater, loose blue jeans, and black boots, Gina said cheerfully, "The first group is called The Identicals, and the second are The Fractured Fraternals. Japhy's band is headlining."

Soon, both warm-up bands ran through their set, receiving polite, respectful rounds of applause from the audience. But it wasn't until a portly teenager approached the microphone and yelled, "All right, Tooferville! Making their first appearance in town, please welcome Mirror Image," that the place finally loosened up. The kids bounced excitedly as Japhy, Hawke, Atomic Aaron, and Looney cranked out their opening number. Three hundred kids cheered, clapped, danced, and spun in circles as the band gave them everything they wanted and more.

From our position at the hall's far wall, we could barely see the band through the throng of teenagers. We weren't concerned, but Gina found a more suitable vantage point near the front. I was content to watch the way kids handled themselves these days. Although I rarely attended dance parties, sock hops, or discotheques during my youth, I doubt they held the same type of behavior that unfolded before me. These kids flailed their arms maniacally, dodged headfirst into others, formed human chains that violently whipped past their peers, and generally acted in an uncivilized manner. I may be dating myself, but it seemed incredibly self-destructive. The kids didn't appear to mind. They laughed, whooped loudly into the air, slapped hands, and encouraged the band to push them to new heights.

While I watched the crowd dance with increased abandon, Ukiah stared at a petite young lady whose appearance differentiated her from the others. Standing five foot tall, with shoulder-length blonde hair and bangs, this young lady's attire consisted of a one-piece mini-skirt, beige stockings, and brown high-heeled shoes. As everyone else danced or cheered the band, this petite little lady stood away from the crowd, smoking a cigarette.

"Look at her," Ukiah panted, absolutely captivated. "I've never seen a girl like her in my life. She's all alone. Incredible!"

Ukiah kept shifting his attention from Japhy's band to this mysterious young woman. I became more jealous with each passing glance, infuriated that his sexual curiosity was once again focused in another direction. Honestly, though, I couldn't blame him. This delicate lady was spectacular in every sense - detached, mysterious, and rebellious in that she didn't follow the pack. I'm sure Ukiah's brain did back flips as he stared at her.

Mirror Image whipped the crowd into such a frenzy that, after three spirited encores, they still clamored for more. The band didn't disappoint them, ferociously diving into a final number called *Knocked Up*. Amid a pounding, tribal drumbeat and Japhy's superb guitar work, Hawke leaped about the tiled floor, inspired the crowd with exaggerated antics, and belted out the song's refrain:

> Please don't tell me that you're knocked up
> Please don't tell me that you're knocked up

How could any song directed at a teenage audience be more direct? Every kid's worst nightmare was held in that refrain - don't tell me that you're pregnant. By song's end, every person in that hall (except for the blonde in the mini-skirt) chanted the chorus in unison until the band raced from the gray-tiled floor and left the hall. To my disbelief, these kids kept applauding for at least three minutes following their departure.

Sometime later, Ukiah and I met Japhy, Gina, and the band in a parking lot behind the V.F.W. We congratulated each of them, then helped load their equipment into an antique panel truck that belonged to their bass player. Japhy and Ukiah walked away for a few moments before returning, then said goodbye with an extended handshake. Waving to Gina and Atomic Aaron as he drove away in my Gemini, it was clear that Ukiah longed to spend more time with his son.

We returned, with me riding shotgun, to the darkened town of Tooferville, its Victorian lamps and boardwalk lights glimmering off the lake to create a stunning effect. Appreciating this spectacular sight, Ukiah said wistfully, "Japhy told me his band cut their demo tape, and should start mixing it shortly. They want to have it done by midsummer."

"Excellent," I told him happily, glad that at least one of them was having some success.

"Y'know, Mirror Image might have a shot at making it. How cool would that be to have a famous rock star son? I could get all his throwaway groupies!"

Ukiah laughed heartily as he sped from Tooferville, its lazy lake and lilting lights slowly slipping into the distance.

He then asked, "Did you see that girl in the mini-dress? I couldn't believe my eyes. What a fucking turn on! She never spoke to one person the entire time ... just smoked cigarettes, looked bored, and stayed in her own little world. If I could, I'd marry her in a minute. Man, the entire aura surrounding her drove me nuts ... those faraway eyes, the ennui, her cute, tricky hips ... everything about her was tiny ... so tiny and remote. What a cutey pie."

As Ukiah continued his lustful description, I imagined him approaching this young lady in the V.F.W. parking lot.

"Hi. You're the most gorgeous girl I've ever seen."

She doesn't respond, or even acknowledge his existence - as utterly selfish as Ukiah was to others.

"Can't you see, from the moment I saw you, I fell in love."

She stares at him blankly, her calm eyes reminiscent of an untouched pond.

"You draw me nearer, yet keep pushing me away. I can't resist your confusing wishes. Whatever you say, I'll repeat a thousand times. Whatever you tell me to do, I'll do without question. I'm powerless in your presence, unable to break your spell."

Silent - unmoved - eyes unblinking like a mirror.

"Please talk to me, hug me, never leave. I'll be yours until the end of time."

She stands frozen ... disinterested.

"I love you ... please let me love you. Don't make me hate what I see before me. So delectable and detestable at the same time - an angelic demon. Give me a sign, at least a glimmer of hope. Please don't disappear like a shadow when the lights go out. Let me know my love is real and not an illusion. I see your eyes sparkle like mine, yet you don't answer."

Pure frigidity.

"Am I nothing but a meaningless lover, and you a misguided dream ...?"

"Chris, I asked you a question. Where the hell have you been?"

"Oh, nowhere. I was just daydreaming. I'm sorry. What did you say?"

"I wanted to know what you thought of starting our own publishing company. I figure, why should we put up with all the shit those agents give us? We'll bypass them and ..."

"Ukiah, do you know what you're saying?" I asked incredulously. "Folks like us don't start publishing houses on a whim. If they did, every unpublished author in this country would begin one. It's crazy. First you wrote to a single agent for half a year, asking for your own publishing wing. Then you dangled a carrot before some other agents, refusing to appease the one who did take an interest in you. Then today, you asked me to be your agent. But a few hours later, you change your mind again and want to start your own publishing company. Every day you lay something new on me."

"The way I see it," he said, "is that if we can land some quick money, we should have 'er licked. Maybe I'll have to rob a bank after all."

As if trapped in a never-ending nightmare, I recalled how relieved I'd been that our legal entanglements had been erased. Now Ukiah talked about robbing a bank, with me being drawn into the equation. I couldn't let him keep starting these fires. When would I be free of worry, able to sleep at night without the fear of handcuffs, perverted policemen, or depraved inmates? I might not make it through another one of these fiascoes.

Adamant, I yelled through the darkness, "Ukiah, you can't rob a bank to start a publishing company. It'll never work. We'll both wind up in prison."

Failing to see my point, he asked, "Where will we get that kind of money? I don't have any stuffed under my mattress."

Being rattled and on edge, I spoke without thinking. "The only person I know with any money is my father, but he's so damn tight ..."

"Your father, the one you hate?" Ukiah perked with excitement, capitalizing on the subject.

"No ... no, Ukiah. Don't get any ideas."

"Your father, huh? How many times have you wished him dead during your lifetime?"

"Quite a few ... well, not that many. Only once last week."

"I have the perfect solution to our problem," he said fervently. "We'll kill your old man and collect his insurance money!"

"No way," I panted. "It'll never work. We'll get caught."

"Chris, the right answer would have been - we can't murder my father - I love him. But you're more concerned with getting arrested. If I didn't know better, I'd say you considered it in the past."

Too nervous to think, I blurted, "Not that many times."

"Then let's do it! We'll kill your old man and collect his money."

"What about my mother?" I instantly asked, becoming more involved in this hypothetical situation than I ever intended.

"I'll marry her! You kill your father, and I'll marry your mother."

"Listen to yourself," I squealed as Ukiah sped through the night. "Do you know what you're saying? People don't kill their enemies at will. If they did, no one would be on this planet."

Pressing his foot more intently on the accelerator, Ukiah toyed with me. "Enemies! I never called him that, you did. Think about it, Chris. Has your father ever hit you?"

"Yes," I responded angrily.

Traveling even faster - "Has he ever demeaned you?"

I laughed snidely, "Countless times."

Screeching through the night - "Has that old bastard always had the upper hand, holding you down like a worm?"

"Yes! Damn him," I yelled, kicking my feet on the floor.

"Then let's do it! You kill him, we'll collect the insurance money, then we'll buy a printing press and publish *Blank Line*. The plan is foolproof. It'll never fail. How do you want to murder him?"

Becoming frantically wrapped up in both our high rate of speed and the ramifications of patricide, I blathered, "I'm not so sure about this ..."

"You're not sure? I'll bet he called you every name in the book, didn't he, Chris? How about asshole?"

"Ukiah, don't."

"How about good-for-nothin' loser - you'll never amount to anything."

"Please, I hate to think about those days."

"I'll bet he'd still love to put you over his knee and paddle your ass."

"No ... no."

Punching his gas pedal, Ukiah persisted, "Shithead, incompetent, lazy, dreamer ..."

"Stop!"

"'You'll never be as good as me,' he yells, doesn't he?"

"Yes."

"Why don't you let him hit you again, Chris?"

"No."

"I can see him sneering - stupid kid, dummy, underachiever, embarrassment ... Freak!"

"Stop."

"FREAK!"

"STOP!"

Screaming at ninety miles an hour, Ukiah roared, "FREAK! You're daddy's little freak!"

"Okay, I'll do it!"

"How?"

Manic, I snapped, "I'll kill him the same way I murdered Woody Dewar. I want to strangle him. I want to put my knees on his chest and wrap my hands around his throat and watch him beg for life. I want to see the whites of his eyes turn red as his blood vessels burst and his pupils fill with fear."

"Now you're talking, Chris," Ukiah panted, racing along a rural highway.

Suddenly, he pulled his foot from the accelerator as my Gemini returned to a normal speed.

Following a period of silence, Ukiah slammed both fists on the steering wheel and cursed, "Fuck, what am I thinking?"

Still deranged by thoughts of murder, my awareness heightened to its peak, I sat breathlessly, awaiting another outburst from Ukiah.

After grumbling indecipherably, he began, "I've become like all those other asshole writers I despise. Look at me - threatening to rob banks, having people killed ... I've lost sight of publication's true essence. Instead, I want money, women, and material objects. Do you know that while we drove to Tooferville and talked about literature, I didn't mention my Muse or The Word's purity one time? I don't know what's wrong with me. Sometimes I even blame Romlocon for not letting me get published. But who could blame her? I haven't cleansed myself ... I'm still filled with lust, greed, and vengeance. If I don't change my ways, I'll never enter the gates of publication."

Relieved by the prospect of Ukiah changing his course, I blurted, "Does that mean we don't have to kill my father?"

"I'm not sure. I'm so damn confused, I don't know what to think. You still might have to eliminate him. Fuck, everything's a mess. Let's not talk any more. I need time to think."

25

"Miss Ewen."

"Yes, Lola."

"I'm calling to remind you of the agent's meeting in fifteen minutes."

"How could I forget? Thank you, Lola."

Jenny, you'll never make it through another one of those meetings. The other agents despise us … resent us … mock us. Our job is a ruse. You're going to puke again. We can't do it. Call Lola and have her tell them we're sick. Oh, baby, you've made every excuse under the stars. One more absence and Old Man Turner will fire us.

What will you do when the vomit bubbles from your mouth onto the boardroom table? There aren't any more safety valves or possibilities of escape. You can't avoid them. You're trapped. I can already feel the queasiness. I'm sick. Oh baby, make it stop. Do something! Think. What can we do?

I don't feel well. Please stop. I beg of you - whoever - make it stop. I'm sorry for what I've done in the past. Forgive me. I'll change my ways. Don't make me start puking again. I'll die. The back of my throat is raw from all the times I've vomited.

Sweet Jenny, how did we let our life slip away? You're sick. Nobody freaks out just because they have to go to a meeting. It's not normal. Oh honey, what are we going to do? I feel it … just puke now. Maybe it'll be over by the time you leave your office.

But I don't want to puke! I'm going to die one of these times. The fissures in my throat are going to tear at any moment. Then I'll vomit until I drown in a pool of blood.

Why me? I know I'm awful, but why this hellatious sentence? Will it ever end? Every one of those agents knows we're insane. Now they'll see the full picture. We'll sit in that boardroom, pale and filled with fright, trembling like a scared rabbit. They've seen my sickness before, but usually we hid most of the symptoms. But every spell gets worse. Sweety, you can't control them any more. What's wrong with us?

Run Jenn, run right now! Even if you're fired, who cares? Anything's better than this torture. It's so hot in here, the room is spinning. What if I have a heart attack? At least you won't have to attend that meeting. I've never felt my heart beat so hard. My eyes are going to burst from their sockets. I can feel each vein throbbing, expanding, pushed to its limit. Soon, blood will gush from my body. The pressure is too intense. Slow down, honey.

We won't survive this battle. Disaster is imminent, our demise inevitable. You'll sit at that rectangular meeting table, bathed in perspiration, chilled (yet flushed), shaking, spinning, delirious. As usual, everyone will shun us, resentful that we don't carry our weight. While they discuss contracts, marketing strategies, and potential prospects, we'll zoom into a secluded realm of nightmarish proportions - begging not to vomit, praying to any Being that will listen, panting, hyperventilating, lightheaded, blood pressure through the roof. Then it'll happen - the negative forces rise to a head, our body nervous, frantic, so wracked by tension that you'll feel it coming - building - all-consuming fear. Nothing exists except the terror. We can't escape the rising tidal wave of vomit. First, the rapid succession of quick breaths overtakes normal respiratory functions, then your cheeks quiver as the gag reflex is triggered. It's too late. Hell on Earth is now with us. Oh Jennifer, no. But nothing can stop it from happening. You'll gag, close your eyes, then SPLAT, rivers of vomit spew from your mouth, through veinous purple fingers that try to hide it, splashing against the table, your clothes, and the coffee cup of the person seated beside you.

NO, NO, please, I beg of you, help me!

You can't go through with it.

"Miss Ewen, it's nearly time for your meeting. (pause) Miss Ewen, are you there? (pause) Jennifer, do you need help?"

Sobbing, I push the two-way intercom bottom, "Thank you, Lola. I'll be out in a minute."

Do something ... anything! You're running out of time. Oh baby, I can't do it. Think - think! Find an escape. Crawl out the window and jump. Slit your wrists. Swallow a bottle of cleaning fluid. Fake a heart attack. Anything's better than being imprisoned in that boardroom.

Okay ... okay - clear your head. Stand up. So far you're all right. Don't think about puking. You'll be fine. There, on your feet. Now, just walk out the door past Lola. She'll never know anything's wrong.

Agghh - dry heave. No! Please, it's starting. Cover your mouth, hold it in. Okay, there. You're better. Breathe. C'mon, it's getting late. You pull this stunt every time. Don't make yourself go into that room after the meeting already starts. They'll all stare at us.

Phew. Good. You're better.

"I'm leaving, Lola. See you shortly."

"Best wishes, Miss Ewen."

Nothing to it. We've overcome one hurdle. Now walk down the hallway - you're feeling better. There's nothing to worry about.

The hell there isn't. Everyone in that boardroom will stare as Old Man Turner asks, "Jennifer, do you have anything pertinent to add to our discussion?"

I haven't had anything to say in three decades. Every agent glares at me, annoyed by my special treatment. I know what they're thinking.

That dingaling's only here because she's Philip Prince's slut.

Look at that vacant stare. Her mind is like a bowl of oatmeal.

I wonder if she can even fill out a contract? It's not as if she's ever signed an author.

They hate me, burning with jealousy and resentment.

"No, Mister Turner, I don't have anything ..."

At that point I'll gag uncontrollably, trying to cover my mouth with one hand, but nothing will save me. Buckets of disgusting vomit will spew from between my fingers - a gooey, dripping, brown colored substance laced with strands of spaghetti, chunks of soggy bread, corn kernels, undigested apples, and green mint jelly. My associates will shriek with repulsion as they run to escape the smell.

Keep walking - one step after another - you're almost there. Don't think about any-thing, you'll be fine. I can feel it bubbling. Don't gag. Not in the hallway. I'll never make it. Oh Jenny, quick, run to the restroom. You're going to be sick.

Hurry, hurry. Don't puke in the hall. You'll leave a trail. Quick, get in there. Oh baby, hold it, hold it.

Nobody's in here. Thank you. Hurry, hide inside a stall.

Raaaaagghhhh, arrrfff, sphleeew ... stop, stop. Please. That's it. No more. You're better, you're better. No more. Please, I beg. No - no! I'm going to die.

Arrrgghhh, Huuurrrllgg, Roggghhh, Gagggg ...

Catch your breath. Oh baby, it's over. Flush it away. Brown floating chunks of food, strains of creamy white milk - oh no, even blood. All over the seat ... wipe the spittle from your lips and chin. Catch your breath. Quick, wipe off the toilet seat and sit down before anyone comes in and sees us kneeling over the commode.

Sweety, this one was the worst. You're not going to live much longer at this pace. Blood, honey, you vomited blood! I'm glad there's not a mirror on the door of this stall. How could we look at ourself? Eyes watering, cheeks flushed, streams of perspiration seeping from our brow, slobber hanging from our lower lip, and chunks of vomit clinging to our chin. Even your breath must smell horrible.

Jenny, are we this terrible to bring such a fate on ourselves? Who else in their right mind would sit on a commode after barfing their guts out before a board meeting? No one but you. What have we done to deserve such misery?

Don't upset yourself, baby, you'll get sick all over again. Clear your mind. Massage your heart. It's beating much too rapidly. Calm down, honey. Feel the pulse in your left wrist. Throbbing. Squeeze it with your fingers. Relax yourself. Breathe deeply, now exhale. Settle down. Empty your mind. Close your eyes and roll them into the back of their sockets. That's it. Breathe. All right, you're feeling better.

Why must we go to such lengths? Why can't we feel normal? You know why, Jenny. Look at the way you've lead your life. The last time you appeared in public rather than hide, you vomited in a trash can while your lover violently raped ... not to mention the other perverted aspects of our adulterous relationship. Jennifer, sweetheart, you've plummeted into the sewer of existence — anal intercourse, puking, stealing plants, manipulating that naive author into signing a contract. Is it any wonder we're sick?

Damn it honey, look at us! We're inside a bathroom stall, cringing from a world beyond our control. Life wasn't supposed to be this way. We had everything going for us. Remember the hope that filled our heart ... the anticipation? Each day started with promise ... then we met Philip Prince. You never should have let him into your life. The signs your body sent were warning enough - the nervousness, galloping heartbeat, and unbearable nausea. But he drew us in, destroying our future in the process.

Our evening together beneath The Latera Shrine was marked by eeriness from the onset - rolling blankets of fog, electrical outages, and owls hooting from every direction. I should have joined my girlfriends for pizza as originally planned, but instead Philip lured me toward a spot fraught with mystery and danger.

"No, Philip, not now. I'm not ready."

I gazed up at The Breached Circle, its cracked granite surface looming below a yellow light that flickered off and on.

"Let's go back to the dorms. I'm scared."

"Don't deny me, Jennifer. The decision has already been made."

Baby, we should have never continued such a twisted relationship. Every aspect of life from that point forward was tainted by our decision. How could you have acted so foolishly? Look what happened. You're a fifty-four year old woman crying in a corporate restroom.

Oh no! What time is it? Damn, we're already late for the meeting. Get up Sweety, c'mon. I can't. I can't. Here it comes again. Please no. Release me. Uh oh, I felt it bubbling. You'll never make it, honey. You'll die this time - we'll choke to death, or hemorrhage from a ruptured abdomen. Please don't let it end this way. I can't take another round. It's coming. I don't feel well. It's rising, taking control. Breathe. Breathe. Squeeze your wrist. I can't swallow. I need water. Help! Help! I beg of you, whoever you are, save me. I've reached the bottom. I apologize. Changes will be made, I promise. I'm through with my past ways. Please help me. Don't make me puke again. I'll die. I'm not ready for death.

"To destroy, one must turn to creation."

"Who is that? Mother? Who are you?"

"Jennifer, I've been waiting for you."

"You're not my mother. Where are you?"

"I've always been here."

"I don't understand, what do you mean - to destroy, one must create?"

"Jennifer, do you want to eliminate these attacks that are slowly killing you?"

"Of course. More than anything."

"Then turn to creation."

"But I've written all my life."

"No, you haven't. You've merely gone through the motions."

"Who are you? Please, tell me."

"I'm your Muse. I've been here all along, but you've never really asked for assistance until now."

"Please help me. I'm dying. Show me the proper course to follow."

"Jennifer, for an author such as yourself - attaining the state of publication is all that matters. Any other pursuit not related to this endeavor is unimportant."

"But how can I destroy The Sickness? While it's still with me, I'll never be able to create ... or even function for that matter."

> "To create eternal literature, one needs to purify every aspect of their life before being able to discover The Word. Only after they have been cleansed, by beginning a new novel at page one, will they be able to discover that which has always existed. It's now your responsibility to accept The Word."

"I accept it! I do."

Jenny, sweet Jenny, what's happening? It's gone. The Sickness has left! It's gone! Get up, Sweety. You can actually function. Go look in the mirror. Oh baby, you're beautiful. Look at your face. We're radiating! The fear in our eyes has disappeared. You're free, Jenny, free to live your life. C'mon, let's go to that meeting!

They looked at me with the usual measures of suspicion, anger, and contempt. I'm the company freeloader, the one who never pulled her weight. But I'll show 'em.

"I'm sorry for being late. It'll never happen again."

"We've heard it before," one of the men mumbles into his hand.

Finding a chair adjacent to Mason Turner, I sit upright rather than slumping (or melting) into the carpet. Then, as he discusses business, I listen to his words attentively, even scribbling a few notes. Unlike every other meeting for the past thirty years where I concentrated on not trying to vomit, I could actually hear the owner speak with other agents. Some of my associates actually began staring at me with curious expressions, as if I were from some distant planet.

At one point, Mason Turner addresses me, delivering his words with the apathy of a robot.

"Jennifer, would you care to contribute anything this afternoon?"

Expecting to hear my standard response, the owner actually did a double take as I cleared my throat and spoke confidently.

"Thank you, Mister Turner. As a matter of fact, I would like to join today's discussion by saying that, within three months, I'll give you the next millennium's first literary phenomenon."

Sweety, we'll never forget that moment. Without exaggeration, time momentarily froze as Mason Turner's eyeballs bulged from his wrinkled face. He probably thought poor Jennifer had finally lost her mind, or suffered from delusions of grandeur. The other agents gasped, sat with their mouths opened, or laughed sarcastically. But we can't blame them. We sat in the same chair for three decades without saying a word, then BAM, make such an outrageous claim that they thought I was insane. But we'll show 'em.

"Lola."

"Yes, Miss Ewen?"

"How long have you been my secretary?"

"Twelve years next month."

"In those twelve years, how much work have you seen me do?"

"Ma'am?"

"Answer honestly. What have I accomplished in the past decade?"

"Honestly?"

"Honestly, Lola."

"I'm sorry, but not much, Miss Ewen."

"You're right. For the past thirty years I've been out of the loop. But now, I'm ready to get involved in the business of being a literary agent."

Her eyes lit up with the magnificence of a Roman Candle. "Fantastic. I'm so happy for you!"

"Me too. Now, first things first. What does a literary agent do? ... ... It's a joke, Lola!"

"Thank goodness," she laughed, relieved.

"Anyway, have you noticed any prospects who've somehow slipped through the cracks? I don't want any of the standard intellectuals, academians, or pretty boy college graduates Mason Turner usually signs. I need someone special ... someone who stands out from the crowd and sparkles."

Beaming, Lola responded cheerfully, "It's funny you mention it. Do you remember me mentioning an author from Latera Heights?"

"My Alma Mater?"

"Yes. Then you flipped out and threw a fit."

"Not exactly," I replied. "The haze didn't lift very often."

"Well, I got another letter from him today. Ironically, a short while ago I mailed a rejection letter to him, signing your name ..."

"Standard operating procedure."

"Of course. But to his credit, he didn't surrender. He sounds quite unique, even ... nah, I better not say it."

"What, Lola?"

"I'll let you read the letters first. Then, if you come to the same conclusion, I'll verify it. Until then, I think you should check him out. He's written nearly sixty pages to you, even including another photograph in his last letter. You'll be impressed."

"Superb, Lola. What is this author's name?"

"His name is Ukiah Rhymes. Wait till you get a load o' him!"

26

Weeks passed without talking to Ukiah. I did notice him coming and going in Japhy's battered gray van (apparently repaired), or occasionally milling about in the yard. But for all intents and purposes, we went in different directions.

During this hiatus, I constantly worried about being forced to kill my father. The illegal aspect of my relationship with Ukiah had, in the past, been limited to events that slowly slipped by the wayside. Nonetheless, Ukiah could burst through my door at any moment and act like the distance between us never existed. Our separation would be all but forgotten as he'd rant n' rave about whatever occupied his mind. Then, within minutes, I'd once again be sucked into an inescapable universe of madness and absurdity. The ramifications were enormous - how could I eliminate my own father?

Ukiah actually thought we could profit from patricide. Plus, to collect the insurance money, he'd marry my mother. I hadn't realized it, but when they were married, Ukiah would become my stepfather! The idea was preposterous.

In the same breath, the thought of killing my father without repercussion (considering Ukiah's ability to escape from the law) was a tantalizing prospect. For the first time, I would be freed from his tyrannical grip.

> "Chris, you have the common sense of an Indian. You can't even tell the difference between shit and shinola."

> "I'm bored, Chris. Why don't you put on that little flowered cape and skip around like a fairy."

> "You'll never amount to anything."

> "Don't look at me that way or I'll bend you over my knee and paddle your little ass."

The situation would be different if Pus had acted that way when I was a kid, then realized the error of his ways as I entered adulthood. Granted, every person can look back at their youth and pinpoint certain actions that slighted, angered, embarrassed, or thwarted their progress. But my father uttered each of the above quotes within the past six months! He saw no difference whatsoever between my adult life and my childhood.

The memory of him is tattooed on my mind - digging a fingernail into my arm as we prayed in church, a leather strap or metal flyswatter across my bare ass, or the way he humiliated me at every turn. I could forgive him if the degradation had ended at some point, or if he felt remorse. But that rotten bastard leaped at every opportunity to control me … even today. He longed to belittle me, or cuff me across the head one more time. To him, I was a worthless failure - someone who didn't follow tradition by becoming a top-level executive or a successful physician. Instead of accepting me as I was, he considered me a disappointment. But what did my father expect? After being trampled year after year, one gets used to the pavement and the boot.

But I did do something he'd never done – I killed someone! I snuffed Woody Dewar with my very own hands. And now, if Pus didn't play his cards right, I'd murder him, too!

"C'mon, call me a horse's ass now."

"Chris, get off my chest. I can't breathe."

"Can't you? How interesting. I haven't been able to breathe for thirty years."

"For God's sake, what are you doing? Get your hands off my throat this very instant."

"How's it feel, Pus? For once I'm putting the squeeze on you."

"You're choking me. This game isn't funny. You're ... you're crazy."

"That's right, Father dearest. I'm a killer! You never knew, did you? I'm a world-class killer - a killing machine."

"You're no such thing you ... you confused lunatic."

"That's it!"

"Chris, you're killing me. Stop!"

"Say your prayers, Pus. It's time to cash in your chips."

"Chris, please, I'm your father. Let me up. Chris ... Chris ... ..."

If pushed too far, I'd take a second life!

Feeling crazed, I walked around the kitchen while reconsidering my violent thoughts. Who was I trying to fool? I'm not a killer. The one time I did take a life was by accident. In all honesty, I'd rather stay away from the world, hidden like I was this Saturday morning. A gorgeous late April sun slowly rose in a cloudless sky, painting the landscape with vibrant yellow rays. Why couldn't I bask in this peaceful state rather than being tormented by plots involving homicide and torture?

I didn't want to be a member of the mob, or intimidate people who crossed Ukiah. Nor did I look forward to murdering my father, or standing by helplessly as Ukiah married my mother. I never fancied police interrogations, high-speed chases, or hiding dead bodies. Believe it or not, I didn't even enjoy the prison nightmares that made me scream at three a.m. I just wanted to hide ... hide forever. Any person in their right mind would say, "Get out. Just leave this life behind." But I couldn't. If I disappointed Ukiah, he'd never come back. Then what would I have? Nothing but boredom and a broken heart. Why couldn't I enjoy the best of both worlds instead of being cornered by opposing forces?

Torn between two extremes, I decided to visit Ukiah before he left for the day. After pulling a windbreaker from the closet, I strolled past my living room window to see a startling sight. A rented moving van was parked in Woody Dewar's driveway, a metal ramp leading to its storage compartment. As a group of people carried furniture and cardboard boxes from the vacant house, I pondered the situation at hand. Being that his murder investigation had been terminated and the estate presumably settled, these strangers must have been Woody's family. Sighing with relief, I figured that after their packing was done, Dewar would be out of my life once and for all.

I watched from my window as his family loaded lamps, tables, chairs, and even Woody's mattress - the one on which we laid his stiffened body. A tinge of sadness struck me as these folks scurried in and out of his house. There were a few teenagers lugging the heavy articles, senior citizens performing the lighter duties, plus a handful of men and women close to my age who filled in the gaps. Although Woody was a pain in the ass, I felt sorry for the people who had to clean his house.

I hid behind my curtain, watching this solemn procedure. Even at a distance, a touch of sadness filled my soul. I regretted being the one who forced them into this ... no. It couldn't be. My remorse turned to disbelief as I rubbed my eyes, looked again, then averted my gaze. As if thrown into a nightmare, I collected my senses, rubbed my eyes again, then stared with wonder.

Who was it? It couldn't be! WHAT IN GOD'S NAME WAS HAPPENING? Was I losing my mind? Carrying a floppy pillow, the same one we had laid his head on, was none other than Woody Dewar! Woody Dewar! No way. He was dead! I killed him with my own hands. Ukiah and I dragged his corpse from my trunk and set him in bed. I felt the coldness in his limbs, and saw his lifeless eyes with mine. But there he stood beneath an elm tree, clutching a pillow to his chest.

Chris, what is happening? Is this person an apparition - a ghost? No! Ghosts don't exist. Are my eyes deceiving me? No. It's him - Woody Dewar. The only other explanation is that I've gone insane. Did the suppressed guilt hidden in my conscience bring Woody back to life? No. That didn't make sense. This kind of stuff didn't happen in the real world - maybe on TV or at the movies - but not in everyday life.

There he stood - Woody Dewar - wearing jeans and a black-and-blue checkered flannel shirt, pacing back and forth in his front lawn. Worse, he started walking toward me. Damn. Now he saw me lurking behind the curtain. Maybe he's seeking vengeance. What if he tries to strangle me? But how could a murdered man seek his own vengeance? Nothing made sense. Could it all be a dream?

Knock knock.

It wasn't a dream. What should I do? Refuse to answer the door. Hide in my bedroom. Knowing that moron ... sorry, I didn't mean to show disrespect for the dead. I hope Woody didn't add that remark to his list of offenses against me.

Knock knock.

Damn. He had me cornered. How could I escape? I couldn't.

Resigned to my fate, I inched toward the front door, tried to collect my senses, then opened it with a flurry.

"Woody! Long time, no see," I said cheerfully, trying to hide my fright.

He stood on the front porch, the same pathetic eyes dripping with sadness and deviance. To think, this man carried a medical bag filled with dildos, vibrating vaginas, and ... wait a minute. Ukiah planted that evidence inside his bag. I didn't know what to believe any more.

"Woody? Are you crazy? You must be taking his death pretty hard. I understand. You're still mourning. Well, grieve as long as you'd like. Considering your loss ..."

"My loss. What are you talking about, Woody?" I gasped.

He laughed with abandon - that smug, annoying chuckle that never left my memory. For no apparent reason, Woody found this situation particularly comical. Dewar hadn't changed since he rose from the dead - he had the same receding hairline, salt-and-pepper colored mustache, and that whiney, nasal voice that grated through my ears.

"I'm not Woody," he hooted, slapping his knee! "Woody's dead. I'm his identical twin brother, Kenny. But you can call me Always."

"Always? Why?" I asked, almost having a heart attack.

"Because I Always Dewar," he howled, cracking the same corny jokes as his brother. "The only things I like to do are get drunk and fuck!"

What a moron. He might have been dopier than Woody, if that's possible.

"Do you mind if I come in?" he asked.

"As a matter of fact, I'd prefer if you ..."

"Thanks," he snickered, brushing past me as he entered the kitchen.

After looking around nosily, Kenny pointed to an empty can of tuna on the counter and said, "Ya know, if you let that can sit out much longer, you could catch encephalitis through an airborne virus. I'll bet you weren't aware of that, were you?"

Frustrated and impatient, I snapped, "No ..."

Snooping through my cupboards, Kenny added, "In fact, most people think that encephalitis is said with a soft 'c,' like Seph. But in actuality, the 'c' is a hard 'c,' sounding more like a 'k.' So, phonetically, it's pronounced en-keff-a-litis. See, ya learn something new every day," he concluded proudly.

"Thrilling," I sniffed, tapping my foot on the floor.

Kenny walked toward my refrigerator, opened the door, and unbelievably, grabbed a bottle of soda, unscrewed its cap, and drank directly from the container.

After putting it back, then burping, he asked, "Did Woody tell you about the time he got food poisoning after I drank from his bottle of chocolate milk?"

Stunned by his audacity, I shook my head, making a mental note to throw away the soda bottle immediately after he left.

Stepping toward me, he then asked, "Did he even tell you about me at all?"

"No," I told him, a pronounced edginess in my voice.

"That scamp! It figures. Woody was always jealous of me ... worried that I'd steal his piece of ass."

"His piece of ass? What are you talking about?" I screeched, instantly angered.

"Chris, Chris. Don't worry. Officer Idem showed us Woody's medical bag, including your little photograph. You shouldn't be embarrassed about your fling with my brother. He always did have an interest in the bizarre."

"I can't believe you'd even consider ..."

"I understand, Chris. Woody held a special place in your heart. But don't worry. I'm married, but I can be as discreet as the next guy. I wouldn't mind trying what's on the other side of the fence. Ya know that old saying about the grass being greener ...”

“Get out. GET OUT!”

“Wait a second ...”

Grabbing a frying pan from the sink, I threatened, “Get out before I smash your skull! I’ll knock your lights out.”

“But, but ...”

“Get!”

Kenny Dewar fled from my house, his eyes possessing the same sadness that Woody’s had when I got rid of him. The nerve of that man. How could he think I’d ever have an affair with him or Woody? I should have killed the entire family and spared future generations a considerable amount of frustration.

Still upset, I tried once again to visit Ukiah. As the Dewar family continued to empty Woody’s house, I slipped undetected from my porch, then snuck through the back yard, tapping lightly on Ukiah’s hollow wooden door.

“Howdy, neighbor,” he beamed, holding a roll of paper towels in his right hand. “What’re you up to?”

Shamed by my visit with Kenny Dewar, I didn’t even mention it. Instead, I walked into Ukiah’s house, asking what he was up to this morning.

“Cleaning,” he told me, spraying his meager belongings with furniture polish, then wiping them with a rag. I must admit, all doubts concerning Ukiah’s suitability as a tenant, at least in terms of cleanliness, had long since been erased. His cottage sparkled, always filled with the pleasant smell of air fresheners and aromatic sprays. The dishes were washed, carpet swept, and counters sanitized. Even his bathroom, which held the most potential for neglect, was in pristine condition. He came a long way from those pitiful days at Transformer Towers.

While he dusted, I asked, “What’s new? I haven’t talked to you in ages.”

Spraying a rickety endtable, he said, “Well, my TV fried last week, so it sent my life into chaos.”

“Chaos? I didn’t even think you watched that much television.”

“I don’t, but I pattern my morning around the local news.”

“Huh?”

"I get up at 5:30, the same time the news begins. I then cook a couple eggs, finishing them when the announcer segues to a national news update. Next, I brush my teeth as the business report comes on, then shower during their sportscast. I should have the water turned off and be drying myself when the newsman starts his birthday quiz … y'know, where he gives clues to which stars were born that day. Finally, I finish dressing, brushing my hair, and spraying my deodorant when the weather forecast starts, then get my shit together and leave the house during their healthcast. Everything falls into its proper order like clockwork. But now, with no TV, I'm lost."

"Why don't you just look at the clock?" I asked, as if stating the obvious.

"It's not the same," Ukiah told me, dusting a bookcase. "Oh," he then perked, "I went to the library last night, and guess who's coming back?"

"Who?"

"Joan Jett and the Blackhearts! I found it on the Internet. They're playing tonight in Dichaville, New York."

"Are you going?" I asked excitedly.

"We're going," he told me with a smile. "I hope you don't have plans."

"None."

"Super. Guess what else I investigated."

"I can't imagine."

"I started looking into Jennifer Ewen, digging for anything I could find in the literary digests and market reports. I scoured every article I could get my hands on."

Shaking my head, I said, "I still think you're wasting time on that lady, but you know best. Did you find anything?"

Ukiah poured a bottle of bleach into his sink, commenting, "It's strange, but I couldn't find the slightest mention of her anywhere. I mean, I knew she went to Latera University, and was employed at Mason Turner for at least thirty years, but beyond that, it's like she hasn't done anything in three decades. Out of curiosity, I scanned the records of other literary agents, and found who they've signed and represented over the years. But with Jennifer, I hit nothing but dead ends. It's hard to imagine, but it seems like Miss Ewen hasn't signed one author since she started at that agency."

"Incredible," I sighed. "What's her story?"

"Who knows? She's a mystery. I couldn't even find a picture of her except for this grainy photograph I tore from an old magazine when she signed with Mason Turner."

Curious, I asked frantically, "Do you have it? Let me see."

"Here," he said, pulling a folded piece of paper from his notebook.

"Wow, it's hard to make out, but she looks young ... very young."

"My sentiments exactly. I just wish some other information existed, or at least an updated photograph. It's hard to tell what she looks like."

"You have a point," I agreed, returning the aged piece of paper.

"Hey," Ukiah perked, switching topics. "I noticed a moving van in Woody's driveway. I suppose the Dewar's are finally emptying the old homestead."

"I guess so," I said softly, turning away.

"Did you meet any of them?" Ukiah asked, now cleaning his stove.

"Yeah, Woody's brother."

"A brother? What was he like?"

"Ah, y'know, a jerk like Woody," I cringed, biting my tongue.

"So, we're on for the concert tonight?"

"Sure."

"Great. I'll catch you this afternoon. For the time being, business calls. It seems 'ol Charley from the lumberyard is skipping on his debts again."

Inexplicably, I asked, "Do you want me to ride along?"

Luckily, Ukiah told me, "No, I have other plans for you."

Other plans for me? What did he mean? The thought bothered me all afternoon until Ukiah arrived (sporting a black eye), saying he'd drive my Gemini to the concert.

Relegated to the passenger seat, I asked, "What happened to you?"

Pulling from the driveway to start another journey, Ukiah sneered, "'Ol Charley got rambunctious when I put the squeeze on him, so he took a swing at me. I have to admit, that old bastard can pack a wallop."

"Oh no," I said with a start, "I hope you didn't ..."

"No, Charlie can still roll his dice. But he won't be playing hopscotch for awhile."

"Ukiah, you ran his foot through the saw?"

"Not exactly," he smiled.

Leaving his answer open-ended, Ukiah cruised along a highway leaving town, fiddling with the radio. I was afraid he'd finally say what plans awaited me, but instead he dangled another carrot.

"Guess what I got in the mail a few weeks ago?"

"What?" I asked excitedly.

"Another request for material."

"Why didn't you tell me? You do this every time! That's great! Who asked for it? What did you send them?"

"Calm down, Chris. If I didn't know better, I'd think you were excited," he chuckled, his shiner looking sinister as he did so.

"Tell me," I urged, squirming in my seat.

"I got a letter from an agent in New York wanting material. Finally, someone with vision!"

"You did? Your plan is finally working. Who was it?"

"The lady's name is Sandra Spratt, and she works for Myron Liebowitz and Associates."

"They sound like lawyers," I commented.

"Actually, you're not far from the mark. On Sandra's letterhead, beneath Myron Liebowitz' name, was the title, 'Attorney at Law.'"

"Wow, that's weird. What does it mean?"

"Who knows? But I retyped seven pages from a novel, wrote her a letter, and mailed it the next morning."

By this time we hit a four-lane highway, cruising steadily toward the state line.

"What did you say in the letter? No. First, which novel did you excerpt? *Blank Line*? Wait; let's start at the beginning. What did Sandra say in her letter to you?"

"First of all, I sent another mailer to ten more agents, but haven't heard anything from them yet. Anyway, I came home one night after bailing a few hookers outta jail. I looked in the mailbox, and there's a letter from Myron Liebowitz. Since I'd been getting nothing but rejections from my query letters, I thought it was the same."

"But it wasn't?" I perked as the sun began to set.

"My name was typed beneath the letterhead, which was a good sign; then below it were the words 'Re: Representation.' I thought - damn! They want to represent me! I started losing my mind."

"What did the letter say? Quit beating around the bush."

"Sandra started by thanking me for my query letter, then apologized for not responding sooner. Hell, it only took her two weeks. Anyway, she continued by saying that due to an increase in submissions, they recently become backlogged. But the uniqueness of my letter caught their attention, and they wanted to see my work."

"She actually said uniqueness?" I asked.

"Uniqueness," Ukiah smiled, brimming with pride. "Then, Sandra told me to send the first three chapters of a book I considered my best work."

"When will you get an answer?" I triggered, pumped with adrenaline.

"Sandra said it normally took four to six weeks to review and discuss someone's material. Almost a month has passed since I mailed the package, so I should be hearing from her any day."

"Ukiah, you're doing it! You're actually going to be published."

"Not so fast," he told me, driving casually along the interstate. "Let's not jump to conclusions."

"I'm not trying to, but this is the best news ever. What kind of material did you send? What did you say in the cover letter?"

"Well, I started by thanking Sandra for her letter, then assured her that my introduction would be brief so she could get acquainted with my novel."

"Which one did you pick?" I asked anxiously.

"That was my main problem - selection. Over the years, I've written so much stuff. Hell, even over the past twelve months, while working fifty hours a week for Tattoo Blue, I wrote 1,050 pages. I've written novels, a screenplay, a horror story, fairy tale, short stories, and a study of Romlocon and The Word. So, to choose ONE sample which was indicative of the whole was almost impossible."

"What did you decide on?" I inquired, nightfall consuming the countryside as we crossed the state line.

"After considering all my options, I finally decided on a book I wrote years ago called, *Crocodile Tears*."

"I never read that one."

"I'm not even sure it's my 'best' novel ... whatever that means ... but the beginning reflects one of my main philosophies toward writing."

"What's that?" I asked, keeping in step with Ukiah.

"Get to the point without wasting time or boring the audience. In other words, start with a BANG. In *Crocodile Tears*, I did that both figuratively and literally!"

"How does the story begin?" I pleaded, consumed by curiosity.

"Without any background, I'll give it to you like I did to Sandra. *Crocodile* starts with a naked woman tied to a bed by two socks and a headband ..."

Oh no. I already doubted his selection.

"Then a man enters the picture holding a hair brush wrapped by two socks and a cellophane bag, held together with tape. This character proceeds to fuck the woman with this contraption while she willingly accepts it."

Oh my God. He couldn't be serious. What was Ukiah thinking? He may have plunged over the deep end.

"For the next seven pages, these two characters begin a relationship - the woman falling in love with a man who is cold, distant, and aloof."

Trying not to put a damper on Ukiah's spirit, I asked in a reassuring tone, "How do you think Sandra will react to your story?"

"I hope she doesn't get the wrong impression. *Crocodile* wasn't meant to be a gauge by which all of them should be judged. I just hate being cornered into one specific writing style. So, *Crocodile* is only one piece of the puzzle ... a piece that's connected to all the rest. I could have sent her more material, but decided to keep it short and sweet."

I felt a profound uneasiness as Ukiah's explanation continued.

"I could have written twenty pages about the state of literature in this country, and how I planned on improving it. But, being that her time is valuable, I concluded by saying that if she believed in me, I'd guarantee that both of us would become incredibly rich and famous. I'm no ham n' egger who can't back up his words. If Sandra doesn't worry about the status quo, or the way things have always been done, we could set the world on its ass."

A naked woman tied to a bed? He really was deranged.

Without warning, Ukiah howled, "I'm going to get published! I'll be famous. Do ya hear me, Chris? I'll be the hottest fucking writer in the country."

Afraid of stealing the wind from his sails, I asked, "Who did you write this story about?"

Tapping his fingers on the steering wheel, Ukiah began, "I used to live with an ex-stripper in Los Angeles. We were one helluva couple."

Trying to convey my doubts, I asked, "How do you think Sandra will react to your submission?"

Turning the radio up and driving faster, Ukiah said loudly. "I'm not making any apologies for *Crocodile Tears*, but I will say I'm sorry if it offended her in any way. I wasn't trying to put Sandra in an uncomfortable position."

"But what if she gets the wrong impression?" I suggested.

"I'm not a smut peddler."

Ruffled, I shot back, "Then why did you pick such a provocative piece?"

Pushing the Gemini harder, he snapped, "There's going to be plenty of choppy water ahead of us. I wanted to be up front about these things, and not spring any surprises on her."

"What if Sandra thinks all your material is this cold?"

"Some of my stories are so tender ya'd think they were written by an angel. Chris, I want this agent to know the extremes, because my books hit every point on the literary spectrum."

All of a sudden I saw Ukiah's ultimate goal, and the risks he was willing to take. At first I thought his choice of materials was ludicrous. But now I understood his live-on-the-edge attitude. How many authors would submit such outrageous prose, especially when they were unpublished and unknown? None. No one would take such risks. But Ukiah approached literature the same way he lived life - all the way, balls to the wall, with no holding back.

Invigorated, I asked, "Tell me more about *Crocodile Tears*."

"Even though it starts with a chilly premise, the tale is ultimately one of redemption. The main character eventually falls in love with the dancer – then recounts the joys and hardships of their romance. It ends, though, on a tragic note that'd make any Greek playwright cry. Their relationship was like F. Scott Fitzgerald and his crazy wife Zelda,

r Sid Vicious and his girlfriend Nancy. The only difference was that they weren't
ne-dimensional, cardboard cutout characters like Sid and Nancy. Instead, the story
hows the complexities of their hedonistic lifestyle."

'Do you think their crazy sex lives will turn Sandra off?"

'It that doesn't, their alcoholism will!" Ukiah laughed. "I did tell Sandra that I've been
nown to get wild in the past, but now I'm clean and sober!"

'How many pages did you send?" I asked, unable to remember.

'Only seven. Being that this novel didn't use standard chapters, I wasn't sure how
nuch to submit. I just wish I could be there when Sandra and the others at her agency
ead this material. I'd love to meet them face-to-face. There's so much to say about
ur collaboration that I can't hold it in. Besides my vast arsenal of material, I know a
nillion ways to set the world on fire. I'm aiming for the limelight, baby," he boasted,
and I won't settle for anything less. With Sandra's help, I can make the literary
vorld's head spin. All she has to do is give me a shot. I'm going to be fucking
amous!"

'You will! You will!" I concurred.

'Then I'll show that asshole Philip Prince how an author is supposed to act. Hey look,
ver there, a sign for Dichaville. That's where Joan is supposed to play."

'I can't wait!"

'It'll be good to see her again. She's going to be great." Ukiah paused a moment,
urned from the interstate, then continued. "Speaking of Philip Prince, let's hit The
plycer Center next Tuesday. I heard his fan club ...."

'Prince's Minions?"

'Yeah, Prince's Minions have been having rallies every Tuesday night, just like every-
vhere else in the country."

Are they still looking for Atropos?" I chuckled gaily.

'Supposedly. It should be a hoot." Relying on an innate sense of direction, Ukiah
eered through Dichaville until finding a fairground that was cordoned off by brightly
olored flags. Pulling into a bumpy field, he bragged, "Wait until I get famous. That
diot Philip Prince'll run for cover."

'It is going to be a howl," I added. "You're lucky to have your Muse."

'My Muse?" Ukiah snorted. "You mean Romlocon?"

"Of course. She's guided you the entire way."

Backtracking, Ukiah spat, "I'm not sure Romlocon had anything to do with my success. In fact, the whole concept might be an illusion. I'm not even sure she exists."

Startled by this turn of events, I asked, "How do you explain your sudden good luck?"

"It's ME, baby, ALL ME. I'm all that exists. I don't need anybody's help but my own. I'll even be on *The Tonight Show.* That's a sure sign of success. Now c'mon, let's watch Joan rock n' roll!"

The opening band had already completed their set as we entered the darkened fairgrounds to find thousands of fans milling about drinking huge quantities of beer which was sold from circus tents. Somehow, we managed to push through the crowd and wind up only ten or fifteen feet from the stage.

The crowd, due to its rampant alcohol consumption, rumbled with anticipation - pressed tightly together under a sinister looking moon. As Ukiah vibed with anxious energy, I looked around, getting an uneasy feeling from what I saw. The people near the stage were pent-up, potentially explosive ... contained like gunpowder in a barrel. The alcohol continued to flow, spilling, bubbling, flowing down greedy throats as roadies set up their equipment under the cover of darkness.

"Ukiah, do you think we should move toward the back?" I suggested, overtaken by claustrophobia.

He either didn't hear me, or refused to answer. It was the type of setting that inspired such behavior. Members of the crowd spontaneously emitted wild whoops and hollers, hoisted plastic beer cups, and shoved those around them. One group of bald-headed hooligans especially caught my eye, their belligerence far surpassing the others. They looked dangerous, ruthless, as if they'd welcome a fistfight. These derelicts seemed like the type who'd enjoy being punched in the face just so they could return the gesture. What were we going to do? If they went berserk, who'd stop them? I didn't see any Security personnel. Unlike a typical nightclub where bouncers in yellow shirts made their presence known, this open-air venue reminded me of a Roman coliseum, or an old West town where lawlessness prevailed.

I tried in vain to draw Ukiah from our crowded spot, but he was impervious, intently eyeing his surroundings. He then started whispering to a tall, bearded man with intense eyes who also looked suspiciously at the frenzied atmosphere. I became terrified when the audience chanted in unison - We Want Joan - We Want Joan. Their volume increased as they stomped, clapped, and guzzled beer and whiskey from plastic cups. A buzz permeated the grounds - a violent, electric charge that swept across all those in attendance.

Meanwhile, The Baldly Sours (the men with shaven heads) increased their rowdiness by shoving, bullying, and intimidating anyone who neared them. If only the concert would start. Then, maybe ... hopefully, this negativity could be forgotten and everyone ... damn it ... The Baldys were out of control - elbowing innocent people in the darkness, lifting their psychotic girlfriends in the air, and screaming bloody murder. Where was security?

"We Want Joan! We Want Joan!"

Shrill, deafening whistles shot through my ears as the crowd stomped, hollered, and clapped - their intensity and anticipation building to a fevered pitch. My heart skipped madly as people in front of the stage started shoving everyone in sight, creating a ripple effect that slammed toward me. Why couldn't we stand somewhere else? I wanted to ask Ukiah, but his attention was focused on The Baldy Sours.

"We Want Joan!"

The crowd soared toward delirium - whistling, screaming, hollering like rabid animals.

Pandemonium broke loose when the stage lights were dimmed. A primitive bass drum resonated through my chest as my ears pleaded for relief - ringing as young girls shrieked with excitement.

Then WHAM! A torrent of brightly colored lights exploded with brilliance as Joan Jett and her band barreled into their opening number. A dizzying mass of bodies shoved us from behind, pushing forward toward an already unmovable sea of people. I saw us getting knocked over, then trampled to death as drunken maniacs stepped on our bodies.

Joan appeared in her usual stage attire - short-cropped blonde hair, dangling jewelry, a black, low-cut rubber vest, skin-tight leather pants, and black boots. With her dark, mascara-lined eyes on fire, she growled her lyrics while ferociously strumming a white guitar. By now, due to crowd shifts beyond our control, Ukiah had moved away from me. I caught glimpses of him bouncing in place as fistfights broke out near the stage. The Baldy Sours were out of control, flailing their arms and elbows as those in their line of fire looked on helplessly or ran for cover.

Nervousness overtook me as I tried to keep my balance. I had hoped that Joan's appearance would calm the crowd, but instead, they only grew wilder. I tried moving toward Ukiah when WHACK, a flying elbow caught my upper lip and sent spasms of pain through my mouth. Momentarily dizzied, I regained my senses to taste blood on my tongue. Panicked, I wiped my face with the back of my hand, only to find the blood from my mouth smeared across it.

The entire place was swallowed by bedlam - waves of momentum sweeping bodies about like rag dolls, the Baldy Sours creating havoc, while drunken revelers stumbled around madly. I anticipated a riot when Joan stopped playing midway through her second number and berated the audience.

"All right, motherfuckers," she bellowed, eyes like a wildcat. "If you don't stop this craziness, someone's gonna get killed up front. And you," she pointed at one of The Baldy Sours. "Your fighting is starting to suck the big dick. Do ya know what I mean? It's like, real offensive! Now cool it, or we're outta here."

Magically, as if following an order from above, the crowd settled into a calm, yet excitable state. Joan, all five foot, two inches of her, tamed a raging beast. Ukiah, along with the bearded man beside him, no longer appeared edgy – both of them finally able to enjoy the show.

Joan delivered a performance for the ages. Energized by the crowd, she tore through her set with abandon. In no time she had taken possession of her spectators, lifting them to new heights. Joan became the only woman in existence for that short period of time - steam rising from her sweaty body into the cool, crisp air. I'd periodically turn to see Ukiah fixated by her presence - her compact breasts nearly peeking from the skimpy rubber vest ... her narrow, compact hips wrapped by tight leather pants ... and her eyes - wild, focused, and absorbing.

Joan churned out a number, bantered with the audience, then counted down the following number, holding up her fingers ... one two three four. She bounced around, flicked perspiration from her chin onto the audience, or winked at someone that caught her eye. At one point, a number of women, hoisted atop the shoulders of different men, lifted their blouses to show their breasts to Joan. She, in return, smiled and pointed, obviously delighted by their affectionate displays while barreling into a new number, carrying each fan until the concert ended with three impassioned encores.

Afterward, as the drunken crowd dispersed, I found Ukiah beaming with an intensity I had never witnessed. Even though he'd seen this show four times now, it still sent him into a different world. As for myself, I was both relieved (that I hadn't been trampled to death), and exhausted (from ninety minutes of pure exhilaration). My ears rang, legs ached, upper lip was puffed and sore, while my hands stung from clapping. It was one helluva performance.

Afterward, we reached the Gemini, this time with me handling the driving duties. Luckily we were able to sneak from a rear exit, soon finding the main highway out of town. Beside me, Ukiah radiated enough electricity to light a small city.

"So, you survived the melee?" he asked, still buzzing.

"For the most part. Someone bashed my lip with their elbow, but what the hell! I had a blast."

"Did you see her? Did ya? Joan has to be THE most beautiful woman on earth. She knocks me out."

"She is incredible," I agreed, soon consumed by darkness as we hit the interstate.

"Every time I see Joan, she gets even cooler, if that's possible."

"I'd give anything to be that cool," I said absently, as if in a dream. "How did she get that way?"

"I'll tell ya - by being her SELF. Joan pops on stage, and in her opening number tells the world - I don't give a damn what you think of me. Once a person gets to that point and calls their own shots without regret, then they're able to define their identity. I know a girl named Trudy who works at the makeup counter at a department store. She's so obsessed by appearances and image that it astounds me. It's a shame, because I used to have a crush on her, but Trudy's whole world revolves around show. I could give endless examples, but essentially this gal wants to be a society queen - Miss Mademoiselle - with her chin in the air and clothes from the high fashion rack. It's pretty sad. She pretends to be a movie star in one of those grocery store scandal sheets, when in reality she puts makeup on the faces of old women. The job is actually cool in and of itself, but Trudy acts like she's married to a Hollywood actor and has won an Academy Award. Her entire universe is based on phoniness. But Joan chops off her hair, dyes it blonde, and dresses like she'd kick your ass up one side and down the other. She presents herself to the world and says, 'Here I am! Take it or shove it.' Man, I could watch Joan every night of the week."

"Who would have ever guessed?" I laughed, cruising along an empty highway.

"Yeah, speaking of cool, I'm reminded of my cat Deuces," Ukiah said softly. "The thought of that little feller's death still gnaws at me."

"I would have loved to seen him."

"Deuces said to hell with the world and ran all day, doing who knows what. He'd be gone for hours - racing through the woods, roaming about the field, or stalking small animals he never caught. He'd then rush into the house, grab a bite to eat and a drink of water, then zoom back out. A lotta people said, 'Who needs a pet like that?' They want one that slavishly craves their affection. But Deuces called his own shots and made his own rules. He came and went as he pleased, did what he wanted, and created his own world. I sure do miss that little boy."

With those tender words serving as an end to our conversation, we drove the rest of the way home in silence.

Tuesday finally arrived, the night of our planned venture to the Bryce Splycer Center where we would see Prince's Minions in action. I counted the minutes at work, then rushed home to eat supper and prepare for the evening's activities. When readied, I strolled through the backyard, knocked at Ukiah's door, then entered.

Once inside, I noticed him, wearing a black T-shirt with an indecipherable symbol across his chest, dragging a vacuum sweeper from the closet.

"Did I interrupt?"

"No," he assured me. "I can do it later. I'd rather watch Prince's Minions trying to emulate their hero."

"We're still on?" I asked.

"Of course. Just let me grab a box. I'll be back in a minute."

After he left, I walked toward Ukiah's television set, pulled the knob, and found that it still didn't work.

Upon his return, I said, "I see you haven't fixed your television set."

"No, not yet," Ukiah responded, carrying a plain brown cardboard box.

"You should go to Tattoo Blue's pawn shop," I suggested, "and get a new one ... even a color model. This is the modern age!"

"Color? Nah, I'll stick with black-and-white. I like it a lot more. Are you ready to roll?"

"Sure. What's in the box?"

"You'll find out," Ukiah said mysteriously, carrying the cardboard box as we left his house and walked to my car.

Riding shotgun, Ukiah put his unmarked container in the backseat, then told me to swing by his mailbox after I started my car. I did so, following Reflection Alley to a solitary box that stood along a dead end. Ukiah reached through the darkness, opened the lid, then momentarily froze.

"What is it?" I asked, my heart suddenly beating faster.

"A letter from Sandra," he said, holding the envelope in his right hand after rolling up his window.

I looked across the seat to see "Myron Liebowitz - Attorney At Law" printed on the envelope's upper left hand corner.

"This is it," he said unemotionally, almost lifelessly.

"Holy Shit! I can't believe it," I interjected frantically, turning on the overhead light. "They wrote back! You're going to be famous. Open it. Hurry!"

Ukiah silently tore the envelopes flap, pulled out the letter, then unfolded it. Squinting in the low light, he read for less than a minute, then swore as he flung it to the floor.

"Shit. Son of a bitch. Fuck," he burst angrily. "I knew Jennifer and S.W.A.N. were behind this travesty."

"What did Sandra say?" I panted, wanting to grab the letter, but thinking better of it.

Ukiah picked up the letter, then read:

Dear Mister Rhymes:

Thank you for the letter and for sending us a copy of your manuscript, *Crocodile Tears*, which we have all read and discussed.

While we agree the manuscript is unique, and a most interesting choice for a first-time submission, we don't think it works as written. The plot appears to be driven by an exaggeration of a single idea, rather than a strong story line. We feel it would be difficult to find a place for it in today's trade market, and unfortunately, we don't currently have the necessary time to help you develop this project.

We thank you for thinking of us in connection with your work, and wish you the best of luck.

Sincerely,

Sandra Spratt

"Damn it! What happened to Sandra's vision?" Ukiah sneered, sitting on the edge of his seat. "She's thinking small time. Didn't I tell her to forget about how things were done in the past? We're starting from page one. Why is she even worried about a single book? There are so many possibilities in front of us, especially when she's only read SEVEN pages. Shit, I have fifty-seven pounds of material ready to hit the presses. She hasn't even met me. Then she'd change her mind. Sandra's intellectualizing things. That's where she made her mistake. She needs some street smarts."

"I'm sorry, Ukiah. You can always try somewhere else ..."

"Sandra's playing by the old rules of literature - all this shit with a bunch of jerk-offs sitting around a room discussing the merits of chapter one. How boring. She shouldn't worry about that crap. Sandra's decision should be based on a face-to-face meeting with me. I'll change her mind and show her the light. I know human psychology better than anyone. Here's what she should focus on. The whole package. Me! And even though I believe in myself whole-heartedly, it doesn't really matter. The American public will choose form over substance any day."

I slowly pulled from the mailbox, sure to shy away from any sudden movements that would disrupt Ukiah's seething monologue.

"Look at Madonna. Is she a star because of her musical abilities? Hell no! She succeeded because somebody had the foresight to capitalize on her vision and exploit the cult of personality concept. That's what we need to do. Name one writer who can excite people like performers in other fields such as music, television, sports, or movies. There aren't any because everyone in the literature business keeps perpetrating the same backward mentality that's in Sandra's letter. Shit, how is she ever going to hit it big if she keeps thinking like it was yesterday, or letting those eggheads at Liebowitz make up her mind? It's time to push the envelope into tomorrow."

"What do you have in mind?" I asked, driving toward the Splycer Center.

Ukiah crumbled the letter in a ball, threw it to the floor, then continued. "Here's the plan. I've written eighteen books so far. Instead of putting all our eggs in one basket by publishing a single novel, Sandra should call a press conference and say we plan on publishing one book a month for a year and a half straight! Wouldn't that set the literati on their asses? It'd be unprecedented. We'd also tell 'em that I got an ungodly amount of money as a signing bonus ... the largest in history. Then I'll hit the podium and say something provocative - even offensive - that will generate tons of publicity."

I weaved through town, listening to Ukiah's peculiar views of the publishing industry.

"Right after this conference, we'll launch a four year book tour, hitting every major market and small town across America. But this won't be your standard book-signing venture with some stiff, boring dickhead in a tweed jacket talking about plot structure. No way. I'm going to storm into these bookstores with a rock n' roll band - maybe even Mirror Image - charge admission, and sell T-shirts, CDs, and other stuff. Y'see, with the band, we'll attract an audience ... the kids, who are non-readers, while I'll draw the literary clique. It'll be a riot, completely wild and exciting. The possibilities are endless."

So were the limits of Ukiah's imagination. Now he wanted to rope Japhy's band into his plan and haul them around the country. He might be completely nuts.

But Ukiah rambled on madly. "Check out how much money we could make. If we did three hundred dates a year, with two shows a day at different stores, that equals six hundred. If I sell one thousand 'pieces' a gig at only five bucks a pop, that comes to three million. If multiplied by four years, that totals twelve million dollars. And this doesn't even include what can be made off the band and from promotional items. We can make a killing, and that's just from the tour. We'll also be selling books and CDs all across the country. I'm not just a writer," he boasted, "I'm an industry!"

Seeing the Splycer Center, I asked, "What do you think Sandra would say about your plan?"

Agitated, Ukiah hissed, "Because of S.W.A.N.'s brainwashing, she's already written me off as a crackpot, or a dreamer. But if we played our cards right, and generated interest and controversy, we'd set the world on fire. I GUARANTEE that within five years, we'd roll over every other writing team in America. If Sandra would only forget about story lines and what will sell in the 'Trade Market.' She should flush that shit down the commode, along with any ideas about developing my projects. The books don't need development, our marketing strategy does! She has to think big, like Kiss does. We'd steamroll across the country, kicking every other writer's ass out the door, then laugh all the way to the bank. We can do it! All Sandy needs to do is quit thinking about all this mundane bullshit. I can make the world hers! I'll be the next Prince of the Earth! All she needs to do is setup an appointment in New York. After Sandra SEES and HEARS me, she'll agree that my package can sell. I'd convince her. Why not throw caution to the wind? What does she have to lose? One lousy meeting with me. Why won't Sandra give me a shot? I'm a fighter, and I ain't afraid of ANYTHING. Why should I be? Throw your dice, baby. You won't be sorry. What else is she going to do, develop some flunky who'll sell five thousand books? Screw that."

I pulled into the Splycer parking lot, aghast that Ukiah truly believed these thoughts.

"When I write back to Sandra, I'll tell her I'm so confident that I don't want any more letters. I'm not settling for anything less than a direct phone call. I want to personally hear her voice. Why should Sandy sell herself short? All she based her last decision on was the bottom line - money. And who could blame her? Not me, 'cause I could make tons of it. But I've only touched the tip of the iceberg. I don't know what she's waiting for." Ukiah paused for a second, then commented, "Holy shit, look at the size of that crowd. C'mon, park behind that cluster of trees. We don't have time to waste."

Ukiah's tone didn't settle well with me, but I did as he said, pulling behind a thicket of pine trees.

After turning off my lights and stepping outside the Gemini, I said, "Look at them. It's amazing."

Gathered between the Splycer Center and football stadium were approximately seventy-five of Prince's Minions. Holding placards that read, "Atropos must go," these folks wore normal street clothes except for their heads, which were concealed by frighteningly garish homemade masks supposed to represent Bubos Virginianus - The Great Horned Owl. The sight of these masks sent chills through my body because it looked like some tribal uprising was at hand. Bathed by fluorescent yellow light, the masks assumed a distinct wickedness with their brown feathers, tufts of fur, pointed ears, beaming yellow eyes, pointed beaks, and open, fang-baring mouths. As a boom box blasted tribal drum music, Prince's supporters danced in small circles, lifted their signs in the air, and chanted, "Long Live The Prince."

Enraged, Ukiah snorted, "Look at those idiots. They don't even know what they're supporting. It's because of them that I can't find an agent. S.W.A.N. controls them just like they do the entire industry. The scariest part is, their numbers grow every day. Someday, Prince will rule the whole publishing world."

The Minions stomped around in circles, then stopped when one of The Owls (with distinct, pointed ears) hopped atop an elevated platform and addressed the crowd.

"Tonight we're gathered to praise The Great Horned Owl, and to make plans for capturing Atropos, the hooded attacker. Bubos ... Bubos - spread your wings over us ... over the entire planet, and place us under your control. Assume, and rightly inherit once and for all, your throne as true Prince of this Earth!"

While the crowd applauded robotically, then lit torches and swung them through the air, Ukiah's mood grew fouler.

"Can you see what's happening?" he asked, focusing intently on the proceedings.

"I'm not sure, but it's weird."

"It's obvious," Ukiah sneered. "The Minions pretend to be a benevolent group whose only purpose is to capture Atropos. But in reality, once their veil has been removed, The Minions are a front organization for S.W.A.N. – intent on undermining those who have true literary pursuits."

"I don't understand," I told Ukiah as the protesters produced a scarecrow with a black hood over its head.

Frowning at this display, Ukiah began, "S.W.A.N.'s primary goal is to control every reader's mind by destroying our language to such an extent that people won't be able to differentiate between quality literature and pulp."

"I still don't see your point."

"Look at S.W.A.N. and O.W.L. What do their opening letters stand for? Single Word and One Word. Don't you get it? Those eggheads want to boil our language down to nothingness. Then, when we can't tell good writing from bad, nothing exists except gray areas in between. There won't be any more absolutes. Over time, as readers become accustomed to inferior writing, they'll lose sight of creation's true aim. Authors will focus all their attention on the unimportant aspects of publishing such as fame, wealth, women, and influence rather than on The Word's purity. In the end, instead of trying to enter the gates of publication, readers will start worshipping characters like Bubo Virginianus. Eventually, The Word will be entirely eliminated, replaced by a language without meaning or substance. Philip Prince and his likes will reign supreme, while Romlocon The Muse will fade from memory."

I wanted to ask Ukiah a few questions, but was distracted by The Minions, who nailed an Atropos scarecrow to a plank of wood, then began urinating on it.

Disgusted, Ukiah snarled, "It's time to teach those fuckers a lesson. Listen closely, Chris."

"To what? Oh no."

"What time is it exactly?"

I checked my watch, then said, "7:12."

"Okay," Ukiah panted, opening the Gemini's back door, then motioning for me to look at his cardboard container. "Here's the plan." He unfolded the box's flaps, exposing an enormous battery-powered spotlight - the kind used to spot deer, only bigger. "At exactly 7:22, put this light on top of one of those car roofs ... let me see ... how about that white Javelin over there. Then wait a minute to see if anyone's spotted you. If not, at 7:23, aim it at that perch below the scoreboard. Do you know which one I mean?"

"That place with the metal grating?"

"Exactly. Now this part is crucial. After you turn the light on and aim it, crouch behind that Javelin and wait for approximately sixty seconds. At first, a few of The Owls will search for the light's source. But after I divert their attention, you'll be in the clear."

"In the clear? I don't understand. Ukiah, what's going on?"

"All your questions will be answered in no time, so pay attention. After you wait for a minute, sneak back to the Gemini. Being that we're parked behind these trees, you'll be able to pull away undetected."

"Where am I going?"

"Drive down Kontra Lane, around the stadium, and park at the Latera Memorial Wall. Don't drive straight past the stadium. If you do, The Owls will see your car, then write down your license plate number. Is everything clear?"

"I think so, but ..."

"Okay, be ready at exactly 7:22. I'll catch you later."

With those parting words, Ukiah crept through the darkness, leaving the Gemini and me in our secluded spot behind the pine trees. What was happening? Without warning, I was involved in another one of Ukiah's harebrained schemes.

I looked at my watch - 7:18. Only four minutes until the plan was to begin. I held the spotlight in each hand, then snuck toward the white Javelin. While doing so, The Owls propped Atropos' mannequin (still nailed to a plank) against a street sign, doused it with gasoline, then set it on fire. I couldn't believe my eyes. They were burning Ukiah in effigy!

7:20. I neared the Javelin as Prince's Minions danced in circles around the flaming, hooded scarecrow.

7:21. I stared intently at my watch, then set the spotlight on the Javelin's roof.

Ten seconds ... nine ... eight ... no one noticed me due to the burning scarecrow ... three ... two ... one ...

I aimed my spotlight at the scoreboard's perch, then pressed its ON button, instantly producing a bright streak of light. At first, The Owls didn't notice, but they soon followed its beam toward the scoreboard after one of them hollered and pointed in that direction. Meanwhile, I did as Ukiah instructed, crouching out of sight for the time being.

While doing so, I looked between the cars to see a fantastic sight. Standing atop the scoreboard in front of the light was none other than Ukiah (as Atropos) wearing his symbol-laden T-shirt and a black hood with two eyeholes! Ukiah had turned into the character who attacked Philip Prince. The sight was incredible. Dozens of vigilantes wearing owl masks and brandishing torches surrounded a burning scarecrow while a black-hooded man stood atop a scoreboard, illuminated by a spotlight. I almost pan-icked while crawling toward my car, but luckily my actions went undetected.

As Prince's Minions rushed toward the scoreboard, Ukiah (still hooded) pulled a bullhorn from behind his back, then taunted the crowd:

> "My name is Atrophy, the hooded spook ... No, I'm Apathy, the boogie man. Ooooh, look out. I'm scary. Yeah, right. Get a life. If I'm so scary, why don't you little hoot owls flutter up here and catch me? Ooops, I forgot. Birds don't fly very well with their heads stuck up their asses! Whoo-hoo. What a riot. I crack myself up. I'd love to stay and play all night, but I have shithead authors to track down and assault. Before I leave, though, since you're all Owls, and birds of a feather flock together, why don't we play a game called Turkey. I'll shit, and you morons can all fucking gobble. Later, suckers!"

As flashbulbs exploded like fireworks and a resounding chorus of jeers emanated from the crowd, Ukiah sped from sight as I slithered to The Gemini and pulled from behind the pine trees. I'm sure none of Prince's Minions saw me, for they clamored about the scoreboard, then rushed toward the stadium to find Ukiah.

As instructed, I followed Kontra Lane, circled the stadium, then pulled behind a granite wall with the words, "Latera University" chiseled across its face. I kept The Gemini idling in our prearranged spot, my heart beating frantically. What in God's name was happening? I saw fanatical vigilantes wearing homemade owl masks burn a scarecrow in effigy, while Ukiah climbed atop a scoreboard and harassed them. Now I sat in a getaway car, ready to have a heart attack.

Where was he? Did the mob capture Ukiah outside the stadium, then beat him to death or set him on fire? Or worse, had I misunderstood his directions and parked in the wrong place? What if I were the cause of his death?

"Hurry, go, go!" Ukiah demanded, hopping from nowhere into the passenger seat. "Turn your lights off. They won't be able to read your license plate."

Without question, I turned my headlights off, then sped from the Memorial Wall through an ocean of darkness. While doing so, I looked in the rear-view mirror to see dozens of fiery torches in the distance.

After escaping our pursuers, I flicked on the lights, then gazed to my right. Beside me, Ukiah's smile nearly leaped from his face.

"Did you see me?" he asked excitedly? "What a hoot ... no pun intended! I thought those people were going to kill me. Man, did I piss them off. They would have ripped me to shreds," he said, holding the mask between his fingers.

"Ukiah, what possessed you? Are you nuts?" I yelled. "I saw them. You could have been burned alive."

"Oh, man, what a rush! I felt like a fucking conquistador riding his stallion into an Indian village."

"What did it look like up there?" I panted, still brimming with adrenaline.

"What a sight. With the streetlights, the fire, torches, and your spotlight ... it was like being in a different world."

"Oh no," I gasped, pulling into my driveway. "I just thought of something. When the cops find that spotlight on top of the Javelin, they'll dust it for fingerprints. We're busted."

"We," Ukiah laughed, still beaming with life. "I wiped my prints off before I put it in the box. Did you really hold that spotlight without wearing gloves?"

Frazzled, I stuttered, "Yes, yes ... why did ... didn't you tell me? Every ... everything went so fast. Oh shit. The cops are going to get me. I'm through."

Stepping from The Gemini, Ukiah said, "Slow down, Chris. Have you ever been arrested?"

"No."

"Then there's no need to worry. How could they find something that doesn't even exist?"

As if the world had been lifted from my shoulders, I got out of my car, laughing as we walked along the driveway.

After entering my house, Ukiah said playfully, "I might go back next Tuesday and torment those imbeciles again."

Removing my shoes, I warned, "That's not a good idea. Did you see the flashbulbs? You'll probably be front page news tomorrow. Plus, the cops will be out in full force."

After taking off his shoes and sitting in my living room, Ukiah agreed. "You're right. I would love to take one more shot at those idiots, though." Ukiah's mood then switched to one of bitter resentment. "I don't know why I'm laughing about that rally. Those assholes are the reason *Crocodile Tears* was rejected by Sandra."

"They were?" I asked doubtfully.

"Them and S.W.A.N. If they weren't brainwashed into adoring Philip Prince, there'd still be room for true literature. But those illiterate Owls can't even read the back of a cereal box."

"They did look stupid in those masks."

"It's no wonder I feel like building a wall around my house. It gets to the point where ..."

"Where you hate people?" I interrupted.

"I don't hate mankind," Ukiah replied, "I just rarely feel 'of' them. We have nothing in common. I'd love to fade into oblivion, insulated from the world. I'd have no contact with society at all - no friends, no news reports ... it'd be like solitary confinement." Ukiah paused, then continued. "Isn't it ironic? The severest form of punishment - an isolation ward - represents the purest aspect of freedom to me. Maybe I wasn't meant for this world."

While Ukiah stared out a window into the darkness, I thought about his predicament. Externally, he exhibited a jaded, cold personality; yet internally, Ukiah melted with sensitivity. It seemed like his need to escape mirrored a fear of being hurt by the world. After repeatedly being knocked on his ass, rejected, and disappointed, he'd simply disappear into nothingness where the world couldn't touch him any more. In all honesty, how could he be faulted or criticized? Look at the world around us - the backbiting, gossip, petty bickering, jealousy, arguments, and resentment that complicate our daily lives. Plus, there were the silly games, commitments, and responsibilities that provided little reward. It's all nonsense. I understood Ukiah's search for a purified remoteness where he could be alone, removed from this madness.

Turning to face me, he seethed, "Why didn't Sandra accept my manuscript? Damn! I hit another dead end."

Uncomfortable, I blurted, "What about making me your agent?"

Bitterly, Ukiah snarled, "I forgot about that stupid idea ages ago. I only have one job for you."

Oh no. Please. No.

"You're going to kill your old man and collect his insurance money."

"No, Ukiah, I can't. I'd never be able to do it ... I wouldn't know where to start. How could I murder my own father?"

"He's killed parts of you, hasn't he?"

"Yes, but ... but maybe he'll change."

Ukiah laughed halfheartedly, then said, "Chris, let me explain something. Do you see this living room?"

"Of course."

"If you wanted to change its appearance, what would you do?"

Thinking for a moment, I said, "I'd rearrange the furniture, lay new carpeting, paint the walls, or get a few knickknacks."

"But after you're done, when the bells and whistles are gone, what do you have?"

I shrugged my shoulders.

"The same old room! Can't you see? My outlook might be pessimistic, but rooms are the same as people. Once the decorations are gone, the former trappings remain. People love to make others think they've changed - they lay new carpeting, hang wallpaper, and rearrange their furniture. But beneath these alterations, they're still the same."

"Ukiah, what are you saying? Your philosophy is so bleak and depressing."

"It is on the surface, but only because you didn't answer my question the right way."

"I don't follow."

"When I asked how you would change this room, you gave symptomatic solutions. But to really change something, it must be destroyed, then created anew. So, instead of rearranging furniture, break down the damn walls and start building from scratch!"

"Then the relationship I have with my father will never change?"

"Correct. For you to become a new person, he must be eliminated. Only by destroying him can you create a new life for yourself."

"I'm not so sure ..."

"Chris, it's the only solution. Think about it. For now, I'm going to scoot next door. I'll catch you later."

Time slipped by slowly that evening as I thought about Ukiah's suggestion. To begin anew, one must first destroy. The implications of this idea troubled me, but in all honesty, I had to admit that the concept of murdering my father crossed my mind numerous ... even an infinite number of times. As a child, I dreamed of his death, then replacing him as Mother and me lived happily ever after. But now, when actually faced with patricide, I doubted my ability to pull it off. In fact, there was no way I could kill my father.

To reinforce this position, I looked from my back window, saw Ukiah's lights, then decided to end this scheme once and for all. Putting on a hooded sweatshirt, I left my house, then remembered the other times when I snuck to Ukiah's cottage during the twilight hours. His walls bounced with insanity, sex, torture, and emotional break-downs. While recalling these events, an aspect of my SELF emerged which truly frightened me. I decided to once again lurk behind Ukiah's lilac bush rather than knock at his door and talk to him face to face.

Why did I choose this method over a more conventional one? Was cowardice an explanation? Partially, but I think it was more directly related to excitement - the rush of prowling through a darkened yard, sneaking behind the bushes, then exploding with fright as my heart beat out of control. The thought of watching people without their knowledge was wildly appealing to me. I remembered being a kid and hiding behind a couch in the living room when no one was there. I'd wait for hours until someone came into the room and sat down. None of them knew I was there, so they'd act completely natural - discussing things that weren't meant for children's ears. The excitement I got from this activity - somewhat related to No-Sho's fantasy world - never left me. I can't imagine anything being more exciting than hiding ... hiding from everyone.

So, knocking on Ukiah's door was no longer an option, at least at this point. Instead, I'd lurk in the shadows, stealing glimpses of life rather than directly confronting it. Deciding on this plan of attack, I ducked behind an elm tree, crawled beneath a row of bushes, then crept toward the rear of Ukiah's cottage. As usual, when the weather was nice, his window was partially open, giving me a perfect opportunity to eavesdrop.

I felt alive - blood gushing so intently that each vessel was ready to burst - brain speeding wildly, heart on fire, limbs tense, eyes darting. As I crouched beneath his lilac bush, I realized this was my greatest joy in life. If Ukiah found me, though, he'd beat me senseless. But the risk was worth it. I needed to feel the rush, the adrenaline, the excitement.

The sight confronting me as I peeked over the windowsill was riveting. Ukiah laid on top of his foldout bed, begging to his Muse.

"Romlocon, Please! Every day becomes more than I can endure. I'm not good enough to enter the gates of publication. I've tried to write literature of the utmost purity, but it still ends up being nothing but smut. I'm trying my best, but what does it matter? I'll never be united with you. I'm not good enough. I'm a shit writer. Why should I continue this lie? I'll never get any better. I've been faulted since day one. I feel myself slipping away from you. I'm stuck in the middle, can't you see? I hate S.W.A.N. with every bone in my body, yet I'm not worthy of your good graces either. What can I do? I climb this mountain every day, then the ground starts shaking and I end up at the bottom. I'm sick of starting from the lowest rung. If the gates of publication were to open this second and welcome for the last time every author who had enough merit to enter, I wouldn't make it. Oh Romlocon, why? I've tried so hard. I love you with all my heart. But each day, when trying to write quality prose, I end up defiling the page with filth from my demented mind. Where can I turn? S.W.A.N. is my archenemy, while you're distant and unattainable. Please help me. Guide my pen. I can't keep being trapped in limbo. Don't force me into S.W.A.N.'s arms. I want to be with you. Romlocon, embrace me. Show me the proper path. I'll do anything to purify the ink that drips from my pen. Cleanse me, wash me with your Word. Oh please, I beg of you."

Ukiah then rose groggily, stumbled toward a window adjacent to mine, then saw his reflection as he peered into the distance.

"Why have you left me?" he pleaded. "Let me lay my tired eyes on you. I'm starving. Isn't it obvious? Nourish me. Why, oh gorgeous love of my life, do you keep neglecting me? Am I so hideous that it sickens you? All the hookers adore me, but you, who I truly love, look at me with indifference. I crave the thought of your arms around me ... to kiss your lips - but every time I try, you run ... shattering my dreams. All I need is one kind word ... or an answer to my call. But no ... no. You won't give me these simple pleasures. Why? What would I see? I know! That I've treated others the same way. Yes, that's it! I'm on fire to be with you ... but what I see with my own two eyes is out of reach ... unattainable. I know I should leave ... to forget this silly infatuation ... but I can't let you slip away. I'll do anything ... anything to make you mine ... but I know, only by destroying myself will I be able to ignite that special bond between us ..."

Inexplicably, Ukiah yanked a silver knife from his hip pocket, then raked it across his left forearm, letting the blood drip toward his wrist.

Freaked out of my mind at this sight, I raced from Ukiah's window with the urgency of a wildfire consuming a forest. Ukiah had lost touch with reality.

27

Ukiah Rhymes - my little boy, look at you before me. I never thought it would happen, but today you stare back at me from this photograph. I'm sure it's you. It has to be. Your face is mine. If I didn't know better, I'd swear this picture was a mirror. We're finally reunited after all these years. This is how you turned out. A writer, just like your father and mother. It's miraculous, but you've found me, probably without even knowing it. Your letters are so desperate ... tortured, ego-driven, clawing and scratching for a shred of recognition.

Oh Jenny, sweet baby, what are you going to do? He didn't die. That poor, innocent child actually survived. Not only did he cling to life, but look at what he accomplished. Eighteen full-length books. I wonder what he's written about us? Philip Prince and I ... Oh God, if Ukiah didn't know I was his mother, he couldn't possibly be aware of Philip's identity ...

"Miss Ewen?"

"Yes, Lola."

"May I enter your office? I have something which should be brought to your attention."

"By all means. Please come in."

"Miss Ewen, something bizarre happened last evening in Latera Heights. Here, it even made *The New York Times*. The photograph is incredible."

"Oh no - it's Atropos ... that hooded man who attacked Philip Prince. Amazing. Thank you, Lola."

Could it be? There he is, in black-and-white – Atropos, the hooded fiend. Beside him, in this photograph, is my son Ukiah. His letters are angry, conceited, reactionary. How many times did he mention Philip's name in his correspondence? Countless, as if he were obsessed. You were inside that dressing room, Jenny. We saw him ... looked into his eyes for a frozen moment. Could our son actually be Atropos the attacker - The Latera Lunatic?

Jenny, what's happening? If it weren't for our intervention inside that dressing room, your abandoned son would have murdered his father. Worse, now he's taunting him ...

"Miss Ewen, line seven."

"Thank you, Lola. Hello."

"Did you see the newspaper? That son of a bitch is taunting me."

"Philip ..."

"What if he drives to New York and stalks me? Jenny, I'm scared."

Should I tell him? It'll only make matters worse. Think. What should we do?

"Jennifer, are you there? Are you even paying attention? This is serious. My life is in danger."

"Philip, settle down. Just lock your doors and keep a low profile. Maybe you should buy a disguise."

"A disguise?"

"Yes, you could dress like a candystriper, or that Lion from the Wizard of Oz. If Atropos plans on stalking you ..."

"You bitch. After he kills me, I hope he kills you, too. You weren't any help. Go burn in hell."

Ukiah's on a mission. I can sense it. He'll murder Philip with his own hands. What if our son uncovered the truth? He'd be furious. We've allowed him to wallow in poverty and obscurity for over thirty years. Rather than opening doors and nurturing my poor sweet child, I discarded him.

Oh Sweety, dear Jenny, for the first time in ages we're on the road to recovering our sanity. The sickness has been eliminated. Thank you, whoever you are, for helping me. If it weren't for your guiding light, I'd probably be dead. But now, with hope filling my future for the first time, this unexpected predicament confronts us.

Jenny, your son has lost his mind. He's a rampant psychopath pulling publicity stunts to torment a man he doesn't even know is his father. He actually tried strangling him to death. Now he's standing on a scoreboard wearing a black hood. What will we do, baby? You surrendered him once. You can't possibly lose him again. You're his mother, for crying out loud! Save him! He needs help. What can we do?

"Lola, could you please come in here?"

"Yes, Miss Ewen, what is it?"

"Please, have a seat. I need to discuss something with you in the strictest of confidence."

"Of course, ma'am."

"I assume you've read those letters from Ukiah Rhymes?"

"Over and over."

"You've also seen this article concerning Atropos."

"I have."

"Well, I remember you assuring me that if I came to a conclusion concerning a certain matter, you'd verify it."

"I did, indeed."

"Lola, this subject is very touchy, but do you think ... could Ukiah Rhymes be The Latera Lunatic?"

"Miss Ewen, I've reread his letters half-a-dozen times. In all honesty, I'd bet my life on it!"

"Oh God! I thought so. Why? Why Ukiah?"

"Miss Ewen ..."

"Lola, please, this is serious. Have you told anybody ... a single soul ... of your suspicions?"

"No."

"Nobody?"

"Miss Ewen, you know how I feel about Philip Prince. That arrogant bastard treats me like a barnyard animal. He's a condescending pig. I wish Atropos, or Ukiah, or whoever it is, would have killed him in Latera Heights. No, I assure you, I'd never say a word if it meant sparing Philip Prince's life."

"Thank you, Lola. I appreciate your honesty."

Jenny, he's our child. Considering the obsessive thread that runs through this family, you know he's not going to stop his vendetta. Ukiah's been forsaken, neglected, left alone in a terrifying world. But somehow he survived without our help. Now look at him. His eyes burn with vengeance. You saw them. We were inexplicably connected that dreadful afternoon. Did he know his father's rescuer was actually his own mother? How could he know? He was possessed by hatred, revenge, and insanity. My son has wanted to lash out since birth. He won't be satisfied with taunting those Tuesday night fools wearing Owl masks. He'll be drawn to Philip right here in the city. What can I do to change this situation? An impending death is certain - maybe even a blood bath. Honey, we can't let it happen. You've been saved, Sweety. As a result, we have responsibilities to uphold. We have to intervene. But how?

Darling, we're in a rent-a-car only ten miles from Latera Heights. We actually rented a car! Oh baby, you rarely left Manhattan for thirty years, now we're creeping toward the place of your downfall. We never should have abandoned our newborn baby, let alone carry through with such an atrocious act. You're the lowest form of human being. So unconscionable. A mother ... Oh sweety, how could we forget our own mother's torture? Despite her affliction, she adored you. But how did we act when given the chance to love our own child?

Jenny, oh precious baby, don't think about that horrendous episode. But we have to. We MUST! After six or seven months, when the baggy clothes couldn't cover our pregnant belly, we hid in a newly rented apartment. Philip would deliver the food ... and we stayed out of sight. We hid our baby, ashamed of the precious life held inside our stomach.

Our baby kicked and moved ... we could feel him. The only thing he wanted was love ... and we wanted to love him. But Mommy, what if he was sick like you? I hated to see the pain in your eyes - the vomit, helplessness, and hopelessness. I wanted him to die inside my belly ... but he wouldn't surrender. I loved him, Mommy, I did. But I'd never make a good mother.

Oh Jenny, quit lying. You didn't want to be bothered with a child. The whole world awaited you - an influential position at a publishing house, a wealthy, mannered husband, yachts, diamonds, and prestige. A newborn infant didn't fit into that scenario. What kind of man wanted a slutty eighteen year old with child?

But Philip raped us. He did. We begged for our virginity beneath the shrine. But that lust-filled monster wouldn't listen. He ravaged our body with a primitive ferociousness, then planted a seed that screamed with wickedness.

Oh love, we felt it growing - developing - tangling like a vine inside our stomach. I knew he was special - chosen - destined for an honored seat among the greats. But what about the sickness? It had to be considered. What if it happened to him like it did with Mommy and her ancestors? The thought of those latent, nausea-tainted genes growing inside him appalled me. Baby, little Ukiah, can't you see? I wanted to spare you. Of course my selfishness played a role in that decision, but ... but we suffer from a plague. Our ancestors, from the earliest times, from the dawn of creation, were marked by the sickness. I wanted to see it skip a generation, but that monster, Philip Prince, wouldn't let us be free. He ruined everything.

Baby Ukiah, I'm coming back to you. Please forgive me. If I could change the past, believe me, I would. But what can I do? Oh Jenny, hug him upon sight like you should have did at birth. You remember. How could we forget? Your belly grew even larger as the weeks went on until ... the urgency became undeniable. Struggling to Philip's car, we drove a hundred miles to Forsacan Hospital in the town of Ad Patres. There, no one would know us.

Sweety, we were awful, like a criminal covering their tracks after hiding a murdered corpse. But our thoughts weren't so clear at the time. A child was begging to enter the world ... water gushing along my legs ... indescribable pain. I didn't want him to enter the world. Inside my body, I could protect him, shield him, preserve his purity. But he wouldn't stay inside me.

Darling, how could we ever forget that glimmering, radiant sunrise peeking above the weeping willow trees as we parked behind a cluster of dangling vines in the woods? The car windows were clouded with moisture as our screams and pleas filled the morning air. Then we saw him, Sweety ... an untouched angel gently sliding to a virgin white sheet laid across the front seat. The placenta and blood filled me with horror, especially the umbilical cord attaching him to me. It slithered snake-like from my vagina - a grotesque noose wrapping my baby's body as he lie with Edenic purity on the seat while a crimson tentacle crept from my womb and tried to strangle him.

But Ukiah, my Sweety, I saw paradise that morning as yellow rays filtered from the sky. I wouldn't let this slithering serpent ... one that tangled from the depths of my polluted body ... hurt you. It could never deprive you of life's glorious gift. Despite myself, I loved you ... cherished you. I wanted you so badly, my dear. But instead, with your gentle whimpers echoing through my ears, I drove to that cold, faceless hospital and ... I held you so closely ... my precious baby. I loved you - such a gorgeous face, eyes flickering open to see mine. Oh baby, little Ukiah, it broke my heart to leave you. I wrapped you as warmly as possible in those blankets ... kissed your tiny cheek, then cried goodbye for the last time after setting you in a basket on those granite steps. Baby, I know you could never forgive me, but I did love you. I did. How could I have abandoned you?

Oh Latera, I remember those splendid days when you were mine - the whistles and adoring looks when we walked across campus, the gaiety of our dorm room slumber parties, and the joy of being free for the very first time. Oh baby, how different the world seemed back then when we looked in the mirror. Our eyes sparkled, seeing the future in terms of promise, not regret. Our smile brightened any room, while our words weren't tinged with suspicion or fear. Today, Latera hardly resembles that special place. Instead, it has become a land of remorse, lost possibilities, and squandered hope. Mostly though, it reminds us of a time we'd rather forget ... when our innocent child was tossed aside to lead a life he hadn't requested or created.

Jenny, should we really try to find him? We have his address from the letters, and located it on a map. Sweety, if we leave this gas station and drive two blocks to Reflection Alley, we could meet him. Ukiah won't be hard to recognize. Just drive there, honey. We've traveled this far.

I wonder which place is his? The large house in front, or the cottage to the rear? There's nothing we can do but wait. There aren't any cars in the driveway. Maybe we should leave a note and get a hotel room. But baby, we know ourself too well. All we're doing is delaying the inevitable. Just stay here and wait.

What will Ukiah say when we finally tell him who we are? I dread it, Jenny, I truly do. What if I tell him I'm a literary agent from New York City who has arrived to discover him. It could work. But baby, you see what happens every day at Mason Turner. Only yesterday you passed an office where another naive author signed his name on the dotted line. More tragically, you heard the screams that came from Old Man Turner's office. Whoever was on the receiving end of that deal finally discovered the publishing industry's true colors. How could I introduce him to such a disgusting environment? We already betrayed him once; twice would be inexcusable.

Whoever rescued me from my sickness, please return. I need help, can't you see? Spare me from this torment. Please guide me along the proper path. I know you're there, because even the plants in my apartment, which had been dying for months, now sprout with life. They thrive, as does my body, once you removed the illness. Now I need special assistance. I squashed my son's hope at birth. Will you let me return it? Please grant this one request. Where are you? I beg of you ...

Ukiah! It's you! My beautiful precious boy. There you are, beneath a tree, alive before my eyes. It's actually you. I'm so glad you survived.

Oh Jenny, he's waiting for you. Don't blow it. Don't chicken out. Just walk over to him, hug him dearly, and tell him the truth. Just open the door ...

No! Wait. Who's that? An intruder. Where'd they come from? They shouldn't be here. Go. Go! Hurry! Drive away. It wasn't meant to be.

You're worthless. A coward. Jenny, your son stood across the lawn, and you didn't make contact. We drove hundreds of miles - now look at us. We're back at this lonely penthouse in New York with nothing more than when we left. How could you have denied our son a second time? You're a failure. Pathetic.

What's the use? I'm going to kill myself. Where are my magic markers? We'll write our suicide note on the wall for the world to see:

I'm despicable

       Lowly!

           I HATE MYSELF!

   I've ruined everything * * *

         He Despises Me.   WHO

     COULD

           BLAME

                HIM??

     ???? I'm Sorry -

I Should BE DEAD!

BZZZZZZ.

No! Someone's at the door. Who could it be?

Where's the intercom button? Push it Jenny. Maybe it's Ukiah.

"Hello."

"It's Philip. Buzz me in."

"Get out of here. I don't ever want to see you again. I hate you. You've ruined my life. I'm going to kill myself ..."

28

"Ukiah, did you notice that woman watching you from Reflection Alley?" I panted, rushing across the lawn with a newspaper in my hand after leaving the Gemini. "She was spying on you," I stressed, still in my work clothes.

"Who?" he replied, staring at a squirrel scampering from a tree.

"A woman ... I didn't know her, but she looked familiar, as if I'd seen her before."

Wearing black jeans and a short-sleeved T-shirt, Ukiah continued to follow the squirrel. "She was probably lost."

"No, Ukiah, she might have been with the cops, or the Secret Service." I then pulled the newspaper from beneath my arm and unfolded it. "Look at the stir you created last night."

ATROPOS: Authentic Or Impostor?

"Wow!" Ukiah laughed, "I made the front page. What does the article say?"

Frantic, I replied, "The police are staging a huge investigation, and promise that the next time somebody pulls a publicity stunt, they'll be arrested on the spot."

"That's it?" he smiled proudly.

"The reporter also questioned your credibility. He even implied that whoever wore that hood may have been nothing more than a drunken imposter."

"Great," Ukiah beamed with satisfaction. "Those fools don't have a clue."

"Not so quickly," I told him, grabbing a twig from the ground. "The police found our spotlight, and made it their prime piece of evidence. Damn, I should have grabbed that light before I ran to the car. How stupid of me."

"Don't worry, Chris," Ukiah assured me, looking to the sky. "I'm sure they dusted it for fingerprints, and if you keep your nose clean, the cops will never find you."

"That's what worries me," I said dejectedly, remembering one last item from the article. "As the story ended, the reporter used a quote from Philip Prince's publicity agent."

"You're kidding? What did that chump say?" Ukiah asked excitedly.

"I'll quote: 'Mister Prince is saddened by this recent episode, and promises to increase his patrols in order to apprehend his attacker.' What a crock," I laughed.

"You said it," Ukiah smiled. "We should drive to New York City and torment that phony face-to-face."

"It would be a howl," I added, tossing my twig, "Prince'd probably piss his pants." My mood then turned serious as I lamented, "I am worried about those fingerprints, though."

We walked across the lawn when I said, "Where's your van? I just noticed it's gone."

"The fuel filter was clogged, so I ran it to the garage. I should get it back tomorrow."

As he spoke, I saw an extended gash across Ukiah's left forearm, the result of slicing a knife across it the previous night while pleading with Romlocon.

Feeling courageous, I asked, "What happened to your arm? It looks nasty."

Frowning, Ukiah snarled, "It got cut. Do you have any more questions?"

"No," I said meekly as we stepped to the porch. "I was just curious."

Angrily, he triggered, "I'm curious about something, too."

I gasped, biting my lip.

"Did you snuff your old man yet?"

I froze, quivers of fear causing my leg to feel temporarily paralyzed. "No, not ... not yet ... I ... it's only been a short - short while. I don't ... can't work well under presh ... pressure."

"Well, you better quit lollygaggin'," he demanded, "because time is running out ..."

Time is running out?

"I'd hate to see your father, or even both of you, involved in an accident."

An accident like Mister Doublet?

"Oh, by the way," Ukiah finally smiled, easing the tension, "Joan Jett is playing tonight in Hershey. We'll leave around six o'clock. I'll see you then."

As Ukiah walked behind my house, his veiled threat lingered like a curse. I stood motionless, terrified by our brief time together. Why should I tolerate his rude behavior any longer? First, he hints at not only hurting my father, but also me if I didn't follow orders. Who did he think he was? Then, Ukiah didn't even ask if I even wanted to go to the Joan Jett concert. The nerve! I just finished another day at work, and now, with barely enough time to eat and change clothes, I'd have to ride two hours each way in my Gemini. Plus, I probably wouldn't get home until three a.m., then have to work the next morning. I couldn't believe his audacity. In the same breath, though, I had been the one who made Ukiah mad by asking about his arm. If only I had minded my own business, this situation wouldn't have arisen.

Chris, no one in their right mind puts up with this kind of behavior. Get rid of him! Tell Ukiah that you're not going to put up with these shenanigans. But his power over us has increased to such an extent that even when we do get an original thought, it's quickly replaced by his control. Our mind is quickly becoming overgrown with vines that creep from Ukiah's tainted garden.

I remembered an event from the not too distant past where I saw Ukiah dancing by himself in his room at Transformer Towers. Although he already controlled me at that point, things seemed much more innocent then. Now, all Ukiah cared about was getting published, or getting revenge on those who interfered with his plans. Regrettably ... my name was on that list. Worse, with my fingerprints on the spotlight, Ukiah could tell the cops about my involvement in Atropos' publicity stunt. By itself, such a disclosure wouldn't indict me, but I recognized a domino effect that could lead to Woody Dewar's murder. If I crossed Ukiah, he'd stop at nothing to bring me down. Hell, he tortured a schoolteacher, attacked Philip Prince, and terrorized people who didn't pay their debts. There's no way he'd let me skip from his web.

Ukiah wanted me to murder my father, and, considering his sense of immediacy, I'd have little time to waste. That's why I failed as his literary agent - sheer immediacy. He wanted instantaneous results instead of delays and excuses. To remain unpublished must have filled Ukiah with such frustration that each passing day became tantamount to torture. So, he intended to attain this goal by any means necessary, even if it included murdering my father.

While pondering these thoughts, I gazed upward to see a setting sun and rapidly approaching clouds that, due to their ominous nature, signaled an inevitable spring rain. The prospect of being bathed by these invigorating showers filled me with delight. In fact, at that very instant, I realized that a new season - spring - had begun. Of course, such a process did not occur instantly, but there is often a precise moment when certain seasons suddenly begin.

That afternoon, such a realization dawned on me. My nostrils were enticed by a swirling, fragrant breeze, while I absorbed the pleasing sights around me. A variety of trees flaunted their leaves as tiny animals reappeared to frolic about the grounds. I remembered those times during my youth when spring's eternal promise filled me with hope, as if winter's frigid, paralytic burden had finally been erased. As greenery replaced the barren tundra, my spirits soared with the robins that returned en masse. I'd skip through mud puddles, romp about the woods, or twirl in circles among the blossoming buds. Although my childhood was frequently characterized by bouts of suffocation brought on by my father, during spring I could finally breathe ... my lungs drawing on the aromatic freshness held within this season's glorious grasp.

Conversely, the darkened clouds that rolled toward me produced a frightening reminder of the horror that plagued me the previous evening. I saw the clouds converging into the abstract shape of a dagger - its grisly blade thrust toward me by an unseen hand from the heavens. As a result, I recalled a dream where my father, with yellowish fluid oozing from his face, was strapped naked to an operating table. I loomed above him, wearing a flowered hospital gown and black combat boots while holding a silver knife.

"So, father dearest, your virility lies before me," I chuckled, waving the dagger near his flaccid manhood.

Terrified, Pus squealed derisively as antelope horns sprouted from his forehead.

"Should I dismember you, or ...?"

Delirious, my father grunted, "Chris, you deformed Siamese Twin. Quit acting like such an idiot."

Without warning, I thrust the knife through my father's heart, geysers of blood gushing into the air and onto my smock. My natural reaction would have been to scream, but during this demented dream, I simply stood and watched as crimson rivers flowed from my father's chest. While Pus slowly ... agonizingly ... died before my eyes, I reeled in horror as an unexpected figure sprung from his wound."

"What a splendid day for murder," the Being giggled, its face smeared with blood.

"Who are you?" I gasped, stumbling backward.

Inexplicably, the red fluid disappeared from the intruder's face, revealing his true identity.

"No! Not you again," I cried. "Why won't you leave me alone?"

The trespasser was none other than Woody Dewar, his face and shoulders dwelling in the blood that bubbled from my father's chest.

"Are you my Mommy, or are you my Daddy?" Woody smirked, pursing his lips.

"What?" I cried, horrified. "I'm not your parent."

"Mommy, Daddy," Woody chimed, coagulated blood surrounding his lips. "Why did you molest me?"

"Are you crazy? I never touched you," I panted as Dewar squirmed inside my lifeless father.

"Don't you remember that day I smiled when we left the playroom together?" Woody laughed. "That proves that I was abused."

"No! It's not so ..."

"You touched me, Daddy. You felt me, Mommy. I cried that time when you left me alone in the car. That proves you ... Please hold me, Mommy. Please hug me, Daddy. That's all I ever wanted," Woody begged, extending his rubbery arms.

Unable to endure these images, I raced inside my house, overwhelmed by the thoughts inside my mind.

Afraid that I was losing my sanity, I rapidly changed clothes and ate in preparation for tonight's concert. Still, despite my efforts to erase it, I couldn't ignore the implications surrounding my hallucination. I actually considered visiting a psychiatrist who could analyze my dreams. I realized that one of the inherent qualities of any altered state was the element of absurdity. But me as Woody Dewar's child molesting parent went beyond absurdity, bordering on full-blown psychosis.

What made my unconscious mind think that I was Woody Dewar's abusive parent right after it produced images of me murdering my father? Could it be rooted in the violation of Dewar's body when I strangled him? Or, did Woody represent me as a child, cursing my father's tyranny and my mother's inability to prevent it? In all honesty, I couldn't find any answers. Whatever the case, the memory of this episode would not be easily forgotten.

At six o'clock, Ukiah stepped onto my porch, primed for another adventure. Noticeably anxious, he bounced in place as I tossed him my car keys.

"All right! Joan Jett. I can't wait," he perked. "Let's get this show on the road."

I sat in the passenger seat, then hesitantly told Ukiah, "Um, the Gemini needs fuel before we leave."

I may have been mistaken, but when informed of this delay, Ukiah actually emitted a GROWL. But this diversion was not enough to sour his mood. Rather, he whistled while driving to a local convenience store. After he filled the tank, I followed Ukiah into the mini-mart, where we both bought drinks (him a bottled water, me a soda). What ensued would remain forever cemented in my mind. Despite its subtlety, this incident painted a perfect portrait of my sidekick.

After grabbing our drinks from a cooler, Ukiah and I wandered to the checkout area where a bespectacled, middle-aged woman wearing a pillbox hat and a leopard-skin jacket stood before us.

"Did you purchase gasoline, ma'am?" a cute, blonde-haired girl behind the counter asked.

"Why, yes I did," the lady replied in a bird-like voice. "Now, which pump was it? Six? No, maybe seven. Wait, I think it may have been number fourteen."

"Ma'am, there is no pump fourteen," the cashier told her.

"Oh, I thought there was."

I heard Ukiah cursing beneath his breath.

"How much gasoline did you get?" the girl asked. "I'll be able to find your total that way."

"How much? Oh my. I think eight dollars and twelve cents."

The cashier repeatedly pressed buttons, then told her apathetically, "Nobody pumped that amount, ma'am."

"Heavens to me," she squeaked, giggling. "Lemme see ..."

Ukiah's tapping foot resonated like a metronome off the convenience store walls.

"Which car is yours, Miss?" the cashier next asked.

"Lordy to Betsy, what did I drive today? Oh yeah, it's that white Oldsmobile," the woman chirped.

Making progress, the cashier punched more buttons, then said, "You pumped twenty dollars and twenty cents."

"Twenty-twenty. Tee hee. Just like my vision. Oh my my, and like that television news show. What a coincidence. Why do these things always happen to me? Just last week ..."

Tick tick tick - the time bomb slowly ticked inside Ukiah's brain.

"... so my cat climbed a tree, and must have been thirty feet in the air, when ..."

Out of his mind, Ukiah handed me his bottled water and a wad of money, then stormed out the door.

Delighted by this display of frustration, I laughed aloud as the woman kept talking about her kittens. In contrast, I'm sure Ukiah boiled with rage inside the Gemini, so totally id-oriented that when he was denied, insanity ensued. He may have been, without exaggeration, the most frustrated man on earth. And, although this affliction was a constant source of irritation, Ukiah wore it like a badge. His displeasure with the world was undoubtedly a major source of creative energy. Whereas others may have been troubled by this delay, Ukiah soared into orbit, his blood searing through each vessel.

I eventually paid for our fuel and drinks, then walked slowly through the parking lot to my Gemini. There I saw Ukiah, both hands gripping the steering wheel, staring vacantly into space.

After getting in the car, I looked at Ukiah, who remained fixated by rage. Unable to contain my amusement, I let loose a joyous snicker at this preposterous situation. After completing this good-natured release, I feared my laughter would further fuel Ukiah's wrath. Instead, I peeked across the seat to see a sheepish grin form on his face.

Somewhat embarrassed, Ukiah confessed, "I don't care. I want the whole world to revolve around me."

And with those telling words, our journey to Hershey began. After leaving the city limits and hitting another four-lane highway, we burned across the horizon as a lazy sun set beneath the treetops.

Following a period of silence, Ukiah broke the ice by telling me, "I wrote another letter to Sandra last night."

"Sandra? Oh, the woman who rejected *Crocodile Tears*," I replied. "What did you say?"

"It was a last ditch effort urging her to reconsider my work. Her rejection still boggles my mind. Why can't she see I'm not some ham n' egger who's written one book and thinks it's The Great American Novel? This may sound brash, but I'm the one she's been waiting for. Isn't it clear that I'm the real thing?"

While speeding through the darkness, I wondered if Ukiah actually believed this stuff. He probably knew more about manipulating words, or the entire English language for that matter, than any person I had ever met.

He continued, "Sandra confuses me. In her first letter, it looked like she could cut through the world's bullshit. All of us have to put up with so much phoniness every day that it makes me wanna scream. That's why I can't give up on her. Instead of following the same path as everyone else, Sandra should throw caution to the wind and find a new course. I know we could hit it big. All I need is one person to believe in me."

"Do you think she'll give you another chance?" I asked.

"Who knows? But to move beyond the mundane, we need to think big, Big, BIG! We can't develop a single novel like everyone else does. That strategy is much too blasé. Instead, we should tap into Andy Warhol's philosophy of segueing into different fields. With my body of work, and Japhy's rock n' roll band, we could take a stab at book publishing, magazines, music, movies, and video."

I had to give him credit. Ukiah never surrendered.

"I'm not gonna be a nickel-and-dime writer. Hell, I could generate millions of dollars. All Sandra needs to do is believe in me. Why can't she see things that are larger-than-life? I know it's hard to take this leap of faith because sometimes even I underestimate my vision."

"You?" I coughed with disbelief. "How so?"

"Well, I'm thinking about starting a literary rock n' roll circus that would barnstorm the country on a promotional tour. But after one year, I know we'd be wasting our talents, especially the band, who could be playing in arenas rather than bookstores."

Feeling relaxed as Ukiah drove at eighty miles an hour, I said, "You do have a point. The money ..."

Interrupting me, Ukiah proclaimed, "Can't Sandra see the opportunity I'm laying in her lap? If I were her, I'd be dancing across the skyscrapers! I know my ideas can work! I'm sure of it. I can feel it like the heart beating inside my chest."

"Why are you so sure?" I asked tentatively.

Tapping his steering wheel with both hands, Ukiah bragged, "Because nobody in the literary field is taking risks. They've left the door wide open. Can't ya see? Wimpy strategies, like namby-pamby people, only last long enough to be buried in the ground. I'm not playing it safe. I don't give a damn if her co-workers at Myron Liebowitz were offended by my submission. We're all big boys and girls, aren't we? What kind of person would mail the first seven pages of *Crocodile Tears* ... all of them dripping with sex and booze … especially when they had fifty-seven pounds of material to choose from? Somebody who's planning on being cautious? Hell no! Then, after getting a rejection letter, he doesn't hesitate in biting the hand that could lead to a huge payoff. Does this sound like a person who would cower from ANYTHING?"

"Hardly."

"If I only knew what the folks at Liebowitz were working on before they pushed me out of consideration, then I could understand."

The ominous clouds I noticed earlier that afternoon finally caused a slight downpour. While raindrops splashed against our windshield, I observed, "Maybe your vision was too off-beat."

"Maybe," Ukiah said. "But after one meeting, my ideas wouldn't sound crazy at all. I KNOW what turns people on. In fact, deep inside, I'm sure Sandra is asking, 'Who is this crazy man from Latera Heights? Could he really be on to something?' Well, she can quit wondering. I've said it before and will say it again. Why won't somebody give me a shot? I've studied popular culture for the past twenty years, and am sure I can peddle a shitload of books, plus an assortment of other products. Do you know the recipe?" he concluded, directing his question at me.

Stumped by his inquiry, I shook my head back and forth.

As if expecting this response, Ukiah continued, "It's not very complicated. Toss in a dose of professional wrestling, a dash of rock n' roll, a pinch of Sunday morning preacher man theatrics, then a final dab of media manipulation. And welluh, what do we have? Pure excitement! We could take my traveling literary circus across the country and have people flocking to us quicker than ...."

A literary rock n' roll circus. I almost laughed out loud when hearing the details of this scheme, then decided to shift our conversation to a more realistic prospect.

"Ukiah, didn't you mention writing a letter to ten literary agents? What did you say to them?"

"Hmmm, let me remember," he answered, refusing to slow down as the rain changed from light sprinkles to an actual downpour. "I think I started by doing away with a sappy introduction and shooting straight for the jugular. After describing my output, and how I wasn't genre impaired like Philip Prince, Jackie Collins, or Charles Bukowski, I ... oh wait, now I remember. I sent those letters to small agencies outside of New York City."

"A wise choice," I assured him. "But won't they wonder why you're not targeting the big city firms?"

"I'm one step ahead of you, Chris. See, I told them that if the truth be told, I dangled a carrot in front of those folks, but walked away disappointed."

"Won't they wonder why?"

"Sure, and I'll tell 'em that trying to meet those bastards is harder than finding The Wizard of Oz. With the New York literary Mafia, ya get nothing but phonies, bureaucratic run-arounds, or complete silence. I don't have time for their shit."

"But I thought you were aiming for the top."

Unfazed by this contradiction, Ukiah explained, "I am, but I'm also looking for an agent I can connect with on a personal level. Then I could play it straight with them every step of the way. Head games don't interest me. Hopefully, they'll find my attitude refreshing. But with the world today, I'll probably have to wallow in the gutter before capturing the public's imagination."

With torrents of rain drilling the Gemini, I said nervously, "That's an interesting point, but what if these agents mistake your stance as self-righteousness?"

"They might at first, but after reading my books, they'll see that each novel is wild - WILD! The point I'm trying to make is that although I've lead a crazy life, I've also worked my ass off, and am the straightest shooter in town."

"How do you think they'll react?"

"I'm not sure, but I ended the letter by saying that if I piqued their interest, I can only ask two things of them. Don't chump me out, or make me jump through hoops. I know I'm good, maybe even the best around. Just give me a chance."

"You really believe, don't you?"

"Chris, with a new millennium around the corner, I know that not only will my books be published, but a new literary movement will be founded in the process."

"I remember ... you called it ... it starts with S ..."

"Solipsism."

"Yeah, Solipsism. But what is it? I don't understand."

Blankets of rain pummeled our windshield as Ukiah tore along the freeway, our visibility limited as humidity clouded the car's interior.

Pulling a folded sheet of paper from the back pocket of his jeans, Ukiah urged me, "Read this."

I took the paper, then read aloud as Ukiah turned on the Gemini's overhead light:

THE SOLIPSISTIC CREED

Who defines your Identity? Not the Sleepwalkers who have been buried under blankets of deceptive conditioning. The only way to wake from our comatose state is by dismissing their illusions and finding a path leading to the truth. Follow your Muse. Scream like a newborn child ... completely infantile in your needs ... the only living person in your own self-created Utopia. Get rid of the programming that limits your freedom, and ignore their veiled realities. Your philosophy is all that matters. Push your boundaries with psychopathic glee, releasing your rage to escape their control. Nothing is true except what WE decide is true! Everything else must be eliminated. Once we've freed ourselves from their suffocating imposition, we'll thrive with Life - differentiated and self-sufficient. Who defines our identity? We do when Art becomes a mirror and phoniness is destroyed by Creation!

In the dim yellow light, I squinted at the typed black letters on crinkled white paper and wondered who in their right mind would produce such an exaggerated manifesto. I didn't even understand "The Solipsistic Creed," yet my partner's bombasity leaped from the page with unrivaled confidence. Ukiah was either a certifiable visionary, or a desperate dreamer with delusions of grandeur.

After returning the document, I asked, "What does it mean?"

Bursting through the rain, he explained, "To become a Soloist, every distraction must be eliminated in favor of Creation. Consider how many things distract us in life. The list is endless. But by removing everything that diverts our attention, every Artist can focus on their ultimate goal - entering the gates of publication."

"I understand that part of the equation, but you also mentioned your Muse. The last time we spoke, though, you had doubts about Romlocon's very existence ..."

"Look, can you see it?" Ukiah pointed. "The exit sign for Hershey. We're almost there!"

Hershey, as its name implies, is a quaint community whose existence revolves around chocolate production - candy bars, devil's food cake, heart-shaped Valentine boxes, and other sweets. The village streets have names like Brownie Road and the Hershey Highway, while their streetlamps are shaped like chocolate kisses. But none of these things mattered to us. Our only concern was finding "Tremblers," which was (much to our surprise) a neighborhood tavern that sat beside a grocery store.

After parking along a suburban street, we zipped through the rain past manicured lawns with hokey, chocolate related lawn ornaments (M&M wind chimes, bird baths shaped like a candy dish), then entered "Tremblers" - a nondistinct sports bar. Considering Joan's bad girl reputation, I expected this place to be a sleazy biker bar with three hundred pound gorillas flaunting chains and brass knuckles. Instead, I saw scores of shorthaired men wearing button-down dress shirts, and women sporting the latest college fashions. Waves of relief swept across me as visions of a violent melee were erased. A repeat performance of Joan's previous concert, with drunken delirium, flying fists, and bloody lips, was the last thing I wanted.

After meandering past the bar and through crowds of cheerful people, Ukiah and I stood near the stage where I noticed a group of young women who had been at each of Joan's previous concerts. I could tell because these women staked out their spot directly in front of the stage at each show, clamoring around Joan's microphone like adoring worshippers at the pulpit. In addition, their hair was styled in either one of two ways - the short, blonde, spiky look that Joan currently sported, or her former hay-stack style with locks of black hair cascading like tumbleweeds to her shoulders. As they joked and giggled in front of her monitors, it was easy to see that these women idolized Joan. If imitation was the sincerest form of flattery, these girls made their intention very clear.

As the bar lights dimmed, I was once again filled with an incredible surge of anticipation. Words cannot describe the excitement that buzzed through my body as darkness settled across the bar and the hum of electric guitars being plugged into an amplifier ricocheted off the walls. I turned to see Ukiah, who likewise experienced the same sensation. An uninhibited power resonated through the air - electricity, rebellion, and the joy of rock n' roll. Yes, I had slowly become a Joan Jett devotee - bouncing in place nervously as the crowd chanted for the band to take the stage. "Tremblers" shook with anticipation as the lingering aromas of alcohol, perfume, cigarette smoke and perspiration filled the air. But nothing struck me like the electrical buzz radiating from the amplifiers - a riveting, powerful, addictive sound ...

The lights then flashed with blinding brilliance as Joan raced before us. With wide, intense eyes streaked with black makeup and her standard stage apparel, Joan attacked a white guitar while delivering her signature song - "I don't give a damn 'bout my reputation ..." With trademark attitude and a rebellious sneer, Joan took control of her audience, leading them on an exhilarating ninety minute ride. Ukiah showed such appreciation for her performance that at times I expected him to rise into the air. Such an occurrence would not have surprised me, for Joan Jett, rock n' roll's most beautiful woman, lifted the entire crowd to new heights.

29

The following day at work, with fatigue slowing my motions and ability to enter data into the computer, I remembered something that Ukiah said the previous evening.

When I asked why he kept going to Joan Jett concerts, he said, "There aren't many things in life that excite me. When I do find something that makes my blood flow, I'm drawn to it wholeheartedly."

Such an insight summarized Ukiah's obsessive nature. I knew this self-absorption in relation to his work produced many detrimental side effects, none the least being an inability to focus on anything other than getting published. Ukiah's dedication became so absolute that we rarely discussed anything other than writing. Unlike most people who talked about news, sports, the latest dress styles, or even the weather, we concerned ourselves with literature, or the consequences facing those who crossed Ukiah.

Unable to arrange the numbers on my computer screen into any logical order, I slowly slipped into another daydream. For some reason, I pictured the piece of paper containing Ukiah's manifesto - "The Solipsistic Creed" - and imagined what someone else would think of this document. Ukiah rarely had a chance to discuss his ideas with others. But if he did, how would they react? Many would call Ukiah a rampant egotist or an unhinged dreamer. Considering the volatility of his statements, it'd be hard to disagree with them. But as I heard more of his literary monologues, I came to see them as products of a complete belief in his vision. He only had one way to escape the world, and that was through his writing.

In light of the frustration and worry Ukiah caused me, some may be surprised by my apologetic tone. I can't blame them, because, due to Ukiah's bravado, most people reading his manifesto would get the wrong impression. Maybe my naïveté's to blame, but Ukiah was nothing more than a lost child who stumbled into the world. To compensate for being alone, he blew his own horn and stomped around like the most brilliant creature alive ... yet I saw his true essence. Ukiah grasped at life with the aimlessness of an unanchored ship, or a tumbleweed rolling across the open plains. Of course he had numerous faults, but when I heard him talking to Japhy, or reminiscing about his grandmother's farm or his cherished white Persian cats, an unguarded aspect of his personality emerged. He became a different person - one whose softness took center stage as he fed the squirrels or whistled to morning doves.

In the same breath, Ukiah's literary obsessions lead to increasing bouts of delusional behavior. I worried that Ukiah's departure from Romlocon, his inspirational light, was a step in the wrong direction. It seemed that Ukiah's one true duty, to follow his Muse, had been dismissed in favor of more immediate rewards.

Although I tried to understand him, Ukiah's world consisted of complex contradictions and never-ending struggles. Who else would limit their entire existence to the dream of publication? I could still see him sitting in his cottage, scribbling madly in a notebook under an uncovered lamp. It didn't seem to make sense. But in Ukiah's mind, he was sure that a savior would arrive at any time, recognize his talents, then rescue him from this torment.

How could a person walk around plotting the lives of five or more different characters every time they wrote a book? He dwelled on these Beings until each was fully developed. Or else he'd say, "How about this scene for a movie. Wouldn't it be great?" Lately, Ukiah spoke of patterning a character after Jennifer Ewen, his first failed literary agent. But his attempts were thwarted because he didn't know her. This shows how deeply he was absorbed in his fantasy. Life was nothing more than source material for his next novel. Even when mentioning his works in progress, or the films to be made from them, Ukiah lived life as if it were a tale, his role being that of the famous-author-to-be.

His escapes from reality would not have involved me if Ukiah were simply a tenant renting a cottage. But my association with him led to the planned murder of my father. Speaking of which, a phone message waited on my answering machine after I returned from the Joan Jett show.

> "Chris, this is your mother. Pus wants you to visit some time. He's been bored lately, and wants to know if you'd stop by and wear a few different costumes, then skip around the living room. Pus said he loves when you make a horse's ass of yourself. I'll see ya, honey. Love, Mom."

The thought of that man belittling me again filled me with rage. I didn't care if Ukiah wanted me to murder him. I'd go ahead with the plan on my own! What could be going through Pus's mind? Plus, my mother added fuel to the fire by relaying these humiliating messages. I swear, one of these days Pus will push me too far, then ....

"Edwards," my boss bellowed. "I've been monitoring your activities for the last fifteen minutes, and you haven't entered one bit of data into that computer. If I have to reprimand you one more time, you're fired. Now get busy. Chop chop!"

Following weeks of boring work and mundane evenings spent home alone, I felt a surge of excitement late one Friday afternoon when Ukiah bounced along my driveway in his dilapidated gray van.

"C'mon," he yelled from his window, a gorgeous yellow sun shining in the sky behind him. "What're ya waiting for? We have places to go!"

So, without further information, I hopped into Ukiah's van and reached for the seatbelt when, thinking twice, decided to forget the safety strap and take a ride on the wild side. Feeling dangerous and free, I wiggled with excitement as Ukiah spun from Reflection Alley onto the highway.

Before I could speak, he began, "You always complain that I never tell you what's happening with my writing, so I have a hot one on the front burner."

"What? What! Tell me. This's great."

While approaching the bypass, Ukiah began, "Do you remember those ten letters I mailed to agents outside New York City?"

"Of course."

"All I got were rejection letters."

"Congrat ... hey, wait a minute. I thought you were going to say one of them wanted ...."

"Nah. None of 'em wanted anything to do with me."

"Then what's your good news?" I asked as we sped along another endless highway.

"At the same time I mailed those letters, I also found the address of an agent in Pittsburgh."

"Pittsburgh? Where all the factories closed down?" I asked, noticeably confused.

"The same place," Ukiah said, tapping his fingers on the steering wheel as a song crackled from his speakers.

"What are literary agents doing in Pittsburgh?" I continued, sensing good news.

"Who knows? But I wrote to a woman named Mindy Silver at The Nina Ocean Agency, and believe it or not, she replied within a week!"

"A week? Those places usually take forever," I replied. "What did you say to her?"

"Nothing different than every other letter ... an explanation of my output, styles, and vision."

"What did Mindy say?"

"In all honesty," Ukiah stated matter of factly, "her response was a form letter."

"Huh? I don't get it."

Unabashedly, he explained, "Y'see, Nina Ocean is a pay-to-read agency."

"You mean ....?"

"Exactly. If an author wants them to consider their work, they're charged a fee for their services."

"I don't mean to sound critical, but it sounds kinda shady."

"I said the same thing to Mindy in my return letter."

"What did you tell her?"

"I thanked her for such a quick response, saying it was good to know my letter was taken seriously, and not shuffled under a stack of unopened mail. But not being one to beat around the bush, I told Mindy I was disappointed by the content of her envelope."

"Because of the financial aspect?" I asked.

"Partially, but the gist of my first letter was about VISION. All I got in return was a form letter urging me to send $125 as a reading fee. So, after thinking about it, I realized my major gripe wasn't about money."

"What did disturb you?" I asked as a calm, partially hidden sun hung in the sky.

Without blinking, he told me, "The cheapening of my self worth. A good analogy would be a man going to a whorehouse. The odds are he'll get laid, but will it satisfy his ego? Of course not. The same principle applies to their reading fee. Someone will read my manuscript, but will it be enough?"

"You have a point. What did you do?"

"I drove to a bookstore, then started researching the pay-to-read industry. The general consensus was that a literary agent should never be paid before they sell your book. They should earn their money by getting a commission from the novel's profits. No respected agent will ever ask for a fee before the book's publication."

"I'm confused. Are you telling me that the whole concept is a scam?"

"Well, I didn't know enough about them to say they were rip-offs. I did tell them, though, that I'm not a piece of shit writer with one book under his wing, thinking it's The Great American Novel. That's why I refused to pay their reading fee."

"You're confusing me more every minute," I confessed.

"Well, I didn't completely rule out The Ocean Agency. I just didn't want to be grouped with those other hacks who mailed checks for $125. I'm sure Mindy has heard every story under the sun, so I shouted mine loud and clear!"

"Which was?"

"That I'm hot shit, the one she's been waiting for. Mindy can keep pussyfooting around with those nobodies who were willing to mail a reading fee, or she could roll the dice with me. She had to make a decision. Did she want to keep swimming in a little pond, or sail The Seven Seas? I guaranteed we could take the world by storm. She only had to do one simple thing - personally invite me to her office. Then we could talk about the future."

A lazy spring sun laid low in the sky as we exited the interstate and followed a bucolic two-lane highway. With mountain laurels blossoming along a hillside and the sound of birds whistling in the breeze, I listened to the rest of Ukiah's tale.

"Being that you didn't send any money, did Mindy write back?"

"Sure, and this time it wasn't a shitty form letter!"

"Super. What did she say?"

"Mindy apologized for disappointing me in her first letter. She said they get close to thirty queries every day, and can't personally reply to each. She then showed some honesty by saying that if they didn't feel like representing me, she would have said so, saving us both a lotta time and trouble."

"That's interesting," I commented, trying to gauge her angle.

While passing through sleepy hamlets with picturesque streets, Ukiah painted a portrait of Miss Silver's response.

"Mindy told me that, like most agencies, they do charge a reading fee."

"Most agencies?" I asked curiously.

"Who knows? She also said many people in the industry have mixed feelings about this practice, but it's common for an agency to charge them."

"I see. What happens once they get your manuscript?"

"Supposedly it gets an honest and thorough evaluation. The novel is given to a freelance editor who prepares a written assessment, considering such areas as point of view, characterization, plot structure, and grammar."

"How long does that take?"

"Surprisingly, only a week or two."

"Then what?"

"Mindy gets the manuscript, then reviews the critical comments herself, making her own suggestions. At this point, she'll come to a decision about the work, contacting the author by phone if it's accepted."

"Tell me! Have you heard from her?" I bubbled, still not knowing where we were going.

"No, but Mindy guaranteed their evaluations are very honest, and sometimes harsh, but anything less would be an injustice to the author. She also said they won't just tell me what's wrong with my manuscript, but ways to improve it."

"That sounds fair enough."

"The best part was, Mindy ended by saying they didn't want to 'cheapen my self-worth,' but to educate me to the realities of the publishing industry. I can still hear her final words echoing through my ears - 'This business is extremely competitive for new writers, and editor expectations are very strict. So, their policy was to charge a reading fee. It was my decision whether I'd pay it or not.'"

"So ....."

"Although I wasn't thrilled with paying them, Mindy's promptness and no bullshit attitude outweighed my misgivings. I appreciated her effort. To take that extra step goes beyond the realm of publishing. Yeah, I could see her behind the scenes, saying, 'Okay, hot shot, it's time to put up or shut up. Let's see what you've got!' So, I mailed a copy of *Glitter Ghetto*."

"Now it's the waiting game, huh? When do you think she'll call?"

"That's what I like to hear," Ukiah laughed, "a positive attitude. Instead of sending a rejection letter, you're sure Mindy will call."

"I read *Glitter Ghetto*, and it's definitely better than anything on the bookshelves."

"I agree," Ukiah said, nodding his head as he drove through another nameless town. "But do you know what I've been thinking?"

"Oh no, what?" I asked hesitantly.

"Why can't we start an agency like Nina Ocean's?"

"You want to start a pay-to-read company?"

"Not necessarily, but something like that. The only problem is, we need moolah to get this show on the road."

A lump formed in my throat while acid boiled in my stomach. I had avoided the subject of murdering my father for at least a month. Now Ukiah was moving in that direction.

He continued, "I wonder why we haven't been able to get any start-up money."

Trembling, I tried to appease Ukiah. "It's a difficult process."

Not pleased with my wishy-washy response, Ukiah bellowed, "Don't bullshit me, Chris. We had plans to start a business, and what have you done? Nothing!" Ukiah's eyes bulged as his face turned red. "Am I just a joke to you? Don't you take me seriously? I'll bet you laugh behind my back after every one of these conversations. If that's where you stand, fuck it. I only asked one simple thing of you - kill your father and collect his insurance money - but what do I get in return? Nothing. Do I have to rob a fucking bank? You know how hard that is in this day and age. I rely on you for one minor part of this plan, and what happens? You disappoint me again."

Shaking, on the verge of a nervous breakdown, I gushed, "Ukiah, I'm so confused. I don't know what you want from me. I ... you keep changing your mind. Being with you is like riding a roller coaster."

He sat silently, gripping the steering wheel tensely between both hands.

I continued hysterically, voice squeaking and uneven. "First you only wrote to one agent, then to many. Before I knew it, you made me your agent, then fired me so I could murder my father. You're always changing your mind. One day you have a full-proof plan, then the next you're veering off on another tangent. I can't keep up with your ... your ..."

Calmly, Ukiah said, "It's called evolution, Chris. Pardon my marketing skills, but I need to keep progressing if there's any chance of making it in this rotten business." Then, as if our argument was over, he returned to the subject of starting his own business. "The way I see it, we'll call our company 'Sisyphus Press.'"

"Sissy what?" I bumbled, fumbling for words.

"Sisyphus. He was a character from Greek Mythology condemned by the Gods to eternally push a boulder up a mountain. Then, when he neared the top, the Gods forced his stone back to the bottom, where Sisyphus started all over again. The metaphor hits pretty close to home, don't you think?"

Ukiah always mentioned these obscure figures in his daily speech - lesbian poets, goddesses from Greek folklore, lost authors of the nineteenth century, or psychological experiments that were used to prove a point.

Relieved that our confrontation had not gotten worse, I smiled, "Sisyphus Press. I can't imagine a better name to describe your struggle."

Showing a stark understanding of his predicament, Ukiah confessed, "If we cut through all the bullshit, here's where I stand. I'm not the best technical writer in America. I have no connections, and my name has never been in print. To my credit, though, I have compiled a vast arsenal of material. So, at this point, writing has become a secondary pursuit."

"Secondary?" I asked. "What's first?"

"Selling ME! I'm nothing more than a product to be marketed, like soap powder. A perfect example is the fairy tale I wrote about my Persian cats. How many children's books are submitted to publishers each year?"

I shrugged my shoulders.

"Amazingly, the juvenile market gets more submissions than any other genre. Hell, how many sweet old ladies and jerk-offs come up with the bright idea to write a kids book, complete with pictures and fancy characters? There must be millions. So, to differentiate myself from them, I need to draw attention to my product. Chris, pretend we're in a supermarket, and my fairy tale is sitting on a shelf beside 20,000 other books. We're all boxes of soap powder, and the shopper is the head of a publishing house. This bigwig is pushing a cart down the aisle, browsing at a sea of manuscripts. Of those 20,000 boxes of soap powder, how does mine leap from the shelf? How do I draw that customer to me, especially when my product is sitting on the bottom rack behind a display for tampons and pickled beets?"

Ukiah's mind was always at work. He epitomized the quintessential "little guy" who never had three nickels to rub together, but always plotted to hit it big. Being a television junkie as a kid, Ukiah reminded me of Ralph Kramden, Archie Bunker, and Fred Flintstone. All of these men had blue-collar jobs (a bus driver, dockworker/taxi driver, and quarryman); but they always thought up new schemes that would send them over the top and end their struggles. All three men were working class heroes ... heroes who never advanced beyond their everyday jobs when their shows were canceled. I saw Ukiah as an extension of these characters, destined to dream, but never privileged enough to succeed.

"How DO you catch their eye?" I asked as the sun peeked behind a tree-lined hillside.

"With my fairy tale, I see a Persian Cat craze ... y'know, like those toys at Christmas that make people stand in line for three hours. Being that Deuces was the most gorgeous cat in creation, what better way to sell books? Kids would fall in love with this poor little feller. I can see it now; Deuces would be on cereal boxes, lunch boxes, t-shirts, and underwear. Plus, the publishers could sell the rights for stuffed animals, slippers, and an afternoon cartoon show. Hell, we could even make an animated movie. How's that for a box of soap powder?" he smiled cheerfully.

"If you could only get your box on the shelf," I moaned. "Your ideas are great."

"I'm sure it'd be a huge hit," Ukiah agreed, pointing to a sign. "Look, we're only ten miles away."

Ten miles from where, I wondered?

"In all honesty," he said softly, his voice suddenly filled with defeat. "I wonder if my efforts to get published have been worth it."

"Of course they are," I said as we passed posters tacked to telephone poles advertising a county fair.

"I'm not so sure," Ukiah lamented. "Look at my life. I've given up EVERYTHING for this dream, and what do I get in return? I think I'm having a mid-life crisis. Look at what's around me. I don't have a family, a wife, a house, or any money. The world has passed me by. All for Art! All for this dream! I look back at the last fifteen years and shudder. I've sacrificed my entire fucking life to create this Legend. And now I ask, was it all worthwhile? Maybe I'm just crazy, or deluded. Whatever the case, I'm getting desperate."

"Don't worry, Ukiah. You'll make it," I said confidently.

Suddenly outraged, Ukiah stomped his gas pedal and vowed angrily, "If I'm not published in the next six months, I'll start drinkin', druggin', and smoking again. I'll get so fucked up someone will find me dead in a sewer. I'm not pissing around any more. Time is of the essence. Entering the gates of publication has become a life and death struggle! I can't rely on anyone but myself. The only one who'll help me is ME. It's me, baby, me against the world!"

As Ukiah stormed along the highway, I trembled with fright. His mood changed so drastically that I thought he'd drive into a fence, or ... it couldn't be. In the distance, chugging perpendicular to the highway, was a freight train. At first I didn't worry as it clawed along the track, spewing smoke from its bowels. But as Ukiah screamed toward the crossing, I realized he didn't intend to stop!

"Ukiah," I shrieked, "if you don't slow down, we're going to crash head on into that train."

Rather than realizing the importance of my plea, he sneered, "You'll never know how hard it is being an Artist. I'm possessed!"

Pushing his van to seventy, then eighty, with rock n' roll music bouncing off the walls, he continued, "Artists always have to cater to and pamper their egos. I have a vision, but who am I to think that what I have to say is important enough for others to read?"

"Ukiah, stop! You're going to kill us."

We were on a collision course with the train - closer, nearer ... two wooden arms with red flashing lights descended to cursorily block the road, but at our speed, we'd barrel through them like balsa wood. The freighter, its destiny clearly defined, churned along the tracks - clanging, spitting smoke, and urgently blowing its whistle.

"Please, hit the brakes," I cried frantically. "I'm not ready to die. I've done too many things wrong that I need to pay penance for."

The gate was only a hundred yards away when Ukiah slammed his right foot on the brake and brought his van to a screeching halt. Pushed forward by the momentum (and not wearing a seatbelt), my head bounced off the windshield as we stopped only inches from the gate with flashing red lights - the freight train tearing past with destructive fury.

Perspiring, panting, and out of my mind, I whimpered, "Why, Ukiah? Why? I can't keep living this way. One of these days you won't stop in time, then you'll look back and regret it."

Laughing insanely, Ukiah turned up the music, tapped the dashboard with his fingers, then yelled, "I don't care about the past. There's only one way to go - straight ahead. I'm always looking forward, baby. Now c'mon, get your shit together, we have a Thrill Show to attend!"

Still jittery from Ukiah's daredevil driving, I stewed as he pulled into a decorated parking lot. Angered that I had been duped once again, I sat silently as his van bounced through a rutty field.

"Here we are," he announced cheerfully. "The Kundalini County Fair featuring Joey Chitwood's Thrill Show. Now c'mon, are ya ready to have fun?"

Sullen, I feigned a smile, then followed Ukiah past an endless row of vehicles.

"Where are we going?" I eventually asked, trailing behind him.

"To the pig barn," he replied, walking at a rapid clip.

"The pig barn? Why?"

"We're going to meet Japhy and Gina. Oh, I guess I forgot to tell you."

"Japhy and Gina are coming!" I exclaimed, my mood immediately improving.

My change in outlook could be attributed to one thing - relief. Although I was used to Ukiah's company, he still made me nervous. With stunts like the one he pulled at the railroad crossing, plus his intense, fiery personality, I always felt like I was walking on pins and needles. I likened myself to a talk-show host who always had to be ON. In Ukiah's company, I guarded every reaction and observation – just like I did with my father. Their presence was so intimidating that I never felt comfortable ... always crawling in my own skin. But due to Japhy's calm nature, I not only felt more at ease, but Ukiah's attention was also drawn away from me. I realize this observation sounds pathetic, but Ukiah's fire burned with an incredible intensity. To be with him was wildly exciting, yet also challenging and exhausting. I just prayed I didn't get too close to the flame.

As these thoughts filtered through my mind, I walked alongside Ukiah into the heart of Kundalini's county fair. As dusk settled across the sawdust-laden grounds, I marveled at the activity surrounding me. With brightly colored lights lining the game booths, rides, Midway, and telephone poles, the sensation was like entering a kaleidoscopic maze, a wonderfully exuberant throwback to my youth when the traveling carnival represented an entire week of indulgence. Surrounding us were the mouth-watering aromas of candy apples, hot dogs, cotton candy, hamburgers, roasted peanuts, fried onions, and melted chocolate. I actually thought I could eat the whole world.

But my attention was quickly diverted by other attractions at the fair. I saw three different Ferris Wheels spinning like huge technicolor wheels ... a penny toss game booth where children filled with piss and vinegar flung coins into slippery glass bowls hoping to win stuffed animals ... a straw-bottomed petting zoo where curly tailed pigs, bushy sheep, fawns, miniature ponies, and even an imported koala bear awaited the caring touch of human fingers caressing their fur. A plethora of activity unfolded in every direction - a magnificent merry-go-round where life-like horses spun in musical circles while sideshow barkers tempted curious onlookers with the lure of headless men, fire breathers, sword swallowers, two-headed gophers, twelve-toed cannibals, pygmies, and bearded ladies.

What more could any person - young or old – ask for? There were games, rides, flashing lights, incredible sights, delightful smells, smiling faces, and an overall playfulness that triggered memories of childhood's idyllic nature. Similarly, Ukiah bounced happily along each row of amusements, filled with curiosity and excitement.

After wandering past a makeshift castle that served as the backdrop for another hair-raising rollercoaster ride, Ukiah pointed jubilantly, "Look, over there! It's Japhy and Gina."

Sure enough, both of them had their heads stuck between the wooden slats of a pig pen, oinking boisterously at a group of sow who looked at them as if they were insane. Without warning, Ukiah rushed toward his son, then pushed his head between the fence - all three of them making silly noises at the obese creatures. While I laughed uncontrollably, Japhy, Ukiah, and Gina pulled their heads from the pen, then hugged dearly. After extending a round of hellos, we strolled through a sheep barn, past cow corrals, and gazed at horses that flaunted blue and red ribbons.

After asking if Japhy and Gina were hungry, Ukiah lead us to a large tent filled with picnic tables and vendors of every sort. In no time, after ordering mountains of food, we all grabbed from baskets of french fries, chicken fingers, and deep-fried cheese sticks. We also ate pizza, shish kabobs, and steaming chili cheese dogs. After finishing this feast, I thought we'd all burst. Remarkably, we still had room for gigantic glasses of freshly squeezed lemonade teeming with ice cubes, pulp, and even the rinds and seeds.

Afterward, we returned to the fairgrounds, engaging in an array of playful activities - we shot water guns into a clown's mouth, tossed darts at balloons, tried to knock over metal milk bottles with a softball, flung plastic rings at pegs on a board, and drove mechanical cars around a slotted race track. The four of us laughed riotously - Japhy's smile beaming through the night, Gina's voice squeaking excitedly, and Ukiah clapping his hands after we won stuffed animals or cheap throwaway prizes.

Then, after spinning on a few rides, we once again walked along The Midway, where Ukiah noticed a haunted house. Without hesitation, we entered the spook house and were soon confronted by moaning bogeymen, dangling rubber spiders, severed heads that sprung from the wall, and distorted mirrors that made us look taller, skinnier, shorter and fatter.

Overjoyed after leaving the funhouse, Ukiah spotted a neon sign that flashed:

Come One - Come All
Amazing!
Mind-boggling!
Spectacular!
Half Man - Half Woman
Live On Stage!
LEE/LEANA

Ukiah bought four tickets, then lead us toward the sideshow entrance. Without time to object, an uneasiness gnawed at my mind. The thought of a half male, half female Being was abysmal ... not something I wanted to see. Who cared about such an anomaly? What was the big deal? Why should society exploit these genetic misfits? Why couldn't they just look at Bug-Eyed Billy, or Lana The Leprechaun Lady? I didn't want to gawk at this oddity. So what - partially woman and partially man. Anyone could think of more interesting attractions. We shouldn't have even wasted our money on it.

But here we were, waiting in the dark to see this freak. And then, there he, she, or it stood. I was instantly fixated by the figure. Wearing a sequined dress that cut across its chest like Tarzan's jungle clothes, Leana/Lee's face had a thick black beard on the right side, while the other half was clean-shaven and smeared with bright pink lipstick. In addition, Lee's head was covered by short black matted hair, while Leana's side tumbled with luxurious blonde locks. But the most bizarre aspect of this creature was its chest. On the right side, Lee's pectoral region was flat and hairy, while beneath Leana's gown flopped a ... I couldn't tell, but it looked like a sagging water balloon.

What in God's name could it be? Was it a man, or a woman? I couldn't tell. The droopy breast looked phony, and when Lee/Leana pointed provocatively to his or her groin, the crowd erupted with laughter, whistling and making catcalls that echoed against the walls. But Leana/Lee didn't mind. He/she simply pursed their lips, blew kisses at the men, and winked at the ladies. The entire performance made me sick. Why was humanity so obsessed with sex? Who cared? I didn't. In fact, I wouldn't care if the subject were never mentioned again. Why did I even come in to see Leana/Lee?

Luckily, we were quickly ushered from the room, emerging into a calm spring evening that had finally been consumed by darkness. The carnival lights sparkled with such brilliance that I thought I was on another planet. Ukiah then asked Japhy to check his watch, and suddenly we zipped toward the speedway where Joey Chitwood's Thrill Show would soon begin.

After racing through the crowd, we sat on a row of bleachers beside the track. Once again, Ukiah landed premium tickets (second row) for one of the greatest shows of all time. We all watched attentively as souped-up muscle cars sped and weaved between each other with precision accuracy, nearly trading paint with each pass. They ramped through walls of fire, rode on two wheels, skidded through the dirt, and did barrel rolls that miraculously didn't demolish their cars. I always thought Ukiah was the craziest driver I'd ever seen, but Joey Chitwood and his daredevils were way outta his league. The crowd gasped with nervousness during each stunt, then held their breath as Joey and his troupe flew through the air or screeched toward walls.

While Japhy and Gina applauded, Ukiah stood with a look of awe on his face. I know, like the nose on my face, he would have given anything to be in one of those hot rods screaming around the track. As I pictured Ukiah leaping through the air at fifty miles an hour, a rocket-powered dragster pulled onto the track and fired its engine. I lunged backward as blinding, BLINDING orange flames burst from the machine's tailpipe, a fiery ball so intense I actually felt the flesh burning on my face. Plus, the blast's deafening roar drilled through my eardrums with such ... the sensory overload was incredible - atomic level flames, earthquake rumblings, and a vibrating excitement that filled the darkened air with exhilaration, alcohol fumes, and overpowering fury. If this monstrous rocket had been allowed to krank itself into gear, I swear it would have barreled through every wall in Kundalini County.

Sweating from the heat's intensity, the four of us stood anxiously as a steep wooden ramp was positioned before us. It seemed Joey Chitwood himself, who could barely walk (due to a lifetime of stunt-related accidents) was going to leap eighty feet into the air through a wall of flames, over ten parked cars, then land atop an adjacent ramp. A hush blanketed the crowd as Joey hobbled to his car, waved in all directions, then sped out of sight. Feeling the collective nervousness, we waited anxiously as Joey stormed toward us, then hit the ramp as fireworks exploded around him. Joey flew violently into the smoky air, burst through the wall of flames, then descended ... no, for some reason Joey's car veered to the left, then crashed into the last car positioned before his landing ramp. Shrieks and screams burst from the bleachers as twisted metal, smoke, and sparks shot across the speedway.

I thought Joey died in this collision, but incredibly, as flames erupted from his gas tank, the daredevil crawled from his passenger side window, then stumbled from the wreckage toward his fans. Spontaneous waves of applause erupted from every spectator, each of them on their feet, clapping with encouragement. Somehow, Joey had survived and was still able to walk, yet no doubt adding another broken bone or torn muscle to his list of injuries.

So, as plumes of smoke swirled toward the stars, we left the grandstand, consumed by waves of wonder. Joey Chitwood and his cohorts had staged such a magnificent performance that none of us could even talk. Only then did we realize that, as this wonderful evening drew to a close, Ukiah would be forced to part company with his son. During their visit, I heard them talk about the band, schoolwork, Japhy's two jobs, his car, and every other detail in between. Plus, after playing all those games and spinning on the rides, it seemed as if a lifetime of fun had been crammed into the span of four hours. Luckily, Japhy would soon end another school year, being free to spend more time with his father during the summer. Regrettably, we finally reached the animal barns where we originally met. With a distinct sadness looming in the nighttime air, Ukiah walked toward Japhy, hugged him, then bid a tender farewell to Gina.

As we parted ways, I heard Japhy yell, "Love ya, Dad."

Ukiah replied, "I love you too, buddy."

Our return trip to Latera Heights in Ukiah's van was somber at best, the sorrow of separation so strong that silence persisted for much of the journey. A respite didn't arrive until Ukiah spoke about a topic that had apparently been bothering him for quite some time.

While driving along the darkened interstate, he snapped, "It boggles my mind that I'm not famous yet."

He once again turned silent, making me wonder what, or how, I should answer. Not wanting to say something stupid, I kept quiet until Ukiah continued this thought.

Minutes later, true to form, he readdressed the topic. "It's all my fault. Maybe I haven't been working hard enough. But my laziness will end tomorrow."

"What are your plans?" I asked evenly.

"I'm going to mail 150 letters to every agent in New York City. Because time's running out, they'll have to be generic, but if only one of them bites, I'll be IN. Plus, I'm going to send letters to a few dozen agents in the children's market telling them about my fairy tale. Between these two efforts, I should land something."

"Or else Mindy will call from The Ocean Agency and tell you that soon every person in America will recognize your face!"

"If it were only that easy," Ukiah said softly, shaking his head. "I'd love to make Solipsism the greatest literary movement of all time."

"I know this sounds silly, but I still don't know exactly what Solipsism is. Could you explain it again?"

"Better yet, I'll give you an example," Ukiah told me as his wrist rested casually on top of the steering wheel.

"An example?"

"Sure - a routine. I'm not very good at dialects, but I'll do my best."

So, with no preparation, Ukiah launched into the following conversation between a fast talking taxi driver and his fare - a chubby, forty year old droopy-lidded man with a Frankenstein-type forehead and monotone voice.

Driver: Hey Danno! Where ya goin'?
Danno: 444 East Latera.
Driver: Oh, I know what that means.
Danno: What?
Driver: You're going to see your psychiatrist.
Danno: Psychologist.
Driver: Yeah, psychologist. What're ya gonna talk about today?
Danno: Suicide.
Driver: Oh yeah? Ya finally had enough o' the world, huh?
Danno: Yeah, but I probably won't do it.
Driver: That's good. I had a good buddy who offed himself about
        thirteen months ago.
Danno: How'd he do it?
Driver: He swallowed a shitloada pills, then tied a plastic bag
        around his neck with a cord. Do you remember that
        suicide cult that waited for the UFO's to return? They
        all wore the same colored sneakers.
Danno: Yeah.
Driver: He stole the idea from them. The stupid bastard planned
        it for months, and no one knew. The authorities even
        found a checklist in the motel room where they
        discovered his body.
Danno: I tried suffocating myself once, but I kept breathing.
Driver: I hope you don't try it again.
Danno: I won't. I hate people who try suicide just
        to get attention. You're not going to
        call the cops, are you?
Driver: Hey man, we're all responsible for our own actions. It's
        your life, and your death. I don't care what you do.
Danno: Tomorrow would've been my 14th wedding anniversary.

Driver: You still got it bad for her, huh? How long have you been divorced?
Danno: Ten years. I called her again.
Driver: Oh no! What'd ya say this time?
Danno: I got her answering machine.
Driver: What'd ya say?
Danno: I told her - Happy Anniversary you motherfuckin',
　　　　cocksuckin' whore.
Driver: Oh man, you're going to get arrested, you crazy bastard.
　　　　I don't know why you let that broad get you down. I've
　　　　had my heart broken a hundred times. Ya just gotta get up &
　　　　find another one.
Danno: That's just it. I can't find a new one. I'm going to buy
　　　　a hooker tomorrow night.
Driver: Where ya gonna find a hooker?
Danno: At The Still Hunt Inn, or at that tittie bar on top o' the
　　　　mountain.
Driver: Those girls are dancers, not prostitutes.
Danno: Then I'll check at The Still Hunt Inn.
Driver: I never heard o' no hookers at that hotel. But who
　　　　knows? I hope ya bring lotsa money.
Danno: I will.
Driver: So, what else're ya gonna tell your psychiatrist?
Danno: That I'm afraid I'm becoming psychotic.
Driver: Psychotic! Y'mean like a serial killer?
Danno: Yeah.
Driver: What're ya gonna do, kill someone?
Danno: Kill someone, or rape them.
Driver: You're gonna rape someone?
Danno: I'm considering it.
Driver: Who're ya gonna rape?
Danno: Anybody.
Driver: If you're gonna rape anyone, it should at least be your
　　　　ex-wife. She's the one who ran off with your best friend.
Danno: Then I'll get arrested.
Driver: Shit, ya can't rape some innocent gal who never did
　　　　nuthin' to ya.
Danno: I probably won't even do it at all. You're not going to
　　　　call the cops, are ya?
Driver: Hey man, it's your life. I don't give a damn whatcha do.

At that point, Ukiah finished his story, staring straight ahead as he drove along the bypass leading to Latera Heights.

Meanwhile, I tried to figure out how this story related to Solipsism. Unable to connect the two, I asked, "I'm sorry, but I still don't get it."

"What's not to get?" Ukiah began. "Was this routine a real life story, Art, or a product of my imagination?"

"I don't have the slightest idea."

"Exactly," Ukiah proclaimed. "To become a Soloist, Creation should be the same as Existence. Life imitates Art, and vise versa. It all boils down to blurring the lines between reality and fiction until one becomes the other. Shit, there are so many people I'd love to pull into this movement."

"Like who?" I asked.

"Before telling you, first I wanna clarify one point. I'm not the first Soloist to ever write a book. There were many others before me, but under different labels."

"Such as?"

"The most obvious example is Jack Kerouac. That poor guy's entire life was contained within his pages, as is mine. Another candidate would be Marcel Proust, who wrote, *Remembrance of Things Past*. More importantly, there are people I've met who could write books a helluva lot better than mine."

"Are you serious? Tell me about them," I asked with obvious interest.

"One would be a person I've talked about many times - Mack Keegan. He lives in Pittsburgh, and could write the funniest memoir ever about partying. Tattoo Blue could write about life on the streets, plus I know a girl who could tell a horrifying tale about mental illness and nervous breakdowns. Hell, even my ex-girlfriend from *Crocodile Tears* would make a great author. But, because I can't get published, none of these people believe in me, so they don't write about their lives. It's a shame, because if they faced their demons, or had an ounce of initiative, we'd start a new literary movement that'd set the world on its ass. But none of them are going to dig into their souls and see what's hidden. This's why I have so much respect for a woman who recently wrote about her battle with bulimia and anorexia. Her stories were so gripping that I'd call her book *Wasted* a masterpiece of pure Solipsism."

With those rare words of praise for another author hanging in the air, Ukiah pulled onto Reflection Alley, then asked, "Did you check the mail today?"

"No," I told him.

"Neither did I. Let's swing by."

After positioning his van so I could reach into our mailboxes, I opened Ukiah's door to find a yellow manila envelope with The Ocean Agency's return address in the upper left hand corner. I momentarily froze, remembering Ukiah's explanation of their policy. If Ocean accepted a manuscript, they would personally phone the author. But if the novel was rejected, a letter would be sent. Obviously, they opted for the latter.

I considered telling Ukiah his box was empty, but knew he'd catch on. It didn't seem fair. After our wonderful evening at the fair, the potential existed for another disappointment. Feeling beat up, I reluctantly grabbed the envelope, then handed it to Ukiah. Even in the darkness, I could see his face turn a ghastly white. But rather than open it, Ukiah shifted his van into drive, then pulled into our driveway.

As we stepped out, I said softly, "I'm sorry, Ukiah. Something will turn ....". My words then trailed into nothingness.

I thought he would return to his house and face the bad news alone. But instead, he followed me into my kitchen, then opened the manila envelope.

After waiting a short while as he read, I couldn't contain my curiosity, blurting, "What did Mindy say?"

Ukiah held a thin, blue covered pamphlet in the air with the words "Nina Ocean Literary Agency, Professional Review" on its front. Beneath the heading, I read:

Author: Ukiah Rhymes
Title: *Glitter Ghetto*
Page Count: 194 - single-spaced
Approximate word count: 80,000

He then said, "According to their Blue Book, here's what's wrong with my novel:

Characterization: Protagonist is not three-dimensional, possibly
                   because of the diary-like way this is written.
                   Characters are stereotypes. No antagonist.

Point of View: Although POV is first-person, you never get to really
                 FEEL what the characters are thinking or feeling.

Plot: There is no plot. This is written like a diary, not a novel. A
      novel needs a compelling event, rising plot action, and a
      climax/resolution. This goes nowhere.

Show vs. Tell: The entire manuscript is told, rather than shown.
                 There are no chapters or developed scenes.

Dialogue: Very little dialogue. Develop complete scenes with dialogue.

Setting: Setting is not established due to telling instead
          of showing and lack of description.

Description: Writing is flat and awkward because of the lack of
               adequate description.

Voice, Tone and Theme: All lacking due to undeveloped protagonist.

Grammar and Mechanics: Check spelling, punctuation. Paragraphing needs work.

Presentation: Unprofessional

Length: Genre category was not indicated, and this doesn't fit any established categories.

Suggestions: Please familiarize yourself with the literary marketplace.

After reading the pamphlet, I yelled, "Bullshit! That lady must not have read the same novel as me. *Glitter Ghetto* is one of the wildest stories ever. It's no wonder no one ever heard of her agency? What ....."

Unexpectedly, Ukiah laughed, "Yeah, I get the impression Mindy liked my work!"

Becoming angrier, I snapped, "What are you going to do? I'd write that lady a letter and give her a piece of your mind."

"Ah, what's the use?" Ukiah replied with obvious resignation, returning The Blue Book to its envelope. "Mindy's not interested, so why waste my time? I'll bet those agents dread getting letters from authors after they've been rejected. Hell, I can't blame 'em. We're all disappointed, angry, and resentful because they don't understand our 'vision.' Y'know what? I hate writers. To hell with us. Nothing's worse than a cry baby artist."

"That's it?" I said.

"What should I do?" Ukiah asked, sitting on a couch. "I'm not going to change anything in the book. Shit, with this attitude, odds are I'll never get published. But what the hell. The world won't stop spinning. It's what I deserve for being such a bullhead."

Surprised by Ukiah's defeatist attitude, I snarled, "I thought Mindy might've been cool. But she's nothing but a bitch. She can be real fiery when it comes to a Blue Book, but I'll bet she'd cringe in person. I'd love to ask her about Ocean's position in the literary field. Then we'd hear a little indecision in her voice, showing her insecurity. In fact, I'll bet Mindy feels slighted by not being further ahead in the literary world."

Ukiah smiled as I paced about the room. "Chris, you're taking this decision harder than I am."

"*Glitter Ghetto's* good enough to sell," I yelled, swinging my arms through the air. To augment these histrionics, I stomped both feet on the floor, then asked, "Why didn't

Mindy accept your novel? What's happening to the publishing industry?"

Fueled by my question, Ukiah's temper finally erupted. "Do you know what those assholes in New York City want? Notoriety! Look at that toe-sucker Dick Morris, or Marv Albert with his backbiting and sodomy. Both of them are worms - perverts. But worse, each will have triumphant comebacks and earn millions of dollars from their wretchedness. Remember Chris, Americans will take form over substance any day. How else can you explain The Spice Girls or Jerry Springer? They're nothing but schlock, but they've somehow captured the public's attention."

"I see what you mean."

"This's the angle Mindy missed with my novel."

"Now I'm lost," I told Ukiah as I paced around the living room.

"It's clear from Mindy's comments that she thinks I don't know the proper 'structure' that established publishing houses want. She spoke at length about this shortcoming. But this lack of mainstream sensibility is what we should capitalize on. Ocean could become the 'anti-formula' agency!"

"Perfect!" I exclaimed.

"There's a strong current in this country where the little man - the daily worker - hates his elitist controllers — those who live in ivory towers and are out of touch with their concerns. But I could storm onto the scene and bash the critics, intellectuals, hoity toity authors, and academians. I'll tell this country that ANYONE can do what I'm doing! Naturally, the establishment, and all those who enable the formulaic writers, will hate us. But guess what? That's what we want! We WANT them to despise us! That's our angle. It's very Machiavellian, but effective none the less. Ultimately, we'll create instant notoriety for ourselves. The common man will relate to the pot shots taken at writers like Philip Prince and John Grisham, because they feel the same way about their bosses, the tax man, and their government. The 'us versus them' stance is very prevalent in this nation. If we play it to the fullest, we'll take off like a rocket."

Finally taking a seat, I said, "How can you make it without the critics on your side? They'll write nothing but negative reviews. It seems impossible."

Standing, Ukiah began, "Look at Kiss. The critics hated them more than any band in history. But 25 years later, they're still rocking stronger than ever."

"Why?" I asked, becoming very involved in this discussion.

"Because of outrage, flamboyance, and theatrics. The same concept applies to professional wrestling. Why do folks go to these choreographed matches? Because of the competitiveness? Hell no. It boils down to one concept - the cult of personality. A character is created and developed, then the audience accepts them as one of their own."

"I get it. The same could apply to you."

"Why not? Following a wild press conference, and the interviews that'll follow, the public will get to know me ....."

"Through your public relations campaign."

"You're catching on. The most crucial element of this plan involves excitement. Almost invariably, writers are the most boring people in the entertainment field. Other than Hunter S. Thompson, the last one to pique the public's interest was Truman Capote, and he was nothing but a sniveling, pill-popping, pathetically drunken fag. Today, the only author I see who somewhat interests me is Camille Paglia, but she's too wacky to bond with the common man."

Excited, I leaped to my feet and shouted, "Ukiah, you're right! We need to get into the book publishing business! To hell with Mindy Silver. We'll push our own products, then go on a book signing tour that'll blow everyone out of the water."

My enthusiasm became contagious, for Ukiah added, "The entire literary field will say, HOLY SHIT, get a loada those crazy bastards. We can pull it off! With Japhy's band tagging along, we'll show the writing world how to ACT. There's a huge market waiting to be exploited. We can walk in and make a killing. Rather than being a boring author on some lame talk show, we'll barnstorm the country creating a buzz and setting everyone's imagination on fire."

Feeling more alive than I had in ages, I gushed, "In no time, we'll be the NUMBER ONE team around. To make it all the way, we need a scheme, and you already have one."

"I know I can differentiate us from the rest."

"All we need to do," I cheered, "is put our heads together and get the ball rolling."

"That settles it," Ukiah snapped, clapping his hands. "By tomorrow, I'll come up with a plan for you to kill your old man, then we'll collect his insurance money!" Smiling broadly, Ukiah walked toward the door, then said, "Y'know Chris, at times I doubted your dedication, but tonight you've proven yourself. You'll see. It'll all be worthwhile. We can set the world on fire."

Ukiah opened the door, then turned and said the most puzzling words I'd ever heard. He told me, "When the final spasms of pain shoot through my body and I gasp my last breath of air, I want to cry with joy and meet Romlocon. That'll be the happiest moment of my life."

Alone at this late-night hour, my mind did somersaults as I thought about Ukiah's parting words. Was his reference to Romlocon an omen, or a not so subtle death wish? By the tone of his voice and that knowing expression, it seemed Ukiah was hinting at things I preferred to ignore. Speaking of which, Ukiah said that by tomorrow he would come up with a plan to eliminate my father. Most of his schemes fell by the wayside, but this time he spoke with conviction. Desperation was replacing sanity as we soared toward madness.

The prospect of murdering my father struck me as absurd, perverse, dreadful, and invigorating. On the one hand, what type of person murdered their own father? The answer, of course, were those people filled with bloodlust and ingratitude - a monstrous aberration in conflict with humanity itself. In the same breath, why would a man bring a child into the world for the sole purpose of destroying it? I thought about the times Pus prodded, belittled, and deliberately prevented my advancement. The sadistic glee he derived from this abuse astouded me. As Ukiah correctly perceived, I had effectively been programmed. My identity - each insecure nuance, neurotic foible, and fearful reaction - became a product of my father's tyrannical hand. To kill him wouldn't make up for the past - that was clear. But it would allow me to finally move ahead. Whether I could actually bring myself to commit such an act, though, remained to be seen.

While I considered the ramifications of patricide, I also wondered about Ukiah. I realized that every time he got bad news, he melted down inside his cottage. I don't know if he dropped his defenses and finally cracked, or if he acted this way every night. Whatever the case, I was sure of one thing. I would once again sneak through our yards and spy on Ukiah - the notion filling me with both terror and unbridled excitement.

With the sensibilities of a fox, I crept from my porch through Woody's backyard, past a row of shrubs, behind a tree, along a vine covered fence, then to the lilac bush which started blossoming alongside Ukiah's cottage. Securely out of sight, I crouched beneath his windowsill, heart thumping madly within my chest. As I knelt, a strange notion entered my mind. Over the past few months, I noticed a dramatic change in me. Rather than living in No-Sho The Hero's fantasyland and hiding from the world, I actually confronted those aspects of life that made me cringe. In the past, spying on Ukiah terrified me. But tonight, I anticipated it. Even if detected, I could face the consequences. I'm not sure what this transformation was attributed to, but the ability to flourish rather than flounder inspired me to new heights.

This burst of confidence was soon replaced by visions of outrageousness as I peeked inside Ukiah's window. Sprawled before me was the most bizarre sight I had ever seen. Ukiah, wearing only red underwear and a black bandanna covering his eyes to serve as a blindfold, laid face up on his sofa bed, which was covered by a white satin sheet. Even more peculiar was the fact that both of Ukiah's wrists were attached to the bed frame by extended pieces of black cloth. From my perspective, it looked as if Ukiah actually shackled himself to his bed!

Then it struck me. Being that Ukiah could not see through his blindfold, I didn't have to worry about being detected. Even better, he couldn't take off his blindfold because both hands were tied. So I stood without fear, staring through the window at this freakish sight. Ukiah had lost his mind. What a maniac. I actually hopped about anxiously while watching him, possessed by this macabre vision. Not only did Ukiah act crazy when he was with me, he also did so in private! He really was a lunatic.

To certify his madness, Ukiah flailed his arms in the air, clawing at an invisible foe. He then moaned in a grievous voice, his words swirling about the room.

"I beg you, let me out of your web. Who could ever be consumed by such cruel, unrequiting love? Nobody pines away like me. I have what I adore, yet I cannot see it. Why do you keep denying me? My passions fall upon the eyes of blindness ... I'd rather be eaten alive than stay in this frustrating maze. My unhappiness gets worse each day. But it isn't a canyon that separates us, but instead a mere chasm ... such a petty distance to prevent our blissful union."

Ukiah kicked his feet defiantly while kneading the air with his arms.

"Whisper the secret that will let me escape this terrible fate," he pleaded pathetically. "You vowed to return my love, to fill me with hope, but all you do is stare at me as if we were one. Please, show some sympathy for my tormented soul. I promise to repay you in hearts by winking when you do, or blowing kisses when you do. But the words I long to hear coming from your lips will never be heard, because your denials have made me go blind!"

Ukiah tossed and turned, the black restraints wrapping his arms like tentacles.

"Can't you see? We were meant for each other! You are me, and I am you. I'm sure of this every time we look at each other. My eyes never lie. My heart is seered by your beauty. Why can't we burn together? This torture must end! What I long to hold is so close, within inches, yet virtually unattainable. But by staying trapped in this web, you and I will never embrace. If only you would leave forever, but such wishes are laughable. How odd for me, the one whose infatuation will never die, to beg for the removal of that which he adores. But who can fault me? Sadness saps my vigor and vitality. But I pray - I pray that our time together will last a short while longer. But aren't such hopes merely the futile wishes of a brokenhearted mistress? We'll never embrace ... nor will we ever kiss or make love. I'm not even allowed to look at you. But please, if I can only have one wish - take this veil from my eyes and let me see your beauty. If you don't, I'll be forced to lead a lifetime of misery and madness."

Inexplicably, Ukiah twisted into such a variety of contorted positions that I actually thought he'd levitate from his bed. And although his restraints kept him anchored, they didn't keep him from writhing until the pain was unbearable.

He concluded his soliloquy by groaning, "You don't even care about my unrequited love. I'm crushed by these vain stabs at fulfillment while you laugh at my grief. Lift this mask and stare into my eyes. You know I would cherish you until my dying day. Why won't you accept me? I've torn the clothes from my smoldering body to prove my love. What else can I do - burn my heart with a torch? Would the blood dripping to my fingers be proof of my devotion! I'll never know, because you'll never embrace me. The only way I can escape your torment is by ripping my eyes from their sockets. Is that what you want? I refuse to fight with you, for only through blindness will my aching infatuation cease to exist. I only pray that when my sight has been permanently destroyed, you will still be able to see. But dearest love, we both know the truth. When I am no longer able to see you, we'll both vanish together - two related, yet unconnected lives destroyed as one."

Breathless, Ukiah slumped to his mattress, lying in a fetal tuck after his dramatic performance. Afraid that he would remove his bandana, I tiptoed from the cottage, then raced to my house. Ukiah was CRAZY ... a certifiable lunatic. And at that moment, as I spun in circles and jumped wildly toward the sky, I wanted to be crazy too, just like him!

30

While I dreamed of saving the world with No-Sho The Hero, my peaceful Saturday morning was ruined as a phone call from my mother echoed from the answering machine:

> "Chris, wake up. Quit sleeping your life away. Pus is very upset that you haven't done a Skip-To-The-Lou-My-Darling for him yet. He needs to turn his frown upside down. Now call, or I'm afraid he'll paddle your fanny one of these days."

The blissfulness of flying through the air with my cape flapping in the wind had been shattered by my mother's denigrating comments. I didn't want to dance in circles for my father, or be badgered by annoying messages. Why couldn't they leave me alone? I wasn't asking for much. I just wanted to be left alone ... no hassles, demands, or involvement in their harebrained schemes. Why couldn't they understand that I didn't need them interfering in my life, or feeling sorry for me. I only asked one thing of the world - leave me alone.

But now that I was awake, I got out of bed and wandered through the house, relieved that I didn't have to work. So, wearing a pair of sweatpants and a loose t-shirt, I sat on the couch and watched television while clearing the cobwebs from my head. Flicking through the channels, I clicked past cartoons, infomercials, old movies, and reruns before seeing a fascinating image. Overcome by excitement, I raced barefoot from my house to Ukiah's cottage, where I found him sitting on his porch step wearing black shorts and a tank top.

Dismissing pleasantries, I blurted, "You should have seen who was on TV."

Ukiah remained silent, staring at me from his perch.

"I was clicking through the channels, and I saw Philip Prince!"

Ukiah's gaze remained blank and distant.

Enthused, I continued, "That big phony was sitting at Fenway Park reading a book when the cameras caught him. Prince looked so bored that I thought he was asleep. I don't know if this was a commentary on the state of baseball, but it definitely said something about the book industry. The most interesting thing Philip Prince could do on national television was read a book and fall asleep. Ukiah? Are you listening? I'm telling you about Prince's appearance ....."

"I heard," Ukiah told me, his wrists red and bruised, a reminder of the previous evening's insanity.

"Don't you care?" I asked, my excitement waning.

"Not particularly," he said blandly.

"Why? What's wrong?" Then it hit me. Maybe he knew about me standing outside his window last night.

"Nothing," he responded. "I stayed up all night writing letters to those agents in New York. All I need to do is make copies, address the envelopes, stamp them, and shove 'em in the mail."

Ukiah's face appeared haggard and fatigued, while his voice was lifeless.

Worried, I asked, "Is there something I can do?"

Rubbing his eyes, he looked drearily at me. "There sure is. Get ready for the last weekend of this month, because that's when we're snuffing your old man."

The world literally stopped turning (at least from my perspective) as his words trickled through the air.

"The last ... last weekend? How ... where?"

Ukiah's head slumped to his chest, hair hanging over his face, as he muttered to the ground, "We'll do it at a stock car race in New York." He remained sullen for a moment, then added, "I keep moving further from Romlocon each day. But at this point, things are spinning so far out of control that I can't keep a handle on them."

"Why are we doing it at a stock car race?" I asked nervously. "It sounds far fetched."

Still slumped over, Ukiah sounded tired. "C'mon inside. I'll fill you in on the details."

Ukiah's idea was so bizarre that I questioned his sanity for even considering it. He wanted to invite my father to a stock car race, then murder him sometime during the trip. Nothing I had ever heard sounded more ill conceived. The only point that made sense was how we were going to get rid of my father's body. Every Sunday evening, my mother played Bingo at the Legion Hall. Being that we would kill him on race day - a Sunday - we'd be able to return the body while she was away, making it look like Pus died of natural causes.

I was sure of two things. One, we wouldn't be able to keep running from the law after this weekend; and two, I dreaded a trip where my father humiliated me endlessly in front of Ukiah. As a result, in less than a week I would be imprisoned, while any hope of keeping my self-esteem would be lost (due to Pus belittling me). After reexamining this plan, I knew nothing good could come of it. Instead, my life would crash land once and for all ......

I tried to change Ukiah's mind one evening while he cooked supper, but he rambled incessantly about calling the vice president of Barnes and Noble with his ideas about a traveling literary rock n' roll circus. I wanted to talk about the obvious flaws of his murder plot, but Ukiah ignored every word I said. Over time, I noticed this annoying habit of his - rather than paying attention to what was important, he'd come up with crazy schemes, or play video racing games. It didn't make sense.

Anyway, resigned to being a marionette in Ukiah's puppet show, I listened to his latest escapade while he prepared an alfredo sauce.

"After talking to Ron Belly at Barnes and Noble, I realized I forgot to tell him the most important part of my plan."

Before he could continue, I asked, "What possessed you to call the vice president of Barnes and Noble? How did you even get through to him?"

"I did some research at the library, and found that Mister Belly had the most influential position at his company. I'm not sure if you know this, but Barnes and Noble, along with selling books, also has a separate publishing wing. So, instead of getting a literary agent, who then has to find a publisher, why not go straight to the source? If they already own hundreds of bookstores, why not let them publish my book? We could eliminate the middleman!"

"I'm still amazed you were able to talk with him."

"Ya gotta be a con man in this world," Ukiah laughed while stirring his sauce with a whisk. "A little smooth talking can get ya anywhere."

"Did Mister Belly sound interested in your ideas?"

"No, but that's because I forgot to tell him all the best parts."

"Which are?"

"Well, there's the press conference, then the literary tour … I don't know … I wrote a letter telling him about all my ideas."

"Ukiah, your ideas are what scare me. What did you tell him?"

"I told Mister Belly that my traveling literary circus will not only have a rock n' roll band, but also a Live Alien Brain, and a menagerie of hand-picked freaks from every town."

My jaw nearly dropped to the floor when hearing this outrageous scheme.

"A Live Alien Brain?" I asked. "What could you be thinking?"

Excited as he poured alfredo sauce over his chicken and vegetables, Ukiah began, "I'll be the greatest showman since P.T. Barnum. You remember him, don't you?"

"Yeah, a sucker is born every minute," I said.

"Exactly! This tour won't be your typical debacle where a boring author sits in a corner and signs books. Hell no. This spectacle will attract people from everywhere. We'll be a rolling freak show, with a Live Alien Brain and other oddities on display."

"Ukiah, what exactly is a Live Alien Brain?"

"We'll have a hundred gallon aquarium filled with bluish green fluid, then inside it will be an oversized clay brain that was supposedly removed from an alien. It'll be hokey as hell, but once advertised, people will flock to see it, only to prove that it isn't real. We'll cloak the aquarium with a black cover, then WAM! The veil will be taken away while the brain sits mysteriously as bubbles are pumped through the fluid. Imagine how cool it'll be. Plus, we'll advertise for freaks in every town - oddities like the human pincushion, rubber skinned women, monkey boys, albinos, and dog-faced Siamese Twins. Once the public gets a load o' me, they ain't ever gonna forget!"

I could only imagine Mister Belly's reaction. Over the years, Barnes and Noble established itself as a respected bookseller. Now Ukiah wanted to attract rebellious rock n' roll fans, sideshow miscreants, and those drawn to alien brains. Riots would erupt, with Barnes and Noble's books being burned by heavy-metal teenagers, or trampled under the feet of carnival freaks.

Laughing, I asked, "Won't everyone know the Alien Brain is fake?"

"Of course, but that's the main attraction! People love to not only be right, but they're also filled with morbid fascination. Everyone will know the Alien Brain isn't real, but they need to see it with their own eyes. It's the same with professional wrestling. Everyone knows it's fake, but the WWF sells out arenas for one reason - they put on one helluva show! This is what I plan on doing - bring excitement back to the field of writing. Literature actually enjoyed a heyday at one time, but now I only see cardboard cutouts that have the pizzazz of houseplants. How boring! The industry is wide open to be exploited, and I can do it."

"I'm convinced, Ukiah, but I'm sure Mister Belly is wondering how this plan would benefit his company."

"Isn't it obvious?" he declared. "What is a bookstore's primary objective?"

"To sell books."

"Exactly. And how do they do this? By bringing people into their store. I guarantee customers will come to every Barnes and Noble store along the tour." Ukiah paused for a second, then continued. "To stand out, someone has to be an innovator, and have the balls to do something different. That's why this rock, writing, n' oddity angle is a sure-fire combination. It'll differentiate us from the rest."

"Did you get an answer from Mister Belly?" I asked, hoping not to upset Ukiah.

"Remarkably, I did."

"You're kidding? A man like him actually took the time to write back?"

"Of course," Ukiah told me.

"What did he say?"

"He wasn't real pleased that I sent a letter after my phone call."

"What did he say? Tell me."

"Well, Mister Belly said that he patiently tried to explain on the phone how I might approach potential publishers, but he didn't think we could work together."

"Did he give a reason?"

"Only that with the glut of media focus on celebrity publishing, he wasn't surprised that I mistakenly thought content was secondary to promotion. So, I suppose another road has been blocked off."

"What are you going to do next?" I asked, fearing that Ukiah had burned all his bridges.

Undaunted, he replied, "Being that I'm almost done with *Blank Line*, it's time to start pushing it all the way. Y'see, I figured out what I've been doing wrong all this time."

"You did?"

"I was selling an idea, or concept, or package deal to these agents when I should have been promoting a specific, salable book. So, it looks like I'll be starting all over again from scratch."

With these words giving him hope, Ukiah served us dinner - chicken and vegetables smothered in a tantalizing alfredo sauce.

As the final weekend of July arrived, I realized that a man who planned on taking a Live Alien Brain to bookstores around the country was also preparing to kill my father. With each passing hour, I thought about disappearing without a trace from Latera Heights. I wouldn't sell my house, notify work, or even disconnect the utilities. I'd just hop in my Gemini and drive until I was free of Ukiah, my family, and life in general.

Regrettably, I didn't follow through with my plans, for as a hot summer sun rose that Saturday morning, I was still a reluctant partner in this preposterous scheme. Why did I let Ukiah involve me in his plans? I was given free will at birth, but I never used it. I tried convincing myself that I was changing. But was I? No. I still shied away from confrontation. Rather than facing my problems, I let them sweep me away without protest. Now the time arrived to murder ... yes, murder my father. I understood the connotations surrounding that word, but I still didn't object.

"All right, let's roll!" Ukiah beamed with enthusiasm. "I'll drive."

Slowly walking toward his dented gray van, I asked, "Ukiah, what's going to happen this weekend? I'm still confused."

After hopping in the van, firing his engine, then pulling onto Reflection Alley, he said, "The plan's simple. We're going to pick up your father, then drive to Watkins Glen, where we'll meet Japhy and Gina."

Appalled, I snorted, "You're not going to involve Japhy in this scheme, are you?"

"Are you kidding? Of course not. Tonight we'll park at the overflow area of a campground and rough it under the stars, then watch the race on Sunday. After Japhy leaves, we'll get rid of your old man. There's nothing to worry about."

"I'm glad one of us thinks so. When are we going to do it?"

"Who knows? Everything'll be fine. I have it under control. Now, where do your folks live?"

Much to my dismay, twenty minutes later the three of us (Ukiah driving, my father riding shotgun, and me sitting on a lawn chair between them) began our trip to Watkins Glen.

"Ukiah," I said nervously, "this's my father, Norb Edwards."

"Nice to meet you, sir," my friend said cordially.

"Likewise," Pus replied unabashedly. "So, what do you do?"

Undaunted, Ukiah told him, "I'm an independent contractor of sorts, but in my spare time I write."

"A writer, huh? Have you ever been published?"

"Dad, maybe Ukiah doesn't ....."

"No, I've never been published, but I have tons of great ideas."

"You do?" my father asked. "Fantastic. I'm an inventor of sorts myself."

He was?

"You are?" Ukiah responded. "Has anything ever been copyrighted?"

"No, but I have ideas flying out the yin-yang," my father told him.

"Like what?" Ukiah asked.

As we neared an interstate highway, Pus said, "I'm designing a personal helicopter that'll let people fly through the air. I got the idea from Chris one day as ..."

"Dad, must you?" I interrupted.

"What? I was telling your friend about my invention. Y'see, the flyer would wear a helmet with helicopter blades coming out of its top. Then, after pushing a button, the blades would rotate and the person would hover above the ground."

"Wow, it sounds fantastic," Ukiah replied cheerfully.

Fantastic? Nobody will ever fly with a propeller sticking out of their head.

"I tried to give some of my practical knowledge to Chris, but that stupid kid doesn't have any common sense. Maybe you could turn my child into a writer."

"Possibly," Ukiah answered.

"Tell me about your ideas," my father then asked, uncharacteristically jovial.

"I want to tour the country with a Live Alien Brain."

"No kidding? Superb! Y'know, it just might work," my father said enthusiastically.

It might work? Was he crazy? If I mentioned Live Alien Brains, Pus would have called me a horse's ass. But now he encouraged Ukiah. What was happening?

"Well, I'm thinking about inventing a waterless washing machine," my father added. "That way, people would never need laundrymats!"

"I hate doing laundry!" Ukiah gushed with joy. "Maybe we should go into business together, Norb."

Were my ears deceiving me? Was I in *The Twilight Zone*? Ukiah and my Father had formed a mutual admiration society.

"That's an interesting proposal, young man. We could also develop a new form of literature — 3-D novels!"

"Three-D writing. You're a genius," Ukiah told him. "We'll be famous! I never knew Chris had such an intelligent father."

"I've been telling Chris that for years," Pus laughed, "but that damn fool kid o' mine never listens. Chris is too busy dancing around in that flowered ...."

"Dad! Please."

So, for two hours, as we passed apple fields, finger lakes, rolling meadows, and expansive farmland, Ukiah and my father discussed their plans for becoming multimillionaires. As for me, I sat slumped on a teetering lawn chair that tipped in one direction or the other every time we made a turn. Not only had I been excluded from their conversation, but my father periodically took jabs at me, or made reference to my faults. Meanwhile, I sat quietly, stewing that I let this event take place.

The weekend quickly became a disaster. We met Japhy and Gina at the campground, pitched a tent, then milled about our site tossing a Frisbee, chopping wood, and cooking hot dogs and marshmallows over a fire as Japhy strummed an acoustic guitar. That night, Ukiah, his son, and Gina slept in the tent, while Pus and I crashed on a mattress in the back of Ukiah's van. Even the next morning, as we cooked bacon and eggs over a campfire, my father and best friend bonded as if they were lifelong companions. I remembered Ukiah once telling me about his ability to read people ... his perceptiveness. But from my perspective, he may have just been a starry-eyed dreamer who played me for a fool. Why couldn't he see that my father was a control freak ... someone with a despicable mean streak? But there they were, each with a frying pan, laughing and swapping stories as Japhy and Gina relaxed beside them. Once again, Pus ruined another part of my life.

After eating, then washing ourselves under a row of faucets which sat in the field, Ukiah said, "C'mon, it's time to rock n' roll."

As the five of us strolled to Ukiah's van, I took my friend aside and asked angrily, "What's the big idea?"

"The big idea?" Ukiah shrugged. "What do you mean?"

Whispering, I said, "I thought we were supposed to kill my father. Now you two are the best of friends."

"We are! Didn't you hear? Next weekend, Norb and me are gonna get that old stock car of mine running and take her to Duality Speedway. He's the coolest man I've ever met."

During the bouncy ride in the back of Ukiah's van, I felt miserable beyond words. The only way this situation could get worse was if Woody Dewar rose from the dead and sat on the spare tire beside me. I got so depressed that I felt like breaking down and crying. Why was my life so awful? I stared at the others around me - Gina sitting on Japhy's lap atop the wheel well, while Ukiah drove and my father sat beside him. All four were laughing, chattering, smiling ... filled with anticipation over the beautiful day's upcoming events.

In contrast, my gloominess lingered like a rain cloud. Why couldn't I develop a meaningful relationship with my father like the one Japhy and Ukiah enjoyed? I saw how they interacted with each other - the kind gestures, handshakes, pats on the back, words of encouragement, and inside jokes that made them laugh. There was never any tension or nervous energy between them - just a lasting love that bonded one to the other.

Although Ukiah thrived on his loner lifestyle, he knew there was at least one person who loved him unconditionally. As for me, I felt more alone than ever. I recalled the previous evening when my father and I crawled into Ukiah's van to sleep on a frayed, musty mattress. We hadn't visited in months, yet for the first ten minutes, not a word was whispered between us. I laid alongside my father ... touching him ... I could hear him breathing, and feel the movements of his body as he tossed and turned. But there was nothing between us except silence. I wanted to reach over and hug my father, to say "I love you," or to ask why he hated me. But I remained frozen, my heart thumping ferociously.

I had never slept with my father ... not even as a child. That type of behavior was frowned upon. Now my arm rested against his, separated only by a thin blue blanket. Although I could hear other campers partying outside, a distinct, eerie silence enveloped the van. My father's breathing got slower as he relaxed ... mine increasing as the emotional chasm grew between us.

Then, when I mistakenly thought my father had fallen asleep, he sneered in a gruff voice, "Y'know, this weekend would have been a disaster if those other three hadn't been here - a total bore."

That comment was my father's way of saying good night. His words stung my pride. I was this man's child, his offspring, and he truly despised me. What had I done to merit such a reaction? I never became what he expected, but was I so unworthy of affection that he couldn't say a single kind word all day?

I experienced an array of emotions this weekend, the least of them being a hope that my father would act cordially toward me. In the back of my mind, I prayed we would finally reunite and end the strife that had persisted all our lives. Then I could have rationalized not taking part in his murder. But as things stood now, I actually wanted to take a pillow and smother the bastard. In reality, it looked like his murder would never take place. Hell, him and Ukiah became such quick friends that all thoughts of homicide had been replaced by future business ventures. Instead of killing my father, Ukiah wanted to become his partner. The world was becoming so absurd that each passing day became a battle against madness.

We bumped and bounced to an open field beside the racetrack that was filled with so many cars and trucks that they stretched further than the eye could see. It was impossible to even count all these vehicles. I thought this event would be somewhat subdued, but my perceptions had been drastically wrong.

After grabbing plastic coolers filled with ice, hoagies, bottled water, sodas, and beer, we wandered, along with thousands of others, toward the track.

Being unfamiliar with this sport, I asked Ukiah to fill me in on the details. But before he could answer, I was traumatized by a snide remark from my father.

"Quit badgering Ukiah with your stupid questions." He then excused me by saying, "Please pardon Chris. That damn kid's partially stupid."

Unable to tolerate these personal attacks, I snapped, "I am not."

"You are too, Chris. You're practically retarded."

Luckily, Japhy and Gina were out of earshot, but Ukiah heard him loud and clear.

After walking through a ticket gate, Ukiah inadvertently answered my question by pointing to the crowd and saying, "Look around. This's the last place in America where people can still be free! We can bring our own food, our own drinks, and our own booze. People can even smoke in public. Check out the freedom! This's the way we should live. Every other sporting event in this country dictates the way their spectators behave. But here, it's wide open."

"How big is the track?" Japhy asked.

"It's a 2.6 mile road course. Every year there's at least 120,000 fans - all of them having fun, partying, and watching race cars go 170 miles an hour."

Ukiah was right about this spectacle. Thousands of people (wearing race car t-shirts and hats which promoted their favorite drivers) milled about the track, or gathered around RV's, campers, and buses parked in every direction. Judging from the number of emptied beer cans and whiskey bottles that overflowed from the trashcans, these folks had been drinking for days. I had never seen such good-natured fun in one place - multi-colored pendants and flags blowing in the wind ... the aroma of hamburgers, chicken, and spare ribs cooking over barbecue grills ... alcohol guzzled by the gallon ... countless vendors hawking their wares to a willing public ... kids tossing footballs ... and women dancing to old-fashioned rock n' roll music.

We circled the road course, Ukiah horsing around with Japhy and Gina, then listening to my father's raunchy jokes. I tried to enjoy the jovial atmosphere, but beneath the surface I still ached. I felt betrayed by not only my father, but also Ukiah. We had been friends for nearly a year, yet he rarely spoke with me at this event. Instead, he buddied up to Pus with the intimacy of a long lost confidant. I think Japhy sensed my alienation, for he periodically talked with me or pointed out various sights. I appreciated his concern, but the sight of Ukiah and Norb practically joined at the rib made my blood boil.

At one point we passed a rowdy section of partiers who stood between a row of RV's and motorcycles. My father grabbed another beer from the cooler, at least his sixth, then stood with the rest of us as an amazing display of uninhibited craziness took place. It seemed there were two types of race fans - an upscale crowd who manned the RV's, then the bikers standing across from them. Rivers of beer flowed between them when a gorgeous, obviously drunken woman climbed atop one of the campers and began dancing. Each group cheered her on until ... I couldn't believe my eyes - the woman removed her skimpy tube top to expose loose hanging breasts.

The crowd erupted with applause, especially my father, who cheered drunkenly, "Shake it baby, shake it for Poppa!"

I cringed with embarrassment, but Ukiah, Japhy, and even Gina howled at the dancing girl.

Not to be outdone, the bikers urged one of their motorcycle mommas onto the roof of a RV. In no time, this plump, wide hipped woman began dancing to the music, slowly peeling her t-shirt to reveal large, round, saggy jugs.

An explosion of applause, laughter, merriment, and insanity ensued as both women danced across from each other, vying for the crowd's approval. The pretty girl danced a little jig, then held her nose while pointing at the competition. In return, the biker momma stomped about, made obscene gestures at her foe, then baited the audience for a round of applause.

I managed to laugh for the first time all day as hundreds of men and women clapped, whistled, and made cat calls at the dancers.

My father, meanwhile, started dancing in circles, hollering to the biker gal, "Hey, big momma, why don't you let Poppa take ya for a ride on this hog!" He then pointed to his groin while doing a lewd pelvic thrust. I wanted to die, but Ukiah encouraged Pus by patting his shoulder and popping another beer for him.

By now, as a radiant sun hovered above us, race time arrived. The five of us scurried to a row of bleachers, then waited anxiously as the green flag dropped and forty rainbow-colored stock cars screamed by at 120 miles an hour. The visual impact and aural sensation was mind boggling - gleaming blurs of color ... thunderous, deafening engines blasting waves of alcohol fuel and exhaust fumes through the air ... screeching tires and burnt rubber ... incredible passes along the straight-stretch, then the furious crunch of twisted metal and flames as the racers blasted into a concrete retaining wall ... sparks flying ... smoke rising, and fans oohing and ahhhing as they rose to their feet.

I couldn't tell one stock car from the next, but the fans around me voiced their approval with waves of applause and ear piercing whistles. The experience was overwhelming - a burning sun delivering its heated rays in our direction ... the lingering aroma of fuel alcohol hanging in the air ... forty engines roaring past like a herd of stallions, or a battalion of tanks ... and drunken spectators screaming in each ear. At one point I nearly fainted from inhaling the exhaust fumes, but no one else seemed to mind. Each time the racers flew past, it appeared as if the crowd sprung a communal hard on. It was an odd, invigorating experience.

The race finally ended with the Number Three car, a menacing, pure black Chevrolet, nosing-out a rainbow painted Chevrolet. The crowd voiced its approval (and disapproval) for all the racers, then slowly filed from the bleachers ... the hillsides ... from lawn chairs and blankets ... and from campers, buses, and RV's. The race grounds became a mass exodus of sun-baked fans carrying coolers and folding chairs back to their vehicles - each discussing the day's collisions and passes. I'm not sure how Ukiah chose these attractions, but once again he picked one that was loud and violent.

After reaching our van and returning to the campground (where Japhy's car was parked), we bid farewell to him and Gina, then drove in separate directions. Once again, Ukiah and his son spent a fabulous weekend together, then parted with extended hugs and sorrow-filled words. The contrast between their relationship and that which I had with my father was enormous.

The three of us, with me still sitting in the middle on a rickety lawn chair, began our return trip when Ukiah suggested that, rather than fight traffic, we'd visit a local gorge. My father, silly from the booze and sun, agreed on the spot, prepared at that point for anything.

As we drove, Pus blurted drunkenly, "I ... I wanna thank you ... thank you for a wonder-wonder ... a great time this weekend. Uke ... Ukimah .. I wish that my wife and m .. m .. me would have had a ch ... child like you rather than this ... fr ... beside me-me. Chris has been a .... dis .. disappointment."

"Thanks, Norb," Ukiah smiled, "or should I say Boss? From now on, when we start our business, you'll be calling the shots."

I couldn't believe my ears. Not only had my father disowned me, but now Ukiah called him Boss!

"You got that ... that right Ukiser ... Ukelele. And we'll hire Chris to sweep the shit shit shit from our elephants. What should we call our company, anyway?"

"It's up to you, Norb. You're the man in charge," Ukiah replied meekly.

What was happening? I had never seen Ukiah demote himself to such a submissive role. Now he welcomed this subservience to my father. At that point, I wanted to murder Pus on the spot, without delay.

We climbed a steep dirt road that apparently lead to The Gorge. Shortly thereafter, Ukiah parked and the three of us hopped from his van.

"There it is, up there," Ukiah pointed. "All we need to do is climb that hill."

"Let's ... let's go," Pus snorted, sipping from his beer can.

I wanted to drive home and be finished with this disastrous weekend, but I followed my father and Ukiah for a few feet until our journey was abruptly aborted.

Clutching his chest, my father panted, "Ulena, I .. I can't climb this damn ... damn mountain. I'm too ... too tired. I need a resss ... rest."

"Sure thing, Boss," Ukiah said, helping Pus to the van, where he laid him to rest on a mattress in back. "There, Chief. You sleep tight."

"Thanks ..."

After we pulled from the dirt road (my father's snores resonating through the van), I cursed, "Damn it, Ukiah ... or is it Uminah? What's the big idea?"

Tapping his fingers merrily on the steering wheel, Ukiah said innocently, "Big idea? I don't know what you're talking about."

"Don't give me that shit! Why did you ignore me all weekend to buddy up with my father?"

"Are you kidding?" Ukiah smiled. "He's a fascinating man, with the most brilliant mind I've ever seen. Considering his genetic makeup, you should have been a genius. He even said so."

Aghast, I spat, "I'll bet he did. What else did your Boss say about me?"

"Only that you never reached your full potential in life. And if the truth be told, I can't say he's wrong. Norb seems like a perfect parent and role model. I don't know why you became such a ... well, such an underachiever. With a father like Norb, I'd be President of The United States by now."

Enraged, I stammered, "Why you ... you ... I can't believe ...."

"What is it, Chris? Are you jealous of Norb? That's it! You're jealous because you couldn't fill that poor man's shadow. You're very ungrateful and inconsiderate after all he's done for you."

"Shut up! Just shut up. I can't take another second of this insanity!"

Ukiah was unaffected by my outburst, opting to drive in silence while listening to the radio for nearly two hours.

After we reached Latera Heights and neared my house, Ukiah finally asked, "Aren't you even curious about our business venture?"

"The one you and my father connived?" I said grumpily.

"Of course."

"I suppose. What is it?"

Smiling broadly, Ukiah said, "Norb came up with this idea. He said we should travel around the country showcasing a person wearing a funny costume and cape that'd twirl around in circles. And guess who this dancer would be? YOU! Norb said we'd dress you like a horse's ass, just like when you were a kid."

"He said that! I can't believe it," I yelled, the blood vessels bursting inside my brain. "What a bastard. I'll ... I'll ..."

"You'll what?" Ukiah asked vehemently.

"I'll kill that son of a bitch."

"Then DO IT! He shows you less respect than a worm. Norb called you a freak all weekend. Now do it. Finally destroy him and start all over again. Kill him like you killed Woody Dewar."

Without delay, I bounced from my seat to the rear of Ukiah's van where my father was still passed out. Seething with rage, I pounced atop the ratty mattress, each knee straddling Pus's chest. I grabbed a pillow and tried to think of one reason not to kill this monster, but all that flashed through my mind were images of him beating me with a leather strap, humiliating me in front of family and friends, or demeaning me to such an extent that I accepted my status as a feeble know-nothing. About to commit patricide ... to see each steely pupil pop from its socket ... I looked at my immobile father through tear filled eyes to see a horrifying sight. Rather than being asleep, or unconscious, my father's face had turned an ashen gray ... his lips blue and puffy.

Incapacitated, it felt as if I actually hovered above his body, viewing it from not only inches away, but from the van's roof. The situation became otherworldly - this figure before me, with cold blue lips, refused to move ... flesh devoid of color ... no breath ... no pulse ... a lifeless lump. My father was dead!

As Ukiah drove along a residential street, I yelled, "Pull over! My father quit breathing. He's dead!"

With that morbid statement lingering through the air, Ukiah pulled to the roadside, then hopped in back with me.

After examining the corpse, Ukiah stood, crawled back to the driver's seat, then said calmly, "It looks like my plan worked better than expected. I guess we should drive to the hospital."

Shaking, teary-eyed, and nauseous, I struggled to the passenger seat, unable to view the hideous sight any longer.

With quivering lips, I whimpered, "What do you mean? What plan worked better than expected?"

"Are you kidding? You couldn't tell?" Ukiah asked with amazement as he sped through suburbia.

"I don't know what you're talking about," I said, checking behind my shoulder to see if the body had miraculously regained life.

"This entire weekend was a scam. I was putting you on."

"Ukiah, I'm in no mood to play games. Just tell me what you're talking about."

"Chris, I never buddied up to your old man. That guy's a moron ... the most egotistical idiot I've ever met."

Relieved, I beamed, "Then you weren't best friends with him?"

"Not at all. Norb is worse than I ever imagined. He is pretty smart, but he doesn't know how to treat people, especially his own family. So, everything worked out perfectly!"

Realizing I'd been duped, I snapped, "But my father's dead."

"That's what we wanted."

"Is it?"

"Chris, if Norb hadn't suffered a heart attack, you were going to strangle him to death."

"Only because you worked me into such a frenzy," I said defensively.

"That was the plan."

"It was? I still don't get it."

"Okay, listen. I knew you'd never murder Norb on your own. You haven't developed your killer instincts yet. So I figured, how could I get Chris to perform such a horrendous act? Then it hit me. I'd be friends with Norb, making you jealous in the process." Ukiah paused a moment, then continued. "But ya see, I still hadn't come up with the final part of this scheme."

"I don't follow," I told him as we entered Latera's business district.

"I planned on having you push Norb over a ledge at The Gorge, but then knew the authorities would get involved. So, I thought that with the amount of alcohol Norb had consumed, coupled with the exertion needed to climb that hill, he'd pass out from exhaustion. Finally, I had to trigger your rage so you'd really WANT to snuff him, which I did by mentioning the cape and dancing routine. So, after you smothered Norb to death, we'd put him inside your house while your mother played Bingo. Your mom would then come home to find her husband dead on the couch, attributing it to a heart attack."

As Ukiah basked in his accomplishment, I snarled, "Yeah, but now my father is dead."

"C'mon, Chris, don't play coy with me. We both know you wanted to kill Norb since you were a kid."

Embarrassed, I admitted, "That's true, but it still doesn't excuse your actions, especially when double-crossing me."

Veering through traffic, Ukiah laughed, "Chris, let's get rid of the phony sentiment. I was the one who came up with a way to kill your father. Sure, I pulled a few strings ... but guess what? Do you know what the key to good writing is?"

"No," I said testily. "How did we get on the subject of writing?"

"The key to writing fiction is an author's ability to manipulate his audience! Can't you see? That's why so many writers are self-centered creeps. They're natural manipulators! Sure, I had to twist you around a bit. So what. The end justified the means. This is a perfect example of Dialectics at its finest."

"You're losing me," I moaned.

"A Dialectic consists of contradictory attributes - bearing on the same agent - being reduced to an abstract resolution."

"That explanation helps me a lot," I stated sarcastically.

"Look at it this way. I devised a plan that, like my marketing ploys to get published, evolved over time. In terms of Dialectics, we have thesis number one - our desire to collect Norb's insurance money. In opposition, the antithesis involves your innate fear of being arrested for a criminal act. Plus, thesis number two involves your hatred for

Norb. In contrast, the antithesis revolves around your inability to actually kill him. So, to save the day, I came up with a synthesis that solved our problems. Norb is dead, we'll collect the insurance money, neither of us will go to jail, and you don't have to live under that man's thumb. Can't you see this plan's beauty?"

"You make it sound so sterile ... so cut and dried."

While meandering through town toward the hospital, Ukiah continued, "Chris, everything pertaining to human interaction reverts back to language and communication. It's like William Burroughs said - Words are a virus."

"A virus? Now you've completely lost me."

"Try to imagine a virus. What is its primary goal?"

"I don't know."

"Every virus wants to survive! So, if the human body is its host, the virus wants to flourish ... to stay alive within that body. In relation to Language, what would you consider the best form of communication between human beings?"

My father lay dead in the back of a sweltering van, and Ukiah was talking about word viruses. I couldn't believe it.

"I don't know."

"Pure honesty! How perfect would our world be if everyone was absolutely truthful?"

"Things would be different than they are now," I replied.

"They sure would be. Just think - how do we manipulate others, divert their attention from the real issues, or deliberately mislead them?"

"Through language."

"Yes! How long has Man lived on this planet? Plus, how long have we communicated through an oral or written language? The two go hand in hand. But have we been able to do away with this virus that keeps deceiving us? No, because we continue to be an enabling host. The word virus loves its home. What if someone steals from work ... to lessen the blow, it's called 'misappropriating funds.' Doesn't that sound more sterile and less injurious? Look around us. The virus flourishes because we intellectualize our language. Words become a veil ... an illusion. But I want to strip this phenomenon to its core."

"How so?"

"Let's look at one particular example - human beings killing other human beings - and how Language not only justifies their act in certain instances, but also removes the horror."

"I still don't follow," I confessed, convinced I could smell my father's body beginning to rot.

"If a 'religious' man shoots another man on the battle field, causing his brains to spill from his skull onto the blood-soaked ground, it's called a Holy War. When an old man feels sorry for his invalid wife because she's hooked to a respirator, then takes her oxygen tank and bashes it through the top of her head so the hair and blood stick to its metal casing, the media label it a Mercy Killing. How about a wife who finds her husband having sex with another woman, then crams a dagger through his chest. This is called a Crime of Passion. Having a guillotine chop off a man's head, causing it to plop into a basket with the eyes still open, is Capital Punishment, while strapping this person to a gurney and filling his blood with poison is Lethal Injection. Deliberately shortening a senior citizen's life is referred to as Euthanasia. Or, how about this one. When a beautiful, precious child is still inside the mother's womb and a doctor pierces its brain with a pair of scissors, then sucks its brains out with a vacuum, it's entitled Late Term Elective Discontinuation. The Virus keeps growing, and I've only listed a few examples. Imagine how we fuck with semantics and play word games in the world of politics, sex, or the work place. Any reprehensible act can be made to sound happy, fun, or inoffensive. I'll even go so far as to say that every spoken word ... every word we say is a form of brainwashing."

"Brainwashing? I think you've carried this idea too far," I told Ukiah. "It's starting to sound crazy."

"Is it? What does being brainwashed mean?"

Nervous, I replied, "A person is made to think like another person, or persons, wants them to think."

"Correct! One person wants to control the thoughts of another person. If I tell you - I believe the sky is green - I'm doing it to sway your perceptions in my direction. The concept is much too complex ...."

"How about a person telling their spouse, 'I love you'? How is that considered brain-washing, or a function of ulterior motives?"

Ukiah chuckled knowingly, then said, "On the surface, those three words — I LOVE YOU — are the most harmless in our vocabulary ... a repudiation of my theory. But in actuality, when uttered with insincerity, 'I Love You' is the most manipulative phrase in our language. Even when one person tells another that they truly love them, a form of brainwashing occurs."

"How, Ukiah? I don't understand," I told him with obvious frustration.

"Humans are like a virus in that their primary goal is preservation. They want to preserve their very LIFE, and that which most benefits it. So, if a woman truly loves her husband, she wants to preserve that relationship. By telling him, 'I Love You,' she wants him to know without question that his presence is an integral part of her life. She's conditioning him to act in a certain way due to her use of Language. I'm telling you, Chris, every word we say, along with its tone, nuance, and expression, is a form of brainwashing. This discussion itself is an exercise in brainwashing. I want to convince you of my thoughts. It all boils down to Control ...."

"I'm not sure about Control, but I do know that in a few days, I'll have to attend my father's funeral ... the father that I almost murdered."

"There you go again," Ukiah yelled, bashing his palms on the steering wheel. "You're letting a societal Virus control you."

"I am?"

"Of course. You need to deprogram your SELF ... to erase all that has been conditioned by external forces. Who wants to stare at a dead body? Name one person."

"Other than necrophiles, I can't think of any," I told Ukiah.

"Then why has this silly, outdated custom of staring at dead bodies continued? I understand mourning, but does sadness mean showing a corpse that is filled with formaldehyde? It doesn't make sense. Funerals have become another virus ... the most ironic of all systematic perpetuations - Death itself is fighting to keep itself alive! Think about it. Funerals and wakes are by far the most absurd human rituals of all time. Not a single person enjoys them, yet they persist as a viral entity. Go figure. Let the dead bury their own fucking dead. I'll never look at another rotting corpse as long as I live."

As these words slid from Ukiah's lips, he pulled his van toward the hospital's emergency room entrance and said, "Well, let's find somebody who'll pull your old man's body off o' that mattress."

While waiting at the registration desk, I thought about Ukiah's statements and felt a huge amount of respect for him. Here was someone who shunned the phoniness of Christmas, believed birthdays were for the birds, and refused to wear rose-colored glasses when viewing the world. Not only did he speak as an iconoclast, but he acted on his words by refusing to bow before these socially erected idols. It was exhilarating to see someone forging a new path rather than following the age-old customs of our ancestors. At that moment, Ukiah became A Modern Man - one who denied mamby pamby worlds of delusion in favor of Truth and Realism ... where others bowed to cowardice in their refusal to bury the silly systems and customs of yesterday, he strode forward toward a new day ... a new era.

As we waited in the entrance area, another thought entered my mind. Was the Old

World ready for this Modern Man? I saw Ukiah standing at the bow of an ancient clipper ship, long hair blowing in the breeze. As his vessel neared a New Frontier, about to burst through the barriers of our past and enter new seas of advancement, he yelled into the wind, "Will you accept The Word, or will you reject me? I'm a mirror that reflects your decision. Please don't make me live without you."

Ukiah looked toward the waters, took one final glance, then rammed a sword through his chest, crying, "So long, my love."

As his body fell into a raging whirlpool, an ocean breeze whispered, "So long, my love."

While his corpse disappeared, Ukiah's blood seeped between the wooden slats of the ship's deck, dripping to the naked body of a Virgin maiden who slept in the galley. As the crimson fluid rested on the young girl's stomach, a flower began to grow ... a magnificent flower with white petals, a clear red center, and a budding head at the end of its stalk. The Virgin woke to find this flower dancing on her tender breasts while a slight kicking was felt within her stomach. From destruction, a new creation had arisen.

Interrupting my daydream, a nurse asked urgently, "Yes, how may I help you?"

I cleared my throat, then said evenly, "My father suffered a heart attack, and is dead in the van outside."

31

I beg of thee, whoever you are, please help me. I've decided not to destroy myself, but to live ... to live a life that becomes more confusing each day. If you are watching, please look at my sorry situation. I'm sadder than I've ever been ... even sadder than when I abandoned my baby so many years ago.

Little Ukiah, I'm so sorry. I wanted to apologize in person, but at the last minute I lost my nerve. But honey, the sight of you made my heart flutter. For three decades I've wondered about my tiny, special child. What did he look like? What went through his mind? Now, miraculously, your letters are spread on the desk before me, while I actually had a chance to see you.

My tender baby, you've grown into such a handsome young man, but your letters trouble me. I'm afraid you'll kill your father, then spend the rest of your life in prison. Oh Sweety, how can I blame you for feeling betrayed? What kind of parents have Philip and I been? We're despicable role models ... the absolute worst type of people. It's a wonder you survived this long. If I only knew what you were thinking ... I'm sure you'd refuse to speak with me face to face. I can't blame you.

Oh Ukiah, little darling, run home to mommy and give her a hug. Sit on my lap and we'll sing songs while I rock you to sleep. I want to cradle you in my arms — kiss you — brush the hair from your eyes and clean your knees after you fall down a hill. My little boy, can't you see? I love you ... I've missed our time together ... Oh, those wasted years ... the squandered opportunities to develop a meaningful relationship.

Instead of lending a helping hand, I ran from my problems, leaving you to fend for yourself. I never helped with homework, cooked you pancakes for breakfast, or told bedtime stories under the glow of a soft yellow moon. Baby, I've missed so much ... ruined so much. Please forgive me. Whenever I lie in bed thinking of you, I try to picture what you're doing. Are you happy, smiling, and content ... or filled with crazy ideas? Just run home to your mommy and I'll make everything better.

If only life were that simple. I'm sure Ukiah could never forgive me. How much different would life have been if I had nurtured my son instead of leaving him on those hospital steps? Sweety, after all these years, I can still remember you lying in that basket. There you were, covered with blood, when I cleaned your face with a tissue, then covered your tiny body with a blanket. Despite what would happen, you remained calm - staring at me with huge blue eyes, trying to form an innocent smile.

Following such a sight, how could I still abandon my child? Sweety, I looked at every inch of your body - your knowing eyes, miniature nose, the tiny dimple on your chin, and those tiny fingers flicking through the air toward me ... the unspoken message was very clear - "Mommy, hold me, hug me, give me your love." But rather than holding you to my bosom, I turned my back and ran down those steps ... forced to lead a life of misery and regret.

Oh Jenny, why does our torture continue? Life was already sorrowful enough ... now Ukiah re-enters the picture after all these years. Oh unseen Being from beyond, why did you initiate such a reunion? Please speak to me. First you made Ukiah write those letters, then you drew me to him - not only in thought, but also in Latera Heights. I'm sure none of these events - even the attempted murder of Philip Prince - could have happened by chance. You somehow drew us together. Why? Who are you, and what hidden meanings am I to decipher from this mysterious collision of opposing forces? I beg of you, speak to me ... speak through me. I promise to listen, to become a conduit for your words. Please reveal your identity.

Yes, I hear you! The words are clear. You are who? My Muse! You're my Muse! But why ... why have I been chosen to receive these messages? Now I understand. You've made your presence known to guide me along the proper artistic course. Now everything makes sense! To create, one must first destroy. I ruined a substantial part of my son's life, but now, with your assistance, we can create anew! But how? What should I do to begin this creative process? Yes! Now I see. Ukiah Rhymes will be the undiscovered literary prospect that I bragged about at our last board meeting. Thank you ... these insights are invaluable. I'll immediately start working on the proposal to be given at next month's session.

Dearest Muse, I can't thank you enough for cleansing my past imperfections and filling me with renewed hope. I know yesterday's indiscretions cannot be repeated. You've rescued me from a life sentence ... an eternity of angst, guilt, and reckless indulgence. On any other night, I would lie naked in bed, hands massaging my pathetically neglected breasts ... fingers exploring my moistened realm of pleasure ... panting and moaning with desire through the darkness ... my mattress transformed into a gyrating trampoline of self-love, the sticky white sheets smothering me with lust.

But dearest invisible love, you've shown me that I can escape the depraved ways of yesterday and follow a more meaningful course. Yes, sweet Jenny, we must become pure ... untouched ... washed by gentle hands that lead us toward the morning light rather than a darkened night. My loving Muse, thank you ... I promise to remain true to your calling ... I'll never disappoint you again.

32

After Ukiah left the emergency room, I phoned my mother at home.

"Mom, this's Chris," I whispered sadly. "I have terrible news. Dad died this evening ...."

Half an hour later, my grieving mother leaned against my chest and cried until her eyes were puffed, veinous, and tear-stained.

"Chris, what am I going to do?" she sobbed. "I'll never make it alone."

"Sure you will," I assured her.

"No, Chris. I'll wind-up in the poor house, or debtor's prison."

"Don't be silly. Dad always made lots of money. I'm sure he socked some away in the bank, or invested in stocks."

"No ... no," my mother bawled. "We don't have a nest egg."

Alarmed, I asked, "How can that be? Dad was a successful businessman. There has to at least be a life insurance policy."

"I'm afraid not," she whimpered, twitching uncontrollably.

"Mom, something's not right," I exclaimed. "How can you be broke?"

"Chris, I never told you this before, but your father's been gambling away our life savings for years. There's nothing left."

Overcome by queasiness, I felt my legs turn rubbery as a stark moment of realization struck. My mother and I were alone, and she couldn't support herself.

I sniffed weakly, "Mommy, why? How could you let such a disaster happen? Isn't there anything left?"

"No ... nothing. You know your father. There was no stopping him. He blew money on football games, horses, poker ... plus he squandered what little was left on crazy inventions, or far-fetched investment ideas. Near the end, he canceled our life insurance policies, sold the stocks, and took the cash out of every account. Chris, all I'll have is my social security check. I'll have to live like a pauper. Oh Lord, why do I have such bad luck?"

As my mother slumped in her hospital chair, I cringed from the guilt that suddenly overwhelmed me. I had indirectly killed my father, and as a result, my mother would live in poverty the rest of her life. Of course, I hadn't been the one to run up an insurmountable gambling debt ... but if Pus were still alive, at least mother could cling to the status quo. Now, due to Ukiah's outlandish plan, not only would my mother die penniless, but she was also forced to bury her husband.

As tears ran along my arm, I felt floods of regret wash over me. Yet again, by becoming entangled in Ukiah's web, I watched helplessly as the world collapsed around me. Worse, what could I do to alleviate this situation? I certainly couldn't support my mother. After paying my bills each month, plus a mortgage, I barely had enough money to buy groceries. Now my mother would be forced to eat crackers three days a week, and freeze during the winter because she couldn't afford fuel oil. Life was a mess.

In hindsight, the fallacy of Ukiah's scheme infuriated me. He wanted me to smother my father! More incredibly, I let myself be manipulated to such an extent that I kneeled on my father's chest, consumed by rage. If he had not already died, I would have killed a second person. How could I take part in such a preposterous plan? Even more absurd was Ukiah's belief that we could get my family's insurance money. Who would fall for such a convoluted notion? The only person foolish enough to be duped by this ruse was me!

As I paced about the rooms of my house, my mind rambled senselessly. I wanted to wake up and find that life had returned to normal. But in this brutally frank world, my father lay dead in a morgue, my mother fretted over her debts, while I almost committed a second murder - all because of Ukiah's twisted schemes. Considering the trouble he created, I wondered what he was doing right now - probably sleeping, or dreaming of new ways to ruin my life.

Unable to handle the pressure, I stomped toward Ukiah's cottage, determined to rectify this situation. I would ask Ukiah ... no, demand that he vacate the premises within thirty days, thus making room for my mother, who would live in his tiny house. As I stormed through the backyard, a lump of uneasiness formed in my stomach. The source of this fear, of course, was Ukiah. I dreaded his reaction when hearing he'd been evicted. In all likelihood, he would either accuse me of betrayal, erupt with dramatic histrionics, hurl a litany of threats, or attack me with a knife. I pictured even worse scenarios - Ukiah kidnapping me, throwing me in a vat of battery acid, or setting me on fire.

Whatever the case, I had to stand my ground when confronting him. So, near noon that day (I had taken a brief leave of absence from work due to my family tragedy), I rapped on my neighbor's hollow wooden door.

Each passing second felt like an eternity until Ukiah, wearing tight black jeans, a white t-shirt, and black boots, answered the door. "Howdy Chris," he smiled, rock n' roll music blaring in the background. "C'mon in."

I stepped inside his kitchen, my heart thumping with irregular beats that made each blood vessel feel as if they would burst.

Overwhelmed by dizziness, nausea, high blood pressure, and Ukiah's music, I blurted, "Could you turn that racket down? I need to speak with ..."

Ukiah lowered his music's volume, then said, "Did you hear who bought Woody Dewar's house?"

Confused, I replied, "No. I didn't even know it sold."

"Yeah it sold, and Kenny Dewar bought it. I talked to him this morning. He told me to start calling him Always, as in he'll Always Dewar!"

I became so disoriented that I was afraid I'd lose consciousness and fall to the floor.

"You've met Kenny, haven't you? He looks just like Woody. If I didn't know better, I'd say they were the same person. Now he's going to be your new neighbor ...."

Any chance of controlling the world around me was futile. Five minutes earlier, the future seemed rosy ... Ukiah would be gone and my mother and I could return to normal lives.

" ... the weirdest part was, Kenny started asking a lotta pointed questions about you and his brother. I got the impression there was more going on between you two than met the eye ...."

With this information in mind, how could I let my mother move into the guesthouse? Knowing how Kenny Dewar ran his mouth, he'd tell my mother about our supposed affair ... the photos ... and the medicine bag filled with pornographic devices. If my father's death and bankruptcy hadn't already killed her, this news would.

" ... I hope Kenny doesn't get on your bad side," Ukiah laughed. "If he does, look out! I wonder how long it'll take for you to kill him."

Ukiah paused, then reached into his pocket and pulled out a thick wad of bills, handing them to me. "Here's next month's rent, neighbor."

Confused beyond description and shaking terribly, I reached for the money, then let it fall to the floor once the greenbacks touched my fingers. Oddly, the money floated in slow motion, each bill fluttering like snowflakes falling from the sky.

Embarrassed, I stooped to the carpet, scooping the money into my quivering hands. Once I collected each bill and set them on Ukiah's counter, I stuffed the wad into my shirt pocket, much to Ukiah's dismay.

"What are you doing?" he demanded, a cross look on his face.

"I'm ... I'm putting your money away," I told him.

"You can't put it in your pocket like that," he said, eyes open wide with disbelief.

"Like what?" I asked, unable to comprehend how this situation had taken such a turn for the worst.

"All the bills are out of order ... plus, some are upside down, and others are crooked. Here, gimme it. I'll show you how they're supposed to be."

Ukiah took the money, then said, "See, the twenties are on the bottom - face up - then the tens ... fives, and finally the ones. Every face is pointed in the same direction, and none of the edges are dog-eared or crinkled. Everything is in its proper order." Ukiah returned the sorted wad to me, then said, "Wait here. I'll be out in a second. We'll go downtown and goof around."

I stood motionless, unable to determine how my plan had gone awry. In terms of making things happen, I was a fumbling stumblebum. Ukiah had not only skirted eviction ... he also paid for next month's rent! Shaking my head in defeat, I noticed one of Ukiah's opened kitchen cupboards. Curious, I peeked over my shoulder, then crept toward it. Filling his cupboard were a variety of canned goods such as vegetables, gravy, and soups. Amazingly, each can's label faced perfectly straight forward, uniformly aligned with those stacked above and below them. The cans were also arranged according to group, with all the beans together, etc.; plus, if two items were identical according to brand name, every letter was perfectly lined with the ones above and below them ... each A in line with each A ... etc. He definitely had a strange affinity for things being in their proper order.

"Are you hungry?" Ukiah chuckled after reentering the kitchen.

"Oh ... no. I was just admiring your shelf-stocking technique."

Ignoring my response, Ukiah said softly. "Y'know, when I was in the bedroom, I realized I had never lived this long in any one place since I was a kid. I wanna thank you for showing such hospitality. I appreciate your kindness." Ukiah grabbed his car keys from the counter, then continued with feigned concern.

"How's your mother handling Norb's death?"

"Fine, other than being on the verge of a nervous breakdown," I said dejectedly. "Ukiah, she doesn't have anything. My father squandered their savings on gambling, foolish inventions, and crazy investments. She's broke ... there weren't even any insurance policies to bilk ..."

"Oh, that," he replied vacantly. "I changed my mind anyway. Tell Mrs. Edwards to hang on awhile longer, 'cause once my next idea catches hold, we'll be rolling in the dough. C'mon, let's go."

Once inside Ukiah's van, he changed the subject by speaking about his youth while we drove toward town.

"It's funny, but I remember one of my foster mothers talking about me running away from home as a kid."

More at ease, I asked, "As a kid ... y'mean a teenager?"

"No," Ukiah howled, "when I was three years old!"

"You ran away as a three-year-old," I laughed. "Why?"

"This lady said I was never content ... never satisfied ... so I'd grab a paper bag and fill it with cookies, clothes, and toys, then stomp across her lawn until I got to The Super Duper Grocery Store. I never went any further. A couple of hours later, I'd walk home and eat supper, then run away the next day. Isn't that strange, a three-year-old runaway?"

"It sure is," I told Ukiah. Surprisingly, I was glad I hadn't evicted him. I still worried about my mother, but we'd find a way for her to survive.

"I even put a version of that story in *Blank Line*," Ukiah said as he entered town.

"Are you still making progress on the novel?"

"I'm almost finished. I just haven't come up with an ending. At times like these, I wait for Romlocon to intervene ... but since I've been neglecting her, I think she's ignoring me. Who could blame her? I've been selfish beyond words. How do I expect to enter the gates of publication? I haven't devoted myself to her in the least. What's the use?"

Ukiah pulled into a parking garage, found an empty stall, then zipped into it with frantic speed, stopping only inches from a brick wall.

Catching my breath, I asked, "Where are we going? What are we doing this afternoon?"

"Who knows?" Ukiah replied casually. "Maybe we'll wander to that magazine stand ..."

"Where they sell ice cream?" I asked happily.

"Yeah, that one."

"Great," I smiled, mouth watering.

While we walked along the sunny streets of Latera Heights, I inquired, "So, what's your next big idea?"

"You remembered? Very good," Ukiah said with a hint of appreciation. "I'm sure this plan will put me over the top."

"What is it? Come clean."

While passing a variety of storefronts with college students walking to and fro, Ukiah began, "I wrote a letter to Vince McMahon."

"Who's he?"

"Vince McMahon! He's president of the WWF Wrestling Association."

"And ...?"

"I want him to publish *Blank Line*."

Flabbergasted, I shook my head and said, "You want a wrestling promoter to be your publisher! Oh my God. Now I've heard everything. Sure, this idea will make us rich. Man, we really are in trouble," I laughed, slapping my knee.

Unamused, Ukiah told me sternly, "Actually, you're the one who put this idea in my head."

"Me! How?" I asked quizzically.

"Do you remember telling me about Philip Prince at that baseball game on television?"

"Of course. He almost fell asleep while reading a book."

"Exactly. Now, try to remember that wrestling match at The Splycer Center. Not one fan brought a book to that show, did they?"

"No."

"Can't ya see? That event was nonstop excitement at its finest. Vince McMahon has filled a vacuum in American entertainment with the WWF. This same vacuum exists in American literature. When was the last time you saw a writer with personality ... who expressed outrageous opinions and kicked ass? It's been so long that I'd fall off my dinosaur trying to remember. So, to fill this vacuum, we need two mavericks, Vince McMahon and me! We'll prove that the same concepts used in the sports entertainment business also apply to literature. That's why HE should be my publisher!"

"I don't know, Ukiah. It sounds crazy."

"It does, but crazy is all we have. I could keep trying the traditional route with established literary agents, but I want this plan to go beyond their parameters ... to be something special. None of the commonplace agents want to take risks, or stray from the status quo. But if Vince entered the publishing business, just think of the possibilities. Through Solipsism ... The Soloists ... we could CREATE wild new personalities in the literature field that it currently doesn't have. Imagine it, Chris ... rather than a bland science fiction writer at a baseball game on TV, we could promote heroes and villains, like Vince does with his wrestlers. No publishing house is trying anything close to that today! We'd be hated by the critics and tight asses, but damn, what a show it'd be."

Unconvinced, I didn't say anything that would upset Ukiah. Instead, I kept quiet until we entered the magazine store/ice cream parlor. Once inside, I instantly melted as the aromas of hot fudge, caramel, sugar cones, fresh milk, whipped cream, and strawberries filled the air. As Ukiah wandered toward a magazine rack, I scanned the menu, then ordered a banana split smothered with extra chocolate syrup.

After sitting at one of the small white circular tables, I indulged my appetite by shoveling huge scoops of ice cream into my mouth. Somewhat later, Ukiah took a seat beside me, a copy of *The New York Times Book Review* in hand.

Ukiah stared at my sloppy ice cream concoction, turned his nose, then opened his newspaper and leafed through its pages, mumbling and making comments while doing so.

"Hmmm, it looks like the furor over Atropos and Philip Prince has finally died down. His Minions still meet every Tuesday though ... dressed like goofy Owls." (pause) "Chris, did I ever tell you about my idea once I get published? It'll be a challenge to all the hotshot authors in this country. I'm going to call it a Write-Off."

"A Write-Off? What's that?" I asked after swallowing a gooey cluster of bananas, chocolate, and peanuts.

"At my initial press conference, after saying I'm the greatest writer alive ... amid the pomp and circumstance ... with Japhy's band blasting tunes before I arrive ... a huge banner hanging behind me ... and I'm ranting n' raving about getting the largest signing bonus in literary history ... I'll reiterate my claim of being the best writer in town, backing up this stance by challenging the Bestsellers to a Write-Off at Latera University. I'll invite Philip Prince, Jackie Collins, John Grisham, Tom Clancy, Camille Paglia, Hunter S. Thompson, Tom Wolfe, plus a few poets, ethnic authors, short story tellers, a horror aficionado, and whoever else fits the bill. I'll even send an invitation to J.D. Salinger. Try to picture the media drooling over this spectacle. They live for that shit. Here's a nobody challenging the greatest writers of our day to a contest. Even if none accept, I'll be linked with them in the public's mind."

As children walked past licking ice cream cones, I said, "I still can't picture a Write-Off. Tell me what it is."

Enthused, Ukiah began, "First, we'll gather all the authors at Latera University's new library wing - the one named after their football coach. Then, these writers - maybe a dozen or so - will be given the guidelines for the competition."

"Which are?"

"Follow along. First, the focus of this contest will revolve around three separate boxes. One box will be filled with slips of paper listing every type of writing style, or genre. A second box will have slips of paper with an assortment of characters. Finally, the last box will hold plot development angles. It'll look like this."

Ukiah took a red pen from his back pocket and scribbled on a napkin:

Genre	Characters	Plot Setting
Science Fiction	Elderly 80-year-old female	Cruise Ship
Romance	Four midgets	Revolutionary War
Horror	A dog and cat	The year 2021
Fairy Tale	Businessman	Shopping Mall
Historical	Divorced woman	Stranded in desert
Travelogue	A thief and corpse	Carnival funhouse
Suspense	Four-year-old boy	Bus ride
Mystery	Taxi driver	Farm
Experimental	Asylum patient	Hell
etc.	etc.	etc.

"Each list's length would be determined by the number of authors entered in the contest, with the topics chosen by an arbitrary panel of judges. With this framework in mind, each writer is given an hour to write a story after they've chosen a slip of paper from each box."

Fascinated by this concept, I asked, "The authors won't be allowed to write about whatever they want?"

"That's the beauty of this contest. None of them will be able to rely on what made them famous. They'll have to explore foreign territory, and use their natural talents to master The Word's purity. So, science fiction writers won't be able to find sanctuary in their specialized genre, nor will those who write romance novels. Let's take Philip Prince, for example. After reaching into all three boxes, he might have to write a children's story about four midgets on a farm - a far stretch from his usual outer space crap. Or how about Camille Paglia writing a detective story about an eighty-year-old woman in the year 2021. Wouldn't that be a hoot?"

"I'd love to see it, but writing isn't the most exciting spectator sport."

"But it could be! See, each writer, after making their selections, would sit at a library carol that is equipped with cameras that'd project their writings onto large overhead screens. So, whether they use a manual typewriter, word processor, computer, or pen and paper, their results would be instantly shown on a gigantic movie screen. In terms of audience appeal, they could watch each author's output to determine their progress, story line, and writing style. The suspense would be incredible."

"There's only one problem. How would a winner be determined?"

"Being that each author is only given an hour, a clock would hang from a wall above them as they wrote. More importantly, these writers could only produce X amount of pages during that sixty-minute span. After they're finished, each work would be delivered, without name, to a panel of judges who were not present during the Write-Off. These scholars, literary experts, and regular people off the street, would read each piece and grade it on a scale of one to ten. Whichever author got the most total points would be declared the winner. Their prize would be called The Golden Quill - a golden feather pen inside a golden inkwell. It would be more prestigious than The Pulitzer Prize, based on an author's ability to write under pressure in any given genre on any subject under the sun. Imagine the purity of our craft - sheer Creation - exposed for the world to see - each author typing, writing, sweating and editing to complete their story before the deadline! I can't wait to announce this concept at my press conference!"

Ukiah bubbled with excitement, then his mood changed in the bat of an eye when he noticed an article in *The New York Times Book Review*.

"What is it?" I asked, scooping ice cream and chocolate syrup from the sides of my dish.

"He's a load of shit," Ukiah snapped in a hushed tone. "I can't believe my eyes."

"Did Philip Prince make another crack about Atropos?"

"Worse. The Mason Turner Agency signed Matt Weston Annus as one of their clients."

"Who's he?"

While continuing to read the article, Ukiah sneered, "Matt Weston Annus is a Brat Pack hack from the early 80's who couldn't write a legitimate suicide note, let alone a novel. This guy is such a schmuck that last month he resorted to writing about cartoon characters. No one would publish him for a decade, now Mason Turner accepted Annus's new novel, *Dramarama*."

"*Dramarama*?"

"It's about a jaded playwright who can't decide if he's straight or gay. To compensate for its lack of artistic merit, plot, and substance, Annus reverts to writing about fashion, discotheques, and other banalities. In this excerpt, the lead character is talking with his father, calling him 'dude.' What a load of shit. There's no purity in this man's writing ... no mastery of his craft."

"How does he get published?" I asked, almost finished with the banana split.

"Who knows, but Annus was also interviewed for the article. Listen to this quote:"

"I had an intimate, closed-door meeting with Mason Turner, who showed me the ins and outs of the publishing business."

"The ins and outs of the publishing business!" Ukiah spat. "I wonder what that means? Fuck! It's not fair. I get so frustrated with this industry that I wonder if it's worth the effort. Maybe I'm nothing but a shit writer ... even lousier than Matt Weston Annus. Time keeps slipping away, and I never get any closer to my goals than the day before. With every passing second, I inch closer to death. There, ten more seconds just slid into the past ... now ten more. Each lost millisecond - the very passage of TIME itself - equals my ultimate demise. I'm not sure if anyone appreciates this concept, but I feel it intimately. Ah, what's it matter?"

I became alarmed by Ukiah's tone, his usual bravado replaced by an unnerving lack of confidence. Worse, he seemed to be alluding to his ultimate destruction. If Ukiah's faith in Creation wavered, or was given up completely, it'd mean the end was near.

Frightened by my friend's morbid thoughts, I asked, "Ukiah, you'd never ....."

"Take my own life?" he interrupted. "No. There are three kinds of suicide, none of which apply to me. The first is an innate compulsion, or genetic predisposition, to the act of self-annihilation. Many artists, both male and female, fall into this category. The second, less noble form, concerns pathetic despair."

"Pathetic despair?"

"Y'know, Oooooh, my girlfriend left me, I lost my job, and the dog ran away, boo hoo. I have no respect whatsoever for those losers."

"And the third?"

"I call it existential suicide, where an individual is so completely consumed by life's absurdity that the game becomes nothing more than an exercise in futility."

Ukiah stood, crumbled *The New York Times Book Review* into a ball, then threw it on the floor, snorting, "C'mon, let's go. I'm tired of reading about these people."

I scooped the last drops of chocolate syrup from my dish, licked it greedily off the spoon, then pictured my mother sitting in a frost-covered house, her moth-eaten robe clinging to a skeletal frame as her icebox sat empty. I shook my head guiltily, thinking about the tenuous, fragile threads that attach us to life.

Weeks passed as my mother and I tended to burying my father and settling his estate. In opposition to summer's bright, flourishing beauty, I felt dead inside. Ukiah was right about the death business. Wakes, viewings, and funerals were, without argument, the most preposterous traditions in our society. In addition to this grueling calamity, I made an assessment of my mother's finances. Luckily, it appeared as if she would survive her golden years, albeit without extravagance. Pus had run my mother into the ground, but at least he hadn't dug the hole so deeply that she couldn't crawl out.

Otherwise, the circumstances surrounding my father's death struck me with a remarkable amount of melancholy. I had always equated his death with an incredible burden being lifted from my shoulders. But in actuality, I felt incomplete ... the absence of his continual antagonism leaving me frustrated ... unable to ever again be whole. In this life of fleeting reactions and rollercoaster emotions, I could always rely on Pus to denigrate, belittle, humiliate, and abuse me. Without such a lingering cloud of negativism and permanence, I slowly slipped into depression.

Also, the thought of Kenny Dewar moving into Woody's house was killing me. How could I tolerate year after year with that moron living beside me? I was never a big fan of murder, but if Kenny kept hitting on me, I saw myself jabbing an icicle through his temple and making it look like an accident.

My life trudged along drearily until an unexpected knock at the front door lifted my spirits one Saturday afternoon. Waiting to greet me was none other than Japhy Rhymes, smiling widely while radiating anxious energy.

"C'mon, what're ya waiting for?" he said impulsively, reminiscent of his father. "We're going to a concert!"

"A concert? Who?" I asked, always glad to see Japhy.

"Bob Dylan's playing at The Entendre Amphitheater later this afternoon. It's going to be great."

"Bob Dylan?" I asked with bemusement. "Why is he playing there? I can't believe it."

"It's true, Chris," Japhy said before singing in a nasal, Bob Dylan voice - 'The answer, my friend, is blowin' in the wind.'"

"Wow!" I panted. "I've never been a huge music fan, but Bob Dylan's my favorite. He's really playing today?"

"In a few hours. Gina, me, and my Dad are going. Stop over in about an hour."

"I wouldn't miss it," I promised, feeling more excited than I had in ages.

A slight drizzle fell from the clouds, but the precipitation didn't dampen our spirits as we drove in Japhy's Celebrity along Entendre Mountain. The four of us bustled with anticipation as a Bob Dylan greatest hits tape blasted from the cassette player. As we hummed along to these songs, I found Japhy's familiarity with Bob Dylan's music quite astonishing. When asked how he knew these songs, Japhy said that not only had he been listening to Dylan for years, but Mirror Image actually played three of his tunes. And, although they never performed these numbers in concert, Japhy described how they had mastered the harmonies and nuances of each song. In an era when many kids listened to music that was, quite honestly, shit, it was refreshing to find someone who still appreciated a true master.

Traffic leading to the amphitheater slowed to a halt, which made me glad Japhy was driving instead of Ukiah. I sensed his antsiness and displeasure with this delay (a symptom of Ukiah's rampant immediacy), but there was no avoiding the congestion. Entendre Mountain was primarily a ski lodge that diversified during the summer months with a par three golf course, driving range, batting cages, and a go-kart course. The only way to access the resort was via a narrow, winding, two-lane gravel road not equipped to handle 6,000 cars.

Japhy eventually parked in, of all spots, one that guaranteed we would be the first to leave the area. Miraculously, a parking attendant chose our car to occupy the first stall facing the exit, unblocked by any other vehicle. Every driver following us was motioned toward an isolated lot more than a mile away. I was pleased by our good fortune, but my reaction couldn't compare to Ukiah's. He was so elated that ya'd think we won the lottery. Events like these tickled Ukiah in the oddest way, as if The Graces had deliberately given us a supernatural gift.

Ukiah beamed with happiness as we trooped up the mountain to the stage area. Along the way, he spoke happily with Japhy about his band, and their progress in cutting a long awaited demo tape. Ukiah's encouragement, advice, and comments had a positive impact on Japhy, for the two spoke with the ease of best friends. Even more gratifying was Japhy's disclosure that the Mirror Image tape would be finished in a few weeks - ready for shipment to a slew of record producers. Ukiah nearly floated off the ground when hearing this news.

After handing four tickets to an elderly man at the gate, we entered, with rain still falling, the open-air amphitheater to discover a scene reminiscent of a 1960's Be-In. Entendre Mountain had turned into a gigantic gathering of hippies, yippies, freaks and partiers. We saw a sea of tie-dyed t-shirts ... the pungent aroma of patchouli ... young women twirling in granny dresses ... men with long, unkempt, matted hair falling about their shoulders ... beach balls being batted through the misty air ... stoned casualties lounging on blankets ... rivers of mud ... booze and marijuana ... and thick swirling plumes of marijuana smoke. Nearly everyone we saw passed joints or smoked bowls - teenagers, yuppies, burnouts, even a circle of senior citizens with long, straggly hair. If a light rain had not been falling, Entendre Mountain would have been consumed by a huge cloud of smoke.

Then, without fanfare at the foot of the amphitheater, Bob Dylan and his band walked on stage and launched into their opening number. Although we had a spot halfway up the hillside, I could still feel this man's energy radiating about the grounds. How does one describe a legend ... a true original? Bob Dylan commanded the stage wearing a stylish white Stetson hat, a black Bolero tie, a white button-down dress shirt with ruffled sleeves, black pressed slacks, and brown cowboy boots. While strumming a white electric guitar, he personified, at least to me, the ultimate in cool. Even with gusts of rain splashing across his weathered face, he stood firm - knowing - alone ...

The crowd, as one would expect, applauded, cheered, and danced during each number, enjoying the performance to its fullest. Dylan, meanwhile, rarely spoke or addressed the audience. He simply smiled, bowed, then sauntered into his next song. The audience's enthusiasm mounted during the show, peaking at the encore, then erupting with merriment as Bob Dylan sang his rousing anthem: "Everybody must get stoned" ...... nearly everyone puffing on joints and blowing their smoke toward the wet, gray sky. The experience was dramatic in its debaucherous, hedonistic glory.

Amid scores of bleary-eyed, wobbly stoners, we returned to The Celebrity, then pulled onto the curving gravel road without delay. Ukiah bubbled with such excitement over this prospect that he and Japhy spoke non-stop until we reached the base of the mountain. I simply sat quietly, thanking the powers above that we didn't have to drive with the stoners.

"Hey man, let's get this bus rolling ..."
"We're not in a bus, dude. This's an Army tank rolling through Vietnam ..."
"You're both crazy, man. We're inside a rocket ship ready to blast off into outer space."
"Oh yeah! Far out, man."
"Don't wait for those cars in front of us, man. Just fly over them!"

Shortly thereafter, Japhy pulled into our driveway. He and Gina planned on going downtown before returning to spend the night. Ukiah gave them his best wishes, then smiled as his son pulled onto Reflection Alley - a free spirit ready to spread his wings and soar through the wet, breezy evening.

After they left, Ukiah and I walked to my porch, where he made a startling revelation.

"Guess who I got a letter from this afternoon."

Brimming with excitement, I gushed, "One of those literary agents?"

"Shit. All they send are rejection letters," Ukiah said despondently. "No, do you remember that story *Crocodile Tears* that I sent to one of those agents?"

"Of course!" I beamed. "Did she change her mind?"

"Nah, I haven't heard a word from her ... shit, I can't even remember their names any more. Anyway, the girl that I used to live with ...."

"Do you mean that ex-stripper ... the main character?"

"Yeah! Demi wrote me a letter ... I don't know how she found my address ... but she wants to visit sometime this fall."

As Ukiah bent to pick up a pebble from the ground, I felt as if a wrecking ball rammed against my chest. If Demi visited Latera Heights, I knew she'd dig her claws into Ukiah and steal him away. I'd been subtly pursuing him for nearly a year, tolerating his shenanigans and crazy schemes. Now this floozy, who'd let anything be crammed into her vagina, was moving into my territory. Why did so many unexpected elements keep popping up in my life? Sensing his lingering affection for her, I knew Demi would turn up the heat and seduce Ukiah, luring him into her web. Damn! Even though I had never seen her, I knew I couldn't compete with an ex-stripper. She was probably tall and gorgeous ... oozing pure, unbridled sexuality. I already hated this woman ... her flirtatious glances, a knowing wink of the eye, and the way she cocked her hip to draw Ukiah's attention. Demi would then whisper in Ukiah's ear, reminding him of the sexual tricks she used to perform. Her attack would be brutal ... beyond my control. How could I prevent this situation? I needed help ... a plan. Maybe I'd meet Demi at the bus station, ram a knife through her stomach, then toss her body in the weeds. Or else I'd cook supper for them, sprinkling poison over Demi's dish until she gagged to death on her own vomit.

Oblivious to my thoughts, Ukiah tossed a pebble through the air, then said, "It's been five years since I've seen Demi. In fact, when my cat had kittens, she was the midwife. That was one of the happiest days of my life. You shoulda seen it. Japhy and all the neighbors crowded into this tiny room with Demi and me to watch the delivery. There were kids, adults, and even grandparents all crammed together watching this miracle. But it wasn't all smooth going. After the mother cat cleaned her three kittens, we noticed the umbilical cords still attached to two of them. This was a problem for the third kitten, because he kept getting strangled by the other two when he tried to nurse. At one point, this little fella could barely move, the cord completely wrapped around its neck. Afraid it would die, Demi, Japhy, a girl named Nina, and me performed minor surgery. While Nina petted the mother cat, who thought we were going to kill her kittens, and Japhy held a lamp, I untangled the cats while Demi snipped their umbilical cords. We were really nervous, but in the end, all three kittens survived."

Ukiah paused, then said sadly, "At least for awhile. I really loved those cats, but ... after being shuffled from one foster family to another, and not really being loved by anyone as a kid except my Gramma Moo, I remained guarded for years, never allowing myself to love. But then these beautiful kittens were born, and my heart melted like butter. I was finally able to care again, but every one of them died. I loved those little babies with all my heart, but they were decimated by disease. I can still see their faces today ... especially as they lost consciousness and slipped away."

Ukiah paused again, then finally said, "Oh well. You don't need to hear me belly aching. Anyway, I have to cook supper for Japhy and Gina. You're welcome to come over, Chris."

Saddened, I said softly, "Thanks, but I'm going to call it a night."

"All right. Take care, neighbor," Ukiah said as he walked behind my house.

As he left, I saw a rain puddle mixed with drops of gasoline in a low spot of the driveway. As my porch light reflected off the glimmering body of water, I stooped to see a fascinating set of images. I clearly saw Ukiah's body shimmering in the water, then falling in a lump as he plunged a knife through his chest.

As he lay bleeding in the pool of water, Ukiah's shadow leaped from his body and moaned, "My beloved Creator, the time has arrived to finally die. No one can adore me more than you, so I'll lie beside you as we breathe our final breaths. We may have learned about the whole world, my love, but we'll die without ever knowing our Self. Dearest object of adoration, our love was all for naught. Goodbye forever."

As I continued to stare into the puddle, an unseen voice chirped from the distance, "So long, my sweet gentle image of love. My affection for you grew like weeds in a desert."

While these words echoed through the rainy night, I watched Ukiah and his shadow floating along a trickle of water, each trying to catch one last glimpse of themselves as they drifted away.

33

One page of the calendar flipped to the next, and before I knew it, summer slowly turned to fall. As the sun hung lower in the sky and temperatures dipped at night, another important date arrived. One year ago today, I picked up a stranger named Ukiah Rhymes walking along the highway. It seemed unbelievable that only a year had passed since we met. I thought about all we had done together - the good, bad, and downright hideous - and felt overwhelmed by our activities. I did more living in the past year than I had my entire life. I only wished these experiences had not pushed me so close to the edge.

Being a rainy Sunday morning, I wanted to spend a few extra hours lounging in bed. In addition to relaxation, my agenda included cooking a big breakfast, enjoying an unrushed shower, then browsing through stacks of magazines. Naturally, my wishes didn't come true, for an urgent rapping at the front door made me crawl groggily from bed. Pulling on a pair of red sweatpants and an orange, zippered warm-up jacket, I hobbled to the kitchen, wondering who would intrude at this hour.

Regretting that I hadn't stayed in bed, I held my breath, then opened the door to discover ... no, of all people ...

"Good morning, Sunshine," Kenny Dewar smirked, his crooked, shit eating grin filling me with disgust.

"What do you want?" I snapped, guardedly zipping my jacket.

Without warning, Kenny walked into my kitchen, rubbing closely against me as he did so. Then, after looking around, he turned to face me.

"Chris, I hope I didn't interrupt your beauty sleep," he laughed slyly, "because if I did knock at an inopportune time, I'd be glad to join you in the bedroom and work on burning off a little energy, if ya know what I mean!"

"That's it. Get out of my house," I demanded, so enraged that I balled my right fist and picked up a frying pan with the other.

"What?" Kenny asked oafishly, refusing to move. "I'm sorry if I offended you. I was just trying to be neighborly."

Realizing that Kenny Dewar (like his brother) lacked any redeeming social skills, I almost felt sorry for him.

But Kenny couldn't leave well enough alone.

He continued, "I'm gonna move in next door pretty soon, so I'll probably be over here all the time." Kenny inched closer, his bad breath making me sick. He then said, "I don't know what happened between Woody and you, but if it had anything to do with size ...."

"Size!" I gasped, filled with horror. "What are you talking about?"

Kenny's laugh was identical to Woody's as he told me, "My brother once told me he read a survey that said 93% of sex partners aren't concerned with penis size, but that he always got stuck with lovers who fell into the other seven percent!"

"You idiot ...."

"Chris, if that's your beef with Woody, no pun intended ..."

"Get out!"

"C'mon, my brother admitted he wasn't the most endowed man to ever ....."

"Just shut up," I yelled, raising the frying pan above my head.

"But I'm different. I'm gifted with girth."

Irate, I screamed, "You and Woody are the biggest morons I've ever met. Now get out or I'll bash your brains in."

Walking hurriedly toward the door, Kenny chuckled, "Okay. I was just trying to be friendly. I didn't know the subject of sexual equipment would get you so flustered. Woody must have been a real disappointment in the sack ...."

"Get out!"

"Okay, neighbor. I'll see ya in a couple weeks," he promised, blowing me a kiss.

Rattled, defeated, and infuriated by his intrusion, I paced through the rooms of my house for nearly an hour trying to burn off my frustration. When this didn't calm my nerves, I changed into a pair of jeans and a sweatshirt, then decided to visit Ukiah. Being that we hadn't seen each other since the Bob Dylan concert, I figured this would be a nice time to visit. I also wanted to tell him that today was our one-year anniversary, but knew Ukiah would frown on such trivialities. So I strolled through the back yard, remembering how we had raked leaves together last fall. In no time, I'd be doing it again.

Moments later I stepped to Ukiah's porch, took a deep breath (our conversations still made me nervous), then tapped lightly on his door.

"Come in," a voice echoed through the air.

Turning the knob slowly, I opened his door, stepped into the kitchen, then asked, "Ukiah, are you there?"

He didn't answer, so I stepped into his living room where I saw a female figure skater spinning in circles on his black-and-white television set.

"Ukiah, are you home?" I asked loudly.

I then looked to my left to see Ukiah, long hair falling about his face, sitting on the floor in a corner, a stack of envelopes surrounding him, a silver letter opener near his bare feet.

Alarmed, I asked frantically, "Ukiah! What's wrong? What are you doing?"

Lifting his head, then brushing the hair from his face, I gazed fleetingly into his eyes, which burned with demonic intensity. I instantly averted my gaze, unable to stare into his desperate, animalistic pupils. In fact, I even took a step back, afraid that Ukiah would leap to his feet and attack me.

Terrified, I asked (hoping to save my very life), "What happened? Can I help?"

Spontaneously throwing a handful of envelopes into the air, Ukiah snarled, "Look at these rejection letters. No one wants me!" Ukiah tossed more mail through the air, his eyes wild and unfocused. "How did I ever expect to enter the gates of publication? It'll never happen. I'm not worthy. They'll never accept me. Damn. Motherfucker! None of these agents even read my material. They're rejecting me outright. Shit! What am I going to do?" Ukiah paused for a moment, tore a letter in half, then proceeded with blistering rage. "It's all Jennifer Ewen's fault. I know it. She's black-balled me within the industry. None of these people will touch me because she's sent a memo, telling them to shun me. I know Jennifer's working for S.W.A.N. They're ruining me, and I can't fight back. I'm powerless. Damn - damn!"

With spit dripping from his lips, moisture dampening each eye, and sweat oozing from his forehead, Ukiah pounded his fist on the floor, kicked at the letters, swore, pulled his hair, and even spit on the wall.

"Damn her. I'll get even with Jennifer if it's the last thing I do. How dare she deny me," Ukiah screamed, completely out of his mind.

Then, as if losing touch with reality, Ukiah grabbed his letter opener from the floor, held it with both hands, then lifted it toward his chest.

Ranting uncontrollably, he began, "What's the use? I probably am a worthless artist. All this talk about how great I am is bullshit. Even Matt Weston Annus can write better than me. At least he gets published. What do I have to show for my efforts? Nothing but a fucking wooden crate filled with stories that are worth less than toilet paper."

He fell silent for a moment, twitched his fingers nervously on the letter opener, then sneered, "Maybe it'd be better if I ended my suffering right now."

Watching him grip the silver object between his fingers, I initially reacted with panic, then mysteriously controlled my emotions.

Staring him in the eye while keeping my cool, I said evenly, "What are you going to achieve by shoving that letter opener through your chest?"

Livid, he blurted, "I'll erase the pain I've been forced to live with every day of my life."

Remarkably settled, I responded, "All of us have pain. I always thought life's positives outweighed the negatives."

"Quit playing the role of calm, cool, and collected," Ukiah bellowed, his eyes sizzling with fire. "I don't want to hear this suicide hotline shit. Do you see this letter opener? I'll ram it right through my fucking heart - right before your eyes. Do you wanna see a bloodbath?"

My emotionless facade rapidly crumbled as Ukiah placed the letter opener's tip to his tongue, licked it, then ran it along his chin.

"Ukiah, please. There has to be a better way. You have so much to live for."

"I DO! Tell me what?" he demanded, the silver spear pressed against his heart.

Nervously, I stammered, "How about your ... your writing?"

"Not good enough!"

"You could change the literary world."

"Not good enough!"

"What about Japhy?"

Ukiah paused, looked away, trembled slightly, then boomed even louder, "Not good enough! You better give me a reason to live pretty fucking quick, or I'll ram this bastard so far through my chest it'll come out my spine!"

Without thinking, I spontaneously triggered, "If you kill yourself, you won't be able to look in the mirror every day ..."

In all honesty, I don't know where those words came from, but they had a dramatic affect on Ukiah. Like a lightning bolt, he dropped the letter opener between his knees, then said curtly, his eyes burning into mine, "I'm giving those bastards one more chance to accept me. If they don't do it on my terms, I'll have to get their attention another way as I go out in a blaze of glory. But I promise you one thing – I'll take a few of those fuckers with me when I go."

Ukiah then turned his head and said softly, "Chris, why don't you stop over later on. Japhy and his band have a huge gig tonight at The Rock in Kundalini. If ya want, we'll ride together."

"I'd love to," I said, walking toward the door, thoughts of a potential suicide washing across my mind.

Unable to predict his moods, I was relieved when Ukiah walked to my house that night with a smile on his face. He soon led me to the Gemini, where he took over the driving responsibilities. As if a prerequisite for our times spent together, we fishtailed onto Reflection Alley, then began another journey into the arms of destiny.

As Ukiah burst onto the bypass, with the autumn sun (now setting sooner than usual) shining in our eyes, he told me how important this performance was for Japhy's band. He said The Rock was the area's premier venue for up-and-coming bands, a proving ground where booking agents from established clubs like The Dies Infaustus (where we saw Joan Jett perform) regularly hung-out in search of new talent. If Mirror Image could impress this crowd, they'd be primed to ride into the future on a wave of glory. Plus, their demo tape would be ready this weekend, a definite plus in that they could give a copy to each of the club owners. Needless to say, it would be a definite boost if the stars were in perfect alignment tonight for Japhy's band.

With darkness settling over the mountain highway, Ukiah's excitement soon turned sour as he mentioned his frustrating literary prospects.

With his wrist lying on the steering wheel, he began, "Last week, I wrote four different letters to 54 publishers."

"Publishers?" I asked. "I thought you were focusing on agents."

Angered, Ukiah spat, "I've washed my hands of literary agents. They can all take a fuckin' walk. From now on, I'm going straight to the source." Ukiah paused, then laughed uneasily, "There's an old saying in this business. To get published, a writer needs an agent, and to get an agent, a writer needs to be published. Well, to hell with them. I'm doing things my way."

"As always," I chuckled.

"There's no other way," he reiterated, a grin forming on his face.

"What did you tell these publishers?" I asked, the darkness making me nervous.

"I didn't just send them letters, I made each package a work of art," Ukiah boasted.

"What do you mean?"

"With each letter, I included a two-inch by four-inch manila packet that held a tiny zip-lock plastic baggy. Somehow, I needed to get their attention."

"I still don't follow."

"You'll see," he told me before exiting the interstate, then following a narrow two-lane highway.

"Tell me," I asked impulsively. "What did you say to them?"

"In the first letter, which I mailed to eighteen publishers, I told them if they're looking for a polished, professional 'poseur' who has a ton of contacts and has won literary awards, they should throw this letter away immediately! I'm none of the above. As a matter of fact, I don't know a damn thing about their industry, or how it works. I'm just an asshole writer who's written eighteen books weighing 57 pounds."

"They're probably thinking, 'what's he doing with this mountain of material?'"

Ukiah laughed maniacally, "Nothing. Nothing because I can't even find a fucking agent."

"Y'know," I said cautiously, "I'm sure your revelations won't paint you in the most favorable light ...."

"But it's the truth! I don't have a clue how their game is played. So my work - this menagerie of madness - gathers dust when it should be ALIVE ... unleashed on the masses ... devoured by greedy readers looking for a RUSH. Chris, I don't have a SOUL fighting for me, but that doesn't phase me."

"It doesn't?" I asked tentatively.

"No, because I have the BALLS and WILL to claw my way to the top. I'm not content being some ham n' egg author who ekes out a living. Hell no! I plan on fighting until I'm bigger than F. Scott Fitzgerald. And I'm willing to surrender every drop of blood, and every breath in my body, to do it."

"Ukiah, they're going to wonder why you sound so urgent."

Irritated, Ukiah snapped, "I'll tell you why! Because 99.9% of the literary world is made up of sleepwalkers who so willingly toe the line and accept the status quo that it makes me want to claw their eyes out."

"But not you," I said appeasingly.

"Hell no! I could have easily written a letter just like those in the L.M.P."

"L.M.P.? What's that?"

"The *Literary Market Place*. This book gives advice on marketing plans, formatting, and so forth. But screw them. I'll break every rule there is, and show those zeroes how to kick some ass. I'm so ready for fame that my head is gonna explode!" Ukiah, breathing rapidly, added, "Inside these envelopes were packets ..."

"The packets and baggies you mentioned earlier?" I interrupted.

"Exactly."

"What did you put inside them?"

"For the first letter I poured some vacuum sweeper dust, chopped cucumber skins, gooey tomato seeds, and glue inside the zip-lock Baggies, with a label pasted on the outside of each saying, 'My brains when they explode,' written in red ink."

Confused, I couldn't even form a sentence, simply saying, "Huh?"

"Don't you get it?" Ukiah asked excitedly. "In the letter I said - 'I'm so ready for fame that my head is gonna explode!' Then, as a P.S., I added, "I hope this packet gets your attention. I don't wanna pull a Vincent Van Gogh and mail part of my ear!"

"I get it ... like that painter who cut off his ear and gave it to a prostitute. That's funny. I can't believe you actually mailed that packet with cucumbers and tomato guts."

"I sure did."

"You're crazy, Ukiah. Certifiably insane."

"Wait until you hear about the other letters."

"Oh no. You didn't pull more stunts ......?"

"Even better," he smiled. "I started the second letter by saying:

1) I'm the best writer since Marcel Proust.
2) If you don't publish me, the world will stop turning.
3) I'm destined to become the most famous author in America.

> 4) The human race cannot survive without my
> insights, revelations, and sparkling prose.

And finally:

> 5) I'm the greatest thing to happen since God!"

I howled hysterically at Ukiah's audacity as he explained, "I'm sure that, being in the business long enough, these publishers have heard every claim in creation. So, I'd go completely over the top! I figured, why approach them like some creep in a bar with a cheesy come-on line? I'd lunge for their jugular and bash 'em with pure absurdity and satire. I then described my output, and made two guarantees."

"Which were?"

"First, I wouldn't waste their time, and secondly, they wouldn't regret taking a chance with me. I concluded with this guarantee - by hook or by crook, I'd set the entire literary world on fire ... see enclosed packet."

"I'm afraid to ask, but what did you put in this letter?"

"I drove to a bookstore near the mall, bought a Philip Prince novel, then, after getting home, ripped out every page and set them on fire."

Alarmed, I asked, "Why?"

"I let the pages get charred, then stuffed a few pieces of each into the Baggies, which had this label:

R.I.P.
(in distant memory)

Philip Prince
John Grisham
Jackie Collins

"You're too much," I howled, wishing I could be a fly on the wall when the publishers opened Ukiah's letters.

Not wasting any time as he sped through the darkness, Ukiah continued, "I leaped into my third letter by saying, 'I'm so sure I can sell more books than any other writer in America that I vow, from this point forward, to ... wait a second, let me finish with my other hand ... there ...   ... that I VOW to abstain from both sex AND masturbation until you contact me and agree to read my material .... See enclosed packet.'"

"No ... no way. You didn't ....?"

"Yes, I did! I filled every baggy with mayonnaise and glue ... with this label on the outside:

> Please don't make this release
> my last
> CAUTION: use sanitizer
> after handling

Then I put one of those moist towelettes in each letter to add the final touch!"

"They're not going to think you're crazy, Ukiah, those publishers are gonna call the nearest loony bin and have you committed."

"I don't give a damn. Let 'em."

"You really are a riot, but I can't fathom your nerve. How can you find the nerve to pull these outrageous stunts?"

"How?" he asked seriously, zipping along a backwoods highway. "I don't see any alternatives. The mainstream book market suffers from such a glut of boring authors that it sickens me. The new lions are even worse. It's a shame because there's a VAST audience waiting for a breath of fresh air - someone from the streets who is young and confident, and willing to surrender every drop of blood to make it. I just wish ONE publisher could recognize my POTENTIAL. We'd rile-up the status quo, create instant notoriety, and rub against the grain of every person who didn't bring excitement to the printed word. I know unpublished authors are a gamble these days, but it won't cost them anything to ask about my vision. What do they have to lose? I'm sharp as a fucking tack. I know they wouldn't be disappointed."

"I'll bet they've never spoken with anyone like you. What treats did you put in your final letter?"

"The last was a real gem. I began by asking:

> Question: How many publishers does it take to discover a
> goldmine?
> Answer: Hopefully just one!

"I then drew an outline of The United States, with the middle of our state highlighted by a star with a red arrow pointing to it and the word 'Jackpot' scribbled in yellow. I then introduced myself with the standard bullshit, followed by an explanation of the map."

"Then what?"

"I said – as you can see from the above 'graphic,' I'm a no frills, no bullshit kinda guy. To compensate for my lack of fanciness, I'm willing to push every barrier to its limit.

In fact, the literary world rips my HEART out a little more each day with what it passes off as product. Where's the EXCITEMENT? I'm ready to shake things up! If these people feel like rolling the dice, why don't they throw 'em in my direction? Ya never know where Lady Luck might be hiding. I'm like the Dark Horse in a race. The odds are stacked against me, but WHAT IF I turn out to be a winner? The payoff would be enormous! All they have to do is give me a shot."

"How about the surprise packet?" I asked with anticipation. "What did you put in that one?"

"Well, I bought a steak and a bottle of red food coloring ...."

"Let me guess. You filled each packet with a piece of meat, and the dye to make it look bloodier and gorier."

"It's scary, Chris, but you're starting to think like me!"

"What did you write on the label?"

"It said: Piece o' my heart. So fresh it's almost still beating."

"You're hilarious, truly out of your mind" I said. "So let me see. In these four letters to the publishers, you mailed your brain, heart, sperm, and burnt words. It sounds like some kind of bizarre offering to the gods."

"That's who those bastards think they are - minor gods who control my destiny. Isn't it clear? Every publisher in this country is controlled by S.W.A.N. They're running the show and calling the shots. But what chance do I have unless I sell my soul, or bow down and beg for mercy? I've given these people so many ideas over the past year ... how about this angle. On my book tour, where Mirror Image would add a party atmosphere - think of the marketing potential. A father and son artistic team - one an author, the other a musician. There'd be articles about us in every magazine from *People* to *Vanity Fair* ... and all the while we'd be selling millions of books, CD's, and souvenirs. But do the publishers and agents listen to my ideas? No! None do. They send fucking rejection letters because Jennifer Ewen took a dislike to me and blackballed me throughout the industry."

"Why do you think Miss Ewen turned against you?" I asked as total darkness enveloped the country road.

"The best answer I can think of was recently given by Sean Penn."

"The movie star who used to be married to Madonna?"

"Yeah. When asked why certain Hollywood types frowned on him, he said, 'Because some people don't like when I tell the truth. They shun me because I disrupt their comfortable little lives. They'd rather hide behind illusions than face the realities of life.'"

Ukiah stopped speaking, bashed his fists against the steering wheel, then continued, "It's the same thing I'm facing. I want to strip the literary world - especially language - down to its core. I want to climb every fucking mountain on this planet and yell to the people - open your eyes! Look around you. We're being controlled ... brainwashed ... led astray. Can't you see S.W.A.N.'s ultimate goal - their purpose for existence? They want to abolish The Word ... its potential for FREEDOM ... so that in the future we won't have any identity at all. Rather than choosing who we will be through free will, they'll define our identities. Human beings and baboons will become indistinguishable. As The Word is obliterated, humanity will slowly lose its uniqueness, transformed into robotic illiterates ... automatons without the ability to transcend their states of slavery. The Word is our only path to salvation, and I'm its messenger ... the one who is preparing the way. That's why Jennifer targeted me as an enemy of the industry. S.W.A.N. chooses writers who are like river stones ... y'know, nice and smooth, with no rough edges. But once she got a load o' me, and felt the threat I presented to their ultimate goal, she blackballed me. So what's left? I keep writing like a madman. But why? Why? Because of fear. I liken myself to a Machine. If I don't keep creating, I'll be like a gear without oil, or The Tin Man in Oz. If I don't keep squirting oil into the joints ... creating my legacy ... I'll seize-up and quit functioning. Plus, I'm always afraid that, like my parents, Romlocon will leave and never return. If my Muse decides to do that, I'm finished as a writer."

Nearly hyperventilating after his rousing monologue, Ukiah said, "Look, there's a sign for Kundalini. We should be there in ten minutes."

Needing advice on a non-related topic, I asked Ukiah, "I hate to change the subject, but will you help me with a problem that's been bugging me?"

"Sure, Chris, what is it?" he said earnestly.

"As you know, Woody Dewar's brother plans on moving in next door. In all honesty, I hate him more than I hated Woody. What should I do?"

"Well," he began, rubbing his three-day beard as city lights shone in the distance. "I was talking with a girl the other day who loves Jack Kerouac. After discussing our appreciation for his work, I asked if she read a new biography called *Subterranean Kerouac*. Lorena said no because every magazine and newspaper review warned that it didn't present 'ol Jack in a favorable light. So, Lorena refused to read it because it wouldn't elevate Jack in her eyes. This is where we disagreed, because I need to see the world in every conceivable light, not just the pleasant ones. I don't want to live in a namby-pamby world where everyone smiles and our fangs are never shown. Ugliness is as prevalent as beauty, so to deny it or shy away is foolish. I'll keep my eyes open to every part of life, acknowledging the thorns alongside the roses."

"Ukiah," I said irritably, "I asked about Kenny Dewar."

"I know," he laughed. "I was getting to that. What I would do is kill him, just like you did Woody. Ya see, I'm a realist. To hell with the world's lily-white illusions. Gimme truth ... gimme honesty ... don't whitewash the landscape. If Kenny is a problem, handle it. Eliminate him."

With those words, Ukiah drove my Gemini into the sleepy hamlet of Kundalini. His advice was so inhumane that I couldn't even respond. This man mentioned murder in such an off-hand manner that it sounded like he was talking about squashing a cockroach. I hated to admit it, but Ukiah had a very prevalent thread of evil living in his body ... coursing along his veins like water through a series of canals. He could be downright wicked and malicious ... an aspect of his personality that so repulsed me that I wondered how I could even be friends with him. Ukiah proved he could do anything, and when it came to the darker side of existence, he never flinched.

I was genuinely frightened as Ukiah wove through town in search of The Rock. To him, at least in terms of human interaction, good and evil were undifferentiated ... each having a distinct and separate purpose. In other words, if a negative deed ultimately benefited one's situation, it was justifiable for those two poles to intersect. The thought troubled me immensely. To casually mention murder, or to fuck someone over because I could, was not my idea of leading a proper life. But Ukiah viewed life in terms of masters and servants ... dominance and submission ... a brutal collision of strength and weakness, with the result being a struggle for power and control.

Ukiah once told me that I hadn't developed my killer instinct. Well, if that meant I didn't have such cold, brutal opinions of the world like he did, then so be it.

Suddenly, as if to distract me from these troubling thoughts, Ukiah slammed his foot on the brake pedal, propelling me toward the windshield.

"What is it?" I yelled hysterically. "Did you hit something?"

Sighing desperately, Ukiah crammed the gearshift into park, then leaped out his door to pick up a frightened kitten that stood shivering alongside the road.

Returning the little feline to my Gemini, Ukiah purred softly, "It's okay, little baby. We'll stop at the store and get you some milk. Then you can sleep in the backseat and stay nice and warm. Yes, you're a good little girl. I won't ever let anything hurt you."

As he spoke these words, I saw a neon sign flashing from the roof of an ominous gray building that read "THE ROCK".

Unbelievably, Ukiah tossed the tiger-striped kitten in my backseat, then circled the block until finding a convenience store. Without saying a word, he rushed into the market, returning moments later with an armful of cat care products - a cardboard box filled with litter, a plastic bowl that he poured bottled water into, plus a paper plate on which he scooped a can of food. This feline, frisky and glad to be alive, voraciously ate the soft morsels, lapped water from her bowl, then squatted in the make-shift litter

box.   Ukiah watched these proceedings from his rear-view mirror as he wheeled
through Kundalini, shrieking with unbridled joy.

"Look at that little girl, just look at her," he gushed, keeping a closer eye on the kitten
than he did the road. "That little baby looks like she's filled with love. I'm going to
name her Mary."

"Why Mary?" I asked, laughing at Ukiah's silliness.

"Because when I was a kid, shuffled from one foster family to another, I always tried
imagining my real mother ... y'know, what she looked like, how she smelled, the type
of clothes she wore. Even though these variables changed, her name, for some reason,
was always Mary. So this 'lil girl's name is Mary ... my precious little Mary."

As we drove through the sleepy streets, the neon sign flashing "The Rock" once again
came into view, the building on which it sat filling me with dread.

After pulling into a pothole-laden parking lot adjacent to this dark granite structure, I
said, "This place looks like a prison."

"It is," Ukiah informed me. "Or should I say, it was."

"A prison? Are you sure we're at the right place?"

"Yeah. This building used to be The Kundalini County Prison, but a few years ago the
legislature shut it down when they built a new jailhouse. So, some guy got the idea to
turn it into a teenage nightclub. The weirdest part is, even though The Rock doesn't
serve alcohol, quite a few adults come to these performances. That's how professional
these bands are. Some are even better than the ones in Latera Heights."

With that introduction in mind (and following a tender farewell to Mary, who stayed in
the Gemini covered by a blanket I got from the trunk), Ukiah and I entered The Rock.
While climbing the wide, white marble steps leading to a dungeon-like door, I found it
amusing that we were entering a prison. Even more bizarre were the windows of this
ominous gray structure - each still had black metal bars and chiseled iron daggers to
prevent escape. What kind of torture chamber were we entering?

Once inside, after paying a cover charge, we encountered hundreds of the zaniest
teenagers I had ever seen. Quite literally, these kids appeared to have fled from the set
of a vampire movie, or an insane asylum. Many had choppy, dyed black hair, pale
(ghostly) complexions, their noses, lips, ears, tongues, and cheeks pierced with hoops,
studs, and diamonds. It's hard to even describe their clothes. Instead of regular blue
jeans, t-shirts, and sneakers, these young men and women sported black leather, fishnet, capes, spikes, brightly-colored mini-skirts, stilettos, stylish canes, floppy hats,
feathers, studs, torn denim, tattoos, body paint, and loose clanging chains. Although
their attire reminded me of the human oddities who toured with a sideshow, they did
have a certain style - cool, detached, and very personal. Ukiah and I actually looked

like the oddballs wearing flannel, corduroy, and cotton. Maybe we needed a touch of spandex and glitter!

While the teenagers hung out and smoked cigarettes in two different rooms - one a large den with couches, chairs, and television sets, the other an arcade cluttered with video games, pinball machines, and a pool table - Ukiah and I checked out the club's interior (where Mirror Image would soon perform), to discover the music hall was actually an old cell block! The sight was truly frightening. At the far end of the narrow corridor sat a six-inch high stage teeming with amplifiers, drums, microphone stands, and a variety of wires and other electrical equipment.

Any semblance of normalcy ended there. Lining both sides of the concrete corridor were actual prison cells, their heavy, iron-barred doors opened to the public. If a night watchman actually had the keys to these locks, I'm sure someone could be imprisoned for the night. In all honesty, it would have been hell to be trapped in this repulsive universe. Ukiah and I stepped inside one of the cold, barren rooms, and to say I shuddered with fear would be an understatement. The cells still had a stained brown commode, an even grimier sink, and one steel framed bed with rusty springs that hung from the wall. That's it! The chipped, concrete floor had a single drain ... and I imagined at night, when the lights were dimmed, every conceivable type of creature crawled from their underground holes - cockroaches, rats, mice, moles, and centipedes that'd make even the most hardened criminal cry in his sleep.

After looking around for a minute, I hurried back to the cellblock. There, at least, an iron gate wouldn't slam shut and imprison me for eternity. As Ukiah returned to join me, we looked about this incredible structure, both of us shivering and cold. The lower cellblock's all-consuming presence was magnified by a second tier of cells above us, lined by a black, iron-grate catwalk. I closed my eyes for a moment and pictured a sunglassed prison guard patrolling level two, slapping a night stick against the palm of his hand while prisoners raked tin cups against the bars of their cell.

Returning my focus to the ground level area, I noticed an array of sayings engraved into the chipped, cinder block walls. Could these messages - words such as "I didn't do it," "Let me out," "My knees are calloused," and "I'll kill again" - be the pleas of prisoners from the past? In some areas, flaked, faded paint covered their cries for help, but most were left intact for the world to read.

Other objects of interest which caught my eye were "The Rock's" logo stenciled on the dance floor inside a blood-red circle, beside it the painted outline of a human form that resembled the chalk diagram police officers drew around a crime victims dead body ... admittedly morbid, but with a cool sense of humor. I also laughed at the opening in a red brick wall that had the words "Soup Hole" painted above it. I assumed this slot was where the prisoners got their daily meals - the hole now used to slide slices of pizza from a kitchen to the teenagers who bought them. I had to admit, I'd never seen pizza served in such a unique manner!

By this time a group of adolescents staked their territory on the dance floor, a signal for

Ukiah and me to seek safer ground - namely the catwalk on level two. There, at least when the craziness began, we'd be removed from harm's way.

Shortly after we climbed a set of steep black iron steps and took our place near a metal rail overlooking the floor, a short, mustached man set a video camera on top of a tripod beside us.

Interested, Ukiah asked this man, apparently the club owner, "What's the camera for?"

Preoccupied with his equipment, the proprietor answered, "Two reasons. First, we like to capture the moment for each band in case a talent agent is interested."

"And the second reason?" Ukiah inquired.

The man quit fiddling with his knobs and wires for a moment, then looked at us and said, "If one of those animals maims or kills someone down there in The Pit, I want it on film."

With this disclaimer setting the mood, every light inside The Rock was suddenly extinguished as the tribal rhythm of pounding drums resonated against the cold, cinder block walls. What a sensation - absolute blackness inside a prison!

As my heart raced frantically, a deep, unseen, phlegmatic voice growled, "Let's raise some fucking Cain for Mirror Image!"

While blinding, multicolored stage lights illuminated the band, the crowd stormed toward them as Japhy, Atomic Aaron, Hawke, and the remaining band members cranked into their opening number.

The sight below us was sheer chaos. The kids, blasted out of their minds with wildness, thrashed about the dance floor (or Pit) in such reckless states of abandon that I realized why a security camera was needed. Japhy's audience slammed into each other with unleashed fury - heads bucking, shoulders used as battering rams, elbows flying, and bodies hurled without fear or consequence. The activity was so intense that it reminded me of a battle royale ... bodies flung with insane disregard, bashed off the prison walls, or hurled violently to the floor.

Mirror Image, meanwhile, played a brand of music that was angrier and edgier than when I had previously seen them. Atomic Aaron's drums filled the cellblock with earth-shaking anger, while Japhy created ear-splitting feedback by grinding his guitar into an amplifier. Hawke, on the other hand, pushed the crowd into a state of frenzy ... urging them to go further ... taunting ... leading ... manipulating them into realms of insanity.

As the show progressed, a dizzying panel of red, blue, and purple strobes sent swirling triggers of light about the floor, producing a hypnotic affect that made my head spin. The music changed from simple entertainment to an otherworldly presence that took control of The Rock ... Hawke's unleashed antics ... bodies colliding ... sensory over-load ... throbbing drums ... screams of sodomy and rape from yesteryear echoing through the corridors ... shrieks ... applause ... dripping blood ... sonic power chords ... sweat - adrenaline - sex - aching ear canals ... bodies pressed tightly against each other ... harmonic synchronicity ... buzzing electricity ... volume - feedback ... delight - dancing - fantasy and dreams - steam-heat - unbridled lust - rock n' roll - rock n' roll ... squealing guitars, primitive rhythms, piercing vocals, a throbbing bass line ... faster, louder, wilder ... sex unleashed - mania released - pure pop, pure energy - uninhibited ecstasy ...

Kids actually leap-frogged over other bodies, flying ten feet in the air, landing with a crash, then zipping in whatever direction was needed to produce the necessary rush. As they did so, the metal catwalk shook beneath us, producing concern within me. What if this throbbing, pulsating, energetic crowd became so wild that we cracked the support girders and plummeted twenty feet toward the floor, crushing hundreds of teenager who danced below us?

I couldn't get a grip on the experience ... the music - rough and raucous - refused to stop ... pounding, grinding - needling through my ears. The kids around us soared into orbit, so possessed by exhilaration that their spells couldn't be broken. Although I was proud of Mirror Image's ability to transform their audience, I also felt an unseen force descending upon us, exerting an influence beyond our control.

The metal grate continued to shake, Japhy's guitar transmitted needle-like shards of electric torture, while Hawke commanded the crowd to fly outta sight.

I thought the entire madhouse would erupt when Ukiah pointed to a female who stood across from us. Looking closer, I realized she was the same one we had seen at an earlier Mirror Image show - the one who stood silently, hip cocked, smoking cigarettes. Ukiah was transfixed as she lit a tar, blew her smoke into the thick, stifling air, then looked our way. Without saying a word, the two communicated on a level only they understood.

The girl, standing 5'2" at best, with straight, shoulder length blonde hair and bangs, wore a slinky V-cut blouse, a red mini skirt without nylons, and brown high-heeled shoes. Unlike the other freakily dressed adolescents, she didn't need to be outlandish. Rather, she simply inhaled, blew grayish blue smoke above her head, then waltzed in our direction.

The sexual energy radiating between these two, when coupled with the maniacal music, overpowered me. This little lady, wearing candy apple red lipstick, strolled to Ukiah's side, put her back against his chest, then bounced provocatively as he hugged her waist with his arms. I watched enviously as she rubbed up and down, shaking her ass against Ukiah's thigh. Something was happening beyond the mere trappings of a rock n' roll show. The kids below us were going insane, so violently out of their minds that bloody casualties hobbled from the floor every few minutes. I almost pleaded with the club owner to stop the show, but such an interruption would have caused a riot.

So, I simply watched in shock as the strobes, volume, and Ukiah's lustful reaction to the young woman all increased exponentially.

Luckily, as I was about to meltdown, Mirror Image blasted through the final chords of their set, nearly setting The Rock on fire. Dizzy, light-headed, and ready to collapse, I sighed a breath of relief as my eardrums rang with fury. The crowd below, although they had virtually crippled each other, applauded for minutes on end, congregating around the band to congratulate them.

Meanwhile, Ukiah told his petite acquaintance to wait in the lobby while we rambled down the steps to find Japhy surrounded by throngs of sweaty, bloody teenagers. Minutes later, we meandered toward a backstage prison cell where Gina and all five members of Mirror Image sat exhaustedly.

When seeing his father, Japhy's eyes twinkled with the brilliance of a morning sunrise.

"How were we, Dad?" he asked excitedly.

"Fantastic! You took me to another planet," Ukiah told him, patting Japhy's shoulder.

"Here, check it out," the youngster then said, tossing a cassette tape to his father. "We finally did it."

"Your demo! Super!" Ukiah beamed. "I can't wait to hear it."

Gina then exclaimed frantically, "You shoulda seen who talked with Hawke after the show."

"Who?" Ukiah asked.

"Some guy from The Dies Infaustus!"

"You're kidding?"

"No," Gina continued, bouncing in place. "He wants Mirror Image to play at his club some night!"

"Plus," Japhy interjected, "he took a copy of our tape and said he'd mail it to a record producer in New York City."

"Holy shit! You guys are going to make it," Ukiah cheered, shaking his son's hand. "So, what are you up to tonight?"

"There are a few guys from the opening bands ... what were their names?"

"'The Mechanical Ego's' and 'The IDiots,'" Gina told him.

"Yeah, they want us to meet 'em at an arcade in their hometown to talk about jamming together sometime. So, after we load our gear, we're going to follow them."

"Cool," Ukiah said to Japhy. "Well, have fun tonight. I'll give you a call tomorrow and we'll talk more about your good news. Congratulations again. You put on one helluva show. Oh, before I forget," he then concluded, "the circus is coming to town next week. You and Gina should make a road trip to Latera Heights. Just think - trapeze artists, clowns, tightrope walkers, tigers and elephants, plus the human cannon-ball. It'll be great. Okay, see ya. Love ya buddy."

"Love you too, Dad."

After shaking hands with his son and hugging Gina, Ukiah and I said goodbye, then strolled through The Rock one last time before finding his little vixen waiting in the lobby.

Immediate feelings of animosity rolled through my body as I saw Ukiah lay a passionate kiss on this girl's ruby lips before leading her to my Gemini. As they whispered and giggled, I burned with jealous anger. Why couldn't I be the one holding Ukiah's hand, or laughing at jokes mouthed into my ear? First I found him screwing that prostitute ... then Demi's letter came in the mail. Now he was with a silly little girl who probably didn't even know how to tie her shoelaces.

When we reached the Gemini, Ukiah raced to the backseat, then yelled to his girl-friend, "Come here, look what I found."

"Oh my gosh, it's a little kitty. She's so cute. What's her name?"

"Mary."

"I just love her," the girl chirped while hugging Ukiah.

As she did so, Ukiah reached in his pocket, found the car keys, then tossed them to me.

"Here Chris, I'll let you do the steering."

After sliding into the driver's seat, I was overpowered by the aroma of urine and defecation that rose from the cardboard litter box. Mary, meanwhile, had upset her water bowl, overturned the cat food, and made tracks on every window. Ukiah, considering his situation, didn't notice. Rather, he motioned for the little lady in the mini-skirt to sit on his lap, rubbing her legs as I gunned the engine.

"Where are we going?" I asked, backing out of The Rock's parking lot.

Before Ukiah could answer, his sidekick quipped, "I don't care where we go, let's just go!"

"Yeah, let's go," Ukiah reiterated, his mood jovial and lively. "By the way," he added, "What's your name?"

"Nikki," she purred, crossing her lean, sexy legs.

"It's nice to meet you, Nikki. I've always loved that name. I'm Ukiah, and Chris is driving."

Not knowing which way to go (being that I didn't have a destination and couldn't remember how to leave Kundalini), I simply turned left and let The Gemini drive itself.

While I drove aimlessly through the barren streets, Ukiah popped Japhy's demo tape into the cassette player and whooped with joy as their music blasted through the car. Nikki tapped her hands on the dashboard while Mary zipped beneath the seat, through my feet, across my lap, and over the steering wheel. I had hoped for a relaxing journey back to Latera Heights, but from all appearances, this evening's craziness would never end.

After listening to Mirror Image's first song, Nikki blurted, "Let's get some beer!"

"All right! That sounds like a plan," Ukiah chimed in, pointing to a six-pack shop.

Unable to believe my ears, I pushed the cassette player's stop button, then snapped, "That's not a good idea."

"Why not?" Nikki whined, a pout forming on her tiny mouth.

"Yeah, why not?" Ukiah repeated.

Nervous, and in no mood for confrontation, I replied, "She's probably not even of the legal drinking age."

"How old are you?" Ukiah immediately asked.

"Old enough," Nikki responded cheerfully.

"That's good enough for me," he quipped. "Now pull into that beer joint."

Following his instructions, I bounced into an asphalt lot, angrily shifting my Gemini into park.

As Nikki slid from Ukiah's lap and he scooted from the door, I felt a tremendous urge to intervene ... to stop this situation before it careened out of control.

After hopping out of the car and rounding a darkened corner, I caught Ukiah before he entered the six-pack shop.

"What's up, Chris? Do you wanna booze it up, too?"

"No, Ukiah, I don't," I told him forcefully. "And you shouldn't either."

"I shouldn't, huh? Since when did I need a babysitter?"

Disappointed by his reaction, I stood silently for a moment, then stared at him directly.

"You don't know what day this is, do you?"

"Other than a day when I feel like getting blown away, no I don't."

"Ukiah, we met one year ago today. Don't you remember what condition you drank yourself into? You were a mess."

"It's been an entire year?" Ukiah moaned, hanging his head. "I can't believe it. I did promise Romlocon that if she let me keep living, I'd never smoke or drink again. Damn!" he then cursed, kicking his foot through the dirt.

"Don't go in there," I pleaded. "Think of the consequences. You could get popped for giving alcohol to a minor, and by the looks of Nikki, who knows what other trouble."

"Hey," Ukiah said, lifting his head, "booze and young women have always been my downfall. And anyway, what has Romlocon done for me lately? She should prove her loyalty by letting me get published."

"You shouldn't make demands of your Muse," I replied quietly.

"Why not? I could be standing on top of the world at this very moment."

"There's more to life than what we can see."

"Well shit," Ukiah snapped, "I'm so poor I can't even buy a decent meal half the time."

"It takes more than food to keep people alive," I said, amazed at my responses.

Frustrated, Ukiah grumbled, "I don't care what you say. I went an entire year without drinking. Doesn't that count for something?"

"Of course," I said sympathetically. "You'll never know how proud I am of you. But think about your commitment to Romlocon. Wasn't it worth anything?"

"The only commitment I care about now is the one I'm gonna make with that 'lil philly. So don't try to stop me, Chris. Not only am I going to buy beer, but I'm also gonna buy a pack of cigarettes."

Mustering every ounce of courage, I fixed my gaze on Ukiah and said sternly, "I can't interfere with the decision you're about to make. So that means I'm going to have to make some decisions, too."

"What are you trying to tell me?"

"I'm at a crossroads, Ukiah ... a place I don't want to be. But now that you've decided to take this drastic plunge ... damnit Ukiah, we've been through some wild times together, and I've stuck by you every step of the way. But I can't let you destroy yourself. So, regardless of what you decide to do this weekend, I promise to stay by your side, through thick or thin, until you've finished this jag. I hope there aren't any hard feelings, but right now the decision is yours. If you don't go in that liquor store, everything can return to normal. But if you do go in, we have to go our separate ways after this weekend." I paused a few seconds, voice cracking and noticeably choked-up, then concluded by begging him, "Ukiah, you're the best friend I've ever had. Please don't do it."

I couldn't tell if my words had an impact on him, for he turned from me, then said softly, "Whatever I choose, there won't be any hard feelings?"

"None whatsoever," I replied evenly.

"Okay then, I'll meet you back at the Gemini," he told me, entering the six-pack shop like a gust of wind.

Emotionally crushed, I returned misty-eyed to my car, only to find Nikki and the kitten bouncing around with glee. More water had been spilled, the litter box completely overturned, food strewn in every direction, and my blanket torn and frayed. My Gemini smelled worse than an animal's cage, but Mary and Ukiah's little mistress didn't mind in the least.

As I sat in the driver's seat, Nikki chirped merrily, "I gave this kitten a new name. I'm going to call her Mee-Mew."

"Wonderful," I said dejectedly, dreading every second spent with her, especially when I had to start work at eight a.m.

Each passing second felt like time spent in a maximum-security penitentiary. As Mary hissed at Nikki, pissed on the floor, and clawed at my neck, I considered walking in front of a train to end my misery. I literally couldn't stand this immature vixen ... her baby talk when speaking to "Mee-Mew" ... the way she primped in a hand-held mirror, brightening her already ghastly red lipstick ... or her habit of humming nonsensical songs. I actually wanted to shift the Gemini into drive, race to the highest cliff in Kundalini County, and push her over a ledge.

Shortly thereafter, as visions of Nikki's cold blue corpse filled my mind, Ukiah returned with two brown paper sacks containing four six packs of beer and three packs of cigarettes. His decision had been made ... and like everything else in life, he didn't plan on doing it halfheartedly.

After patting Mee-Mew on the head and letting Nikki sit on his lap, Ukiah reached into his sack, popped two beers, then exploded with glee.

"Whoo hoo! Here we go - just like the olden days!"

Nikki and him chugged in unison from their bottles of beer, each spilling trickles of yellowish-brown fluid down their chins.

"Let's go, Chris - onward to Latera Heights," he chuckled. "No hard feelings, right?"

I remained silent as Ukiah tore the cellophane from a pack of smokes, stuck a cigarette in Nikki's mouth, lit it with a match, then removed it from her crimson lips and inhaled deeply, exhaling the smoke over his shoulder.

Ukiah sipped from his beer again, then roared, "I wanna make a toast ... a toast to promises."

"To promises," Nikki cheered, sipping deeply.

"I wanna make a second toast," he then declared. "A second toast to broken promises!"

Disgusted by Ukiah's behavior, I followed a poorly lit two-lane highway out of town, soon encountering the darkness of rural America.

With Japhy's cassette playing lowly from the tape player, Ukiah and Nikki drank, smoked, joked, giggled, and horsed around with each other as Mee-Mew slept in the backseat. Their inane, drunken conversation digressed to such a level of idiocy that it was like being with lobotomy patients.

"Ukiah, when I grow up, I want to be a princess."

"I'll make you a princess, trust me."

"No, a real life princess that stands on a balcony," Nikki snickered, "waving to her subjects. Do you think I'm pretty enough to be a princess?"

"Baby, you're the cutest gal I've ever seen. If you were a princess, I'd never take my eyes off you."

"Really? I'm that gorgeous?"

"I've never met a prettier girl than you."

"Tell me what you adore about me," she demanded giddily.

"First," Ukiah said, rubbing his hand along her thighs, "are your legs and ass. Perfect. Absolutely perfect. I wish you could see your ass."

"I do see it! I stare at it every day in the mirror after I'm done showering. I love my ass. It's gorgeous."

"It really is, baby."

"What else? Tell me. I love being complimented."

"You're so thin, with no stomach, and beautiful, perfect little tits. Then there's your face. Oh my ... if I were your mirror, I'd spend eternity smiling back at you ... those eyes ... dazzling .. and your hair, it's so cute ... especially the bangs. But nothing compares to your lips ... I love that red lipstick. Here, let me kiss them again." (during an extended make-out session, with both groping at each other, Ukiah slid his hand along the young lady's legs .. then beneath her mini-skirt). "You're so hot, Nikki. I can't wait until we get home."

"When we're done screw ... I mean making love," she cooed sassily, "I want you to tell me how perfect I am. Then we'll pretend I'm a princess. You can describe how my subjects fawn at my feet, showering me with rose petals and expensive gifts as I walk in front of them."

This type of banal dialogue continued for over an hour as Ukiah and Nikki guzzled huge quantities of beer and filled the Gemini with thick clouds of smoke. As they occupied themselves with booze, lust, and the fantasy world of make believe royalty, I kept my eyes on the road, burning with resentment. In less than two hours, Nikki took something I had secretly pined away for during the past twelve months. Even worse, tonight she would let Ukiah inside her body ... groaning and panting as he drove his love toward her burning core. I wanted to black out and never think again ...

Finally, relief arrived as I pulled into the driveway, feeling more neglected than a sideshow freak at a high society ball. Sadly, I realized the rest of my evening would be spent alone, while Nikki and Ukiah's sweaty bodies became indistinguishable from one another.

Stepping from the car, Ukiah added insult to injury by grabbing his kitten from the backseat and asking, "Chris, can I ask a favor? Is it all right if Mee-Mew spends the night with you? I don't have time to mess with ......"

"Sure, anything," I said despondently. "Bring her in the house. I'll make a new litter box and scrounge up some food."

"Thanks. C'mon Nikki, we'll drop Mee-Mew inside, then walk to my place."

Similar to Ukiah's habit of never locking his door, I simply turned my handle, then walked inside and flicked on the kitchen light. After removing my coat, I looked toward my answering machine to see its red light flashing. Without thought, as Ukiah and Nikki hugged and sipped from their beer cans, I pushed its play button to hear the following message:

> "Chris Edwards, this is Detective Morbus Eschara with The Kundalini County Sheriff's Department. I'm calling in hopes of contacting Mister Ukiah Rhymes. We have some terrible news to report. His son Japhy, along with the other members of his band, were killed tonight in a horrible traffic accident ...."

34

The ultimate frozen moment - stone-cold silence and shock, stopped time, our stares glassy as the phone message hung in the air like a dirigible. As Nikki shrieked and started to bawl, I crumbled lifelessly on the couch, overpowering bursts of nausea bubbling in my stomach, slowly sliding to my throat. Japhy Rhymes, a seventeen-year-old teenager, was dead. His entire band, for that matter, had died in a traffic accident. Japhy Rhymes, a boy who didn't smoke, drink, or do drugs, died alongside a highway in ... who knew where? What in God's name happened? How could such a tragedy befall these youngsters? Japhy wasn't dead - it couldn't be true.

While trying to convince myself that this news was nothing but a dream, I looked at Ukiah to see him frozen with fright ... motionless - eyes unblinking, fixated on a distant point in space. For a moment I actually thought Ukiah, paralyzed and rigid, had turned into a statue. But then, when noticing my concern, he snapped from his lethargic state, reacting with the rage of a caged cobra.

"No," he snarled violently, throwing his beer bottle across the living room, smashing it against a brown paneled wall.

Fishing in the right pocket of his jeans, he pulled out a silver knife before sitting on the couch. As Nikki lay sobbing on the floor, Ukiah opened the knife blade, then raked it across his left arm without warning or delay.

Events spun out of control - Nikki screamed, I leaped to my feet, and streams of blood ran from the bulging veins of Ukiah's forearm.

"Stop," the young girl squealed, makeup staining her face. "It's already bad enough."

"She's right. Don't do anything else," I added.

But Ukiah wasn't finished mutilating himself. He again sliced the knife through his flesh, this time perpendicular to the first incision, his blood now seeping from two sources.

"Is that what you want?" he begged, staring straight ahead. "You've already stolen my son. But you need more. Why didn't you take me? Japhy never hurt you. I'm the one to blame. I'm sorry for breaking my promise. But why him? He's all I had in the world. Now I'm alone. Why? You should have taken me. I'm the rotten one. Why, Romlocon, why? Who else do I have left to love?"

Pushed beyond my limit, I sped to the bathroom where bursts of vomit shot from my stomach, splattering the commode with such force that drops of cold water splattered against my face. As each violent regurgitation spewed forth toward the porcelain bowl, my mind rambled with images of the accident scene - fractured skulls thrust through a splintered windshield ... detracted eyeballs ... gasoline mixing with blood and glass ... twisted, shrapnel-like metal ... flashing police lights reflecting off a glistening roadway ... broken limbs, shattered headlights, gnarled guardrails ... matted, bloody hair attached to a rearview mirror ... nocturnal eeriness ... and silence - the troubling silence of life being lifted from this planet and taken to an alternate realm of existence. Also, I pictured the nightmare occurring in my own home - Ukiah's arm dripping with blood ... Nikki's tears ... and my own broken heart barely able to beat.

After catching my breath - stomach aching, lungs heaving, eyes moist and cloudy - I wanted to lie on the bathroom carpet and cry ... cry until time had stopped and loss became a concept removed from human knowledge. I longed to quit right there, to curl up in a ball and join the others who had passed before me - Woody Dewar, Mister Doublet, my father, plus Japhy and his band mates. Life, at this moment, seemed empty, hollow, and devoid of substance or meaning.

On second thought, I realized my world wasn't the only one crumbling to pieces. In fact, I couldn't even imagine Ukiah's reaction to this tragedy. What awful thoughts tumbled through his mind? I needed to pull myself together and be a rock who Ukiah could rely on. So, after flushing my sickness and trying to forget the entire episode, I gargled with mouthwash, then washed the forlorn look from my ashen-colored face.

Trying to put up a brave facade, I walked into the living room to find Nikki lying like a rag doll on one couch, while Ukiah sat stoically on another. With a living room lamp serving as their only light, a spooky stillness settled over my house.

Standing beside Ukiah, I summoned enough courage to ask, "How are you doing? I brought some bandages for your wound."

An eternal silence filled the air as Ukiah remained seated, blood dripping from his forearm onto each leg.

Then, without warning, he leaped to his feet and said urgently, "Chris, get ready. We're driving to New York City!"

"New York City? But I have to be at work ..."

I then remembered my vow to Ukiah. I would stay by his side until this episode ended. In the context of what had just happened, going to the data entry firm and punching numbers into a computer didn't seem very important.

So, as Ukiah stared blankly at me, I told him, "Sure thing. Whatever you decide, I'll stick by your side. When are we leaving?"

"In ten minutes. I'm going to track down Jennifer and kill her ... the same way she killed my son. I'll be back in a few moments."

Ukiah zipped frantically toward the door, then stopped and turned to us.

"Chris, call that detective in Kundalini and find out what happened tonight. Be sure to get every detail. And Nikki, after we leave, I want you to walk to that convenience store up the road and buy some food for Mee-Mew. I'll leave some money for you to get home."

Nikki nodded her head, then continued to cry. In contrast, I sprung into action, replaying the phone message (albeit lowly) to get the sheriff's number. After writing it on the cover of a notebook, I dialed the number, and was soon connected to Detective Eschara. I listened intently as he relayed the details of their crash. By the end of his explanation, Ukiah returned, bursting into my kitchen with a can of gasoline in one hand and a black pistol in the other.

"Let's go," he hollered, kicking a half empty beer bottle that sat on the floor, his left arm wrapped with a hastily prepared bandage. Still wobbly and drunk, Ukiah waved his gun through the air, declaring, "It's time to do some killing!"

After setting the gas can on my kitchen floor, he pulled a wad of perfectly arranged bills from his pocket, set them on the counter for Nikki, told her to take care of Mee-Mew, then motioned for me to follow.

Like lightning bolts flashing from a thundercloud, I soon found myself pulling from the driveway onto Reflection Alley - Ukiah by my side, his collected writings (crammed into a wooden crate) sitting on the seat between us.

As I rolled along the darkened streets, a slight drizzle fell from the sky while Ukiah bent to pick up a bottle of beer that must have fallen from his satchel.

With the smell of soiled cat litter still evident, Ukiah raised his beer bottle toward the windshield, then suddenly became lugubrious.

Speaking softly, he said to no one in particular, "Was it all worthwhile? Look at this fucking bottle of beer. I killed my son because of it. DAMN! For a fucking lousy buzz, I broke my promise to Romlocon, murdering Japhy in the process. Son of a bitch."

After tossing the brown bottle over his shoulder into the backseat, Ukiah sat quietly for a moment, inhaled, then asked, "Well, tell me what happened."

Making a left turn onto the bypass, I was overtaken by sadness. With tears dripping from each eye, I said in a choked up voice, "Detective Eschara told me that Japhy and his band were following the other cars to a town called Remontant when ... Oh Ukiah, do you really want to hear the details?"

Biting his lip, Ukiah sniffed, "I can't believe he's gone. I'll never talk to him again, or watch him laughing at cartoons on TV. What happened?"

Unable to hold back the flood of emotions, I bawled, "Japhy was driving The Celebrity ...".

"Was Gina with him?"

"Right beside him?"

"Did she get killed?"

"No. Somehow ... it's a miracle ... Gina was the only survivor."

"Is she all right?"

"I'm not sure. She's at the hospital in critical condition."

"I hope she survives. How did the others die?"

"Detective Eschara said that Japhy was cruising along route 88 when ... you're going to go nuts ... some drunken asshole fell asleep at the wheel, crossed the double yellow lines, and smashed into the front of their car. The detective told me they estimated the drunken driver's speed at eighty miles an hour ... his blood alcohol level at .314. Ukiah, they didn't stand a chance."

With tears soaking my cheeks, chin, and chest, I blathered, "I'm so sorry. They shouldn't have died."

Ukiah coughed, wiped his eyes with the back of his right hand, then said, "No, they shouldn't have. I hope their murderer fries in the electric chair. (pause) I appreciate all your help, Chris. You've really stuck by me every step of the way. There aren't many friends like you in the world. Even now, you'll miss work today just to drive with me to New York. And why? To kill a literary agent who has such little regard for me she doesn't even know I'm alive. I should track down that fucking drunken driver and run over his head with a steamroller. My entire life is a fucking mess. Why did Japhy have to die? He's the only person I loved with my entire heart and soul. Man, his band was so close to making it ... a gig at The Dies Infaustus, their demo tape, record producers. They would have been a smash. See, that's the difference between us. Japhy had natural talent, where mine is ... hell, I probably don't have any at all. I've been fighting and clawing every inch of the way, while Japhy could pick up a guitar and play without even trying. I used to love how he made up songs right on the spot." Ukiah paused, then said drearily, "It's hard to believe I'll never hear him play again, or race against him at the video arcade. He turned out to be a nice boy ... not frustrated, embittered, or constantly struggling like his old man. Y'know, at his age I was so confused I couldn't tell up from down ... all the pills and dope and booze ... the crazy wild women. But Japhy never needed that shit, or fell into those traps. He even made the honor roll his last two semesters. But look what I did because of pure selfishness. I broke my promise to Romlocon. And why? To get drunk and score a piece of ass. Now look at my life. Japhy's dead, and I'm riding to New York City to kill a literary agent. I don't know why you stick by me, Chris. You should have dumped a loser like me ages ago. Shit, you'll probably even get fired from work so you could keep your word to me."

Not knowing how to answer, I kept driving along Route 80, which would eventually lead into the heart of New York City.

Sounding tired, Ukiah continued, "If I had only stayed faithful to Romlocon. Do you know how scary it is to spend every hour wondering if you'll enter the gates of publication? As each day passes without me making my grand entrance, I realize I'm not any closer than I was the day before. Worse, as things stand now, it looks like I'll never ... ever enter the gates of publication. Chris, all I've ever wanted was to lay my eyes on that glorious entranceway ... but I blew it. I try so hard to purify myself, but my efforts always fall short. Do you know what it's like to be so obsessed with an ideal ... to try and satisfy, or attain a specific goal, yet be disappointed at every turn? I try to please Romlocon, begging that I won't let her down ... that I'll be allowed to enter the gates of publication, but in the end, whenever it's convenient, I slip-up and fail her. Tonight was a perfect example. Just because I wanted to momentarily escape myself, and to nail that 'lil philly, I said to hell with the big picture and indulged my appetites. My actions were inexcusable."

As the miles rolled by, Ukiah continued to let his vulnerabilities show. I'm not sure if the alcohol caused him to drop his defenses, but I'd never seen Ukiah so open and unguarded.

"Despite having a terrible father, Japhy still turned out fine. I don't know why. I abandoned that poor kid, ran around, wasn't a proper role model, and paid more attention to my own satisfaction than his. I was a drunk, a drug addict, and a chain smoking loser ... Japhy had all the cards stacked against him - the illegitimate son of two wild teenage kids. But despite these negative forces, he matured into a hard working, talented young man who could have had the world by its ass. But look at what I did. Instead of giving Japhy a fighting chance, I betrayed Romlocon and started a domino effect of bad luck that killed my son." (a slight pause, followed by an extended yawn which conveyed his fatigue) "I can still remember moments from Japhy's life as if they were yesterday, like the day he turned four months old. His mom and me propped him against a pillow, then put a Four of Hearts beside his head when we took the picture so we'd remember how old he was. It's like all those seminal moments are still alive - the first time he crawled across a room, became potty trained, or walked and talked. I remember tossing a baseball in the yard with him, buying Japhy his first electric guitar, and how proud I was when he passed his driver's test on the first try. I could list a zillion memories, but what's the use? Japhy's dead. All he ever asked from me was one thing - to be loved. And although I loved that kid with every bone in my body, I wasn't strong enough to keep him alive. Now he's lying in some morgue, blue and lifeless. I'll bet his poor mother is dying of sadness ......"

On this sorrowful note, Ukiah stretched his arms, then laid his head against the window. Being exhausted myself, I decided to pull into the first roadside rest area I saw and catch a few winks before the sun rose. I couldn't see any benefit in adding our names to a list of traffic casualties. So, after passing a marker that read "New York City - 30 miles," I swerved (while Ukiah snored) into a roadside rest facility that would serve as our resting place until daybreak.

35

I slowly opened my eyes to see an intricately woven, all encompassing spider web looming above my head like a planetarium star show. But unlike most spider webs, at the center of this silky maze was a discolored vagina - its chapped, leather labia opened wide to expose a swirling black hole of creation. Terrified by this surreal image, I struggled to escape, but was inexplicably stricken with paralysis. Unable to move or divert my gaze, I watched in horror as a two-headed serpent with tentacles burst from the vagina, then crawled toward me.

Upon closer inspection, I noticed that each face - one glimmering with translucent brightness, the other sinister and dark - looked identical to those of the man sleeping beside me. Ukiah was the two-headed snake slithering from the core of creation, imprisoning me within his inescapable web.

Unable to flee, I laid motionless as each head displayed its individual personality. The light-colored serpent took a secondary role, its mouth constantly saying words that could not be heard. The darker half of this Being was more immediate in its actions, hissing and showing its fangs while coming toward me. Then, without provocation, the more sinister of the two snakes opened its bloody red mouth to expose a coffin. As it zeroed in on me, I realized that this opened casket, lined with blue velvet, held the body of Japhy Rhymes — his eyes closed in tranquil repose. Rows of mourners walked past to pay their final respects, each face marked by grim disbelief. I could smell the roses that lay at his feet, plus the incense that filtered from a swinging golden urn. I saw close-up the makeup applied to each eye, and the putty-like substance used to fill the gouge in his forehead.

The black serpent descended toward this scene, gleefully shrieking, "He's mine! He's mine! It's only a matter of time before you're all mine!"

Crazed, the snake slithered toward the mourners, exposing its fangs while they scrambled for cover. Everyone raced to safety except one fallen individual who lay face first on the funeral parlor's marble floor. Overjoyed, the serpent pounced on its victim, whose identity was finally revealed.

It was me!

I screamed wildly as the serpent howled with delight while its alter ego, the fair-skinned snake, babbled an endless string of unheard words.

The Beast drew closer, its squalid breath swirling toward my nostrils ... "You're about to enter an unknown world," it hissed, smiling with pleasure. "A domain where dungeons of doom are our only rooms."

The serpent showed its ghastly fangs ... inching closer ... toying with me ... certain to take another victim ...

About to be eaten by this beast, I squealed at the top of my lungs, then woke to find Ukiah still sleeping beside me, his wooden crate filled with stories sitting between us.

Panting for air, I groggily rubbed each eye, stretched my arms, then realized that the casket, serpents, and spider web had been nothing more than a dream. Relieved, I squirmed about the driver's seat to get comfortable, shivering due to the brisk autumn temperature. To my right, Ukiah was sleeping, curled in a ball and snoring while the world spun in endless circles. It seemed this was the only time he'd find peace ... while sleeping … unconscious, unaware, untroubled by circumstance and imposition ... the burden of existence temporarily lifted from his shoulders.

Still feeling cold on this overcast morning, I gunned the Gemini's engine to generate some heat, waking Ukiah in the process.

Yawning, Ukiah tossed slightly, turned to one side, then opened his eyes, mumbling, "Ahhh, where am I?" Unaware of my presence, he asked, "What day is it?"

Not wanting to alarm him, I said softly, "Ukiah, we're in my car at a roadside rest."

Gazing drearily in my direction, his makeshift bandage peeling away, he focused his eyes, then started to shiver.

"Where are we?"

"About thirty miles from New York City."

"What are we doing here?"

"You don't remember?"

A moment passed before Ukiah's memory returned.

"Fuck. Son of a bitch. How could Japhy be dead? Damn. Last night was a fucking nightmare. Where did you say we were?"

"Thirty miles from New York City."

"Man, if I woulda drank any more beer last night, I'd really feel shitty today. What time is it?"

Checking my watch, I said, "Ten o'clock."

"Perfect. We won't have to deal with rush hour traffic. Man, my neck and back sure hurt. These weren't the most comfortable sleeping arrangements."

"Nothing worked out very well last night," I told him. "I'm a little stiff myself."

"I sure could go for a long, hot shower," Ukiah commented vacantly, "or a soft mattress and pillow."

"I agree."

"Shit. I can't believe what happened last night. Is Japhy really dead?"

"I'm afraid so."

"Well then, I suppose we should go ahead with our plan."

Hesitant, I asked, "The one concerning Jennifer Ewen?"

"You got it," Ukiah yawned.

Walking on shaky ground, I bit my tongue and said, "Ukiah, I hope you know that killing that agent won't bring Japhy back from the dead."

"I know that," Ukiah replied testily. "Do you have any other brilliant ideas?"

Disappointed, I shook my head from side to side, dreading what awaited us.

After splashing handfuls of cold water on my face in one of the rest stop facilities, I wandered across the parking lot to find Ukiah urinating behind a tree. Laughing at his audacity, I sat in the Gemini's passenger seat, knowing full well Ukiah would drive.

Within minutes, the sun nowhere to be found, we resumed our journey toward New York City, Ukiah silent and contemplative as he rolled along the interstate.

Bursting with anticipation as the two-lane highway fanned into four, I asked, "Are you hungry? I bought a few packs of crackers from the vending machine."

"Sure. Thanks," Ukiah said graciously, grabbing a jalapeno cheese on wheat.

While we munched noisily, I said, "I've never been to New York City. I can't wait to get there."

"It's one helluva place," Ukiah told me unemotionally, his mind on other matters. "Japhy and me used to go there every summer. Last year we even took Gina."

Unable to take the suspense, I finally burst, "Ukiah, what are we going to do? Did you come up with a plan?"

As if he hadn't heard a word, Ukiah commented, "I remember when Japhy was three years old, and he ran through our living room with a *Dukes of Hazzard* car in his hand. For some reason he stumbled and WHAM, bashed his cheekbone off the corner of an endtable. There was blood gushing everywhere, he was bawling ... man, it was wild. He still has that scar to this day. It looked cool as hell, along with his cleft chin ... just like a movie star."

Ukiah kept telling stories about Japhy's youth when suddenly the gloom which had thus far monopolized the day parted and fantastic needles of sunlight burst through the clouds to illuminate The George Washington Bridge.

"Holy shit! There it is," I squealed with delight, "New York City! Wow. What a sight. It's more incredible than I ever imagined. Look at the buildings."

Ukiah crossed this tremendous bridge, then followed The Henry Hudson Parkway toward the city. By all appearances he knew where he was going, for soon we zipped from the parkway, turning left on 52nd Street to pass a sprawling waste management facility. As Ukiah maneuvered through hordes of snarling traffic, I marveled at the maniacal drivers honking their horns ... taxi cabs darting like eels ... buses, moving vans, delivery trucks ... merging lines - pedestrians ... one way streets – and more honking horns. For the life of me, I didn't know how he stayed so calm amid this sea of insanity.

Rather than worrying myself to death about the traffic, I gazed at the surroundings – New York City in all its majestic glory - the apple of this country's eye, the greatest city in the world. And what a wallop it packed - skyscrapers kissing the clouds ... graffiti, homeless wanderers in shabby clothes - splashy signs ... upscale storefronts - famous landmarks - statues ... eye-catchers ... pollution ... steam rising from heating grates - litter - police cars ... and people — people everywhere - driving, walking, running, loitering, waiting for buses, begging for change, sleeping on sidewalks, washing wind-shields, traipsing aimlessly, sipping booze from brown paper bags, soliciting prostitutes, planning robberies, going to work ... yes, the people were everywhere - in every direction - inescapably present - a fixture, akin to the skyscrapers - like ants in an anthill - countless - multitudinal - tall, short, white, brown, thin, crippled, fat, young, aged, freakish, normal - people everywhere ... everywhere - living their lives, telling stories, being ... being and epitomizing New York City - filling its spaces, causing it to thrive - creating energy ... people everywhere - along the porno shops of Times Square, read-ing newspapers on a park bench, waiting to enter movie theaters and subways, pur-chasing food from sidewalk vendors or in tiny markets whose produce spilled out onto the streets - tossing crackers to pigeons - carrying shopping bags, looking sinister, laughing and conversing ... New York City - a magical painting of life - vibrant colors and aromas, signs in foreign languages ... flashing neon lights (even during the day) - storefronts glittering with diamonds, electronic equipment, watches and souvenirs - radios and boom boxes ... car horns, hustlers ... people everywhere - people who took for granted the bustling, thriving, glorious surroundings of their fascinating city.

Intrigued by every vision that confronted me (even though I feared what would soon ensue in regard to Ukiah and his target), I could not help but burst with excitement. My heart throbbed joyously inside my chest, pumping blood and adrenaline like water from a fire hydrant. Why couldn't we just sightsee all day like regular old tourists? We'd visit statues, museums, skyscrapers, restaurants, glitzy stores and parks, taking in all that the city offered. But rather than enjoying these activities, Ukiah drove with the determination of a man possessed. Feeling no need to explain his plans or our modus operandi, he simply meandered through traffic, passing taxis and ambulances while zipping between skyscrapers.

After an apparently aimless excursion around the city, Ukiah pulled alongside a curb on Vengier Avenue, then pointed to a ten-story building with crimson trim that looked like a glistening white temple.

"There it is," he grunted, a sneer forming on his lips.

"What?" I asked, expecting the worst.

"That," he said resentfully, "is the infamous Mason Turner Agency - America's most elite literary cesspool."

"I wish you'd change your mind ..." I began before being interrupted.

"Damn," Ukiah cursed. "I forgot that gas can at your house."

"Why do you need it?" I asked with surprise.

"I wanted to find Jennifer, drag her behind a dumpster, douse her with gasoline, then set her on fire. It would have worked perfectly — no bullets for the ballistics experts, no fingerprints, no evidence. Damn. Now I have to come up with another plan."

While we sat along Vengier Avenue, I secretly watched as Ukiah squinted, his eyebrows hardening into a furl as his face tightened and lips pressed firmly together. One might think that any man plotting to murder a literary agent he had never met would be a lunatic, or a raving madman like actors playing a role on TV. But in reality, Ukiah was far more dangerous than any wild-eyed psychopath prowling the streets in search of a victim. Why? Because Ukiah was smart, calculating, bright, and conniving ... an emotional chameleon. Sure, he could lose control at any second, but as it stood now, I could see the wheels of his mind determining his next move. Unlike crazed killers who needed victims to satisfy their bloodlust, Ukiah could care less about the thrill of taking a human life. Death didn't interest him ... that's why he was the worst type of criminal. No, death wasn't his forte ... justice was. When the scales of equality needed balancing, at least within a sociopath's mind, these individuals became the most dangerous to walk among us. Ukiah could smile, pat a kitten on the head, help an old lady cross the street, then slit an enemy's throat. I dreaded what laid before us.

Ukiah sat motionless ... thinking. The time arrived for him to make a final decision. The culmination of his struggles during the past year had been reduced to this moment. Sitting inside my Gemini in front of The Mason Turner Agency, he mentally put every piece in its proper order, like parts of a puzzle, or chessmen setting on black-and-white squares. At that moment, the only people that mattered were him and Jennifer Ewen - the king and queen, predator and victim, hunter and target.

While a variety of images passing outside the car window caught my attention, I couldn't ignore the monotonous passage of time I had to endure as Ukiah mapped his strategy ... seconds sliding into minutes ... minutes moving without motion. I felt like screaming, or running into the streets and disappearing among the millions of pedestrians who strolled past my view.

"Decide ... just decide," I wanted to yell ... anything to get things moving along.

Finally, after a seeming eternity had elapsed, Ukiah checked the pistol in his pocket, then said calmly, "Okay, I guess we're ready."

"Ready? For what?" I gasped. "What are we doing?"

"I'm going to walk into The Mason Turner Agency and find Miss Ewen," he said lackadaisically.

"Do you even know what she looks like?" I asked. "That seems like a good starting point."

"I have this," he answered, pulling the faded magazine photo of Miss Ewen taken thirty years earlier.

"That's it?" I exclaimed, unable to believe my eyes. "Jennifer must have been in her early twenties when that picture was taken. How can you base everything on a crinkled, worn out magazine photo?"

Ukiah stepped from the Gemini, locked the door, then whispered, "Follow me."

While we waited at a crosswalk, instead of telling me the details of his plan, Ukiah said, "Y'know what we should have done with Japhy and Gina? Gone to a gymnastics meet, or a figure skating exhibition. I think that would have been a good time."

An overhead traffic light turned red, which allowed us, along with scores of other pedestrians, to cross the street.

"Y'see, in practically every other sport, the participants chase balls, catch balls, throw, hit, shoot, or kick balls. But in women's gymnastics and figure skating, the girls are objects of beauty - perfect examples of the human form. Look at a top-level female figure skater sometime ... absolute perfection ... a body without rival - her legs, chest, flat stomach and glittering costumes. While other sports, or aspects of life in general, overflow with brutality and ugliness, it's refreshing to see a skinny young woman skating around a rink, or tumbling across a mat - the purity of their lines, the absorption into their routine, the concentration, discipline, and orderliness. It has everything - elegance, sex appeal, and pure physical prowess. I could watch those princesses skate and tumble all day."

In all honesty, my mind did back flips as Ukiah spoke of gymnasts and figure skaters. Here he was talking about purity and lines while we walked across a street toward The Mason Turner Agency. The two of us stood at the foot of this glistening white temple ... this red rose palace with light blue doors. Once we entered this elegant castle, it was safe to say our lives would never be the same.

Without uttering a word, Ukiah grabbed one of the golden handles, pulled it open, then motioned for me to lead the way. Gulping deeply, I stumbled through the door toward a yellow brick wall with a roster board of names. Following me, Ukiah gazed at the list, then pointed to one in particular:

Jennifer Ewen - 10th floor

Pushing the up button on an adjacent panel, we stood silently for a few moments as the ringing and buzzing of an elevator resonated through the corridor.

Then it opened and we walked inside. Never at any time had I experienced such trepidation and fear. Aware of the gun in his pocket, the bitter resentment over his rejection letter, and especially Japhy's tragic accident, I pictured Ukiah springing from the elevator on the 10th floor and shooting everyone in sight. He'd kill employees, innocent bystanders, and any literary agent who crossed his path until Jennifer Ewen had been eliminated ... gunned down not in cold blood, but in warm blood, the type one sees oozing from a wound, the kind that stays alive as it drips from a victim's clothing onto the floor ... blood that is still warm as a crazed gunman sticks his finger in it, then slowly licks it with his tongue. To hell with cold-blooded murder, Ukiah wanted the more intimate, personal form of vengeance.

I watched the overhead numbers click in sequence - 1 ... 2 ... 3 ... 4 ... 5 ... 6 ... please stop ... please let a policeman step inside the elevator and notice Ukiah's gun ... 7 ... where are mechanical failures when we need them ... 8 ... change your mind ... please come to your senses ... 9 ... just press the emergency button and run ... 10 ... RING ...

The door opened to an immaculate reception area, vacant except for a solitary woman seated behind a marble desk. Ukiah stepped from the elevator, then strolled confidently toward the woman as I self-consciously followed. Although the distance between the elevator and desk was only a few yards, it seemed farther than a football field.

"Yes, sir," a woman with a bouffant hairdo and garish makeup who appeared to be in her late forties asked disinterestedly, the nameplate on her desk reading, "Myra Goldstein." "How can I help you?"

Ukiah smiled broadly, placed both hands on the top of her desk, slowly leaned forward, then asked congenially, "Is Miss Jennifer Ewen in her office today?"

"Yes, she is, sir," Miss Goldstein replied, not bothering to look up. "Do you have an appointment?"

"No, ma'am, I do not," Ukiah replied sweetly.

Preoccupied by matters of importance on her desk, Myra responded robotically while fingering a silver necklace. "Who may I ask is requesting her services?"

"My name is Vincent Dagger. I'm an author," Ukiah declared boldly. "I have an entire case of material waiting in our car downstairs."

Miss Goldstein scanned a list of names, then snapped, "I'm sorry, Mister Dagger, but Miss Ewen is currently with a client. She cannot be interrupted."

"How about when she's finished with that client?" Ukiah asked politely. "Could I see her then?"

Tapping her fingers impatiently, Myra finally looked up, telling Ukiah brashly, "Miss Ewen plans on leaving the office at noon today, and will not be returning until tomorrow. Good day, sir."

I instantly looked at my watch, which read 11:50 a.m.

"Thank you for your courteous assistance," Ukiah smiled, adding, "Have a nice day."

Then, anticlimactically, he returned to the elevator while I followed, sighing a huge breath of relief.

36

As our elevator dropped toward the first floor, I smiled with relief, grateful that an explosion of gunfire hadn't erupted inside the marble tiled lobby. In fact, I found it odd that Ukiah exhibited such restraint when being ushered away by Miss Goldstein. I even looked toward him in the elevator, expecting to see an angry scowl on his face. Instead, Ukiah glowed with satisfaction, an aura of pleasantness radiating from his body.

After reaching the ground floor, Ukiah bound from the elevator, scurried through the lobby, then burst excitedly onto Vengier Avenue.

Following behind as we approached the street corner, I finally asked, "Why are you so happy? Now you'll never get to see Jennifer. We can't hang around New York City forever."

"Are you kidding?" Ukiah panted while we waited for the light to change. "My plan worked better than I ever expected."

"It did?" I asked as we crossed the street.

"Of course. Isn't it obvious? Rather than being completely blown off, like I thought would happen, Myra gave us specifics."

"She did?"

"Weren't you paying attention? The receptionist, trying to get rid of us as easily as possible, said Jennifer was leaving at noon. What time is it now?"

I stared at my watch, replying, "11:57."

"Super," Ukiah exclaimed as we reached the Gemini. "We'll just loop around the block and park in front of the Mason Turner building until Jennifer leaves. It's a good thing Vengier Avenue is a one-way street. At least we'll be pointed in the right direction. I'll just throw on the four-way flashers and wait."

Satisfied with his plan, Ukiah unlocked the driver's side door, then slid in and unlocked mine. As he did so, I looked to the top floor of the glistening white and red temple.

There I saw the receptionist, Myra Goldstein, peering down at us through a pair of opera glasses, scribbling something on a notepad while doing so.

"C'mon, we don't have time to waste," Ukiah hollered, swinging open the door.

After hopping inside, I told Ukiah in a flustered tone, "I might be imagining things, but that receptionist was staring at us through a pair of opera glasses from a window overlooking the street. What do you think she wants? Maybe she wrote down our license plate number."

"I don't have time to worry about that old bag. Listen. Do you hear those church bells ringing twelve times? We have to circle the block before Jennifer leaves the building. I hope she didn't decide to sneak out a few minutes early. Then we'd be screwed."

With the aggressiveness of a panther battling through a pack of boars on a cactus-filled prairie, Ukiah snarled and clawed through traffic, hurriedly circling the block until he pulled in front of The Mason Turner Agency.

Tapping his fingers on the steering wheel with the impatience of an expectant father, Ukiah frantically asked, "What time is it?"

"12:02."

"Damn. I hope we didn't blow it."

As cars, taxis, buses, and trucks flew by my passenger side window, we sat with our emergency lights blinking, waiting for Miss Ewen to make her appearance.

During this excruciatingly suspenseful hiatus, Ukiah took the wrinkled magazine photo from his pocket and held it in the air near his steering wheel.

"Chris, look at this picture," he told me. "If you see anyone that looks even remotely like Jennifer, point her out immediately."

So we waited ... waited as businessmen carrying briefcases exited the building, along with high-heeled women, bearded senior citizens, people with large noses and small noses, bald men, made-up ladies wearing the latest metropolitan fashions, and a young man (possibly an aspiring author), who was hunched over and hobbling as if he had just finished riding a horse. But nowhere, not high or low, left or right, did we see anyone resembling Jennifer Ewen.

As this waiting game continued, I broke the silence by asking, "Ukiah, why did you say Vincent Dagger when the receptionist asked for your name?"

Keeping his gaze fixed on the doorway, he said, "I figured one reason the publishers and agents were overlooking me was because of my name."

"Ukiah Rhymes?"

"Yeah, I mean, it's adequate, but I needed a name with some punch - a name like Vincent Dagger." He paused a moment, peered intently through the crowd, then continued, "I also thought of another marketing angle to get the public's attention. I'll buy advertising space in *The New York Times Book Review*."

"An ad?" I commented. "What will it say?"

Eyes darting like a coyote, Ukiah told me, "First, I'll have an outline of mid-town Manhattan, with skyscrapers reaching to the sky. Beside them, standing at the same height, will be the profile of a longhaired man supposed to be me. The caption above this picture - printed in boldface, capital red letters - will say:

'VINCENT DAGGER IS COMING'

Finally, walking along the streets will be a group of pedestrians, each carrying umbrellas above their heads. Get it? Vincent Dagger is COMING, and they're shielding themselves from the shower! It'd be a riot."

"You're always thinking, huh, Ukiah?" I laughed.

"Chris, look!" Ukiah yelled. "It's her!"

Emerging from the doorway was a petite, dark-haired woman with pronounced cheekbones, languid eyes, and slender, pursed lips. I quickly looked at the picture, then again at her, and imagined an additional thirty years.

"Y'know, it could be Jennifer," I gasped excitedly. "But it doesn't look like she's aged more than ten years. What are we going to do?"

"Just keep watching. Don't let her out of your sight," Ukiah insisted, leaning forward against the steering wheel, literally only yards away from her. "No matter what she does, we can't lose sight of her."

The woman stood motionless for a moment, then moved toward the curb, where she flagged a taxi.

"Okay, baby, I'm right behind you. Taxicab number 888. Chris, hang on tight. I'll run every stoplight, bowl over pedestrians, and ram smack dab into a bus if it means keeping a bead on Jennifer. It's now or never, so don't let 'er outta your sight."

Pulling directly behind the checkered yellow car, Ukiah continued his rambling monologue, all the while clutching the steering wheel between his white knuckled hands.

"So, the infamous Jennifer Ewen zips around the city in a taxi. I'm glad she didn't pick the subway. That would have been disastrous. Did you see her, Chris? Not bad looking for a woman in her fifties. Maybe I'll get a chance to score with her! Where are we goin', honey? I see, into the bowels of the city. Hey look, over there - CBGB's - the most famous punk club in the world. I would've loved to have seen some of those shows in the late 70's. Joan Jett even played there once with 'The Runaways.' (pause) "I wonder where she's going? If that cab stops and Jennifer hops out, I might have have to follow on foot, so Chris, get behind the wheel quick and stay on our trail. Okay darling, nice n' easy. No drastic turns. It looks like we got lucky. That taxi driver ain't darting around like a fucking jackrabbit. Where are we going, baby? Lemme know. Hmmmm, over to Saint Mark's Place. That's interesting. Let's see, there's Washington Square Park. This's so weird."

"What?" I asked as we trailed the taxi.

"When Japhy and me come to Manhattan every summer, we hang out in this exact neighborhood. There's Subterranean Records ... and over there is Bleecker Bob's. If ya cruised down that street ya'd find See Hear, the coolest magazine store ever. Then along one o' those roads is Generations Records, and this other punk record store. Plus ... where was it? I think at 7th & 2nd, or 7th & 3rd, there's this fry joint that cooks the best burgers in town. Right down the street there's also a little breakfast cafe that's real cool. I love this part of the city. I wonder where she's going? Okay, outta Saint Mark's Place. Wow, don't tell me she lives in The Village?"

"The Village? What's that?" I asked, hanging on dearly as Ukiah zipped between cars, staying on the taxi's trail.

"Greenwich Village. It's where the hippies hung out in the 60's. Y'know, peace n' love, flower power, all that crap. Who would imagine that one of the most influential literary agents in the city lives in The Village? It's mind-boggling. ... That hack is starting to pick up the pace a bit. Hey, he's starting to drive like me. I don't like when people drive like me. I wonder if Jenny knows we're on her trail?"

Ukiah dodged left, then right, barely avoiding a tractor-trailer that abruptly stopped.

He then uttered the strangest words I'd ever heard come from his mouth. While looking directly ahead, he said, "In all honesty, I don't even hate Jennifer."

"You don't?" I asked with amazement. "Then why are we even following her?"

"Don't get me wrong. I still might have to murder her, but I have a feeling that meeting this woman will somehow lead to my publication."

"You can't be serious," I gasped, unable to believe my ears. "You're essentially stalking a literary agent - planning to set her on fire, murder her, or snatch her from the street. I'm sure when we finally meet Miss Ewen, she won't welcome us with open arms."

"You're probably right, but I feel excited ... I can't explain the sensation. But here I am, in the middle of Manhattan, tracking a literary agent who I've been pursuing for the past year. Last night, inexplicably, my son was taken from me. It seems like destiny has drawn me to this place. Look around. The pieces have fallen into their proper order. Japhy's death pushed me toward Jennifer Ewen. Why? Why has this woman, who lives in the same neighborhood Japhy and me visit every summer, exerted such influence over me? She's the one who blackballed me within the industry. But for some reason, my rage has turned to anticipation. I can't wait to meet Miss Ewen, to find out what makes her tick, and to see how she reacts when the object of her torment finally confronts her. This's it, Chris! We've all been chosen to be at this precise place at this precise moment in time. I'll finally meet Miss Jennifer Ewen, whoever she is."

The taxi suddenly flicked on its right turn signal, veered onto a residential street, then hit its four-way flashers.

"Look, they're pulling over next door to that flower shop. Jenny must live in that apartment building. Holy shit. Keep an eye on what entrance she uses."

While Ukiah parked behind a billboard, we watched as Jennifer paid the driver, then stepped from her cab. Wearing a knee-length black leather jacket fastened at the waist by a loose black belt, Jennifer scanned her surroundings, then ducked inside a doorway as her tangled locks furled in the wind.

Tapping the steering wheel with each hand, Ukiah said proudly, "All right, here we go."

"Here we go? What are we going to do?" I asked.

"In all honesty," Ukiah laughed, "I don't know."

"You don't know? How can that be?" I demanded.

"I haven't thought anything through beyond this point," Ukiah said whimsically. "From here on out, we wing it and see where the chips fall. These are the only things I brought along."

Ukiah pulled his pistol from a hidden coat pocket, along with two black masks.

"See, I made you an Atropos mask," he said while pulling my Gemini into a parking lot. "That way, we can hide our identities."

The notion that I, a mature adult, would be wearing a mask was so bizarre that, if the circumstances weren't so serious, I would have laughed. But charges such as breaking and entering, conspiracy, rape, and murder hung over our heads. With every passing second, Ukiah's plan drew us closer to doom.

"The way I see it, we'll leave the car unlocked in case we have to make a quick getaway." As we stepped outside the Gemini, Ukiah continued, "Once we enter her building, follow me. And remember, don't make any brash decisions unless our backs are against the wall. It shouldn't be hard to subdue a woman."

With those prophetic words ringing in my ears, I followed Ukiah toward Jennifer's building, a sign on the lawn reading, "Hamettan Plaza". But after walking through the door, we faced our first stumbling block. Hamettan Apartments was a security building where visitors were only allowed to enter after being buzzed in by a tenant.

"Now what are we going to do?" I whispered as an elderly couple strolled past on a sidewalk outside the door.

Ukiah stepped toward a board that listed the name of each renter.

"Let's see. Ah ha. There she is. Jennifer Ewen. Apartment 3-D."

Impulsively, without making a plan, Ukiah pressed the button beside Jennifer's name.

"Ukiah! What are you going to say?"

He shrugged his shoulders.

"Yes, who is it?" a voice blurted from the miniature speaker.

"What are you going to tell her?" I asked nervously, my words rapid and tense.

"I don't know," Ukiah replied urgently.

"Quick! Think of something," I told him.

"Hello? Is anyone there?" the voice asked impatiently.

Ukiah pushed a white button, then said, "Flower delivery."

"Flower delivery?" I asked.

"Flower delivery?" the voice asked suspiciously. "From who?"

"She doesn't believe you, Ukiah. Think of something else."

"What else?" he asked frantically.

"I don't know."

"Hello. Who are the flowers from?" the voice asked again.

"Quick, answer, or she'll call the cops."

"But I don't know anyone in New York."

"Then make up a name ... any name."

"Hello ... who are the flowers from?" the voice asked yet again.

"Ukiah, say something!"

"Yes, ma'am, they're from Philip Prince."

"Philip Prince?" I blurted.

"Philip Prince?" the voice asked. "Are you sure?"

"She doesn't believe you, Ukiah. Tell her a different name," I urged.

"I'm sure, Miss Ewen. It says so right here on the card."

"Well, wasn't that sweet of him. I'll buzz you in."

"She believed you!" I gasped with excitement. "Maybe she knows Philip Prince."

"Who knows, but we're in," Ukiah smiled as a buzzer opened the magnetic lock.

After rushing through the door and scurrying down a hallway, Ukiah reached into his coat pocket and pulled out both black masks.

"Okay, here's the plan," he said. "Once Jennifer opens her door, I'll barge in waving my gun while you search for something to shove in her mouth before she starts screaming. Damn. I should have brought a hanky or something. Are you with me?"

I nodded my head as we neared the sequence of doors beginning with 3 — 3A ... 3B ... 3C ... I felt a lump in my throat as ... wait a second. Instead of being closed, door 3D was ajar, welcoming our intrusion.

"Okay, good. This'll keep us from drawing attention to ourselves," Ukiah whispered. "Now put your hood on. Ready? On three — one - two - three!"

Wearing a black hood and holding his pistol overhead, Ukiah burst into Jennifer's apartment, then abruptly stopped when finding her seated on a couch, legs propped on an end table, pointing a revolver three times the size of his directly at our heads.

"Hello, Atropos. It looks like you forgot my roses," Jennifer said slyly. "My gun's already cocked and aimed. I'd drop yours if I were you."

"Wait a minute, lady," Ukiah snapped, frozen in his shoes.

"No, Atropos, or should I call you Vincent Dagger? I'd say you should wait a minute. Y'see, all I need to do is punch the final 1 of this 911 number, and the cops'll be here in two minutes. Now drop it!" she demanded forcefully.

"Shit!" Ukiah cursed as he set his pistol on an endtable, then stood open mouthed, unable to speak.

Jennifer, wearing a low-cut black dress slit up one side and hiked above her knees, rose from the couch and told us both to sit down ... all the while aiming the barrel of her gun at our heads.

After we sat at opposite ends of a purple couch, Miss Ewen, her dark hair not showing a trace of gray, laughed playfully.

"I always thought the Atropos routine was kind of amusing ... but Vincent Dagger? Myra told me all about it. That name reminds me of a B-grade actor from a 1940's horror film. You can do better than that."

Digging his fingernails into the couch's arm, Ukiah, still wearing his hood, as did I, snarled, "Lady, I don't think you know who you're messin' with. I almost killed that asshole Philip Prince."

"I know," Jennifer laughed. "Don't you recognize me? I'm the one who walked in while you were strangling him."

"Shit! I knew I'd seen you before," Ukiah said rapidly. "You're the one who barged into his dressing room."

"Yes, it was 'lil 'ol me," Jenny laughed daintily, executing a curtsy.

"You still don't know who you're dealing with. I'm a ......"

Before letting him finish his sentence, Jennifer interrupted, "You're what? Let's see. Your name is Ukiah Rhymes. You're 37 years old. You live in Latera Heights, and you've written 18 books which weigh a total of 57 pounds."

I sat in amazed silence, as did Ukiah, who couldn't form a response.

"Ukiah, you can take off that silly hood," Jennifer told him. "I'd like to get a look at you."

After doing as she said, Ukiah mumbled, "How'd you know my name? I guess you plan on calling the cops?"

Still wielding her weapon, Miss Ewen spoke softly, extending her left hand.

"Come here, Ukiah. I want to show you something. And tell your friend to take off that silly hood. It makes me nervous."

"Chris, ditch the get-up," Ukiah demanded. "She already knows everything. I don't know how, but she does."

As I sheepishly pulled the hood from my head, Ukiah rose and held Jennifer's hand, following her to a mirror that hung from a wall.

As Ukiah stood before the looking glass, staring at his reflection while removing his jacket, Jennifer moved closer, putting her face beside his.

"Ukiah, I've been waiting for you," the woman said softly.

Not able to understand her message, Ukiah said, "I don't know what you're getting at ...."

"Look," she demanded urgently. "Look at us. What do you see?"

"I don't know ....."

"Yes you do. Look!"

Ukiah gazed intently into the mirror ... deeper ... nearly through their reflections.

"What do you see?" she repeated.

Shaking his head, Ukiah turned to the literary agent and said, "No ... it can't be?"

"Look, Ukiah. You can see it, can't you?"

Frustrated, Ukiah blurted, "I don't see anything, lady!"

"Ukiah, your face is mine, and mine is yours."

"No they're not. You must be crazy."

"Baby, look at your nose, and then mine ... how about the eyes?"

Jennifer ran her red painted fingernails along Ukiah's cheek, then toward his parted mouth.

"Look at my lips, and then yours. Your mouth is mine, and mine is yours. When my eyes peer into yours, it's as if they're seeing their own reflection. We don't even need a mirror."

"No, it can't be!"

"Ukiah, it is," Jennifer exclaimed, tears running along her cheeks. "Thirty seven years ago I had a child, then abandoned him on the hospital steps. Ukiah, sweet baby, you're that child. I'm your mother!"

Reeling backward, then stumbling clumsily, Ukiah roared, "You're not my mother! You're nothing but a lousy literary agent who blackballed me within the industry because I'm a threat to the status quo. You're not my mother. You could never be my mother!"

Sobbing uncontrollably, Jennifer inched toward Ukiah, crying, "Baby, I'm so sorry. I could never apologize enough for what I've done to you. The thought of abandoning you has haunted me every second of every day since I walked down those steps. I know you might never forgive me, but please try ... try to find a place in your heart for me. I love you so much. I truly do. I miss you, baby. Please take me back."

Unable to keep standing, Ukiah plopped onto a reclining chair, his eyes characterized by the same glassy stare he had last night when hearing that his son had been killed.

"Mom, why'd you do it?" he asked, moisture welling in his eyes. "And who's my father?"

"Baby, my actions were inexcusable," Jennifer bawled, sitting on the arm of Ukiah's chair. "I admit it. But I've changed. I've discovered The Word. My Muse talks to me every day."

"Damnit, who's my father!?"

"Baby, you don't want to know." Jennifer then noticed the bloody bandage on Ukiah's arm, asking, "Sweety, what happened?"

"Nothing. It was an accident. Now tell me the truth! Do you know what it was like growing up without parents? I've written an entire book about it, if you could ever find time in your busy schedule to read it," Ukiah sniffed. "Do you know what that book is called? Huh, do you?"

Jennifer cried into her hands.

"It's called *Blank Line*. And do you know why I called it that?"

"No, baby, I don't."

"Because at the hospital where I was born, do you know what the nurses typed on the dotted line of my birth certificate where it read <u>NAME</u>? They typed BLANK LINE. That was the fucking name I was born with - Blank Line! You abandoned me, Mom ... why? Now tell me who my father is!"

With a torrent of tears flooding from her bloodshot eyes, Jennifer bawled, "Baby, your father is Philip Prince ...."

37

In little more than half a day, Ukiah's already-frazzled world had been disrupted to the point of utter chaos. Not only did Japhy's death steal his last grasp at love, but the following day he discovered the identity of both parents - each targets of separate murder plots - the same parents who abandoned him at birth without trying to reveal their identities or initiate a reconciliation. He now sat on a couch in his mother's living room, paralyzed by shock when hearing that Philip Prince, his literary nemesis, was his father.

The atmosphere in this parlor, which flourished with shrubs, greenery, houseplants and flowers, felt icier and more surreal than a wax museum. While Jennifer excused herself to freshen up in the bathroom, her face drenched by tears, remorse, and guilt, Ukiah leaned against a throw pillow, his unblinking eyes seeing, but not registering. As for myself, the tension permeating this room caused such discomfort that all I could hear was a hollow ringing in my ears. Nothing moved, silence persisted, gazes were fixed and lifeless, while time didn't seem to exist. The living room was so far removed from normal life that I was afraid we'd be permanently trapped inside this bubble with no possibility of escape.

The scene became a bit more normal as Jennifer emerged from a distant room carrying a tray of sandwiches.

"You're probably famished," she said tenderly, setting her silver platter on a mahogany endtable.

Although none of us moved toward the tray, the preparations did serve as an icebreaker.

Not mincing words, Ukiah began, "Mom, of all the men on this planet, why Philip Prince? He's such an asshole. You must know that. Why him? How did it happen?"

Sitting beside Ukiah, her slender features and feminine mannerisms quite noticeable, Jennifer explained, "Baby, I don't know where to begin." Her unwrinkled face appeared youthful, yet pained. "In a nutshell, during childhood, my mother suffered from a horrible affliction that caused her to commit suicide. I mourned for years, but by the time I entered college, it felt as if the entire world were mine. At Latera

University, I met Philip Prince ... then a struggling, unpublished author. One evening, near The Latera Shrine ... Oh darling, he raped and impregnated me."

Leaping to his feet, Ukiah yelled, "I knew that creep was rotten to the bone. Not only am I a bastard, but I'm also the by-product of rape."

"Sweety, after seeing my mother suffer all those years, the concept of parenthood ove ⚬ helmed me. I know this doesn't excuse my actions, but I've literally been dying for the past three and a half decades ... so consumed by The Sickness that I've barely been able to function."

"You expect me to believe that cock-and-bull story?" Ukiah roared, pacing about the room. "You're a literary agent at the most prestigious agency in America. Yeah, it really looks like you've wallowed in misery," he concluded sarcastically.

Visibly hurt by this assessment, Jennifer sniffed sadly, then said, "Honey, do you want to hear the truth about my position at Mason Turner?"

Ukiah turned toward a hanging spider plant, pretending to smell it.

"Baby, after Philip found out about my pregnancy, and how I refused to get an abortion, he freaked out, refusing to take responsibility for the child. Shortly thereafter, his first science fiction novel, *Spacek*, was accepted by Mason Turner."

"I know the story, Mom. It was about an insecure, telepathic alien girl. At least the movie impressed me, unlike the novel itself, which was shitty like all his other writing."

Unaffected by Ukiah's comment, Jennifer continued, "Anyway, from that day forward, Philip's been the hottest author around. How do you think I got such a cushy job at Mason Turner? Philip arranged it." Jennifer stopped for a moment, then stressed dramatically, "Ukiah, during my thirty-year tenure at the agency, I haven't discovered a single writer! Not one. I've been stuck in a back office, encouraged to stagnate so that I'd keep quiet about you. We couldn't let the public learn that the esteemed Philip Prince was a rapist who abandoned his child. One time, during an argument, I even threatened to expose him, but Philip told Old Man Turner to buy my silence with a raise. Baby, for the past three decades, my life's been nothing but a downward spiral of wasted talent."

Touched, Ukiah turned to his mother, saying, "That explains why, after researching you, I couldn't connect a single author to you. Mom, was it worth the price you had to pay?"

"No, baby, it hasn't been a wise decision ... until today. I look at you now, after reading your letters, and am so pleased with your development. But instead of letting your resentment devour you, think about one thing. How did you become who you are? Who defined your identity? Allow me to answer. In terms of nurturing, Philip and I had no impact whatsoever on your development. You truly became your own person in that regard. But sweety, look in the mirror. You're handsome, confident, and from all appearances, a literary force to be reckoned with. How do you explain this phenomenon? Was it an accident? Of course not. Philip Prince may write substandard prose, but he is dedicated, and a master at telling stories. With his natural abilities and my literary talents, you were gifted with sheer genius. It's all in the genes, honey. Never forget, genetics is destiny."

Ukiah's face brightened with realization as if a hidden secret had been exposed.

"It does make sense," he replied. "Every piece now fits into the puzzle. I always wondered why I was bestowed with these talents. Now everything is clear. Nothing happens due to randomness or chance. Everything has to be in its proper order." Ukiah paused, collected his thoughts, then asked, "Mom, did you mention your own literary talents? Do you write, too?"

Jennifer smiled with a hint of embarrassment, then replied, "I'm certainly not as prolific as you, but yes, I've been exorcising my demons for years."

Intrigued, Ukiah returned to the couch, grabbed a finger sandwich from the silver tray, took a bite, then said, "Has anything ever been published? Knowing Philip Prince, you should be a shoe-in."

Before answering this question, Jennifer turned to me, saying, "Chris, eat ... eat. You must be starving." She then faced Ukiah and began, "Y'know, that's the weirdest part about our relationship. He gave me this position and offered money if I ever needed any, but adamantly refused to read, publish, or even acknowledge my literary output. I could never understand why."

Increasingly interested, Ukiah asked, "I hate to be forward, but do you have a sample of your writing that I could read? I need to figure something out."

Unnerved, Jennifer replied, "I suppose ... if that's what you'd like."

"I wouldn't ask if it weren't so important," he told her.

"Okay, wait a second. I'll dig out my latest project," she answered, leaving the room.

Less than a minute later, Miss Ewen returned with a stack of typed pages.

"Here," she said obligingly, "I'm not sure if it's any good or not. No one's ever read my material except me."

Ukiah hurriedly grabbed the white sheets of paper, scanned the first few pages, then exclaimed, "It's amazing! Your writing style is almost identical to mine. You scribble three-dot Flash just like me ... complete with dashes, hyphens, and ... and everything."

Puzzled, Jennifer asked, "Flash? What's that?"

Excited, Ukiah told her, "Come here. Look. Do you see this string of words attached by dots and assorted punctuation? I call it Flash."

"Honey, I still don't understand," Jennifer admitted.

"Try to imagine a tattoo parlor," Ukiah began. "Every wall is lined with designs called Flash. The tattoo artist could have hearts, serpents, anchors, an Indian feather, and a blazing sun all positioned next to each other. Can you see how I formed an image in your mind with this description? Picture it like this," Ukiah said, grabbing a pen from the table and scribbling:

hearts ... serpents ... anchors ... an Indian feather ... blazing sun ...

"Flash is a technique where the regular grammatical guidelines are eased, or eliminated all together, so that a set of images can more fully reflect the world around us ... just like the designs on a tattoo artists wall."

As Jennifer smiled proudly, Ukiah proclaimed, "I'll be damned. You're a Solipsist, just like me. That's why S.W.A.N. won't publish you!"

"Solipsist? S.W.A.N.? What are you talking about, Ukiah?"

At the mention of these words, I smiled inside, pleased that I would finally be able to gauge someone else's reaction to these concepts.

In his prime, Ukiah kept talking without delay.

"Solipsism is a title I came up with to describe my writing style."

"But what is it?" Jennifer demanded, the literary agent in her emerging.

Scratching his head to think of the proper words, Ukiah explained, "Solipsism, in simplest terms, is Narcissistic Literature ... the transference of one's Creative Self through their Art. I can tell from reading this story that you're conveying the essence of your life — sickness ... guilt ... frustration and loss. That's why S.W.A.N. won't accept these stories. You've discovered The Word ... something they want to monopolize."

I almost laughed out loud as Jennifer's eyes darted with confusion - her reaction similar to mine when first hearing these concepts.

"Ukiah, I don't understand a word you're saying," she told him, shaking her head. "First, who is S.W.A.N.?"

Focused and intense, Ukiah admitted, "I could talk about them until tomorrow, but essentially, S.W.A.N. - the Single Word Authorial Nation, and its sister group O.W.L. - One Word Literature - are secret cabals whose primary goal is to control the mind of every reader until we devolve into little more than illiterate cavemen. By instituting this plan, which is already in progress, they'll get complete control of The Word, which is language's most fundamental component."

Rather than writing her son off as a crackpot, as I had expected, Jennifer showed a keen interest by asking, "How will this scheme be implemented?"

Animated and alive with excitement, Ukiah sat on the edge of his seat, explaining, "By controlling language, S.W.A.N. has politicized, mangled, confused, and perverted The Word to such an extent that nobody says what they really mean any more. Listen to television newscasters, or read a magazine like *Newsweek*. Not only are these people diverting our attention away from their ultimate plan, they're brainwashing us in the process."

"Brainwashing? How?" Jennifer asked, a troubled look on her face.

"Philip Prince accomplished this feat in the pages of his last novel, *Prince Of The Earth*. Y'see, he inserted subliminal, implant-like word devices in the body of his prose which caused readers to react in bizarre ways."

"Do you mean like 'Prince's Minions'?" Jennifer inquired.

"Exactly! Who in their right mind would dress like an Owl and parade around town every Tuesday night? No one, unless their brain had been infiltrated by ideas that caused them to react in ways contrary to their nature."

"Oh baby," Jennifer fretted, a troubled look causing her face to go white. "Most people would consider you insane, but I can't quit thinking of those two groups you mentioned - S.W.A.N. and O.W.L. Both were in *Prince Of The Earth*, weren't they?"

"Yes, you see! This's how they communicate their symbols and ideas to one another."

"You're starting to scare me," she admitted, moving closer to her son. "What are their ultimate goals?"

Absorbed by this discussion, Ukiah told her, "Since the inception of Man's artistic sensibilities, his primary goal has been to emulate his creative inspiration ... to become a force like that who made him. So, to become like The Original Artist, we have to become Creators. Look at the world and universe around us ... plus all the people in it. What are we the products of? A Creator! So, we also need to Create! But as time passed, Man somehow lost touch with his creative spirit, choosing to dawdle along a worn out path like a robotic automaton. Our creative inspiration - The Muse - has been lost, replaced by more immediate trappings of the modern world. That, in a nutshell, is S.W.A.N.'s true aim - to eliminate Romlocon, The Muse, and any memory of her so that Bubo Virginianus - The Great Horned Owl - can arrive to exert total control over our language ... reducing The Word to a mythical, long-forgotten image."

Frantic, Jennifer demanded, "What did you call The Great Horned Owl?"

"Bubo Virginianus," Ukiah instantly shot back.

"And who, exactly, are these people who control S.W.A.N.?" she asked impulsively.

Wavering for the first time, Ukiah replied, "I know Philip Prince is involved, along with Mason Turner ... but as for the other members, or an ultimate Architect, I can't give you an answer."

Radiating with intensity, her burning eyes mirroring Ukiah's, Jennifer hastily replied, "I might be able to fit the final piece to your puzzle."

"You can? How?" Ukiah asked excitedly.

"I hate to admit it," she said with embarrassment, "but until recently, I've kept up a relationship with Philip Prince, allowing him to sexually denigrate me. Luckily, since discovering my Muse, I've ended that pathetic chapter of my life. Anyway, when Philip used to visit, he'd call a man named Richard Evadoo ..."

"Who's he?" Ukiah interrupted.

"I'd only met him once at a Mason Turner board meeting, but he's a shadowy, extremely powerful figure who makes Old Man Turner shake in his boots. At this meeting, Evadoo spoke of his visions for the future of literature ... how it should all fall under one umbrella. But, being that my sickness so monopolized every waking thought, I couldn't focus much attention on the actual content of his presentation."

"How does Evadoo relate to S.W.A.N.?" Ukiah asked with bated anticipation.

"I'm getting to that. Whenever Philip worked on his novel at my apartment, he'd phone Evadoo and ask him about plot development and philosophy. To make a long story short, instead of calling him Richard, or Mister Evadoo, Philip referred to this man as Bubo!"

"Holy Shit!" Ukiah roared. "Evadoo's the key! He's the one calling the shots for S.W.A.N.! Damn. Now every piece has fallen into place. Evadoo's vision is to destroy the true Words provided by Romlocon so that the book-buying public is never allowed to re-create themselves and advance to a more knowledgeable level."

Burning with energy, Jennifer hugged her son dearly, then confessed, "I've worked in this business for three decades, and never knew how corrupt it was."

"Mom, it's been scaring the hell out of me for years. That's why I hated you. I thought you were one of them ... one of the one's who refused to publish me because I was onto your trail. Yeah, a dark, sinister underworld lurks around us, but S.W.A.N. has so conditioned the reading public to ignore the warning signals that most can't see the true aim of these organizations."

"How do they do it?" Jenny asked somberly.

"By diverting the reader's attention. Y'see, instead of serving Romlocon through hard work, dedication, devotion, and artistic creation, we're told through various book reviews and critical studies to be happy ... to smile and be content with the way things are. Romlocon has been replaced by a slew of gurus and false literary movements that draw us away from the true path of expression. And the worst part is, we've all been duped. The game is over."

As Ukiah and Jennifer sat dejectedly on her sofa, ruminating over their depressing discovery, I finally saw that Ukiah had been right all along. Rather than getting satisfaction from this insight, though, I realized that the literacy we had strived so long to develop would soon be nothing but a distant memory ... a future right granted only to the vindictive, literary elitists.

Outraged, I spoke for the first time since entering Miss Ewen's apartment, demanding, "All right! You two figured everything out. Now what are you going to do about it? Knowledge is useless unless it's acted upon to make things better."

Ukiah sat silently for a moment, then exclaimed as the fire returned to his eyes. "Y'know, Chris's right. We can't lie down and let S.W.A.N. turn us into idiotic machines that march to their orders. We need to wake the reading public from their deep sleep and show them the lies being perpetrated by these bastards."

"But how, Ukiah?" Jenny pleaded. "If the publishers won't print your books, how can we inform the public?"

Oozing with enthusiasm, Ukiah said, "I have a plan." He then turned to his mother and asked, "Does Philip know where you are right now?"

"Not that I'm aware of," she replied. "Why?"

"And he has no idea that I'm his son, is that correct?"

"Of course not."

"Great! Here's what we'll do. Mom, when everything is finalized, I need you to call Philip on the phone ... ... and be in a real panic. Tell him that Atropos has kidnapped you."

"Kidnapped me? I don't follow," she answered with a tinge of suspicion.

"Wait until you hear the whole plan. First, you'll have to stage the greatest performance of your life - freaking out while telling Prince that Atropos is holding a gun to your head and plans on taking you to Latera Heights."

"Ukiah, this's too weird," she responded. "I can't fathom your ..."

"You will, trust me. After you finish telling him the details, begin protesting, like 'Hey, wait a minute, I'm not done ...' I'll immediately take the phone from you and growl into the receiver - 'I'm killing her first, then you second, fucker.' With this seed planted in his mind, I'll hang up."

"Baby, what is this plan supposed to accomplish?" Jennifer asked.

"Can't you see? We'll cruise back to Chris's house in Latera Heights while Philip, out of his mind with fear, will instantly call the authorities, who'll in turn leak their story to the press. By the time we get to Latera Heights sometime tonight, we'll get a good night's sleep and be ready for tomorrow's activities. As we do so, the news organizations will scramble to send cameramen and reporters to our town. They won't know exactly where to send them, but at least they'll be prepared. So, when we get up Tuesday morning and call the cops, filling them in on the 'Atropos Kidnaps Literary Agent' scoop, they'll flock to our front yard."

"Okay. I see the picture so far," Jennifer replied. "But then what? All the cops need to do is storm Chris's house and arrest you. I don't see the point to this plan."

"That's because I haven't laid down my trump card," Ukiah declared, seizing the moment. "After calling the cops, we'll once again phone Philip in New York. If he knows I'm in Latera, it's the last place he'll want to be. Anyway, I'll sneer into the receiver - 'Hey asshole, I heard about your rapist activities beneath The Latera Shrine, and how you abandoned your illegitimate child. I'm ready to invite one of these reporters into my house to broadcast your story LIVE for the whole world to hear, along with a few other juicy tidbits.' You'll then grab the phone and frantically scream, 'I'm sorry, Philip, but Atropos tortured me. He forced the confession ....' Now do you follow? The whole routine will be choreographed like a soap opera, all to force Philip into playing his trump card."

"Which is?" Jennifer panted nervously.

"I'll tell him we intend to blow his cover unless he has Richard Evadoo call us. If he reacts as I suspect, he'll have Evadoo on the horn in five minutes."

"And then what do we do?" she asked.

"I'll tell Evadoo I want fifteen minutes of LIVE network coverage to speak my peace, or else I'll kill the literary agent and spill the beans on Philip Prince to every tabloid in the country. This way, he'll at least be able to partially control the setting." Ukiah paused for a split second, then concluded, "There's only one thing I'm not sure of."

"What's that?" Jennifer asked.

"How will I know it's Evadoo on the phone? Being that I've never spoken with him, I won't be able to tell whether it's him or an impostor."

Excitedly, Jennifer blurted, "I can help. Do you remember that meeting I told you about? I'll never forget that man's voice."

"What was it like? This's crucial to the plan."

"Whenever Evadoo said a word ending in 'S,' he drew it out and extended it, like a hissing snake. So, if he said Boss, it'd sound like Bosssssss. The sound was so distinguishable it could never be copied."

"Terrific!" Ukiah cheered. "So, what do ya think? Is it a go?"

"I'm in," his mother cheered, clapping her hands.

Ukiah then looked at me.

"Well, Chris, whatta ya say?"

I rose from the sofa, gathered every ounce of courage, then said, "Let's show the world what we're made of!"

The three of us hugged, laughed with nervous energy, then collected our belongings and began implementing the plan.

38

The three of us crowded into my Gemini, then began another journey. With Ukiah, there was always movement - he basked in the concept of moving from one location to another, regardless of where those points were. So, after placing his wooden crate filled with manuscripts in the backseat and covering the kitten odor with air freshener, I drove while Ukiah rode shotgun and Jennifer sat between us. New York City soon faded in the rear view mirror as my passengers caught up on their lives - Ukiah describing Gramma Moo's farm, his various foster families, a drug-induced youth that stretched into an alcoholic adulthood ... his marriage and divorce ... the life, joys, and tragic death of his son Japhy ... the subject matter of his novels, and the frustrations he faced with the publishing industry. In return, Jennifer elaborated on her mother's condition ... her college days and eventual pregnancy ... the years of sickness, being brutalized by Philip Prince, and her stagnation at The Mason Turner Agency.

While they caught up on their lives, I thought about the first step in implementing Ukiah's plan - the staged phone call to Philip Prince. After Jennifer found the author's number in a message book that had two identical fish on its cover, she dialed his number, then talked frantically into the receiver.

"Philip, this is Jennifer..." (pause)

"I'm here at home ..." (pause)

"Atropos, that crazy man who attacked you, broke into my apartment and plans on kidnapping me ..." (pause)

"Yes, right now! He's holding a gun to my head ..." (pause)

"He's going to take me back to Latera Heights ..." (pause)

"Do something! Call the cops! He's going to kill me ....!" (pause)

Using a technique called Method Acting, Ukiah grabbed the phone from his mother, then growled, "Listen, fucker. First I'm killing the broad, then I'm gunning for you. Watch out!"

After slamming the receiver down, the three of us ran out the door before Prince could notify the authorities. As I raced from the parking lot, I felt satisfied with our performance, laughing heartily as we dashed through The Village.

We eventually reached Latera Heights late Monday evening, stopping along the way at a convenience store to buy bacon, eggs, and juice for breakfast the next morning. While Ukiah and Jennifer waited inside the Gemini, I entered the market, my attention drawn to a stark black headline that leaped from the front page of a newspaper:

Five teenagers killed in automobile accident;
Sixth in critical condition

Incapacitated by this horrific reminder, I stood frozen for a minute, staring at a color photograph of the twisted wreckage - complete with fluids of unknown origin streaming down the highway. As I reminisced about the wonderful times spent with Japhy, I found it hard to believe that these five innocent beings – all who had their entire lives in front of them - could be so unjustly removed from this planet.

I read the adjoining article, scanning ahead to the following paragraph:

> ... the pick-up truck driver, who crossed the double
> yellow lines and had a blood-alcohol level of .314,
> was uninjured in the collision ...

The ramifications were absurd ... Japhy had to die, while this moronic drunk would be sitting on another bar stool next week after getting a suspended sentence.

> ... a wake for all five victims will be held Wednesday
> evening at The Formalin Funeral Parlor ...

While grabbing a few things from a refrigerated cooler, I pictured Japhy's casket lying beside four others, their blue-lined interiors and colorful bouquets masking the tragic realities of life. As tears welled in my eyes, I wanted to run screaming toward the county jail and strangle the man who caused this disaster ... to rip his eyes out ... claw at his tonsils ... smash a cinder block through his skull ... then squash his body with the front wheels of my car. If he were still alive, I'd cover him with gasoline and set him on fire. How dare he drive a vehicle in that condition. Murderer!

After paying the cashier, I returned to the Gemini, my eyes puffy and moist.

"Chris, what's wrong?" Jennifer asked with concern.

"Yeah, you look terrible," Ukiah added.

"Oh, nothing ... must be allergies," I lied, turning onto Reflection Alley, then parking beside Ukiah's van.

After entering my house, Ukiah immediately called, "Mee-Mew, come here little girl. C'mon."

But after making kissing noises with his mouth, he realized that both the kitten and Nikki were gone. Her disappearance didn't surprise me, but Ukiah seemed troubled by the loss. I knew Nikki was trouble from the start. She was the kind of girl who wreaked havoc with a flurry, then vanished into the wind. After searching through each room, Ukiah gave up hope of finding either party, resigning himself to join Jennifer and me as we sat in my parlor. For security reasons, we decided to spend the night together under one roof, sleeping in separate quarters until daybreak. While I lay in bed listening to crickets chirp outside the window, my mind and body ached from the unrelenting excitement and endless miles. I desperately needed some rest and relaxation. But after all that had happened during the past 24 hours – finding Mee-Mew, a manic rock n' roll show, Nikki's introduction (or intrusion) into our lives, Ukiah's drunkenness, Japhy's horrendous death, and a road trip to New York City where Ukiah discovered the identity of his long lost parents - I wondered how we ever survived. It'd seem that after such a dizzying array of activity, I'd be able to rewind. But as fatigue washed over me, giving way to sleep, I realized that whatever tomorrow held, I'd be worrying about it all night long.

As sunlight filtered through the curtains, I woke to find Ukiah sleeping on a couch in the living room, while his mother slept on a cot in the spare bedroom. After attending to a few matters in the bathroom, I tiptoed through the house toward my kitchen, looking forward to cooking the bacon and eggs I bought the night before. But upon reaching the kitchen, I noticed the five-gallon gasoline can that Ukiah forgot before our trip to New York. Not wanting it around, I lifted the can by a loose metal handle, then lugged it across my kitchen. After opening the door and pushing it open with my foot, I looked across the lawn to see two police cars and a Channel 10 news van sitting at the end of my driveway on Reflection Alley.

Immediately filled with alarm, I slammed the door, dropped the gas can, then raced to the living room.

"Ukiah, quick, wake up! We have trouble," I told him, rustling his shoulders with each hand.

"What ... huh?" he mumbled groggily. "What's going on?"

"There's two police cars and a news crew waiting outside the house on Reflection Alley. They're on to us."

Springing to an upright position, Ukiah tossed aside his blanket, then rolled to the floor, where he crawled toward my picture window.

Peeking through a crack in the curtains, he exclaimed, "Holy fuck! They tracked us down. Shit. How the hell did they find us?"

He slowly retreated from his vantage point, a look of fear settling across his face.

"They're smarter than I gave them credit for being," he moaned blankly. "This whole time I thought we were one step ahead of them. How'd they find us so quickly? I wanted time to feel out our situation before calling Philip Prince. How'd they do it?"

As I paced around the living room, Ukiah rose, stepped toward me, then whispered while placing one finger to his lips. "Where's my mother?"

Getting the hint, I said softly, "Still sleeping in the spare bedroom."

"Did you hear her leave last night? I wonder if she could have double crossed us by calling the cops?"

The notion never occurred to me, so I replayed every possible scenario in my mind until WHAM, it hit me.

"Ukiah," I burst excitedly. "I know how they found us!"

"How?" he immediately responded.

"Do you remember me telling you about that receptionist watching us when we left The Mason Turner Agency?"

"Vaguely."

"Well, while watching us, she scribbled something on a notepad ... probably our license plate number."

"Oh no," Ukiah responded. "I'll bet S.W.A.N. has a few policemen on the payroll. All they had to do was run your number through the computer, and BAM ...."

"That lady was wicked anyway," I added. "It all makes sense. After we left, I'll bet she told Mason Turner that two suspicious characters were asking for Jennifer Ewen ...."

" .... And then Philip called and told them about Jennifer's kidnapping. Shit. I didn't want to give them this much time to form a counter strategy."

My counterpart fell silent, his eyes lost and confused.

"Ukiah, the walls are closing in. We're trapped. Maybe they have snipers back in the woods, or sharpshooters behind the bushes. There's no escape. What are we going to do?"

Before he could answer, Jennifer emerged from her bedroom, shuffling listlessly along the hallway. Wearing nothing but a dress shirt unbuttoned past her tiny breasts, with ringlets of tousled brown hair falling about her face, she appeared before us with the youthful exuberance of a 25-year-old girl who didn't need makeup.

"What's the commotion?" she asked tiredly, rubbing her eyes.

As Jennifer stood beside the couch, her lean, exposed legs begged for attention. Inexplicably, I began sweating and trembling, then had to look away.

Leaping into action, Ukiah rushed toward his mother, then escorted her away from the window and couch.

"What's going on?" she protested, shivering in her skimpy attire.

"There's two police cars and a news van at the end of our driveway," Ukiah explained.

Interrupting him after peeking between the curtains, I said, "You better update that report."

"Update? What do you mean?" Ukiah asked manically.

"Now there's four squad cars, three news vans, and a flock of Owls ..."

"Owls?"

"Of the 'Prince's Minion' variety, plus some spectators cordoned-off behind a yellow police line. I can see spotlights, video cameras, and flashbulbs."

"Where'd they come from?" Jennifer asked timidly. "How did they know we were here?"

Radiating nervous energy, Ukiah told her, "After we left the lobby at Mason Turner and walked to Vengier Avenue, Chris saw a receptionist watching us through a pair of opera glasses. She probably scribbled our license plate number on a sheet of paper, then gave it to someone at S.W.A.N., who had it traced through the police."

Sitting on the couch where Ukiah had slept, then covering herself with his blanket, Jennifer said assuredly, "Myra's S.W.A.N. all the way. She's been infatuated with Philip for ages. She's practically obsessed with him. I'd guarantee she ratted on us."

"The only question now is, what are we going to do?" I asked. "They definitely have the upper hand."

At that moment, the ringing of my telephone made all three of us leap with fright.

"Who could that be?" Ukiah inquired.

"I don't know," I told him. "Maybe it's my boss. I haven't been to work in two days. Should I answer it?"

"Hit the speakerphone button," he said sharply.

After three more rings, I punched the appropriate button, saying, "Hello,"

A terse voice began, "Chris - Officer Idem ... Latera P.D. Put Rhymes on the line."

"It's that asshole Idem," I coughed, filled with apprehension. "He's been out to get me ever since Woody Dewar's mur .... unfortunate death."

Not bothering with details, Ukiah strolled toward the phone, answering, "Yeah Idem, I'm here."

"Rhymes, what's going on in there?" the officer snapped.

"You tell me. Whatta ya know?" Ukiah returned.

"I got a call from The N.Y.P.D. They said you're holding a literary agent ... a Miss Jennifer Ewen ... hostage. Is that true?"

Amped with intensity, Ukiah snarled, "Idem, tell whoever called you from New York that I need to speak with Prince. They'll know what I mean. If he doesn't get a hold of me in twenty minutes, I want you to send in Medina Spiller from the Channel 10 news. Make sure she has a camera. Over and out," he finally said sarcastically.

"Medina Spiller, the weather girl?" Idem asked suspiciously.

"You got it. If my demands aren't met in twenty minutes, I'm killing both hostages - Chris Edwards and Jennifer Ewen - and it'll all be on your head. Later."

Ukiah abruptly hung up the phone, then turned to face us.

Looking uncomfortable, his confidence wavering, Ukiah said softly, "Well, here we go." After wandering aimlessly around the kitchen like of a caged animal, Ukiah asked his mother, "You brought that gun, didn't you?"

"It's in my purse, baby," she replied lovingly.

Ukiah next turned to me. "Do you have any guns or weapons in here?"

Embarrassed, I mumbled, "No ... nothing but kitchen knives."

"Well, go grab a couple and stick 'em in your pocket. And Mom, you better get that cannon. If those bastards decide to barge in, we need to defend ourselves."

As Jennifer, still wrapped in a brown blanket, shuffled toward the back bedroom, I asked Ukiah, "I'm curious. Who is Medina Spiller?"

Suddenly beaming with cheerfulness, Ukiah walked into the living room, then turned on the television set.

"I should have thought of this earlier," he said. "Maybe the local stations are reporting on us. I'll check Channel 10." After flicking through the stations, he returned to my question. "I watch Medina Spiller every morning when I get ready. She's this gorgeously thin weather girl with brown hair ... she got it cut short a few weeks ago ... that is so cute it drives me mad."

As Ukiah spoke, his mother, now dressed in tight blue jeans and a loose tank top that revealed part of her bra, returned to the living room, her revolver dangling from one finger. As she sat on the couch, a male broadcaster segued into the sports segment of their show, reading scores that meant nothing to me.

Ukiah continued, "Medina's a knockout, with a tricky little body, and she has this fiery sense of humor. She's hilarious. One morning, the female anchor mentioned an animal shelter that was giving away free dogs and cats. Along with your pet, then, came a free pedicure. After hearing this news, Medina joked, 'A free pedicure! Okay, I'll be down there this afternoon with my feet in the sink, telling them to paint my nails red!' The female anchor then told her, 'Uh, Medina, the free pedicure is for your pet.' 'Oh well, that's a horse of a different color,' she responded, giggling viciously. She's such a doll. I love how she'll have her head turned sideways, then face the camera and open her eyes real wide and smile. What a turn on. If anyone interviews me, it'll be her."

Then, as if we were on *The Twilight Zone*, the female anchor just mentioned by Ukiah appeared on screen, reporting, "Just in - a young lady named Nicole Arlot recently contacted the Latera Heights Police Department with chilling news concerning the Atropos hostage situation."

Nikki's face appeared on my TV, a microphone near her mouth. With wild-eyed deceit, she spoke frantically to the camera, "He's crazy, I'm telling you."

"Crazy? In what way?" an unseen reporter asked.

"He kidnapped me Sunday night from a club in Kundalini, then forced me to drink alcohol and tried to rape me. That maniac wanted to sacrifice a little kitten, then make me lose my virginity. He's completely out of his mind ... capable of anything."

"That lying bitch!" I cursed. "What is she trying to do?"

Alarmed, Jennifer asked, "Ukiah, who was that young girl?"

"A mistake," he said curtly.

The male anchor suddenly blurted, "Breaking news. We have verified The Latera Lunatic's identity." As Atropos' hooded image appeared on the screen, the announcer continued, "According to police investigations, Atropos is none other than Ukiah Rhymes, aged 37, described as a vagabond and street-level criminal."

As a photo of Ukiah taken from an outdated driver's license appeared on screen, I watched as he paced frantically about the living room.

"How do they know so much?" he asked vacantly, obviously infuriated.

"It's okay, baby ... settle down," his mother said encouragingly.

"Ukiah! Look. There's even more of them out there," I gasped, peeking between the curtains.

"How many?" he snapped.

"At least ten cop cars, plus spotlights everywhere. I even see a couple network news vans."

"Honey, maybe we should surrender," Jenny told him.

Ring ... Ring ...

Ukiah bolted toward the phone, pushed the speaker button, then said, "Hello."

"Listen you son of a bitch ......"

Ukiah immediately hung up the phone by re-pushing the speaker button.

"Baby, what are you doing?" Jennifer squealed. "That was Philip!"

"That bastard isn't going to talk to me like that."

Ring ... Ring ...

Ukiah replayed the scene from a few moments earlier, answering, "Hello."

"If you ever hang up on me again, I'll ....."

Click.

"Ukiah - Stop!" his mother pleaded. "Philip's a dangerous man."

"He needs to learn some respect."

"Baby, I don't think you know who you're dealing with."

The female anchor reappeared on my television screen with a further update.

"It has been brought to our attention that Ukiah Rhymes, The Latera Lunatic, also known as Atropos, is the father of a boy killed in that horrible automobile accident Sunday night in Kundalini County. Our reporter is at the crime scene in Latera heights."

"Yes, Marsha, I'm here on Reflection Alley with Officer Idem from the Latera Police Department. Sir, what details can you add to this unfolding situation?"

Stern faced, Idem responded bitterly, "It looks like Ukiah Rhymes was the direct cause of his son's death."

"The direct cause? Could you elaborate?" the reporter asked with eager disbelief, realizing he had a scoop.

"Yes. Throughout his life, Mister Rhymes continually abandoned his child with such reckless disregard that it eventually lead to Sunday's terrible tragedy. I may be out of line, but Rhymes, in my book, is a coward ... a worthless piece-of-trash father who should be held directly responsible for his son's death. I'd even go so far as to say he should get the electric chair."

"That fucker! I'll kill him!" Ukiah roared. "What the fuck is he talking about?"

With a rabid look on his face, Ukiah stomped about angrily, shoving chairs, kicking walls, mumbling indecipherably, and waving his arms about crazily.

"How dare he say I killed Japhy! I loved that kid more than anything in the world."

Equally enraged, Jennifer rose from the couch and walked toward the telephone.

"Give me the number of the police department," she demanded to no one in particular. "They have no right making those accusations."

As she picked up the receiver, I interceded. "Wait. What if Prince returns our call? We can't tie up the line."

"That's right, Mom ......"

Ring ... Ring ...

Before either of us could react, Jennifer punched the speaker button and cried, "Hurry, Philip, do something! He's planning on killing ...."

The agent turned actress abruptly stopped, a huge smile on her face as she motioned for Ukiah.

"Jennifer, don't worry. I won't let them hurt you," the voice said frantically, obviously belonging to Mister Prince. "Okay, Rhymes, I'll play it your way. What do you want?" he demanded.

Ukiah moved toward the phone and spoke hurriedly. "All right Prince, let's cut through the bullshit. You know that I know everything - how you raped this lady and fathered a child that was abandoned. I'm ready to tell every news organization, gossip sheet, and tabloid television show what a creepy bastard you are."

"I get the picture," Prince muttered. "What do you want from me?"

"I want to speak with Richard Evadoo ... pronto. If I don't get a call in twenty minutes, I'm inviting one of those reporters in with a camera and broadcasting live for the world to see. Do you get the picture?"

Snarling with ferociousness, Prince replied, "I get the picture," then hung up.

"Yes!" Ukiah cheered, overjoyed with the outcome. "I'll bet his fucking head is ready to explode. And do you know the best part? He still doesn't know I'm his son! What a riot. Prince's under the impression that I'm some demented stalker named Atropos. What a howl!"

"Ukiah, sweety, I don't think you should underestimate these men. I've seen how they operate. They didn't reach the top by being pushovers," Jennifer warned.

"Don't worry, Mom ...."

Ring ... Ring ...

"Holy shit! It's Evadoo already," Ukiah bolstered, pushing the speaker button. "Hello."

"Chris, this's your mother. What in God's name is happening inside that crazy house?"

"Get her off the line!" Ukiah demanded.

"Mom, hang up," I snapped, moving toward the phone. "We're expecting an important call."

" ... I saw it on TV. Oh my God. How did you get involved with that rapist crazy man?" she cried hysterically.

"Mom, please hang up ....."

"Your father is probably rolling over in his grave ...."

"Get her off the line, damnit," Ukiah cursed frantically.

"Mom, just watch the TV. I'll call you later."

"I always knew you'd turn out for the worst. Your father was right. We should have burned that super hero cape of yours ...."

After hanging up on my mother, I turned to see the female anchor from Channel 10 interrupting normal programming by declaring, "Late breaking news in The Latera Lunatic hostage case. We have recently received news from an unnamed source in New York City that the primary suspect in this case - Mister Ukiah Rhymes - is also an aspiring author. Our undisclosed source, speaking on information received from an anonymous literary agent, stated that after reading material submitted by Mister Rhymes, concluded that he had the talent of a fourth grader. Repeat - fourth grader. We'll now return to our regularly scheduled programming."

I thought Ukiah's head would spin off his neck as he erupted, "A fourth grader! I have the writing abilities of a fourth grader? Holy fuck! Who told them that shit?"

"Ukiah, settle down," his mother protested.

"Yeah, don't let 'em get to you," I added without success.

"Which one of those bloodsucking fuckers is trying to undermine me? Chris, try to remember the agents I sent material to. I can't even remember their names. Shit, I wish I could look through my files. A fourth grader! How dare they? They're not allowed to badmouth me like that? Mom, aren't there laws against defamation of character?"

"Yes, honey ....."

"Which one do you think did it? Maybe Prince tipped 'em off. But how would he know? What if that bitch Myra told them?"

"She could be the culprit," Jenny interjected quickly.

As these two rambled madly about the latest news update, an insight struck me.

Pumped with adrenaline, I interrupted, "Ukiah, what if the entire report was a ruse?"

"A ruse? What do you mean?"

"Don't ya see? They're trying to get your goat, like that segment on you being responsible for Japhy's death. They figure if you're crazy enough, you'll lose control and mess up."

"Yeah ... yeah, you have a point. S.W.A.N. is cunning enough to pull such a stunt ... and the local news affiliates wouldn't be bright enough to figure out what's going on."

The male news anchor interrupted the *Regis and Kathie Lee Show* to announce, "Latera P.D. plan to investigate a string of recent deaths which may be linked to The Latera Lunatic. Details at noon."

"Now what?" Ukiah burst with exasperation. "Is this a ploy, too?"

Shocked, I remembered Ukiah's involvement (directly or indirectly) in the deaths of Woody Dewar, the high school teacher, Mister Doublet, and my father. With a crafty D.A., and Officer Idem's ability to trump up charges with false evidence, I quickly freaked out, even picturing my own imprisonment.

"This's serious," I blurted, clearly rattled. "With public sentiment so clearly against us, those bastards could railroad us with anything."

"Ukiah, what's this all about?" Jenny cried. "Are you a murderer?"

I envisioned all the men Ukiah tortured while extorting money to cover their gambling debts suddenly turning state's evidence ... the attack on Philip Prince at The Splycer Center ... and now Jennifer's kidnapping.

"Ukiah, we're doomed!" I yelled hysterically.

"Settle down," he demanded. "You two don't have anything to worry about. As far as they're concerned, I kidnapped both of you. You're nothing but victims. I'm the only one facing charges. I'm the culprit. Now c'mon, let's put our heads together. What are we going to do?"

Ring ... Ring ...

"Shit, who is it?" Ukiah snapped. "I can't fucking think ..... Chris, push the speaker button."

Frantic, I stumbled while rushing toward the phone, eventually doing as he told me.

"Who is it?" Ukiah yelled across the room.

"Thissssssss issssssss Richard Evadoo," the high-pitched, lisp-ridden voice answered.

While I pushed the mute button, Jennifer squealed, "It's him! He's hissing his esses."

"Holy shit! We have the head of S.W.A.N. on the line," Ukiah burst triumphantly. "I'm finally going to get my chance to face the world! Damn! Okay Chris, push the speaker button."

"I'm here," Ukiah said confidently.

"And I'm lisssssstening," Evadoo replied evenly.

"Here's the deal," Ukiah demanded. "Either you get a network news crew to set their equipment up inside this house and broadcast live for fifteen minutes, or I'll call in one of those schmuck tabloid reporters and give them an exclusive. At least with the network, you can destroy the tape after it's been broadcast. And don't try any funny stuff, like a fake feed, 'cause we'll be watching our TV. It's either that, or I start killing the hostages. Get it?"

The voice whinnied with high-pitched laughter, its tone so mockingly evil I swore it could have cut through concrete.

"Oh Rhymessssss, you sssssilly boy. Did you actually think I'd fall for thissssss esssscapade?"

Turning ghastly white, Ukiah stammered, "Fall ... fall for ... for what? I'm ser ... serious."

"About what?" Evadoo responded.

"I'll murder 'em. You know I'll do it. I'll kill both Jennifer and Chris."

"Go ahead and kill 'em. Ssssee if I care."

Eyes bulging wide with disbelief, Ukiah snarled, "You don't care? I'll do it. Then this fiasco will be on your head."

"Sssssilly boy," Evadoo chuckled effeminately. "If you kill your hosssssstages, what further ammunition will you posssssesssss? None!"

Surprised, stupefied, and noticeably off-guard, Ukiah retorted, "Imagine the headlines, you bastard – 'New York literary agent ... Mason Turner employee ... killed.' How would that look?"

"Ssssssonny boy, issssssn't it better to sssssacrifice one life for the good of the whole?" Evadoo fell silent for a moment, then continued, his voice confident, defiant, and direct. "You lissssen to me, you cocky bassssstard. I'm ssssssending The Latera P. D. in there with gunssss-a-blazin' twenty minutessss after we hang up. If you don't ssssurrender by then, I'll kill the whole damn bunch of ya. And don't get any bright ideasss about calling a newssss conference. Every reporter on the sssscene hasss been told to hold their ground. I control every one of them. Now, how do you like thosssssse rotten fucking applesssss?"

"You fucker, I know all about S.W.A.N. ......"

At that instant, the line went dead.

Even though it felt as if time suddenly stopped, we had less than twenty minutes until Richard Evadoo sent in his storm troopers. Realizing that each minute was vital, Ukiah zipped into the kitchen as his mother followed.

"Baby, what are we going to do?" she cried, devastated.

"I have one last plan," Ukiah said boldly, looking out the front window to assess the situation. "It's my only chance."

Desperate, Jennifer bawled, "Sweety, I don't want to lose you. We've only known each other one day. I love you so much. It can't be over already."

Jennifer rushed to her son, hugged him dearly, then slumped against the wall.

"Ukiah," I said, rushing to his side. "If there's anything I can do, let me know."

Smiling weakly, Ukiah looked at me sadly. "You've always been there for me, Chris. Even though I may not have said it enough, I appreciate your support. I've never had a friend like you."

Touched by his admission, I replied softly, "What are your plans?"

Without looking at me, he said, "Do you really want to keep Kenny Dewar from moving in next door?"

"Kenny Dewar? I hate to sound critical, but in fifteen minutes, Evadoo's going to bombard us. What does Kenny Dewar have to do with this?"

"Do you see that gas can?" he asked hurriedly. "I'm going to slip out a back window, crawl behind your shrubbery, pour some gas around his house, then set it on fire. Do you see where I'm going?"

Enlightened, I gasped, "You'll start the house on fire to create a diversion!"

"Chris, you're starting to think like me even more than I think like me," he laughed, grabbing the gas can. "We better get this show on the road. Which window should I use?"

"The one in my bedroom is the most hidden," I said in a hushed tone, leading him along the hallway. "But what if they have snipers in the backyard?"

"If they do," Ukiah said, straight-faced, "let's hope their aim isn't very good."

With those ironic words, Ukiah crawled from my bedroom window, then grabbed the gas can that I handed to him. Racing to an adjacent window, I watched as he snuck behind the bushes, haphazardly emptied the container near the rear of Kenny's house, then pulled a pack of matches from his hip pocket. As planned, like Hell's gates being opened wide, flames leaped from the base of Dewar's foundation, crawling along his siding like twisted ivy. Not taking time to admire his handiwork, Ukiah scrambled back to my window, a look of accomplishment beaming from his eyes.

Reentering my house through the opened window, Ukiah smiled, "That should side-track them awhile. Now it's time for my getaway."

"Getaway? What are you talking about?" I asked.

"Getaway?" Jennifer shouted, joining us in the bedroom. "Where are you going, baby? You can't leave now. You can't abandon me. No. Please, Sweety. I want to know you. I've endured a lifetime of separation. Don't go now. Stay with me. I'll protect you."

Jennifer hugged her son tightly, smothering his cheeks with tear-drenched kisses.

"No ... don't go. You're the only person I have in the world. I love you, honey. Stay here. I'll keep you from harm. I need you. I've missed you so much. Be my little baby. Hold me. Don't go. I want to rock you in my arms. C'mon, hug me. Kiss me. Stay by my side."

Ring ... Ring ...

"Get that, Chris," Ukiah demanded, alarmed by the intrusion.

I ran into the living room, pressed the speaker button, then heard Officer Idem bellow, "What the hell are you maniacs doing? A fire! Tell Rhymes he'll pay for this."

As the distant echo of fire trucks grew louder, Ukiah grabbed his mother, then held her at arm's length.

"Mom, I love you, I really do. But listen. Those bastards are going to break down our front door in five minutes. I need to get away, or I'll spend the rest of my life in prison. They have enough charges to send my ass up the creek until the end of time."

"But baby," she sobbed. "What am I going to do without you?"

"Mom, you'll see me again. Once I blow outta here, I'll lay low for awhile, then meet you and Chris on the sly. Don't worry, everything'll be cool."

Jennifer stumbled weakly toward Ukiah, hugged him dearly, then said after kissing his forehead, "I can't bear to watch, Sweety. I'll wait in the bedroom. I love you."

As his mother limped down the hallway, wailing with remorse, I watched the flashing lights outside our window as two fire trucks pulled onto Reflection Alley. Looking next door through the curtains, I saw orange flames of fury crackling amid thick plumes of noxious smoke.

"Okay, Chris, I suppose this's it. The diversion has been created."

"But how are you going to get away?" I asked with marked confusion. "Things are happening too fast. I can't get a grip on them. I wish everything would just slow down. .... Oh Ukiah, what're you going to do?"

Focused, he replied while pulling the pistol from his jacket. "I'm going to run outside, then jump in my van through the back doors. After gunning the engine, I'll blast through their barricade. See – look over there," he pointed, ushering me to a corner of the window facing the front yard. "Do you see those news vans?"

I nodded my head.

"Now look to the left. What do you see?"

"Two police cars."

"Right. Now, between them and that group of people is an opening. It'll be simple. I'll duck in my van, crank the engine, then BLAST through that crack. With Kenny's house in flames ... the fire trucks ... and all those crazy people running around ... by the time they know what hit 'em, I'll already be on the main highway."

Choked-up, I coughed, "Are you sure there isn't any other way?"

"None that I can see," he smiled, feigning confidence. "Now remember, after I'm gone and the cops burst in, convince them that you and Jennifer were both hostages. I kidnapped you and held you at gunpoint. Agree to cooperate, and you'll get off scot-free."

I nodded my head, tears clouding my vision.

"Oh, before I forget. When Idem asks about Woody Dewar's death, I'm the one who killed him, not you."

"But ...." I couldn't even speak, for Ukiah had already moved toward the kitchen door.

Holding the handle between his fingers, Ukiah turned and said, "Remember, to create, one must first destroy. If I'm destroyed ... if I go out in a blaze of glory, it's your responsibility to create something. Got it?"

Unable to hold back my sadness, I burst into tears, hugging Ukiah tightly. "Good luck. I ......"

Before storming from the door, Ukiah lowered his head and said, "I'm not ready, Chris. I haven't purified myself enough yet. I dread what will become of me."

Like a flash, he fled onto my porch, scurried to his van, and fired its engine. I raced to my living room window, then watched as Ukiah barreled along the driveway while a hail of gunfire rained down on his van, causing him to veer wildly onto Reflection Alley, then abruptly stop as the nose of his vehicle careened into a utility pole.

39

Pandemonium unfolded in my front yard as steam rose from the grille of Ukiah's demolished van ... the piercing wail of sirens reverberated through the thick, smoky air ... police officers, paramedics, and ambulance attendants rushed to drag Ukiah from his van ... Jennifer screamed hysterically, flailing about the house in a panic as undercover detectives burst through the front door ... a helicopter circled above my roof, its whirling blades cutting the air to create a swishing sound that echoed across the land ... billowing smoke poured from Woody's roof as fire engines raced to the scene ... Prince's Minions, dressed in feathers and sporting Owl masks, chanted "Death To Atropos, Long Live The Prince" while brandishing torches and plastic swords ... flashbulbs erupted ... curious onlookers scavenged Ukiah's van in hopes of stealing a souvenir ... a metal stretcher was wheeled from the rear of an ambulance ... red spinning lights sent splinters of terror in every direction, while yellow suited firemen aimed water cannons in a valiant attempt to douse the flames next door ... television announcers delivered catchy phrases and buzzwords such as "Terror In Latera," "Atropos Tragedy," and "Hostage Inferno" ... Officer Idem drilled me with questions while Jennifer required medical attention ... screams ... sirens ... brilliant flashes of light ... sensory overload ...

I managed to momentarily flee from the insanity taking place inside my house, bursting through the front door in time to see Ukiah's limp body being placed on a silver gurney, arms folded across his chest like a corpse.

In the ensuing chaos, while bumbling Latera detectives dashed about without rhyme or reason, I lead Jennifer to my Gemini, where we frantically dashed from the driveway toward the county hospital. During the melee, when investigators, medical personnel, and reporters trampled about the grounds, I tried to determine Ukiah's condition, but no one could give me any details. For all I knew, Ukiah may have survived the gunfire and his collision with the utility pole, or he could already be lying dead in a morgue.

Whatever the case, I knew Officer Idem was infuriated by our decision to leave the crime scene, especially after the Gemini's rear tires spat gravel and dust across my driveway. So, wracked by paranoia, I drove along the side streets and alleys, sure to avoid any major arteries or thoroughfares on my way to the hospital.

As we crept toward our destination, Jennifer sobbed lightly into a tissue. The sadness that consumed us was so great that I needed every ounce of strength to keep from joining her.

Following a period of silence, she finally said, "I only knew him one day. It's hard to believe, but I wasted an entire lifetime for a few lousy hours. You must think I'm horrible."

"Miss Ewen, I don't care about the past. I just hope Ukiah survived his ordeal."

"Thanks for not making me feel worse. Ukiah's lucky to have a friend like you." Jennifer paused a moment, then asked tenderly, "Chris, you knew my son better than anyone. Was he happy with life?"

"At times," I laughed uncomfortably, "he soared to the highest highs. But at other times he was so dissatisfied with the world that it ate him alive."

"I never should have left him on those hospital steps," she cried. "Isn't it strange that both times I've been with Ukiah, a hospital has been involved? For the past 37 years, a day hasn't passed that I haven't blamed myself for being an unloving mother. Now, if Ukiah dies, I'll never be able to live with myself. I should have taken those bullets instead of him."

As Jennifer cried uncontrollably, I zipped into the hospital's main entrance, parking in a circular lot that faced its front doors.

"Here we are," I said softly.

Jennifer sat solemnly for a moment, then told me, "Chris, I can't take any more bad news ... it'll kill me. Could you find out if Ukiah survived, or if he's already dead. By that time, maybe I'll have pulled myself together. I'm sorry ....."

After consoling Jennifer to the best of my ability, I inched along the sidewalk, each step drawing me closer to a verdict that I might not want to hear. I tried to weigh each possible outcome, but was too confused to concentrate. I wanted life to be an extended blank ... a complete nullification of thought, perception, and decision.

A set of sliding glass doors opened automatically as I stepped on a black fabric mat, the reception desk appearing directly in front of me. Feeling dizzy and nauseous (due to the smell of antiseptics in the air), I gulped deeply, closed my eyes for an instant, then walked toward the desk.

As I fidgeted neurotically, a dough-faced woman in a white uniform turned to me, her expression conveying an unbothered acceptance of life.

"May I help you?" she asked tonelessly.

"Yes ... yes. I'd like to visit Mister Ukiah Rhymes, or at least check on his condition."

"Madge," the receptionist snapped impulsively, "page room 1001 - stat."

"What does that mean?" I asked with fright. "Is Ukiah all right?"

The receptionist didn't answer as she tapped her fingers on the counter top.

As she did so, I looked around frantically, noticing a newspaper vending machine with the following headline:

Veteran Rocker Bob Dylan Hospitalized
- seriously ill with respiratory infection

The implications startled me, for I remembered that rainy day when Dylan played at The Entendre Amphitheater during a rainstorm. Could he have contracted this life-threatening lung infection while we stood watching? Could we be indirectly responsible for the death of rock n' roll's most influential poet?

Before I could unravel this mystery, a police officer grabbed my shoulder from behind, asking in a gruff voice, "Are you Chris Edwards?"

"I am."

"Officer Idem has instructed me to take both you and Miss Ewen to the station downtown."

"But I need to know Ukiah's condition ....."

"Edwards, Officer Idem has every right to arrest you for fleeing a crime scene and disregarding your responsibilities as a witness. Don't make me cuff you."

"Sir, that won't be necessary. I'll go along without incident. Just please tell me, how is Ukiah?"

The policeman looked around suspiciously, then whispered, "He's still alive, but in a coma. Now c'mon, let's go."

After substantiating Ukiah's story that Jennifer and I were hostages under his control, we were allowed to leave the station pending further investigation. But at this point, nothing mattered except a glimmer of hope — Ukiah had survived his ordeal and was lying comatose in room 1001 at the Latera County Hospital. The biggest roadblock now facing me was what method I would use to meet him. It definitely looked suspicious that, after being held hostage by Ukiah, I would rush to check on his condition. But I bypassed this strategic pratfall by explaining that Ukiah had, over time, engaged in a concerted effort to brainwash me ... even now I still felt controlled by him. I'm sure the authorities knew I was lying, but if they could sweep this matter under the rug in a timely fashion, everything could return to normal. With this in mind, if I were caught trying to visit him again, our story would undoubtedly start to crumble.

But I had to ... NEEDED to see Ukiah! The only question was - how?

There was no way I could enter the hospital's main lobby and walk to his room. First of all, after hearing small talk at the police station, I knew an armed guard stood watch outside his room 24 hours a day. Why shouldn't he? Ukiah would eventually be charged with arson, kidnapping, assault, murder, and attempted murder. He tried to kill America's most famous author, plus held a literary agent hostage, transporting her across state lines. The future didn't look bright for my friend.

How could I make contact without jeopardizing our situation? I paced through the rooms of my house, then saw No-Sho The Hero's cape hanging from a hook in my bedroom closet. During the past few months, I had become so entangled in Ukiah's web that I'd nearly forgotten about this once important part of my life. But then an idea struck me with such magnitude that I had nothing to thank but the multi-colored cape. In my fantasies, No-Sho could save the day by becoming whoever he wanted. That is exactly what I would do to meet Ukiah. I'd temporarily create a new identity!

Before implementing this plan, I had to make sure that Miss Ewen, who was staying with me and understandably crazed with concern, would not interfere. So, as she tossed and turned in the spare bedroom one night, I crept from the house, then drove to the hospital. Rather than park in the main lot and enter through the sliding glass doors, I circled the building until seeing an unattended rear loading dock. After parking the Gemini and scampering past an unlocked gate, I scrambled through the darkness in hopes of finding an essential ingredient to my plan - a clothes hamper where the hospital orderlies discarded their uniforms. If I couldn't locate one of these laundry bins in a reasonably short period of time, the entire plot would be foiled.

Completely paranoid and on-guard, I snuck past furnaces and boilers, through a dark-ened kitchen, along vacant hallways, then into a rehabilitation room. I was even forced to duck into a storage closet at one point as a few nurses shuffled along an otherwise empty corridor. My heart beat so fast that I was afraid of having a heart attack, then being wheeled into an operating room after passing out. Luckily, such a disaster did not occur, for there, outside a laundry facility, I discovered a goldmine - mountainous stacks of fresh uniforms folded in neat piles.

Overjoyed, I rummaged through the clothes and selected the appropriate uniform - a white V-necked buttonless frock (complete with a sewn-on name tag), along with light blue slacks, white shoes, and a white cap. Satisfied that I fit the role, I returned to the maternity ward where I noticed an abandoned pushcart filled with cleaning supplies and medical apparatus. Everything was falling into place. I would become ... wait a second, I better look at the name tag on my chest to see who I was. Okay, I had suddenly become "C. Mensplotch." I couldn't tell from the label whether Mensplotch was male or female, so, after pulling the cap over my brow, I resigned myself to playing either role, depending on the situation.

With push cart in hand, I rolled into the hospital's west wing, a clock on the wall reading 1:10 a.m. Realizing that my plan's success depended on my ability to avoid people at all costs, I hurriedly located an elevator, pushed the tenth floor button, then waited as lighted numbers flashed during my ascent.

"Please hurry," I silently begged, prepared to turn away if the elevator did come to a stop at one of the floors.

2 ... 3 ... 4 ... 5 ... 6 ... DING.

Shit. Somebody was getting on the elevator.

With head bent low and eyes directed at items on my pushcart, I tried to remain anonymous as the doors opened and a man and woman entered.

"So she said, I don't care what he does as long as the economy is good."

The man replied, "That's right. I mean, if any of us did what he's accused of doing, we'd be imprisoned, or at least fired from our jobs. But that's all right with me. He's superior to us."

"And you must admit," the woman added, "he really does care about us and our interests. I mean, he's working tirelessly for us. It's no fun and games for that man. So what if two or three floozies are in his office every day down on their knees."

"Just keep talking," I thought, hearing the chime of another lighted number on the overhead display.

"He really does love his wife and daughter," the man reiterated. "It's so easy to tell. Who cares if he committed adultery every year of their marriage with hundreds of other women? All I care about is extra money in my pocket."

"You're right, Joe," she responded giddily. "I don't even care if he forced himself on some of those ladies. I mean, my husband would go to prison for doing that, but business is booming."

8 ... 9 ... 10 ... DING.

Thank goodness. I made it without being detected.

After rolling my cart between these people and exiting the elevator, I breathed deeply, then turned to notice a uniformed security guard lounging outside room 1001. Here it was - now or never.

Playing the role of a hospital orderly for all it was worth, I moved toward the guard, only to find him fast asleep in a padded chair that was propped against the wall.

"Room duty," I said softly, already halfway through the door.

"Hum? Oh ... yeah, uh sure ... go right ahead," the sleepy eyed man replied.

After closing the door behind me, I looked across the low-lit room to see Ukiah lying unconscious in his bed, an array of tubes and wires running from his body to a panel of machines that monitored his bodily processes.

Pretending to clean, I moved closer to my comatose friend, whispering, "Ukiah, it's me ... Chris. Can you hear me?"

Nervously, I shuffled toward the door, then peeked from the window to find the guard sleeping once again.

Returning to the bed, I sat on a chair beside Ukiah, his eyes closed, face bathed by tranquility.

"Ukiah, wake up. Please," I begged. "I don't have much time."

But he remained unaware ... unable to communicate. The sight of respirator tubes, I.V.'s, bandages wrapping his head, the aroma of cleaning fluids, and the complete dependence on devices to keep him alive filled me with unbearable sadness. Ukiah would never let himself live in such a manner. He needed to be alive ... moving ... thinking - plotting and planning ... to have one foot on the gas pedal ... flying from here to wherever. But now, with him helpless, passive, and catatonic, I nearly broke down and cried. Lord only knows what happened during that shoot-out and collision. Ukiah may have suffered permanent brain damage, paralysis, or an injury that confined him to a wheelchair. In all honesty, though, none of these factors affected his ultimate fate, because once he recovered, the authorities would convict him on a score of charges, forcing my friend to spend his remaining days in jail.

The irony was unavoidable. Here lay Ukiah Rhymes, a man who epitomized freedom of both movement and thought ... now confined to a hospital bed ... incapacitated ... comatose ... destined for prison. Yet again, the world did not make sense.

While I sat in a wooden chair beside medical machines that beeped and whistled, I reminisced about the times I spent with Ukiah ... how he hounded Mister Doublet to let Japhy's band play at a high school assembly ... how he went nuts after the grocery store clerk forgot to bag his apples ... his sit-down strike at the post office ... the way he slaved away at this typewriter, sweat rolling from his forehead as pages unfolded onto the carpet ... his refusal to back down at a Joan Jett concert when a drunken spectator tried to shove in front of us ... then sticking to his word by attacking Philip Prince (without noticeable fear), even though every card was stacked against him.

Ukiah refused to be controlled, yet he lay only inches away, completely dependent on these machines. If conscious, he would have freaked out at his helplessness. Him a vegetable! Reliant! Weak ... attached to a life-support system. Such a scenario didn't paint a proper picture. Ukiah needed to soar – to run - to fly along a highway. How could I let him get bed sores as his mind and body rotted away ... unable to properly function? He couldn't even breathe on his own ... every inhalation a desperate grasp (or gasp) at life.

Leaning beside him, I whispered, "Ukiah, please wake up. I don't know what to do."

The sight of white bandages wrapping his head with drops of blood seeping through made me sick. Had brain matter actually dripped from his head after a string of bullets entered his skull?

"Ukiah, it's Chris. Can you hear me?" I whispered.

Miraculously, Ukiah's eyes flickered as he moaned, "Ah ... where am I?"

"Ukiah," I said a bit too loudly. "You can hear me!"

"Of course," he mumbled tiredly. "I have to finish writing my book."

"Sure you do," I replied with a smile.

"How's Japhy?" he then asked, his mouth coated with spittle.

"Japhy? He's fine ... doing great," I lied. "His band is playing next week at The Dies Infaustus."

"Super," he coughed weakly. "Are we going?"

"We wouldn't miss it," I told him softly, grabbing his left hand.

"I don't ... don't feel so well," he moaned. "Something's wrong with me."

"No, no, you'll be fine. Just hang on."

"Are we still going to the circus with Japhy and Gina?"

"Absolutely!"

"And we'll invite my Mom and Dad."

"Of course."

The EKG machine beside him started to react violently, each of the electronic gauges losing their peaks and valleys before settling into an even flat line.

"Chris," he then said with near inaudibility. "I can't have the unattainable, even in my dreams."

"Shhhhh ... be quiet, Ukiah. Save your strength," I told him, spasms of fear filtering through my body.

Ukiah winced, held his breath, then closed his eyes, panting, "It looks like I'll never enter the gates of publication, huh?"

Cringing, I knew I needed to free Ukiah from his pain. So, as if guided by an alien presence, I changed from a passive, wavering do-nothing into a person making the first conclusive decision of their life.

Peering through the shadows, I followed the ventilation hose from Ukiah's nose to the respirator, then whispered good-bye before pinching the tube between my pointer finger and thumb. Resting my other hand on his chest, I felt him twitch three times, heard a faint cough and gasp for air ... then sat in silence as he died quietly beside me.

As Ukiah's body fell limp and began turning cold within the span of a few minutes, I rose from the wooden chair, kissed his lifeless cheek, then snuck from the room, returning undetected to my Gemini. After firing its engine and turning on the head-lights, I looked into the rear view mirror ... my clouded, veinous, tear-drenched eyes seeing the eyes of a killer.

Days and weeks passed by drearily as the reality of Ukiah's death hit me. It seemed unbelievable, but I'd never again walk across my backyard and tap at Ukiah's door to hear music crackling from a cheap set of speakers, or rake leaves by his side. In fact, a number of changes took place after he died, none the least being my mother's relocation to Ukiah's cottage. Considering her impoverished state, I couldn't see any alternative other than selling her house, paying the creditors, then letting her live behind me. Mother's company didn't fill the vacuum left by Ukiah, but at least we could rebuild a relationship that had been strained over the past few years.

Other than raking leaves that fall, I also tackled a chore that had gone unnoticed since I moved into this place. This job consisted of cleaning my house ... to get rid of every item not absolutely necessary to my existence. Anything that cluttered my life (those items not in their proper order) were throw away for good. I no longer needed useless objects lying around - reminders of a past I wanted to forget.

While performing this time-consuming task, I thought about the deaths and burials of Japhy and Ukiah. In regard to the latter, in accordance with his wishes, Ukiah was laid to rest in a simple pine box without a funeral or wake. None of us, Jennifer included, were present to watch his body being lowered into the ground. By all counts, he had been a vital member of society one day, then vanished the next. Regrettably, the most noticeable token of Ukiah's existence was the videotaped footage recorded during his attempted getaway, when a hailstorm of bullets rained down on his van and caused him to career into a utility pole. This scene was rebroadcast so often on the local stations that I quit watching television.

As for the tragic passing of Japhy and his band mates, a funeral service was arranged that epitomized everything Ukiah despised - extensive media coverage, elaborate arrangements, theatrical mourning, needless expense, and unnecessary pomp and circumstance. Although I felt compelled to pay my final respects, I realized that this virus was spreading impurities with such disregard for what benefited mankind that I couldn't attend the service. Ukiah was right in assessing the horrors of this awful custom. How could people gawk at five deceased teenagers, their bodies lying solemnly in blue-lined caskets, hands folded over their stomachs, smeared with ghastly pancake makeup, while incense and formaldehyde filled the air? Even though I didn't go to this atrocious spectacle, I did see a few newspaper articles covering the event that confirmed my suspicion that it escalated into an overblown display that perpetuated the least desirable aspects of society. We should, as a collective whole, eradicate this virus once and for all by abolishing the practice of staring at dead bodies. The only bright spot resulting from this tragedy was that Gina would recover from her injuries and be able to lead, considering the circumstances, as normal a life as possible. As for the drunken driver who collided with Japhy, it appeared his lawyer would arrange a plea bargain, keeping him from serving any jail time. The idea of this man enjoying his freedom while the rest of us suffered for the rest of our lives sickened me.

I continued to throw away items from my closets, corners, drawers and storage rooms, amazed at the volume of worthless material I had gathered over the years. To even describe these objects would be an endless task. All I can say is that when all this junk (for lack of a better term) had been pulled into broad sight, I noticed most of the boxes had been shuffled from one location to another without ever being unpacked.

While putting everything in its proper order, I wondered about those people who had touched my life during the past year. For starters, Bob Dylan recovered from his near fatal respiratory infection, then released another record album.

Following a cursory investigation of Philip Prince's attack, Mister Doublet's suicide, Woody Dewar's death and arson case, and the New York hostage situation, the Latera Police Department closed the books on Ukiah Rhymes, making him responsible for each of these criminal acts.

Being cleared of any involvement in this mess, Jennifer Ewen returned to her apartment in The Village, then retired from the literary industry to pursue other interests. At a farewell dinner together, we discussed Ukiah's life, his writings, and every other facet of his existence that she had missed over the years. As we parted, I did ask Miss Ewen for one thing. I planned on doing an intensive study of her son's works, and asked if she could send me her writings from the past few decades. In return, I would copy Ukiah's manuscripts and mail them to her in New York. In no less than a week, I received pounds of short stories, articles, novels, poetry, and miscellaneous writings. With this collection in hand, I formed a complete picture of their fractured family.

In regard to Philip Prince, Jennifer never told him that Ukiah was his illegitimate son. Without this information, Prince kept bad-mouthing, libeling, and degrading Atropos at every turn, using the tragic affair to further his already healthy career. In fact, spurred on by hype surrounding The Latera Lunatic case, *Prince Of The Earth* sold more copies than any other novel of the twentieth century, assuring its adaptation to the silver screen and nominations for numerous literary awards. I even read in *The New York Times Book Review* that Mister Prince was developing a television mini-series chronicling his involvement in pursuing, capturing, and bringing about Atropos' downfall. I couldn't help but laugh at this article, wondering how many more black eyes, bruises, and contusions Prince would add to his face in the screenplay.

After loading tons of useless objects into the backseat and trunk of my Gemini, I drove to the local dump, basking in at least one bright spot to my otherwise sad state of affairs. By all appearances, Kenny Dewar would not move into his brother's house, for the fire had caused such extensive damage that the entire structure had to be leveled. With any luck, Kenny would forget about becoming my neighbor and invest his insurance money elsewhere.

Finally, after missing days of work while The Latera Lunatic fiasco unfolded, I was forced to face the question of employment. Specifically, when meeting with the General Manager of my data processing firm, I needed to decide what I'd do in the future regarding my livelihood. Should I stay with my current firm, or relocate to another line of work? So, after being reprimanded for a string of absences related to the above matter, I reacted in a way that seemed foreign to me. Rather than assuming the mild persona of Chris Edwards, I felt Ukiah's presence in me. Unbelievably, by the end of this meeting, not only had I been promoted, but I became Business Manager of the entire data entry operation.

The news thrilled me. I would no longer need to enter numbers into a glowing green computer screen. Instead, I'd finally be challenged – stagnation becoming a thing of the past. After familiarizing myself with the position, I confronted an employee named Tom Twinson who continually undermined my authority as night shift supervisor by making barnyard noises over the intercom. During our meeting, I explained that I would not tolerate him behaving like an eighth-grade child with a CB radio. Regrettably, Twinson challenged me during the following shift by oinking like a pig and quacking like a duck. Needless to say, Mister Twinson was fired that evening, setting a precedent that essentially said that the former Chris Edwards no longer filled these shoes. From now on, every employee was expected to perform their duties in a professional manner without the immature shenanigans displayed by Mister Twinson.

By this time I reached the city dump, where I threw dozens of boxes over a ledge into the landfill. Yes indeed, yesterday's Chris Edwards was moving ahead into uncharted territory ... the first sign of this transformation being a properly maintained household. Disorder would no longer prevail. Instead, I vowed to start fitting pieces into the puzzle rather than letting them lay strewn across the table.

After adjusting to this new routine, life passed without incident. I worked a normal shift, dined at night with my mother, then tried to finish a daily crossword puzzle before going to bed. On the surface, I should have been satisfied with my situation. First and foremost, whether it was due to luck or good grace, I still couldn't believe I wasn't in prison. Considering what Ukiah and I got away with, freedom in and of itself should have been enough to please me. Plus, I had been promoted at work, my raise finally providing me with an adequate level of comfort.

But none of these factors, including the renewed relationship with my mother, satisfied me. Quite frankly, I missed Ukiah. I figured these feelings of sadness, lethargy, and reminiscence would pass, but in actuality they only grew worse. Something special had been taken from me ... a burst of life that filled me with such exuberance that, without it, each new day seemed commonplace and blasé. Even if we just sat on the porch or raked leaves, Ukiah's ideas about the world were unlike any I had ever heard.

Thoroughly depressed one Saturday afternoon, I raced to my Gemini, cranked its engine, pushed a Joan Jett cassette into the tape player, then drove to the bypass. This was more like it! Ukiah and I must have spent half our time together on one highway or another. Now, I'd finally hear his voice whispering in the wind, or see his face in the passing clouds. I even considered going to a Joan Jett concert if she returned to the area, but knew it wouldn't be the same without Ukiah. Even trying to drive my problems away was just an attempt to recapture the olden days. It seemed promising in theory, but when I actually drove along the highway, I felt lost and lonely ... so lost and lonely.

Plummeting into the cradle of despair, I exited the bypass, then cruised along a rural highway, so dejected that I longed for an approaching freight train, or a treacherous cliff without guardrails. Sensing I would soon cause a traffic accident, I bounced onto an unpaved path leading into the woods, then parked beneath a thicket of trees with radiantly colored leaves. There, a peculiar thought entered my mind. I remembered one of the last things Ukiah said to me before entering his van and drawing a volley of gunfire. He confessed that he was the one who murdered Woody Dewar, not I as he led me to believe. During this time, Ukiah's lies were so convincing that I actually believed I strangled that man. Now the notion seemed absurd, but while under his spell, anything was possible.

I laughed with embarrassment at being so easily swayed. How could I have been so gullible and naive to let him lead me astray? Ukiah must have laughed every step of the way, seeing me as a simple, uncomplicated mark. But we did have some fantastic times together. If only he hadn't burned so brightly, maybe his candle would still flicker at times such as these, illuminating my darkened life.

Frustrated and angry as I sat beneath these picturesque trees, I slammed my palms against the steering wheel, closed my eyes, then cried like I had never done before.

While tears streamed along my cheeks, I yelled at the top of my lungs, "Why? Why did you leave? You're so selfish. You always took, but never gave in return. Now look! You're gone, and I'm forced to spend the rest of my life without you. I hate you for being so self-centered!"

Bawling hysterically, I opened my eyes to see the most perfect creature of all time walking in front of the Gemini. Amazingly ... beyond belief ... here - in the middle of nowhere - stood a pure white Persian cat with such an elegantly manicured tail and cottonball fur that I nearly choked from the shock. The feline's beauty was so radiant and complete that I started crying even harder. Why was this magnificent animal walking in a forest when it should have been standing atop a pedestal? The sight — this glorious vision — didn't make sense. Why was he here with me?

I actually wanted to die at that moment, The Being before me so absolute in its beauty ...

"Chris ...." a soothing voice of unknown origin suddenly said, its message echoing through the wind. "The time has come for you to start living with a single-mindedness ... to discover the proper path leading toward Creation."

"Who are you?" I whimpered, my bottom lip trembling, tasting like salt.

"Please listen," the female voice continued as the white Persian cat scampered from sight. "You no longer need to be a hostage of your past. Discard those elements that exert undue control and impede your progress. Chris, define your own identity! Do you want to enter the gates of publication?"

Suddenly realizing who the voice belonged to, I exclaimed, "Romlocon! Is that you?"

"Chris, if you want to enter the gates of publication, all you need is an unwavering belief in your Muse. After that, everything will become clear."

"I will! I'll do anything to join Ukiah."

The wind whistled eerily for a moment, then The Voice said, "I'm sorry to inform you, but Ukiah never entered the gates of publication."

"Why? Please, tell me. He tried harder than anyone I ever met. Ukiah gave his entire life for Art."

"Yes, he certainly did try, but his efforts alone weren't enough to grant him this privilege. You see, Ukiah knew WHAT the proper path was, but he didn't follow this narrow trail. He heard The Word, but refused to act accordingly. Ukiah never discovered the Purity of which he so often spoke. This poor man recognized Order, but he deliberately chose a chaotic lifestyle. Chris, open your eyes and ears. Entering the gates of publication cannot be a hobby, past-time, or sideline affair ... something to simply occupy one's time. Instead, you must be drawn to me with an intense, burning focus. Can you hear my message? The Word has always existed, even before Man invented language, or found the ability to communicate. You've been given The Word ... genetically predisposed ... destined, if you will, to absorb this gift and Create under the guidance of your Muse. Isn't it evident? ... ... Ukiah was delivered for a purpose. He showed you the path, but was incapable of following it himself. Please, I beg of you, don't let your actions mirror his. Don't retrace his footsteps. Rather, absorb this concept of single-mindedness ... epitomize it — hear The Word, then Create ... Ukiah has been destroyed ... now find the ability to Create from his destruction. Tell the artists of this world one thing – that they CAN enter the gates of publication, even though those in control lead them to believe otherwise. They don't need fancy degrees, prominent titles, awards, or contacts to gain entrance into these hallowed halls. Ukiah proved this by conveying a glimmer of hope through his Art. Despite his faults, he truly believed that any of us ... ALL of us ... can realize our dreams. Chris, follow THAT lead - Create ... tell the factory workers, the waitresses, the gardeners, janitors, dishwashers, secretaries, taxi drivers, and everyone else to throw away their chains and get rid of the elements of control that govern them. Every artist can be drawn to me - the painters, sculptors, poets, musicians ... The Gates are OPEN — don't be deceived ... we're waiting ... all you have to do is follow my lead ... believe ... Create ... and purify yourself. Chris, become PURE ... this gift is available to ALL!"

Then, quicker than it had arrived, The Voice disappeared, slowly carried away by the wind.

Intrigued, inspired, and consumed by trepidation and awe, I was sure about one aspect of my newfound existence. The past confusion and indecision that plagued me would be discarded in favor of a new beginning. Romlocon would be my guide, drawing me toward a purpose my life had otherwise been lacking. Yesterday's emptiness and loss were replaced by a meaning that transcended the ordinary.

While driving home after this incredible experience, I looked back on how my impressions of Romlocon had changed over the past year. In all honesty, when Ukiah first mentioned this mysterious Muse, I thought he was insane. But over time, as I grew more familiar with her through Ukiah's repeated references, I realized Romlocon did exist as a source of creative inspiration for the artists of this world. Then, unbelievably, I also heard Jennifer allude to The Voice. Could she have been communicating with the same visitor who contacted Ukiah and me? By all appearances, this business of voices and messages from beyond sounded insane ... even ludicrous. But I heard this Muse, the same one who became an integral part of other people's lives. Even more extraordinary was the content of her words ... that I, Chris Edwards, needed to follow a path of creation begun by Ukiah Rhymes. I felt confused, yet honored at the same time. How had I become involved in a process that began over a year ago when I picked up a solitary man wandering along the highway?

After returning to my home on Reflection Alley later that afternoon, I instantly went to my bedroom, locked the door, sealed the curtains, and stood before a full-length mirror that hung from the wall. Ukiah, and now Romlocon, told me to get rid of past instruments of control that conditioned and molded me into my present form. Now, although this concept disrupted my preconceived notions, I decided to dispose of the past and define my own identity. I understood that such an undertaking promised to be a daunting affair, but as I removed my shirt and tossed it aside, I vowed to eradicate those forces that controlled me - my parents, the educational system, peers, media, advertising, and every other peripheral source. I next pulled-off my jeans, intent on becoming my own person. Standing in full-view of the looking glass, wearing only socks and my underclothes, I wondered what it would be like as an autonomous individual ... a being shaped in its own chosen image rather than a ball of clay molded on an assembly line.

Then I heard The Voice echoing again through my mind ... not the soothing tone of Romlocon, but my Father's indignant words blasted with machine gun intensity.

"You're worthless! You'll never amount to anything. Why can't you be more like me? I'm logical. I have common sense. You can't tell shit from shinola. Stupid ... idiot ... lamebrain ... no good for nothin' ... I oughta kick your ass ....."

"But, Dad, all I ever wanted was your love. Is that such a terrible thing to ask for?"

While each sock, then my underclothes, were peeled away, I stood fully naked in front of the mirror as Pus's words continued to haunt me.

"You're a disappointment ... not at all what I expected ... look at you ..."

At that moment I glanced to my left, noticing No-Sho The Hero's flowered cape draped over a hanger in the closet. The sight of this object sent shivers through my unclad body.

I tried to deny the scene countless times, but it finally entered my mind with the urgency of a locomotive. I was a toddler, barely able to walk, when my Father had the following conversation with me.

"Chris, please listen carefully. You're not like other children. You're different. See - look at yourself. LOOK. You're not normal. You're freakish ... an abnormality. But you'll be able to survive if you remember one thing. Around other people - NO SHOW your body. NO SHOW is good. NO SHOW is a hero. Always cover up. Never show. Do you understand? NO-SHO!"

At that moment, No-Sho The Hero was born ... a make believe fantasy figure who saved the day on numerous occasions, at least within the recesses of my deluded mind. But now I was being guided by a more prominent and real Being who promised free-dom instead of fantasy. Romlocon urged me to do away with every element from the past that denied my advancement. So, I lifted No-Sho's cape from the hanger, looked at it one last time, then tore it in half and flung it over my shoulder.

So there I stood, naked and in full-view. Admittedly, I was different ... abnormal ... conceivably a freak. My condition was certainly unique ... not one of a kind ... but highly irregular. But instead of hindering the progress of my life, I accepted myself for who I was without embarrassment or fear. No-Sho was an illusion, a crutch I relied on to balance the shattered emotional state created by my Father. But I could no longer deny who I was. My destiny had been sealed ... I would now create my own identity and stop pretending to be what Pus and everyone else wanted me to be. I had to become ME ... to become REAL ... the end of fiction had arrived.

With those sentiments fueling an inspiration that nearly burst from every conceivable seam, I raced, still naked, toward the closet, retrieving Ukiah's wooden crate filled with stories, plus the package Jennifer sent containing her works. Then, gushing with joy as

Romlocon's words echoed through my mind, I pieced together my best friend's notes and novels, Jennifer's tortured writings, and my own recollections ... then began writing the bittersweet saga of Ukiah Rhymes.

Written: September 7, 1998 (Labor Day) — February 14, 1999
          (Valentines Day)

ORDER FORM

- ❖ Telephone Orders:　Call (814) 237-2853
- ❖ Online Orders: victorthorn.com
- ❖ Postal Orders:　　Sisyphus Press
　　　　　　　　　　P.O. Box 10495
　　　　　　　　　　State College, PA 16805-0495

❑ I would like to order _____ copies of THE END OF FICTION @ $12.99.

Mailing Address:

Name _____

Address _____

City _____ State _____ Zip _____

Telephone Number _____

Sales Tax:

Please add 6% for books shipped to Pennsylvania addresses.

Shipping:

$2.99 for the first book and $2.00 for each additional book.

Payment:

❑ Check

❑ Money Order

❑ Credit Card: ❑ Visa ❑ MasterCard

Card Number: _____

Name on card: _____ Exp Date: _____

ORDER FORM

- ❖ Telephone Orders: Call (814) 237-2853
- ❖ Online Orders: victorthorn.com
- ❖ Postal Orders: Sisyphus Press
                      P.O. Box 10495
                      State College, PA 16805-0495

❏ I would like to order _____ copies of THE END OF FICTION @ $12.99.

Mailing Address:

Name _____

Address _____

City _____ State _____ Zip _____

Telephone Number _____

Sales Tax:

Please add 6% for books shipped to Pennsylvania addresses.

Shipping:

$2.99 for the first book and $2.00 for each additional book.

Payment:

❏ Check

❏ Money Order

❏ Credit Card: ❏ Visa ❏ MasterCard

Card Number: _____

Name on card: _____ Exp Date: _____